T0366164

PITFALLS
OF *Young Love*

PITFALLS
OF *Young Love*

MAMTA CHAUDHARI

PARTRIDGE

To order additional copies of this book, contact
Partridge India
000 800 10062 62
orders.india@partridgepublishing.com

www.partridgepublishing.com/india

Contents

PART ONE

PART TWO

PART THREE

To My Husband

PART
ONE

1

Sight of an Angel

There was light. But the brightness seemed to be unnatural, the glare incredibly harsh and there appeared to be no source or origin for the unearthly brilliance. Is this how heaven looks?

'Oh God! . . . I am dead . . . I don't want to die . . . I am just a 13-year-old kid . . . I can't be dead . . . I want to live. . .'

Suddenly everything turned dark. There were black, menacing clouds swirling in the wind, some of them rushing to meet some emissary, a few twirling around as if spun by a giant playing some macabre twirling-the-fluff game and many marching towards me in a hurry, in order to envelop me in their ghastly embrace. I couldn't see anything in the gloom except the murky, dark shapes, suddenly dissolving, suddenly assuming gigantic forms. A roar emerged from the chaos, as if a fire was raging nearby.

'I am in hell . . . I am indeed dead . . . and I have been consigned to purgatory . . . I don't want to die. . .'

The dark clouds dissipated, as if blown away by a strong gust of wind. And there emerged a face. An angel!

'God she is so beautiful . . . She is an angel . . . If this is heaven, I want to stay here forever . . . It is good to die . . . What is she saying? . . . Where is she going? . . . Please don't go . . . I can't live without you . . . But I am dead. How can I live, with or without her?'

I woke up dizzy, my mind swimming in whorls, to Bindu's desperate cries, 'Sanjay, Sanjay. Wake up. Your fever is down. How do you feel?'

I felt miserable and there she entered. I turned towards Bindu and enquired, 'Are you dead too?'

'No silly. I am very much alive and well, thank you. And we are at my home. Have you forgotten that, too?'

'Then how come she is here. She is an angel in heaven.' She was so radiant.

'Don't be absurd. You were delirious. She is no angel. She is Pratima Pandey from class 9. You must have seen her in school, sometimes.'

My mind cleared bit by tiny bit. The fuzz vaporised and the swirls disappeared in slow, checkerboard motions. I recalled catching fleeting glimpses of her in the corridors of Raman Block—only glimpses. I hadn't given a second thought to it then. She was two classes senior and looked much older than me. And, we were in a boys-only school, with a few girls studying with the multitudinous boys.

And here she was, this beautiful angel, bearing a bowl. She came closer and stood beside the bed. She looked down at me and for the first time I saw her face up close. She had such beautiful eyes, I felt as if I would drown in spiral eddies. Her milky white complexion shone with radiance as the dying sun's rays bathed her. Her jet black hair were kept open and floated down to her shoulders in a graceful flow. Her black piercing eyes were glowing with a sublime softness, and that impression of going down in winding spirals returned when I gazed into them; it was with some will that I was able to extricate myself, by drawing my eyes away from hers. Her naturally red lips were curled in a pout and it seemed as if she would give me a kiss any time. The round shapes of her jawline converged onto a soft oval chin, which contained the sole blemish on her angelic visage, a small scar at the centre of her chin, giving the appearance of a dimple (it was the result of a clumsy fall as a toddler, she told me later). She held her chin in a slight upward tilt.

I was drawn to her face like a bee to nectar. I wanted to just keep on looking at her till eternity.

She broke into my reverie, 'Hey, hey. Aren't you listening? Where are you? (Turning to Bindu) I think we will have to prop him up. (Chuckling) I hope he has not gone back again into his dream world. Next, he will turn me into a goddess.'

Both of them lifted my upper body and braced my back against the wall to make me sit up. I remained lost in admiring her face, turning my head all around, as if there were an invisible string running from her face into my eyes and would not let me shift my gaze. After I had been made comfortable, she handed the bowl over to Bindu and said, 'You feed him. I am off.'

Bindu stuck a spoon full of warm soup into my mouth. I mumbled and gurgled inside my mouth, as Pratima approached the door. She paused and turned towards me, 'What was that?'

I gulped down the thick broth, choking on it, cleared my throat and croaked, 'Please stay.'

She smiled a sweet charming smile, the soft regions around her mouth dissolving into attendant dimples, and asked, 'Why? Don't you want me to remain a human?' She chuckled at Bindu again.

'I feel good when you are around. You made my sickness vanish,' I seemed to have got my normal voice back.

She walked up to me and said in an accusing tone, 'And what was that you were mumbling while drifting in and out of your consciousness? "God, I am dead . . . I want to live . . . she is an angel . . . I can't live without her." I was here the whole time and my presence did not make your sickness vanish. The medicines and passage of time did. You need to rest and not work yourself up by looking at me like a lost child who has just found some hidden treasure.'

I lowered my eyes and squirmed at her insinuation. She glowered down at me and I whimpered, 'But I don't get worked up in your presence. As a matter of fact, you have the opposite effect. When I look at you I feel a blissful peace enveloping me in her calm. Check my heart. Its beats are normal.'

She softened her scowl and said, 'Okay. I will stay till you finish your soup.'

I grabbed the bowl from Bindu's hands as Pratima sat down on the bed next to her. I willed time to stall, I took tiny sips from the bowl, I chewed nonstop on each morsel, even if there was no vegetable; I tried everything to prolong her stay.

We chatted, we talked, we chortled, we laughed, we played stupid number games; I enjoyed it all and basked in this exquisite young maiden's company. Bindu's presence was not felt at all, she seemed like a ghostly presence, detached from the proceedings.

Pratima did most of the talking and I did my besotted-teenager-staring-nonstop-at-his-paramour act—when she asked me about my House (the building in which the students stayed in barracks-style dwellings) I got lost in her eyes, drowning in the twin pools; when she enquired about my friends, I wanted to hold her hands and talk friendly boy-girl talks; when she wondered about the hostel matron I wanted her to take on the mantle of the sweet maiden who ensured that we seventh graders lived appropriately; when she gushed about the books she had read I wanted to turn into all those knights in shining armour and save my damsel in distress; when she questioned me about my preparations for the forthcoming final exams I wanted her to turn into my teacher and help me pass the tests; when she examined the tiny puncture wounds on my arms and speculated on the pain I must have felt when they had poked the needle into my arm that noon, I wanted her soul to enter my body and relax my throbbing tissues.

Her voice had a singsong quality to it and she delivered each sentence in an uninterrupted flow, without pausing to think or fend for an appropriate word—in distinct contrast to my motor-mouth fashion of delivery and deliberate halts while speaking a sentence, as I searched for the correct term. Each sentence of hers was spoken as if every word were attached to the next by a transparent thread and the words glided into one another in a continuous motion. Her brain seemed to work with a constant churning motion, whereas mine worked in jerks and jolts. Her chortles and cackles were throaty. Her laughter seemed to emerge from deep inside her belly; her pretty nose crinkled and her eyes closed when she laughed.

She left much after the sun disappeared below the ragged hill tops silhouetting the Western horizon, and the world outside had turned pitch dark. And my bowl was still half full. When I complained that I had not yet finished my soup, she replied that if I had my way, she would have to stay till eternity to keep her promise, and slipped out with a grin on her face.

After devouring a sumptuous meal, lovingly prepared by Bindu's mother, I skipped and hopped my way back to my House, happy and contented, despite the lingering pain in my arms.

2

The Message Inside a Towel

It was the spring of '82 and I had completed more than a year and a half at Sainik School Ghorakhal. Situated on a plateau—with a marvellous view of the lower valleys and mountains of Bhimtal and Saat Taal, the map-of-India-shaped Bhimtal lake's pristine blue waters distinctly visible from its Parade Ground—the school was located fourteen kilometres from the hill station of Nainital. It is a boarding school established on 21 March '66, in the magnificent estate of the erstwhile Nawab of Rampur; the name of the place was derived from one of the two small ponds where, in 1857, a British general's horse had died while drinking water from it, the general having strayed into this area in a desperate bid to escape the revolutionaries of Awadh. The school's campus was huge and at that time composed of five Houses (two Holding Houses for the junior students and three additional houses named Singh, Kumaon, and Kesri houses for the seniors), Raman Block which housed the classrooms and laboratories, an administrative block which comprised the offices of the staff and the library, a huge parade ground where we had our morning parades and practiced drill, numerous playgrounds, a huge newly built mess for the students, a long barrack where old black-and-white Hindi movies were screened on a six-by-six-foot white screen using an ancient sixteen-millimetre projection system operated with extreme care by our arts teacher Noor Muhammad Sir (the new auditorium was still under construction then), a long row of double story apartments, called the Staff Quarters, where the teachers and other employees of the school resided, three isolated bungalows where the trinity of principal, headmaster, and registrar of the school stayed (all three were defence services officers), and an evergreen tree hanging over the steep slopes of a hillside leading down to the main sports ground of the school, which bloomed with different varieties of leaves and flowers with each changing season. Within the school premises, the famous temple of Golu Devta is located atop a small hill, where numerous bells are hung by those devotees whose wishes had been granted by the deity and where animal sacrifices are also conducted— the entrance archway to the temple grounds, sitting on top of a flight of stairs leading to it, is dominated by a huge, monster of a bell which let out a gigantic boom accompanied with echoes of its lower decibel cousins, whenever the iron chain attached to its clapper was swung, bringing it in a thundering contact with the bell's lip and mouth; we could virtually see the sound waves colliding and colluding, swimming and dancing, merging and dispersing within its waist, if we were brave enough to stand directly below the bell, when it was struck. The reverse slope of the hill on which the temple stood was also used by the school's senior students as a secret destination for trysts with their paramours, if they ever got lucky with the daughters of the school's teachers or staff, or in case one of the women employees felt an urge for the company of an adolescent youth. There was one canteen, Shahji's, where we could eat omelettes and drink his especially brewed, spicy, milky, sweet tea, which was a hundred times better than the brown, thin, bland affair they dished out at the students' mess. The other shops located just outside the school premises were out of bounds for students but were frequented by the rebels amongst us, just for the thrill of it than to enjoy the delicacies. There was a small town, Bhowali, located four kilometres away, which serviced the bare minimum needs of the school. For other requirements we had to depend upon either Nainital or Haldwani, the penultimate railway station before the rail head at Kathgodam, located two hours away.

I had joined the school in June '80 after a tough, three-stage selection procedure and having not stayed away from my near and dear ones a single day in my entire life till then, I was constantly homesick from the first day of joining the school. During my first year I missed my home a lot and cried often, whenever I grew desperate for Mother's loving care.

Always craving for Mother's affectionate embraces, I had been extremely sad and gloomy when I had first entered the main gate of the school, one and a half years back. I only found solace in the welcoming arms of Dwivedi Sir's family, especially Mrs Dwivedi, my Aunteeji, when I was invited to their home by Dwivedi Sir a week after I had joined the school. She had an affectionate manner and would give me a huge motherly hug every time I met her. She also prepared delicious meals and loved to feed me up to my gullet. I was particularly fond of their youngest child, Bindu, who was three years younger than I, and whom I considered as the sister I have never had. Their two sons and Bindu's elder sister also loved me a lot and would constantly indulge me, so that I could overcome my longing for home. Soon their home became my home away from home. Dwivedi Sir bore my frequent presence in his house with a grudging acceptance and never objected to my being there, presumably at the behest of Aunteeji. It was only when I had almost completed two years at the school that I myself imposed a semipermanent ban on visiting their house, but the reasons for that were different. Thereafter, I went there only on special occasions—to celebrate a birthday or during festivals and such like events.

That fateful day, in the spring of '82, I had been inoculated with TAB, TT, and Tetanus vaccines, and due to my propensity to fall sick at the drop of a hat, I was running a high fever within an hour of having been administered the dreaded injections. Instead of the school's medical personnel, I reposed faith in Aunteeji's abilities to revive me and after downing a Crocin tablet I was sleeping out the fever, when I had those visions of heaven, hell, and an angel I couldn't live without, in my semiconscious state.

After that auspicious beginning I could not meet Pratima for a long time. I sighted her, as earlier, while moving around the hallways of the Raman Block during class breaks and whenever we rushed from the classrooms to the laboratories to the arts class, pursuing our separate education curricula. But, where earlier I used to rarely venture out of the classroom, preferring to plop my head upon the desk and snooze for those ten minutes of class breaks, now I would be the first one out of the classroom to roam those same corridors, hoping to catch a sight of her, even just for a few seconds. But those were just fleeting glimpses and after a week or so she shifted to the fringes of my thoughts and would only occupy centre stage for those few infrequent moments whenever I saw her talking to Monisha, her classmate, hurrying from one class to another. Whenever I saw her thus, I would not be able to concentrate on anything else for the next couple of hours, as her beautiful face would float in front of my eyes endlessly.

In the past couple of months I had discovered the pleasures of reading novels. Out went the comic strips, *Champak, Chandamama, Nandan, Lotpot* et al., which I used to devour earlier and now I entered the fascinating world populated by the likes of Oliver Twist, David Copperfield, Hardy Boys, Tom Sawyer, and heroes of the other English classics. For my regular feed I visited the school library frequently and borrowed books to read during my spare time.

One day, as she was again beginning to fade from my imagination, I was caught short while entering the library. She was coming out, with *A Tale of Two Cities* firmly grasped in her hands and I stood rooted to my spot. She sauntered over to the entrance of the library and almost ran into me.

'Hello Sanjay,' she beamed and flashed a charming smile. Silent as a rock, my feet glued to the ground, I stood staring at her fascinating smile and the familiar sensation of drowning in spirals returned when I looked into her eyes. I was barring her way and she tried to step around me unsuccessfully.

'Let me pass please,' she frowned at me.

My heart was doing somersaults; 'she remembers my name, she remembers my name. . .' was repeating like a litany. It took me some time to register her request and I moved aside to let her through. She grinned, flashing a neat row of her pearly white teeth and chimed, 'See you again later.'

The entire episode must have lasted a minute or so, but it remained imprinted upon my mind for the next twenty-four hours, her charming smile and parting grin coming up from my subconscious uninvited, at odd hours. I spent the balance of the day in a restless commotion. Turning endlessly in my bed after lights out, I spent the entire night in sleepless fits of recollection of the scene at the library.

The next day, desperate to meet her again, I walked over to the children's school located within the school premises, to seek Bindu out, who was studying in class 5 there. I had skipped the library period of my class, reasonably sure that no one would miss me there. Bindu was busy in her class and I waited, impatiently stomping my feet, for her class to have a break so that I could speak to her.

After a considerable amount of time, the duration inflated by my restiveness, she emerged from her classroom. I rushed over to her and blurted out in a breathless tone, 'I want to meet her.'

'Hello Sanjay. Where have you dumped your manners? Is that the way to greet a girl? Anyways, let it be. Whom do you want to meet?'

'Pratima. Please ask her if she too wants to meet me. Please persuade her, tell her I want to see her alone. It can be at your house, when your father is away.'

'Wait, wait, wait. Time out! Not so fast. Isn't she a bit old for you? Come on, she is your senior by two classes.'

I decided to open up further, wanting to make her my confidante. 'I can't get her out of my mind. I will go crazy if I don't meet her again. I can't meet her at school. But you can arrange it at your house. Please, please, please.'

She considered my request and ultimately gave in, unwittingly entering into a secret, silent pact with me. 'I will see what I can do. But no assurances, Okay! Meet me again tomorrow.'

I spent another restless day and sleepless night, my mind swimming with myriad possibilities, 'Will she say yes? If yes, what would I say when I meet her? If no, will I cry at another missed opportunity? If yes, then when? If no, should I try again, will I have the will to continue with my wooing? If yes, will she meet at Bindu's place or some other location, maybe behind the Temple or some other stupid location like the Washerman's Point.'

The next day I skipped lunch and rushed straight to Dwivedi Sir's house, immediately after the last period. Sensing that I must have not had lunch, Aunteeji insisted that I have the meal inside her kitchen. She served copious helpings of daal and vegetable curry accompanied with an endless supply of chapattis till my tummy bloated and distended. Bindu had also arrived from her school and sat eating with me. I could not get confirmation of my request in front of her mother. From time to time she threw sheepish glances at her mother or looked with indirect peeks towards me, repeatedly nodding her head to convey an affirmation, whenever her mother was not looking at her. Slowly the house filled, as her brothers and sister streamed in from their respective engagements. The kitchen crowded over and I couldn't get an opportunity to corner Bindu all by herself. As the time came for me to realise that I was overstaying my brief visit, I excused myself to go to the toilet and discreetly nodded at Bindu. She got up with me and said that she would get me a towel. When I came out of the bathroom she was standing outside the door, a towel in hand. I took the towel and felt a piece of paper under it. I slipped the paper into my pocket and bid farewell to Dwivedi Sir's family (fortunately he had not yet arrived) thanking Aunteeji with profound gratitude for the lunch.

'*Saturday evening, 4 o'clock, this house*', the note read. And I walked on clouds the next two days till Saturday. The world around me changed its sounds, its colours, and its tones; the high-pitched scream of the school siren in the wee hours of the mornings bidding us out of our beds sounded like peals of hundreds of bells; the barks of our seniors to hurry with our ablutions fell on my ears like love songs; the morning runs felt like strolls in a park, its pathways strewn with flowers; the soggy bread at breakfast tasted like a warm, fresh loaf straight out of the oven; the boorish, boring monotone of our History teacher sounded like sweet music; my belligerent classmate Manoj became my best friend, as I repeatedly hugged him, heaping undeserved praise upon him; the blows of our seniors, when they punished us for our silly misdemeanours, felt so much like being assaulted by a cloud of cotton balls.

3

The Lowly Serf and the Martyr's Widow

I spent the next two days in a warm cloak of anticipation and was sitting in Bindu's room come Saturday, from three o'clock onwards, twiddling my thumbs and shaking my legs in nervous excitement, shivering with impatience. Bindu tried to becalm my fraying nerves initially, but gave up after a few attempts and left me to my own devices, joining her siblings who were studying in the living room or sleeping. The day and time had been carefully chosen by her (or by Pratima) as Dwivedi Sir had gone visiting an acquaintance at Bhowali and Aunteeji was taking her afternoon nap, and I had the afternoon and evening all to myself, it being a half day at school.

At two minutes to four—from the grandfather clock lounging in a corner, which, had it been a living being, would have run away by now, from the numerous stares I had thrown at it in the past fifty-eight minutes—Bindu walked in bearing a tray containing two cups of tea, steam curling above the rims in delicious white curves and a plate piled with biscuits. I promptly stood up and saw Pratima entering with a confident gait, head held high. She was resplendent in a peach coloured Salwar Suit, the stole hanging down both sides of her neck like a tippet, its hems almost touching the ground. She looked as radiant as ever. She walked up to me and stood staring at my face, with a look conveying equal amounts of amazement and curiosity. And I could also read a sign of approval in her eyes, as if she had contemplated me and accepted what she saw. Even though we had conversed freely and frankly the last time, the clandestine nature of our current meeting affected my nerves; my knees turned into jelly and I went weak in my legs. I staggered and held on to Bindu, as she straightened herself up after placing the tray upon the coffee table. My eyes were glued to that lone blemish on her chin and I did not dare to look into her eyes, where I was

13

certain to drown in spirals. She was the most beautiful girl I had ever seen in my life and I didn't know what to do, now that she had come responding to my summons. I seemed to have forgotten all those well-rehearsed sentences I had practiced in the past forty-eight hours. Bindu pried her arm out of my grip, leaned over with a gleam in her eyes, whispered conspiratorially, 'Best of luck,' and touching the arms of Pratima left the room.

I dropped like a stone into my chair. She sat across the table in another chair, crossing her legs gracefully and straightening her stole and tunic. I stared at her nose for a long time and losing all self-restraint peered into her eyes and the by-now-familiar sensation of being caught in a spiral whirlpool and getting sucked in, inch by delightful inch, entered me. I couldn't pull my eyes away after that.

After sometime, I heard her voice, sounding as if emerging from a deep well, filtering through layers of liquid, before reaching my ears, 'Sanjay, Sanjay. Snap out of it. Come out from wherever you are and stop staring at me like that. You look besotted. Bindu told me you wanted to meet me.' 'Alone,' she added after a pause, in an accusing tone.

I nodded dumbly in reply.

'Stop staring please and say something.'

'I . . . I . . . You are so . . . so . . . beautiful,' I stammered.

'Is that all?'

I shook my head and protested, 'No . . . No . . . there is more.'

'I am all ears.'

I pushed my head down and stared at the cups of tea, the contents now covered with a brown, wrinkled layer of cream. I picked up a cup and gulped down a sip, scalding the roof of my mouth, and I opened my mouth in reflex, to draw in cool air.

She chuckled and said, 'I presume you don't drink tea like that in the mess.'

I muttered, 'I don't know what to say.'

'You were quite chirpy the last time.'

'That was different. I have never been with a girl like this before . . . alone.'

'Well, this is the right time to start. What do you want to say? Either you come out with it or else I am leaving.'

'No, no. Please wait. Let me . . . let me . . . okay.' Taking a deep breath, I took some time in composing myself. 'Tell me about yourself, your life story.'

'Is that the best you can come up with?' she asked disbelievingly, as if she had expected something else. 'I have never been asked about my life before. Why don't you tell me about yourself?' she mimed.

'But I asked first.'

Most probably coming to a conclusion, rightly so, that she won't be able to get a single coherent sentence out of me in my nervous state, she said, 'Okay. Let's start from the start. I was born in a village called Bhojpur, fifteen kilometres from the town of Pithoragarh.'

'But you are not a *Pahari* (one from the mountains), from your features,' I interjected.

She leaned back, resting herself on the back of her chair and went back into the mid nineteenth century.

As per family lore, her ancestor from back then was a lowly serf living the life of a bonded labourer for a landlord family which owned huge tracts of land in the *terai* (marshy, lowland area south of the Himalayas) area of modern-day Pantnagar. He lived a desolate life, having run away from his original place of domicile, far to the South, in a village near Cawnpore (now Kanpur), to escape the law for having committed the murder of an Indian *sepoy* (soldier) in the military garrison of Cawnpore, over a dispute involving the locality's belle. Upon arriving at modern-day Pantnagar, then a village, he had taken up residence at another nearby village and had disguised himself by adorning the local clothes, changing his appearance and working in penury, even though back home his father was a *Munshi* (secretary) in the East India Company's employ. After spending a few months at the village, he fell in love with a widow of another *sepoy*, who had attained martyrdom with Elphinstone's army, which was massacred by the local Ghilzai warriors in that disastrous retreat from Kabul in 1842, amidst the treacherous gorges and passes along the Kabul River. The widow was bereft and was staying with her twin offspring (a boy and a girl) at her dead husband's parents' house in the heart of the village. She was well respected in the area as a martyr's widow and the daughter-in-law of a loyal retainer of the landlord.

But love changed her destiny and she eloped with Pratima's ancestor, six generations back, taking the twins along with her. The couple, with the toddlers, couldn't stay in the *terai* region, as the entire population was desperately searching for them and would have lynched the perpetrator of this ghastly act—Pratima's ancestor—and the widow, if they were ever found.

They couldn't go south, so they trekked northwards, climbing mountains after mountains till they reached a small hamlet in the midst of the Himalayas. There the generous Kumaonis provided them shelter and work for the able-bodied man. Miraculously, the twins survived and within a year of their arrival their mother gave birth to a bonny son (they had passed themselves off as a family escaping the clutches of the Britishers in the South). The seeds of the Pandey clan were sown by this eloped couple, and six generations and many branches later, Pratima was born at Bhojpur, as the third child of a school teacher and his diminutive, subservient wife. Pandeyji's wife, her mother, had taken a vow of celibacy after delivering two sons and a daughter and Pratima grew up in a patriarchal society reeking of misogyny.

Her father was deeply religious and strongly influenced by the age-old customs and traditions that guided his large clan and the society at large. As per these beliefs, daughters were supposed to be married off by the time they reached puberty and the groom and his family had to be given a huge dowry, depending on the stature of his family. The dowry was supposedly given to assist the groom and his family in providing for the additional member who would be joining their numbers after the marriage. Because her birth meant that a father had to start scrounging around to amass the dowry, a girl-child was considered a burden, first to her parents and after marriage to her husband's family, as she became an additional mouth to be fed.

'It's a surprise that I was not killed at birth. There were tales going around, of abandoned babies found frozen to death on the slopes of the hills or their half-eaten carcasses lying strewn around. Sometimes their bodies remained undiscovered, buried deep under the snow, till the ice thawed in the following spring and revealed the well-preserved corpses. And all of them were girls,' she said in a melancholy tone. 'From my own family, numerous aunts would mysteriously claim stillborns, whose infant, blue bodies, they said, were buried immediately after birth. I once saw one of my uncles and his teenage son taking an infant new born, bawling for love and life, towards the neighbouring hills and returning empty handed an hour later. My uncle's mother and his sisters had kept a malicious eye on the goings-on during the delivery of the child and goaded the males of the family to dispose off the girl-child. Sanjay, it was so miserable, you can't imagine. I was 6 years old then and had gone searching for the little child that night, hoping that I could save her life. I could never find her in the thick mountain jungle surrounding our village.'

She further added that since the people perceived a girl-child as a liability right from her birth, her parents had not to be additionally burdened with having to spend their meagre resources on her education. She was married off as soon as she reached puberty. She earned her real and only worth when she gave birth to a son herself. Most of the first-time mothers were children themselves, barely in their mid-teens, when they gave birth to their first child. And if that first child happened to be a girl, then she would have to give birth again and again till she produced a brood of male children. The fate of the mothers who birthed only girls (many of whom were abandoned) was miserable as they remained ostracised by their in-laws as well as their husbands, who, after a few births, having concluded that their wives' wombs only produced girls, would invariably marry again in pursuit of a male heir.

'And what happened to the ones who couldn't give birth?' I asked in sheer disbelief.

'They spent their lives as servants. Worse than servants even. They were branded as barren and would live in penury at their husbands' homes. He would remarry and all this would be ascribed to having been permitted by the religious scriptures and blessed by the Brahmin priest. So he had the spiritual right to marry again. But to treat the first wife as a servant, that is demeaning.'

'Why didn't the first wife return to her parents' home?'

'After her marriage a girl is the property of her husband. Post marriage she is not considered to have anything to do with her parents. Till 1956 she did not even have any right over her ancestral property. They have a saying in North India for girls, '*Doli Yahan Se, Arthi Wahan Se*' (you go from here on a palanquin, you will leave from there on a bier). In a world permeated by such prejudiced attitude, there is no life for a sterile woman. She is as good as dead.' My heart went out to her, hearing the despondence in her tone.

She looked at the clock, stood up suddenly, and said, 'It has been more than an hour and a half. I better get going.' I looked at her like a pupil admiring his favourite teacher. 'You must be wondering how I got here, with my father so mired in rigidity and stuck with those old traditions. That we will leave for tomo . . . for the next time. And loose that reverential look. I am not as beautiful as you make it out to be.' If only she knew how much beautiful she looked in my infatuated eyes. And this on our first date!

She turned and walked away. I called out as she was nearing the door, 'When shall we meet again?'

She halted in her stride, turned her head, sending her tresses in a long shallow arc and beamed a bewitching smile, 'I will let you know. You are a good listener.'

I picked up the barely consumed cup of tea left by her and gulped it down in a single swallow. Imagining her lips on the rim of the cup, I ran the tip of my tongue along the fringe, presuming that this was the very spot where she had pursed her lips to take sips. Is there another heaven? I immediately gagged on the thick layer of cream, the tepid, foul-tasting beverage, and the dregs I had swallowed. No wonder she had scarcely touched her tea. It appeared to have been made by Bindu and she had established that she was no gourmet cook, which she had often boasted of.

Bindu was snoozing on the couch in the living room, her siblings were nowhere to be seen and her mother was still inside her bedroom. I tiptoed out of the house and out on the road I strutted like a peacock with his feathers spread out while he performed his mating dance.

4

The Rumination: Plight of a Girl-Child

I had listened with rapt attention to Pratima's fascinating narrative of murder and love, of sad beginning and happy ending, of birth and death and for the first time in my life I felt angry at a world which treated its women with such disdain. Up until then I had been living in a cocooned world created by the social circle my grandparents and parents had weaved around me, where everything seemed hunky dory. But there was a different realm out there, another dimension of our own world, full of male chauvinists who were so consumed by their fanaticism that they would kill a fellow human, their own child. They must be thinking that abandoning a child at a desolate slope, on a chilly night, was not as bad as killing her, thus absolving themselves of the sin, but I think it is one and the same. The very people, who curse *Kansa* for killing his infant nephews and celebrate Lord Krishna's triumph over his evil uncle, go on killing their own children. Which religion permits this? A pervert mind might still be excused, if he found a sinister motive in *Kansa* killing his sister's infant sons, as he had believed in that divine pronouncement of his impending death at the hands of his sister's eighth-born son. But what is the purpose in killing your own newborn, except sheer malevolence. Who authorises it? Is religion their vindication? But whose religion? My religion definitely does not allow it. Or does it? Male preference maybe, but killing your own child? A shiver ran through my soul as I pondered such draconian practices. A ghastly thought crept into me, 'Do these people mutter prayers as they abandon their child? Do they ask God to forgive them after they returned home?'

I recalled a recent conversation I had overheard between Mother and *BB Mausi*, during the last vacations, when they were discussing a woman from an upper caste family in Agra. She had just given birth and her mother-in-law, after snatching the wailing, newborn girl from her exhausted but jubilant mother's bosom, had placed the infant on the ground and after planting a leg of an empty cot upon her tiny, almost nonexistent throat, she had sat atop the cot with her 100-kilogram bulk and shouted vehemently, 'Go, go . . . go away. Send your brother in your stead,' while the enfeebled mother of the dead infant pleaded all the time with her mother-in-law to let the child live. Which God would ever forgive that?

I shuddered in dread.

The lesser ghoulish amongst such she-devils of mothers-in-law are known to have poured tobacco leaves down their sons' infant daughters' throats to get rid of them and the father of the child was invariably a collaborative onlooker.

Nature is made in a manner that parents take care of the well-being of their children, ensuring their safety and grooming them to be prepared for the future challenges of their lives, as they grow in years. This enables the next generation to take on the world on their own when their time comes. Look at the animals and birds. A lioness never abandons her cubs, she moves them around clutched in her powerful jaws till they are able to walk by themselves, she feeds them first before feeding herself. A cow crocodile moves her hatchlings clamped in her jaws, from the place where they hatch to the safety of the water. A bird feeds her chicks from her own mouth, never swallowing the food herself, even if she might be suffering from severe pangs of hunger. Parents not only have the responsibility to look after their offspring, to ensure their well-being, but it is also their debt to nature (God!) for having given them the ability to reproduce and procreate. That debt is not repaid till they have ensured that their descendants have learned the ways of the world and can live with absolute independence. And here we have humans who kill their children just because they are born differently, not according to their stereotypical mindsets! For the first time in my life, I felt sorry for the human race.

God created woman after his own image. That's why she is so beautiful. Modern woman is the most beautiful creature amongst the hominids. Right from the time our ancestors climbed down from their lairs amongst the trees (not that I subscribe to Darwin always) and started walking on their hind limbs, leading to the humans diverging from the chimps some seven million years ago, till the modern age, there has been no species that has produced any female equivalent as beautiful as the modern woman. Not the hominines, not the Neanderthals, not the Cro-Magnons or the early modern humans. And it is such a pity that there are people in our society who kill their child, this wonderful being who would grow up into a beautiful woman—just to ease their burden? Morbid, morbid, and morbid.

But who created this burden? Is it only because, by their very birth, they carried the tag of dowry, that girls are discriminated against? God did not create the practice of dowry, but he did create that child (here Darwin takes a beating—I did not know then how babies were created, but there was God's hand in it, no doubt; Mother always used to say that babies are born by God's grace). Dowry, as a custom, is the handiwork of humans. And since mankind reposes such faith in God, why extinguish a God-given gift when you can easily destroy a human-created ritual?

No, Pratima's explanation was too simplistic for this gender discrimination. The actual interpretation was much more complex, sinister even, than Pratima's version. Should a man kill his own child just because he would have to give dowry in the future? (I always presumed, in my musing, that killing, or abandoning, if that sounds better, his daughter would always have the tacit approval of her father). No, he will not do that just because he is apprehensive of an uncertain future. After all, what is dowry but an exchange of money and property? A father could earn the money or acquire the property in his lifetime and pay the dowry.

But what about the plight of the father? He would have slaved all through his life to save that money, to amass that property, which he could have used in his old age, when he would require it the most, as he would have reached a stage of nonproductive existence then. And in that old age, or well before that, he would have to dish out his life savings to gift his son-in-law and his family. For what? For agreeing to marry his daughter!

That was dismal.

Lost in my thoughts, arguments, and counterarguments, I had involuntarily reached the base of the stairway leading to the famous Golu Devta Temple. Arriving at a decision, I climbed up the steps. The peals of the thousands of bells which devotees had left tied to the branches and trunks of the trees, to the strings strung on the walls and around the pillars in the temple premises, strengthened my resolve with each step. There was a large group of people who were sounding these bells, invoking the deity's blessings.

I pushed through the throng and knelt at the threshold of the door opening on to the small shrine of the deity and vowed that neither my family nor I would take dowry in my marriage.

That was the first of many such decisions I have since taken in my life, which today define my principles and beliefs and guide me in my struggles through life. They are my keystones which define my way of living in this prejudiced world. They contain the answers I seek whenever I am mired in doubts about the ways of the world.

5

The Rumination: Bereft of Choice

I found a secluded corner in the temple premises and sat down. The sun was hanging low on top of the jagged peaks dotting the western horizon, which was filled with layers of myriad colours ranging from orange to yellow to pink to red to magenta and I was once again filled with thoughts of the wonders of nature. As I sat contemplating the various types of animals, their lives, their habitats, their offspring, I noticed the sudden silence that had descended upon the surroundings. The group of devotees had left and their chimes and chants were slowly replaced by the chirps of the mothers returning to their nests from a hard day's labour spent in foraging, to feed their chicks.

I returned to the predicament of girl-child and the gender discrimination in our society.

An image emerged in my mind of a person clad in a black cloak, completely covered from head to toe, with a net sewed into the cloak to cover an opening in front of the eyes, crossing the street in front of our house, as I sat discussing mundane things with Mother, waiting for Father's return from work, one evening some five years back, at Hospet. I had enquired from Mother about the cloak and she had replied that the person was a Muslim woman and the cloak was called *Burqa*.

'But how could you make out that she is a woman?' I had asked in my puerile innocence. 'And why should she wear a *Burqa*?'

She had replied that it was a custom amongst the Muslims to make their women wear *Burqa* whenever they ventured out of their homes. It was done to ensure their own safety, so that the men folk do not see their faces and bare limbs, and be tempted with bad thoughts to hurt them. If men can't see their faces no harm would come to them.

'What bad thoughts would the men be tempted with? What harm would men do to the women if they saw their faces?' I had asked earnestly.

She had said that men would beat them and hurt them in other ways.

'But men can beat them still, even if they are in *Burqa*, because they would know that there is a woman in there, as men do not wear *Burqa*. What are the other ways in which women can be harmed by such vicious men who beat women?'

Getting fed up with my inquiries, she had chided me for being too inquisitive, told me to wait till I grew up and understood the world better and had shooed me off to go complete my homework.

Now, as a 13-year-old, I still didn't know what those other ways were, in which a man could physically harm a woman. I had heard a classmate of mine mentioning something called rape—a bad deed which vicious men do to docile, nubile girls, but did not know what it encompasses; must be some kind of physical torture. I had not yet seen *Premrog* and did not know much about a woman's honour and prestige and its loss. What Moushumi Chatterjee had suffered in *Roti Kapda Aur Makaan* had seemed more like a physical torture by three villainous men covering her in flour, to my 7-year-old mind when I had seen the movie in '76?

Now that I thought of it, another image came to my mind—that of Mother and my married aunts wearing saris and covering their heads with the loose ends of their saris (*Pallu*). In the presence of my grandfather (when he had been alive), or other elders of the family, or when outsiders came calling to our house, or whenever they themselves ventured out of the house, they would pull the *Pallu* down and cover their faces like a veil. It was not as if they were clad in a *Burqa* but the effect was something akin to it; hide the face. Mother did not cover her head when we used to go to her father's home at Jaswantnagar or when we were staying at Dalmiapuram and Hospet away from my hometown, but always covered it and hid her face in the presence of elders and outsiders, whenever we were at Shanti Bhavan in my hometown or when Father's brothers used to visit us down south.

That had seemed strange whenever I witnessed it but I had never enquired about it from Mother. I knew that she would give the same reply as for that *Burqa* clad Muslim woman.

I was not aware of the temptations that bothered the women, that would make men fall prey to, if they a saw woman's face, which forced them to cover their faces with a *Burqa* or a sari's *Pallu*, but I could never imagine that my kind-hearted uncles, or my stern, strict grandfather with a genial heart or the extremely polite visitors to our house, would ever lift a hand to harm the women of my family.

There has to be more to it. There was a deliberateness in forcing women to behave in a particular fashion. As a young, unmarried girl, she was allowed to wear a salwar suit or a sari. In some middle class families, young girls, till their early teens, were even permitted to wear skirts and frocks. But a married girl or woman has to always wear saris. Even girls married off in their teens, or even before, have to wear saris. I have never seen Mother or her sisters or my aunts from my father's side, married or unmarried, ever wear anything but sari, in my entire life. They even have a 'sleeping sari', the one they would wear when retiring for the night. Mother wore a sari when she went to the bathroom to bathe and change into her fresh clothes inside the small cubicle, before emerging freshly bathed, a sweet scent of motherly aroma redolent of fresh water, soap, shampoo, and Pond's talcum powder drifting in her wake—it was the one thing I used to get up early in the morning for, as a kid; to revel in the mesmerising fragrance of Mother after she emerged from the bathroom. I used to feel so much love and affection for her that it sent shooting pin pricks into my belly with attendant soft aches.

Another macabre thought struck me. This straitjacketing of women, by limiting the choice of clothes they could wear, by forcing them to cover their faces or their entire bodies so that men do not get bad thoughts (but why get bad thoughts in the first place?), by restricting them from viewing the outside world in its entirety, had a sinister design. Women are being cowed down by not allowing them to choose. And it starts right from their birth.

A midwife spanks a child so that it can open its airways by inhaling its first breath in the crying process and thereby opening up the mucous membrane covering its nose and mouth. This gives it the choice of either to breathe and live or to remain inert and perish. If the father or the child's grandmother discovers that it is a girl and doesn't want her to live, he (she) could ask the midwife not to open her airways and in the process take away the child's right to choose between life and death.

Even if he (she) does allow her airways to be opened or if the midwife is not pliant enough to abide by his (her) wishes, he (she) takes away the child's choice of living a life by abandoning her on a lonely hill slope, left there to wither away and die or be consumed by the wild animals.

A child, if she decides to live, would suckle her mother's breasts for her first feed or could choose to die by refusing to be nursed. By leaving her abandoned at the mercy of the elements and wild animals, she is being denied her right to choose between life and death. She is left for dead.

Later as she grows in years she is denied the right to choose education (in certain societies, like Pratima's). No school for her, no knowledge of the outside world, no exposure to the wealth of wisdom contained in the books, no right to choose her station in life. She will forever remain dependent upon the men in her life, hoping for generosity from the domineering males, always living a life of servitude, lest the men be offended by her and consign her to poverty.

When she becomes a mother herself, she can't even choose whether her infant girl would live or die. She herself lies exhausted from the efforts of the child birth, with no strength left in her to defend her new born, as the males and geriatric females of the family dispose of the child. Hell! Even animals have the right to defend their infants.

She can't choose what she wants to do with her life, hers is not to choose but to do and die. Where is the right of choice in a life which follows an unbroken pattern—as an infant she is tolerated (if she is allowed to live at all) whereas her male siblings are indulged in, their every whim met (I have seen this discrimination in my own household, after the fourth girl-child was born in our family, to another of Father's younger brothers two years back); as a toddler she is just accepted as part of the family but not allowed to engage in the games the boys indulge in, not even permitted out of the house to play with the neighbours lest she be kidnapped, if she has sisters or female cousins in the family she can afford company, otherwise it is dolls and sticks for her; in her preteens she has to be groomed for a future life of a dutiful wife, an attentive daughter-in-law, a caring mother, an indulgent sister-in-law, whereas her brothers go to school, get educated, be knowledgeable, seek recognition, secure jobs, shine in life; by the time she reaches puberty, she is married off to a boy who is himself an adolescent or, if she is unlucky, to a much older man, chosen and selected by her parents, a process in which she has absolutely no say; at an age when she should be going to school and playing with other children of her age, she becomes a mother, and if the child is a girl herself, she can't even choose whether the child will live or die, others choose for her; as her children grow she doesn't have a say in their destiny, her husband and other male members in the family decide her children's future; if her husband passes away while she is still alive, she can't choose a different life for herself, she would have to spend the rest of her life in mourning, consigned to an isolated corner of her house, wearing a white sari, her shorn head permanently hanging in docile subservience; and when her time comes, she would get a pyre and a fire, memories of her too consigned to the roaring flames eating away her flesh and bones—no family tree mentions the maternal lineage, it's always the paternal links which are drawn.

Women in our society, right from their childhood till they breathe their last, always eat the leftovers of the meals consumed by the male members. Mother always ate the remains of the food after we had had our fill. And sometimes, especially during my school vacations when I would eat like a glutton, only few morsels would be left for her, barely enough to sustain her, but the poor soul never complained.

It all boiled down to denial, repudiation of a woman's right to live her life on her own terms, abrogation of her capacity to choose what is right for her. She has to conform to the rules set for her by the men.

I shook my head to clear my mind off such gloomy thoughts and walked over to Golu Devta's shrine again. I prayed for daughters in my future and pledged that I would never treat my daughters the way the rest of the society treats theirs, I vowed that I would give them the same opportunities others give to their sons, I promised that I would let them choose what they would want to do with their lives, including the husbands they would want to take as their soulmates.

That seemed a bit overblown for a 13-year-old, but it cheered me up and I sauntered back to my House, whistling a merry tune, the charming visage of Pratima floating in front of my eyes.

6

The Scrofulous Society in the Future

I waited impatiently for a message fixing our next meeting. It didn't happen for one full week, which seemed like an eon, time crawling at a snail's pace. I often caught glimpses of Pratima in the school and wanted to walk up to her, but that would have embarrassed her. I went to the library on frequent occasions so that I could meet her there and get a word in, but to no avail, as she never visited the library that entire week. I met Bindu daily at her school, during the tea breaks, but she did not have any fresh message. I even went to Dviwedi Sir's house on Wednesday and when Bindu shook her head in negation, I asked her to pass a message to her from my side, but she replied that Pratima had told her she would let her know herself, when the time was right.

By Saturday, pessimism set in: 'She doesn't want to see me. She has decided I am too young for her. So stupid of me to ask her to open her heart and talk about her life. What had gotten into me to ask her that? Sanjay you are a fool. You were so nervous she must have concluded that you are not suited for her. You will never be successful with girls. You are an utter failure. You are just a kid. She doesn't want anything to do with you anymore.'

I was chiding myself thus disdainfully, as Dwivedi Sir was explaining the formula to derive compound interest in our maths class. The bell chimed, signalling the end of our class and Dwivedi Sir beckoned me over, 'Sanjay, what's wrong with you today? You were not paying attention at all. You look glum and aloof. Anyway, Bindu asked you to meet her at four. She said you had forgotten something at our house the other day. Do come over. I will not be there, as I have to go to Nainital with the class trip of tenth class students.'

A cheer went to my heart and I beamed at him, 'Thank you sir. I will be there sir. I think I had left my handkerchief during my last visit.' I almost hugged him.

'You are acting strange today. One moment you were as sad as a shrivelled rose and now you are beaming like a Christmas tree,' with that he strolled away.

I was at Dwivedi Sir's place at half past three and waited impatiently in Bindu's room. At four she entered the room. Bindu did not accompany her this time and there was no tea—she must have warned Bindu not to serve that vile concoction, if it was prepared by her.

'You first today. What did you do in the past one week?' was her opening sentence.

I told her that I had spent the last seven days in anticipation of today's meeting, that I had visited the library so often that even the librarian had gotten suspicious, that I had lost interest in my studies Wednesday onwards, that I had been filled with gloomy thoughts the entire seven days that she would not see me again, ever. Then I told her about my reflections on our earlier conversation.

After I had finished narrating my ruminations, a prescient thought occurred to me. I said, 'A society that kills its girls would suffer one day. What happens if, after all these killings, they can't find enough brides for their privileged sons? Today the sex ratio in our country is not so skewed, but in a not-so-distant future, maybe in the next generation itself, there will be lesser girls and more boys. Where will they get the brides from, so that their next generation is born? I don't know how babies are born, but they do not come out of thin air nor do they drop from the heavens. And they are born only to women. So, take a group with, hypothetically speaking, 1,000 families, who only marry within their own social circle. Barring a few families, let's take a figure of 300 families, which decide to bring up a girl each, the rest of the families only have boys. I think 30 per cent is a fair estimate.'

'I am liking this. I love the way you put it across. Go on,' she said enthusiastically.

'The balance 700 families will each have four to five boys. And those 300 families, which despite their preference for boys, decided to have a girl each among their brood, will also have two to three boys each. So they will have thousands of boys of marriageable age but only 300 girls, give a few more as some families may have two girls. And then, they will stop killing their girls.'

'You are oversimplifying with your figures; the effect of Bindu's father is rubbing off on you I presume. By your hypothesis, this society should realise within one generation that the sex ratio has gone awry and put a halt to the ghastly practice to set matters right. But killing of girls at birth has been going on for the past so many generations and nobody has vehemently called for a public outcry to put a stop to it. There have been activists, but they are few and far between and no one pays heed to them anyway. Taking your scenario, most of those 1,000 families will have sons who could not marry for various reasons: they maybe imbecile, born with a defect, too mired in poverty that no one would give them their daughters, so grotesque looking that nobody in his right mind would consider them a suitable match, afflicted with some deformity which would eliminate them from the marriage market and some who would prefer to stay single all their lives. In my own larger family, there have been five great-great and great uncles, whom I know of, who died a bachelor. Currently there are three uncles in their fifties but single; one is imbecile, the second is hunchbacked, and the third has taken a vow of celibacy. So no, I beg to differ. This mathematical analysis of yours does not hold water.'

'What is celibacy?' I interjected. 'You mentioned it the other day too, but I forgot to look it up.'

'It's a condition where a man does not take a wife,' she replied.

'But if this killing continues unabated, sometime in the distant future, if not in the not-so-distant future I mentioned earlier, the ratio will get skewed and then the elders would realise that enough was enough and would ostracise those families which kill their daughters, because the very existence of the future generations will be affected if they couldn't get enough brides from within their own rigid social circles, for their sons. They will listen to the mother's pleas to let her daughter live, grant her the right to save her child, which is every mother's bounden duty. They will give women the due respect they deserve.'

'Who says they will restrict themselves to their own social circle or caste in search for the brides?' She retorted in excitement.

'What do you mean?' I was really enjoying this, all the nervousness of last Saturday having evaporated in the warmth of her company and in the heated discussion.

'I do not believe in crystal-gazing, it's a worthless exercise. But I can make predictions based on cool logic and raw statistical data at hand. People are fanatics and maniacally radical in their mindsets and too stereotypical in their attitudes and beliefs. They will never change. Women have always been treated with disdain and contempt over the past so many millennia. The misogyny of the present-day modern society has deep roots; in our history, in our customs, in our traditions, in our rituals, in our scriptures, even in our modern laws and the constitution. Look at the Hindu Succession Act; I don't even have equal right on our ancestral property, as my brothers have. So, to say that people would have a dramatic change of heart and would start considering us women as equals; that's an idea which is too far-fetched, too absurd to even ponder over. Men have always loved to keep women under their thumb and feet, to treat us as second-class citizens, to consider us too lowly, too inferior to them. And they are not going to let go of that feeling of superiority, of haughty arrogance. People are too pertinacious to change.'

She shifted forward in her chair and raised her hands up to her chest, palms facing towards me, as if she wanted to push her arguments into me.

I made a mental note to look up 'pertinacious' in the dictionary. 'God, she is brilliant, she has such a fine vocabulary.' I also moved closer to her and we sat within sniffing distance of each other. My olfactory senses picked up a whiff of a glorious lemony perfume. 'Did she wear that for me? That's progress! Surely she couldn't have worn it in the morning for the classes, else the teachers would have admonished her for acting too pretentious.'

'So this is my prediction,' she continued while my mind was churning with an unlikely possibility. 'In the distant future, maybe in the next two to three generations, certain sections of our society, a few of those castes within castes, possibly my own people, will start feeling the pinch, so to say, of this deplorable practice of preference for boys and in turn killing their infant girls. As you so succinctly put it, they will not find adequate number of girls within their own social circle to marry their well-generated and preserved huge population of boys. They will then get girls from outside their own rigid society and marry them off to their sons to procreate.'

'You mean to say that they will change their age-old traditions of marrying within their community just to assure themselves of their superior status over women?'

'You have drawn up to a conclusion in your own convoluted way, but you are dead right. Yes, that's what I think will come to pass, ultimately.'

'That people are too per . . . perti . . ., what was that word you used? . . . Too pertipacious to change.'

'Pertinacious. It means holding on tenaciously to one's beliefs or opinions. It's a synonym for obstinate. And there is no word called pertipacious. And yes, people will not change their psyche with regards to treatment of women.'

'What is the statistical data for your prognosis?'

'What do you mean?'

'You had said earlier that you base your predictions on cool logic and raw statistical data at hand. Your cool logic was brilliantly analysed and commendable. So, what is the statistics on which you have based your forecast?'

'You do pay attention to everything I say. You repeated my exact words.'

'And I won't let you off so easily.' I chimed.

'True enough. I have based my prophecy on the sex ratio of our country. As per available data, since 1901 till 1971, the figure for number of women per 1,000 men has hovered between 930 and 972. Over the decades, there has been a steady decline of 6 women per 1,000 men every decade. The highest ratio of 972 was in the decade ending 1901 and the lowest of 930 in the decade ending 1971. It has not always been a steady fall of 6 women per 1,000 men over the decades. The highest declines were of 11 women per 1,000 men in the decades ending 1921 and 1971, whereas there was an increase of one woman per 1,000 men in the decade ending 1951. But the average works out to a decline of 6 women per 1,000 men, every decade. So, including the previous decade, the census of which I have not been able to access yet, and continuing this trend of decline, by the end of the fourth decade from now, that's two generations hence, the sex ratio will drop down to 900 women per 1,000 men, by the year 2021. That's not as bad as that scientific analysis you put across, of thousands of boys for a mere few hundred girls.'

'My God! You have such a brilliant mind. How do you retain these figures?' I exclaimed.

She seemed abashed, a faint blush creeping up her cheekbones. She had suddenly gone silent and was staring at her toes, as if lost in her thoughts. A frown creased her forehead, as if her mind was in turmoil. Her mental discomfort put a strange thought in my mind. Here was a beautiful girl sitting in front of me, who possessed the most brilliant mind I have ever come across in my life, her exceptional vocabulary and her ability to recall figures instantaneously testimony to that, who seemed so interested on reading any and every thing on earth (else how should she be knowing these census figures), who appeared to crave knowledge as an infant hankers for her mother's milk, who puts such persuasive logic to her assertions—and she still felt ill at ease upon being praised for her supreme intellect. She had by now demonstrated that she did not agree with the way the society behaved, but she was not comfortable at being commended for her intelligence. When I had commented abruptly, the other day, on her beauty, she had taken it in her stride, but when appreciated for her brains, she exhibited disquiet; as if she was concerned of anyone finding out her brilliance. If this gifted girl is so disturbed, think of the others who are not so talented. I presumed she would never be raising her hand in class to answer a teacher's question voluntarily, even when she knew the answer. Her reluctance in acknowledging her own brilliance affirmed my conclusion that this prejudice is too ingrained in our society to be erased easily. It is not the men only who are oppressive; the women are at fault too, for accepting their male counterpart's arrogance. God! If this bigotry has sunk in to such deep levels, it will take centuries to transform the society for the better. I decided to change her mentality for a start, and said, as she continued looking down at her toes, her mouth clammed shut, 'Pratima, you don't have to be ashamed of being so intelligent. You should flaunt your brilliance. You are the most amazing girl I have ever met; so beautiful, so smart. Let the entire world know how brilliant you are.'

She looked up and beamed a hesitant but dazzling smile, 'Thanks Sanjay. You do know how to cheer me up. You are the third person in my life to have commented upon my intellect. I have never been complimented for my brains by anyone else because of my elder brother, not so much the younger one. He is more like you: "Tell everyone you are smarter than them," the younger brother asserts. But the elder one says that I have a photographic memory, that I can retain vivid impressions of any and every thing I examine. And after he had discovered this ability of mine he had said not to ever let it be known that I was so intelligent. He warned me that if Father ever found out that I was supremely talented, he would marry me off without a second thought, as in our caste it is extremely difficult to get a suitable husband for intelligent girls. The moment it came out that I possessed such intellect, all boys in our community would shirk away and Father wouldn't risk that. So if it came to his notice that I was smart he would immediately terminate my studies and send me away in marriage. Hence no raising of hands in class for me, I deliberately give wrong answers if asked a question, I answer as many questions in the tests and exams that I am barely able to achieve pass marks, I flunk in my class tests and half yearly exams so as to make Father request for grace marks from the class teacher to get me promoted, year after year. I continue the charade at home, too. No reading books in front of Father, locking myself up in my room to read and study, goofing up on the homework so that the teacher has to complain to my father about my shoddiness, going to the library on the pretext of borrowing a book for one of my brothers; all to hide my brilliance from Father. Oh Sanjay! It's so miserable, but it is essential too.'

The warmth of her emotions washed over me like a waterfall. I moved my chair closer to her and held her hands, softly squeezing them, and in walked Bindu. I did not notice her gawking at the tableau on display. She cleared her throat and I released Pratima's hands with a start, upon hearing her sound and slid back into my chair, a rush of crimson filling my cheeks. She smiled in a sheepish manner at us and asked, 'Shall I get some tea? Rekha *Didi* has agreed to brew it for all of us.'

I raised an eyebrow at Pratima who shook her head and I said, 'Thanks Bindu, but no thanks. We are comfortable.'

'Okey-dokey. You are indeed comfortable,' she chimed and shrugging her shoulders, slipped out.

We looked at each other for a long time. I drowned in her eyes. Gasping for breath, I drew my eyes away and said, 'But I won't let you leave me in the lurch.'

She relaxed. 'What do you mean?'

'You still haven't explained that statistical data of yours. We diverged.'

'All your fault. Anyway. Where was I? You broke the chain, now reattach the links.'

I retraced a few steps and said, 'You had found a glaring fault with my arithmetic. You had brought out that by 2021 there will be 900 women to every 1,000 men.'

'Oh yes,' she took up the refrain there onwards, 'while the all-India percentage of women will be 47.4 per cent of the entire population (she was just too brilliant, she had worked out the percentage in a jiffy, while I had only reached the 9-divided-by-19 stage), there will be certain sections in our society, the ones who are obstinately involved in the vile practice of killing their infant girls, whose women will number 30 per cent of the entire population. So there will be 20 per cent more men than women in that section of society. Now imagine that this section is confined to a geographic region, say a state or an area like my village and other adjoining villages. They will have more boys of marriageable age, than girls. The future of their group will be at stake. If there are no brides, there will be no babies, and they will become extinct sometime in the future. But there will be other regions and states in the country where the sex ratio will not be so skewed, especially in the Southern states. So the elders of this depleted section of society would decide to get brides from the South. How will they accomplish that? They would buy brides, kidnap them, lure girls from poor families, give bride price to the girl's family and such like. And these procured brides will ensure that their future generations flourish.'

'But aren't marriages fixed between specific groups? Caste, subcaste, lineage, and clan play a big role in nuptial arrangements.'

'That's true for now. But rules, customs, traditions, they all get hammered on the anvil of convenience and moulded to suit necessity. That is how societies evolve. If a particular custom becomes too tiresome to maintain, it can be discarded. Modern Western influences have, in the past few centuries, had a great influence in the banning of certain barbaric traditions, like the practice of *Sati*. Even widows are allowed to remarry now. History has been witness to earth-shattering changes in the way people live, especially with the spread of Christianity and Islam. How did Islam evolve and spread as a religion in Asia? It had come about in the early seventh century AD because of the dogmatic way of life in the Arabia, which was divisive. It expanded because it propagated the message of universal brotherhood in a world stricken with the menace of divisions by caste, creed, race, colour, etc. People turned to Islam because their own circumstances were threatening their way of life; their very existence was at stake. When the Muslims first came to India as Arab traders in the seventh century and later as Afghan and Turkic invaders in the twelfth century, thus establishing the Delhi Sultanate which from the thirteenth century lasted till the Mughals came in 1526—they influenced the social structure prevailing in those times. These Muslims carried the message of universal brotherhood, which particularly appealed to the lower caste and outcaste Hindus who converted en masse to Islam to escape a life of drudgery and slavery which gave no assurance of survival of their future generations.

'Going by this analogy, I predict that in the distant future, maybe in our own lifetimes, the rigid marriage rules will be renounced by certain sections of our society. Today marriages are arranged between same caste families, where the families of the prospective bride and groom are scrutinised by one another in great detail, which includes the examination of their ancestry, their subcaste, their lineage, their standing in society, their financial status, and myriad other parameters. But due to the necessity of ensuring their group's survival, these niceties will be done away with. The only criteria for the selection of the bride will be that she should be able to bear children, and that too, only boys. They still won't abandon their misogynist attitude and will go on killing their daughters at birth. That's Darwin's theory for you, in its convoluted form, in the badlands of North India. A scrofulous society in the future,' she almost spat out the last sentence.

I stared spellbound at her for a long time, amazed at the flush of energy which had made her face even more enchanting, if at all that were possible. I shook my head to escape those spiral pools of her eyes, swallowed a huge gulp and said, 'That was brilliant. If I could I would applaud loudly,' and I clapped with soft hands.

She stood up and gave a dramatic bow as if she were on stage having just delivered a stupendous performance and was drinking in the adulations of the audience.

I also stood up and added, 'And that is why I took two pledges last Saturday.'

'What? Where? When? To whom?'

Then I told her that, to clear the gloom that had descended upon me like a dark ominous cloud, as a consequence of my preoccupation with the thoughts of the plight of a girl-child and the denial of choice to girls, right from their birth, I had approached Golu Devta and taken the two vows.

After listening to the solemn promises I had made to the deity, she said, 'My, my. What age are you, again?'

'Thirteen.'

'I am impressed. Keep this up and you will grow up faster than you notice. Will you really not take dowry? Will you defy your father if he did not agree with you and took it on the sly?'

'I will never take dowry. If Father takes it, I will return whatever portion he gives to me to my wife's father and the balance which my father would keep, I will return from my own earnings. If he takes it clandestinely, for keeps, I will find out from my wife and do the needful. But I won't let the girl's father suffer.'

She leaned across and touched my hands softly. This was the first time she had voluntarily touched me and it sent shivers up my arm. She must have felt it too for she shrank back and sat down.

'By the way, what does that word *scrofulous* mean?' I asked while I was also taking my seat.

'It means morally degenerate, corrupt. It is also related to scrofula, a form of tuberculosis most common in children, affecting the lymph nodes, especially in the neck, and is usually spread by unpasteurised milk from infected cows. I like to use the word to describe someone's vile character.'

'How did you improve your vocabulary?'

'From the moment I was eleven I have been fascinated with the English language. I had asked my younger brother then to get me a dictionary and he had purchased the third edition of the *Oxford Advanced Learner's Dictionary* from Nainital. Father had refused to dish out the money for the purchase, so both my brothers saved their entire monthly pocket money Father used to give them, never a pie to me, for six months, and having accumulated the cash, my younger brother went to Nainital one Sunday and bought the dictionary for me: so sweet of my brothers. Father was told that it was for their own use. But, despite my eidetic memory, it was difficult to remember all those words in the dictionary. So I chalked out a strategy. Each day, locked inside my room, when Father was not in the house, I would look up ten new words in the dictionary and write down five sentences each, incorporating the words I had read. That way I remembered the words and learned to use them too. By now I have completed fifteen thick registers, with my words and sentences. And it's a work still in progress.'

'Can I borrow those registers? I want to improve my vocabulary too.'

'I keep the dictionary and the registers in my brothers' room, away from my parents' prying eyes. The registers have got the words in alphabetical order. I will give you the one containing A and B the next time we meet. You should copy those and make your own registers; you will have to go through the words again and again in future to refresh, that's how they will get cemented in your mind. When you finish with the first register, give it back to me and I will give you the next.'

My heart filled with profound gratitude for the readiness with which she had accepted to share her private possessions with me.

7

The Month Long Hellish Ordeal

She looked at the clock and said with a sigh, 'Time slips by so fast. I love talking with you. But now it's my turn to continue my monologue . . . What? Have you forgotten that I had not yet commenced my life story last Saturday? Where did we leave the other day? Ummmm . . . got it. I was born in a patriarchal family amidst a misogynist society which killed their girls at birth to avoid the burden. That was seventeen years back. I am grateful to my father for not having consigned me to my fate and abandoning me, like so many others. Maybe he had thought that he already had two sons and he could afford to raise a daughter. But what I think must have gone through his mind was a surge of emotion which would have overwhelmed him on seeing me suckling my mother's breasts—that's a comfortable thought and that's what I see in him, sometimes. Despite his dogged adherence to rigid societal norms, many a time I have seen such warmth in his eyes when he looks at me that I get this prickly feeling that he adores me. He is a good man, despite his many shortcomings. But life was no stroll in a park for me.'

As a toddler she was proclaimed the most beautiful child ever born in the village. Her brothers doted upon her; they used to always accompany her, whenever she ventured out of her house, when they were home. She used to only feel safe when they were around her.

Back in the village, her father was a teacher in a school at Pithoragarh. Her brothers studied in the same school and would walk the fifteen kilometres' distance with their father every weekday, leaving their house in the wee hours and returning late in the evening. On school days, Pratima's life was tedious and lonely. She was not allowed out of her house and remained under the strict vigil of her mother. She spent the day confined to her room or roaming around the house, while her mother was occupied

39

in domestic chores. On rare occasions, when her mother had to go out to make some purchases from the only shop in the village or go visiting her relatives and acquaintances, she would take Pratima along with her, lugging the little toddler on her hip or dragging her through the winding lanes. Pratima loved those occasions when she used to meet and play with her cousins. Sometimes they also used to come over to her house, along with their respective mothers, for fun and frolic. On weekends and holidays, she could go out and play with her brothers, with strict instructions that she would never let them out of her sight. Whenever her brothers used to get engaged in playing with the other boys—'How long could two teenaged boys keep themselves occupied with little me, they had other temptations'— she would slip away and go to her cousins' houses to play. Late in the afternoon, the brothers would locate her after frantic searches from house to house, admonish her jocularly for abandoning their company and hoisting a cackling Pratima upon their shoulders they took her home; but they never let it out to their parents. It was a secret the siblings kept to themselves.

Her elder brother was of a serious nature, right from his childhood days. He was the studious kind, always buried in books when at home, fastidious in his homework, meticulous in keeping his routine devoid of any turbulence and simply adored his 'little princess'. When she had reached the age of three, he commenced her tutorials. She loved the pains he took in explaining the English alphabet to her and the secret nuances in pronouncing the words, which 'strangely followed their own deviously concocted pattern', unlike the Devnagari script of Hindi in which the words were pronounced the way they were written. She had initially found it extremely difficult to understand why 'put' and 'but' and such like words were spoken differently, even though they had the same vowel. After learning the Hindi alphabet and its usage she had concluded that the English-speaking people were too miserly, 'they had put only five vowels and twenty-one consonants, so they invented different ways in which these meagre letters were used to construct a word. And why have they got this fixation for long words by adding all those silent letters? Knowledge could easily be written as n-a-o-l-e-j. He used to smile at me and exhort me to learn harder, whenever I let go of my frustrations.'

Her mother always objected to these tutorials and often grumbled about, while kneading the dough: 'What use will all these lessons be to her?

Her fate has been destined by God; betrothal at nine, marriage at twelve, and children by thirteen or fourteen. I never touched a book in my life and I am none the lesser for it.' She used to hate her mother whenever she spoke thus. By the time she reached five, it had become amply clear to her that God had nothing to do with her destiny, that it was her parents who had designed it.

She had often whispered, in secret tones, to her brothers that she wanted to study, that she desired to explore the world contained in those books, that she wanted to learn new things like them. She often saw a fire of determination in her elder brother's eyes, whenever she used to express her wishes and she wondered about the cause for its intensity.

'Father was obstinate. I could learn as much as I wanted from my brothers, but there would be no formal schooling for me. He used to declare that none of his brothers and cousins had had their daughters educated in any school whatsoever and he did not want to be the first in his family to start a nefarious trend and be an object of ridicule in the village and society. Despite my brothers' numerous pleadings to send me to an all-girls school at Pithoragarh, he was relentless and never budged an inch from his staunchly held belief, supported enthusiastically by my mother.'

Things came to a boil one day when, a few days short of her sixth birthday, Pratima had boasted to one of her cousins about her knowledge of the English language and had added in good measure that she would become an English teacher when she grew up. The cousin's mother had overheard the conversation and word spread like wild fire. 'That evening Father had been summoned by the community elders and chided for indulging his daughter when it was forbidden. Chagrined, Father had returned home in a fury and forbade my brothers from holding any further tutorial lessons for me. 'This girl is polluting the atmosphere in the village, very soon other girls will also demand education', were his exact words. I was chastened by Mother and the next day onwards my practical lessons on domestic chores commenced, under her strict vigil; I was made to scrub the floors of our home, spread cow dung paste on the sun-baked mud walls of the house with my bare palms, wash dirty linen, learn sewing and knitting, apprentice with Mother in the kitchen, clear the dung and urine of our cows and calves tethered in the front yard of our house, prepare the feed for the cattle, lubricate and prepare the teats of the cows for milking by my mother every morning and evening, hold on to the leash of the bucking and mooing calves as they craved for their mother's udders during the milking and numerous other tasks I was expected to perform as a future wife and daughter-in-law, after my marriage. This process normally started for girls in our village after their betrothal, but for me, it commenced early, as punishment for bringing shame upon my father.'

Her brothers used to be mortified whenever they saw the consequences of her practical lessons; the bruises on her knees and elbows from the scrubbing of floors, the tiny punctures on her finger tips from the sewing and knitting, the burns on her arms from the kitchen, the stink of cow dung and urine, that had become her constant companion, from her tending to the cows and calves. She had only two days of respite, on Sundays and Wednesdays, that too at her brothers' bidding. The first Sunday after her ordeal had started, her younger brother had asked her to come out and play with him; 'there was a sly twinkle in his eyes when he had beckoned me. A satchel was hanging from his shoulder'. Her mother forbade her from leaving the house and he had wailed that even servants at the big houses in Pithoragarh got breaks on Sundays and that Chhutki had slaved the entire week, so she deserved rest. Mother had lamented that she herself never got rest on Sundays, so why should Pratima be privileged? Then the elder brother had reasoned with Mother that Pratima had looked exhausted and tired the whole week and she would be wasted away if she continued toiling like this, day in and day out—'Then who will marry a feeble girl, since she would not be able to help out in her in-laws' place.' He had further added that two days' break in a week would rejuvenate her and keep her energy levels high.

'Mother had understood the logic of I becoming emasculated by twelve and fearing that she would have a spinster to care for, if I was not sent away when I came of age, she had reluctantly relented to two days of break in a week, the other being Wednesday, when I could rest as much as I wanted.'

But that was a sly strategy concocted by her brothers to continue her studies. The younger son picked up a few apples, wrapped some chapattis and pickle from the kitchen inside a piece of paper and declaring that they would return late in the evening, he sauntered off, swinging hands with Pratima. A few moments later elder brother followed, grumbling that he needed a break too. He soon joined his siblings and the three of them trudged up a hill where elder brother continued her tutorial while the younger one sat atop a boulder or loitered nearby, keeping a watch for any intruder. She had spent the first hour of that Sunday crying copiously and loudly into her elder brother's lap, in violent sobs. He stroked her head all that time and had promised that things would be okay shortly.

That shortly came after a long period of one month. In that period, Pratima had lost her entire weight; never a plump child—what with having had to feed on the leftovers of her brothers and father, she had never had her fill during her entire life till they came to Ghorakhal, even though Chhotu always used to leave a few extra morsels for her—now she had become debilitated, her cheeks had sunk in, her arms hung like useless appendages, her ribs had started showing through her ash white skin, she was left with no waist virtually, her hips had vanished and she had two stumps for legs. She started fainting during the day, from which she would be revived by her mother with sprinkles of water splashed upon her face and her mother used to threaten her from narrating the episode to her brothers. She used to spend her days in a somnambulant state. The brightest sparks in her life were the four Sundays and Wednesdays she spent with her indulgent brothers. They would pilfer money from their father's pockets, buy savouries from the lone shop in the village, and stuff her with food, till she vomited. They tried to continue her lessons but she would spend the entire day sleeping in their laps, oblivious to the world and deaf to the words of knowledge emanating from her elder brother's mouth. She would often whimper in her slumber and her brother would softly stroke her head, as she travelled from nightmare to nightmare. The brothers took turns providing her their laps, to keep her head in, as she slept from morning till late into the evening, opening her eyes only to wake up when her stomach grumbled in protest and nodding off soon after she ate. She could never eat enough to satiate her perennial hunger and fed like an infant, waking up every two to three hours to eat and then doze off. She had taken to sucking her thumb lately.

She only felt safe and secure in the company of her brothers. Life at home had turned into a hellish ordeal with no end in sight.

The end finally came in an unexpected manner.

'Father arrived home one night in a jubilant mood and announced that due to his sheer perseverance he had been appointed as a teacher at Sainik School Ghorakhal. I later learned from my elder brother that Father had paid money to some university officials to get the mandatory bachelor of education, B. Ed., degree and that he had greased the palms of a greedy government mandarin to be appointed as a teacher at this prestigious school.

'Then he dropped the bombshell.

'He further added, "I have arranged for Chhutki to continue staying at this village. She will move in with Bhago." Bhago was his spinster sister who lived in a dilapidated, lonely hut at the village outskirts, as she had been shunned for being barren, due to a genetic condition discovered early in her life.

'I stared aghast at my elder brother, dread written all over my face, silently mouthing repeatedly, "I will die . . . I will die . . . I will die. . ."

'Father continued, "I have spoken to her. She has agreed to take full charge of her training and will care for her till she is nine. I have my eyes set upon a couple of boys and once I have decided upon the right one, she will be betrothed to him in three years." Rubbing his hands in glee, he added, "Time is very short and there is a lot to do. I have to take on my new assignment within a week. So we would better go to bed early. We will start packing and winding up our affairs here as soon as day breaks tomorrow."

'My elder brother was still sitting in his chair and said in a calm and sombre tone, "We won't be going." He glanced at Chhotu who nodded his assent and at me, his little princess. I stood staring at him with my spindly fist shoved into my mouth, suppressing a sob.

'Father retorted, "What do you mean you won't be going? Do you mean both of you?" and he jerked his head towards Chhotu, who stared back at him defiantly.

'"Yes, it means both of us will not be going if Chhutki does not come along with us. We won't leave her alone here. She is our responsibility."

'"What do you mean she is your responsibility? I am her father. She is my responsibility. She will do what I deem fit for her."

'"Exactly. That's what I meant. She is your responsibility." He replied craftily, discreetly drawing Father in, as if in a boxing bout. "You can't palm off your responsibility to some old hag."

'"That old hag is your father's sister. She had an unfortunate malady that resulted in her current condition."

'"It was no malady. It's an open secret in the village. She used to fool around with boys as a teenager. When her promiscuity came out in the open, no one was stupid enough to marry her. Even her betrothed snubbed her. You and your brothers had her uterus removed, so that she wouldn't bring shame onto the family."

'Father gaped at him in disbelief. Mother had the ends of her sari inside her mouth and was looking down in shame. Younger brother was staring with admiration at elder brother, rejoicing at his courage in taking on Father like this. I was too stunned by grief to understand even a single word of the confrontation. The whole episode was narrated word by damning word by my younger brother much later. When I had asked him what promiscuity meant, he had replied that I need not need to know.

'Father responded, after collecting his senses, "I don't believe a word of what you just said."

'"Who cares whether you believe it or not? The whole village talks about it."

'Father appeared to be trying desperately to regain lost ground, "But she has a good heart. She will look after Chhutki."

'"She will not look after Chhutki, she will drive her mad. Have you seen her lately? She coughs like the old hag that she is. She smokes *bidis* (a favourite of smokers in India) inside her house. She scares the children away with her devilish visage. She is bent over double with some bone disease. She shuffles when she walks. Her house stinks of human excreta, vomit, and urine. They say she passes urine in her sleep and is also incontinent. Chhutki will die if she stays even one night there. By sending her to that place and putting her in that bitch's care you are carelessly absolving yourself of your prime responsibility as a father." The argument was getting heated up and my interest grew in the verbal conflict.

'Father rose from his chair and raised his voice, "How dare you? You can't speak to me like that. I am your father."

'"Then act like a father of your daughter for once in your life." Elder brother raised his voice too and stood up, towering over my diminutive father. He was nine years older than me and topped my father by good six inches. I had never seen him raising his voice and speaking in such a nasty manner to Father before. "And don't you dare 'How Dare' me. How dare you? How dare you turn a blind eye to Mother exploiting her like a slave? Have you seen her condition?"

'He strode over to me and touched my face, "Look at her face, looks like a witch's child's visage, all bones and sallow skin," lifting my arms, "all bones and no flesh," lifting my bodice, "her tummy has vanished," poking my ribs, "sticking out like bent twigs," turning me around, "she has lost her hips," lifting my skirt, "all flesh and muscles gone from her thighs. This is what both of you have done to her and now you want to send her to that witch. No, both of you go. Chhotu and I will look after her here." When he said that, I wrapped my arms around my brother's hips and buried my face into his stomach, letting my tears flow in a gush, wetting his shirt.

'My younger brother, the imperious Chhotu, walked over and placing his hand over my head, declared, "I will stay at home with Chhutki while brother attends school. I won't be going to school."

'That was a body blow to Father. Being a teacher himself, he took immense pride in the education of his sons, particularly elder brother, who excelled in all subjects and scored 100 per cent marks in all the exams. Younger brother is not particularly bright but he could manage to scrape through. And he is a brilliant athlete. Father had beamed at his achievements in the then recently concluded district athletics meet at Ranikhet. Having one of his sons not attending school would be a huge dent to his carefully cultivated reputation of a father with two sons anyone would have been proud of. And there was that added fear that, without a well-qualified son, he won't get enough dowry in his marriage. All of his brothers' married sons were nincompoops, who had never studied beyond class six, if they studied at all, and had got very meagre dowries in their marriages.

'Seeking a suitable retort, he shouted in desperation, letting loose his last shot, "But it is an all-boys school. She might come to harm there."

'Elder brother mocked at him. "Father, open your eyes to the real world. Not all boys are like your brothers' and cousins' sons. Most of the boys in the world are decent and honourable, primarily interested in their studies and concerned about doing well in their exams. And the Sainik School is a prestigious institution, where boys come from reputed families from all over the state, after a tough selection procedure. Either you are making this up or your perception about boys at large has been damaged by the evil deeds of your brothers' sons."

'Most of my male cousins had been thrown out of school, those who went to school at all, due to their poor academic performance and other misdemeanours, including molesting a female teacher. They always used to loiter in the neighbouring villages, eve-teasing teenaged girls and young, newlywed brides, in the bargain earning a reputation of thugs and hoodlums. Two of them are still in jail, serving prison sentences for molestation and rape; one for molesting that teacher and the other for raping the young wife of a low caste soldier in the Army.

'Father had doggedly continued with deflated belligerence, "They are your elder cousins. You should speak of them with respect and dignity. Not all of them are bad."

'"Dignity my foot. They are all devil incarnate. They terrorise the girls in the neighbouring villages and beat up any one who interferes, including the married girls' husbands. They have no shame and hang around in gangs. They are tarnishing our ancestors' name and the family's image. Don't you ever tell me to respect them? I don't want anything to do with them henceforth. I break all relations with them. Now it's up to you. Either all five of us go or only you two go. The decision is yours. We will be wherever our little princess will be."'

Sensing that the tables had turned and accepting the battering his immense ego had taken, her father had conceded, and a week later Pratima and her family had arrived at Ghorakhal.

Life changed for the better. Her training was still on, but there were no cows and calves and cow dung paste, and she could visit the houses of her father's colleagues, those who had daughters. She made new friends and the undivided attention of her brothers filled her up. There was no dearth of food now, as her brothers ensured that she ate with them, after their father had eaten alone. She regained her colour, growth of new tissues, flesh, muscles and some rare fat brought her back to her original self, her vibrancy returned, the spring in her steps was restored and within a month of her arrival she was adopted by the entire Staff Quarters as 'their little princess.' She gained the right of uncontrolled access to any household in the colony, a right which even her parents could not deny her, as every mother in the colony wanted to feed 'their little princess' with unlimited quantities of delicious cakes and cookies and fatten her up.

She sniffled, her voice breaking, and I saw a tear roll down her cheek. My heart ached seeing that tear. I wanted to wrap my arms around her and wipe that tear away. Her shiny eyes no longer felt like a pool threatening to drown me, although I loved the sensation of drowning.

'What happened when you turned twelve?' I asked, when that lone tear waited and waited for its absent and reluctant cousins, before dropping off her jaw when the other tears ignored its summons. In reflexive motion, I shot out my arm and caught the teardrop in the bed of my palm, before it descended upon the silk fabric of her sky-blue salwar suit and dissipated into anonymity. The droplet retained its semispherical shape in my palm. I dipped my head towards my palm and sipped the lone tear with my puckered lips.

There was reverence in her shining eyes when I looked up, after quenching my thirst. 'What does it taste like?'

'It tastes of . . . I don't know . . . salt, a bit of tang in it, watery. Well . . . it is very tasty.'

'What happened when I turned twelve?' She repeated my question. 'That's way into the future.' With that she looked at the clock and sprang up, bolting me out of my chair, so sudden was her movement. 'Oh my God! It's way too late. Mother would have sent my elder brother to search for me. If he finds me here with you, there will be hell to pay. I should get going.'

She turned around, walked a few steps towards the door, turned back towards me, looked at me straight in my eyes, and said with a sweet smile shining on her wet lips, 'I like you Sanjay. You may not be much to look at, but you have a beautiful mind and a kind heart. I want to know more about you. Where did you get such noble thoughts from? What drives you? We will meet every Wednesday and Saturday, if that's okay with you. I will be here at four. Just make sure Dwivedi Sir is not home before you enter. Bye, bye.'

My knees went weak and she walked out of the door. I dropped like a sack of potatoes onto my chair and lay sprawled with a satisfied grin on my face. I was still dreaming about her parting smile and her 'I like you' remark was singing in my ears, when I heard Bindu shouting loudly, 'Seeing you sprawled like a contented tiger, smiling like a Cheshire cat, I presume that it was very satisfying.'

'Shhh', I whispered, 'lower your volume, everyone in the house can hear you.'

'I saw you holding her hand,' she whispered back. I turned crimson.

She continued, 'Be careful the next time you hold her hand. Even though Rekha *Didi* has promised not to enter this room when both of you are here, you never know she might have a sudden change of heart and venture in unannounced.'

I asked her, suspecting the worst, 'Does she know?'

She nodded and said, 'This is her room, too. I had to tell her.'

'Who else knows?'

'Everyone except Father.'

'What?' I exploded, feigning indignation. 'Your brothers and Aunteeji, too? Oh God! What will they think of me? Who will it be the next time? Dixit sir on the first floor, Kapoor sir next door, thereafter! And after some time the entire Staff Quarters! Her brothers will kill me if they ever find out.'

'Don't worry; your secret is safe with us. But isn't she a bit older than you?'

I replied in a pompous fashion, 'Age, caste, and creed are no barriers in matters of the heart.'

'Are you in love?' she enquired in an incredulous tone.

This was a serious question and deserved a sincere response. I replied, after thinking it over, 'I don't know anything about love, Bindu. I know that I like her. Her image floats in front of me whenever I close my eyes. She is a constant presence, even when she is not with me. The mere thought of her warms my heart. I feel the same way as Rishi Kapoor felt for Ranjeeta in *Laila Majnu*. If that is love, then I am in love', and grinned at her.

She stared at me with admiring eyes and Rekha *Didi* entered the room. 'So Sanjay, how was the evening?'

I stood up and said, 'It was extremely good *Didi*.'

'I thought so, from that broad smile lighting up your face. What is it called . . . the Cheshire cat grin, right?'

I blushed again as Bindu chimed in 'he touched her hand.'

Rekha *Didi* raised an eyebrow.

'And he is in love. Like Rishi Kapoor and Ranjeeta.'

I blushed a deeper red when the twin of her raised eyebrow joined its other twin to appreciate me from their conjoined elevated state, and she said, 'My, my. In only two meetings?'

I corrected her. 'No, this was our third meeting. I fell for her during our first meeting.'

'When you were delirious with that miserable fever?'

'Yes and she appeared as my guardian angel and I was sunk hook, line, and sinker.'

'It is "hooked, line and sinker". Isn't she too old for you?'

I shrugged in a nonchalant manner, as Bindu repeated my earlier declaration, 'Age is no barrier in matters of the heart', miming my pompous tone.

Rekha *Didi* regarded me with an intense look and said, 'Take an advice from your elder sister. Don't confess your love to her unless you are absolutely certain that she loves you, too. You will spoil the effect. Girls like her don't fall in love easily. And if she feels too much under pressure because of your obsession with her, she might break up with you. Give her time, don't hurry her up. If she has similar emotions she will open up to you surely, but from what her younger brother has told me, she has suffered a lot in the past. She is bound to take her time. And the age difference is likely to rankle her a bit. She is from a deeply conservative family and this situation of yours, her being almost four years older than you, is unacceptable in their circle. But if she truly loves you and her brothers support her decision, then there is no stopping.'

'Oh how much I wish that my father had married four years earlier,' I said, with a forlorn look.

'And how much I wish I had wings to fly,' she chuckled. Then sensing my self-pity, she laid a warm palm on my cheek and said, 'Don't think of the ifs and buts. Think only of the present. Forget the past and dream of a future you wish for.' After a thought, she added in an incredulous tone, 'Are you sure you are thirteen?'

This lesser age of mine was becoming an irritation and I said in a firm tone, 'Thirteen years and almost two months.'

'I have never seen a 13-year-old fall in love before. Not to a 17-year-old girl. Never even heard of it. And here I am proffering you advice as an adult. Are you sure you are not infatuated?'

'I am not sure *Didi*. After today I don't think I will ever be able to sleep comfortably. She will exist with me as an invisible presence, her face a permanent imprint on my mind. I am attracted to her in a way I have never felt before in my life. I don't know whether that is infatuation or love.'

'Will you stop seeing her if she asks you to?'

I considered her question for some time and then replied, 'If that be her most sincere desire, I would. I will never do anything that will break her heart.'

'You are truly in love. Keep at it and you will get your love. One last piece of advice: be careful of her brothers. They dote on her. They will never allow any harm come to her. They are extremely devoted to her and can never see her unhappy.'

'I know *Didi*. She has already told me that. She also says that there will be hell to pay if they ever see me with her.'

'Then she doesn't know them so well or she is imagining it. They are extremely amiable boys. The elder one, who used to study with me, is very friendly, good-natured, and likable, though too sober for his age; he is here on a spot of leave for a few days. If they come to know you two are good friends they will accept it as long as it is her desire. They will get her the moon if she wished for it. But break her heart or harm her in any way and they will kill you. The age difference may irk them some, though.'

The damn age difference! I had to accept it as an inalienable reality and get on with winning her love. That was the sole important objective for me henceforth.

Aunteeji entered and a few minutes later her two sons sauntered in. All five of them bombarded me with questions simultaneously and I could not make out anything in the incoherence. After sometime, they started talking to each other and to me; I could only catch snatches of their conversations— 'she is so pretty. . .', 'you are so lucky. . .', 'will you marry her. . .', 'isn't he too young. . .' Thereafter, I bid my goodbyes; politely refusing their invitation for dinner—I did not want to be reminded of my meagre 13 years and 2 months plus age anymore—stating that Dwivedi Sir would have my hide if he found me at his house this late in the evening. I hopped and skipped back to my House with a love song in my heart, her 'I like you' repeating in my ears like a stuck needle on an LP record, her lovely face dancing in front of my eyes and that night dreamt of bright sunshines heralding a future full of optimistic desires; flying angels giving company to Cupid as he let loose his golden arrow towards Pratima and when the arrow pierced her heart he morphed into me; marriages of 12-year-old girls, their tearful eyes burning with juvenile fear of an uncertain life; Golu Devta bestowing his blessings on other faithful, ignoring me, as I knelt before him beseeching his divine approval; wailing infants left on dark hill slopes shivering and shrivelling into nothingness, as night dew and mist smothered them. I woke up in a cold sweat in the middle of the night when Pratima' brothers were bludgeoning my inert body.

8

Her Initiation

The next couple of weeks I dutifully arrived at Dwivedi Sir's place at five minutes to four on Wednesdays and Saturdays. In the following few sittings, she narrated the circumstances leading up to her present day. One of those visits was cut short by Dwivedi Sir's abrupt arrival, which had forced Pratima to hide in the bathroom, as I had slipped away quietly.

Another mini crisis developed in the Pandey family a month after Pandey Sir had taken up his maths teaching assignment, an event which transformed Pratima's destiny forever.

Sainik School Ghorakhal, due to its remote location, has an extraordinary feature. Since the school and its associated infrastructure is located within its own grounds, with the nearest big city, having English medium educational institutions, being fourteen kilometres away at Nainital, the staff of the school, including the trio of defence services officers, the teachers, the clerks, the peons, the laboratory assistants, the drivers, the cooks, the waiters, and even the washer-men and women were permitted to have their wards, including their daughters, educated at the school, despite it being an all-boys school. The classes were from sixth to twelfth, and for the younger children of the staff, there was a children's school, Bal Vidya Niketan, located next to Shahji's canteen, which also catered for the young children of the villages located nearby, like Shyamkhet, Nagrigaon, Mahargaon, and even Bhowali. The teaching staff at Bal Vidya Niketan comprised the wives and elderly daughters of the teachers of the Sainik School and a few came from Bhowali.

So, in each class of the Sainik School, there were sprinklings of two to three fair-skinned, pretty girls, amidst the sea of moderately brownish or dark complexioned boys, and these damsels were the objects of whispered comments, surreptitious glances, stammered responses, and subjects of scurrilous rumours amongst the teenaged, adolescent youngsters, especially from the junior classes. Even the young, unmarried female teachers and the Holding Houses' hostel matrons did not escape the discreet stares and blabbered wisecracks of the starstruck, shy, and inept-in-talking-to-girls boys.

Upon their arrival, the Pandey boys had taken admission in classes 6 and 10 and Pratima used to spend her time with her mother at home or pranced around in the Staff Quarters, visiting house after house, like the darling of the masses that she had become within a week of her arrival. She was the prettiest amongst all the girls in the school, even in the scrawny state that she had arrived in initially and as she filled up, with colour returning to her cheeks, her beauty surpassed everyone else's.

All this while, an intense desire was brewing in her brothers' hearts. In each of their respective classes, two girls were studying with the other boys. Rekha *Didi* was in the class of the elder brother. This was the first time the bothers were exposed to girls studying side-by-side with boys, having been schooled in a boys-only school at Pithoragarh earlier in their lives. Seeing the girls studying diligently in class, replying to the teachers' questions with alacrity and supreme confidence, drawing books from the school library with a sense of purpose, their faces glowing with an aura that only fills a person who has an unquenched thirst for knowledge, their perceptive and intelligent brains—particularly Rekha *Didi's* who excelled over all the other boys in her class—testimony to their willingness to learn, witnessing the other girls' personality blossoming, which only comes with the ingestion of the wisdom buried in the books; the brothers were burning with a fire in their bellies. They wanted their little princess to attend school, to acquire the hunger for learning, to see her personality too, to bloom.

One evening, as her father sat reclining in the living room couch, musing over the events of the past one month since he had moved to Ghorakhal, her elder brother had approached him and broached the subject of how interesting it was to see girls studying with the boys in the school. Father had looked at him suspiciously, having fathomed the secret purpose behind the seemingly routine conversational tone of his son; he was still smarting from his defeat at the house in their village and often remained guarded in his responses whenever confronted by his sons, particularly the elder one.

'Father replied, "Yes, Son. The other teachers here have this belief that educating their daughters would enable them to seek employment later in life. But why should a girl be working on a job after marriage, since she will have a husband who will be the bread-earner? Her task will be confined to mending the hearth and breeding and bringing up his kids. And women working alongside men outside their homes, that's an abomination. No sane person will ever entertain such vile thoughts. These other teachers have been living away from their larger families, from their clans; hence their minds are muddled with these strange notions of educating their daughters. They lack the sobering advices of their family members and village and clan elders. Why spend money on educating daughters when they will go away to another house after marriage?"'

Elder brother had continued relentlessly, listing out the benefits of educating girls—they would be able to understand the ways of the world better, they would be empowered to teach their own kids, they would be able to stand up on their own feet in case some misfortune strikes upon their husbands, they would be able to take on the world with the confidence that knowledge bestows upon them, they would get better husbands.

'Father was unwittingly being drawn in now, "But Son, in our community, if a girl is better educated she would never get a husband, as she would be overqualified. In our own family, none of your male cousins have studied beyond class 6. Imagine if any of them had had to marry an eighth class pass girl. She would boss over her husband. Which man would ever accept that?"

'"But in your family, all these cousins of mine are twerps. They never took any interest in their studies. They always used to skip classes and jump over the walls of the girls' school to gape and gawk. And when the girls' school's watchman used to approach to shoo them away, they ridiculed him and even beat him up. They have always been good-for-nothing numskulls with vile intentions. Had they taken their studies seriously, they would never have to feel ashamed of their educated wives."

'"But in our community, we don't educate our daughters."

'"Why can't we make a start? Your elders cannot influence you here. We can send Chhutki to Bal Vidya Niketan and commence her education. She is not too old to start."

'"Chhutki will be betrothed in another three years. Three years hence she will be the responsibility of her husband and his family. So, even if she starts her classes today, she will only be able to study till class 4 or 5, by the time she is 12."

'"She can study further."

'"That would be for her husband and his family to decide. And I don't want to waste my money on her education. I have to arrange her dowry and the pay here is marginally better than what I used to earn at Pithoragarh."'

Her elder brother had then reasoned out that Father did not have to pay any fees since she was a girl-child and also a ward of faculty. As for her uniform and books, he had offered to work as a guard or any other lowly job after school hours, and on Sundays and holidays, to pay for that from his own earnings.

'Father had taken serious offence to that suggestion. "No son of mine will work as a guard. You can't demean me. What will the other teachers think of me? Chhutki will not be attending school and that's final. No girl from our community has ever gone to school and I don't want to initiate a ridiculous trend." He had added after a pause, "Don't you go on filling her stupid mind with such fancy ideas."'

Elder brother had taken offence to that and had told Father that Chhutki had never been stupid; rather, she was very sharp and intelligent.

'Father derided him, "That's what I mean exactly. You have been teaching her back at the village and she has been getting these stupid ideas. She goes flouncing around the Staff Quarters, as if she is the country belle. She will remain in the house, learn from her mother about her wifely duties and leave at twelve for her new home."'

'"But it is against the law. She can't marry before she is 18," Brother had responded heatedly. The decibel level of their conversation had risen by then and the other members of my family, including me, had joined in by then. I was holding the hand of my impulsive younger brother, who was seething in frustration that the conversation was not heading in the direction planned earlier by my two brothers and that it was now mushrooming into a full blooded heated argument.

'"That is the problem with getting you people here at the first place. Away from the influence of our elders, you start getting such notions like law. The law, the constitution, they are for the others. We follow what our customs and traditions allow and what our elders dictate. Chhutki will marry as soon as she reaches puberty."

'"Your elders allow the boys of our clan to eve-tease girls, make merry, roam in gangs terrorising others, molest and rape girls and women. Your customs and traditions permit female infanticide and forbid education of girls. The law on the other hand catches these perpetrators of evil and confines them to jail. The constitution gives rights to women. And Chhutki need not marry at twelve. She is a toddler now. She will be just a child in six years."

'"She will marry at 12," Father had insisted obstinately.

'"And I will inform the police. They will put you in jail. Child marriage is unlawful in our country."

'A deathly silence descended upon the room. The new refrigerator's soft hums and the silent hisses of the pressure cooker could be clearly heard in the calm. Father's face went pale and he sat gaping at his elder son, in sheer shock and disbelief. Mother had incredulity writ large on her face and tears started welling up in her eyes. Elder brother was staring with sheer defiance at Father, without blinking an eye. Younger brother had a smug look on his face. I had only admiration for my saviour—my elder brother had grown in stature in my eyes.

'Father stood up from the couch after a long period of brooding, walked up to Mother and said, "This is what you have given me—a son who will put me in jail. This is entirely your fault. It was you who had insisted on coming here. Had you not nagged me so much, none of this would have ever taken place. These brats would have been studying in that school at Pithoragarh and not be getting these revolting ideas. He says he will put me in jail."

'Mother started sobbing and said plaintively to elder brother, "You can't be serious son."

'Big brother walked up to where I was standing with my younger brother and placing a reassuring hand upon my head, he said, "Have you ever heard me utter one word without genuine purpose, Mother. I swear over Pratima's head that she will not marry till she is 18 and anyone who forces her will have hell to pay."

'Chhotu put his palm over his brother's hand and declared, "I will not go to school till Chhutki joins Bal Vidya Niketan."

'Faced with such hostility and open defiance from their two sons, my parents walked out of the room, heads hanging down in dejection. The three of us stood in a huddle, hugging each other and letting out a sob I enquired from elder brother, "Big Brother, what will happen now?"

'He kneeled down, cupped my tear-stained face in his palms, and wiping the tears from my cheeks, said in a calm, confident voice, "Everything will be okay, little princess. Don't you worry?"

'No one had dinner that night.'

Her voice broke at this point in her narrative and she took a pause. I was so absorbed in this fascinating tale of brothers standing up for their sister, of open hostility and rebellion against parental authority that I couldn't wait for more.

I blurted out impatiently, 'What happened next,' and looking up I saw her wiping her cheeks. 'Oh! Sorry, take your time,' I said. I looked away towards the curtained window, unable to stand her anguish. Yellow light of the dying sun, streaked with a pinkish hue, tried desperately to enter the room through the curtains.

When I looked back at her she smiled at me through her tears and nodded.

'The next day younger brother took me to the Golu Devta temple as soon as Father and Big Brother left for school. There he opened his satchel and took out a nursery class book of Bal Vidya Niketan, which he had borrowed from a peon, whose daughter had 'jumped' mid-session to the Lower Kindergarten (LKG) class. We started my lessons under that huge tree in the temple premises. We returned home for lunch after which Big Brother took up my lessons at home, right under the eyes of Father. This continued the whole week. On Sunday, we took packed lunch, climbed to the top of Water Tank Hill, and I was tutored by both of them there. This time around, there was no need for any of them to keep watch and they repeatedly argued over the correct method to conduct my tutorial. I loved the bickering and bantering going on between them. At mid day, I told them that I was fed up of reading and studying the whole week. We played and they told me stories of the fairyland and tales from the Upanishads. They lifted me, threw me into the air as I giggled and cackled and enjoyed the feeling of flying before gravity would drag me down into their upturned arms, swung me between them holding my arms and legs, ran with me as I slid down the pine needles ridden slopes, attended, with feigned worry, to the scrapes on my knees when I fell, kissed me a lot, indulged me in whatever fancy overtook me, took turns in providing their lap for me to snooze and as the sun hung low over the hills to the West in a blaze of orange, pink, red, and yellow colours, Big Brother hoisted me upon his shoulder and carried me down the hill, all three of us singing merry songs. It was the first of many such wonderful and peaceful days of my life.

'Father had still not relented when we entered the second week of my younger brother's ultimatum. On the first day of the second week, Big Brother didn't go to school and declared that he would be taking up a peon's job within the next ten days and send me to school from his earnings. He didn't accompany Father when he left for school and took me to the temple to resume my lessons. The next day, younger brother declared hunger strike and refused to eat. I also joined him and said that I won't eat anything if he did not. By the third day I had stomach cramps for not having consumed a single bite in the past twenty-four hours. Big Brother tried to persuade me to eat an apple but I shook my head and told him to give it to Chhotu, who in turn also shook his head. Big Brother walked up to Father after his lunch and told him that I would die if he did not relent.

'Father came to my room in a hurry and seeing me writhing on the bed, clutching my stomach, a look of grief and pity passed over his face. He went into the kitchen, piled a plate with the leftover rice and daal and fed me with his own hands. When I had refused initially he promised that he would put me in Bal Vidya Niketen the very next day. I threw up the first morsel, my stomach rebelling in frustration, and splattered his shirt. He laughed and wiping his shirt, apologised to Big Brother for his obstinacy.

'Big Brother was not surprised by Father's sudden change of heart as my brothers' protests and his decision to don a peon's uniform must have been a big blow to Father. Father sets great store by his reputation and having two sons—one insisting on working as a lowly employee at his place of work and the other refusing to attend school, would have been an immense disappointment to him. I had initially thought that Father had agreed to my brother's insistence out of his love for me. Later events revealed how wrong I was.

'I started attending school. Around my ninth birthday, Big Brother had caught my parents discussing my betrothal and had thrown such a fierce look at them that they never deliberated upon the issue any further. When I had turned twelve, younger brother had spied a photograph of a man in his twenties, which was the topic of a whispered conference of my parents and a relative from our village, who had come over for a few days. When Big

Brother heard of it, he had walked up to the assembled trio in our parents' bedroom, where they were discussing that man in the photograph as a suitable husband for me, snatched the glossy paper with a black and white image of a fat, ugly character with a treacherous look on his face, snarled "never" and had flushed it down the toilet. That relative of ours slunk away like a beaten dog, as my parents stared aghast at Big Brother.

'Big Brother took his promise very seriously. When I had turned nine, I was still studying at Bal Vidya Niketan and he had joined the university at Nainital for his graduation. He had taken a month's break from his studies, feigning illness, and stayed home twenty-four-seven, never letting me out of his sight, even once, after my school hours. By the time I had entered my twelfth year he had finished graduation. He wanted to continue his studies to become an educationist. But, since younger brother had by then left for the National Defence Academy, NDA, Big Brother decided to take a sabbatical of one year.'

I jumped into her narrative. 'All this to ensure that your father did not bump you off, so to speak. He had not promised that he would not marry you off at twelve. He had only relented to allow you to study. So, when you reached the ages of nine and twelve, your elder brother conjured to stay at home, to never let you out of his sight a single moment, thus preventing your father from arranging your betrothal or marriage. That was very thoughtful of him. But why was he so distrustful of your father? Was your father so . . . so. . .' I was searching for a polite word to replace the euphemism I had in my mind.

'Malicious, you mean,' I nodded and looked at her, surprised that she could use such a derogatory term to describe her own father. 'Don't look at me in that manner. I had lost all regard for him when he had decided to desert and dump me with that crone of a sister of his, all those years back. I had lost faith in him pretty early in my life, when I had first listened to him discussing my future with Mother and planning to bump me off, as you said, as a child. My brothers must have lost it earlier. Father never did anything positive to regain our trust, and having gauged his vile nature accurately, Big Brother had decided to sacrifice a year of his life to ensure that I was not sent away permanently. Not only that, throughout his graduation and postgraduation years at the Kumaon University in Nainital, he stayed at home. He never lived in any hostel at Nainital. He used to walk to Bhowali, leaving our house at six in the morning, catch a bus from there to Nainital, attend his lectures and come back by bus in the evening; day in and day out, except Saturdays and Sundays. He used to ensure that my parents could never take advantage of my loneliness, by asking for me the moment he was back from Nainital, every day. My parents dared not defy him. In his twelfth class, before he shifted to the university, he befriended a pot-bellied, middle-aged police inspector from Bhowali and would often invite him to our home, just to put a scare in Father. Once when Father refused to pay his bus fare, so as to force him to take up residence at Nainital, he brought the application form to seek employment as a watchman at the school gate, on Saturdays and Sundays. Father tore up the form and never brought up the bus fare again.

'But whatever be my father's intentions, his decision to let me join school changed me forever. The eleven years since have been a revelation for me. I joined LKG as a 6-year-old and "jumping" a class or two, mid-session, now I am the oldest student in my class, where others are 14 or 15 years old. As you have so marvellously stated, I was bright and smart, and I have this photographic memory. I could always finish the entire syllabus of the class within a month of the start of the academic session, with my brothers as my tutors at home. After that first month I used to explore the school library and read whatever I could lay my hands upon. In class 3 I had asked my younger brother that I wanted to learn the words in the dictionary, since I knew all the words in the book. Big Brother had then learned about my propensity to absorb whatever I read and had warned me never to let Father know that I was brilliant in my studies. In his heart of hearts, he had never felt confident that he would ever report on Father to the authorities, despite his threat. And he was pretty sure that if Father came to know that I was intelligent, he would have surely had me married off. He had sat me down and chalked out the strategy—never raising hand in class, giving wrong answers, shoddy homework, studying in my room after securing the door properly, scoring bare minimum marks in the exams so that I could barely scrape through. As an 11-year-old I loved devising these devious schemes with him as a co-conspirator. The very thought of getting the better of Father excited me. And I wholeheartedly participated in these charades and Father remains safe in his assumption that I am a dumb girl.'

9

En Route to a Fascinating Journey

'We used to follow a daily routine which was so predictable that its very duplication, day after day, made it interesting; it's a paradox, I know, but that's the way I felt it. We would set off for school in the mornings, both my brothers walking on each of my side as my bodyguards. They would drop me at Bal Vidya Niketan and walk on to their classes in the main school. Initially, when my classes finished a good two to three hours before theirs, I would wait at the canteen for them and after they arrived we would march back to our house—everyone took to calling me the "princess with her sentinels".

'When I joined the main school, on the first day after each vacation, my younger brother, before he left for NDA, would leave the house early and before I arrived for the classes, he would address the boys in military style clipped tones. Monisha, who is in my class, once heard him and told me verbatim the text of his speech:

Welcome to your new semester. What I am going to tell you is to be followed in letter and spirit. Any divergence from my instructions will invite severe punishment on the perpetrator. So listen carefully and commit them to your memory. Anyone who doesn't have the capacity to retain memory can note down these instructions. In a short time from now a very pretty girl will enter this class. She is my sister and you are fortunate that she is your classmate. I know you jokers have very high regard for the daughters of the school staff members. But still, to reinforce the age-old traditions of this great country of ours, with respect to the way our women are revered— there is a hidden paradox in that statement which you imbeciles will never understand—I want to leave certain instructions with regard to my sister.

No speaking to her directly; if you want to convey something to her, use Monisha as a conduit. No staring at her. When she climbs the stairs no one is to stand below to look up her skirt. She is a bit dumb, so don't let any noble notions enter your hearts to help her in her lessons. She will be able to manage. Don't you even dream of touching her, ever. No one will approach her, asking for any kind of help from her. When you go on your class trip to Nainital don't ask her out for a treat or a movie. That's all and commit these diktats to your memory.

'In fact whenever I used to go for the class trips from Bal Vidya Niketan or the main school, both my brothers, or one of them would take a bus from here an hour earlier and be there before our school bus reached Nainital. Then they would accompany me to a movie or some eatery or to China Peak or take me boating in the lake. When Big Brother shifted to Kumaon University, he would meet me at the bus parking and take me to the university, marvelling at my amazement on seeing such huge buildings and humongous halls. When the trips ended, they would ensure that I had boarded the school bus before taking a separate bus to our home. Both of my brothers never took the school bus when I went for these school trips, as the bus was meant for my classmates only. They always took a separate bus saying that they did not want Father accusing them of taking advantage of his position.'

I butted in again. 'Didn't it get irritating? This constant attention, it almost seems like they never allowed you a private moment.'

'Oh Sanjay! You can't even begin to imagine how my life was earlier. Mother has always treated me like an outsider, as if I am a tenant who has stayed overlong without paying the rent. Father is so steeped in his fanatic zealotry that he has never paid any attention to any of my needs. It was my brothers who would always notice my skirts getting shorter, my bodice getting tighter, my toes growing larger, my toothbrush bristles fanning out, my nails getting longer and then they would get me new clothes and shoes, replace my toothbrush, clip my nails, even brush my hair when it became too unkempt to manage on my own. They are the brightest spark of my life. They would do anything for me and I basked in their company, never thinking of their presence as an intrusion. They had become such a permanent fixture in my life that now that they are not here, I miss them a lot. Big Brother is a lecturer at a university in Lucknow and he can barely manage to come home. Younger brother is at NDA and he is home only twice a year. I was feeling so lonely and then I met you.'

'What do I make you feel?' I ventured a diagonal question.

'I. . .'

A heavy noise, of someone clearing his throat harshly, intruded and then we heard Dwivedis Sir's bark of a voice, 'Bindu, Bindu. Where are you?'

I forgot my oblique question and the warm emotion that had crept into her voice as she had set out to answer, and both of us bolted out of our chairs. I looked around, saw the open bathroom door and told her in urgent whispers and wild gestures to hide there and not to come out till Bindu came calling for her. She darted in and closed the door. I searched frantically all over, picked up the first book available, an English grammar book of Bindu's, and sat down in the chair, as if preparing myself to give a tutorial to Bindu. Bindu peeped in, put a finger to her lips, frowned at not seeing Pratima anywhere, noticed the closed bathroom door, gave a nod of acceptance and went out. I sat there breathlessly, listening to Dwivedi Sir discussing routine domestic matters with his family members and slowly the drumbeats of my heart receded and were replaced by the regular lub-dub rhythms of a human heart. When silence was restored in the house, interrupted by infrequent conversations emanating from different rooms, I presumed that the crisis was over. I dared not go to the bathroom door. Bidding a silent good bye to Pratima, I tiptoed past the living room and slithered out of the house.

We met the next Saturday as the intervening Wednesday Dwivedi Sir was at home and Bindu was standing outside her house at ten minutes to four, to warn me off.

As soon as we sat down sipping tea, prepared thankfully by Rekha *Didi*, which was why it tasted so much like Mother's tea—warm, milky, and sweet with a hint of ginger and cardamom—she said, 'That question of yours?' I raised an eyebrow in anticipation, my heart shooting thunderbolts and my mind running over and over again, 'She remembered the question, she remembered the question. . .' Here it comes.

She continued, 'Ever since I have started narrating my life to you, I have been recollecting our conversations every night, as I lie in bed waiting for sleep to engulf me. And I relive my entire life, each episode merging into another, reminding myself of how fortunate I am to be blessed with such fine brothers who are so devoted to me and I suddenly feel alive, the loneliness dissipating, and I feel their presence around me, their genial smiles lighting me up, their cackling laughter filling my ears, their amiable ways reassuring me, their confident stares giving me the strength to take on the world, their noble beliefs reinforcing my resolve, their strength of character renewing my unsaid promise to live up to them. That lifts my spirits up. And it is all because of you.'

I shrank back into my chair, my hopes deflated. And here I was thinking that she would say, 'I can't get you out of my mind. You have replaced my brothers. I think of you often when I am alone and your mere thought cheers me up. You crawl out of the niches of my heart on unexpected occasions; when I am reading, you would suddenly spring out of the pages, when I am listening to the teacher's instructions you would peep over his shoulders, when I am in the library you would drop down from the tallest shelf.' Thirteen-year-old hearts can be so impatient. There was always the next time. I was ready to wait.

To hide the disappointment writ large upon my face, I got up and walked towards the peach and yellow curtains of the window, to close the imagined gap in the tightly drawn drapery and said to the window, 'I am so lucky that you have such extraordinary brothers.'

'Every night I pray to God thanking him for giving me this rare opportunity of being taken care of by my virtuous brothers,' then she caught on, the first time that I had her on the wrong foot, 'what do you mean you are lucky? I thought you were commending my luck.'

'Had it not been for them I would have never met you. When I was shivering with fever, I would have never seen my angel standing there to rescue me. Instead you would be squatting in front of a hearth blowing into the embers to coax a flame, coughing miserably into the daal simmering in a pan on top of the fireplace, your numerous, bawling infants and toddlers lying discarded on the kitchen floor or hanging onto your tails crying for attention, your domineering mother-in-law towering over you cursing your mother for foisting her inept daughter onto her, your jobless, imp of a husband drifting around with a bidi dangling from his foul mouth, impatient for the next meal, your stingy father-in-law bickering about the measly amount of dowry brought by you, your brother-in-law, a twig in his mouth, staring at you with that Jaggu look from *Roti, Kapda aur Makaan.*'

She was chuckling in mirth. 'Oh Sanjay. You paint such a vivid picture of a dreary existence I have dreaded so much. Where do you get all these images from, I wonder? Why that Jaggu simile?'

'Jaggu is a thug in the movie who is villainous towards Moushumi Chatterjee and gives her these dangerous looks. You are much more beautiful than her. And if your husband is impish your brother-in-law might fancy his chances.'

'I don't think any brother would hanker after his sibling's wife.'

'With what you have told me about the men in your clan and caste, amongst whom you would have been married, but for your brothers, I couldn't come up with a more appropriate analogy.'

She grinned at me and said, 'I am happy that my registers are having their effect. Your vocabulary is showing a distinct improvement.'

I grinned at her, contented that she was happy and said, 'But we digress. You have come to your present but I guess that you are not finished yet. I get a sense that you have something more to say, before you end your life story.'

'I cannot complete my story, especially to you, without talking about the greatest influence upon my life, after my brothers. It is the books; all kinds of books. I started reading books to keep myself occupied, since I would complete the entire school syllabus within a month. And it initiated me into a fascinating journey. I started devouring books like a hungry lion on his first meal after a fortnight's unsuccessful hunting. It became an obsession. I lived in the fantasy world of *Alice in Wonderland,* took pity on *Oliver Twist*'s travails, roamed amongst the stars with Dr Bowman in *2001: A Space Odyssey,* marvelled at the strange marriage rituals of the Garo and Khasi tribes, stood atop the Eiffel Tower and screamed into the howling wind, dove with the marine creatures till the deepest depths of the Mariana Trench, searched for the ships lost in the Bermuda Triangle, rode with Babur in 1526 as he came to conquer India. I loved transporting myself into these strange and exciting worlds the books contained. I loved reading each and everything—novels, journals, glossy film magazines, comic books, newspapers, anything I could lay my hands on. And whatever I read I could retain and recall. It changed my life, turned my world upside down. That is what I had left for the last.'

'What happens when you turn 18? You must be a few months short now. Won't your father try to marry you off then, as you would have reached the legal marriageable age?'

'I had discussed it with my younger brother the last time he was home. He had said that Father would dare not go against my wishes, as I will be an adult then and can take decisions for my life in an independent manner. And if Father tries to bump me off, I can complain to the police and put him in jail.'

'Will you go to the police against your father?'

'I don't have to do much. That police inspector from Bhowali, whom Big Brother had befriended, is a genial fellow. He comes to our house once in a while to enquire after Big Brother and he has let it slip to me that if I ever felt threatened here I should send a message and he would leave a couple of policemen to guard me. If ever that time comes I will just tell Bindu's brother, who is in class 6 now, to go to Bhowali and deliver the message. The mere presence of policemen here would put the fear of God inside my father.' She ended wistfully.

After a moment's pause, she added, 'That was my life story. Now it is your turn. But I won't listen to you from here. It's better sitting next to you. Let us sit on that couch.'

With that we both got up and walked over to the couch, sitting next to each other, a discreet distance between us like a chasm. A thrill went through my limbs as I inhaled the aroma of her lemony perfume. 'She does wear it for me. Not all is lost. There is hope.'

We turned towards each other and I started from the start, my birth.

10

Birth and Its Consequences

30 January 1969. This was the day I was born. Marked as the Martyr's Day, 30th January is also significant as Mahatma Gandhi's Death Anniversary. I entered this world exactly twenty-one years after the Father of the Nation left for his heavenly abode, his life mercilessly undone by an assassin's bullets. At the stroke of eleven in the morning, all my fellow countrymen were observing the customary two-minute silence in honour of those heroes who had laid down their lives in sacrifice to the nation's cause. They paused in their endeavours, standing up in reverence, head piously hung down. Many were calling out the names of Mahatma Gandhi, Bhagat Singh, Chandrashekhar Azad, Rajguru, the Unknown Soldier and others, in silent prayers. Some were thankful for the few moments of peaceful quiet in a chaotic world, millions engaged in private contemplation of a life full of drudgery. Schoolchildren sniggered to themselves, holding each other's hands behind the desk, out of the teacher's spying eyes and throwing furtive glances all around, the shakes of their shoulders betraying them. Amidst all this silence and inert activities, I was swimming and pushing my entry into the mortal world, defying all laid-down norms. My birth was not so uneventful and these series of not-so-uneventful events left lasting physical and psychological effects on me.

Born in a small town in the North Indian state of Uttar Pradesh, I was lucky, in that, our small town was also the district headquarter. Though the district hospital had an edifice, it was not on the government's high priority list, in terms of staffing the hospital. On that providential day, the hospital could only spare a young, recently recruited midwife, who had cynically taken the job for the sake of the meagre remuneration she received, to support her poverty-stricken family back in her hometown, amidst the backwaters of Alleppey in Kerala. For my birth, she had been summoned by my grandfather, an influential personage in the town due to the umpteen occasions he had been imprisoned by the British government during the struggles for India's independence in the Thirties and Forties, thus earning him an exalted stature and the supplementary privileges of a Freedom Fighter. Miss Mary, the midwife, was there to assist my mother in bringing me forth into this world, that too at my parents' home and not at the hospital. No C-section, if anything went horribly wrong or forceps-tugged delivery for me, if I got stuck.

And get stuck I did. At the exact moment when my compatriots were all reverentially paying homage to our great country's martyrs, I was engaged in frantic motions, pushing and swimming my way through into this world. How dare I? (I have always wondered, as I grew up and started understanding such things; what would secret lovers, meeting clandestinely, be doing if they chose that exact time of day for their dalliances. I myself always ensured that I was standing at attention in my undressed glory whenever I was engaged with Meena as an adolescent, in my later years). So, I firmly believe that God did not take too kindly to my shenanigans, even though it was in a worthy cause, and he conjured such circumstances that I carry the consequences of my Dare into my mortal life; as I did not have any capacity to retain memories of the circumstances of my birth, I had to be left with these physical and psychological effects as permanent reminders of the repercussions of going against the established norms. So, while I was assisting in the assistance of Miss Mary to deliver me from my mother's womb, I seemed to have spent all of my energies at the exact time when my head and eyes had just emerged. There I remained stuck, with only my round head sticking out: 'It was a difficult birth,' was the wry comment of my aunt later. She was witnessing the miracle of my birth, complacently standing next to Miss Mary, overseeing the entire episode. The midwife stared dumbstruck at the round mass of my head with the twin slits, seemingly horrified at the sight and started waving and flailing her arms in helpless and futile gestures, babbling indecipherable gibberish in her foreign-sounding Malayali tongue. After accurately judging that Miss Mary was utterly incompetent of doing anything helpful and also sensing that Mother was at the end of her tether and not in any positive position to bring me forth anymore, my aunt gently took hold of my head at the temples and applying gentle pressure, pulled me out. As she was pulling me out, my cheekbones got compressed and elongated; which in later life enabled me to conjure a deadpan at will, whenever my superiors in my adult life doubted my intentions and questioned my actions. This very expression has, many a time in my life, been my saving grace from landing in deeper trouble during my pranks-ridden school days. But, in my later life as an Army Officer, it also leaves my superiors frustrated. This frustration of some of my senior-ranking officers has not always been taken too kindly by them and has subsequently led to greater inconveniences for me. And equally disappointingly for me, my various attempts at establishing romantic relationships in my adolescent and adult lives have often met with abject failures due to the way I looked: most of the girls whom I have approached for dates have turned me down stating that I was not handsome enough; then, most probably taking pity at the disappointment that would descend upon my face, they would add as an afterthought, 'But you are good looking in a good-looking sort of way'—whatever that may have meant—girls and women . . . unfathomable! The elongated cheekbones and the deadpan are God's way of telling me to be in tune with my fellow countrymen and follow the customary norms of society. But was it my fault that Mother decided to bring me forth at the exact moment when everyone else was calm and quiet? God, what a dare, to swim and push for your own birth.

The second of the not-so-uneventful events occurred as soon as my nose and mouth emerged. The changed ambience, from the cocoon of the quiet, warm, dark, and peaceful environment of Mother's womb to the expanse of the loud, cold, bright, and harsh surroundings of the real world, coupled with the pull on my temples and the pressure on my cheekbones, immediately prompted me to do something to make my presence felt. Maybe it was the pain caused by my aunt pressing my temples and the consequent crushing of my cheekbones, or the desire to fill my deflated lungs with oxygen or enough oxygenated blood was not being transferred from Mother through the umbilical cord; whatever the reason, I felt the need to cry. I cried even as I was emerging into the world. Since I had already commenced the process of respiration, there was no need for the midwife to deliver the customary slaps on my back or buttocks, by holding me upside down. But Miss Mary was young, trained to do this particular act as a matter of routine and she was despondent, because it was her birthday too and instead of celebrating the occasion with the Keralite nuns at the only convent school in town, she was on her third at-home delivery of the day and there were two more to come. She was also frustrated at not having been able to take the requisite prescribed action on my having got stuck earlier, thus exposing her incompetence in front of these 'North Indian Ignoramus' (her choice of words to collectively describe those of us dwelling in the North Indian states, since the literacy rate in her home state of Kerala was the highest in the country and that of the North Indian states, specifically Uttar Pradesh and Bihar, was among the lowest: she even had the gall to quote Mark Twain: *'A person who won't read has no advantage over one who can't read'*, as a parting remark when she had finally left our household, ostensibly to tide over her own incompetence). All these frustrations and despondence of Miss Mary led to the next event. Having emerged in my entirety, I was bawling away to glory to get my lungs pumping properly, but she still held me upside down by my right leg, holding me by my tender ankle and registered a tight slap on my pink, newly-born, pristine, unblemished, still-covered-in-slime right butt-cheek. My aunt swears till this day that the midwife had used considerable force in the spank, as if she was furious that I had dared to cry even before she could administer her ministrations. Whatever the reason for that slap, I had to bear its consequence, in the form of an angry, red, distinct Question Mark (minus the dot at the bottom) on my virginal, pristine, and unblemished right butt-cheek. Till this day, that angry, red Question Mark is misconstrued as a birthmark, by those who have been privy of a peek or when it was at full display at NDA. I have never related the circumstances that led to the birth of that Question Mark to anyone, except to Meena and my wife, of course.

The last lasting effect of the series of not-so-uneventful events of my birth is more psychological. The shenanigans of my own swimming and pushing and the pulling out by my aunt led me to be aware of the changed surroundings—from a quiet, warm, dark, and peaceful enclosed place to a loud, cold, bright, and harsh real world—a few seconds earlier than what is normal. As I have grown over the years, any change in the environment and surroundings or climate leads me to become more nervous and anxious, than it is usual for others. Climate changes lead to immense physiological reactions and I constantly suffer from common cold during the season changing days. I have never known anyone else sneezing continuously, during the searing, hot summer months.

During my narration, Pratima caressed my cheeks with her fingers to reassure me that they were not so bad looking. I melted at her touch. I did not mention the question mark on my butt cheek—that would have been forbiddingly intimate.

11

The Tivaris and Dixits

My birth was an event of celebration in my family. I was the pinkest, healthiest, and the most robust child born amongst the substantial number of children bred in the entire Tivari family, which included Father, his six siblings and the brood of four of these siblings. Father was the second son of my grandparents, but he had only got married after three of his younger brothers had already been bonded in conjugal union earlier than him. My uncles had got married at very young ages (between 16 and 18), as was the norm then, and what with the wandering hormones kicking in and having a willing, legally wedded mate, who had similar heightened sensations coursing through her body and similar desires to satisfy the urges; two of my uncles had implanted their seeds on their respective wedding nights itself and as a result their wives had hatched and bred a screaming male Tivari scion each within nine months of their respective marriages, and by the time I came into this world, they had brought in two more, one of them a female, which had been cause for a great deal of consternation in the Tivari household, as she was the third girl child born in the family, since the time my grandparents had sown the seeds for the Tivaris to proliferate. The third uncle, who had also got married before Father, had continued the convention set by his elder brothers and though he had just been married, six months before the fateful day of my arrival, his wife was also heavily pregnant.

The Tivari family contained, in addition to the youngest bachelor brother of Father, a younger unmarried sister too, my *Bua*. I also have three elder cousins (one female amongst them) from the firstborn of my grandparents. The entire Tivari ménage at the time of my birth composed of my grandparents, four married uncles and their respective spouse, one bachelor uncle and an unmarried aunt, Father and Mother of course, and seven cousins (five males and two females) with another one on its way. This substantial population of Tivaris thrived on the produce and proceeds from the huge acres of ancestral agricultural land surrounding our farmhouse, constructed by my grandfather and located sixteen kilometres from my hometown. My eldest uncle, with his school-going children and the unmarried uncle and aunt, stayed in an expansive, sprawling house, again built by my grandfather, in the town, and the others, including Mother, stayed at Premnagar, the name lovingly coined by my grandfather for the farmhouse, ostensibly in memory of his first wife, who had passed away pretty early in their married life, without giving him an heir. Grandfather had named the expansive, sprawling house in town after his second wife, whom he had married during his days as a Freedom Fighter, before independence.

Family legend has it that during one of his escapades, while thwarting the authority of the local British officials, he had been given shelter by a reputed Brahmin family in the nearby village of Jalaun. During his stay there, he had happened to lay his eyes upon the diminutive, shy, and vivacious youngest daughter of the family; my grandmother in her youth was the village belle and her beauty outshone the plain features of her two sisters. 'She exuded great deal of charm and grace when she sashayed into my room, fetching me my meals during the three days of my incarceration'— grandfather's very words, whenever he was in a rare, generous mood and narrated the circumstances of his marriage to his starstruck grandchildren, all of us staring in rapt attention at his animated visage as he went about narrating the different incidents in his life as a Freedom Fighter. So enamoured was he with the beautiful maiden that when the period of his confinement ended, he had, the very next day, propositioned his father to approach my young grandmother's parents for her hand. Grandfather had built up a strong reputation of a noted Freedom Fighter, in addition to being the sole surviving scion of a landlord family, which could trace their illustrious lineage six generations back to Trilok Singh, a *Jagirdar* (feudal lord) of glowing repute of 1,162 villages in the mid nineteenth century; he was equally notorious for his philandering ways. My great grandfather, giving in to repeated requests of his son, had distributed his large, inherited land holdings to the lesser fortunate family retainers and other minions whose families had served ours with loyalty and dignity over the years. Despite all these and his widower status, my grandfather was still a prize catch and my grandmother's parents had promptly agreed to the match. My grandparents were joined in matrimonial union four days later. As per family lore, grandfather, on his wedding night, had amorously promised to his newlywed wife that he would build a palatial home in the town and name it after her, 'Shahjehan built for a dead wife, I will build for a living one,' he is presumed to have declared—was he on his knees when he had announced thus to his beloved, I love to think so; it would be in keeping with the charming circumstances that led to their marriage and would be a testimony to the way he was so captivated by the allure of grandmother. He definitely had the personality to give rise to such speculations. Twenty-five years later, seven births and thirteen miscarriages and stillborns hence, when the edifice of his dreams had been erected, he had named the house *Shanti Bhavan*, fulfilling the word he had given to his newlywed bride that fateful night.

In addition to being the pinkest infant, I was also the chubbiest, even at birth. My aunt, the one who had pulled me out, says that I was very heavy at birth, 'I could make out that you had weighed about four kilos, even though we could not measure the weight, as we did not have any of these modern weighing machines back then. Now of course babies are born in hospitals and weighed there itself.' Perhaps that is the reason I had to swim and push my way through, like a fish making its way down a progressively constricting pipe, to assist Mother in bringing me forth. It may also have been the reason for my having got stuck and thus having to bear the consequences of that happenstance for the rest of my life.

There was great rejoice on my mother's side, too, since I was the first male child born in my maternal grandfather's family. He belonged to a long line of patriarchal, Brahmin businessmen, who took particular pride in their male heirs. It is to the credit of my grandfather that, despite having fathered four daughters and Grandmother having had to suffer multiple miscarriages later on, he was never despondent of his fate. He had always taken immense pride in his four daughters and ensured good education for them; in the small rural town of Jaswantnagar, education of girls was unheard of. My mother was an intermediate pass prior to her marriage; in itself a huge achievement, for that small, rural town did not have a school for girls and grandfather had had to make special arrangements for all of his daughters to study till class 8, in an all-boys school. After eighth class they had continued their studies at Agra, living with a distant relative who ran a shop there. It was indeed a sad reflection on the societal norms of the Sixties that there was no encouragement for girls' education in rural areas (even today, in the 'modern' twenty-first century, our country suffers the same malady). My maternal grandfather had to face a lot of ridicule, even from his brothers, who had objected to him having sent his adolescent, teenaged daughters to live with a far off relative more than 100 kilometres away. But he had complete trust in his relative, that he would care for his girls, and more than that, he had full faith in his daughters. He had never cared two bits about the prevailing sentiments in the rural, agrarian-based town. Society at large, then, used to consider the birth of a girl-child as a nonevent. A boy's birth was celebrated by the families with full gusto in a festive atmosphere, whereas a girl's birth was acknowledged with mute acceptance of fate having served them a raw deal; more often than not, the mother was blamed for the calamity. The girl-child was considered a burden to be married off as soon as she attained puberty. Sadly, even after the gallant efforts of numerous activists in this field and the modernising influence of Western thoughts, there are sections in our society who still treat a girl-child in similar vein as in the yesteryears.

But my maternal grandfather was of a breed apart. Even though he was born and brought up in a strict patriarchal family and society, his beliefs were never swayed by the prevailing misogynist attitude and consequently, he took the responsibilities of fatherhood seriously. None of his daughters married below the age laid down by the laws of the country: that in a society and era when child marriages were rampant, especially in the rural areas. All of them attained education till intermediate level, with the youngest daughter going on to pursue a graduation degree, at the time of her marriage. By virtue of his family's lineage and his steadfast, ironclad, and unyielding beliefs and values, he was an icon of respectability in the town and had a solid reputation in the district. So much so that there were marriage offers galore for the Dixit daughters from reputed families with well-settled sons, which was unheard of in those days; it was always the bride's family which initiated the proposals, grooms were always in great demand. My paternal grandparents' and my parents' marriages are the proverbial exceptions which proved the rule. My maternal grandfather had even refused a proposal for Mother from a hugely respected Brahmin family, with the son a rising star in state politics, before agreeing to Father's proposal.

My parents' marriage had beaten the existing trend, in that Father married after his younger brothers were already well ensconced in marital bliss, with children to boot. Back then and even today, the hierarchal structure in a family was always followed when it came to marriages of sons. Younger sons could only marry after the elder ones' marriages. But Father had joined the Army in '63, immediately after his graduation. It was the aftermath of the '62 debacle and the Army was in the midst of tumultuous transformations and severe changes. Father could never get adequate leave to even consider marriage, as within a year of his commissioning he was shunted to the Western border to fight in the deserts of Rajasthan in yet another confrontation with the Pakistanis in '65. After the war ended with the Tashkent Agreement in September '65, Father was finally granted leave and he relented to the continuous coercion of grandmother and repeated requests from grandfather to agree to send his marriage proposal to the respectable Dixit family from Jaswantnagar, for their eldest daughter's hand.

My parents got married in December '65. They again went against the well-established practice in the family. All of my aunts had conceived during their respective wedding nights or shortly thereafter and delivered an offspring nine months later. My parents waited for long, way too long; one might also say that they didn't get many opportunities. Father had got only three days of leave for the marriage ceremony and there was such a frenzy of frenetic activities that they would have been dead tired by the end of it and in all probability must have slept off their wedding night. Father had left for duty the very next day, away to some distant border post amidst the hills and jungles of the North-East Frontier Agency (then Arunachal Pradesh) leaving his young wife with his parents. He got limited, infrequent leaves during the intervening period leading to my conception and those occasional periods of leave he would spend at Premnagar, assisting Grandfather in tending to the vast acres of farmland. The house at Premnagar was big, but had very few rooms. There was one huge room for my grandparents and another one for exclusive use by my eldest uncle; even though his wife and children stayed at Shanti Bhavan, he often spent his days at Premnagar. There was a 'cool room', used by the womenfolk only, for their siesta during the sweltering summer months (the room's roof was covered with inverted coconuts shells, its ceiling lined with *khas* shoots and its walls and floor coated in thick paste of cow dung; all these measures ensured that it remained cool during the hot summers). There was a small, tiny as a tin shed, room meant for the newlyweds. That was where Father and Mother spent their nights during his leaves. And in keeping with his amorous ways I should have been conceived during those sporadic periods of leave. But maybe they were using contraceptive measures or it was always the wrong time of the month; whatever be the reason, it was only after two and a half years of their marriage that I was routinely conceived in the spring of '68.

12

The Younger-by-Eight-Months Uncle

Even though my maternal grandfather was extremely devoted to his daughters and brazenly abhorred the misogynist attitude of his brothers and other acquaintances, he still yearned for a male heir. He owned a shop in the Main Bazaar of the town, selling footwear, male undergarments, and the ubiquitous *Bidi*, a favourite of the smokers of rural India. The shop was often frequented by the citizenry of the town as well as the inhabitants of the nearby cluster of villages, earning him a handsome income. He wanted a son to pass on the business after him. Many were the times when he would look with concern and anxiety at his three younger brothers, who all had sons being groomed to take over their respective enterprises. And he craved for one too.

After Mother had informed her mother about having conceived me (missing her menses was the sole indication, with the lone district hospital not equipped to conduct pregnancy tests), my maternal grandparents came over to Shanti Bhavan on a visit. That day, the district hospital had a visiting gynaecologist from Agra. Mother was taken to the district hospital by her parents for a routine check-up, since the doctor came only once a month. After many miscarriages, her parents were eager for another child and they too consulted the doctor about the chances of my grandmother conceiving another child. The doctor advised them to further consult his senior at the government hospital at Agra, which they did a few days later. There they were advised that due to earlier miscarriages, my grandmother's uterus lining had become weak and the chances of another child were low. Gauging the earnestness and anxiety of my grandfather, he prescribed some medicines and permitting a conception warned them that this was the last chance for my grandmother to ever bear a child again.

Buoyed by the treatment and reposing her unwavering faith in God, my grandmother ultimately conceived eight months after Mother had conceived me. To today's generation, this scenario is akin to the frolics of Steve Martin as a prospective father and grandfather, at the same time, in the 1995 Hollywood movie *Father of the Bride Part II*. However comic the scenario depicted in the movie, simultaneous conception by a mother and her married daughter in our country was a common phenomenon in the Sixties and early Seventies. Daughters were married off young when their mothers were barely past their twenties, males never lost their virility, the desire for a son or for sons galore never abated in patriarchal families, women of child-bearing age were always expected to keep on reproducing till their menopause set in and which they meekly accepted as their way of life—so much like factory assembly lines—people in rural areas had never heard of contraception and ascribed every new birth to God's wish, society at large never reproved or censured anyone for having numerous progenies, well-to-do and not so well-to-do families never felt the compunction of raising a large brood, population growth was welcomed—such were the conditions in the country in the Sixties and early Seventies, which permitted large families. It was only with the draconian compulsory sterilisation programme initiated by Sanjay Gandhi in September '76, that the government considered addressing the issue of population growth—the move was not only devilish but lost its appeal due to its unpopularity.

So, I have a maternal uncle who is younger than I am by eight months. On Father's side too, his youngest brother is just a year older than his eldest brother's son. Such was the permissiveness in those days.

Even after the birth of my uncle, I remained the cynosure of all eyes at my maternal grandparents' home. Not only was I the eldest male child in the family, my soft skin, its pinkish hue, and my chubbiness made me a hundred times more appealing than my dusky-hued, reed thin, younger-by-eight-months uncle. He had just been conceived when I was born, so it was my image which was imprinted upon my grandmother's mind whenever she brooded on her unborn fifth child. As a result, she bestowed lots of love and affection upon me. As a toddler, every time we visited Jaswantnagar, she was the one who would plant the most kisses on my cheeks and clutch me close to her bosom at every opportunity. Her fragrance lingered on me for hours after we returned from our visits. Later, as I grew older, this affection continued and she has always been more attentive to my wants and desires than she had ever been to her son.

'Though I was not given the sobriquet of a little prince, there is one parallel between our lives.' 'I hope you are not making this up to draw a similarity with me?' She asked jokingly. 'You don't believe me? Wait.' I dug out my wallet and pulled out a black and white photo of a 2-year-old me I always carried with me. I handed it to her. 'Oh my God! You were so cute! Can I keep it,' she cooed in that girlish sort of way, dragging the 'quooooot' endlessly. I nodded, passing over my first private possession to her with a relish.

13

BB Mausi

I do not recollect the exact date, but it must have been when I was about 4 or 5 years old that I fell in love for the first time. My days till then were spent in the fragrant and affectionate company of the women of both my paternal as well as maternal households. Father was serving in the frontier posts in NEFA and later along the Cease Fire Line in Jammu and Kashmir. He could never take his family with him. Mother alternated between Shanti Bhavan and Premnagar, with frequent trips to Jaswantnagar. All my cousins were either school going or staying at Premnagar. My grandfather, being a strict disciplinarian and a staunch patriarch, left rearing of toddlers to the women of the household. I was the centre of attraction, the cynosure of the entire womenfolk of both the households and the raison d'être for the single women. Even though I basked with enthusiasm amidst such concentrated affection of the female species, the constant pecking, smooching, patting, and cuddling at times took its toll. Ask any pink hued, chubby toddler and you will understand my irritation. When it used to get too much, I would let off my steam and start throwing tantrums. It was during these moments, when I would be flailing my arms about, ranting in infantile rage, which were more frequent at my maternal grandparents' (what with five affectionate women there) that I was consoled by *BB Mausi*, Mother's youngest sister. She would pick me up, all thrashing and shrieking and kicking and spitting and crying (tears streaming down my plump cheeks) and whisper sweet nothings into my ears to assuage my rage,

'Be quiet Sanju . . . You are so lovely . . . Please stop kicking . . . Oh!. You have hurt me now. Please stop . . . You are so good . . . Oh! My lovely son . . . Look your mother is coming. Now she will give you a nice whipping . . . Oh! Please be quiet . . . Oh! You are so good . . . This is not the way to behave, my good son . . . You are so lovely. . .'

She was a classical Indian beauty, my *BB Mausi*. Her dusky complexion accentuated her allure. She had long, flowing, black hair which ended at her waist. The sari that she wore (I never saw any woman I knew wearing anything other than sari) draped her frame in a voluptuous manner (what did a 5-year-old know about voluptuousness, but still). Her broad forehead was indicative of a perceptive and intelligent mind, how else would she have earned a graduate degree in a boys-favoured education system. Her thick eyebrows and lush, dark eyelashes never required any visit to a beautician for trimming or attenuating; not that Jaswantnagar could boast of a beauty parlour then. She always applied *kajal* (kohl) to her eyes, which lent a mesmerising effect to her big round eyes. She had a small nose (compared to us Tivaris—my grandfather, father, and three of my uncles had huge flaring noses which never seemed to stop growing), well suited for her pretty face. Full red lips, high cheekbones and a rounded chin completed the countenance of an angel. It was a pretty face, not overly beautiful, but pleasing to the eyes and enough to arouse desire in a hot-blooded young male (what did I know of such desires; I was just a 5-year-old kid, but still).

Whenever she used to pick me up in a tantrum, she would press me close to her chest. That was what calmed me down. She had a mesmeric sweet fragrance which always relaxed my frayed, infantile nerves. During our visits, she usually would be the first person I would gravitate to, upon entering the household. And if she happened to be away from home, I would be inconsolable and my laments would go on and on till she was back home.

Why have you sent *BB Mausi* away? Where is she? Why isn't she here? I want to meet her now, now, now . . . I will not enter the house if she is not here. I am going (Mother running after me as I sprint out of the house). Go and get her from wherever she is. No, I won't drink milk. I will only drink it from her hands. You are all very bad to send *BB M*ausi away, when you knew that I would be coming.

Once, she asked me in a teasing tone, 'Sanju,' she is the only person other than my *Bua* who always calls me by the shorter version of my name, 'what will you do if I get married today?' Another person in my future would also be using this shorter version of my name to refer to a portion of me, but I will come to that later.

My 5-year-old self never registered it as a tease and considering the question with all seriousness, I replied, 'If you are so desperate I will marry you.'

'But you are so small. It won't be proper to marry you now.'

'Then you wait for me till I am as grown-up as you.'

'But I will also grow up simultaneously and by then I would be too old for you.'

That had put me in a spot. After searching desperately for a retort, I reluctantly gave up and said, 'If you go away I will come with you.'

'How can that happen? Your mother will never let you come with me.'

'I will persuade her. She has *Kaalu* and she does not need me now. You have nobody, I will come with you. I will give you company at your new home.'

'Oh Sanju! You are so sweet', and she enveloped me in a huge, fragrant, bear hug.

By the time I was six, Mother's two younger sisters had got married and *BB Mausi* was the only daughter left in the household. Father had by then quit the Army service and was seeking alternate employment. He was invariably away from home in his hunt for jobs and we got ample opportunities to visit Jaswantnagar during his periods of absence. Mother was very attached to her brother—my dusky-hued, reed thin, younger-by-eight-months uncle—and would cook up one pretext or the other for such visits, mostly during the weekends. With the strength of women in the house having reduced to three, I was pecked, smooched, patted, and cuddled lesser and lesser. Now I could not throw tantrums and draw attentions of *BB Mausi*. She was also invariably busy with her studies and would pay increasingly lesser attention towards me. She only came for weekends from her college at Agra and I would get fewer opportunities to be picked up and hugged and kissed by her. I missed inhaling that sweet fragrance of hers and would grab at any opportunity to gain her attention. I devised new, devious, and ingenuous methods to generate reasons to throw tantrums.

While taking my first sip from a glass of milk, I would start crying, 'This milk is hot. Why did you give me hot milk. Now look, my lips are

*burning' and would throw the milk away: throwing the milk was central
to this strategy which I had learned the first time I tried this trick without
throwing away the milk. Mother had checked the milk by dipping a finger
in and had given a tight slap to me for lying. Subsequent episodes always
culminated with throwing away the milk and always when Mother was not
around. And BB Mausi had to be close by—perched on a chair, reclining
in a couch, lolling on her bed musing over some unsolved maths problem,
sauntering around the house in languorous fashion, coming out of the
kitchen, her hands covered in white flour, forehead damp with perspiration,
strolling out of the bathroom freshly bathed, a sensational aroma of wet
clothes, soap, shampoo, and Pond's talcum powder intermingled with that
sweet fragrance of hers, trailing her as she passed me by with a cheerful smile
on her face, her hair piled up on her head, wrapped in thick cotton towels
soaking up the water from her tresses.*

*The milk-throwing event would invariably be succeeded by BB Mausi
picking me up and pecking and smooching my 'burnt' lips. That was
heavenly. Now that I look back, I suspect that BB Mausi must have definitely
caught on to it after I had repeated the trick once too often. But she used
to go on with the charade and would always kiss my 'burnt lips', maybe
just to indulge me. Or maybe she felt stirrings of motherly affection and a
premonition of her own inability to bear a child (she never gave birth after
marriage—Oh! How cruel can God be?) Whatever be the reason, I loved
those pecks and smooches and would resort to this prank on a regular basis.*

My younger brother, *Kaalu*, who by now was 3 years old, also craved for
such singular attention from *BB Mausi*. Without understanding the deeper
machinations at work, he tried emulating my trick. After two to three sips,
he suddenly realised that the milk was 'hot' and slammed down the glass
on the floor (spilling a portion of the milk in the process) in the presence of
both Mother and *BB Mausi*, and started bawling. His tomfoolery suffered
from numerous disadvantages but the glaring ones were his plain features
and dark complexion for one and for another the presence of my dusky-
hued, reed thin, younger-by-eight-months uncle in the near vicinity, who
promptly shouted, laughing gleefully, 'He is crying after drinking half of
the glass.' Mother turned around, picked up the glass, dipped a finger in,
glared at the spilled milk on the floor, picked up *Kaalu* by the scruff of his

shirt, and registered four tight, sweet-sounding (to my ears) thrashes on his nonexistent rump, 'You liar. You have started aping your brother. He also did the same thing, but never spilled the milk. Now who will clean up the mess? Vanish immediately . . . Come back, finish this remaining milk first. If you ever repeat this I will be very bad with you. (Turning to *BB Mausi*) I don't know why ever should he be doing this? If he doesn't like drinking milk, he should say so. But why tell lies.'

I stole a glance towards *BB Mausi*, as she turned her face to look at me. She had a faint smile on her lips and as soon as our eyes met she stared at me for a few seconds and gave a conspiratorial wink before turning away.

The other tricks to garner her affections were of the everyday variety— *tripping down the stairs; slipping in the bathroom; pretending that my plain-featured, dark-complexioned, nonexistent-rump-bearing brother or my dusky-hued, reed thin, younger-by-eight-months uncle had been harassing me; getting yelled at or whipped by Mother; hurting myself while playing with my brother or uncle; painting a finger or lips red and feigning an injury and such like antics.* Each of these 'hurtful' episodes were followed by *BB Mausi* picking me up, pecking and kissing the 'injured bruise' and whispering sweet nothings into my besotted ears. I especially loved the way she used to crush my face into her bosom to cajole me—I would immerse myself in her sweet, alluring aroma. That was all I needed. That was all that was divine. There is no other way to describe the feeling. What did a 6-year-old know of other feelings?

As I grew older and outgrew my penchant for those childish tricks, I developed a fascination for *BB Mausi*. Till my parents stayed at Shanti Bhavan or Premnagar, before moving down South, Mother got numerous opportunities to visit Jaswantnagar. I always luxuriated in *BB Mausi*'s company during our visits, which happened only on weekends or holidays and suited us both, as by the time I was 4 years old I had been attending school and she was studying in a college at Agra. She used to take my education very seriously, significantly more than hers. Even before I began my formal school education, she would sit me down in her room, lock the door, and open a few elementary books on English and Hindi alphabets, and numbers. She would laboriously explain forming up the various shapes to write the Hindi alphabet, how to differentiate 'tha' from 'ya' and 'bha' from 'ma' in the Hindi script. For the world of me I could never fathom, till I was nine, when 'C' is used sounding as 'S' and when sounding as 'K'.

I often cursed God for making English so hard to understand. But it had its pluses, too; it had lesser number of alphabets to mug up than Hindi. By the time I entered school, she had already taught me rudimentary of the English and Hindi alphabets, one word for each letter, and counting till fifty, both in English and Hindi. When I started my formal education, she kept tag of my class work and would demand inspecting my school notebooks, which I always carried for our visits, and would tut-tut whenever she glimpsed any shoddy marking by the nuns at the convent school, urging Mother to go to the school to complain against the crummy manner in which my efforts were being treated at the school. Mother, of course, never heeded such advices; she thought that it was the school's job to ensure that I became literate. She just made sure that I went to school every day, wearing clean clothes and was on time when the school gates opened in the morning. I used to travel to the school, a good three kilometres from Shanti Bhavan, in a rickshaw ridden by Gafur, a stringy fellow with coal black skin; brown crooked teeth resembling a muster of terracotta soldiers—of varying heights, waiting for the command to get them in order; a permanent, three-day-old stubble shadowing his face; a huge flat nose constantly dripping in the winters, which he used to wipe with the sleeves of his black checked shirt, leaving a smear of a transparent, shiny, gummy fluid across his cheeks in the process; a bidi dangling from his drooling mouth as a permanent appendage. He used to pile up his rickety cycle rickshaw with twelve children, sitting in three rows from the floor of the decrepit vehicle to the rear. He later added two wooden slats to each flank, increasing the carriage capacity to sixteen.

After I turned six and *BB Mausi* got busy with her twelfth board exams towards the spring of '75, we started drifting apart. With my school commitments and Father insisting that Mother stay at home during the weekends, our weekly visits to Jaswantnagar became too infrequent. I started looking forward to our visits days in advance; where earlier visits seemed to be regular and routine and there was no anticipation, now I would wake up early on the appointed Saturday and would fidget impatiently and squirm and fret and twiddle my thumbs till we had boarded the bus for the short journey.

14

The Secret Conversation

When her board exams were over and she came to stay at Jaswantnagar, because her graduation course would be commencing two months hence, Mother took us visiting for a week. The initial few days were spent in blissful existence, as I followed *BB Mausi* wherever she ventured. The third day, distraction manifested in the form of the other two sisters of Mother. Mother had organised this visit in consultation with her married sisters to transform the occasion into a rare family get-together. I was still the centre of attraction for the giggling, babbling sisters and was shared by them all. But after I had tried my childish pranks once too often, I was discarded as an irritating brat. Even *BB Mausi* got preoccupied, attending to her sisters, reliving their past singleton days and whispering secrets with them, locked inside her room.

One day I decided to hide in her room and eavesdrop on one of these private conversations. Inside her room I was frantically searching for a hiding place when I heard a pair of footsteps approaching the room and simultaneously heard *BB Mausi's* voice, giggling and demanding in an urgent whisper, 'Tell me Mona, tell me please. I will be married some day, I want to know.' My heart beating like a railway engine's pistons, I dove under the bed in desperation. The bedspread hung low over the sides and I was fairly certain that I would not be noticed, unless I made a sound. I covered my mouth with a shaking hand, as I lay prone under the bed, breathing into the cool marble mosaic of the floor. The bed sagged as the two sisters dropped on it and the portion of the bedspread hanging down the nearer side of the bed vibrated, as if blown by a gust of wind. Mona *Mausi* was the third daughter of grandfather, recently married six months back and this was her first visit to her parents' home, post marriage.

They were conversing in low whispers, as if they were aware of a ghostly presence inside the room, but were not sure of its whereabouts. I panicked, thinking that they had discovered me and gasped with a sudden intake of breath, holding it in for a long time. I let my breath out slowly, when there was no movement on the bed and the pitch and tone of their silent conversation did not change. *BB Mausi* had a husky voice and her whispers were audible, but her sister spoke very softly and I could barely make out any sense from her hisses.

BB Mausi exclaimed, 'He asked you to undress fully, no lifting the sari?' . . . 'Oh my God . . . He unhooked the brassiere with his teeth!' . . . 'He sucked them? How did it feel?' . . . 'How did it feel when you held it?' . . . Mona *Mausi* had a habit of speaking in long sentences and her inaudible replies to *BB Mausi's* queries took forever. *BB Mausi's* loud whispers returned with an urgency: 'What happened after your husband got on top?'

There was a sudden sound of a knock on the locked door from the outside and I abruptly jerked, my head almost hitting the underside of the wooden bed. Mother's voice, sounding as if emerging from the watery depths of a well, muffled as it was by the heavy wood, enquired frustratingly from outside the door, 'Chhotu? Have you seen Sanjay?' The bed straightened out as the sisters slid out of it. I heard the swishing sound of their saris, when the pair hurried to the door and opened it. Mother stepped in and continued in an exasperated voice, 'He seems to have disappeared again. I think we will have to search in our neighbours' houses too. I am going out, while both of you search the attic and the roof. This boy gives me the creeps when he does these vanishing acts. The other kids are sleeping inside the house and he goes missing.' The trio moved out, closing the door and I heard the bolt sliding into the hasp, when they locked the door from outside. I was trapped inside the room and they were searching for me all over. I sniggered at the irony of the situation and rolled out from under the bed, climbed atop it and closed my eyes to sleep. I dreamt of lifted saris, huge hooks stuck in the gaps between the white teeth of a giant monster, hundreds of suckling babies making sucking sounds, Mona *Mausi's* husband sitting atop a cupboard, refusing to climb down; all vivid imaginations of my subconscious mind as *BB Mausi's* whispered questions roamed the confines of my mind.

Mother and *BB Mausi* found me later in the evening, sleeping soundly in *BB Mausi's* bed, after the sisters had searched the entire house and had enquired from all the neighbours. My mother hugged me for dear life. *BB Mausi* had stared at me with a puzzled expression, no doubt trying to speculate the reasons for my presence inside her locked room. The rest of the visit went off without any noteworthy incident and we returned to Shanti Bhavan at the end of the week. *BB Mausi* never got a chance to enquire from me the puzzling question that was no doubt plaguing her.

A few days later I got a godsend opportunity to spend a luxurious month alone with *BB Mausi*. Father had finally landed a job in Tamil Nadu and had taken Mother and my brother with him there, leaving me in the care of my maternal grandparents, till he could arrange suitable accommodation for all four of us. Accustomed to sleeping in my mother's arms at night, I expressed my severe disappointment, by throwing my usual tantrums, at my grandmother's insistence that I sleep with my dusky-hued, reed thin, younger-by-eight-months uncle. Finally I had my way when *BB Mausi* agreed to my proposal to arrange for my sleeping in her bedroom. That first night was blissful as I lay snug in her arms, listening to her narration of stories of fairy lands and episodes from the epics, Ramayan and Mahabharat. She dozed off well into the night but sleep for me took a long time in its coming, as I lay awake inhaling her sweet fragrance and listening to her soft breaths, her sudden murmurs, her sharp intakes when she was disturbed by some monster in her nightmares, her gasps as she turned in her sleep. In the middle of the night, she fended me off for being too intrusive in my attempts to wrap my arms around her when she turned her back to me. She immediately apologised in a sleepy whisper and I slid closer. I drifted into sleep only after she had gotten up for her morning ablutions.

The second night she asked me in a sombre tone, 'Sanju, that time when all four of us were here, did you overhear Mona and me talking in this room.'

I was lying clasped in her arms and shook my head into her chest, clucking a negative response, afraid to let her see my face, lest she spy the lie in my eye. I had instantly figured out which conversation she had been meaning.

She pushed me away, crooked her forefinger under my chin, and lifted my face up, 'Look at me and answer' she said in a stern voice.

I lifted my eyelids, sheepishly looked at her, and replied hesitantly, 'No *Mausi*, I didn't hear any such conversation.'

'Don't lie to me. I know that expression of yours. Come on, come out with the truth.'

'That's the entire truth, God promise!'

'Don't' you go getting God involved in your lie? I won't speak to you and send you off to sleep with Guddu if you don't tell me the truth.'

My 6-year-old heart couldn't bear being rendered incommunicado and the dread of having to sleep with my dusky-hued, reed thin, younger-by-eight-months uncle forced the truth out of me: 'But I only heard what you spoke, for Mona *Mausi* was speaking with such low whispers that she was inaudible.'

'I had suspected as much. I have since wondered, "How had you got inside this room when it was locked, the bolt unreachable for you kids." What did you hear?'

I told her about the lifting of sari, the unhooking of something called brassiere, the sucking, the holding of something, and Mona *Mausi*'s husband on top of something.

'Did you understand any of it?'

I shook my head and added, 'I had thought about your questions and even had strange dreams.' I told her about my dreams.

She chuckled at the part when Mona *Mausi*'s husband sat on top of a cupboard, reluctant to come down. She sat me up and said, 'We women lift our saris to squat and pee, like you pull down your shorts to do the job. The rest is too inconsequential and you should not think about those matters until you are old enough.'

This was not the first time that my age had been brought into the equation, as far as my relations with the women and girls in my life is concerned; I recalled my earlier conversation with *BB Mausi* when my age was a hindrance in cementing my relations with her, and it definitely would not be the last, as later events would reveal.

But I was not convinced by her explanation. I couldn't, for the world of me, understand what pleasures Mona Mausi's husband would be seeking in watching her squatted, with nary a stitch on her body, urinating in a thick flow of golden liquid. But I didn't express my doubts to *BB Mausi*, keeping them to myself.

15

The Parting

That period of a month passed off in a jiffy, as if Father Time was pumped up on steroids and had decided to convert its leisurely stroll into a 100-metre sprint. But I relished every moment of it, as I had uninterrupted attention of *BB Mausi*, with nobody to share it with. I do not recall much about that time except the daily routine, from morning till evening, and definitely the nights. In the mornings I would play with my uncle and the other boys in the neighbourhood, the afternoons would be spent with *BB Mausi*, when she continued my lessons for the next academic session and in the evenings I would shadow her from room to room and house to house, as she went about completing her chores or visiting her aunts and cousins at their homes. My great aunts and aunts (her aunts and cousins) had taken to calling me 'her tail', after observing that I would never leave her side during such visits and do her bidding as an obedient lapdog. In my fascination, I had almost become her slave, anticipating all her needs before she would even express her desires; placing a towel in the bathroom as time approached for her evening baths, replacing the run down soap, standing with a towel at the sink when she came out of the kitchen after kneading the dough, getting her a glass of water after she finished her meals, fetching her slippers at the appointed time for the visits to the neighbouring houses, bringing her 'sleeping sari' as she changed her clothes for the night (she never bothered that I was present in the room when she changed her clothes, after all I was just a 6-and-a-half-year-old kid), getting her dried clothes from the terrace and folding her undergarments and petticoat to stack them in her cupboard (that's when I learned what a brassiere is and an image of Mona *Mausi*'s husband placing her dried brassiere's hooks in his mouth before stacking them in the cupboard, flashed through my mind; why would he do that?).

I had one morning got up before her and gone to the bathroom to squeeze out her toothpaste and had run the thick, gooey, white mush along the bristles of her toothbrush, holding the prepared brush proudly for her as she entered in a dishevelled state immediately after waking up (brushing her teeth was the first activity of hers after waking up in the morning). She had guffawed and told me off, 'Thanks Sanju, but don't do it again, I can manage it myself.'

At the end of that month-long period of blissful existence, Father suddenly arrived one hot afternoon, when I was snoozing in *BB Mausi*'s lap, having given up on my own attempts in unravelling the mystery behind the process of subtracting 18 from 34. Father was greeted with enthusiasm by *BB Mausi* and my grandparents and I looked at him with suspicion. The noon wore on and when *BB Mausi* went about switching on the numerous globe shaped bulbs, filling individual rooms with golden brightness as the sun died, Father announced that it was time for me to go. Go where, I had enquired.

'With me. You are going to live at Dalmiapuram. Your mother and brother are waiting for you there.'

'But I don't want to go. I am happy here.' I resisted, my mouth screwed up in a petulant pout.

BB Mausi came over to me, picked me up in her arms, and carried me to her room, sitting me up in her bed. There she told me the importance of staying with my mother and father, the necessity for me to get good education, the fun I would have at the new location, the joy I would feel at making new friends at school, the camaraderie I would generate playing with kids my age.

'But I don't want to leave you,' I persisted in dogged defiance.

Then she dropped the bombshell: 'But I won't be here for long. Come next month and I will be staying at Agra.'

'Why are you leaving?'

'I want to continue my studies further and get a graduation degree. That's what you should also do. Go with your father and study at a good school.'

My 6-and-a-half-year-old self had never realised that she too had ambitions in life. By now tears were streaming down my face and I wanted to persevere, by arguing that I could stay with her at Agra and go to a good school there, but realised the futility of it all. I threw myself into her arms and sobbed inside her bosom. She wrapped her arms around my plump body and I cried my heart out, feeling so heartbroken that I thought my life would pass away.

Over the next few years, we made occasional trips to the North, for durations of a month and a half during the yearly summer vacations and an odd week during other times, to participate in any family event at Shanti Bhavan. During the longer vacation periods, Father would leave after a week and Mother would take us to her parents' for a span of seven to ten days and that was the high point of my vacations. While my brother used to throw frequent tantrums and pester Mother to return to Shanti Bhavan, so that he could play with our cousins, I always urged her to stay longer or leave me there for the entire vacation period. In addition to retaining my cynosure status amongst the women in the Dixit household (though the Southern sun had erased, to some extent, my pinkish hue and I had lost my chubbiness due to my vertical growth, I was still cuddly enough), I was indulged in by *BB Mausi* often. Though the kisses, smooches, and pecks lessened in their intensity and frequency, she still at times clutched me to her bosom, especially upon our arrival and while departing.

I was growing up and she must also be experiencing the growth pangs of her late teen years. She was my much adored aunt and I was her favourite, plump, pinkish, now-blemished-by-the-Southern-sun, nephew. Black-and-white photographs of my images from 6 months old to 3 years, adorned the walls of her room, as if she wanted an imprint of my images as an infant and a toddler etched permanently in her mind, and my lanky, growing-up-everytime-I-returned, not-so-pinkish, chubbiness-discarded, form was losing its charm.

BB Mausi always saw in me the child she dreamt of having, in her future. Her affection for me was that of an indulgent aunt, aspiring for motherhood, who bestowed her extreme fondness upon a nephew whom she desired as a child. She saw her child in me, when I indulged in my childish pranks to gain her undivided attention. She was not eager for marriage and motherhood—she wanted a good education before that—but she looked in me the son she would want in the future.

For me, she was the ultimate fantasy of a 6-year-old. She was beauty personified, as a 6-year-old would perceive beauty. I yearned for constant, undivided attention of this angel. Was I looking for motherly love? No, definitely not. I had Mother for that. Even though I have only covered the whippings my brother and I received from her, she loved both of us a lot. She took immense pride in having birthed two sons and devoted her entire love, affection, care, and attention on us. I, speaking for myself, was completely overwhelmed by my mother's love.

If not motherly love, what was it I craved for from *BB Mausi*? Does a 6-year-old have any cravings other than motherly affection, when he is confronted with an affectionate and beautiful woman of certain age? A 6-year-old does not have any passionate urges, as one would associate with an adult or even a young boy in late teens, but when he feels certain attraction towards an adolescent woman, what is it? I never knew then, I do not know now and I will never know from here on.

But what I do know is that I felt genuine attraction for her, her beautiful features from those years are still vivid in my memory. I always yearned for her attention and affection. I will cherish those memories for eternity and will remain forever indebted to her for having opened my heart towards women so early in my life. Unconscious of the fact then, my beliefs and feelings were being channelised by her to such a degree that when I came of age I started looking towards women in a different light—I luxuriated in her presence and I still enjoy the company of beautiful women; I marvelled at her beauty and I am still drawn towards pretty women; she was absolutely convinced of the power of education and that showed in the zeal with which she sought her own literary pursuits as well as the pains she took in commencing my tutelage well before I joined school and continuing it till she finally parted from me when she went into her nuptial union (during the vacations whenever we visited Jaswantnagar she would spend three to four hours every day for my lessons, the books having been procured by her), and I have always considered that quest for knowledge is the greatest enterprise a human should undertake, woman or man. Her very conduct with me changed my outlook towards women; now that I ponder over it, I admire with fascination how her small gestures, her routine actions, her admonishments, her hugs and embraces, her diktats and requests were camouflaged with a hidden purpose—she would always be well dressed throughout the day, even when she had nothing to do but lounge around, 'a girl should be at the ready at all times' she used to say; she would always say thanks whenever I did her bidding and also when I acted voluntarily to cater for her needs and expected me to do the same to whosoever did some act of kindness for me, especially the women; she would insist that I touch the feet of women first, then of men, as a mark of respect, whenever we went calling on her aunts' or cousins' homes; she always kept me at an arm's length on such visits, 'Kisses and hugs are for our own home and our private moments, not for public display,' she used to insist; she would tell me off for troubling my cousin (Mother's sister's daughter born two years after me) or imposing myself too much upon her, whereas she would never concern herself if I fought with my brother, uncle, or other boys in the neighbourhood; she would always ask me to turn around whenever she changed her clothes in my presence; her bedtime stories would always bring out the noble deeds of the heroes with respect to the women in their lives, especially Sita's equations with Ram and Lakshman in Ramayan and the obligation to restore Draupadi's honour, that led to the Pandavs going to war against their cousins in Mahabharat. Above all else, she programmed and moulded my subconscious mind into treating girls with the respect, understanding, and dignity they deserve, as I approached my teenage years and fell in real love for the first time in my life.

Any regrets? Yes, two of them—one for myself and one for her.

She broke my 9-and-a-half-year-old heart when Mother announced in the summer of '78 that we would be spending twenty days at Jaswantnagar. I whooped in exultant excitement and was about to break into an animated jig when I deflated like a pricked balloon, after she followed it up with the explanation that *BB Mausi* would be getting married during the vacations. And here I was dreaming that I would be spending the rest of my life having *BB Mausi* all to myself, vacation after vacation—9-and-half-year-old minds can be so unimaginative.

Hers was a 'self-arranged' marriage—she had met her future husband, two years her senior, at Agra University the previous semester, during his graduation ceremony and had decided that he was the chosen one for her, after a few discreet meetings. She had thereafter told as much to her elder sister, the one with those inaudible secret whispers, who had subsequently revealed *BB Mausi*'s desire to their mother, who had further convinced her husband to take the marriage offer to the Sharma family from Kanpur, whose youngest son was, by then, working at Agra and who was the most suitable match for Chhotu, without revealing that their daughter had already met and chosen him. On my grandfather's further enquiries she had 'revealed' that the son had come to Mona's notice when she had gone visiting the Sharmas one of these days, as they were close friends of the family of her husband (the one who had declined to climb down that cupboard). The prospective groom had secured a job at a bank at Agra and was earning a respectable salary. And yes, the Sharma family had agreed for Chhotu to continue her studies and finish her graduation after marriage. 'Why the hurry? Let Chhotu complete her graduation and we can arrange for this marriage then,' grandfather had retorted. Grandmother had replied earnestly that if they waited another year, such a marvellous offer would slip out of their hands, as the Sharma family is not likely to wait for so long, which was not entirely untrue. But the real reason was the growing impatience and the fire of passion burning in the young couple's hearts, which was prompting them to enter into conjugal union at the earliest opportunity. And indubitably, they weren't managing well in keeping their hormones in check and the desire to consummate their union was intense in both of them.

The circumstances that led to their love affair, the conversation between my grandparents, and the genuine motive behind their hastily organised marriage were revealed by Mona *Mausi* to me much later, when I had started understanding such matters, including that unchecked hormones bit, which was added as a parting shot by her accompanied with a wicked grin, after I had confessed to her about my eavesdropping all those years ago.

Heartbroken as I was, I had still attended the wedding, with a sullen look all through the proceedings, refusing to meet the groom, even at *BB Mausi's* behest. I had cried the loudest and shed the most tears when *BB Mausi* had ultimately bid her final farewell to the home where she had grown up, in the traditional *Vidai* (farewell) ceremony. With those tears my first love affair (or half love affair) came to a most undesired culmination.

The regret for *BB Mausi*? She was never able to bear a child. More than that heartbreak of a 9-and-a-half-year-old, this tragedy is the one which continuously bites into my interiors, perforating my heart, whenever I think of her as an adult myself. A woman who conferred so much love and affection upon me and who had so many photographs of me, as an infant and a toddler, decorating the panels of her room so that she could retain a lasting image of me, to be passed onto her unborn child while it lay languished in her womb, growing up cell by minute cell, imbibing its mother's very soul, when the time came, and of all the people in the world she was the one who was denied that time, that joy and wonder which only a mother could feel. Till the present day, whenever I ruminate on my childhood and think about her, a sob, fabricated in the deepest depths of my heart, escapes from my lips and I shed a solitary tear. 'My poor, beautiful, enchanting *BB Mausi* did not get an opportunity to get a replica of me.'

But God, in his ultimate wisdom, decided not to be so cruel. While he took away her capacity to procreate, he has given her a great brother. My younger-by-eight-months uncle, when he came of age, gave his second infant child, that too a son, to *BB Mausi,* whom she adopted as her child. And she has proven to be a wonderful mother, by rearing this adopted son of hers. Maybe she sees a pinkish, chubby 6-year-old me in him, in her pensive moods. That's a goosebumpy thought.

16

My Visionary Grandfather

After that goosebumpy sentiment I got to the first mini crisis in my life, when I almost lost my life in an accident, 'but nothing compared to what you had suffered.'

She remarked in astonishment, 'You almost lost your life and you are calling it a mini crisis, nothing compared to my life. That is a gross understatement, I think.'

'It was not as frightening as it sounds. And I didn't suffer much. Not as much as you have. It happened when I was 3 years old. I don't recollect any moment of the incident, so what I am about to narrate is as told to me by others.

'Grandfather had bought a new Willys jeep, one with a right hand side drive-train. He used to love travelling the sixteen kilometres distance from Premnagar to Shanti Bhavan, flying on the metalled road, with the roaring wind cooling his bald pate. That fortuitous day the jeep was being driven by Father's younger brother, with Grandfather sitting beside him in the passenger seat. I was lounging in the back, inside the compartment behind the driver's cabin. The jeep's rear had a foot high tail-board and the back flaps were folded up, leaving a three–by-three-foot opening. We were travelling from Premnagar and had reached 500 metres short of our destination. As we neared a girl's government school, a bullock cart suddenly darted across the road, one of the bulls bucking under the yoke as the cart moved in jerky motions. My uncle applied sudden brakes to avoid the cart and the jeep, after a short rubber burning skid, came to a standstill in the middle of the road. One of Newton's laws of motions came into effect—I don't recollect which one.'

'It is the first one. It happens every time you stop or start movement suddenly—every object in a state of uniform motion tends to remain in that state of motion unless an external force is applied to it. Don't you recollect trains stopping at stations?'

'Yeah that's the one. There was a steel bucket kept near where I was sitting and with the sudden halt of the vehicle I dove into the bucket, head first. And unbeknown to us, a bus driven with great speed rammed into the jeep from behind, propelling it forward from its stationery position. Brother Newton applied his first law again and threw me backwards under the bus.'

She let out a gasp and held my hand sympathetically. I felt the warmth from her hand creeping up my arm.

'But even though Brother Newton so unkindly hurled me around, God, the biggest saviour of them all, was kind to me that day. I shot out of the rear opening of the jeep, flew in the air with my head still stuck inside the bucket and landed on the road between the wheels of the bus which was screeching to a halt. The jeep fresh in motion from the collision, slammed into the bullock cart whose bucking bull had by now come to a halt and was staring at the scene, as if fascinated by these crazy contraptions, driven by humans, banging into each other. The bus came to a screaming halt and crashed into the jeep for the second time. This triple impact of ramming-slamming-crashing had a terrible effect on my grandfather, as the last two smashes—one from the front courtesy the stationery cart and the other from the rear by virtue of the careening bus—had both been on the passenger side of the jeep. He was crushed badly between the bus and the bullock cart. My uncle's neck had been pierced by a flying piece of iron from the bullock cart which had toppled onto its side, its ancient driver, as old as Methuselah, lying unconscious on the road, bleeding from his head. The two bulls were moaning and kicking as they struggled to free themselves from the yoke. The rear of the jeep had been pushed inside, the iron frame jutting in all directions, mangled and wrecked. One of the rear wheels had scooted off and lay discarded to one side. I had been saved both by Newton and God. Had Brother Newton not applied his first law and initially plunged my head into the bucket and later thrown me out, my head would not have been cushioned by the bucket when I fell on the road or I would have been smashed into a pulp remaining inside the jeep. But for God's application of his fortitude, the bus would not have lurched to its left and I would have been crushed into a mush under a wheel. But thanks to them I lay unconscious under the bus, head still inside the bucket. My right leg must have hit the underside of the bus, as it was found broken later. A crowd gathered, as often happens. People lifted my unconscious grandfather out of the mangled remains of the passenger seat. My uncle moved out of the wreckage in a daze, blood dripping down his neck from the iron stuck in it and dropped senseless on the road. After some time, both of them, along with the unconscious bullock cart driver, were moved in an ambulance to the district hospital.'

'What about you?'

'I lay comatose under the bus. Nobody thought, in his right mind, to look under the bus. Only my grandfather and uncle knew I was the third passenger in the jeep. And it all had happened in a split of a second, so no one must have seen me flying out of the rear of the jeep. It was only late in the evening, after they had moved the bus away from the site that I was noticed lying dead to the world, blood, from the bruises I had sustained, having coagulated and feeding the buzzing flies. When a few passersby saw my inert body, they wondered about the parents who had left their child unconscious or dead on the road. Then the gatekeeper at the girls' government school recalled that morning's accident and said that I was from Tivariji's family. Father, who had by then rushed from the village and was frantically asking about his lost son, was contacted. He came over and took me to the hospital.

'There the three of us and the elderly cart driver were treated for our injuries. Grandfather had sustained major injuries in his neck and spine, which had damaged his nervous system, leaving him paralyzed waist downwards. My uncle was operated upon, the iron rod from his neck removed and he was sent home the very next day. I had broken my femur at the top of my right leg; 'near the Pectineal Line,' the doctor had said. My leg was encased in a plaster. Since the hospital was overcrowded and it hardly had enough beds, both Grandfather and I were moved to our home after initial treatment, to convalesce there. There was no treatment existing then for Grandfather's condition, so he spent the rest of his life in a vegetative state, on a cot in the living room of Shanti Bhavan most of the time and in the verandah of our house in Premnagar, whenever he desired to breathe fresh air; where he was moved to strapped to his cot on a tractor trolley. I was placed on a separate cot alongside his in the living room, lying restlessly still to allow the bone to mend by itself. I had this strange habit of turning over and around in my sleep and there was a danger of my falling out of the cot at night. So four planks were erected and stuck to the four sides of the cot to prevent me from diving out of bed. But I could still injure myself with my restless stillness and the crabs on my leg inside the plaster would itch so badly that tears used to come to my eyes in frustration, at not being able to scratch at them. Sensing that my turning over and around in my sleep would not allow me to heal properly and apprehensive that my right leg may become shorter than the left one after the healing, our family doctor ordered that a rod be hung over my bed and my legs be strung to it, leaving me in an upside-down position for a month.'

'Poor Sanjay, all of 3 years old,' she placed a palm on my left cheek and I bent my neck to the left, to trap her hand between my cheek and the shoulder. I felt wonderfully blissful from her touch and didn't want her to let go. She pried her hand out after sometime, more out of fear of someone walking in, I presume.

'So there I lay, my tiny legs pulled over from the hips upwards, fastened to a rod hung over the bed. But I was as fidgety as any other 3-year-old. I would turn in circles with my torso and grumble and mumble and irritate Grandfather, who lay unmoving waist downwards, in the neighbouring bed. Maybe he was more frustrated with the thought that he could not move unassisted due to his paralytic condition, whereas I, equally immobilised by being trussed upside down, could still move in circles—than be disturbed by my incessant grumbling and mumbling. Whatever be the reason, he would often bring the house down, hollering for my mother to shut me up or to stop my circling motions. I was told that I had developed it into an art form, moving my torso in repeated circular motions with high speed, 'whoosh, whoosh, whoosh. . .' in the process tightening the cord securing my legs to the rod, in tight knots, increasing their tensile strength, and thereafter releasing the tension in the knots and 'whirr, whirr, whirr. . .' I would return to my original position like a spinning top. That was what annoyed Grandfather the most, more than my rumbles and grunts, more than the odour of my excretions, more than my baby farts. He breathed a sigh of relief only after I had heeled completely and left his company in the living room, with no shorter right leg thankfully, a month later.'

'How was he like?' She asked. 'Tell me more about him. Mine passed away well before me and my parents rarely talk about him.'

'Grandfather! He was a gem; a gentleman to the core, deeply passionate, steadfast in his beliefs, a strict disciplinarian, a patriotic citizen, a thinker, a great innovator, a visionary ahead of his times, very enterprising and very caring about his family, his friends and his animals. He performed wonders at Premnagar and was a model citizen and farmer for all the neighbouring villagers. When he saw that the nearby villages did not have any medical practitioner and people were largely dependent on the local quacks and hakims whose only interest was in making money from the poor patients they attended to, he learned homeopathy all by himself and used to prescribe medicines for minor ailments to all and sundry, free of cost. There was a constant stream of patients at our house in Premnagar when he was able. Even after his disability in that accident, many people came over to discuss homeopathic treatments and take his advice. In addition to the patients, the farmhouse was invariably full of visitors calling on him for myriad suggestions; fellow farmers to discuss new techniques of irrigation, local businessmen asking him on ways to make more money, poor farmhands requesting for loans, friends and distant relatives eager to renew old ties.

'There was a well outside the house which catered for the needs of the house and the thirst of the livestock. The women of the household used to draw water from this well, trudging through the crowded verandah under the gazes of strangers. When Grandfather observed the visiting men gaping and gawking as the veiled females went about their chore of fetching water from the well to the kitchen inside the house, he had a well dug inside the house, next to the kitchen. When he noticed that Grandmother and my aunts had to wake up well before sunrise so that they could take bath in the open, before the men folk rose, he had a bathroom cubicle erected near the well inside the house, exclusively for women. He couldn't bear watching his family's ladies defecating in the fields well before the crack of dawn, feeling ashamed of it and had a privy built inside the house, solely for their use.

(This in the Fifties! We are now in the twenty-first century and our country still has not been able to provide privacy to its women, even in cities like Bhopal, what to talk of our villages. I live in an 'urban' colony in Bhopal where women going to the fields with a plastic bottle in hand, in the mornings and evenings, is too common a sight; and that when there is a *Sulabh Shauchalaya* (community toilet) constructed just fifty metres away. Many girls don't go to school in the twenty-first century India because there are no toilets for girls there. What a shame? How I wish we had such compassionate visionaries like my grandfather instead of the decrepit, antediluvian elders in grey whiskers, sucking on their hookahs, killing their infant girls and ordering the deaths of young lovers with impunity).

'When he witnessed his household women having endless coughing fits as a consequence of having to blow into the stone hearth to build and sustain the flames, he had a bio-gas plant installed to cater for the cooking. I still recollect with fond memories the quests my cousins and I used to go on as kids, collecting dung from the cattle shed and the fields, for the gas plant—we used to call it *'Gobar'* (dung) gas plant.

'When he got tired of having to depend upon Mother Nature to irrigate his fields and after a particularly severe drought which had halved the yield of that season, he exploited his immense reputation and coaxed the government officials, even petitioning Shri Chandra Bhanu Gupta, the then chief minister of the state, to extend electrical power to Premnagar and went on to dig two tube wells to water his fields. He was the first farmer in the district to buy a tractor and relieve the tormented bull from the agony of pulling the plough—I never saw any bull ploughing our fields my entire life. He had a cool room prepared inside our house so that the women could take their afternoon naps in comfort, during the scorching summer months. Even though he himself had had no formal education, he had realised the power of knowledge and ensured that all of his sons went to school sixteen kilometres away in the town. When the house at Premnagar started filling up with his sons' children, he constructed his dream house in the town, the one he had promised to his newlywed wife as a besotted second-time husband on his wedding night, so that his grandchildren did not have to travel sixteen kilometres everyday to attend school.

'Even after the accident, he never let his enthusiasm dwindle. After the initial period of despondence, made severer by my shenanigans when I had shared the living room with him, he regained his vibrancy in no time and was his usual exuberant self thereafter. His liveliness was contagious, and it used to bathe the entire Shanti Bhavan in tremendous positive energy. It used to seem as if a luminous brightness emerged from the living room and traversed each nook and cranny of the house, filling it with its radiance.

Even after Father took us down South, I used to look forward to our yearly visits to Shanti Bhavan with eagerness, just to submerge in the wash of his positive energy.

'His one last desire was to remain alive till his only daughter's marriage. As his time drew closer, his life was sustained with the help of intravenous drips and oxygen mask. An extreme joy had lit up his wrinkled, weather-beaten face, when my aunt had gone around the holy fire with her groom. The entire family had gone to see the Rishi Kapoor starrer *Hum Kisise Kum Naheen* that evening after the marriage ceremony was over. Later I narrated the film's story to him, enacting some of the scenes and aping the dance moves of Rishi Kapoor. He had chuckled mufflingly from behind his gas mask at my clumsy impersonation. He passed away peacefully in his sleep four days later, a contented man.'

As I finished she looked up at the clock and said, 'An extremely wonderful man. We need more like him in our country to convert the dreams of our forefathers into a reality. The tea has gone cold, the sun is threatening to die and the clock is indicating that our time is up. I feel sorry that we won't be able to continue meeting for another month as Big Brother is arriving this Sunday on a month-long vacation. We will meet after a month on. . .' she glanced at the Ganesh-Lakshmi calendar hanging on the wall and added, '12th May, same place, same time and please finish your story before you leave for your summer vacations. Bye Sanjay, you do know how to tell stories,' and she rose and walked away.

I was not entirely sure of that last assertion of hers. When she told her stories, there was a flow to it, her reminiscences moved event to event in a smooth manner, like water pouring down a channel paved with marble. On the other hand, my recollections were jerky, jumping from one episode to the next, like the grainy, black-and-white newsreels they showed before screening the movies in the cinema halls, the camera hopping from one location to another like a jumping jack.

I had never seen her brothers before and had a desire to meet her virtuous Big Brother who had wrought such tumultuous changes in the life of the only girl in the world for me. Where earlier I used to throw surreptitious glances at the few girls in school, after meeting her, I had lost interest in the Monishas, the Aabhas, the Meenakshis, and the Farahs of Ghorakhal. Even the extremely pretty, convent-school-going girls at Nainital, in their short skirts and mid riff baring tank tops, whom my classmates used to leer at during our Sunday visits there, held no appeal for me.

But I could never meet her Big Brother. He spent his mornings either at Bhowali or at Nainital and would cocoon Pratima in her house after her classes. By now I was besotted with her and had utterly, foolishly fallen in love with a girl four years older than me. I could never get her out of my mind and even thought of going to her house. What would I say to her Big Brother? That I am a friend of Pratima; two classes and four years her junior! He would throw me out. Better to wait him out.

I spent that time immersing myself into my studies for the class 8 syllabus—an impossible task—devouring Hardy Boys, Robinson Crusoe, and the likes, playing cricket with my mates at the Grassy Field, occasionally going for a dip in a shallow pool located at the base of Madhumati Hill (the flat plateau located two kilometres away, where a scene of the movie *Madhumati* was shot years back) and mostly viewing the love stories of last year, imagining Pratima in place of Rati Agnihotri in *Ek Duje Ke Liye*, Vijeta Pandit in *Love Story*, and Tina Munim in *Rocky*, always replacing the heroes in the duets and love scenes with a lanky, baby-fat-deposits-on-face, slightly effeminate, me—I was particularly thrilled imagining Pratima and me in that bathtub scene in *Love Story*. I also went to Nainital one Sunday to enjoy the histrionics of Amitabh Bachchan in the recently released *Namak Halal*.

Finally, the day came when her brother left for Lucknow and we met on the appointed day, a couple of weeks short of the school summer vacations. There was a flush on her face as if she had been rejuvenated. I stared at her, captivated by her beauty and energy as she gushed about the feeling of immense joy she had felt in her brother's company. For the first time I felt envious of her brother for stealing her affections, sisterly though they maybe. She showed me the trinkets he had brought for her and a hardback copy of *To Kill a Mockingbird* he had procured, at some cost, for her. I looked admiringly at the cover of the book; a row of prison cell bars, the walls covered in reflected shades of yellow and orange, a man's right hand peeking through the bars—its wrist resting on a horizontal slat, its pudgy fingers turned towards me, its thumb inclined at an acute angle pointing towards the spine, the man's left hand holding the cell bar closest to me in a tight grip. The title of the book was printed towards the bottom in light blue font in two rows, with the author's name written in smaller, white, capital letters below it. I ran my hand over the glossy finish of the dust jacket, brought the book close to my nose and flipped the pages, relishing the familiar musty odour which can only emanate from the pages of a book read often enough. A sudden urge overtook me and I asked her if I could borrow the book after she had read it. She told me to keep it and return after I had read it. I again felt gratified by her generosity.

Thereafter I picked up the refrain from where I had left off the last time.

17

The Terrific Thespian

Over the next two Wednesdays, including this one, and Saturdays, I related to her the arrival of my brother, our stay in the two Southern states of India, our subsequent return to Shanti Bhavan, and my move to Ghorakhal.

'Father was a hard-working and conscientious man who held strong moral values. Having been brought up by a strict, disciplinarian father himself, he aped him in his beliefs. He had left the Army because he wouldn't agree with his superior officers to fudge the records and show the use of a vehicle for training purposes, when it was actually put to use for hunting. He remained unemployed for long after "chucking the Army"—his exact words—and worked as a farmer assisting Grandfather along with his brothers. But he had a fire burning inside his belly. He did not want to live the life of a farmer. He desired to get out of the rural environment of Premnagar and the semiurban surroundings of our hometown, which had nothing in the way of novelty to offer him. He also wanted to shield us, his sons, from the scurrilous ways of his nephews, most of whom were turning out to be huge disappointments with their vulgar languages, their obscene behaviour, their salacious attitude towards the low caste daughters and wives of the farmhands—specially the sons of his elder brother—and their offensive manners, and wanted to live away from the bad influences of his brothers and their wives at Premnagar and Shanti Bhavan.

'And the most pressing reason for him to get away from there was the depression Mother was going into, day by day. One of the reasons for my mother's frequent forays to Jaswantnagar was to escape the repressive atmosphere at both of my paternal homes, a creation of my grandmother. She was the very personification of the typical mother-in-law enacted in the movies by the likes of Shashi Kala and Nadira. Gone were the charms and graces of her youth which had so besotted my grandfather all those years back. Her diminutive stature had acquired gigantean proportions in the eyes of her daughters-in-law, her reserved nature had metamorphosed into a conceited temperament, her vivacity had transformed into surliness. To my mother and aunts she was finicky to a fault, too overbearing for comfort, relentlessly demanding, very sharp witted and scathing in her criticisms and ran the household like a benevolent dictator: benevolent to her sons and dictatorial to their wives. I used to often witness Mother and my aunts shiver in fright, when being berated by her for minor lapses—leaving the hearth with smouldering coals after cleaning up post dinner, not attending to the boiling milk and letting it foam over the rim of the utensils in thick frothy flows, not sweeping the floors properly—she ran her fingers to pick up dust like a prudish drill sergeant. Her incessant reprimands were taking their toll on Mother and she used to often suffer nervous breakdowns; what with two energetic, sprightly and demanding sons constantly hankering for her attention too. Father used to continuously worry about Mother's deteriorating condition and he was looking for an opportunity to move away from the oppressive conditions at home.

'Help came in the benevolent form of Arjun Thakur, a staunchly loyal friend from Father's college days. He was also the illustrious son of Grandfather's colleague from his Freedom Fighter days, who had gone on to carve a niche for himself in the political domain of the country. Utilising his tremendous clout and influence, Arjun Thakur secured a job for my father with an industrial conglomerate in their cement factory at Dalmiapuram, deep in the southern environs of the state of Tamil Nadu. We moved there when I was 6 and a half years old.'

That was another parallel I had with Pratima's life, even though I did not spell it out to her in as many words.

I told her about my school at Tiruchirapalli, a city forty-five kilometres from Dalmiapuram. About the two Gandhi sisters who had told us not to address Father as 'Papa' as it sounded so much like calling for a baby, and instead we started calling Father 'Daddy'. About the bullock cart my brother used to ride in, to go to his local elementary school. About the battery-operated toy aero plane that Father had bought for me and which, on its first flight, had veered and drifted, landing on the inaccessible roof where it remained lounging till we left Dalmiapuram. About the fat, black woman whom I had spied lifting her sari and urinating from standing position, the amber liquid streaming down like a mini waterfall, splashing all over her *hawai* slippers clad, pudgy feet. About the time when Father had told me not to take the school bus back home after school, as they would come to Tiruchirapalli to pick me up in the family car and the entire family would thereafter go see the multi starrer *Roti Kapda Aur Makaan* and how I had stood outside the school gate in fading light, giving company to the watchman and waiting and waiting, tears streaming down my face, fearing that my parents had abandoned me. 'Mother had felt so miserable at my condition that, when they had finally arrived three hours late, she didn't stop kissing and hugging me till we had reached the movie hall.'

Father had to leave his job at Dalmipuram a year later, fed up of the stench and dust of the cement the factory produced and the unjust demands of his superiors. Brought up by a virtuous father and influenced by the ethically and morally upright culture of the Army, barring a few bad apples, he was finding it extremely difficult to come to terms with the confusion and disorderliness that characterises the civilian world and the loose morals espoused by the civil society at large. What upset him most were the corrupt ways of the functionaries at his work place, who were more concerned for their own individual needs, and their obligations towards the organisation, which provided them for their wants, were sacrificed on the altar of their personal greed. Whereas in the Army he had learned and practiced the principles of putting one's own life in danger, for the sake of his peers and the unit. When his boss had ordered him to overlook the misdeeds of his minions working at the cement factory, Father quit his managerial post.

The fanatically faithful Arjun Thakur came to his rescue again and we moved to Hospet in July '76. It is a town located thirty kilometres from the district headquarters at Bellary, in the centre of the mining operations of a big, family-owned, semiprivate enterprise from Bombay, which had employed Father as a manager.

'The time spent at Hospet was the best period of my life, till I met you (she grinned at that and I thought for the *n*th time, "How lucky I am"). Father had put us in a co-educational school, but I had not yet developed any interest in girls and was busy cultivating the habit of seeing movies. Dalimiapuram did not have a decent movie hall to speak of whereas Hospet was a revelation for my, by now, cinema-crazy mind. It was a big town with several movie halls which screened Kannada and Tamil movies mostly, but also six- to-eight-month-old Hindi movies. Mother was a diehard fan of Amitabh Bachchan; "Amitam Bachchan" she used to call him, no doubt an inflection from her childhood, as she would have had trouble differentiating "bha" from "ma", since they both look almost the same when written in Hindi. I liked the sound of the two *m*'s in the first name and never corrected her.

'To indulge in her obsession for 'Amitam Bachchan', she used to make secret trysts, unbeknown to Father, who did not like movies much. So, she saw movies during the day, the twelve to three matinee shows, when Father would be away at work. And it had to be first-day-first-show for her 'Amitam Bachchan', even though the movies would almost be 6 months to a year old by the time the much-travelled and worn-out reels reached the heartland of Kannada-speaking Karnataka. Come the occasional Friday and she would be standing at the gates of my school at eleven, asking for her son Sanjay Tivari to come home immediately for an uncalled for emergency. I would skip the remaining classes and promptly report to my beaming mother, ready for our secret rendezvous with her 'Amitam Bachchan'. From there we would stroll over to the movie hall or ride on a cycle rickshaw, if the hall was far away. She used to carry my change of clothes in her handbag and inside the movie hall's bathroom I would transfer from my staid school uniform to the colourful floral shirts and dark, striped shorts that she was so fond of me to wear.'

'What about your brother?' She asked.

'He used to be left to his own devices—to board the bus for the journey back home after school finished at its regular time, pull out the cold lunch from the kitchen and after gulping it down, await our arrival from the movie hall. And there we sat for three hours, gaping at the screen with the shining eyes of a starstruck ardent fan and an open-mouthed expression of amazement. We saw most of the movies of Amitabh Bachchan released from '75 to '77, including some re-runs, and would marvel at his histrionics: we cackled with glee at his ineptitude in expressing his feelings to his lady love in *Chupke Chupke*; we clapped and whistled when he closed the doors of the warehouse and threw over the key to Peter in *Deewar*, looking glorious in a blue shirt, his luxurious chest hair peeking through the unbuttoned front of his shirt, a length of white rope dangling from his left shoulder, the 786 badge tied around his left arm shooting off a glare, dazzling our eyes; we seethed in sympathetic rage when he lifted a portly Madan Puri, clad in a U-Brief, and hurled him out of the window, as an avenging lover in the same movie; we shed copious tears as he lay in his mother's lap inside a temple, the don undone by his brother's bullets, and when he was breathing his last, we prayed to God to let Vijay live, again in *Deewar*; we hoped that the coin will, for one time, land 'tails', when he flipped it to decide who will leave to get the ammunition and live and who will stay to defend the bridge and die in *Sholay*; we silently pepped up a depressed Shekhar as he drunkenly lamented about the futility of his life in *Mili*; we sang with him when he crooned 'Kabhie Kabhie Mere Dil Mein. . .' in *Kabhie Kabhie*; we enjoyed his capers with Vinod Khanna, as Vijay in *Hera Pheri*; we detested him for sporting that horrible beard in *Alaap*; we laughed hilariously when, in a drunken stupor, he stuck bandage strips to his reflection in *Amar Akbar Anthony*; we loved his sharp wit as he pulled out his right hand to describe the height of '*Gullu Miyan*', the rooster, in that court scene in *Imaan Dharam*; we willed him to pummel the tiger into a pulp in *Khoon Pasina*, cheering him on all the way; we joined him in his anger as he swung his arms and connected his fists with the villains' jaws in all of his Angry Young Man movies and we chortled at his dance moves when he serenaded with Aruna Irani in the song '*Dil Tera Hai*' from *Bombay to Goa*, wearing an appalling purple and pink floral shirt.' I got up, went down on one knee and lifting my hands in the air, twisted my waist, mimicking his moves in that sweet song and horrible dance routine. 'The dude may be the best actor of his generation, a star even, but he has two awful left feet as far as dancing with his heroines in romantic duets is concerned.' I resumed my seat.

She was giggling uncontrollably as she moved closer, her right thigh touching my left, her warmth seeping into my body like a friendly ghost enveloping my insides in a snug embrace, tendril by delicious tendril. She exclaimed, controlling her tee hees, 'God! You love this guy.'

'Amitabh Bachchan! What is there not to love about him; he is not an actor, he is a complete package. There has never been an actor like him. Take all of them one by one. Raj Kapoor: too Chaplin-esque in his imitation of the Tramp, but he had this boy-next-door charm which titillated some, especially when he was paired with Nargis. Dev Anand: he was a dandy, suave to the hilt with that Gregory Peck style of his. His penchant for tilting and nodding his head while uttering his dialogues, his neck scarves and that puff of his hair made him the Pied Piper of Hindi cinema, leading a horde of swooning women when in his prime, his irritating buttoned-up collar notwithstanding. Dilip Kumar: the tragedy king, they call him. He may be the ultimate method actor—that as per Satyajit Ray—but acting in too many tragedies has left him with a permanently etched morose expression on his face. He was brilliant though, in essaying a subdued Salim in *Mughal-e-Azam*. Rajesh Khanna carried this lover boy image for a long time and was aided in his success by some peppy music from RD Burman, though he excelled himself in *Anand*. Raj Kumar has only one thing going for him, his dialogue delivery—'*Yeh Bachchon Ke Khelne Ki Cheez Nahin, Haath Kat Jaaye Toh Khoon Nikal Aata Hai*' (I mimed his throaty voice, ending up executing a botched imitation). Sanjiv Kumar: he acted in varying genres, ranging from romantic drama to thrillers. He is the most versatile amongst all of them, his portrayal of disparate characters seem the most genuine. Vinod Khanna: here is an actor who not only has good looks but superb acting talent too, but he is stuck with a spate of side-hero (supporting actor) roles lately, even though he started off well with solo leads in *Hum Tum Aur Woh*, *Farebi*, and *Qaid*. He even outshone Amitabh Bachchan in *Khoon Pasina* and outclassed Dharmendra in *Mera Gaon Mera Desh*, though he was the villain in that film. Dharmendra tries to steal the Angry Young Man tag from Amitabh Bachchan, but *Zanjeer* and *Deewar* never happened to him, so he is consigned to hollering, '*Kutte Kamine Main Tera Khoon Pee Jaaonga*' (this time in a perfect impersonation).' I joined her in her sudden explosion of guffaws.

'*Kutte Kamine!*' she giggled to subdue her loud cackles. 'I think that was *Yaadon Ki Baraat*, right?'

I nodded and continued, 'But they all pale in front of Amitabh Bachchan. For one, most of them are well past their prime, especially the trio and Rajesh Khanna. The last great movie of Raj Kapoor was *Mera Naam Joker* and now he is reduced to portraying character roles and promoting his son and brother. Dev Anand, after *Bullet* and *Darling Darling*, is fading and starring in shockers like *Man Pasand* and *Lootmaar*, opposite Tina Munim, who is as old as his daughter. Dilip Kumar; well what can one say of the tragedy king, his hey days are over after acting as old man Sanga in *Kranti*. Rajesh Khanna has to stoop down to *Red Rose* to earn a living, he is a goner, so well past his 'star' days. Dharmendra and Jeetendra can't even hold a candle to Amitabh Bachchan. The Kapoor kid, Rishi Kapoor, excels in bits and pieces like *Bobby* and *Khel Khel Mein*. His uncle Shashi Kapoor will have to be content with side-hero roles, though he may have excelled in *Junoon* and *Fakira*, and he has that once-in-a-lifetime dialogue, '*Mere Paas Maa Hai*' for keepsakes. Shatrughan Sinha is too bombastic, though he excelled in *Kalicharan* and *Kaala Pathar*.

'But Amitabh Bachchan is different. He is here to stay and rule. His baritone is marvellous and it will get deeper with age. He has no fat on his body, though his spindly legs in *Hera Pheri* spoiled the effect. He looks good bashing up those bad guys—although it doesn't seem genuine at all, I love those dhishim-dhishum's. He is an actor par excellence. Look at the fire in his eyes in *Zanjeer*, his dialogue delivery in *Deewar*—nobody else could have implored God with '*Aaj . . . Khush to Bahut Hoge Tum*' like he did—his comic timing in *Chupke Chupke* and *Namak Halaal*, his unbridled anger in all of his action movies. His portrayal of a romantic poet in *Kabhie Kabhie* was superb, he even shines in movies which essay him in negative roles, like *Don*—which other actors could have claimed "*Mujhe Junglee Billian Pasand Hain*" with such panache, standing on top of the stairs holding the balustrade in the 'V' of his right hand, his left hand stuck into the pocket of his bell-bottoms, looking dazzlingly magnificent in a dark grey waist coat, light grey shirt, and a brick-red bow. Who else but Amitabh Bachchan could have gotten the better of Peter Sellers from *The Party* after fourteen years, in the prelude to '*Pag Ghungroo Baandhe Meera Naachi Thi*' song in *Namak Halaal*, with that shoe floating in the water channel?

'And his private life is clean as a whistle. No scandals, no affairs, no rumours. But look at the others. Raj Kapoor had an elaborate affair with Nargis and flings with Vijayanthimala and Padmini, even when he had wife Krishna at home. Dev Anand used to meet Suraiya clandestinely, ultimately married Kalpana Kartik, and has had alleged links with Zeenat Aman and Tina Munim. Rajesh Khanna cannot stop falling in love every time he meets a pretty girl; first Anju Mahendru, then marriage to a 16-year-old Dimple Kapadia, who is thirteen years younger than him, and now there are rumours of his dalliances with Tina Munim. Dharmendra married Hema Malini at the drop of a hat, despite having wife Prakash keeping the hearth fire burning back home. Hema Malini is drop-dead gorgeous no doubt;

there is not a man alive who will not fall for her. But polygamy! He had converted to Islam before the marriage to attain legitimacy.

'Amitabh Bachchan has never been involved in any liaison, any illicit relationship, neither before his marriage to Jaya Bhaduri nor post marriage. All that talk of liaison with Rekha is so much hogwash.'

'How do you know so much about these people?' She asked.

'Mother loved reading about the film stars. The Hindi magazines she used to read gave only sprinklings of information about the various scandals, illicit affairs, and rumours involving the actors and actresses. She read *Sarita*, *Grihashobha*, etc, which were never sufficient to whet her appetite. Once, while flipping through the *Stardust* magazine at her friend's place in Hospet, she was captivated by the glossy pictures and the long stories detailing different romantic affairs between the film stars. But she had one very big complication: she did not know English. Then she started her tutorials, initially from me and later with a friend of father's, who had volunteered to teach her the language. After acquiring the requisite English reading skills, she often spent the afternoons ingesting the latest scandals, the rumours, the innuendos, the interviews, the movie reviews, the Agony Aunt columns, and even the letters from readers. She used to absorb the juicy tidbits, the goings-on at Bombay, the new releases and would later share them with relish, among her circle of friends during the gossip sessions and the ubiquitous kitty parties, especially the latter, where she would circulate graciously from one small cluster to another, guffawing and chuckling at the reactions of her interlocutors.'

'Were those the only movies you saw at Hospet?'

'I also saw many movies with a young college student who had made friends with Father and who would often visit our house. He never refused Mother's requests and upon my insistence, would abide by her wishes to take me to the movies. He is the same one who taught her English. Now that I think of it, I suspect that he might have had a secret crush on Mother, the way he used to look at her with so much reverence—strange why I feel that way, is it okay for a son to feel so?'

'I don't know the mysteries of your mind. Is she beautiful?'

'Not in the sense that I see beauty in you (she never blushed or reacted in any manner whenever I complimented her, she just took my praises in her stride). In my brother's and my eyes, hers was the prettiest face, after *BB*

Mausi, for me. The few photographs of hers, prior to her marriage, show a pretty maiden with soft features.

'So this young man would take me to see English and Hindi movies, whenever I could get an opportunity. Once while seeing *Nagin*, he left me alone in the hall for some time. Seeing the writhing snakes transform into Jeetendra and Reena Roy scared me so much that I shrieked in terror and ran out of the cinema hall, deaf to the hoots of laughter from the other spectators.'

'What about your brother? Didn't he see movies too?'

'He is an odd kind. He never liked movies. Many were the times when the entire family would be in a cinema hall watching a movie and he would get up in the middle of the screening, as if caught up in a fancy, and would demand to leave. If we tried to cajole and restrain him, he would grow fidgety and start creating a ruckus, till the whispered protests of the other moviegoers became a cacophonous dissent, forcing us to beat a hasty retreat. Embarrassed we would leave the theatre, Mother pulling his ears and scolding him.

'Once, after much wheedling and cajoling, I got him to agree to go for a movie on animals, made in Kannada. When Mother said that we would not be able to understand a word, I appealed to her that since the animals too couldn't speak the language, we would be able to understand the movie, Kannada or no Kannada. When we reached the hall, it was empty and the manager would not give us tickets as there was no audience. We said we were the audience and after much finagling he relented, probably taking pity on two kids out for some fun. We entered the cavernous balcony enclosure and sat there for a thrilling experience, the empty space around us sending a deadly chill through our bodies. As the opening credits started rolling, we relaxed and sat back in our seats. The very first scene had a herd of elephants running berserk towards the camera and it felt as if they would break through the screen and trample all over us in that vacant hall. We let out a twin shriek and bolted out of the door, and my brother vowed never to see a movie with me again.'

18

Atithi Devo Bhava (A Guest Is Like a God)

I continued my narrative of our life at Hospet—on how I had learned cycling, borrowing the cycle of a septuagenarian, beanstalk of a man, whom Father had employed as a *Munshi* to assist him at the small office he had set up in the house. I told her about the evening when, while on a family outing at a resort overlooking the immense expanse of the mighty Tungabhadra dam reservoir, Father had been stung by a poisonous scorpion. We kids had been spooked by his rapidly deteriorating condition as he drove our Fiat car like a maniac to the nearest hospital, which was twenty kilometres away, Mother all the time patting his sweating brows with a sodden handkerchief and continuously urging him to remain conscious for another few minutes, as Father's head drooped and lifted in seesaw motions, in his attempts to fend off the debilitating effects of the scorpion's poison. He had been able to successfully reach the hospital, ramming the car into one of the pillars of the gate in the process and had passed out promptly. Fortunately, the car's speed was low and Mother had applied great presence of mind by swinging the steering wheel of the car at the last moment, to avoid running over the watchman who was snoozing in a chair out in the open, a bidi dangling from his drooling lips. We thanked God that no one had got hurt in the collision and Father had arrived safe and sound, although he was out cold.

I recounted the trip we had made, along with one of Father's brothers, who had come visiting alone, as his wife was with child back at Shanti Bhavan. We had stayed at a grand hotel in Bangalore and had visited the Visvesvaraya Industrial and Technological Museum, where we marvelled and ooh-ed and aah-ed in awe at the amazing interactive exhibits on display:

the balls trundling over a roller coaster and after looping a loop bouncing high into a basket, the electro-technical gallery where classical experiments like the Oersted's Experiment, the Barlow's Wheel, the Faraday's Ring, etc., were demonstrated, among others. The best part of the visit was the Fun Science Gallery, where we had joined the throng in operating the large number of exhibits on display there.

The next day we had gone to the Jog Falls, driving through the Bhadra and Sharavati Valley Wildlife Sanctuaries, spying an occasional tiger prowling around deep inside the jungles, hidden amongst the thick trunks of the deciduous flora; often mistaking the yellowed, discarded leaves lying on the carpet of wet black earth, as the stripes of the magnificent cat. We had reached the vast chasm in the bed of the mighty Sharavati River, when the sun was hanging low over the Western horizon, an egg yolk in a sea of blue, and gaped mesmerised at the huge plunge waterfall, divided into four distinct falls. The largest of them, Raja Fall, plummeted with a deafening roar in a magnificent unbroken column from a height of 253 metres. Halfway down its descent it was joined by the Rover which shot out some fifty metres below the summit. The Rocket propelled itself in a series of jets and the Rani moved noiselessly, as its waters poured over the lip in foamy sheets, following the contours of the sheer vertical cliff in a tight, shifting embrace.

We spent two days at Mysore, donating an entire day to the Mysore Palace. We had gawked in admiration at the magnificent blend of Hindu, Muslim, Rajput, and Gothic architectural styles of the marble domes and the 145-foot-high five-storey tower, had stared in reverence at the exquisite sculpture of Gajalakshmi and her elephants above the central arch and had run our fingers in delight, feeling the cold touch of the fine gray granite of the three-storey palace building. Entering the opulent hall of the Ambivilasa, through the elegantly carved rosewood doorway inlaid with ivory, we had bowed our heads in obeisance at the shrine of Lord Ganesha, strolled amongst the ornately gilded columns of the central nave, bent our neck backwards to squint at the stained glass ceilings, glided along on the *pietra dura* floor which was decorated with semiprecious stones and contemplated the huge chandeliers bearing fine floral motifs. We had ogled at the huge collection of dolls and figurines inside the Doll's Pavilion and had tried to estimate the value of the wooden elephant howdah adorned with eighty-four kilograms of gold.

The second day at Mysore, we had gone to the Brindavan Gardens, which lay adjoining the Krishnarajasagara Dam on the Kaveri River. We strolled along the promenade, listening to the soft gurgles of the flowing water, in the magnificent water channels, and feasted our eyes on the opulent spread of the celosia, marigold, and bougainvillea flowers. We fought imaginary battles with the sculptures of animals created out of clipped shrubs. We hummed in a chorus, in tune with the music, as multicoloured waters whooshed towards the sky in splendid arcs in the evening, from the lighted musical fountains, after the sun had dipped below the horizon in a blaze of glory. On our way back, Father had driven our rickety Fiat car like a race car driver, overtaking vehicle after speeding vehicle, gobbling up the miles and covered the twenty-kilometre journey back to our hotel in flat twelve minutes.

'How old were you then?' She asked in amazement.

'I must have been around . . . eight and a half, I think.'

'And you remember all these details so vividly as if you were there yesterday. Have you also got a camera inside your brain?'

I chuckled, 'If I had, you would remain permanently etched inside my head. No, I am not as brilliant as you. Mother had maintained a journal of her own impressions of the trip, to remind 'you boys of the most memorable trip of your lifetime and since you won't recollect much of this when you have grown up, I will give it to you, Sanjay, for keepsakes,' she had said. She had given it to me in a surge of emotions when I first left Shanti Bhavan for Ghorakhal, almost two years back. I had gone through the journal last night to prepare for you.'

I placed my left hand over her right. We had by now got into the habit of touching each other's hands in silent gestures, whenever emotions overtook us during my recollections. Gone were the hesitation, the awkwardness, and the anxieties of the first time when we had touched each other. She made me feel comfortable by never minding my touching her hands and even sat close to me, letting her leg touch mine, as she gazed at me, listening to the words gushing out of my mouth in a torrent, in my motor-mouth fashion of delivery.

I continued my newsreel-type-episode-jumping reminiscences and returned to the night when Father had brought home a bearded, lanky, tall, and handsome foreigner, who had pale skin, light blue eyes and golden hair. 'He had reminded me so much of the German soldiers marching in step, dressed in black, displaying Swastika arm bands proudly as they swung their arms, in those newsreels of the Second World War, I saw in the movie theatres; sans the beard. When he had arrived, he was hanging on to Father's shoulders, walking with a heavy limp, his face caked in coagulated dark red blood, one eye shut as if the lids were glued together, lips swollen up, as if a bloated leach had attached itself to his mouth and wouldn't let go, his free hand hanging like a tattered rag doll. Father later told us that he had found the stranger in a deserted, quiet alley—the result of a mugging gone bad—moaning in pain. Father had somehow managed to push him into his car and had brought him home to give him succour. We had immediately placed him in our guest bedroom and Father had rushed outside to fetch a doctor friend of his.

'Mother, in the meanwhile, fed him warm milk, flavoured with tamarind, and I, with my brother, placed wet towels over his feverish forehead to bring his temperature down, repeatedly changing the towels when heat from his body warmed the cold, wet towels. Father arrived thirty minutes later with his doctor friend, who injected some fluid into the stranger's arm—which gave him instant comfort—arranged for an ambulance and had him shifted to the small government hospital in the town. He was back in our home two days later, as the hospital was understaffed and overworked and had limited beds for the never-ending stream of patients from the town and adjoining villages, and he had nowhere else to go, with his money lost to the muggers. He had bandages covering most of his head and face, his right hand and left leg were in casts and he was clutching his chest in pain, when he was moved from the ambulance into the guest room on a gurney.

'He spent two months at our house resuscitating. Whenever he was in his sleep I would stare at him in amazement—he looked like a creature from out of this world: his exposed skin was as pale as a summer cloud floating in a rich, azure sky, the blue of his eyes was the same hue as the midday sky, his hair was of such a rich golden colour that when the sunlight fell on it a halo would emerge around his head, his beard was of similar golden colour. He spoke to Mother and Father in a thick accented English, no word of which was comprehensible to me, with exaggerated gestures of his sleek, long hands.

'At the end of his two-month period of recovery, he bade farewell to us and presented Father with a Mauseur Pistol. He still has it with him and uses it once in a while during festive occasions, like marriages in the family, *Diwali* and *Holi*, firing into the air with joy and bravado.

'One day, two years back, while digging through Father's address book I discovered his address in West Germany and wrote a few letters. He also wrote back conveying his immense gratitude for our help during a difficult time in his life and how pleased he was to be alive because of my father. He further wrote that he had seen both the evils and virtues of a great country and what he carried back home and which still remains vivid in his memory is the generosity displayed by my family to a complete stranger from a foreign land. My chest had swelled with pride for my parents on reading those lines. That is how we should treat our visitors to win their hearts: not for nothing did our forefathers used to swear by the 'Atithi Devo Bhava' Mantra. His name is Manfred Potter and he is a teacher in Bonn.'

'Did you establish an epistolary relationship with him later'—that was another word to look up in her registers. She smiled a sweet smile and sketched small, skinny squiggles in the air, with two fingers and thumb folded as if holding a pen, when she saw the puzzled look on my face and added, 'like become a pen pal?'

'We wrote to each other sporadically for a few months, but I soon ran out of ideas on what to write about and he also did not know what else to say to an 11-year-old Indian kid. Now I send a card on Christmas and he responds promptly, wishing me and my family a happy new year.'

19

The Steel-Studded Belt

I next jumped to an episode that happened in the summer of '78, a few months before our final departure from Hospet. Father rarely took us to his office buried in the hills outside Hospet. That day, he took us there after a gap of almost nine months. The complex was located deep inside the mining heartland of Bellary district where a mad frenzy of myriad activities used to take place all at once; empty trucks zooming around to collect their loads, loaded dumpers lumbering on the black surface, heavily laden with tons of iron ore, huge hydraulic hammers falling to earth from heights of thirty metres, the constant vibrating cacophony of jackhammers rending the air with an irritating background score, jibs of huge cranes hanging high up in the sky, dragging their cables in enormous arcs, banging large metallic spheres against the sides of the mountains with crashing sounds. Both of us, my brother and I, had always been amazed, every time we came to his office and its surroundings, by this incredible sight of lumbering giants of vehicles, scooting vacant trucks and the huge machineries at work, peeling the mountains tonnage by hungry tonnage. It was a miracle that our puny Fiat had not been crushed amidst all that commotion.

'We somehow managed to reach his office, not without some deft manoeuvring by Father on the churned, black surface of the mud track, and there we saw two burly youth, clad in checked *lungi* (a strip of cloth worn around the waist, the favoured dress of South Indians) and perforated cotton vest, cowering in fear, heads hanging down in feigned embarrassment, their dark faces conveying false remorse. Father told us to remain inside the car, as he disembarked, carrying a thick leather belt. It was a favourite of Father's and he carried it always as a permanent fixture in his car, whenever he ventured out of our home. It was a thick, army-style waist belt, made of

121

dense animal leather and studded with pointed steel knobs which spanned the three-inch width of the belt, three in a row, each row spaced evenly, an inch apart, all around the belt, the shiny, silvery points of the studs catching the sun's rays and shooting off delicate beams. He strode over to the duo, barked a few questions in Kannada and appearing dissatisfied with their stammered responses, started hitting them with the belt in huge vertical thrusts. He beat them black and blue, drawing blood from numerous cuts and bruises on their bodies. He then ordered his other minions to take the 'thieves' to the police station and register a case of stealing truck tires from the company-owned vehicles.

'Both of us were shocked by Father's behaviour. He had never displayed such violence before in our lives. The most he had ever come to was tweaking our ears and registering a slap or two when our childish fights and disputes used to get out of hand and he would get frustrated with our quibbles and quarrels. Inside the car we looked at each other with fear written all over our faces, shook our heads, and I vowed never to flick coins from his pockets, which I used to indulge in at home, whenever Father took off his pants for his occasional siestas on hot afternoons, so that my brother and I could steal away to a shop located some distance away and enjoy a Coca Cola or two, discreetly.'

'You used to steal from your father? Bad boy!' she elbowed my ribs softly, in jest.

'You put a bad ring to it by calling it stealing. You see, there was strict rationing in our house as far as eating or drinking anything from the streets was concerned; one Coca Cola every alternate day, and that too after numerous entreaties and false promises of good behaviour. We liked to sneak away during the afternoons, when Father and Mother were sleeping, and enjoy the fuzzy cold drink with the other kids—throwing around some; hanging the bottle upside down over our mouths till the last resistant drop fell on our still thirsty, hanging tongues, after initially refusing to leave the glassy rim of the bottle; burping out the gas through our nose, bringing stinging tears to our eyes; shaking the filled bottle vigorously and spraying the foam onto each other, in showers of the sweet, sticky liquid. But after witnessing Father in that kind of murderous mood, I did not want to be at the receiving end of that metal studded belt and I promised to myself never to make away with his money, again. Asking for it was much better. As it turned out, I once tried it reluctantly, after a lot of goading from my brother and he calmly, indulgently, pulled out a few coins and told us to "go, both of you enjoy yourselves on a Coca Cola." Kids!' I shook my head. 'While growing up we never realise that the easiest thing to do is just ask. We always feel that whatever endeavour we plan to embark upon, like that peeling out of the house to enjoy a Coca Cola, will meet with instant disapproval of our parents and thus we resort to nefarious means to attain our desires.'

'What next?' She asked in an earnest tone, seeming totally immersed in my narrative, begging for more, as I paused in my recollection.

'Father chucked the job and we moved up North, to Shanti Bhavan, to the utter disappointment of Mother. But I think it's getting late and you will have to go, lest your father comes looking for you.' I looked at her in anticipation, hoping that she would stay longer, not bother that her father would ever concern himself with her whereabouts so late in the evening. But she must have realised that she had overstayed her absence from her home and decided to leave, after a quick glance through the darkened window which showed a curtained blackness outside. A hesitant reluctance was written all over her face. I went breathless and almost folded her into my arms, so immense was my desire.

'You just broke the suspense. A good storyteller always keeps the best for the last. Now I will not be able to sleep, wondering what led to your Father leaving the job. I guess it must be the same that happened at Dalmiapuram. I want the complete story when we meet next.'

20

Return of the Prodigal Son

The next time I told her about the falling out of Father with the son of the top man of the company, who was also a friend of Arjun Thakur and who had been instrumental in Father landing with this prestigious job.

'Father had never bothered about local sensitivities while running the affairs of the company that had employed him. He always placed loyalty towards the company above everything else. But the locals were more concerned with protecting their own turf and promoting their conceited self-interests. To them he was a stern North Indian imposed upon them by a benevolent company and his Army-influenced high moral values did not sit well with the tolerant attitude of the locals towards the criminal elements amidst their ranks. Placing a heavy premium on moral character and ethical conduct, Father dealt with miscreants severely. That was not the first time that he had beaten up the felons working for the company. Whenever he noticed any illegal activity in his jurisdiction, he would demand immediate removal of the culprits, in addition to administering a taste of his own medicine on the offenders—the metal studs of his belt. The locals resented him for that and the union leaders would often complain about him to the top management. The bosses would invariably resolve the issue by giving in to the union's demands and reinstating the miscreants in some other mining operation, away from Father's area of responsibility, the police end of the business having been taken care of by the locals themselves. Father never came to know of such goings-on, kept blissfully unaware of the secret deals between the top management and the union leaders.

'Things came to a head on our return after *BB Mausi*'s marriage during the summer vacations of '78. When he reached his office, Father blew his top when he saw those two thieves, whom he had beaten up in front of us a few months back and whom he had got handed over to the police, back again, working within his jurisdiction. It so happened that the top bosses had not only again acquiesced to the wishes of the union but had also agreed to their further demands of restoring these two goons' former status, within Father's area of authority. It was a rare provocation and Father felt extremely offended.

'He immediately called the union leaders and demanded instant removal of the fiends. The union leaders insisted on retaining them, reinforcing their arguments by stating that it had the blessings of the boss man at the very top. Father returned home in a foul mood and high temper that evening and spoke to the top boss on the phone, explaining the situation and reiterating with sincere conviction that the hoodlums should be removed immediately, else he would quit. For the company, he had been a rare find—with his tremendous zeal and commitment he had transformed the loss making mining operations into an enterprise that had made tremendous profits for the company in the past two years, and this threat of renunciation shook up the top man. He immediately dispatched the scion of the family and his anointed successor to Hospet, to sort the matters out. The son arrived the very next day, in a plane-train combination of mode of travel, and after meeting the union leaders, where he did not achieve any success, he came to our house late in the evening to pacify Father and somehow get him to agree on staying on. But Father's principled stand and strong beliefs, further strengthened with a stubborn resolve, took a toll on his fickle patience and the top man's son had to finally take his leave, after Father issued the ultimatum: 'Either you can stoop to the ground in front of the union leaders or have me running the operations my way.'

'We boarded the train next week, to travel the long two days' journey for one final time. Father sold most of his belongings, including the family's favourite Fiat car, for pittance at Hospet, keeping his loyal Yezdi motorcycle to himself; he had it transported by train.'

Father has always believed in the concept of 'living in the now', and though he used to earn a handsome salary at Hospet, within six months of our return to Shanti Bhavan, he had run through his meagre savings. From a prosperous employee of a prestigious company he had turned into a penniless jobseeker, entirely dependent on his brothers for subsistence of his family, as my grandfather had not left any will (the concept of will was alien in our family then) and it was not in his nature to demand his share of our ancestral property from his siblings. He was a firm believer in keeping his larger family together and maintaining the Tivari name as a mark of respectability and dependability in our town. It was not in his nature to ever indulge in any bellicosity which would lead to separation from his kin. But those kin, in their turn, had not been able to live up to the legacy of their father. After Grandfather's passing away, one year ago, the affairs at the farmhouse had deteriorated, primarily due to the lack of ability and interest on behalf of his descendants. Father's elder brother had suddenly developed an interest in politics and would spend most of his time hobnobbing with the wannabe local politicians. His younger brothers were totally inept at managing the affairs of the huge farm. They were more interested in and were perennially preoccupied in canoodling with their respective wives. 'One lecherous uncle of mine seemed to take greater interest in his younger brother's spouse too and in the wives and unmarried elderly daughters of the few remaining retainers at Premnagar.' Only one of his younger brothers took some interest in farming and his efforts were sufficient enough to meet the daily needs of the Tivaris from the produce of the farm and some spare cash from the proceeds of the harvests. For the money, even the basement of Shanti Bhavan—which Grandfather had meant to be used as a garage, for the umpteen numbers of vehicles he had dreamt of possessing, and which was now reduced to stacking the firewood for the centralised kitchen—had to be rented out to a genial Sardar (Sikh gentleman), to let him establish his automobile workshop.

Father's dwindling financial situation had its adverse effects on the standard of living we had become so used to in the past three years. Gone were the 555's Father used to smoke so luxuriously, emitting clouds of blue smoke through his nostrils, and now he had to be content with the humble *bidi*, its pungent odour permeating the fabrics of our clothes, making us smell like a Paan shop. He couldn't spare cash to even fill petrol in the motorcycle, his most prized possession, and he was reduced to pedalling a cranky Atlas bicycle for commuting to and from Premnagar, where he used to help out his farmer brother, whenever he was not away hunting for a job. We brothers had to rely on his discarded trousers, altered by a benevolent tailor who did not charge any money from Mother to refit Father's trousers to our size, for our 'new' shorts and pants. Our shoes would only be replaced when the holes on the soles widened into receptacles for big stones, small pebbles entering through pea-sized gaps were accepted as minor irritants to be borne with a brave face and occasional tears. Mother had to take up sewing in order to stitch our school uniforms, as we were in that stage of our lives, particularly I, that we used to fast outgrow our clothes, even before the collars of our shirts would start fraying into threads. The pitter-patter of the Usha sewing machine was a constant background score during our afternoon siesta ritual, as Mother sat squatting on our bedroom floor, rolling its wheel with her right hand. Mother had to sacrifice her noon rest for us.

But Father never ran out of cash for two things: education and nutritional requirements of his sons. In a household where his brothers were educating my cousins in government schools, primarily to seize upon the free education scheme for wards of Freedom Fighters, Father had us studying in the only English-medium convent school in town, doling out the money from the deepest recesses of his reserves every month, to pay the exorbitant school fees. When our weakness in maths became apparent, he had even hired a tutor to give us brothers extra lessons at our home. He also paid for extra private tuitions in Sanskrit for me, which I attended with great relish and anticipation, as the tutor was very pretty—by then I was 10 years old and stirrings of attraction towards pretty girls were awakening inside me. 'I still remember the way my heart used to skip a thousand beats when, every Saturday, I stood outside the door of her *Peeli Kothi* (Yellow House) eagerly waiting for her to answer the bell I had rung and thereafter continuously gape at her face, as she desperately and unsuccessfully tried to make me see the sense in differentiating between the nominative a-stems of the masculine grammatical genders of '*ramah*', '*ramau*', and '*ramah*' in singular, dual, and plural, respectively. How could I? All the 'Ramas', from the various versions of Ramayan in our country, wouldn't have been successful in making me understand the nuances of Sanskrit grammar, when I was in the company of such divine beauty. Her prettiness proved to be her handicap and my undoing, as my grades in school never improved and Father, having realised the futility of the entire exercise, cancelled any further Sanskrit tuitions after two months. I had shed a solitary tear when I was told that the *Peeli Kothi* was no more my scholastic destination. Anyway, she had left the town immediately thereafter, having got married to someone in Delhi.'

Pratima chuckled and interjected here, 'Do you always have a thing for females older than you? First *BB Mausi*, then the Sanskrit teacher, now me.'

I shrugged nonchalantly. 'Something to do with me that I haven't been able to fathom. I guess I never will. God has his own mysterious ways in moulding us humans. I leave it up to him to decide for me, where matters of my heart are concerned.'

'Are you implying that what you feel has got nothing to do with you, but it is God who creates those emotions inside your heart?'

I grinned at her and said, 'Well, if something goes wrong I can always put the blame on him.'

'You scoundrel,' and she laughed loudly, her nose crunching delightfully and her eyes closing shut—I noticed a strand of saliva between her open lips and involuntarily, I waved a finger across her gaping mouth to cut the string before she closed her mouth.

'The nutrition part was on Mother's insistence. She knew what was the basic minimum for her sons' growing bodies; two eggs daily, except Tuesdays, a glass of milk three times a day, fresh vegetables, daal, rice, and chapatti topped up with fresh fruits in the afternoons and a sumptuous meal of vegetable curry and paranthas before we went to bed at night, with an occasional chicken dish thrown in once a week—this from a lady who had been brought up in a household where they abhorred eating onion and garlic, what to talk of eggs and chicken. Mother was always at Father's throat for the extra money required to buy the fruits and vegetables, the poultry and the dairy products necessary for our nourishment. Even my maternal grandfather used to chip in often—bringing a sack full of fresh vegetables and fruits on his fortnightly visits every alternate Sunday. I still recall, with a silent sob, his hoarse, *bidi*-affected, throaty voice hollering 'Badi Munni, Badi Munni' from the main entrance of Shanti Bhavan, whenever he came calling. Both of us brothers would run with shrieks of excitement and leap into his arms, Mother following in our wake. He would prop each of us on his lap, as he sat down on the sofa inside the living room and handed over his sack to Mother, surreptitiously slipping in some cash into her grateful, trembling palms and giving lollipops to us. He would only drink water from Mother's hands, politely refusing her offers of tea and biscuits; not for him to consume anything procured out of his son-in-law's pockets, that too when they were almost empty. He would terminate his brief visits with a prayer that God would improve our situation, placing a blessing upon his eldest child's head as she reverentially touched his feet and tousling our hairs as we stood sucking on the lollipops.'

After a brief pause to control the overflowing emotions I was caught up in during my narration, in which time she slipped in closer and touched my face to reassure me, her lemony perfume soothing my nerves, I told her about my first contacts with girls of and around my age, except the cousin born before me on my father's side and the one after me on my mother's side.

'Hasina Khan was in my class. Daughter of the SP (Superintendent of Police) of the district, she had a very fair complexion, a beautiful face with doe eyes and dimpled smile, a small nose and a lanky frame—she was even taller than me. In deference to her parentage, all students in the school avoided her in a respectful way. She carried a forlorn look upon her and did not have any friends; she used to eat her tiffin alone, propped up against a bush in a far corner of the school premises. She never indulged in the "kho-kho" games the other girls played with us boys and was always seen moving around in circles along the school's perimeter during the free periods, talking to herself, lost in a world of her own making. Sometimes, watching her from a distance, as she went on her prowls along the periphery, I used to take an uncharacteristic pity on her and often wondered what was eating into this pretty girl.

'I was particularly fond of her, as she never laughed at my inadequacies in recitation, unlike the other students. Having studied the past three years in Tamil and Kannada language schools, I was out of my depth in Hindi. And our Hindi teacher used to like her pupils read passages from the textbooks, out loud; "To improve your diction," she said. I was never comfortable while reciting these passages and used to draw peals of laughter from the other kids, whenever I stammered through my assignment. Even in English, I once spoke the ampersand as "s". One day while reading out a passage from the Upanishads I pronounced "Om" as "oon", since it was written that way in the Hindi textbook. The entire class, including the teacher, guffawed in mirth. My face reddened and I glanced sheepishly towards Hasina. She was giggling too.

'I cornered her outside the classroom during the break and accused her of hurting my feelings. She apologised to me promptly, feeling genuine shame for her involuntary snigger and added, "I will make it up to you. Why don't you learn Hindi from me?"

'She turned out to be a marvellous tutor. During the tiffin breaks and free periods, we would sit under a huge mulberry tree amidst the school grounds and she would explain to me the intricacies of making out the differences between "ya" and "tha", "ma" and "bha" and how to make words and write sentences. She made me read out entire passages and corrected my diction, bringing out why "Singh" was spoken with a deep nasal "na" and not as "Sinh". I spent six wonderful months learning Hindi from her, listening to the sweet, lilting tone of her voice, which sounded so much like flowing water.

'She was not only my unofficial tutor but became my enchantress, too. Over a period of time, I started developing a liking for her, which had more to do with the attraction I had started feeling towards her. She often figured in the boy-to-boy conversations I had with my brother back home and after some time even my aunts started joking with me, making frequent references of Hasina to elicit a blush from me. But I could never reach the confession stage with her. Six months after my joining the school, she left abruptly one day and after discreet enquiries I found out that she had left for Kanpur, where her father had been transferred.

'I did not wait long to fill up the void left by Hasina. I had never noticed her much, not until Hasina left. She was a presence in the school but best avoided, since she was the daughter of Father's close friend and our family doctor, the one who had had me hung upside down for a month, as a 3-year-old. Neelima was not pretty, but what caught my eyes was her smile, which lit up her eyes and crunched up her nose, just like you. And I found her brilliance in academics very fascinating. When Hasina was there, Neelima used to compete with her for the first position in the class tests, but after Hasina's departure, Neelima acquired the numero uno status and there was no beating her thereafter. But I never got close to her. My frequent sit-ins with Hasina earlier had drawn a lot of ridicule from the other boys in my class, mostly out of envy, I am sure. There was this tall boy, who had overgrown his ten years by three additional years—no doubt with his father faking his date of birth in the records—who was particularly severe on me and often mocked me for being close to the girls; my effeminate nature, bolstered by my fair complexion, soft features, and the baby fat I had not yet expunged, did not help much in removing the impression of a wannabe debonair, an object of ridicule in small-town societies. Ultimately I had to resign myself to admiring Neelima from afar and trying to impress her by performing well in the exams. She was the best in the class and I somehow managed to be the best among the boys, so I got numerous opportunities to share the stage with her, during important school functions. Those were the occasions when I would sit next to her and dream of meeting her alone sometime. But that time never came. Her being Father's friend's daughter did not help matters, as I dreaded the thrashing I would receive if Father ever found out that I was dallying with his buddy's daughter.'

I also told her about the pretty younger twin who used to play with my younger brother, making me go green with envy, as I had to make do with her plain featured elder twin.

21

The Medical Exam at Nainital

My immediate future became a source of constant worry for my parents in the autumn of '79. The next year I would be completing my sixth class and the convent school had not yet been upgraded to a high school status. I would have to leave after March next year, as the school did not run classes beyond the sixth standard. The options for my further education were very limited in my home town—all other schools were government-aided, Hindi-medium schools where Father was reluctant to put me in.

'Hindi-medium for me! I would have never passed a single exam.'

'So your Father decided to send you to a boarding school and you landed up here.'

'But it was not easy. The Army man inside Father liked the concept of Sainik School education and since there was scholarship available, it appealed to him more. He had not been able to secure any employment after having spent close to one and a half years as a jobless wanderer and was short of cash all the time. So he homed on to two Sainik Schools, at Lucknow and here. I spent the next six months studying furiously for my class 6 exams as well as the entrance exams for the two Sainik Schools. The syllabus for the school at Lucknow was very difficult, especially maths. Maths was and remains my Waterloo. Like Napoleon at Austerlitz, Friedland, and Wagram, I can wade through all the other subjects, but the moment I come up against the complications of mathematics I get stumped, faltering and failing in my futile endeavours of unravelling the mysteries hidden in those numbers and their multitudinous formulae. I could never understand the complexities involved in working out the compound interests, converting percentages into fractions, deriving profit percentages from cost price, and selling price and myriad other problems; which were part of the syllabus for the entrance exam for the Sainik School at Lucknow and despite much cajoling by my mother and tutoring by Father—the facilities of the private tutor of last year had been done away with, as we could not afford him—I could never master the syllabus. Compared to that the syllabus for the school here was a cakewalk, with its simple multiplications and divisions and easy equations and formulae. After a month, Father realised the hopelessness of persisting with the school at Lucknow and one day, in a fit of rage and frustrated with my incompetence—which had led to my receiving my fair share of lashes of his other leather belt, not the steel studded one thankfully—he burnt all the books for the entrance exam for the Lucknow school and told me to concentrate on Ghorakhal: "and you better pass or you will end up like all of your cousins, a literate ignoramus," he had warned me.'

'Why the difference in syllabus at both the schools?' she asked innocently.

'Father had explained to me once, after I had complained about the difficulties I was facing. The school at Lucknow is based on the Uttar Pradesh Board syllabus, whereas this school has the syllabus of the Central Board of Secondary Education, CBSE. We have such a complicated education system in our country—each state has respective education boards which prescribe the syllabus of schools under them, mostly taught in the regional or state languages; the CBSE determines the syllabus for the schools run and funded by the Central Government, the syllabus covered in English or Hindi medium; then we have the Council for the Indian School Certificate Examinations which lays down the syllabus of the convent schools and public schools, the classes conducted in English. We have such a complex education system in our country. No wonder people find it so difficult to get a job. And the irony is that, despite such a complex system, we deny education to our daughters. What a shame.'

I continued after a brief pause to restrain my angst, 'With the preparations for Sainik School Lucknow consigned to the pyre, I put my whole and soul for the Ghorakhal exam. In February '80, Father and I came here to appear in the entrance exam. After clearing that, we went to Nainital for the interview and medical tests. We were staying at Hotel Natraj and by the evening I was a nervous wreck, even though the interview was scheduled the next day. While we were listening to Amitabh Bachchan crooning in his own voice '*Mere Paas Aao Mere Doston*', from the tinny solitary speaker of the portable Murphy transistor Father carried with him everywhere, he offered to take me to the movie, *Mr Natwarlal*, principally to soothe my nerves, as the film was being screened in a cinema hall in town. Even Amitabh Bachchan didn't help and I crept into a fitful sleep that night.

'The next morning saw me fidgeting restlessly amongst a cluster of shy, reticent, and anxious 10- to 11-year-olds, assembled in a huge hall at the interview site. A few of the boys tried to break the ice by cracking some dry jokes and gradually I started relaxing in the company of like-minded kids and even cackled at a joke or two. One of them was even related to our situation and went like this:

An aspirant for a job could not commit to his memory the name of the second president of India and instead he committed it to a slip of paper, which he wedged inside his waistband. Lo and behold, in his interview, he was asked the same question and he looked down, as if searching for Sarvepalli Radhakrishnan in his lap. He discreetly inserted two fingers into his trouser's waist, curled over the cloth, read the name of the brand printed on the strip of cloth stitched to the inside of his underwear's waist and shouted, "Young India."

'After giggling obligingly at the joke, I sped off towards Father to enquire about the names of all the ex presidents and prime ministers of our country.

'My interview went off well and later we were measured for our weight, height, chest expansion, and waist circumference. The last event in the medical examination was the colour blindness test. I had never seen the book before and stared at the multicoloured small circles arranged in a haphazard manner. Not understanding what to do, I looked at the bespectacled gentleman who was holding the book open. Looking at my bewildered expression, he told me to identify the number hidden amidst the circles. I bent down to peer at individual tiny circles, to search for the one circle that contained the number. Sensing that I was finding it difficult to understand the concept, he showed me how a few circles of similar shades of colour, amongst the jumble, were arranged in a manner that they formed a shape in the form of a number; the first page contained "3". Realisation dawned and as he turned over to the next page, I read "9", he turned over— "5", he turned over—"8", he turned over . . . blank. I went totally blank. The number of circles on this page had multiplied manifold, they were of numerous shades of green and yellow and their size had become smaller. This was becoming difficult. After waiting for some time, he turned to the next page. By this time the circles had started moving, first the ones along the edges, then the ones in the centre, and they commenced dancing. All the circles went into constant motion and my eyes blurred. No shape of a number could be made out by me and I ventured, "It is 1, sir." "No, son, it is 14," he said. He turned to the next page, the circles on this page also appeared to be executing macabre movements; merging into one another, bouncing off each other, some of them taking off and leaping into the air with toothy glee, some drifting towards the edges of the page and dripping over the sides in mournful sadness, but none of them combining to form any number I could make out. I looked up at the reflection of the tube light in the gentleman's thick glasses and shook my head, tears welling in my eyes. He sighed and gestured for me to leave and I wept into my father's arms, sobbing hysterically. In between sobs I told him how the circles were dancing in front of my eyes and how I couldn't read the hidden figures, saliva strings shooting off with each word. He wiped off my tears with his handkerchief and told me to wash my face in the restroom. When I came out after a good scrub of my face, he was nowhere to be seen. I stood outside the door of the room where the test was being conducted and grew progressively miserable as each aspirant came out smiling broadly, indicating success.

'Finally, the last candidate came out with a confident smile on his face and Father emerged simultaneously, with Dwivedi Sir, from the corner room where we had been interviewed earlier. Dwivedi Sir looked at me sympathetically and walked with Father into the colour blindness test room. After sometime, I was called inside and the gentleman with the spectacles beckoned me over towards a table, where an array of coloured sketch pens was laid out. Father and Dwivedi Sir were standing in a corner. He picked up pen after pen and asked me to name its colour—"red", "blue", "green", "black", "yellow", "blue"—he said, "No son, it is not blue. Look at it carefully." I peered at it; it was definitely not the navy blue I knew of, but it was a shade akin to blue and I did not know its name. It looked like the colour of some vegetable I had seen earlier, but for the world of me I could not recall the name of the damn vegetable. Panic struck me and I looked at him, despair clouding my eyes, and reiterated, "It is blue, sir." He shot a smug look at my father and said emphatically, in a sombre tone, "It is purple. Haven't you seen a brinjal?" The ceiling descended upon my head and I ran out of the room, hiding myself inside a toilet cubicle in the restroom and cried my heart out. My worried father coaxed me out after sometime and we returned home in dejection.

'The next academic session started and after Father had waited long enough, without receiving any letter asking me to join this school, I was taken to the Government Inter College—a Hindi-medium, boys-only school, located at a walking distance from Shanti Bhavan, where most of my cousins had studied or were studying—for the admission formalities. I dutifully reported for my first day at the college on Monday. My seventh class comprised of about thirty-four boys, all of them older and taller than me, with some of them sporting dark fuzzes above their upper lips. No teacher appeared in the first two days. The students joked, played, quarrelled, fought, and pulled my leg. Nobody seemed to be interested in studies and I kept to myself, lost in my own world. On the third day, a rotund, moonfaced, baldish man, wearing thick lenses in his squarish spectacles, which made his eyes bulge, peeked inside the classroom and announced that there would be no classes till the next Monday—all my fellow students cheered—adding that all of us had to get our textbooks when we came on Monday and issued an ultimatum that those of us without books need not come to the college.

'I told Mother that she had to procure the books, else I would not be able to attend classes at the college. She replied exasperatedly that whatever money she had had already been spent on my new uniform and we would have to wait till Father came home. He had mysteriously disappeared that Sunday and remained incommunicado till Saturday. He arrived late at night, when I was asleep, and in the morning I woke up to the best news in my life till then; I had been selected for Sainik School Ghorakhal and since the session had already started I had to leave within the next five days. The following few days were spent in frantic searches for the dresses, underwear, shoes, socks, bed sheets, towels, toiletries, and countless other items required for a boarding school. After bidding tearful farewells to my grandmother, mother, brother, uncles, aunts, and cousins, we left for Hathras by train, laden with a trunk full of my possessions, and hired a taxi from there for the 300-kilometre journey to reach here and I joined sixth class again.

'The first year here was miserable for me as I used to persistently feel homesick, finding succour only with Dwivedi Sir's family here in this house. Things eased up a bit in the second half of last year, after I had cemented my friendships with compatible classmates. Then you appeared as an angel this spring and now I have a feeling that my life will never be the same again.'

'Don't you have high hopes with me? You might end up in a huge disappointment,' she chuckled. 'How did your Father manage it?'

'I don't know the exact details. But after a lot of soul searching I have homed on to two theories. The more probable one is Dwivedi Sir. He is a friend of Father's from his university days and is from my home town. He has assumed the role of my local guardian here and I have had unlimited access to this house since joining the school. Interestingly, his father also taught maths to my father when he was in his school at my hometown. Dwivedi Sir might have used his influence to get me selected despite my "purple patch turning turtle".' I finished with a pun.

'And the second theory?'

'The second probability is a clerk in the administrative office here. He is a Mr Khan, reeks of rotten meat when you are up close to him. In my first year, he used to call me over to his office often, asking after my welfare. I think some money was passed under the table. I have always wondered where Father came up with all that money from; to purchase my uniforms and other items, for the school fees, the taxi ride and for bribing that clerk, if at all it had happened. Imagine my father, always an upright man, having the greatest regard for strong morals and ethics, having had to stoop down to bribing lowly clerks for his son. It must have been very difficult for him to lower his high standards. Had it not been for him I would have been rotting in that Hindi-medium college and would have never met you. Wasn't it serendipitous—our meeting on that first day, while I lay delirious on that bed over there? Your brothers and my father have been instrumental in moulding our combined destinies.'

'You give such a nice ring to our circumstances. Are you always so forthcoming with girls?'

'No, I have never been like this before. I was attracted to Hasina but could never tell her so. Neelima was admired from a distance. That pretty Sanskrit teacher was too old for me. I also found our hostel matron appealing, till I met you, but she is also too elderly. But you make me feel so comfortable. This is the first time I have ever narrated my life to anyone and I felt no hesitation in letting you know all about myself, even my aspirations and secret desires. I have never spoken about my feelings for *BB Mausi* to anyone but you. I feel as if I can even tear open my heart and show you how it beats.'

'I like your candour, Sanjay. I like the way you say things, it is so different from how my brothers talk to me. For the first time in my life I have felt so free, not that I have ever felt confined with my brothers. But you are like the breath of fresh air of the early morning. I would like to continue meeting you and share my thoughts as well as learn from yours. You are leaving for your vacations tomorrow. We will meet again the first Sunday you are back from your home. But not here. It is too restrictive and the time is always short. We will have our sittings at the Water Tank Hill. Towards its south there is a trail strewn with boulders, well hidden from casual observers, which leads to the top of the hill. We will meet at the beginning of that trail at nine on 13 June.'

And I imposed a self-ban on entering Dwivedi Sir's house again, except on festive occasions.

22

The Water Tank Hill

I was there at the base of the Water Tank Hill at seven on 13 June, after having spent the month-long vacations in eager anticipation, bursting with impatience and frequently snapping at my brother for his incessant intrusiveness. I climbed the hill twice, repairing the trail by moving stones and small rocks, so that she would not lose her footing, clearing the pine needles where their density made the going slippery, identifying strong bushes to act as handholds, where the climb became steep and selecting the spot on the roof of the tank where we would sit and talk.

Water Tank Hill is a huge mountain within the premises of the school, which contains a water tank on its summit. The hill runs in a rough north-south alignment, with its base being about 300 metres long, rising up to a height of 300 metres, via gentle slopes towards its west and steep slopes towards the east and peaking in the form of a flattish plateau, 200 metres in length. It is on this plateau that a twenty-metre long, ten-metre wide, and ten-metre deep concrete cuboid had been constructed, to store water. The tank is mostly submerged with its lip protruding five feet above the ground surface and the roof of the tank can be easily reached by lifting oneself up on to it. It caters for the water requirements of the entire school by feeding the water, using the gravity feed principle, to all the taps in the buildings of the school. During the winters, when the steel pipes leading out of the tank are blocked by the water freezing into ice, all students of the school form a 'water chain' to ferry water in buckets from a perennial stream located on the western slope of the larger plateau on which the school stands—400 metres downhill from the students' mess—to the mess and the Raman and administrative blocks of the school. During such times, a water truck fetched water from Bhowali, for the residences of the staff and students, which was collected in bucketfuls by the wives of the staff and the junior students of each House.

The hill is offset from the main road of the school by a flat shrub land of 100 metres width. Its top can be approached through numerous trails on its western slope which overlooks the principal's mansion, the slopes of the ground on which the mansion stands, the main road and the Grassy Fields; an open flat area where cricket, football, hockey, and even *gilli-danda* could be played. A scene of the song '*Tujhse Naaraaz Nahin Zindagi*', in the film *Masoom*, was shot on that very slope that year, when I had the opportunity to see Naseeruddin Shah in person, the one and only time. Towards its north are the school's obstacle course and a reentrant which can also be used to climb up to the summit, albeit a bit longer. Towards the south are the Staff Quarters and a narrow trail, strewn with rocks and boulders, which is well camouflaged and not visible to anyone observing from the Staff Quarters or the Grassy Fields. The steep eastern slope of the hill dominates the Shyamkhet Valley and the trekking route leading up to the humongous Gagar mountain and its minions, located to the north, twenty kilometres from the school, standing like a sentinel guarding the realms beyond or, one could say, acting as a barrier preventing the icy cold winds from the snow peaks of the higher reaches of the Himalayas reaching and biting into the soft sensitive skins of the young children from the hot plains, staying at the school.

The entire mountain is covered with tall pine trees, bushes and shrubs, with shed pine needles and discarded pine cones carpeting the surface. During the monsoons, the slopes become quite mushy and are difficult to ascend, while on sunny days, it is strenuous to purchase traction on the slippery clusters of pine needles.

At nine I spotted two figures approaching the hill from afar. As they drew closer I recognised her and Bindu. Always a sight for sore eyes, she looked enchanting in a sky blue salwar suit, with the stole hanging from both sides of her neck. I had missed her so much during the past four weeks that I wanted to fold her into my arms. Instead I threw my arms around Bindu in a brotherly hug and said a soft 'hello Pratima, missed you a lot', to her. She replied with a dazzling smile—dimples, dimples, and dimples; crazy dimples, deep dimples, shallow dimples, mesmerising dimples, a deep yearning engulfed me making me want to caress them with the tips of my fingers—and extended her hand in a formal handshake. I let my grip on her right hand linger for some time and led her along the path, telling her to be careful at tricky spots and amused her with sweet nothings about the time I had spent at home during the vacations. She didn't say much about what she had done during the long break. Bindu followed us silently.

'Bindu has agreed to act as my chaperone and my excuse to be here, in case someone seeking adventure happens upon us by happenstance. I have become her unofficial tutor, now that she has joined the main school', she said as I pulled her up to the water tank's roof and settled down at the spot I had selected earlier. Bindu sat some distance away under a pine tree, out of earshot, and spent her time reading, snoozing, and chewing a pine needle. I felt I was the luckiest boy in the world, sitting so close to the girl I love, and the clandestine nature of our tryst gave a thrill to me I had never experienced before. I looked up at the pristine blue of the sky with nary a cloud to mar its sterile expanse, snatches of it visible through the canopy of the top branches of the pine trees, swaying and swirling in the breeze travelling all the way from Gagar. The filtered rays of the dazzling sun were casting myriad shifting shadows upon her exquisite face, as I looked at her with reverence and gratitude.

We spent many glorious Sundays on the Water Tank Hill, till the winter of '84, missing only the Sundays of the vacations and the times when any or both of her brothers were home: 'I want to devote my entire time for them, as they come home so infrequently,' she had said. (That was a warning bell I now regret to have ignored then. Who could have thought that her brothers would become my rivals for her affections?). I spent those Sundays at Nainital, seeing movies.

Some Sundays she would miss without due warning, due to some complication at home or with Bindu. Such Sundays I would wait and wait and wait, trudging up and down the hill countless times, seething in frustration, my mind reeling with infinite possibilities to explain her absence; 'she has gone sick, she has broken a leg, she has been sent away by her father to live with his spinster hag of a sister back at her ancestral village, her father is contemplating her marriage and has barred her from leaving the house' and so on and so on, dark gloomy images materialising like unsolicited ghosts. When I subsequently complained to her for missing our date—'it is the one event I look forward to the entire week, you will never be able to gauge my agony when you don't come, I slogged up and down the hill a thousand times'—she would hold my hands tenderly, apologise profusely, explain her reasons and admonish me for working myself up and wasting my energy in plodding up and down the trail: 'Your cheeks have sunk in due to the lack of nutrition from that horrible garbage they feed you in the mess. If you continue like this you will waste away and vanish, your body dissolving in your angst. Where would I ever find another you, to spend my Sundays with?' It was true enough, the food at the students' mess was pathetic, to say the least—soggy breads with cold, oily, thin omellettes in breakfast; runny daal, half-cooked rice, boiled cabbages, and skinny chapattis in lunch; bland, milk-less tea in the evenings; and watery daal, tasteless cabbages, fat rice, and flimsy chapattis again in dinner. As a result, all of us students looked like skeletal remains of our portly selves, from the day we had joined the school.

We used to be there on top of the hill from nine till one, and on occasions Pratima and Bindu would get packed lunches and we would spend time till late in the evening. Pratima's parents were told that she was busy with her studies and tutoring Bindu and they never bothered to enquire about her whereabouts. Bindu's family members, except Dwivedi Sir, were into the secret and they never let it out. Dwivedi Sir was also kept under the impression that she had gone with Pratima to study. 'Gone where?' 'None of your business. Bindu feels comfortable learning from Pratima and it shows in her high marks in the exams. They might be studying anywhere they find peace and quiet,' was Aunteeji's response to his query once and that had shut him up for good.

We were rarely disturbed by any intruders, since other students considered Sundays as breathers from the hectic activities of the week gone by and preferred to spend the holiday in motionless activities, requiring minimum investment of their tired muscles, than to climb mountains. On the occasional occasion when any of us spied a trespasser climbing up the slopes, I would peel off and go hiking, away from the duo, and Bindu would come over to sit with Pratima. I would wait out the interloper or if he decided to stay, I would open a book and read, sitting a respectable distance away from the pair.

We carried satchels filled with books and magazines, which we read or discussed together. Pratima was very fond of the National Geographic and we would spend hours roaming the world contained in the glossy, colourful pages of the journal: admiring the entasis of the columns and the delicate curvature of the stylobate of the Parthenon; gazing at the three-storeyed arcade, surmounted by a podium and topped by the tall attic of the outer wall of the Colosseum; wondering at the gifts of nature which created the magnificent Uluru in Australia, granting the inert sandstone structure the ability to change colours; speculating at what kinds of people were there and which technology they used, to transport for hundreds of kilometres, the stones, weighing up to four tons, to construct the megalithic monument of Stonehenge, almost 5,000 years back; marvelling at the colossal effort gone in recruiting and managing the 20,000 workers and the 37-member creative team, hired from all over the world, for the construction of the Epitome of Love, Taj Mahal—she had a different opinion on the epithet and said, 'How can a man, who put his wife through the painful experience of fourteen pregnancies in nineteen years—she was virtually pregnant throughout her adult life—be considered a great lover. I think it was more a matter of hubris than love for his wife which prompted Shah Jahan to construct the mausoleum.'

She was particularly severe on the modern Indian architects' lack of imagination and vision: 'We are the birthplace of urban civilisation from 2700 BC, but after the Britishers left, we have hardly added any building of note to the immense wealth of architecture we have, right from the fourth century BC.'

'But I won't let you lack where your studies are concerned,' she said after pouring scathing criticism on the very limited portrayal of post independence Indian architecture. 'Tell me what are your weak subjects and topics?'

I told her that maths, as she knew, remained a mystery still. She started my lessons promptly, taking it as a challenge. Learning from her, maths became my favourite subject. Her method of approaching her teaching assignment was fairly simple—'Every maths question can be solved any number of ways. Say, you want to multiply 7 by 24. To solve it you can multiply directly, which will take a long mental exercise. Easier way is to break 24 into 12 and 2. From the table of 12 you get 84 and double of that is 168. Easy, see! Every problem can be broken into simpler steps to reach the solution. Think of the steps. Most of you boys here try to mug up just one way to arrive at a solution. You have to understand the concept. If that is absorbed by you, you can arrive at the solution in any manner.'

When it came to trigonometry, she got an inclinometer and a tape measure, and using them, she showed me how to measure heights of trees using the 'tan theta' formula. She even explained to me how to measure the time of day by using the shadow of a stick; she stuck a four-foot-long stick into the ground at a spot where the sun's rays were not obstructed, barring a short period of thirty minutes, when the sun was over our heads. She kept the stick inclined at an angle of thirty degrees—'to cater for the earth's tilt, the angle should be the latitude of the place'—the head pointing towards the north and placed rocks at the end of the shadows of the stick, every hour. In the evening she compared the position of the rocks with the corresponding time of day noted in a note book. The position of the rocks conformed to the actual passage of time and we did not have to carry our watches henceforth; just looking at the stick's shadow in relation to the rocks (now dug into the ground), we could tell the time of day.

She got a stopwatch and explained to me how to measure her acceleration, by running on the flattish top a distance of 100 metres in 15 seconds and using the formula $S = ut + \frac{1}{2}at^2$. She once borrowed a vernier caliper and a circular nut from the physics laboratory and explained to me how to measure the nut's outer and inner diameter, when I told her about my inability to comprehend the vernier scale, to arrive till the second decimal place in a centimetre. She ran, whistling from one end of the plateau top to the other, to show me how the changes in the sounds of the whistle denoted the Doppler's principle—which is how the radars function.

She explained potential energy and measurement of gravitational force, by climbing a tree and dropping stones from measured heights, telling me to hit the button on the stopwatch when she released the stone and when it impacted with the ground. She was an expert tree climber, wrapping a rope around the trunk and using her hands and legs she would propel herself to climb the tallest of trees—not elegant to look at but it got her to the highest branches of the tall pine trees. When she used to reach almost to the top, my heart would stop beating, seeing her swaying with the motions of the tree, hanging onto the fronds and howling and laughing with glee into the wind. I often begged her not to climb trees but she loved the feeling of holding on to the flimsy branches on top and swinging back and forth with the wind.

There was an adventurous streak in her which was enticing but at the same time made me fear for her life and my future.

One day she pulled out a jar, a one-foot-by-one-foot wooden board, and a box of pins out of her satchel. She pulled out some pins and clamped them between her teeth, like the benevolent tailor master who used to alter Father's trousers for our shorts and pants, back home. Inside the jar was an unconscious toad submerged in its bath of brine. She extricated the toad from its cosy aqueous digs and laid it spread-eagled on its back, on the board, pinning its limbs to the wood. Next she took out a scalpel, a pair each of tweezers, and scissors and started peeling off the skin of the toad. Opening its abdominal and chest cavities, she pinned the skin flaps to the board. It was the cleanest dissection I had ever seen, even more efficient than that of our biology teacher. She went on to explain the various internal organs of the amphibian—its spongy lungs, its still beating heart-shaped heart, its large three-pieced liver, its-pea shaped gall bladder, its serrated pancreas, its distended curved stomach, its rubbery small intestine, its tubular large intestine, its greyish black large rectum.

Later, she tenderly buried the toad's dismembered body under the shadow stick, declaring the slender stick as 'the grave marker of a martyr who gave up his wretched existence in this mortal world towards the worthy cause of making Sanjay Tivari a learned man. Amen.'

She was truly magnificent as a teacher. She employed ingenious ways to explain things. It was a wonder how, with her explanations, seemingly complex formulae and equations became easy to comprehend. She was better than most of the teachers of the school. I think only MC Pandey Sir, our English language teacher, was better than her in teaching, but even his vocabulary was not as diverse as hers; though he could explain the nuances of grammar better than her.

I discovered her one weakness when I proposed to her an innovative method for understanding the characters of our epics and the English classics.

In addition to learning from her, I loved spending time discussing the personalities of different characters of Ramayan and Mahabharat and the English language classics written by Charles Dickens, Jane Eyre, the Bronte sisters, Daniel Defoe, Jonathan Swift, Robert Louis Stevenson, Mark Twain, Walter Scott, and Alexandre Dumas, among others.

One Sunday, while discussing Bhim's character and his role in fomenting the great battle at Kurukshetra, I suggested, 'Why don't we substitute Hanuman in Ramayan with Bhim from Mahabharat?'

She said, 'Good idea. Bhim had almost the same strength as Hanuman. He would have wreaked havoc amongst Ravan's army, swinging his club in murderous rage, while Hanuman rarely got angry and was too devoted to Lord Ram. Bhim may not be as reverential, but being unencumbered by his feelings towards his lord, he would have been a better fighter.'

I retorted, 'but Sundar Kaand would have never taken place, as Bhim would not have been able to leap across the ocean to land on Lanka, reassure Sita by presenting her Lord Ram's signet ring, and Lanka would not have been burned, since Bhim did not have a tail. Also Ramayan would take forever and Lakshman would die.'

'How?'

'When Lakshman gets injured and Bhim is tasked to get the Sanjivini Booti, he will have to travel by foot all the way to the Himalayas, since he cannot fly. And poor Lakshman will perish for want of the miraculous herb in time.'

She chuckled and shook her head. 'We better leave Hanuman be in Ramayan. No need to tamper with our epics, else Ramayan and Mahabharat will never finish.'

'How about deconstructing the classics?' I asked, after pondering for some time. 'It does not fit the exact definition and we are no literary critics. But it will do for what I have in my mind.'

'What is that?'

'It goes like this. We select two books, or even one book, amongst the English classics and alter the characters or stories in a way that's different from the original one. For a start, let's try David Copperfield and Oliver Twist. We will spend the next two weeks reading these books or refresh ourselves, even if we have read them earlier. Then we will place David Copperfield into the place and time of Oliver Twist's miseries and vice versa for Oliver Twist. Take your pick, whom do you want to replace.'

'That sounds interesting,' and after some thought, she added, 'I will take Oliver Twist into David Copperfield's world.'

'Okay. I will deconstruct Oliver Twist. But remember the single rule of the game. You cannot change the character traits of the main protagonist.

However, driven by his personality, you can change the outcome of events of the original book. To amplify, Oliver Twist when transposed into the world and time of David Copperfield, cannot become David Copperfield, he will have to act as if he is the original Oliver Twist.'

Two Sundays later, we played our literary game. She came a cropper in the contest. Her 'David Copperfield' had a relatively happy childhood with his frail mother, whereas Oliver Twist was an orphan. He never got into fights with the other children at the boarding school, Salem House, whereas the original Oliver Twist had a short temper and would have got into fights with the bullies in the school, necessary to build up his character. Likewise, she made many mistakes in her transposition and I had to correct her many times. She gave up in a hurry, when her 'David Copperfield' is renamed as Trotwood Copperfield by his eccentric great aunt Betsey Trotwood. I fared a shade better with my 'Oliver Twist' and she could pick very rare flaws in my version.

To be fair to her, it was my brainchild and it took her some time to get the hang of it. We tried to change the stories of many literary classics, but my favourites were *Robinson Crusoe*, *Ivanhoe*, and *The Count of Monte Cristo*.

23

The Giggling Girl from Vodrumeepfijiksha

It was a warm winter morning on the last Sunday before our winter vacations of '82. There was an incandescent sun glowing with warmth, its rays piercing through the multiple tiers of earth's atmosphere with such ferocity, it seemed the sun would burn away the entire ozone layer. There was a scattering of few snow white clouds across the sky and I spied a few of them marching purposefully towards the glaring orb, as if they wanted to smother the sun for daring to shine so brightly. But there was a chill in the air, the wind carrying the remains of an icy draft from the snowcapped mountains way up in the north. Even the mighty Gagar failed to prevent such winds from reaching us. My nerves and senses tingled with this unnatural mix of a hot sun and the icy cold wind. I was standing at the foot of the trail, waiting impatiently for Pratima and Bindu. They were late. Half an hour passed and I was becoming progressively despondent. My heart started sinking with each slink of the sun, as it started playing hide and seek in the company of the irregularly shaped white puffs of clouds. Suddenly a large shadow fell on the earth, enveloping the hill side in a dark embrace and my hopes began dissipating with the dissolving of the sun's rays. After a long time, the massive cloud, shaped like a mythical dragon, continued on its inane journey, in search of a mate to produce rain, revealing the sun and it once again bathed the pathway leading from the road to my location with light and I saw two figures, tote bags slung upon their shoulders, approaching me.

'What's wrong with you?' I asked with concern, when she drew closer. 'You are so crimson. Your nose, your cheeks, they are as red as an apple.'

'It's the chill silly. I get it every time the air gets icy like this. Mother says it is my curse for being so fair.'

'I like the curse.'

'You are the first person to have said that,' she declared and took hold of my hand, her cold touch sending shivers up my body. We started our climb.

'It will be so cold on top. Let's go someplace else.' I said anxiously.

'That is the whole point. We will drink in the first frosty air of the season, that way no harm will come to us during the entire winter.'

'If that is the little I have to suffer to earn the privilege of looking at those red apples on your face, I am all for it,' I grinned at her.

When we reached the top and parked ourselves at our usual spots, Pratima and I sitting next to each other atop the water tank and Bindu propped up against the trunk of a pine tree, I slipped out a coin from my trouser pockets and flipped it into the air. She yelled 'heads'. The coin landed on the tank some distance away and rolled towards us. After losing its momentum, it danced its spiral jig and lay flat on its 'Tail'. Heads it was. To spice up our game we had not decided beforehand which book would be deconstructed by whom. Whosoever won the toss decided for the other. Today it was her chance to decide for me between *Gulliver's Travels* and *Robinson Crusoe*. She said, 'Let us see how you make Robinson Crusoe survive on that island. It's a tough one, as there is hardly any other character for you to play around with.' It was a solo deconstruction, in that I could not change Robinson Crusoe but I had liberty with the rest of the plot, without losing on the main focus of the story. The previous evening I had given a thought to how I would go about the task. With Gulliver, I had thought of replacing the giants at Brobdingnag with cannibals and pirates and had then gone about how Gulliver converts them into normal humans. For Robinson Crusoe, I had visualised replacing Friday with a skull and how he survives without being spoken to by anyone alive for ten years of his life on the island.

She pulled Robinson Crusoe out of her bag and said, 'Did you know that the first edition of the book, published in 1719, had a longer original title which went like this:

THE

LIFE

AND

STRANGE SURPRIZING

ADVENTURES

OF

ROBINSON CRUSOE,

Of YORK MARINER:
Who lived Eight and Twenty Years,
All alone in an un-inhabited Ifland on the
Coaft of AMERICA, near the Mouth of
The Great River of OROONOQUE;
Having been caft on Shore by Shipwreck, where-
in all the Men perifhed but himfelf
WITH
An Account how he was at laft as ftrangely deli-
ver'd by PIRATES
Written by Himfelf.'

She pulled out a notebook to show me the title written in her neat hand. I snickered, 'God! That is indeed a longish lauauaung title for a book (I spread my hands to indicate the extent of the lauauaung). Daniel Defoe must have been crazy. Why didn't he replace all the other *s*'s with *f*'s, I wonder? Must have been going for some bizarre dramatic effect.'

'He had written a second novel on Crusoe, also published in 1719 with an equally lengthy title (this time she narrated from memory),

THE FARTHER
ADVENTURES
OF
ROBINSON CRUSOE,
Being the Second and Laft Part
OF HIS
LIFE,
AND STRANGE SURPRISING
ACCOUNTS OF HIS TRAVELS
Round three Parts of the Globe
Written by Himfelf

While calling out the title she depicted each line by dramatically waving her hand in left-to-right horizontal motions and calling out, 'in capitals', for the words in uppercase. The two *f*'s, instead of *s*'s, she spoke by pronouncing the *s* sound with her tongue between her teeth.

She added, 'The book is now rendered as "The Further Adventures of Robinson Crusoe". He had written a third book on Crusoe in 1720, which was published in 1729, with a surprisingly "shorter" title, "Serious Reflections During the Life and Surprising Adventures of Robinson Crusoe With His Vision of the Angelick World. The Angelick ended with a *k*."'

'I think I will go under with that much research on Crusoe. Where did you get all this from?'

'After we had decided upon Gulliver's Travels and Robinson Crusoe last Sunday, I had gone to the Kumaon University, where mine is a familiar face since Big Brother's undergraduate days, and had browsed through their library.'

'You are very earnest and meticulous, I must say. But letf start with my verfion of the firft story.' She giggled at my mime.

'Thank God, you did not let Daniel Defoe rub on you too much. Otherwise, the "start" would have made me run for cover, to prevent my nose from being assaulted by a vile, sulphuric odour.'

I chuckled and commenced my deconstruction, 'Why should Robinson Crusoe have a man for a companion? What if we replace Friday for something else? Say a skull.'

'What will he do with a skull? How will he get one?'

'My story goes like this. Friday is caught in his attempt of escape from the cannibals. Crusoe sees him being eaten by the cannibals and realises that he had really liked the man. The pleading expression in his eyes when he had begged his captors to spare him, haunted our hero for days. Not being able to bear much any longer, weeks later, he goes in search of the remains of the man, so that the deceased Friday could be given a proper burial. He arrives at the spot where those vicious humans had consumed the man and sees a pile of bones and some heads with rotting skin and flesh. He recognises the head of Friday and carries it to his dwelling. Instead of burying it, he scrapes off the remaining skin and flesh and retains the skull, naming it Friday. It becomes his constant companion. He spends his days speaking to it. Later when he rescues those other two prisoners, he learns that one of them is Friday's father and hands over the skull to him for a decent burial.'

'Why should it be a man's skull?' She interjected with enthusiasm. 'It could be a woman's skull too. The woman could have been living in a faraway island and must have drowned some time back. Her body was

152 | Mamta Chaudhari

dismembered by the sea creatures and her skull washed up to the shore of Crusoe's island, after the flesh had been eaten up by the fish and other marine animals.'

I asked, 'How would he know that it was a woman's skull?'

'After he finds the skull he is fascinated by it. Unlike the other heads and skulls left by the cannibals, after they had dined upon their original owners, who in our story were all males, this skull looks different. Intrigued he goes to the feasting site of the cannibals and observes that the washed up skull is smaller and more rounded than the longer profile of the male skulls and that it has a vertical forehead. Further, he lifts one of the male skulls and runs his fingers over the two skulls and discovers that the male skull is heavier, has thicker bony mass, its facial bones are rugged and it has more pronounced brow ridges than the skull from the sea. Thus he concludes that, since this skull is so different from the male skulls on the island, it had to be a female's skull.'

I jumped in, 'I have another idea. But first tell me, how are babies made?' I was one and a half months short of my fourteenth birthday and had no notion of sexual intercourse then.

'I don't know,' she replied. 'When I had questioned my mother about it, she had stared at me and snapped, "Had you been married in time you would have found out much earlier," and had clammed up. None of my friends know much about it. Our biology books say that there are male and female reproductive organs which produce babies. I believe that something is secreted by the different reproductive organs, which combine to form babies inside the mother's body. The babies grow below their mother's stomach for nine months and are born thereafter. Why did you ask?'

'In the movies they show that the hero and heroine come close together to kiss on the lips and thereafter they show two sunflowers necking each other, or two birds rubbing their beaks together, or the heroine's dense hair, or the hero's broad back or their feet dancing together, as they lie on the bed and sometime later the heroine becomes pregnant. I think the secretions from the male reproductive organs are transferred to the female's body through that kiss and thereafter, travelling down her food pipe and traversing through her stomach and intestines, somewhere along this journey, they meet the secretions of the female's organs and both of them combine to form a baby.'

I continued with my fantasy, 'Say, the female's reproductive organs are distributed all over her body and this female skull with Crusoe has some remnants of the original woman's reproductive organs or her secretions. Crusoe, after realisation dawns upon him that this is a woman's skull, feels an intense desire to kiss it, as he hasn't had the company of a woman for the past ten years. And when he kisses the skull, "whoosh", his secretions go into the bones of the skull and "whiz", they mix with her skully reproductive secretions and "plop", a baby falls down, since the skull has no stomach to store the baby. This continues for the next ten minutes: "whoosh" . . . "whiz" . . . "plop", "whoosh" . . . "whiz" . . . "plop", and there are 100 babies on the island. They all look like Skeletor's miniature version, from the Masters of the Universe mini-comics. All bones and no flesh, bawling through their mini jawbones, their mini skeletal fingers clutched in mini skeletal fists, their mini eye sockets staring with blank eyeless gazes at Crusoe kissing their skull mother again and again, and their clones dropping to the ground in a deluge "plop" . . . "plop" . . . "plop" . . . "plop".'

She was chuckling and giggling by now.

I was struck with another thought.

'Within an hour Crusoe will have 600 babies at this rate, all bawling on the little island. The cacophony will definitely draw the attention of the cannibals, who will throw the babies into the sea—there is nothing to eat in them—and will eat our hero. This is not a nice ending. Why should we write a story where, after all the struggles in his life, the hero is finally eaten as lunch in the denouement?'

She said, 'The problem is with that female skull which does not have a body attached to it and thus babies fall every six seconds, . . . "plop" . . . "plop" . . . "plop" . . . "plop".' She giggled again. Bindu raised her head from her knees, satisfied herself that it was only Pratima laughing and giggling and went back to her snooze, placing her forehead gently upon her folded knees.

'Let's give him a girl,' I continued. 'Let's name her . . . mmmm . . .' And looking at her chuckling again, 'Giggling girl, since she giggles too much and I like the alliteration. All those *g*'s . . . got it; she is shaped like the letter *g* in the Caroline Miniscule Script, in the lower case.'

'Like the Khoi-san tribe in South Africa, also known as Bushmen. Their women suffer from Steatopygia, a genetic characteristic, where a high degree of fat is accumulated in and around the buttocks, forming a thick layer, reaching sometimes to the knees. So that forms the lower *o* of the *g*. Now for the upper *o*,' she added.

I took the refrain thereon: 'This girl is not from the Khoi-san tribe and has an equally round chest. But what about the thin line between the two *o*'s. The girl has to have a very thin waist. But if it is too thin then her torso would topple over. That is the dilemma.'

I paused to think it over and resumed after sometime. 'Her waist is so narrow that it is composed only of muscles and a cylindrical pipe like structure, like our spine, without the vertebrae. It is a smooth pipe to pass food and blood from her upper body to the lower portion. The pipe is surrounded by dense muscle tissues, which have eight times the tensile strength of human muscles and are called "octa-scles".

'But no human is shaped like that.'

'Exactly, she is not a human. She is an alien.'

Her eyes lit up with excitement and she drew in closer, her entire right flank, from shoulder to calf, touching my left side snugly. That felt heavenly and my nostrils picked up the familiar aroma of her lemony perfume. She had told me some time back that she had purchased it on a trip to Nainital, the day after our first conversation and wore it only when she was with me. That had pleased me immensely; I was making considerable progress.

I continued, after drawing myself out of the sea of sensations I had immersed myself into, with considerable difficulty. 'There is a planet in another dimension in space, millions of light years away from Earth. It is habitable and has a huge supercontinent the size of Europe, Asia, and Africa, combined. This supercontinent is surrounded by a sea, which, roughly translated into English, is called Surround Sea. The supercontinent is called just that, Supercontinent, roughly translated.'

'What's the name of this planet?' she asked.

I tapped the tip of my finger against my brow in deep concentration. I picked up *Robinson Crusoe*, turned to the flyleaf at the end and scribbled on it for some time. Then I showed her the word I had written down on the page. She read the name out loud and enquired, 'How did you arrive at this bizarre name? What did you do with the other alphabets?'

I smiled at her in smug satisfaction and explained: 'This planet has a powerful transmitter-cum-receiver. So powerful that it can send hyperfast radiations into space and receive audio signals, riding atop the reflected radiations, from millions and millions of light years away. Since times immemorial this planet's inhabitants have been picking up the audio signals from Earth. If at all we were able to communicate with these aliens, the biggest mystery of all time would have been solved—how did we come into existence? They have been listening to the noises and sounds of Earth for Earth-equivalent eons; from the prehistoric imitations of the cries of beasts and birds, to the "pooh-pooh", "ding-dong", "yo-he-ho", "ta-ta" language spoken by our ancestors, according to these theories propagated by Max Muller in 1861 and Sir Richard Paget in 1930, to the pidgin-like communication techniques of the Neanderthals, to the creole-like language of the early Homo Sapiens, to the different inflections and sounds of various languages spoken in the ancient civilisations, after humans moved out of their caves and settled into social groups, to the recitations of the hymns by the ancient sages beside the mighty Indus River, as they sat composing the Vedas, to the modern languages spoken the world over. Lately, with the imperial expansion of the British Empire since the sixteenth century, they have been listening to a large number of humans speaking a common language. Where earlier they used to hear the same earthlings speaking a variety of languages restricted within their geographical boundaries, now they could hear a greater number of people from different areas of our world, cutting across regional limits, speaking English. So in the Earth year 1662, the year when this story of ours takes place, four years after Crusoe was stranded on the island, they realise that Earth is moving towards having a common knowledge. Yes, there are people who speak other languages too, but the English-language-speaking people are more in number and their numbers keep growing.

'This planet's inhabitants are supremely intelligent and had done a great deal of research on the English language in the past. They were not satisfied with the phonetics of the language. It is so complicated—*c* can be used to sound as *s* or *k*, and when combined with *h* as a digraph, it sounds like a softer *c* used in "church" or like a *k* when speaking "character". They used to argue, 'Why have a *q* when you already have a *k*?' The consonant *s* when used alone in "sugar" sounds the same as the digraph *sh* in "sheep". The *g* sounds differently when used twice in the same word, like "gauge".

'They were more frustrated with the use of vowels; the *a* sounds differently in different words. The *u* sounds as an *a* in umbrella but in "unique" it is different. They even had problems understanding the use of two vowels together; *ea* combined, sounds like two *e*'s in "meagre" and *ie* combined also sounds the same in "movie".

'And the biggest problem they had was with the silent consonants and vowels. "Why have anything when you don't intend to use it. And what rule says that you will have only *p* with "pneumonia" and *k* with "knowledge". Why not any other alphabet, if you don't want to use it at all? Replace *p* in "psychology" with *z* and it will still remain the same while speaking. And the biggest blasphemy was the use of silent vowels, it is as if you are speaking and no words are coming out. Most of the words ending with *e* have this vowel silent.'

'I think we are in the process of deconstructing Robinson Crusoe and not the English language,' she interjected.

'Okay, okay. These *g*-shaped aliens on a planet in another dimension in space decided to come to Earth for a reason I will give you later, and in order to give a suitable name for their world, which we earthlings could call it by, they devised an ingenious method. They grouped similar-sounding letters of the English alphabet, or those they felt convenient, to give a substitute phonetic, thus reducing the number of letters and then used these letters to form the name of their planet in the English language. Various groups and their substitute phonetics are as follows (I indicated the table I had made on the blank last page of the book, some of the groups having single letters):

English Alphabet	*Substitute Phonetic Letter*
CKSQX	'KSH' as in the Hindi word 'Kshatriya'
GJZ	'J' as in 'jury'
LMN	'M' as in 'mother'
BVW	'V' as in 'van'
DT	'D' as in 'daddy'
F	'F' as in 'father'
H	already used in the first group
P	'P' as in 'pea'
R	'R' as in 'romeo'
Y	discarded as they felt that it served no purpose

'They retained the vowels, with the sole modification that *e* to be used as *ee*. They named their planet in English with these substitute phonetic letters and the original vowels retaining their principal sounds, as "Vodrumeepfijiksha" and called themselves "Vodrumeepians".

'What did they call Earth in their language?'

'Roughly translated into English, Earth was called by them as "Food?", with a question mark at the end, as it was still a mystery to them.'

'What is with this rough translation bit? This is the third time you have used that phrase.'

'You see, they have a very peculiar language, which is the only tongue spoken all over the planet. It has ten alphabets, of which three are vowels and the balance are consonants. And to communicate they use both phonetics and sign language. For example, they have this letter *c*; they pump a fist above the shoulder to denote that they mean *sh* or strike out a claw below the waist to indicate *ch*. Similarly, a vertical slash to the right indicates *k* and so on.'

'How did they convert the sign language into written script?'

'Each consonant in the script followed a set rule; they always went by rules. So a fist above the shoulder, while speaking, became a dot above the letter, in its written form. Similarly, a claw below the waist was denoted by a triangle below the letter, a vertical slash to the right in sign language became a vertical line drawn to the right of the consonant. Each consonant was accompanied with two fists, two claws, and six slashes: horizontal, vertical, and diagonal. Each vowel had four additional signs: one clockwise and one anticlockwise rotation with the right hand above the head, and one jerk of the pelvis forward and one rearward. When you saw two Vodrumeepians speaking, it was a flurry of movements and a frenzy of phonetics; hands darting forward in fists and claws or slashing the air in vertical, horizontal, or diagonal lines or running circles above the head with the pelvis jerking forward or backward, at times. And each word ended with a clicking sound, something similar to the sound created by us humans, when we jerk our tongue down from the roof of our mouth, while making the clip-clop sound to imitate a horse trotting. It is the sound created in the !Kung language, with an exclamation mark before the word to indicate a click, spoken by the !Kung people in Namibia, Botswana, and Angola. Remember that Kalahari bushman in the movie *Gods Must Be Crazy*, where he clicked before speaking each word. The Vodrumeepians used clicks after the words. In script form, the clicks are denoted by exclamation marks suffixing each word.'

'Why the clicks?'

'The clicks depicted their emotions. A single click denoted anger, a double click mirth, a double click in quick succession meant that the word was spoken in jest, a triple click meant that it had to be taken with all seriousness and so on.'

'So they had ten alphabets which could be converted into 112 phonetics-sign language combination, which when further combined would form words, each word followed with a click or series of clicks to denote the feelings. We have something similar on Earth too, the International Phonetic Alphabet, minus the signs and the clicks, created by the International Phonetic Association in 1888. It has some 100 plus letters and more than 45 diacritics and four prosodic marks. It has undergone numerous revisions over the years, with the last one carried out in 1979.' Now that was something I did not know. Her hunger for knowledge was phenomenal.

'Learning the language must be very hard for the kids,' she continued.

'No, no. You forgot the principal sounding alphabets, when used without the signs. In all they had 122 phonetics-sign language combination. As for learning the language, you should understand that they are supremely intelligent beings. Each child is born with a base minimum Earth equivalent IQ of 200, the intelligence transferred from the genes of the parents. They are already Earth-equivalent genius when they come out of their mothers' wombs. They master the basics of phonetics and the written script by the time they are two Earth-equivalent weeks old, and within an Earth-equivalent month of their birth, they are able to communicate without the clicks. At one Earth-equivalent year of age their IQ is 1,000 Earth equivalent. As a teenager, they are somewhere between 100,000 to 200,000. The highest IQ ever recorded is of the Vodrumeepian who invented the craft, a few Earth-equivalent years back, to travel the millions of light years to Earth in exactly one Earth-equivalent year; he has one million Earth-equivalent IQ.'

'You have not yet answered the original question. Why the rough translation?'

'Such a complicated language of phonetics, signs, and clicks cannot be translated exactly into any known language on Earth. Any conversion can only be approximate; hence, they called it "rough translation". It is very difficult to translate their language into a simple word, *Food?*'

'Why *Food?* for *Earth?*'

'The Super Continent is a dry, arid land. Its hinterland comprises of rocks, boulders, mountains, sand, pebbles, and gravel—long stretches of desert land in the south, large mountain ranges with huge peaks, running in a north-to-south alignment towards the east, stony wasteland, dotted with humongous craters, from some celestial event in the distant past, to the north and west. There is no vegetation whatsoever on the entire planet; not on land, not in sea. The Surround Sea is a vast, flat water body; no waves there, as there is no moon for tides, or winds for waves and there is no rotation of the planet—beats Einstein's and Newton's theories there. The Surround Sea has no living being. But the planet has two suns that never set, located exactly opposite to each other, which hold the planet in its place in space. There is no other water body on the planet except the Surround Sea.'

'Then where does the Surround Sea get its water from?'

'From the planet's core. Like Earth's core spews out magma, Vodrumeepfijiksha's core gushes out distilled water, which is as pure as the rainwater on Earth—a product of a chemical reaction between the elements comprising its core and the radiations from one of the two suns, which penetrate the planet's surface right till its heart. The water is what sustains them, in addition to their main source of nourishment, their animals. As a consequence, the Vodrumeepians stay in cities dotting the coastline of the Super Continent. Each city is located exactly 500 kilometres from the other—remember, they live by rules. There is no Vodrumeepian-made structure in the hinterland, except the transmitter-cum-receiver station for the audio signals from Earth and the project site for constructing the craft for the travel to Food? These sites are under the terra firma, located at the centre of the land mass and occupy a combined underground area of three million square kilometres, roughly the size of India. The project site and the transmitter-cum-receiver station are sustained for water through underground pipes pumping water from the Surround Sea and for food they breed their own animals.'

'If the core spews water continuously, don't the coastal cities get drowned?'

'Two reasons for why that does not happen: one, the massive amount of evaporation due to the never-setting twin suns; and second, the channelising of the water emerging from the core. The core only ejects water into the Surround Sea and not into the Super Continent. Millenia ago, the core used to vomit billions of gallons of water in an Earth-equivalent day, and despite the enormous amount of evaporation, once in almost every five earth-years, there used to be a colossal surge of water from the core and the coastal cities would get flooded, causing massive deaths and destruction. So some twenty Earth millennia ago, the Vodrumeepians went under the sea and plugged all the vents through which water came from the core and they also learned to trap the radiations from the sun, which convert the core elements into water. Thereafter, they have been controlling the water as per their requirements.'

'What did they eat?'

'I am coming to that. Patience, patience, my radiance. Since nothing grows on the planet—no plant, no tree, no shrub, no bush, no grass, no algae, no weed—the Vodrumeepians feed on animals. They breed and rear them—huge, big animals for the adult Vodrumeepians and smaller ones for the big animals, the Vodrumeepian infants, and for transportation. The animals are colossal in size, the biggest of them is ten times the size of the largest dinosaur ever discovered, that roamed the Earth 150 million years ago, the Sauropod Amphicoelias, and the smallest is the size of our prehistoric mammoth. They feed only on the bones of these animals. They use the flesh of the bigger animals to make their favourite beverage; they mince the meat and process it with water to brew a thick viscous liquid which gives them the high, like the wine on Earth. The flesh of the smaller animals is fodder for the bigger and smaller animals and for the infant Vodrumeepians, till their weaning and baptism: they called the ceremony "baptism by bone", where the young child got her first taste of bone.

'For the past two earth-years, the Vodrumeepians have been facing their biggest crisis in Earth millennia gone by—their people are at war!

'For the past four Earth millennia, they have been living peacefully: the last Great War had occurred 4,200 earth-years back, which had decimated close to 80 per cent of their population and they had learnt their lessons then. Since then, they have been living in peaceful coexistence. But two earth-years back, sporadic fights between the citizens started erupting, which had assumed gigantic proportions in the Earth year 1662, with cities getting ready to go to war against each other. Some Vodrumeepians fear another Great War, which will decimate most of their population; there are talks of even extinction of their kind.'

'What is the reason for this change in attitude of the citizens?'

'Their animals are dying and their food stock is depleting. They breed and rear these animals in huge pens at the outskirts of their cities. Each enclosure for the big animals measures the size of 200-by-1,000 kilometres, roughly the size of the state of Gujarat. The smaller mammoth-sized animals have their separate pens, much smaller in size.'

'How did they control such huge animals?'

'The animals are mostly very docile. Finicky ones are kept in separate enclosures. Once in a while, as it happens on Earth too, especially with humans, due to some genetic mutation, an odd animal would go berserk. When that happened, in its frenzy such beast would destroy the closest city, kill the Vodrumeepians, and consume the mammoth-sized smaller animals. During such times, help came from the neighbouring cities, which would send rescue forces to kill the mad animal, using their own domesticated big animals.

'Coming back to their dying. A dangerous pandemic has erupted amongst the animals and is sweeping across the planet, killing them in huge numbers. They have lost almost 70 per cent of their food stock to the disease in the past two earth-years. The accurate aetiology of the disease could never be established, but they believe its origin to be extra terrestrial. As per local myth, which changes from city to city, some alien force from a far off planet had ejected microscopic germs, some Earth centuries ago, into the Vodrumeepian atmosphere. These germs had, over the intervening period, mutated by ingesting radiations in the Vodrumeepian atmosphere, and now, the cumulative effect of those mutations has transformed them into dangerous killers, killing the Vodrumeepians' only food source. God, rough translation of their Supreme Being, only knows what further alterations will these germs undergo and their next victims may be the Vodrumeepians themselves. Another theory suggests that some genetic alteration during the breeding process of these animals has been killing their future generations.'

'Didn't they find a cure? After all they are supremely intelligent.'

'The problem is that they are not able to find the source of the disease. All tests done on the dead animals revealed no origin of the mystery pandemic. They are flabbergasted and are worried to death. Almost all of their mammoth-sized small animals are dead and their infants are going without nourishment. The infants' food, till they are a month old, is the flesh of these animals. Their mothers don't have mammary glands and cannot feed their children; they have breasts, whose sole purpose is to differentiate between the male and female Vodrumeepians. Without the succulent meat of the mammoth-sized small animals, soon all their infants will die and there will be no future generations of Vodrumeepians. Their very survival is at stake. All experiments done to feed the infants with bones or flesh of the bigger animals have borne no fruit. The bawling babies would just throw up whatever else was fed to them.

'Fights started breaking out sporadically, inside the cities, one and a half earth-years back. Since then, hoarding of bones has started taking place and prices have soared. Now the prices are at an all-time high. People have been killing each other for some time now. Cities have started amassing armies to launch assaults on those cities which are comfortably better off. Already two cities in the north-eastern corner of the Super Continent have been decimated, as they went to war to capture the other's food stock. There are daily riots in almost all cities. Desolation rules over planet Vodrumeepfijiksha.

'Two inventions paved a way through, provided a ray of hope. One was the "X-ray reflection receiver".

'The audio transmitter-cum-receiver, which they had invented all those Earth millennia ago, has a severe limitation. Using it, they have been able to hear what humans speak in their various languages, the sounds of the earth's movements, its winds, its waves, even the soft whispers of clandestine lovers. They can hear the dogs' barks, the kangaroos' chortles, the anteaters' hrows, the peacocks' screams, the nightingales' pipes, the swans' cries, and even understood what the various animals and birds on Earth meant, when they spoke in their tongue.

'But they had no visual representation of the owners of these different sounds. For the past two Earth centuries, they have been working on some kind of transmitter-receiver, which could be used to get images of Food? and its inhabitants. When they accidently discovered the Vodrumeepian with the one million Earth-equivalent IQ, languishing in the slums of the largest city on the Super Continent, as so often happens on our Earth too, where true geniuses originate from the unlikeliest of sources, he was entrusted with the task of inventing such a transmitter-receiver. After repeated threats and some indiscreet cajoling, he had been able to tap and separate one particular radiation from one of the suns, which travelled much faster than light—Einstein takes a beating again—and which also has the capability to reproduce radiographic images. Just like X-rays, these radiations can penetrate relatively thick objects without being absorbed or scattered and can image the insides of visually opaque objects. And also like X-rays, their penetration depths can be varied by adjusting their energy levels, thus giving desired transmission through the object to be viewed and at the same time get good contrast in the image.

'Next, the Vodrumeepian with one million Earth-equivalent IQ, worked on and successfully created a transmitter to send this radiation to Food? and a receiver to collect the reflected radiation back, loaded with its radiographic image. Thus they were able to get visual X-ray images from Earth. Hence the roughly translated name of the device, "X-ray reflection receiver" or "X-ray transmitter-cum-receiver". This radiation takes one earth-year to travel the 156 million light years of distance from Vodrumeepfijiksha to Food?, that's how fast it is. The other radiation, the one from the audio transmitter-cum-receiver, is even faster; its beams return within one Earth week.

'The first reflected X-ray radiation, with its radiographic image, arrived on Vodrumeepfijiksha two earth-years back, after a long travel of two earth-years, to and fro. Over the past two earth-years, the Vodrumeepian scientists have been analysing these images and have come to two interesting conclusions:

'One, that the quantum of bone marrow in each of the mammals on Food? is more than ten times the bone marrow present in the largest animal on Vodrumeepfijiksha. And bone marrow is their elixir—the cure for all their diseases. In fact, open sale of bone marrow has been banned on the planet and is only available for the infirm and those in the governing council of the planet, the privileged lot. The mammals on Earth, especially humans, who have bone marrow to the tune of 4 per cent of their total body mass, were identified as the ideal food and medicinal source by them.

'The second intriguing conclusion from their observations of those images was more mundane, so prosaic that they often talked of it with chortles and chuckles—they were fascinated by the greater bone density of birds and bats and often wondered how would such small, lightweight bones taste?

'The other living beings on Food? did not interest them, as they were not a source of nutrition for them; like the worms which have no bones, the insects which have a bony coat of mail that did not excite them, the marine animals whose bones, they surmised, would have been badly affected by staying in water all the time, or the amphibians whose cartilaginous bones again were not considered a good nutritional source.'

I was loving this. I was making up as I proceeded, with new ideas entering my brain for the next sentence. My mind was working like a nonstop threshing machine. In flew an idea and my mind churned it into a thought, my words forming that idea into a verbal image.

'The second invention which provided them escape from the imminent disaster, which was going to engulf their planet soon, was the craft that would take them to Food? This task was also given to the Vodrumeepian with the one million Earth-equivalent IQ. He had already made great headway in discovering that super fast radiation and inventing the X-ray reflection receiver. Now he combined this X-ray radiation with the Plutonium-like substance, roughly translated again, found in immense abundance in the higher reaches of the tall mountains to the East of the Super Continent.

'Since there are no nights on Vodrumeepfijiksha, there is no requirement of artificial light on the planet; all the buildings have walls and roofs made of a material which allows light to pass through, but the interiors of the buildings cannot be seen from the outside. There are no self-powered surface transport vehicles for conveyance. The only means of transportation on the planet for the common public are the mammoth-sized animal-driven carts, which move at great speeds, almost equivalent to 200 kilometres per Earth hour. The fastest of these mammoth-sized animals had recorded a top speed of 500 kilometres per Earth hour in a competition for animals they organise every alternate earth-year. For the government officials and those among the elites, they have saucer-shaped flying vehicles, which have solar panels on their flat surfaces, for power generation. They require an energy source for only two things: one for the project site and the transmitter-cum-receiver stations buried deep in the hinterland and the other for the factories-cum-breweries, where the animals, big and small, were converted into chunks of bones to be sold to the population and flesh to be sold to the Vodremeepian infants' mothers, as also to be brewed into that intoxicating liquor they liked so much, and for the other factories which made their garments, their air conditioners, their refrigerators, their ovens, their ice-making machines, et al. And the power source for these requirements was the twin suns. Huge solar panels, erected in the middle of the flat desert in the south of the Super Continent, tapped the suns' powerful energy and converted it into power. This power was thereafter transmitted through a grid of underground cables to the project site, transmitter-cum-receiver stations and the factories.

'So, unlike Earth, the natural, plutonium-like substance found in the higher reaches of the tall mountains of Vodrumeepfijiksha had not been utilised ever since the advent of the Vodrumeepians on the planet, some hundred million earth-years ago, and was therefore, available in abundance. Such a contrast to Earth, where we are eating into our natural resources with such gay abandon, as if there will be no Earth tomorrow—there is so much to learn from these aliens.

'The one million Earth-equivalent IQ Vodrumeepian scientist used this plutonium like substance as the power source and, combining it with that super fast X-ray radiation in a complicated engine, the size of forty Earth-equivalent football fields, he created a craft which can move at the speed of the X-ray radiation and reach Food? in one earth-year. When he declared success, some two Earth weeks back, he was entrusted with the responsibility to create 10,000 such crafts for the invasion of Food?'

'Why didn't he use that other radiation, which is so much faster?'

'That was what he tried initially. But that radiation, when combined with the plutonium like substance, forced the engine to consume the power source at a phenomenal rate. For the comparatively much shorter three and a half Earth days' journey, they would require a craft the size of 5,000 square kilometres. And. . .'

'Got it,' she butted in. 'For the 10,000 crafts they would require an area of 500 million square kilometres, whereas the Super Continent is of the size of Asia, Europe and Africa, combined, whose total area is 84,370,000 square kilometres. So they can only send less than one fifth of the invasion force initially. But why insist on an invasion force of exactly 10,000 crafts? They could have gone with lesser strength.'

She was the most amazing girl in the world. Remembering information is one thing, but recalling it at the drop of a hat was unbelievable. She was not only bewitchingly beautiful; she had the most brilliant brain I had ever read about, let alone knew. That photographic memory of hers must be phenomenal.

'Because, in the ultimate analysis of the Supreme Council of Vodrumeepfijiksha, roughly translated—which is a 2,500-member committee, drawn from the sixty cities of the planet, to govern Vodrumeepfijiksha—the invasion should involve minimum bloodshed as they wanted to take maximum humans alive, to be able to breed future generations of humans out of them and for that they would require the entire population of Vodrumeepfijiksha to subdue the humans, without much fighting. The number of Vodrumeepians on the planet, as per a recent census, was 600 million and since each craft could carry only 60,000 people, with additional space of almost two football fields created in each craft to cram in the three score thousands of Vodrumeepians, they required exactly 10,000 crafts.

'But before the invasion force could go, they needed to carry out preliminary reconnaissance to confirm what they saw on the radiographic images. So they decided to send a two-member mission to Food?, to scout out and pave the way for the main invasion force which would follow two earth-years later, as that much would be the time required for the scouts to report on their findings and for the 10,000 crafts to be manufactured.

'That is how our *g*-shaped giggling girl arrives on the island where Robinson Crusoe has been living a lonely existence for the past four earth-years.'

'Why do you always talk of earth-years?'

'Because the Vodrumeepians don't have any concept called Time, as the planet does not rotate, and since the suns always remain constant, there are no seasons. Hence, they don't have any way to define a day, a month, or a year, except the menstrual cycle of their females which varies with each female Vodrumeepian. Since Earth equivalent 3500 BC, they have been listening to Food?-lings talking of time; first calling time using sundials from some locations called Egypt and Babylon, thereafter they used to hear the faint susurrations of flowing sand and heard humans calling duration of time elapsed using something called *hourglass*, they were even amazed to hear humans using flowing water to measure duration of time elapsed, with a water clock from way back Earth equivalent 3500 BC till the sixteenth century BC. But it was the recent invention of the Pendulum Clock which excited them the most. Invented by someone called Christiaan Huygens, a few earth-years back in 1657, this machine was being used by humans to tell time most accurately, and since they did not understand the concept of time, they took a conscious decision, during last earth-year's annual convention, not to eat the bones of this "magician", they called him in their complicated language.

'For them, time meant the duration of travel from one city to the other or to measure the speed of their animals in their biennial competitions. Any other duration like day, month, or year was based on how Food?-lings defined them. To tell time, one of their minor scientists had invented a digital clock, as big as a modern wrist watch, which was invented on Earth much later in 1883. They wear these watches on their foreheads and tell time by looking at each other's heads. That's how they calculate time in terms of Earth seconds, minutes, hours, days, months, and years. Even interstellar and intergalactic distances were measured in terms of Earth light years and they had accurately measured the distance to Food?'s core, using that hyperfast audio radiation, to an accuracy of one micromillimetre, at 156 million light years away; although this distance varied constantly, due to the movement of Food? in its elliptical orbit around our sun.'

'Why should it take them two years to construct 10,000 crafts? They know the technology and they have the ingredients. Since their animals are dying and their infants won't be surviving long, they should be in a great deal of hurry.'

I thought over it for some time, did some mental calculations, flipping over to the front flyleaf of Robinson Crusoe to do the complicated steps necessary in the arithmetic involved and replied, 'They are in hurry, but those super fast X-ray radiations are limited in supply. You see, the sun which produces that radiation undergoes a complicated series of fission and fusion reactions followed by a final hyperfusion reaction, called 'hy-fu' processing of the sun's core, to produce that radiation. In that process, it loses a lot of its energy. To maintain balance, it sends that radiation in bursts of forty-five Earth minutes onto the planet. And they cannot use the entire radiation which reaches the planet, as the same radiation is absorbed by the planet's core to produce the freshwater for the Surround Sea. They require the water too for their survival, till they leave for Food?, so they have to let go 50 per cent of the radiation to the planet's core.'

She added, 'Taking into consideration that they can tap the radiation bursts every one and a half hours for the engines of the crafts, it would take them 625 Earth days to tap enough radiation for 10,000 crafts and the remaining Earth days they would take to assemble the crafts.'

'And also, that much time would be taken by the Scout team to reach Food?, make their observations, and return with their first-hand report, which is so essential for any invasion.'

'But wait a minute. She was on a scouting mission. How did she arrive on Crusoe's island and where is her partner?'

'Since the Vodrumeepians had only audio recordings and X-ray images of Earth, they did not know much about Earth's gravitational field. They had heard of someone called Aristotle talking of elements returning to their proper place, in the fourth century BC, implying that heavier objects fall faster than lighter ones, a Brahmagupta saying that 'all heavy things fall down to the earth by a law of nature', someone called Bhaskara saying, 'Objects fall on the earth due to a force of attraction by the earth', and a Galileo dropping balls from the Leaning Tower of Pisa, a few earth-years back, but Newton and his falling apple had not happened yet, that will only take place in 1666, so they did not know much about Food?'s gravitational field and had assumed that its gravity would be similar to theirs. But they were mistaken ten times over.

'Earth's gravitational force is ten times that of Vodrumeepfijiksha. So, when this scout craft enters the Earth's atmosphere and is drawn in by the Earth's gravitational force, the craft, which was not designed for such tremendous *g*-forces, comes apart and the giggling girl's partner disintegrates. But she is smarter and is wearing her protective suit, thus splashing safely into the waters, very near to the island where our hero languishes alone.

'Now that we have constructed a planet, let's deconstruct Robinson Crusoe. Here it goes. Crusoe has just witnessed a gory orgy of murder, mayhem, and feasting by the cannibals and they had two women captives this time, whose meat they consumed with great relish. He is sitting on a boulder musing over man's violent nature and staring out at the sea, and in walks a vision. His eyes pop wide open looking at this strange being emerging out of the waters, clothed in a body hugging black apparel made of some kind of leather, the snug embraces of the garment accentuating each curve of her *g*-shaped frame. He is fascinated by this creature, which has such a tiny waist that he can close his right fist around it. She has a tight bunch of hair sticking out like a bent shaft from the left side of her otherwise bald head. That is the comma shaped protrusion from the head of the top *o* of the letter *g* in Caroline Miniscule Script.'

'Why does he call her giggling girl?'

'The first thought that comes to his mind, when he sees her perfectly shaped figure supported on two shapely legs, is the letter *g*, and she can't seem to be able to stop giggling continuously. So he names her giggling girl.'

'Why does she giggle continuously?'

'It is her protective suit and the extremely low temperature of Earth. At Vodrumeepfijiksha, because of the two suns, the usual air temperature is 200°C. On Earth she is at a temperature about ten times lower than that. So she is wearing a protective suit, also designed by that one million earth equivalent IQ Vodrumeepian, which keeps her body temperature at a steady 200°C. But it has Earth-equivalent ammonium nitrate as one of the ingredients. At a temperature of 200°C, ammonium nitrate decomposes into nitrous oxide and water vapour. As she emerges from the water, her suit lets out lot of steam and she is covered in a cloud of the colourless, sweet-smelling laughing gas, which makes her giggle and she can't stop it.

'But for Crusoe, she is a godsend. He immediately realises that she is a girl, from her figure-hugging suit and her protruding breasts, and she is so beautiful, all those giggles revealing a long line of white, sharp-edged teeth. He has not enjoyed the pleasures of a woman's company in the past four years and that morning's witnessing of the cruelty of the cannibals towards their two women prisoners has left him longing for the opposite sex. So, as soon as she steps on dry land, Crusoe rushes towards the giggling girl. He draws himself into the cloud of steam and laughing gas and the sweet aroma fills him with euphoric ecstasy, and he pulls her into his arms and kisses her.'

'Wait, wait, wait,' she puts a finger on my lips. 'There is a "whoosh", a "whiz", and a "plop".'

'Gotcha! For the first time in so many days, I have caught you on a wrong foot. There is definitely a "whoosh", transferring his reproductive secretions into her, and also a "whiz", but no "plop". She has a full body. His secretions travel down to the place where her own reproductive organs are and she feels all of this with her super sensory senses. She knows immediately that she has become pregnant and this bearded, dirty, foul-smelling roughly translated human is the baby's father. And she can't eat him now.'

'She wanted to eat him!' She exclaims.

'Yes. That was her original intention. She had become very hungry after her miraculous escape. The loss of her "bone candies"—her energy source—in that terrible breaking apart of her craft and the swimming of a few nautical miles to reach Crusoe's island had drained her entirely. She had seen in Crusoe an appetising meal of bones and marrow.'

'Then why didn't she? Eat him, I mean.'

'It's her customs. Back at Vodrumeepfijiksha, when a male and a female Vodrumeepian kiss and the female becomes pregnant, the male turns into her husband. There is no marriage ceremony on Vodrumeepfijiksha. She is his wife and he her husband, there onwards. They have to stay together as husband and wife till the baby is born. After the baby's birth, they can separate, unless they kiss again and she becomes pregnant once more, after her first child. So, if a female Vodrumeepian wants to separate from her "husband", or vice versa, they don't kiss again after the first child is born. They can separate from each other and the child remains with the mother.

'That's her dilemma. For all purposes, Crusoe is her husband and she can't eat his bones. If she does eat him her Earth-equivalent God would punish her and confine her Earth-equivalent soul to some Earth-equivalent purgatory.

'And it is also that kiss. Her protective suit covers her entire body, including her face, except her mouth, which she uses for breathing. The exposed lips had by now frozen in the ten times lower temperature of Earth, and when Crusoe closes his lips upon hers, all the blood in her body, or whatever Vodrumeepians call the circulating fluid that keeps them alive, flows in a violent motion into her lips, instantly warming them in a euphoric surge and she goes limp as a noodle all over. She wants him to kiss her again and again and again. Crusoe wraps his arms around her upper body, and when her suddenly transformed supple frame collapses, with her blood surging towards her lips, desire fires him up and he kisses her again and again and again—she gives birth, nine months later, to a set of quadruplets.

'When the euphoria subsides, hunger pangs bite into her and she spies the pile of bones of the animals Crusoe has eaten in the past, the tethered goat and his pet parrot. She rushes over to the heap of bones and gorges on them, with loud, crunching bites.

'Crusoe and the giggling girl spend the rest of their mortal lives on the island, bringing up their numerous—half of them human, half of them *g*-shaped—children, feeding on the animals on the island, rearing more animals, killing the cannibals and their prisoners, including the original Friday, the Spaniard, and Friday's father. Crusoe slowly comes to terms with her and her *g*-shaped children's bone diet. And they live happily ever after.'

'What happens when the invasion force comes?'

'Let us leave that for some other time. My mind is getting tired of thinking up new possibilities. Maybe they also disintegrate when they come under the influence of Earth's immense gravitational field. Maybe, now that he is free from thinking up new inventions, the one million Earth-equivalent IQ Vodrumeepian puts his whole and soul into the pandemic affecting their animals and finds a miraculous cure. Maybe they perish before their crafts are ready, by a sudden dramatic mutation of the mysterious germ which had been killing their animals, and now the germ kills the Vodrumeepians, before they ever got a chance to evacuate their planet. Possibilities are immense when you let your mind soar.'

'Wow! What a story! A planet in . . . what was that you said . . . another dimension in space, core spewing out pure water, super and hyperfast radiations, *g*-shaped Vodrumeepians, two suns, no moon, only days, no nights, a planet held in space by those two suns, coastal cities, arid hinterland, 600-metre long animals, mammoth-sized small animals. Where do you get these ideas from?' She moved her head, I lifted mine, she turned towards me and stared into my eyes.

'From you,' I said.

She didn't say anything, went absolutely mum. The chill had eased out and I could see an unnatural red creeping up her snow-white cheeks. She was blushing. That was a first. She had never before blushed on so many of my compliments about her beauty, which I never tired of expressing. But this time, she looked demure, affectedly shy and modest and even more enchanting, if ever that were possible; exactly like Sadhana in that scene beside the Dal Lake in *Aarzoo*, moist pink lips parted slightly, revealing a glimpse of the white row of her teeth, eyes covered with her dark lashes, chest heaving with heavy intakes of breath. The moment passed in a blink.

'You are embarrassing me,' she said looking up.

'Sorry.'

'Why do you say that? We should never apologise to each other.'

'Pratima. I don't ever want you to feel ashamed because of me. You mean the world to me. I will never be able to look into the mirror if you ever felt that I had caused you any discomfort.' I was a few months short of my fourteenth birthday and was already feeling like I was a grown-up adult. Short of saying, "I love you from the deepest depth of my heart", I had told her every emotion I felt for her, in those three sentences.

Her voice was warm with a swell of emotions, as she said, 'Sanjay, I did not mean it in that sense.' (My heart started hammering large drum beats, blood surging into my ears: 'Here it comes, here it comes, here it comes!') 'My life has been influenced by people who have been close to me. My parents in a negative sense, my bothers positively. But I have never seen myself as someone who can influence others. I love helping out Bindu with her homework. I like explaining science and maths to you. But to imply that I can influence your imagination, that's something new to me. I have never considered these compliments of yours with anything but great seriousness. When you say I am beautiful, more than the words, I like the look on your face. I have never seen that look before. You have reverence written all over you. You look at me with such purity of your heart. I will never know why you credit me with such prestige, but I feel honoured when I am with you.'

'But it is the truth. You inspire me. I had thought up that skull bit last night. But the giggling girl and the exoplanet; I was making it all up as I spoke. Everything came to my mind with each step. Each idea followed the preceding one, building up on it. I have not felt such excitement, such exhilaration in my life earlier. And it's all because of you. Before you came into my life, I was a dull, boring student, learning my lessons by rote. But you have opened a world of incredible possibilities. I feel as if I can explore the innermost reaches of my mind and create anything out of nothing. I can let my imagination soar, give wings to my flights of fancy, finding fresh flashes of fascinating fantasies. Thank you.' 'My lovely', I wanted to add, but remembering Rekha *Didi*'s 'don't hurry her up,' I held back.

We sat watching the shadows wobbling upon the mountain slope in an eerie dance. I looked up, the uppermost fronds of the tall pine trees were weaving in to and fro motions, as if waving goodbyes to a far-away acquaintance. The sun was out in its full brightness, the clouds from the morning having drifted off to some unknown destination, probably to bring down rain to some parched land. And I thought again that I was the luckiest guy in the world, sitting so close to my ladylove, immersing my senses in her lemony perfume.

After some five minutes, she broke out of whatever reverie she was in and said, 'there is one flaw in your story. They have had their audio sensors for thousands of years and their X-ray transmitters-cum-receivers for the past two years. Then how come they did not hear or get images of things falling on Earth, which would have given them an accurate measure of our gravity and consequently they would have constructed their craft accordingly.'

And here I was thinking that she had gone into a dream world of her own making, taking me as her celestial companion. I said after some pondering, 'I can't think of everything when I am making it all up on the run. So let us say that these hyper- and superfast radiations have a serious limitation. They can't detect sounds created by moving objects and can't get images of objects in motion. They would not be able to hear the mesmerising sounds of the winds as the air swirled in twirls and whirls, the soft murmurs of the waves as the water kissed the beaches and shores, the thunder of thousands of galloping horses of the invading armies of all the wars from our history, the heavy breathing of Philippides as he ran 225 kilometres from Athens to Sparta to seek assistance, the screams of an eagle in full flight its wings spread gloriously as it glided magnificently high up in the air on a hot air current, searching for its rodent prey on the surface. Not for them to be enthralled by the susurrations of the flowing waters in the marble water channels of ancient Rome, to be awed by the nature's fury on Earth as the waves rose to dizzying heights and crashed down on land in thunderous deluges, during all those tsunamis right from 426 BC at Malian Gulf in Greece till 1607 at the Bristol Channel in Great Britain, to be able to marvel at the beauty and grace of the expansions and contractions of the muscles of the cheetah, as it chased its prey at phenomenal speed. They can only pick up sounds and images reflected from a stationery source, as reflections from moving sources get dissipated.'

'You do think of a solution very fast. Who is the genius here? You are,' and she poked a finger into my chest.

I stood up and bent down, elaborately executing a bow in dramatic fashion, a la Raj Kapoor in *Mera Naam Joker* and said, 'Thank you my sweet lady.'

As I settled down, she said, 'Hey that's a pun I like, constructing a new planet to deconstruct Daniel Defoe's Robinson Crusoe.'

'I can always make it Venus Woman. Do we have time?'

'Sure, go ahead.'

'There is this slip of a girl, really tiny, who is an aristocrat's daughter living a miserable existence full of nasty comments from her father, who never lets a day go by without tormenting her for being so tiny, and this girl one day decides to run away and join a gang of pirates—as she looks like a small boy she assumes that they would take her as a deck hand—but none of the pirate leaders who frequent the shores of her country want to employ a pint-sized boy; however, eager for adventure, she swims across to a ship anchored off a deserted coast, where she hides as a stowaway, coming out of her hiding days later, when the ship dangerously pitches and rolls in a terrible storm, finally listing to its starboard side, taking the entire crew with it into the bowels of the raging sea, sparing the girl's life—as she is not a crew member, such are the ways of nature—leaving her to hang on to a chest full of gold for dear life and after losing the chest and her clothes to the sea and the fishes, she swims for nautical miles after tiring nautical miles, till she arrives one evening, in an exhausted state, at Crusoe's island, where he is sitting on a boulder, reflecting over the events of his life as a castaway over the past decade, staring at the Evening Star, as the sun bids its goodbye to another dull day in his life and watches Venus materialise into a lovely girl, fully unclothed and he sprints up to her, picks up her tiny body into his arms and with his lips having gone dry for want of a female's company, he kisses her thrice, thus transferring the secretions from his reproductive organs, in three distinct "whooshes", into this apparition of Venus, who, despite being a tiny girl, has fully matured reproductive organs of her own, and nine months later she gives birth to triplets, giving immense joy and happiness to Crusoe who accepts her as his wife, despite the age difference, and they live happily ever after on that island till the end of days, growing rice and barley, raising their children, rearing goats and killing cannibals. End of story.'

She applauded with soft hands and exclaimed, 'Bravo, and all in one sentence. Those registers of mine are showing their effect.' She paused to ponder and said in reflection, 'Vodrumeepfijiksha, isn't it a bit long. We will have to shorten it.'

I said indignantly, 'Why? When they can have Czechoslovakia for a country, why can't I name my planet Vodrumeepfijiksha?'

After some musing, she said, 'Why do all stories, novels, and plays end with a denouement that seems so set piece that it feels as if the author had thought out the end well before she had even started writing the story. After finishing a novel, I always feel empty, as if I was expecting something more. While reading through the plot, as it unfolds and different characters enter and depart, I get so engrossed that I rarely put a book down till I have finished it. But when I reach the end I get this hollow feeling when the hero gets the girl and the villain is vanquished. Even in tragedies, after the customary sniffle at Jennifer's fate in Erich Segal's *Love Story*, I couldn't get over the feeling of something having gone missing. Except *Gone With The Wind*, I have not read a book where the story has not been conclusively brought to a closure; be it a love story, a comedy or a tragedy. The "and they lived happily ever after" feel at the end appears so clichéd.'

'I will write a novel that will be inconclusive. No 'boy meets girl, they fight against the odds and are finally united to live happily ever after' stuff. And I will dedicate the book to you. I promise.'

'So sweet of you. If you become an author, don't start with the end already in your mind. I somehow have this feeling that writers start with the story divided into component parts, in their mind, like different arcs of a circle. But the final arc, the one which closes the circle is there already, with the entire climax, even before she starts connecting the various arcs. So where is the fun then, because she just moves these arcs, these different parts of the story, so that she can form the full circle. Are you getting me?' She asked of my bewildered face.

'Geometry is not my forte, but I can somehow understand what you mean. It is like that Gene Wilder movie, *Stir Crazy*, we saw in the school auditorium last week. I could not understand a single dialogue in the film, because of that horrible nasal, American accent, but I could get the gist of the story.'

She chuckled as the sun winked from its descending path towards the west, that our time was up. Bindu walked towards us, when both of us jumped down from the rear of the tank to climb down the hill. We had been so engrossed in my fantasy that the thought of lunch had never entered our minds. Bindu was smart; she had by now become familiar with our ways and always carried tidbits to munch on, whenever she felt hungry. My stomach growled and Pratima said that her belly was echoing like a barren landscape. I offered to take her to Shahji's canteen for a tea-omelette snack, but she declined with a sweet smile that melted my heart.

24

The High of the World Cup Victory

1983 was the watershed year of my life. Amidst the snowfall in spring, gory deaths in faraway Assam, and the jubilation of triumph, in a David-vs-Goliath contest, I had gone into serious contemplation of my life and had taken a decision which would determine my destiny.

When I returned to the school, after the two long months of winter vacations, spent uncomfortably in longing for Pratima, two events occurred in the country which showcased, in equal measures, the generosity and violence so rampant in our country.

One ended a sordid saga of girl-child exploitation, child marriage, and physical abuse by upper-caste, domineering men to subdue a girl from a lower caste, followed by bloody revenge. Phoolan Devi, of the Behmai massacre fame, and her gang of dacoits, surrendered on 12 February '83, laying down their arms in front of the portraits of Goddess Durga and Mahatma Gandhi, giving themselves up in front of Arjun Singh, the then chief minister of Madhya Pradesh, and a cheering crowd of over 10,000 people, at Bhind, a town thirty-four kilometres from my home. Her life story still sends shivers up my spine, whenever I think of this girl who, in her own abstruse manner, championed the cause of women to a large extent. Married off at the tender age of eleven, to a much older, thirtyish Putti Lal, she was abused on multiple occasions all through her pubescent and adolescent life; first by her husband soon after her wedding, later by her village leaders and the policemen after she had run away from her husband, and much later by a gang of upper-caste Thakurs at Behmai village, who kept her in confinement for three weeks and violated her repeatedly. But she was not a woman who would accept her low station in life, dictated by the men, and bear it too. She had fought back, and how! After fleeing from her village she was kidnapped by a gang of dacoits from the notorious Chambal Valley and she became part of the gang. She stuck a knife into her ex-husband and left a note warning older men from marrying young girls. Later, when inter-gang rivalry led to the death of her paramour Vikram Mallah and her confinement and maltreatment at Behmai, she returned to Behmai after seven months and, in a murderous rage, festered by her hatred for the entire caste of Thakurs, her gang massacred her tormentors and other Thakur males in the village, twenty-two of them, in all. The Behmai massacre had provoked such an outrage across the country that VP Singh, the then chief minister of Uttar Pradesh, had to resign in its wake. Two years later, the dacoit, who had earned a cult status by then—she was called a feminist Robin Hood—had surrendered on her own terms, at the behest of the Indira Gandhi-led central government. (She was finally released on parole in '94 and went on to be elected as a Member of Parliament in '96 and was subsequently assassinated on 25 July 2001 by a trio of Thakurs in revenge for the Behmai massacre.)

What a woman!

The central government had achieved success in the heartland of the country, but famously botched it, in the North Eastern state of Assam, and that too around the same time. The massive sigh of relief heaved by the country, especially in the badlands of Bundelkhand, turned into a shock of horror a week later, when over 2,000 people, mostly women and children, were killed by local tribesmen on 18 February '83 at a village called Nellie and thirteen other adjoining villages. The killings were in retaliation to the central government's decision to hold the state elections despite stiff opposition from the other political parties; yet another example of the government running roughshod over the sentiments of the local populace and its apathy towards their feelings. And there was a sinister purpose behind the decision—the appeasement and winning over of the votes of the more than six million illegal immigrants from Bangladesh, who had settled in the border regions of Assam, displacing the local Lalung tribes and who now had residence and voting rights, thus providing them legitimacy. (A phenomenon which exists even today and has led to numerous massacres over the years).

The next month saw all the nine planets of our solar system in a rough alignment and this wrought tremendous changes in the local weather pattern of Ghorakhal. For the first time in many years, it was the first since 21 March '66, the day the school was established here, it snowed in March. And what a snowfall it was; it didn't let up for a single day of the week. It dropped from the heavens, as if the angels and gods above were indulging in friendly pillow fights and the downy contents of the pillows were descending to bless us mortals, in the form of snowflake after fluttering snowflake. For those of us from the plains, who had never seen mountains before, what to talk of witnessing a snowfall, it seemed like a miracle, watching the jagged flakes melt on our fingers. The individual snowflakes drifted gracefully in the air, executing magnificent dance manoeuvres like a ballerina in full flow, to eventually settle on the earth in a final twirl, joining their cousins and friends, to magically transform the surroundings into a majestic wonderland bathed in white. We walked amongst the snowdrifts with bare minimum clothes on to ward off the unnatural chill of the spring season, wearing slippers and losing them in the snow. We gathered papers in huge tin containers and built fires to keep ourselves warm; some of us plunged our feet directly into the raging fire, after losing the slippers, to warm the numb digits. Many fellow students, who weren't careful enough, had to be treated for chilblain, at the Military Hospital in Bareilly, one of them losing a toe in the bargain. But it was worth the risk. I spent numerous hours roaming in the snow, well clad to ensure that none of my fingers or toes was amputated. Classes had been cancelled for the entire week, and I had plenty of time to myself. I read books, I lay on the snowbanks near the Grassy Fields dreaming about Pratima, I paid my obeisance to Golu Devta, thanking him for bringing Pratima into my life, I played with Rekha Didi, Bindu, and their brothers in the snow piled at the Staff Quarters (Pratima was nowhere to be seen), I participated in the feeble attempts of my classmates in rolling the snow into a snowman. None of the snowmen made by the students survived and would collapse immediately after the stick was inserted to depict its nose, but there was a huge one, erected by some locals, in front of the main gate of the school, which later took seven days to melt. There were also talks about Doomsday, the Judgment Day, the End of the World scenario, and one day, after hearing Appu and Vaibhav talking about the earth imploding and collapsing due to the cosmic phenomenon, I panicked and even contemplated eloping with Pratima and spending our last few days on Earth in blissful togetherness, before our world shattered into zillion fragments. The only thing that held me back was the presence of her elder brother, who had come home on a spot of leave. As it turned out eventually, all the planets moved on along their eternal, elliptical journey around the sun, breaking the alignment. And our Earth did not fall apart, restoring normalcy at the school.

The David-vs-Goliath fairytale event was the unprecedented victory of the Indian cricket team in the Prudential World Cup. Having trumped the mighty West Indies in their first-ever one-day international triumph against the Carribeans at Albion Guyana on 29 March '83, Kapil's Devils continued their marauding ways by trouncing the West Indies again on 09 and 10 June, in their first match of the World Cup. I listened with exhilaration to the radio commentary, extolling the batting exploits of Yashpal Sharma, at my home—as I was on vacations till 15 June—in that game against the West Indies, which was completed over two days. I whooped in excitement when Sandeep Patil completed his half-century off just fifty-four balls, in the next match against Zimbabawe. I cringed in dismay when the Indians fell like nine pins and folded up with a paltry score of 158 runs against the Trevor Chappel championed mammoth Australian score of 320. I listened to the drone of the commentator's voice (now I was at school and listened to a portable Panasonic radio Father had gifted me after much persuasion), and rubbed my palms anxiously as the top five Indian wickets fell for a measly score of seventeen runs and in walked the man himself; with the team's future in the competition hanging in the balance, Kapil Dev wielded the cricket bat like a sledgehammer and bludgeoned the ball to all corners of the Nevill Ground at Royal Tunbridge Wells, turning certain defeat into an unlikely victory—what a match that was, I cried in joy when Kapil caught the catch off Tracois' bat, sealing the victory over Zimbabwe. On 21 June, I gave a treat of omelette and tea at Shahji's canteen to my entire class, in celebration of India's victory over Australia the previous day (it was in fact a bet I had lost to Chachi, but money was spent in a worthy cause, so I had basked in my defeat). After India beat England handsomely, in the semi finals on 22 June, with Mohinder Amarnath, Yashpal Sharma and Sandeep Patil taking the team into the finals, I asked Pratima, the message conveyed through Bindu, to come to the Water Tank Hill and listen to the commentary of the final match with me. She acquiesced after much reluctance (not much of a cricket fan herself)—Bindu had to run to and fro between us, four times. She arrived on top, with Bindu in toe, after the Indians had been dismissed for a pitiful score of 183 runs. She found me despondent and dejected and even her presence did not lift the cloud of doom I was mired in. I recollected to her the way the Indians had fared during their innings, picking faults with each of the batsmen, the way they were dismissed. We discussed the prospects of the likes of Kapil Dev, Madan Lal, Balwinder Sandhu, Roger Binny, Kirti Azad, and Mohinder Amarnath ever being able to dismiss the best batting lineup of the era, below 183. My heart soared when Sandhu rattled Greenidge's stumps with the West Indies score reading 5 for 1. Haynes and Richards left me twiddling my toes and when Haynes fell, I stopped chewing my nails. Seven runs later, Kapil stunned the world by running backwards thirty yards to gobble up Richards' catch, sending me cart wheeling clumsily along the roof of the tank. When Holding fell leg before wicket to Amarnath, as the last wicket, with the West Indies score reading 140, I enveloped Pratima in a huge bear hug and in my euphoric excitement I kissed her cheek; she was equally enthused and did not mind my kissing her. I think she didn't even notice that I had pecked her. It was magical, the feeling I was experiencing. I had kissed her and crushed her soft body into mine for the first time and India had won her maiden World Cup beating the mighty West Indies for the first time in a world cup final match. The three of us were dancing crazy jigs in the middle of the night on top of the Water Tank Hill, oblivious to the world. Pratima could afford to be at the hill that night as her parents had gone visiting some relatives at their village—no doubt again planning some sinister scheme to get rid of Pratima, now that she had completed her tenth class—and her brothers were away, one at Lucknow and the other at NDA. And Bindu had managed to slip off, since it had been arranged mutually that she would be sleeping with Pratima at her home, till her parents got back.

We climbed down the hill, our way lit by our hand-held torches. I slipped my arms around Pratima's waist when she stumbled mid way and I kept her close to me, till we reached the base of the hill. I walked both of them up to Pratima's house, through a shortcut not visible from the other teachers' houses and returned to my lodgings, my ears reverberating with the sounds of fire crackers and cheers of the jubilant teachers and students. I could not sleep that whole night, refreshing again and again, in kaleidoscopic recollection, the feel of Pratima's soft body in my arms and the velvety touch of her pristine cheeks on my lips. It had felt like a dream to me.

At the crack of dawn the next day, I made my first of many such most important decisions of my life; that I would spend the rest of my mortal life and beyond, with Pratima. When the time came, I wanted to feel her next to me first thing in the morning, wanted to smell her presence all through the day, wanted to drown in the spiral pools of her eyes every waking hour, wanted to look at her beautiful face till eternity, wanted to fill her life with eternal love, wanted to close my arms around her to ward off her nightmares, wanted to erase the last lingering memories of her childhood, wanted to be hers and hers alone, every moment of my existence in this world and for the next six lifetimes, and to make that happen, I had to prepare myself worthy of her and her brothers. That could only be achieved if I got a job the moment I left school. Joining NDA would make that possible. In Dec '85, I would be appearing for my first crack at the entrance exam and I vowed that I would clear it in that first attempt itself.

25

The Knight in France

It was a bleak Sunday morning and the wind sang mournful tunes, in mutual harmony with my mood. The eternal sun had hid itself behind a thick curtain of angry black clouds looming over me, swirling in macabre dances, surging this way and that, like a pack of hounds fresh on the scent of a scared rabbit and threatened to dump their burden over me in a heavy deluge. The dull pewter of the ambient light turned the world around me into a gloomy microcosm. As I limped past the two ponds filled with murky water, a film of algae carpeting the surfaces of the waterholes, it started to drizzle lightly. I tightened the belt of my rain cape and shook open the umbrella. I almost gave up on continuing for my rendezvous, but my heart was aching more than my body. Even though my body was not in the right frame of mind to trudge up the 300 metres to reach the water tank, my heart won't let me cancel the date, as she had been away the last two weeks due to some death in her family back in her village and I was dying to see her beautiful face.

Yesterday, Manoj had finally caught up with me. He had been stalking me for some time now and on many occasions earlier too he had been able to corner me at some remote, isolated locations, but before we could progress to a flurry of blows and kicks, some senior or intruder would interfere and break us off. Last evening, he had waylaid me when I was returning from my solitary practice at the obstacle course, situated near the school gate. As I was walking, humming to myself a happy tune in anticipation of my date with Pratima the next day, he had crept up to me and pushed me hard to the ground. Before I could say Jack Robinson, he had rolled me over and sitting on my stomach started pummeling my face with his fists. I had arched my back, pushed him away, tried to kick in his groin, missed it, grabbed hold of his leg which he shook away and by the time I was up on my knees, he had kneed me full in my face. There were stars in my eyes and I regained my senses to a rain of blows on my chest and face, as he sat astride my belly again. The fight, it was more of a battering, had finally got over after he had vented his anger and grudge and left me writhing in pain beside the main road, quite close to my rendezvous point with Pratima.

Manoj had a serious grudge against me. Last week he had dived into a bunch of *Bichchoo Ghaas* (urtica parviflora), a nettle containing serrated leaves and stinging hairs, which stung like a scorpion, hence the name. And the effects of the sting stayed for long. The reason for his dive was not some puerile desire of Manoj to swim into the depths of that shrub, but my push delivered in a jest, to score some brownie points with my other buddies, who had challenged me with a reward of an omelette-treat at Shahji's canteen. Manoj had spent the next twenty-four hours dipped in medicinal oil, scratching all over his body like an old crone. He had never forgiven me for my dare and last evening he had had his revenge.

Fights were a kind of custom in our school; you had to get into a fight in order to be considered as part of the grownups, else you stayed a sissy—a coming of age sort of ritual. And the fights were always with own classmates, on some pretext or the other—a grudge festering like a sore thumb, jealousy for scoring better marks in the exams, some prank gone wrong, a jibe which struck the heart, a joke taken too personally; anything that annoyed anybody, and at times even an imagined affront, just to feel the clash of fist on the other guy's face. I have had my share of fights in the school and invariably I have ended up second best to Appu, Anmol, Manoj, and Om Pal.

Why Appu—the name? It doesn't sound like any Indian male would be named thus by his proud parents. Typical of all boarding schools the world over, where young teenagers live together in close proximity, which makes their character nuances, their idiosyncrasies, their distinguishing facial and bodily features stand out and gain prominence in the eyes of others; our school also has nicknames for teachers coined in the past and for fellow students conceived by their respective classmates, after they joined school. Some of them stuck like a leach, for life. Appu was a tall, brawny, overgrown-for-his-age lad, who got the moniker after the mascot for the 1982 Asiad. There were others too, like 'Haddal' for Malik's skeletal frame and 'Chachi' for my first name-namesake Chaudhari's fair complexion and soft features—the nickname was in reference to the iconic comic book character Chacha Chaudhary's wife, Bini Chachi, of the polka-dotted sari and rolling pin fame and the name remained with him even after he left school; when he went to NDA, his classmates, who accompanied him, continued calling him 'Chachi' there and today, in addition to us, his classmates, even his NDA coursemates, those not from our school, call him by this sobriquet. Some of our teachers who had been granted this privilege were the rotund history teacher *'Aaloo'*, the finicky maths teacher *'Dhampoo'* (its origin remains a mystery for me) and *'Kauva'* for the nasal cawing inflection Dwivedi Sir was blessed with. The most famous of these nicknames was *'Bhadra'*, a seventh-class student with a growth of hair on his face and under his nostrils, belying his official age of 13 years, thus earning him the sobriquet of a 'respectful fellow'. He had been rusticated for getting too amorous with a teacher's adolescent daughter a few months back (Pratima and I had not met for an entire month, as a consequence of that scandal). I, with my Sundays spent on Water Tank Hill and my preoccupation with thoughts and daydreams of Pratima on other days, was never considered popular enough to earn the privilege of a nickname and was simply called 'Oe, Tivari *Gandoo'* by all and sundry.

With these thoughts churning my mind, frequently interrupted by Pratima's cackles and laughter, I reached the foot of the trail and parked myself on a boulder to wait for her. My lips were swollen like a dead hippo, chest burned with numerous aches and bruises, one leg dragged like a dead man's foot and I felt the wind bite into the cuts on my cheeks and above my right eye. I pulled the flaps of my rain cape closer, as the drizzle eased out. After some time, I saw two specks in the distance morphing into miniature versions of two girls as the dots drew closer, finally manifesting into Pratima and Bindu. She was a sight for my sore eyes, a balm for my bruises, a comfort for my aching heart. I stood up wincing when they reached me. Seeing my condition, they exclaimed in unison. Pratima touched my lips with a tender finger. Explaining with false bravado that it was nothing but the outcome of a minor skirmish with a good friend gone rogue, I refused their entreaties for cancelling our meeting, and placing my arms upon their shoulders, I limped up the trail. I was glad that I had given in to my heart's impulses as Pratima's lemony scent softly tingled my nerves with pleasant sensations during the climb. When we had perched ourselves on top of the grey expanse of the

186 | *Mamta Chaudhari*

water tank, Pratima touched each of my bruise with soft hands and ran her fingers over my bloated lips. Had I had a premonition of such tender care, such undivided attention, I would have asked, begged even, Manoj to break a bone or two. It would have been divine, with Pratima holding my plastered hand, her tears leaving wet smudges on its pristine white surface, her voice hoarse from crying, sobs rocking her shoulders, as she kissed my swollen fingers.

The vision vaporised when I heard her admonishment: 'I forbid you from ever getting into a fight with your friends. I can't stand seeing you hurt and beaten up like this, it hurts me here (pointing towards her heart with a dainty forefinger). Either you fight back or don't fight at all.'

'I gave him a beating of his lifetime. The idiot is languishing in the infirmary, moaning in agony.' I puffed up my bruised, aching chest and lied promptly.

She again touched my lips tenderly and chuckled some. 'Poor Sanjay! Does it hurt much? You can't even lie properly. I was at the infirmary in the morning to fetch some medicines for my mother before coming here and there was no imbecile drowning in pain there.'

I looked down sheepishly at my toes and said nothing for a while, the wind howling in my ears.

After some time, she pulled out *The Count of Monte Cristo* from her satchel and asked, 'Have you got your *Ivanhoe*?'

I took out the hardback copy of *Ivanhoe* from my waistband.

'How do we start?' I asked. By now she had mastered the art of deconstruction and we alternated between who will decide the characters to be transposed. Today it was her turn to decide.

'You take on the Knight, I will be the Count,' she laid out the modus operandi. 'Remember the original Ivanhoe was in twelfth-century England, whereas Edmond Dantes lived in nineteenth century France.'

'First the knight.' Last night, lying in pain, my lungs breathing fire, I had thought about Wilfred of Ivanhoe and how he would fare as the Count in France. 'He has a romantic streak, no not a streak, he has it in abundance, he is an adventurer, trusts his friends, is friends with the king, loves jousts and melees, has a heart of gold, will even risk his life to preserve the honour of a maiden, separates from his father for the sake of his love for Lady Rowena and duty towards his king; all in all the ultimate hero.'

'In *The Count of Monte Cristo*, he returns to the nineteenth century Marseille after a voyage, during which he was promoted to be the captain of a merchant ship. The air of Marseille is full of rumours; intrigue is lurking around every corner—even the street dogs' barks sound treacherous— numerous conspiracies dot the night skies like thousand stars, betrayal lurches at unsuspecting strangers like a pack of bandits. But he is happy. He is back with his family and his ladylove sleeps beside him, as he lies contented, having made love to her (I was now close to my sixteenth birthday and knew what a man does with a woman, in addition to kissing her). He is looking forward to a bright future with Mercedes as his wife, and he dreams of sailing to distant lands, in search of new adventures.

'Even though he is a merchant sailor and lives under the regime of Louis XVIII, his heart and mind are with Napoleon. For Ivanhoe, he is the true emperor and Louis just a pretender. He ponders leaving France with his lovely Mercedes, go to Africa, and return only after Napoleon won back his crown.

'But disaster strikes the next day, the very day when Mercedes would have been his, forever. He is betrayed by an envious colleague. Drawn into an insidious scheme of a jealous rival for Mercedes' favours and an overzealous deputy crown prosecutor, he is thrown into the dungeons of Chateau d'If, without trial. There he meets The Mad Priest, who emerges from the floor of his prison cell like a ghost of one of his ancestors, in the dead of the night. Ivanhoe befriends The Mad Priest, Abbe Faria, and learns from him the ways of life, how to use his brains before his brawns, how to use intrigue as a weapon, and also discovers the whereabouts of the hidden treasure.

'He, along with The Mad Priest, digs another tunnel, using his keen senses and observing the goings-on of the rats, to chart the correct course. Five years after being dumped into that prison cell, nine years before the original Count, they emerge out into the open in broad daylight and after a brief fight with the prison guards, he and the old man escape, killing all the guards. But the old man is mortally wounded in the fight and after burying him at sea he escapes to a nearby island, from where he is taken by a smugglers' ship to Monte Cristo, where he again escapes from the smugglers and finds the hidden treasure.'

'You make Edmond Dantes sound ungrateful and bad,' she protested.

'But Ivanhoe has a generous heart. He wouldn't leave his friend to die. Okay, I twisted the original story a bit, but that was to show that Wilfred, now the Count, has good intentions and a noble soul. And unlike the original Count, he would definitely not impersonate the dead Mad Priest, whatever be the circumstances. He would ensure a decent burial for the dead body and pray for his soul's deliverance.

'Continuing further, Ivanhoe returns to Marseille, mourns his dead father and swears revenge upon the three men who were the reason for his incarceration and had in turn led to the death of his father from starvation. But his heart breaks when he discovers that the love of his life, Mercedes, had been taken away by her wily cousin Fernand, that jealous rival who had conspired to imprison him. More than the revenge, his heart burns with the desire to have her back, with him. He also learns that his emperor, Napoleon, was detained at the island of Saint Helena in the Atlantic Ocean.

'Ivanhoe sets about the task of getting back his ladylove and devises a meticulous plan, for which he would need loyal men to work with him. He helps out his former employer Pierre Morrel, who is on the verge of bankruptcy, by paying off his debts. In the process, he wins over the loyalty of Pierre's son, Maximilien Morrel, who leaves the army and joins hands with Ivanhoe.

'Before arriving in Paris, he rescues and recruits Benedetto, the illegitimate child of Villefort, the deputy crown prosecutor who had sentenced Ivanhoe to prison all those years back, and Madame Danglars, wife of his envious colleague who had betrayed him earlier. With the assistance of Maximilien Morrel and Benedetto, he goes on to build an army of close to a hundred men, by enlisting acquaintances of these two individuals from the army and the criminal world, who swear their allegiance to him. He buys real estate outside Paris to house them and puts them under the charge of Maximilien Morrel to train them.

'He goes to Paris, but unlike Dantes in the original version, he does not announce himself. Ivanhoe has a big disadvantage; he has distinctive features and no amount of disguise could hide his broad forehead, his sea-blue eyes, his prominent nose, and his flat ears. The moment he goes public, he would be recognised. So he goes into hiding in Paris.

'But his desire to see Mercedes cannot be suppressed and he arranges to meet her clandestinely, at her husband, Fernand's, palatial house. There he reignites the passion of their love, which had lain dormant inside her heart all those years he had remained incarcerated. He chances upon a portrait of a boy of five, hanging in her bedroom and discovering glaring similarities between his own appearance and the child's, he asks her about him. She confesses that the child was his son from before her marriage to Fernand; in fact, that had been the very reason she had agreed to marry Fernand, as she was carrying Ivanhoe's child inside her womb and did not want it to be born out of wedlock and be labelled a bastard. Ivanhoe vows that he would free her out of the clutches of the sly Fernand and that they would reunite as the family that they were in reality, reassuring her that that time was not far away. He also tells her to keep their son close to her, as turbulent times were ahead.

'He becomes the architect who engineers those turbulent times. He executes his well-thought-out plan and, with his loyal army, trained in the art of warfare by Maximilien Morrel in the forests outside Paris, he mounts an assault on the island of St Helena in the winter of 1820–21, freeing the true emperor, Napoleon Bonaparte.

'And Voila! I change history—Vive la France,' I pumped my fists into the air.

'Napoleon marches back to Paris, frail and infirm from his poor health. But his vitality is restored after he returns at the head of an army whose strength had been bolstered by deserters from the French army. He is greeted by jubilant citizens who had got tired of the rule of King Louis XVIII and his Chamber of Deputies. The Parisians wanted change, they craved the older Napoleonic era and they desired revenge. And Napoleon promised them that and more. Ivanhoe is now anointed as the Count of Monte Cristo and becomes a powerful minister in Napoleon's government. He exacts his revenge by putting Fernand, Villefort, and Danglars in prison. In order to be able to marry Mercedes, he challenges Fernand to a duel, offering him freedom if he defeats the Count. He defeats Fernand, leaving him to die of his injuries. Later, after marrying Mercedes, he buys a ship and sets sail along with his family and his original loyal army of hundred, seeking new adventures in foreign lands.'

She said after an appreciative pause, 'That was an interesting twist from the original. Changing history, returning Napoleon for the second time from exile—Europe will never rest in peace with him as the French emperor, that man had a mad streak, seeking wars all his life. I don't know whether I will be able to match you but I will try.'

Her attempt at deconstructing Ivanhoe fared poorly, as she forgot that Edmond Dantes was a suave gentleman and a sailor, not much of a fighter, and couldn't have won the individual jousting on the first day of the tournament at Ashby-de-la-Zouch, as the 'Disinherited Knight'. Similarly he couldn't have defeated Brian de Bois-Guilbert in the trial by combat, to free Rebecca, as her champion. She came out second best again. In the medieval world full of fighting in the Crusades, jousting in tournaments, close combat in the melee, romance and love, witch-hunting and trials by combat, Edmond Dantes as Wilfred of Ivanhoe would have been a total misfit.

26

The Last Winter

It was the winter I was dreading the most. She was in class 12 and her family's decisions with respect to her future would decide my destiny. Many were the nights when I could not sleep due to frustration that my fate was in the hands of her parents and brothers, where I could not have any say. There can be no feeling more distressing than when you realise that you are ineffective in taking decisions that will guide your future, as those decisions were to be taken by people who don't even know you exist. Come March next year and Pratima's parents might decide to marry her off; will I be able to muster the courage to confront them and tell them that I love her—they will laugh at me, kick me out of their house, and get me expelled from the school; Father would be so disappointed if I got thrown out. Her brothers would definitely insist that she study further and attain a graduation degree, but she will then go away, most probably to Lucknow, where her elder brother was a lecturer in a university and I would not be able to meet her again—the best case scenario for me, as by the time she completed her degree course I would be in NDA and well on my way to becoming a commissioned officer and her family would not be able to refuse accepting me as her groom; that was a pleasant thought. What if her brothers gave in to their parents' wishes, as she was already 20? I shuddered at that. I couldn't confront both her parents and her brothers. The younger one might even kill me.

And she had not yet told me that she loved me!

With such divergent thoughts of despondence, hope, and dread churning my mind and my heart trying to seek some solace somewhere, I reached the foot of our trail. I was late and she was pacing impatiently, clad in green flannel trousers, jacket and jerseys to ward off the chill in the air.

The sun was out in its full glory, but the wind blowing down from Gagar carried the remains of the icy cold of the snow peaks beyond. I was equally dressed in layers of wool. That morning I had taken my weekly bath in ice-cold water and was still shivering from the effects.

I beamed when I sighted her, all thoughts of depression vanishing from my mind—she had that effect on me, having her with me, I could pull myself out of whatever depths of despair I was stuck in. I almost bent down to kiss her as we held hands in greeting. She was alone, Bindu was not with her. I had not seen Pratima for the past one month, and looking at her was enough of a blessing for me.

The frozen overnight dew had not yet melted in certain nooks still in the shadows and the pine needles, strewn all over the hill slope, with droplets of the morning dew shining like diamonds, made the trail slippery and our climb treacherous. She held on firmly to my hand as I marched up the pathway, slipping and skidding.

Halfway up the slope, she stepped on a bed of pine needles sitting atop a small hole. As her foot broke through the false floor, her other leg gave way due to the sudden loss of balance and she carried both of us down the slope, skidding on our backs. Holding her hand in a tight grip, I frantically waved my free hand for a handhold. After bumping and skidding for a fair distance, my hand got stuck in a shrub with sturdy roots and I closed my fingers around a bunch of wet stems, breaking our slide with a jerk. I held on with one hand for dear life, and she crawled up my legs, lying on top of me, gasping with deep hot breaths, the cold tip of her nose tickling my neck. As she lay there panting, faint stirrings of desire crept through my body, goose pimples shot jolts of electricity through my nerves and the hairs of my hands stood up. I let go of the shrub and closed my arms around her, pulling her into me. After a long moment, in which I relived the last three years of my life in seconds, she jerked up her head. Having regained her breath, she slid off me hurriedly and said, 'I am sorry, I shouldn't have. . .' She left the unsaid words hanging in the air.

I said, 'I am sorry. I shouldn't have held you.'

'No, you silly. You saved my life. Had you not been holding my hand, I would have slid all the way down and broken some bones.'

I did not correct her for misunderstanding what I had meant from my apology. For the first time in my life I had intensely desired for the touch and feel of her body, barring that euphoric experience in the post World Cup final victory celebration of last year. Till now I had never wanted to feel her body against me, in the manner that grownups feel with a woman. And the reason was very selfish, strange as it may sound. Just looking at her face filled my heart with such warmth that it felt impure to regard her in any other manner. Whenever I dreamt of Pratima, she always appeared as an angel and her chaste nature in the real world never made me long for greater intimacy. I was content with what we had going between us and did not wish for the next stage of sensual explorations in our relationship.

Till then I had never had a chance to see the private parts of a girl, except that one occasion at Shanti Bhavan, four years back, when I had blundered into a room where a cousin (the one whose birth before me had caused such consternation in the family) was changing her clothes. I still vividly remember that episode. I had stood gaping at her standing there, wearing just her brassiere and underwear and she had said, 'What are you doing? Close the door and come inside, somebody will see me naked. Come in now,' and then she had put on display her body, calling out the names of each of her intimate parts and even explained 'the curse'; she never asked me to show mine as that would have been too embarrassing for me, but my 12-year-old self had shivered with emotions as I stood staring at her in breathless amazement. Later, I had shaken my head in vigorous negation when she had warned me, with a smirk, while pulling on her underwear, 'Now run away and don't tell about this to anyone, not even to your brother, promise me by slapping my hand.'

I have that effect on all the girls and women I know. Where, as a toddler and during my preteen years, I used to bask in the centre of attraction status I enjoyed amongst the women of Shanti Bhavan and Jaswantnagar, now as a lanky, five-and-a-half-feet-tall adolescent, I still get hugs and pecks on my cheeks, from my aunts and cousins, on a frequent basis. I sometimes sensed oedipal feelings from my youngest aunt and that cousin who went buff to explain the female anatomy to me; their kisses lingered longer, their embraces were tighter as they pressed themselves into me fiercely and rubbed their palms vigorously against my back, their breaths were hotter when they whispered their farewells into my ears on the last day of my vacations. During such moments of intimacy, I felt the blood surge into my ears and goose pimples rose at the base of my neck.

But with Pratima, I had never before felt such stirrings. For me, just a glimpse of her beautiful face was sensuous enough to calm my heartbeats, to soothe my nerves, to stop the churns of my mind whenever I contemplated a desolate future without her, to relax my muscles whenever the turmoil in my heart led to physiological reactions.

She broke into my thoughts: 'Why did you feel embarrassed for holding me so close when I lay on top of you?' We had resumed our climb and were close to the summit, walking side by side as the trail widened.

I feigned ignorance. 'But I thought you had meant my holding your hand while sliding down was what made you feel uncomfortable.'

'You are kidding with me, right?'

'No, I am just having a routine conversation.'

'Don't you behave in such a smug manner?'

'We are digressing. You were onto something.'

'Oh Sanjay! At times you run circles around me. Actually I was building up to something ethereal. You must understand that what we have between us is the most beautiful thing that could have ever happened to me. It is divine, it is pure, and it is otherworldly. I want you to know that you are the first and only boy I have been with and talked to. There have been some of them, a few of my classmates and some seniors too, who wanted to be friends with me. There was this prude who had once held my hands and wanted to kiss me.'

'Who was that bastard? Tell me his name. I will kill him.'

'Don't go murdering people just because I am beautiful.'

'What do you mean?'

'Since the time I was in class 8, before I met you, lot of boys used to stare at me. Then I had thought that there must be something hideous about my appearance; maybe my nose or the scar on my chin. Later, Monisha told me that they stared because I have a pretty face. Then you happened. When you confessed that you regarded me as an angel, I started looking at myself differently. I wanted to look beautiful. You know we girls have this strange mindset. When we are told that we are beautiful, we want to look more beautiful. And an unending spiral begins. The more beautiful we look, the prettier we want to be the next time.

'As we grew up in age you grew on me. I loved the rapt attention with which you regarded me, the intense gaze with which you would study my face. I glowed under your gaze. It felt as if you would drink me in with your eyes.

'And then I discovered something fascinating in you. You have a vivid imagination. Who would have thought of a *g*-shaped girl? But you did. As we sat deconstructing Robinson Crusoe, I loved the way you would invent images out of thin air—a mysterious, laws-of-nature-defying planet, 100 kids from a skull just with kisses and plops, slip of a girl turning into a vivacious angel descended from heaven. You were just beautiful.

'Later, when I started understanding such matters, I realised how selfless you have always been. I know boys of your age have these urges, as the hormones start kicking in. It must have started with you a year or so back. But you never thought on those lines, whenever we were together. You always had pure intentions in your heart. I know girls who enter into physical relations within months of knowing a boy; mostly it is at the boy's insistence. But not you, never. And I cherish that.

'Today when I slipped and skid, you held on to my hand. On impulse I climbed over you and lay on top. And when you closed your arms around me I felt so safe, so secure, so protected. But when you apologised I could see the embarrassment written all over your face and I feigned that I had misunderstood.'

After that we fell into silence and walked up the rest of the way, lost in our own worlds. The severe chill at the top pulled us back shivering into the real world and both of us blurted out simultaneously, 'It's so cold out here.' We cackled at the coincidence and I pulled out my faux-leather gloves from my pockets and blowing into them, pulled them over my bloodless fingers. She wore her woollen mittens and stuck her hands inside her jacket, under her armpits. Her cheeks were the colour of strawberries and her lips were quivering. There were tears in her eyes and drips from the tip of her nose were carried away by the gale, which swung and swayed the tall pines in drunken waltzes. I cupped her face with my palms and brushed my gloved thumbs against the tip of her nose and below her eyes.

I felt sorry for her and hoping that she would not say yes, I asked, 'Do you want to cancel it?'

'No way! That slide was exciting. Let's walk over to our usual place. Sit close to me.'

The reticence of our initial days had been overcome with the passage of time. The formal nature of those first few meetings, more out of shyness on my part, had made us maintain our distance from one another. The first few days we had sat on different chairs, opposite each other, as she had narrated her life story in Dwivedi Sir's place. Over a period of time, the initial solemn formality disintegrated into a familiarity engendered by our frank exchanges and deep appreciation of each other's intellect, more hers than mine, which not only overcame my shyness but brought us closer, both literally and metaphorically. If anyone made a kaleidoscope of the images of our postures over the years, it would look like a boy and girl sitting on chairs, each facing the other and as they grew in age and the boy in height, the distances between them shrunk with each new image: from sitting apart on a couch and later on a concrete structure, narrowing the gap with each image, till their legs stuck together, to the arms going around the other's back, initially placed consciously, the hand aware of its limits, to later moving across, till the finger tips then the fingers went under the other's armpits. We held hands on a regular basis and I had subconsciously grown into the habit of cupping her face, especially during the chilly winters, the ball of my thumb and the base of my palm sitting under her round jaw line, my thumbs brushing the joints of her lips, desperately seeking permission to run along her lush red lips, the cup of my palm covering her cold cheeks, the tips of my middle fingers disturbing the ampersand created by her locks, next to her temples.

We settled down atop the water tank, our feet dangling down its front wall, our flanks snugly fitting into each other, our arms around the other's back with the gloved fingertips lodged inside each other's armpits, our free hand holding the other's in a tight clasp, fingers linked with each other like entwined vines, our heads joined together in a conspiratorial huddle with friendly ghosts, so as to be able to hear each other's voice amidst the howling wind.

She spoke about her future plans.

And shattered my heart.

She was going away.

I stared at the swaying pine trees in sheer disbelief, as she told me how her father had selected a 'worthy' match for her, a clerk working in a government office in Nainital, to whom she would be married during the summers, after her twelfth board exams. 'You have had enough education. No girl in our family, in our entire village for that matter, has ever entered a school and you are an undergraduate now. The boy is the youngest son of a reputed family. His father retired as a head clerk from the same office. It is time for you to settle down,' he had said with a finality. She had written to her brothers about her father's choice and the ultimatum. They had taken immediate short leaves from their respective vocations and had arrived three weeks back, in a bid to persuade their father against his decision. It had erupted into a huge row at the house.

'Father was stubbornly defending his decision, saying that the boy belonged to our caste, the family was well known, he had a steady government job, that I would be very happy in that large joint family, that I would be well looked after by my in-laws, that he was fed up of having to listen to the rebukes of his relatives and acquaintances for having an unmarried, grown-up girl, when all his brothers' and cousins' daughters had been married off when they were much younger. He called me a girl and not his daughter. I felt so ashamed. My mother then piped in, timidly saying, 'We have suffered enough ridicule. Had it not been for your insistence, we would have been rid of her burden so long back.' She called me a burden. I felt so miserable that I wanted the earth to open up and swallow me. I looked at my brothers with trepidation, hoping that they would be my gallant saviours once again. Father continued with his tirade that he had spent enough money on my education—even though he did not have to pay a single paisa for my fees with my being a girl-child and daughter of a faculty member—that he did not have any resources for any further education for me.'

Her big brother had then asked a pertinent question, 'How much dowry have they asked for?' And upon hearing a sheepish reply from his hesitant father, that seven lakh rupees had been demanded by the prospective groom's family, he had exploded in fury, 'For a lowly clerk. And you agreed to that! Damn you Father. How will you arrange that much money?'

'"He has a government job." Father insisted obstinately. "As for the money, I have one lakh in savings, four I can arrange by selling a portion of our ancestral land or by mortgaging the entire lot and I was banking on you two for the balance."

'My younger brother said in a plaintive tone, "I have just joined the Army. My pay is meagre. How do you expect me to cough up one lakh rupees?"

'There ensued a deathly silence for a long time as my mind roiled with myriad possibilities—will my brothers be my proverbial knights in shining armour again? I had seen the photograph of the man my father had chosen for me and I had shuddered in terror on looking at the moon-faced, jowly, squint-eyed, flat-nosed Pahari. I had thought, "How could my father agree to such a match, did he hate me so much?" I had never realised that he had never forgiven me, as if it was my fault, for the battering his ego had taken when he had had to relent to my brothers to let me join school and continue my studies further, when I had reached twelve. I was also worried of the future, if my brothers caved in that day. "How can I wed such a lout?" I decided that I would run away after my board exams and stay with one of my brothers—"but would they take me in if they relented today?" Then I thought about you—what would you think of me if I married that clown? In you I saw a glimmer of hope; I would run away and stay with your parents if they agreed, they are such nice people and I was sure that you would be able to persuade them to accept me as their guest, till things cooled down here after my running away. I was feeling so helpless; I did not know where to turn to. Big Brother was looking at me contemplatively, deep in thought and I was hoping that he could read the desperate plea in my eyes.

'The Army man broke the silence and declared in a loud voice, "If you marry off Chhutki to this twerp I will publicly disown both of you," he looked pointedly at my parents. Father staggered a few steps back as if hit by a blast of hot air and Mother let out a loud gasp and started sobbing. But I continued looking at Big Brother with a forlorn look in my eyes, without batting an eyelid. I knew that despite my impetuous younger brother's chivalrous attitude and bravado, it was my level-headed big brother who would decide my future. Would he relent or not?

'He gave a reassuring nod in my direction and I started breathing again. I had not realised that I had not taken a single breath during the whole period of unearthly silence and the staccato declaration by Chhotu. In a cool and calm voice, Big Brother said to his younger sibling, "No one is going to cough up any money. And don't you dare disown Mother. I go with the territory. If you disown her you disown me too."

'Then, turning towards Father, he said, "Father, and this is the last time I am ever going to address you in that manner. After the truth is out today, you won't be deserving of that revered title. You have not spoken a single word of truth during our entire conversation. I tried to give you a chance to be honest, yet you chose to pave the path of your own doom. Not only are you a misogynist maniac, but you have been a chronic liar throughout your life. I will start from the beginning, since now that every truth will come out, let the ultimate truth be out in the open first. None of the three of you have an inkling, so form your opinions about him yourself."

'Then he dropped an atom bomb which shook all faith in humanity I have ever had. Turning to Mother he said, "Have you ever wondered why he had insisted on you giving birth to Chhutki at his sister's hut outside the village. Because Bhago, the witch that she is, had divined that you would be birthing a daughter and she had convinced him, not that he had ever required much persuading in such matters, to get rid of Chhutki immediately after her birth. So he had had you moved to Bhago's decrepit hut the night Chhutki was born, with that rogue of a cousin of mine, who is now in jail for molesting that school teacher, recruited to leave our Little Princess on a far away mountain slope, in the dead of the night; 'smother her if need be', that crone had insisted. And this man had not even let out a whimper of protest. Mother, you were dead to the world, exhausted after the efforts of child birth. It was my good fortune that I had gone with your dinner and standing outside the door I had overheard their conversation; I did not have to put in much effort, the three of them were talking in loud voices about their diabolical scheme." Walking over to me, he continued, "Had I not been there in the nick of time, I would have never known so much joy and happiness in my life," and I slipped into his embrace, as he planted a kiss on my forehead.

'Mother asked next, "What happened thereafter?" "As has always happened since then—this man has an Achilles' heel; his reputation. I threatened to tarnish it by letting everyone at the school know about his desire to abandon Chhutki. He would have not only lost his job, he could have been put in jail too. That was the first time I put the fear of God in him. That nephew of his vanished like vapour and that sly old hag disappeared into some remote nook. I had taken the bawling Chhutki from his arms and had gone in the middle of the night to each house in the village, to announce that a little princess had been born in our family; not only was I filled with immense joy while holding the little bundle of joy who had by then gone to sleep after exhausting herself from crying, it was also an insurance that this demon of a man and his vile sister could not think of some new fiendish scheme to harm Chhutki. He had brought Mother back home late the next morning, denying Chhutki Mother's milk for the first twelve hours of her life. I had fed her goat's milk every hour, all through that night. That is the reason this man has never seen eye to eye with me all my life and despite his gigantic ego, has always relented to my wishes. Little Princess, don't you ever carry even a faint notion that this fiend has something called love for you in any remote corner of his heart. I wonder if he ever knew the definition of love. He has kept his wife as a subservient servant dancing to his tune, poisoning her heart against her daughter, right from the day she was 6 years old. He is diminutive in size but he has a demon in his heart. I now know what you are. You are a degenerate who has such a depraved mindset in relation to women that I detest you. You are too pertinacious in your misogynistic mania and I feel nothing but extreme aversion for you. You might have fathered me and raised me, for which I will pay you back, with interest, but you are nothing to me. Thank heavens I had the forethought to conduct a detailed investigation of the matter at hand today, this sham of a marriage of Chhutki to this clown."

'Looking directly at Father, he continued: "You say that he has a steady government job of a clerk, when in actuality he is just a peon, and that when you had feared for your reputation when I had offered to be a peon for Chhutki's education. You would accept a peon son-in-law, but not a peon son. You say that she would be happy with him; well you know for a fact that he is a homosexual pervert, who likes grown-up men; don't deny it." Mother had let out a gasp at the insinuation. "What you don't know is their real intention and I wonder whether you would have refused the arrangement, had you known about it; knowing you, you wouldn't have. In addition to their pound of flesh, they wanted you to give your daughter to be an unpaid servant to the mother and a sex slave to the father. You look surprised? Ask the police about the circumstances of the death of their elder daughter-in-law. You say that the family is well reputed; well their reputation surpasses them, as two daughters in the family had eloped last year with low-caste do-gooders and are leading comfortable married life, despite having married against the wishes of their parents. You say that she will lead a happy life in that large joint family, you must be surely aware that one of their sons is in prison, convicted for burning his wife, due to their incessant demands for dowry and his parents are still under investigation for being complicit. The truth is that the girl was raped and murdered by her lecherous father-in-law and the son took the blame on the lesser charge of death by negligence and he later pleaded guilty for dowry-related death. Her body was burned to hide the evidence, but unknown to them the police have got a bone from her neck, which has a sharp cut. The moment they get conclusive evidence, the father will be in jail with his son.

'"As for the dowry, you are not giving the four lakh rupees from the proceeds of sale of a portion of our ancestral property. You have shamelessly agreed to transfer half of our entire ancestral property, including the top floor of our house in the village, to this lout's father. You don't have any saving worth a dime. You spend half of your monthly salary on your vice of gambling at Bhowali, Shyamkhet, and God only knows where else and with the balance you barely manage to run this family. There was no cash to be paid in dowry; the dowry was half of our ancestral inheritance, which is worth more than twenty lakh rupees.

'"It's such a shame that being a teacher yourself, in your muddled head, you never gave it a thought what wonders education would do to your only daughter. She is the most intelligent girl I have ever seen in my entire life. You cannot even begin to imagine what brilliance she has inside her brain and she has the purest of hearts I have ever come across. It is such a pity that both of you never saw the real Pratima. And she is not any unmarried grown-up girl, she is our sister; don't you ever forget that. If you ever lay a hand on her or torment her in any other manner, I will have you put in prison for actual and imagined offences and ensure that someone puts a knife into your guts, ending your reprehensible existence."

'Father's face had gone pale, an expression of horror writ all over his visage. Mother stared at him with amazement. She had been taken aback by the revelations. Father was finding it difficult to swallow, as he stammered, "How . . . ho . . . ho . . . how d . . . d . . . did you . . . find out?"

'"Chhotu and I had arranged to go to Nainital and Bhojpur, before coming here, the moment we got Chhutki's letter begging for our help. We had rushed immediately, as there was sheer distress hidden between the lines—our poor princess was in need. We investigated this sham you had arranged in connivance with this buffoon's father. Not for nothing have I made friends with the police. The entire truth came out. You are in debt to him to the tune of ten lakh rupees, courtesy to all that gambling, and drinking too. Mother does not know about the drinking, because you have always been careful to only indulge in it when you were sleeping it off in some dingy dharmshala, during your outstation visits. And when he sent his goons to recover his debt, you quivered in front of him and offered your daughter and our ancestral property. Shame on you, to save your skin you were selling our little princess."'

She halted in her narrative as her voice was breaking. I looked inside her tear-stricken eyes, brushed a gloved finger under each eye, cupped her beautiful face in my gloved palms and said, 'Take your time.' She took deep breaths, soft sobs escaping her lips and resumed after a few moments.

'Then Big Brother announced, "There will be no marriage, neither in the summers nor in the near future."

'A wave of gratitude washed over me and I sagged into his arms. He was my pillar of strength. He saved me again from a life of misery and grief. The Army man also converged and both of them enveloped me in a huge hug, as I wept silent tears into Big Brother's chest. He consoled me, "There, there. Shhh . . . Chhutki. Everything will be fine. Don't you worry, your big brother would have never let it happen. You are our little princess. Have faith in us. We will look after you henceforth."

'Father bleated, "But he will kill me, my son."

'Big Brother stared with contempt at Father and said, "I am no son of yours, I forbid you from ever calling me that. Since you had decided to put a price on our Pratima, the day is not far when you would do the same to us too. So, I have decided to name the price for both of us and be done with the sale process you so prefer, so that you cannot call in your debt for having raised us, anytime in the future. Here is what will happen henceforth. Pratima will continue her studies, staying in this house, till her board exams. Both of you will care for her, as has been going on till now. She will not be put under any pressure or harassment. You will not broach today's episode, her education, or her marriage to her, ever. I will ask Dwivedi Sir and his sons to keep a discreet watch on her, to ensure that my decisions are being followed in letter and spirit. Once a week, a policeman from Bhowali will visit the house to check on her well-being. I will be leaving 5,000 rupees with Mother to cater for Chhutki's needs. Mother, you will keep an account of all expenditures, so that I am assured that the money is not used by this man to satiate his other desires and indulge in his vices. The moment she completes her board exams, I will take her to Lucknow and there, she will join the university where I teach, to pursue her graduation course. She will never come back here or to our village, unless one or both of us accompany her for some important ceremony. During holidays, she will stay with Chhotu, if he is allowed a family member to stay with him; else she will spend the time with me. After her graduation, she will decide whether she wishes to continue her studies or get married, it will be entirely her choice. When the time comes I will select a suitable boy for her.

"'Coming to our price. The ancestral land and the house back at our village had been left to you by our grandfather, as a custodian, to pass them on to your progenies, provided you did not squander away our inheritance on your vices. And it is our good fortune that you have not been able to waste away our bequest. But now that your propensity to splurge your limited resources has come out so starkly, I do not feel confident that you won't fritter away our inheritance. The ancestral property is the right of all three of us, now that we are of age, and not yours to run through. All three of us have equal share in it, Hindu Succession Act be damned. You will be travelling with me to the District Court at Nainital tomorrow, to distribute the land in three equal shares. You will have complete access to the proceeds from the sale of the produce off the land. And our price is the house. You can do whatever you wish with the house. You can sell it for all Chhotu and I care and pay off your debt. But be warned that you will need it in your old age, as you would never be welcome in either of our households. Except, Mother is always welcome, for it is my firm belief that even though she had colluded with you in this vile conspiracy, guileless that she is, hers was not a willing cooperation. You must have wheedled her into it, against her better instincts. As to whether your lender will agree on giving you time for securing the money, now that you will be reneging on the secret deal, that is a cross you will have to bear alone. You will send a letter today to inform him of the cancellation of your unscrupulously contrived agreement.

"'But before I put the stamp of finality, I would require the assent of the one person in this room who has suffered the most, due to this man's devilish mindset. What do you say little sister, should we let him do what he wants with the house? You have one-third stake in that, too." He looked down at me with so much love that my heart ached with gratitude. I immediately nodded my ready acceptance of the proposal, with vigorous up and down movements of my head.

'He placed a loving hand upon my head and said, "Good girl. Now the final question; princess, answer this one with due care and thought. Do you want to study further?"

'I hugged him with all my might and said, "Oh Big Brother! Thank you so much. I don't know how I will ever be able to do anything that would be enough to convey my gratitude. You have saved me, transformed my life forever. Yes, I would love to study further. That is my life's ambition. I want to do BSc and become a doctor, or an engineer. Then I will think of marriage, if at all."

'"One step at a time, Pratima, one step at a time. First pass your board exams with good marks in the science subjects and maths, which I am sure you will. We will see what you want to become as time goes by. But we promise you this (he placed a hand on my head, the Army man following suit): we will ensure that you study as much as you wish and will never force marriage upon you, till you wish for it.

'"And never ever think of gratitude towards us. The thought should not even enter your mind. We are your brothers and we will move heaven and earth for you. In fact, it is the other way round. We are indebted to you, that you had so much faith in us to have confided the truth to us. Had we not received that letter of yours, we would have never come to know about this evil scheme and by the time it had unfolded, it would have been too late. By your very action, you have saved us from dying of shame and disgrace, had this devil been successful in his insidious plot."

'With that he looked at Mother and said, "Can we have food now mother?"

'Mother, who had been silently weeping till now, wiped her tears with the edges of her sari, walked over to us, turned around, looked defiantly at my father and spoke, "Yes my son. But before we eat I want to say something. (She placed a hand upon my head). I swear upon my daughter that it was never my intention to be party to this treachery. He forced me into it, sweet-talking me, threatening me, cajoling me; he had even hit me once when I had objected vehemently. And, as is the lot with our kind, I had to either be thrown out of this house or accept that Chhutki be sent off. I am ashamed of myself that I accepted the latter choice. Take her away son. Take her away from this fiend." And she ambled into the kitchen, her head held high for once.'

I stared at Pratima for a long time, as tears streamed down her face. I wiped them away with my gloved hands and gave her my handkerchief. I swallowed the lump in my throat, which had lain stuck there, like a greasy ball of wool. I cleared my throat, brought my flowing emotions under control, and said, 'Is this really true?'

'What do you mean?'

'I mean this seems like a scene straight out of a Hindi movie. How can a father be so selfish, so steeped in evil practices, so diabolical to even contemplate killing his daughter and be ready to sell her later? There is so much to learn from this world. Anyway,' with that I stood up and dramatically saluted, 'my salute to your brothers, especially the big brother. Where is the prince, the knight in shining armour? I want to touch his feet.'

'He has gone back to Lucknow. If he ever sees you with me, he will kill you. Don't mistake his brotherly love as an acceptance of our relationship,' at last her tears stopped and she smiled at me.

Then it struck like a hammer blow. As I looked down at her angelic grin, the sunlight moving across her face with the shadows, reality hit me hard and shattered my heart into thousand fragments.

She would be going away.

Never to return.

Oh God! What an irony. What a twist of fate. Her brothers had saved her from a life in hell, from where she would have definitely proceeded to her heavenly abode, but they were taking her away permanently, from me. I would never be able to meet her again. She must have also sensed my turmoil, as she stood up and losing her grin, put a gloved palm on my cheek. 'Don't lose heart, Sanjay.'

'Can I ever become that suitable boy? Rekha *Didi* had told me once that you underestimate your brothers, that they have a very affable nature, that they would accept me if it were your desire.'

'Wait till I graduate.'

I looked down at my feet and clammed up. I remained in that position for a long time, my heart despondent and my mind in turmoil. I broke from my brooding with a shake of my head, to discard the dark thoughts that were simmering in my brain.

'Look, I have brought something for the two of us,' she said in a solemn voice, a hint of sadness in her tone. My gloomy mood was affecting her too. She pulled two packets out of her jacket pockets, wrapped in foil, and handed one to me. I took it from her and we sat down. I opened the wrapping, it contained sandwiches.

'I prepared them myself, so don't throw them away if you don't like them. Just swallow the bites and thank God that they are better than the garbage they serve in the mess.'

I ate the sandwiches with a relish, more out of hunger than for the taste. The sandwich was cold and it had gone mushy. She had spread coats of butter and jam and had piled thick slices of tomato, in between the bread. The morsels stuck to the roof of my mouth and I had to curl my tongue to pry the offending pulp off, and thereafter it slid down the roof stickily, in halting motions, till the oesophagus, where I had to take huge gulps of saliva to wash it down. Some small belligerent lumps of gummy bread stuck to the gums and lay there, stubbornly refusing to be dislodged, even when I ran the tip of my tongue to dig them out. Pratima was also experiencing similar difficulties in eating her piece and after some time she scooped out a sticky mush from her gums with her finger, flicked it into the air where the wind carried it away and threw the remaining portion of her half eaten sandwich. 'They are worse than garbage. Don't act chivalrous. You can throw yours if you want to.'

'I have had worse. You should have given that to me, rather than chucking it away. You don't know what they feed us in the mess. You were dead on when you said it is garbage. It is even worse than that sometimes. At least garbage is relished by street dogs.' I hiccupped.

With a contented sigh and in throes of hiccups, I leaned back on my arms, pulled up my knees, and hung back my neck, glancing up at the sky. There was a gap in the canopy of pine fronds and branches and I could see a squarish, shifting stretch of the blue sky. There was nary a blemish in the azure emptiness and I wondered about the miracles of nature which lent such a blue hue to the bleak, blank, and black expanse of space outside the earth's atmosphere. A white mass rushed across the fragment of sky visible to me, followed by more clouds hurrying with great speed from West to East, as if being summoned by the Gods to be consigned to some dark prison, for having the temerity to mar the magnificent view of the heavens for us mere mortals. I looked around for the sun and saw that it was creeping across the Eastern sky, on its ascent towards its zenith. I realised that she had been away from her house for more than two hours now and her parents must be looking for her, suspecting numerous possibilities for her long disappearance, especially after that stern warning from Big Brother. I turned towards her, neck still bent in a transverse arch and asked, 'Aren't you getting late?'

'My parents have gone to the village in connection with the sale of our house there. I presume his lender has been pressing hard on Father to cough up the debt. They will be coming back tomorrow.'

I asked in complete innocence, 'Can I come over and stay the night with you? To keep all those monsters and dark spirits at bay, while you sleep.'

She playfully poked an elbow into my ribs. 'Don't be silly. Bindu will be giving me company during the night. She is sleeping over at my house.'

'Bindu is pliant and in the know. Let her sleep in your parents' bedroom and we will sleep in yours. No hanky panky, God promise (I straightened up and pinched the middle of my neck with my thumb and forefinger). We will just lie there and talk of the uncertain future, well into the night. Then I will leave before the rooster crows.'

She chuckled and said in a mild tone, 'You do dream of improbable possibilities. You are truly growing up; keep this up and your dreams may really come true some day. But for tonight it is a staunch no. I don't want a scandal after the recent happenings in my life.'

'True enough. But it was still worth the thought and the attempt. For a moment there, I got lost in a marvellous dream.' I sighed and quietened. After a couple of minutes of silence, the rushing gale of howling wind flapping our jackets and swinging the tall pine trees in wild swaying motions, I said with warmth, 'Say something.'

She looked at me pensively for a few moments, her eyes locked with mine and the sensation of drowning in those black pools in unending spirals coursed through my veins. She leaned over and whispered conspiratorially, as if we were partners in a crime, 'Sanjay, do you want to touch me.'

I feigned puerile innocence and putting my left arm around her back, said, 'I am already touching you,' my heart bucked like a mare in heat, in anticipation.

She put her arm around my back and leaned in closer, her lips tingling my ears as she murmured, 'You know what I mean.'

Continuing my charade I turned to face her and insisted, 'No, I don't know what you mean.'

'I think you very well know what I mean, it is in your eyes,' she grinned. 'You are what . . . going to be 16, in one and a half months from now. (I nodded). Boys your age do dream of touching girls in that manner. Why only boys? We girls also want to see and feel you boys. In our private conversations, we girls discuss a lot about the boys' private parts, especially that thing between your legs. All I have seen of it, in our biology books, is a limp appendage annotated as "peeniss" (she spoke the first syllable as in pee and ended with a hiss). What about you Sanjay? Do you never have a desire to touch me like this?' and she picked up my free hand and placed my palm over her chest.

An electrifying current jingled my nerves, sending jolts of electricity shooting through my skin, as I felt her through the cushion of the roughly textured wool of her jacket and the thickness of the sweaters underneath. That initial reaction to such an intimate gesture subsided as, after some time, the thick layers of clothing made me feel as if I was cupping a ball of wool. I felt disappointed and pulled back my arm. But there was another vital reason for my hesitation.

'I . . . I . . . don't know Pratima. Since the first day I have been enraptured by your beauty. You enter my dreams, sashay around, talk to me, laugh with me and leave me wanting for more. But more of what? It was neither revealed in my dreams nor have I been able to fathom this unfulfilled desire. Maybe, I just want to look at your beautiful face forever, never letting you out of my sight, maybe I just want to feel your presence when you are with me, maybe I just want to absorb more and more, listening to you as you speak on myriad ranges of subjects, that brilliant mind of yours spewing out what it had itself consumed through your voracious appetite for reading, maybe I just want to revel in the tremendous energy you exude through your positivity, maybe I want to join you and lift my chin too, regarding the world with contempt, for the misogyny it perpetrates, corrupting our society. Whatever it is, I feel that I can never have enough of you. You can't even begin to imagine how I spend my time away from you, especially during my vacations, longing for you every wakeful second and dreaming of you, when I get tired of thinking of you all the time and somehow manage to get some sleep. I don't know how I manage to study at all, when I am not with you. The entire period of the past three years I have only looked at you in the purest of sense. I can't put to words the deep regard I feel for you. You are unblemished and so pristine that I don't want to spoil what we have between us. I can't give a name to our relationship, but I treasure what we have. I have revelled in your company, felt privileged that you allowed me to hold your hands, put my arms around you, cup your face with my palms so that I can drown in your bewitching eyes and have felt immensely honoured that you shared your intimate thoughts, your deepest fears, your private moments, and the occurrences in your personal life, including that family row. But to touch you in that manner, I don't know, Pratima, I am not sure of myself.'

Tears glistening in her eyes, she leaned over and tenderly placed her head on my chest. 'You are beautiful, more beautiful than me.' I looked down upon her head scraping my chin and saw a white bread crumb seemingly lost amongst the flowing strands of her hair. I bent down and licked the soggy piece, her hair smelling of Dabur Amla and a remnant aroma of the shampoo she had used that morning. As I lifted my head, a single strand of her hair stayed glued to the tip of my tongue and I moved my tongue between my lips, like a serpent, to dislodge it. The bread crumb fell back into the dense jungle of her head, as if it hadn't relished the idea of being so unceremoniously moved out of its dwelling. I blew at it and it delved deeper into its abode, amidst the glossy tresses. I gave up.

She continued into my jacket. 'You are so noble. Chivalry hasn't died with the medieval knights after all. Any other boy would have grabbed at the opportunity and pawed all over me. But you, you are different. Will I ever meet someone as thoughtful of me, I wonder. I feel so safe being with you. You give me that strange feeling one gets. . .'

She lifted her head and stared at me with a strange light in her eyes, must be the sun. 'You can kiss me if you want to. It won't spoil the effect.'

I bent my head and placed my lips on hers. They were so moist and soft, I felt my heart skip several beats. It was so sublime. But after the initial euphoria I felt nothing. No fresh feelings were aroused. I pulled back and saw disappointment in her eyes too. 'What!' she exclaimed. After some time she said, 'Let's try again.'

This time I cupped her face in my palms and enclosed her lower lip with mine. I sipped on the moisture and nibbled tenderly. She moaned deep inside her throat and ran the tip of her tongue along my upper lip. It felt divine, as the leathery surface of her tongue scraped the soft skin of my lip. I had never thought that a kiss could have such an effect and blood surged into my pelvis. I felt myself harden when she pressed her chest into me and grabbed fiercely at my head, pulling me down. She closed her lips around my lower lip and nibbled at it with soft bites of her teeth. Her mouth tasted of butter, jam, and tomatoes. A searing pain of intense desire and pleasure wrapped my heart, as I closed my arms around her and crushed her into me. We remained wrapped, drowning in our kiss, when the need for air forced us to break.

'That was nice,' she said. She ran her tongue along her lips, gasping for breath. I just stared at her flushed face and said, 'You have become more beautiful than ever. Is that what a kiss does to girls?'

She rested her head on my chest again and hiked up the hems of her jacket and sweaters, pulling out her shirt from the waistband of her pants. She took my left hand and pulling out the gloves, slid it under all her clothes and placed it at the bare flesh of her waist. I put a finger into her belly button, there was a slight protrusion there, not a dip like mine. I snaked my fingers up in caterpillar motions, touched her ribs and closed my palm. She was warm and soft and round and plump, like the bladder of a football. The touch was so soft, it seemed that if I pressed harder, I would push her breast into her chest; the sensation so magical as if I was floating amongst the clouds. I ran a finger over the coarse texture of her puckered nipple and pinched it with my thumb and finger. She let out a gasp and slapped my hand, the sound muffled by the layers of wool. 'Don't pinch it, just touch it. Feel the warmth,' she whispered into my ear and kissed me again.

As we broke again, she said, 'I heard the daughter of the school bus driver, the one who, it was rumoured, had got pregnant from an affair with a boy from Bhowali and had subsequently had an abortion at a private clinic at Nainital, she says that you boys do something with your hands, playing with your peeniss.'

'Why do you call it that?'

'It's a quirk of mine. Since you use it to pee or piss; I like the play of the words, so I combined them.'

'Peeniss . . . no that's yours, for keepsakes,' I grinned at her smile, 'but penis is such a scientific, bookish name. It sounds as if I am being examined by a doctor. My mother used to call it "koon-koon", when we were small and would refuse to wear our underwear under the pants. She used to say, "your koon-koon will peel off when you open your zipper, wear your underwear."'

She chuckled. 'Koon-koon. Sounds as if it is going to coo.'

'There are other Hindi names for it, but they are all so vulgar and obscene sounding. There is also the proper Hindi name, "ling". But let's give it an unscientific, everyday name and call it "willy".'

'Willy it is then. Do you play with it as she says? She says it gets hard as you caress it with your hand.'

I nodded and didn't say a word, a blush growing over my face. She was talking so nonchalantly about something I rarely spoke of, even with my classmates. I had been ritually masturbating for a year now and enjoyed the release of the sexual tension in performing the act, but I was shy of talking about it.

She sensed something in my silence and looked at me. 'Did I say something wrong? Why are you so red?'

'I am just shy talking about it. But with you I can open up. Yes we all do it. I have been doing it since the past year. It gives me pleasure.'

'Will you show it to me, how you do it?'

I reluctantly pulled out my hand from under her clothes, opened my zip, groped into my underpants and the underwear and pried it out through the slits, with some difficulty. It was stiff as a shaft.

She looked amazed, seeing it for the first time in her life. 'She was right. It does become hard as a rock. Can I touch it?'

I nodded with a wild look in my eyes and she closed her soft hand around it, fingers wrapping it in a warm embrace. 'It is so warm and stiff. How does it become so hard? The biology books show it hanging limp.'

She started moving her hand in a spiral motion and I corrected with my hand to move it in vertical motions. I sighed as she tenderly slid her hand up and down, and I slid my hand inside her clothes again. I explained to her the phenomenon of dilation of the arteries which fills the erectile tissue of the penis with blood, of the extendable nature of these erectile tissues which run the length of the organ, of how these tissues expand to hold 90 per cent of the blood involved in the process of erection, of how the blood is prevented from leaving, by the pressure of another dense tissue which constricts the veins, thus maintaining the rigidness.

After sometime of enjoying the strange sensations coursing through my veins I said, 'Let's lie down.'

'It is cold here.'

'I know a place on the other side of the hill, where we will be safe from the elements.'

She reluctantly let go, as I pulled out my hand from her chest. We got up and I pushed it into my trousers, but it would not go into the slits of my underpants, so I let it be, under the zipper and carefully pulled up the chain.

We walked arms around each other, her head resting on my shoulder, comfortable in our familiarity and recently acquired intimacy, ambling down the steeper eastern slope of the hill, overlooking the Shyamkhet Valley. This slope was rarely visited by any of the students and during my earlier explorations I had discovered a small recess where two people could lay side by side, safe from the wind and cold. There was a rarely used path and the larger gaps between the trees allowed us to walk together, like conjoined twins joined down our flanks. The wind was less harsh here, the rough north-south alignment of the hill was skewed towards the east and the gale from the snow peaks of the Great Himalayas was mostly caught by the opposite western slope.

We reached the cave like recess and lay down beside each other, after I had placed my jacket for her to lie upon. She held me and I closed my lips around her lips, and both of us sighed in twin pleasures. Later I lifted her jacket, sweater and shirt and closed my lips on her chest. Her skin felt like an inflated balloon against my lips and I exhaled hot, wet breaths. She was moving her hand in vigorous motions and I arched into her. I put my hand between her legs. She stopped her hand's movements and guided my hand into the elastic band of her pants and undergarments, placing my fingers on a mound of silky hairs. I slid my finger up and down. I felt the moist, soft-as-jelly flesh, at the base of her cleft and slid a finger in. Her walls yielded and I felt my finger push in, as if inserting into a mould of clay. After sliding it in a few centimetres I felt a membrane pushing against my finger and I pulled it out, afraid that I would hurt her. She put her hand inside again and guided my finger to the top of her cleft. My finger felt around and found a pea sized protrusion. I ran the tip of my finger in feather-touch, spiral motions all around that protrusion. She pulled my head from her chest and kissed me with hot breaths and deep sighs. Sometime later she let out a moan, pulled my head with both her hands into her panting mouth and arched her back. Drowning in her ecstasy, she pressed her pelvis into me and wrapped me in a tight embrace. Her mouth was all over mine, shooting hot breaths into me; I swallowed her bread-jam-butter-tomato-flavoured exhalations. But there was something distinctive in the way she was kissing me. This kiss was different from her other recent kisses. There was an undercurrent, a tremor, beneath all that mixture of the ingredients of her lunch, something beyond description. There was an ethereal sensation, as I drank in her breath. How can you drink a breath? But here I was, gulping down huge swallows. It was the most exhilarating sensation. When her spasm subsided, she laid her head on my chest, panting into my sweater, and I lay flat on my back, enjoying the thrill of her ecstasy.

Blinded by the pornographic depiction of sexual acts in the books we shared in the dormitories and the X-rated movies we saw at Bhowali, running the eight kilometres to and fro distance in the dead of the night, as criminals, I had thought that only the man took pleasure in the act, that the woman's role was to give the man ecstatic delights. How stupid I was. There cannot be a more euphoric experience than feeling your loved one's delight in the thrill she partakes in the act. I am sure what Pratima had felt in her spasm, as she arched her body and moaned, was hundred times more rapturous than what I have ever felt alone, inside the bathroom. It was so delightful to feel her elation and hear her sighs, that what I myself felt a few moments later would never equal it.

Pratima resumed her vertical motions with her hand vigorously and I heard her murmur 'What happens, what happens. . .' and I erupted shortly, shooting thick jets of seminal fluid into the air, which promptly fell back down on to my trousers. She removed her hand before the torrent turned into a trickle. The front of my gray flannel trousers was dotted with globs of the white viscous liquid seeping into the minute holes of the fabric. She dipped her index finger into the thickest lump and rubbed her thumb against it. 'It is oily to the touch. How does it smell?' I cried 'don't', but she already had her finger under her nose, the white glue turning transparent, as she sniffed at it.

'Eee, yuk. It has a peculiar smell.'

'It is not a perfume and definitely not hair oil. It is meant to make babies. How naive we were two years ago, thinking that this comes out of Crusoe's mouth, so much like phlegm, and being transferred into the giggling girl's body in a kiss it travels down to her Fallopian tube or whatever Vodrumeepians call it, to fertilise and create a baby.'

She chuckled and pulled out my handkerchief from her jacket pocket, stained with her tears and sitting up, set about wiping my trousers, after cleaning her finger. I pulled down her sweaters and jacket as she had forgotten to cover her exposed chest. 'Thanks Sanjay, I was wondering why I was feeling so cold suddenly.' She threw away the handkerchief later into a corner of the cave and I looked down at the wet spots left on my trousers, arranged like two semicircles around my zip. How will I ever explain this to the other students?

She slid on top of me and kissed me hotly. I gurgled something into her mouth and she lifted her head to look into my eyes.

'I love you Pratima.' I finally said what I was dying to say since the day I had met her and had later confessed my undying love for her to Rekha *Didi*.

She let out a warm breath and put her cheek against mine.

I whispered into her ear, 'Don't you love me?'

After what seemed like an eternity, which passed in a few seconds, she raised her head and said, 'I don't know Sanjay. I like you a lot, I adore you. But what is love? I miss you when I don't see you for long, especially during the school vacations. Many a night I have woken up from a dream, crying out your name and would thereafter spend the rest of the night, till dawn, thinking of you and dampening my pillow with silent tears. My heart leaps at your very sight. When I see you walking the corridors of Raman Block, I am filled with this intense desire to run up to you and throw myself into your arms. Is that love? I don't know Sanjay. I have not been so unsure of myself ever before.'

A morbid thought struck me. 'Is it my age?'

'No silly. Had it been our reverse age difference I would readily go with you till the end of this world. But it's my love for my brothers. The gratitude and recognition of all the sacrifices they have made for me. I think that's what love is all about. Not the desire, not the passion, but the willingness to give up the one thing you feel for the most in your life. My brothers were ready to give up good education and remain at Bhojpur, so that I did not have to live with that witch sister of Father. My younger brother was ready to forego his education and gave up food for me. Big Brother gave up one year of his life to ensure that Father could not ensnare me in any of his vile traps.'

'I will also give up anything for you.'

'Sanjay, I repose full faith in you. I know that from the way you look at me; there is not only love in your eyes, but something close to worship. I feel so comfortable with you, so safe. Any other boy fifteen minutes back would have taken advantage of me, but not you. You not only have the purest of hearts but the noblest of intentions too.'

'Then what is it my love.'

'It's the real me. When I consider our relationship, I don't know where it will lead to. I will be going in a few months' time, never to come back here again. You have two more years of school and if you join the Army, even if you qualify the next year, you will have another four years of training, before you become an officer. You will be 21 and a half then, I will be over 25. Shall we marry then? Will my brothers allow me to wait so long, despite all those promises of Big Brother? Will they overlook our age difference and the fact that you are from a different subcaste? Big Brother may be all for education of girls, but deep in his heart, he is very conservative. Will your parents accept me? Will I be able to go against my brothers, if they don't accept our match? There is a definite answer to that and that is a big no. I can't, even in the wildest of my dreams, think of negating my brothers' wishes. I will never do that; they are too dear to me to even contemplate the thought.'

That sounded like a death knell. I had to stem the tide before all hope was lost. I said earnestly, 'I will convince your brothers when the time comes, just wait for another five and a half years. I will put my all into qualifying for NDA next year. And in '90 I will be an Army officer. I will then beg your brothers, lie prone before them, and ask for your hand. If they truly love you, they can't deny you happiness.'

'That is so sweet of you. But you don't know them. If they take a stand, they take a stand. They are as stubborn as Angad, will never budge. And they have spent their growing up years in a deeply conservative society, with all its caste rules. They might not be too steeped into it, but their beliefs are affected by it. To such an extent that there are certain things they consider taboo. An inter-caste relationship is one of them.'

'But both of us are Brahmins.'

'I know, but there is the lineage, the *gotra*, which is also considered in marriages. Why is our society so restrictive and rigid, with its rules and conventions?'

I remained silent for some time, lost in my thoughts of despair and despondence. She must have read the anguish on my face, for she said, 'Oh Sanjay! I am so sorry to have led you to this. I had thought. . .'

I lifted my head and kissed her warmly, muffling her thought. 'Don't you ever say that. Never, ever feel sorry for me. I love you so much that I will respect whatever decision you take. I love you with all my heart and I will never accept that I ever become a cause of consternation for you. You are my life.'

'Oh Sanjay! What will I ever be without you,' and she pressed her cheek against mine, her warm tears prickling my skin as she sobbed softly into my ears.

I enjoyed her weight pressing into me, relishing the warmth which was seeping from her, into me. After some time, I said, 'We will wait. We have enough time. Maybe your brothers will change with time.'

From her regular breaths I could make out that she had shut herself off from this world and was deep in slumber, her tears having dried out, her sobs having receded. I wrapped my arms around her and closed my eyes to luxuriate in her aroma and be lost in my thoughts of her.

I was dreaming of Bhishma *Pitamah* lying on his bed of arrows at the battlefield of Kurukshetra, Arjun failing in his attempts to shoot his arrow into the earth, to coax Ganga to flow into the *Pitamah*'s parched throat and quench his thirst with her sweet elixir. I woke up to the pain of the sharp tips of the arrows on my back and a dry throat. She was not heavy but lying on top of me for so long, her deliciously relaxed body supported by mine, I was being pushed into the tiny ridges, and whorls and dents and mounds of the uneven, stony floor of the cave. I was going numb. I also realised that we had not had any water since the morning. I shifted my body to get the blood circulating again and relieve the pressure on my back. Her chin on my shoulder, she whimpered her protest with a soft 'ooon-ooon', moved her lips with chapping sounds and sighed into my ears, her warm breath titillating the soft transparent hair on my earlobes.

I whispered into her ears, 'Pratima, Pratima, get up, it's getting late.' I could see the sun hanging low over the western horizon. It was going to be dark soon.

She seemed not to have heard me and I spied a drool escaping a corner of her pursed lips. In an involuntary gesture I stuck out my tongue and curled it to the left in an attempt to lick the liquid.

'That's gross what you are attempting,' she chided me playfully, her dreamy eyes opening to the world in soft, sensual flutters, her voice a delirious drawl. 'My fluid is my fluid. If you so desire you can have my tears to quench your thirst, whenever they appear.'

I grinned a happy grin and said, 'It's getting late, I am going numb and my back is hurting.'

She slid off me and glided her hand between my legs. 'Did you ever go soft? Why don't we do it again? There is ample time.'

Fifteen minutes later, after I had once again revelled in her ecstasy, I did not so much as shoot into the air but dripped onto her fingers in tiny droplets, till she squeezed out the last drop. She wiped her fingers and mopped up the tiny dribbles on my fly with the discarded handkerchief lying like a lump in the corner where she had earlier thrown it, its folds now stiff and stuck together, as if there were elements of starch in it.

She again climbed on top of me, put her lips on my lips and gurgled. 'What was that?' I asked when she lifted her head to gaze into my eyes.

She kissed my lips lightly and said, 'That was marvellous what you did with your finger. In no time you will become a finger expert.'

'What did you feel?'

'It was the most wonderful sensation. That button-sized protrusion down there has more than 8,000 nerve endings and is the principle pleasure point of us girls,' and she went on to explain the various erogenous zones of her body, which gave her pleasures.

'If you have read so much about the nerve endings and pleasure points of a woman, you must have surely read of men, too.'

She nodded with a shy smile.

'Then what was that you were saying back on the water tank, feigning ignorance?'

'Oh Sanjay! You have always been so reserved in matters concerning girls, and I love you the most for that, that I did not want you to be alarmed by my forthrightness, had I shown overt interest. I had to draw you in without appearing to be overly eager. I feared if it seemed as if I was coming on you fresh, it would turn you off. So I had to pretend that you were leading me on, with my inquisitiveness. And I am thankful for that. I have never experienced such ecstatic euphoria before.'

'And I thought only boys come fresh upon girls. Do you girls also do the female equivalent of what we do alone? Like, finger yourself.'

'Some of the girls do it and boast of it, too. That driver's daughter lets it around during our girly talks, that she does it frequently. I had tried it once and had given up in disgust. I did not feel then what you have made me experience today, this time it appeared as if massive amounts of tiny electricity jolts were traversing through the nerves of my entire body, all emanating from that finger of yours. Thank you Sanjay for the magnificent experience.'

And she kissed me again, nibbling at my lower lip with tender bites of her teeth. It sent tiny electricity jolts through my body too and I could vaguely understand the delight she must have taken earlier.

She lifted her head and smiled at me. 'You are not as hard as they make it out for the boys.'

Offended by her implied innuendo, I said indignantly, 'Have you held others' too?'

'Naughty,' she punched my nose with a tender fist, 'I meant your body. But to answer your crass question, no, I have not held anybody else's, not even seen one before today. And to prevent any further morbid thoughts entering your brain, I have never lain with anyone else, except with my mother when I was small, which I stopped when she put me to task as a 6-year-old and I only found solace in my brothers' laps those Wednesday and Sunday afternoons and the other occasions here, when I was a kid. And I have definitely not rested on top of someone, like this. And I am absolutely certain that I am enjoying this.'

I chuckled, held her head between my palms and brought it down to kiss her from her forehead to her neck, in long sweeping arcs.

'Will we meet again?' I asked after nipping at her collar bones.

Her expression suddenly became serious. 'I don't know Sanjay. We definitely can't meet when you return from your vacations. After that threat from Big Brother, Father would be certain to keep a close eye on my goings-on. It is not beyond him to ask a school employee to shadow my movements, outside our home and after school hours. I cannot risk him finding out about us, not even when he is not here. And I have to ensure that my brothers don't take it as a betrayal of their trust. I will immerse myself in my studies henceforth, though after today, I don't know how I would ever be able to manage that. This, I will cherish forever.'

'So this is our last winter together,' I stated with a despondent finality.

'I am afraid so Sanjay. I feel so sad, for you and for me. We have had such a fabulous time the past three years. You have brought me such joy and happiness. You build such wonderful fantasies with that remarkable mind of yours. You have a heart of gold. You have pure intentions and you respect women, the ultimate quality a man can possess. You are one of those rarest of rare gems one discovers once in a lifetime. And I am going to miss you a lot. How would I ever be able to fill the void in my heart, in my very life, your absence would leave?' By now her warm tears were falling on my lips and I tasted their salty, tangy flavour, my throat constricted with emotions, the lump going this way and that, as I held back my tears.

She slid down my body, placed her face on my chest and wept her heart out.

After sometime she lifted her head, gazed tearfully into my liquid eyes and said, 'Don't hold it in. You can cry if you want to.'

'Oh Pratima. I love you so much. Please don't leave me,' I bawled and cried, as she slid forward and lowered her face, placing her cheek against mine. I wept like a child denied his favourite car, my body shaking violently, my howls of anguish riding on the shrieking wind outside the cave, my tears mixing with hers in a never-ending torrent, my hot breaths swirling her hair in woeful whirls, my sobs making it difficult for me to breathe, my arms pressing her into me as if I wanted her to merge with me, to melt into me, my heart breaking into thousand pieces.

Time elapsed and we wept into each other. After some fifteen minutes, when our sobs receded, our emotions cooled, our shakes faded, our breaths returned to normal, our eyes dried up, she slid away from me and I crawled towards the rear wall of the cave, propping myself up against the wall, my knees drawn up. She crab-walked up to me, placed her back against my folded legs, pried them open and moved in between them to sit against my chest. I folded her into me and asked, 'Can I come and visit you at Lucknow during the summer vacations next year?'

She was silent for some time, and when I had given up on expecting a reply, she said, 'Big Brother will also be having his vacations during that time. Younger brother too is planning to take a long leave during that period and they might have plans to take me someplace on holidays or spend the entire time with me at Lucknow. You can't come then. Even if you came later, during the winters they might wonder what purpose did a 16-year-old boy have, to come visiting their much older sister who was not even in his class at the school? Although we have the purest form of relationship, they might take it amiss as a betrayal.'

'When will you tell them about us?'

'I don't even know whether I would ever tell them at all. If it comes to that, I think it would have to be you telling them the truth.'

'Is it over for us?' I asked with trepidation, fearing her reply.

She went silent. She folded her knees and brought them close to her chest. I pulled her closer inside me. My entire future depended upon her reply.

'Here it is, this is how we will go about it,' she replied with a certain certitude. 'We will continue with our lives as if today never happened. We will not meet each other for another year. Not even once. You will not come to Lucknow on any pretext whatsoever. One year hence, when you come to Lucknow for your NDA entrance exams, we will meet again and then decide what to do next.'

I perked up. She had provided a silver lining in the doom of dark clouds I had just consigned myself to; a ray of hope, a glimpse of brightness. And I grabbed at it.

On our way down the hill, as twilight turned into dusk and then into darkness, she clung on to my arm and we skidded and slid and tumbled down the slopes, laughing hilariously. I asked her for her brother's address at Lucknow. She refused to divulge it for two reasons: she did not want me writing to her and she was not sure that I would not go running to her during my summer vacations. And if I confronted any of her brothers, a heart which had fallen in love as a 13-year-old, with a much older girl, at first sight, might make me act crazy enough, which I might come to repent later. I walked her to her house and kissed her hungrily inside her living room, with Bindu staring aghast in amazement.

27

The Amber Door

I somehow managed to survive the year-long separation. After the two months' long winter vacation, spent in forlorn hopes and desperate deluges of despair, it became difficult glimpsing Pratima occasionally in the hallways of Raman Block, but never being able to meet her or even walk up to her to have a word. I had once approached her in the library, as she sat there going through a journal, but looking up she had admonishingly shook her head, silently reminding me of our resolve with that gesture. I came across Bindu often in the school and even met her at her house during the Holi festival that March and she never mentioned the kiss she had witnessed at Pratima's home last winter; she just smiled at me in a conspiratorial manner and muttered, 'I am so happy for both of you. . .', 'you deserve her. . .', 'you two are made for each other. . .' and words to that effect. After Pratima had finally left Ghorakhal in April, it became easier to live. I had wept through the night when Bindu had told me, after frantically searching for me all over and walking up to me in a dare, as I sat at Shahji's canteen sipping his sweet, masala tea—her arrival had sent my friends into a scattering frenzy—that she had left with her elder brother that morning. I had not been able to even bid her a farewell. But I took heart in our promised meeting at Lucknow that coming winter. Her permanent absence from Ghorakhal, after that year's summer vacation, was a hole in my heart that never healed. But I survived by reliving each moment of our togetherness and walked up to the Water Tank Hill every Sunday morning to reminisce and feel her ghostly presence. I talked and talked into the thin air, redolent with the sweet smell of pine trees, till the sun completed its diurnal journey and vanished in a blaze of glory. Sometimes, Bindu would come and sit with me on the roof of the concrete water reservoir and I would regale her with the stories of the giggling girl and Ivanhoe in France and other fantasies I had created for Pratima. I somehow seemed to have lost the ability to concoct new fancy stories without the inspiring presence of Pratima. It turned out that what I had told her after deconstructing *Robinson Crusoe* was true; it was she who triggered my brain into conjuring those fascinating visions. Without her I am empty—till today I have never been able to create any fresh fantastic fabrication out of my imagination, as I did with her. Bindu wrote to her regularly and she kept me updated on news of Pratima. Bindu also missed her a lot; despite their age difference they had become bosom friends over the years, and Bindu gave much credit for that to me, since she was our confidante who used to accompany her as her chaperone. But Bindu was younger and got over her grief faster, as is the wont of adolescent teenagers. I was in love and it was difficult for me to get her out of my mind. I did not so much as become somnambulant, but my classmates would often catch me giving them vacant stares and snub me for my lately acquired mysterious manners of suddenly clamming up mid-sentence, going for long lonely walks, not accompanying them to Nainital on occasional Sundays to ogle the girls in short skirts, even shunning the monthly ritual of running to Bhowali to see X-rated movies. The only thing that kept me going during that one long year of separation was the preparation for the NDA entrance exams, scheduled in December '85. If at all I had to be successful in getting Pratima forever, I had to be in NDA the summer of '86. I put my whole and soul into it.

After the long wait of a year, I boarded the Lucknow-bound train at Kathgodam, with the other aspirants of my class in mid December. I was nervous, I was excited, I was anxious, I was eager, I was jittery, I was relaxed; conflicting emotions betraying a heart which couldn't sit still. We arrived at Lucknow the next morning and were ferried by bus to our dwellings at Sainik School Lucknow, where I dumped my luggage on my assigned bed and set off immediately to her brother's address next to Lucknow University. The address had been given to me a week back by Bindu.

I travelled by the ubiquitous tempo. It is an ugly-looking, diesel-guzzling, thick-black-smoke-spewing vehicle, used for public transport within cities and between towns and villages all over North India; all of about four metres in length with a single front wheel and a broad rear squatting on two wheels. Its front looked like a pig's snout, its muzzle's base inclined upwards at an angle, a grill in place of the nostrils and a flat bonnet leading to a vertical windscreen. The driver's cabin could accommodate two passengers, who had to be careful of the driver's pumping elbows when he negotiated the bends with umpteen turns of the large steering wheel which grated in protest, its sockets and joints and bearings demanding grease from the miserly owner. But like a faithful canine, it continued to chug with dogged determination, announcing its crawls with large 'bhud-bhud' sounds on the unpaved, potholed, debris-strewn roads of rural and semiurban India, despite its master's inconsiderateness and apathy. The rear cab portion had two wooden or iron slats, which could hold ten to twelve passengers sitting in two rows facing each other; children and dilapidated old women had to invariably make do by squatting on the floor, dodging unsuccessfully, the seated commuters' flat feet and pointed knees. A steel carrier, constructed by welding together steel pipes and angle irons, was placed on top, meant for carrying luggage but used for additional fares and the passengers held their bags and *jholas* close to their chest lest someone flicked them away if placed on the carrier. More travellers were accommodated by making them stand on the fenders of the rear wheels and atop a horizontal plank fitted to the tail of the vehicle, the individuals hanging on to the rails of the carrier for dear life, coughing hysterically, their eyes streaming tears from the thick dark cloud of smoke belching out of the tempo's exhaust pipe. In all, the rickety, swaying vehicle could carry twenty-five to thirty passengers, making decent money for the owner.

I somehow managed to reach the house in a fit of cough, recognising her abode from the name board nailed to the wall beside the locked entrance door; 'Lalit Pandey, Assistant Professor, Lucknow University', it read in three rows. He must be a fast riser having upgraded from lecturer so early in his academic career. Realising that I was too early—she must be away for her classes—I decided to watch *Blue Lagoon* at Mayfair Cinema Hall in Hazrantganj. After ogling Brooke Shields and lusting for her exquisite body, I came to the conclusion that she was no match for Pratima. In any beauty contest, my Pratima would win hands down over Brooke Shields.

After a delicious lunch of *Tunda Kabab* and *Roomali Roti* at Aminabad, I again hired a tempo to the university staff quarters. Standing outside the closed door I heard mixed voices of Pratima, a male, and another female.

I decided to return to my temporary digs as there seemed to be no chance of meeting her alone.

The next day was our first paper of mathematics and I appeared with the others, in a ramshackle classroom of an equally destitute campus of *Kanya Putri Paathshaala*. After three hours of rubbing my pencil's lead onto the circles of correct answers, confident that I would pass the paper and having had my eye-fill of staring at the pretty, young, women invigilators, I set off for her house, immediately after consuming a meal of cold, spicy *samosas* and *kachauris* at the *Paathshaala's* canteen, refusing the bus ride back to the Sainik School. I reached there by three and knocked on the door, nervous with anticipation. I had her brother's gift for her, which she had further gifted to me, the hardback edition of *To Kill a Mockingbird*, to explain my presence, if her brother was home. I had forgotten to return it to her back at the school and she had never asked back for it, presumably pretending that it was her gift to me.

The door opened and there she was. My heart skipped a thousand beats as I looked at her stunningly beautiful face. I had missed gazing into those eyes all these past months and with great restraint I stood at the steps, my limbs itching with an intense desire to take her into my arms and crush her into me.

She smiled a hesitant smile and an alarm beeped inside my head, 'something is not right.'

I shook off the nasty thought and beamed at her when she said, 'Hello Sanjay. You have really grown up. How tall are you?'

'I am a late bloomer. Took me all these years to reach five-eight. The doctor at school says my growth hormones have lived out their lives and I will stagnate. I wanted to be closer to Amitabh Bachchan, but I guess I will have to settle for my meagre 174 centimetres.'

She chuckled (first positive sign). 'It seems you have not got over your Amitabh Bachchan fixation.'

'Oh, he is marvellous. But let us leave him be. How are you keeping, my sweetness? You look as radiant and sublime as ever. Yesterday I had concluded that Brooke Shields does not hold a candle to you. In addition to not possessing the magnetism of your allure, she has no breasts.'

She chuckled again. 'You will never change. Please come in,' and stepped aside to let me in.

I remained standing, regarding her face. God! I missed drowning in those eyes, kissing those lush lips, sipping her tears, running my hands in her hair. She looked resplendent, but a note of worry had crept into her eyes, after the initial shine. I had dreamt of this very moment so often that I had lost count and expected her to drag me inside and throw herself into my arms, after shutting the door to the world. But she just stood to the side waiting for me to get in, her lids drooping with a hint of colour under her eyes; was that a dark ring, I was not sure. It seemed as if she had not been sleeping well.

Another alarm beeped. I shook my head again.

She was smiling but it appeared forced. The dimples did not accompany her grin and I suspected if she laughed her nose would not crunch up and her eyes would not close.

Third beep.

She looked glorious in a lemon yellow salwar suit with flowery designs. She did not have her stole on and I could see that her chest did not heave with the sudden intakes I had expected my sight would engender inside her. It seemed she had not been looking forward to my visit.

Fourth beep.

I still held on to hope, there is no greater motivator than that. I discarded all those alarm beeps as figments of my nervous imagination and said, 'God, it has been so long. I almost died out there looking at you after such a long time. You look more radiant than before. Can I hold you in my arms? I am itching with excitement.'

'Come inside before anyone sees you gaping like a besotted grown-up kid.'

I ambled inside her house and she closed the door behind me. I stood uncertainly in a corridor lined with photographs of a 30-year-old man and his new bride—both their necks adorned in rose garlands hanging down till their stomachs—beaming into the camera, the girl shy and tiny with her eyelashes covering her eyes, wearing a red saree, her blouse sleeves hanging lose around her spindly arms, *menhdi* designs of floral motifs covering the back of her hands from her elbows till her fingertips, where there was a dark, red ring of henna around her nails, her palms held in a 'V' in front of the sari's folds below her small waist. Every aspect of hers was diminutive and her head stood many inches below the shoulder of her husband. There was another photo in which the same man, who I presumed to be Pratima's

Big Brother, now sporting a pair of square shaped, black, plastic spectacles, wearing a light gray safari suit standing with his tiny wife, now dressed in a green salwar suit, faint traces of her menhdi from her marriage still visible on her hands, as she stood gazing into the camera with a look of defiance in her eyes. Where the husband oozed energy and confidence with his handsome features, the wife had a sly look and a curled mouth which sat in a grimace on her face. Hers was not a pretty sight. I also spied a photograph of a tall, young man wearing the olive green uniform of a second lieutenant, with movie-star looks. Both of Pratima's brothers were handsome with pleasing personalities. It was no coincidence that Pratima was so astonishingly lovely. Her grandparents' genes must have skipped one generation, leaving a diminutive father and mother, but emerging again in the form of perfectly endowed, beautiful grandchildren. But what led Associate Professor Lalit Pandey to marry such a creature?

Pratima moved past me while I was surveying the photographs and entered a door to the left. I followed suit into a well-furnished drawing room, whose walls were adorned with four-foot-by-three-foot, framed photographs of the Bara Imambara, Taj Mahal, Fatehpur Sikri, and the Dal Lake at Srinagar. The pride of place was occupied by a beautiful rendering of the famous painting by Raja Ravi Verma—of an enchanting and enchanted Damyanti, clad in a red sari and blouse with golden borders, listening to the tales of Nala's virtues and accomplishments from a white swan perched on a marble pillar, a pink bud of water lily jutting out from the green water at its base. I settled down into a couch as she asked, 'How was your day today?'

'Why only the day? What happened to, "How has been the past one year?"'

'I know what you would say. Your litany will be, "I missed you a lot. I could not live a single moment without thinking about you. I spent sleepless nights this past one year. I have become insomnious." On and on you would go about me. So I thought I would ask of today itself. Any further back and it would be all about me.'

'You are absolutely true there, but only one addition. I have not only become an insomniac, but whenever I do manage to get a nap, invariably close to dawn, I have got into the habit of calling out your name. So I requested our House Master to make me the House Captain, so that I could get a room to myself. But he kicked me out of his sight. And now I sleep with the others, taping shut my mouth every night, lest someone hear me mumbling your name in my sleep or shouting it out in my nightmares.'

I expected her to at least snigger at my poor attempt to lighten her up, as she very well knew that I couldn't be made a House Captain in my eleventh class. But she went silent, as if reminded of a dreadful past experience. We were sitting opposite each other; I had purposefully chosen a couch so that she could sit beside me, but she had dragged a chair and sat across the coffee table. She hadn't even offered me a glass of water. By now the beeps in my head had morphed into an uninterrupted whine and I couldn't help dread the outcome of this meeting. Something was definitely not right.

She sat as if frozen in a tableau—leaning back into her chair, her right forearm lying across her forehead, her eyes closed shut and I thought I heard a faint sniffle.

My ears were playing tricks with me.

After some time I tried to restore normalcy, more for my worrying nerves than for her and said with a great deal of warmth, 'You haven't answered my earlier question. How have you been doing my sweet love?'

That did it. The love bit.

She opened her eyes and the tears trapped by her closed lids gushed out in a torrent and she sobbed. 'Oh Sanjay! I am so sorry.'

'No need to be sorry, my darling. This is the first time you have wept in joy in front of me.'

'They are not flowing in joy Sanjay. It is for the deepest sorrow I have ever felt in my life. My heart is shattering as we speak.'

'What is the matter Pratima my lovely? What has gone wrong?'

'Everything Sanjay, everything has gone wrong. I don't know how to say this, but things have changed. It all started when Big Brother brought this girl to our house.'

And she narrated her life since we last parted with a kiss at her house, more than a year back.

She had been in a state of blissful happiness during that two-month-long winter vacation when I was at my home at Shaktinagar last winter. She spent the entire time reading a plethora of books and studying for her board exams, unmindful of her father's disapproval. 'You will never get a husband if you are overqualified. You will die a spinster,' he used to lament whenever out of her mother's sight. But he dared not stop her. Gone were the pretensions, the appearance of a dumb bimbo. She had mustered the courage to defy him and her mother became her sheet anchor, continuously confronting her father whenever he used to become too overbearing with his scathing reproaches. The new feeling of belonging to me had been the one bright spark in her life that kept her going in my absence, which kept her spirits high. Bindu became her sole partner with whom she used to share her feelings for me.

After I had rejoined from my vacations, she could barely hold herself. Many times she had asked Bindu to take a message for me, to arrange a meeting. But every time she had stalled her, realising that her father had indeed been spying on her, as she had predicted. There would always be some teacher's son or some peon, watchman, clerk, waiter from the mess, who would be shadowing her whenever she was out of her house. Even the librarian was in cahoots with him, as she frequented the library often—that's why she had shunned me when I had tried to approach her that day in March. These people were not discreet and she had discovered them within a few days. She had spent her days in frustration and nights in longing.

Immediately after the board exams, Big Brother had come to Ghorakhal and took her away the very next day. She had wanted to say her goodbyes to me but held back as it was not as if she was leaving me forever. The promise of our meeting in December gave her hope and warmed her heart whenever she used to pine for me.

At Lucknow, her younger brother had also arrived for a long leave and the three of them celebrated her liberation and homecoming. Big Brother's was her only home now. They rarely talked about their father; he had become nonexistent for the siblings. Their mother kept in constant touch with them, through letters written by Bindu, conveying her deep love for them. Sometimes, Pratima used to ponder in melancholy, that her brothers had broken ties with their father for her sake. She would reminisce how they had fought with their parents during different stages of her life to ensure that she got her just dues. She used to shed silent tears of gratitude whenever she thought of those occasions and took a resolution that she would never do anything that would disappoint her brothers. She knew that they had her best interests in their hearts and would never ask her to do anything which was not her desire. So likewise, she would not do anything that they did not expect of her.

She passed her days in the warmth of her brothers' love and the nights in anticipation of the fateful day when we would have our promised meeting. Big Brother had secured for her a place in the Lucknow University for BA in English, as she had finally decided to join the teaching profession. Academics had never been a challenge for her and she had been doing exceedingly well in her studies, which Big Brother acknowledged with immense pride at the university campus. She was the star of his eyes, the spark that brightened him and she was very contented to have done her brother proud.

All was going well—she was studying hard, Big Brother was very caring and loving, younger brother was chirpy and his usual impetuous self, whenever he was home on leave. She loved making different dishes to feed them up to their gullets (her initial attempts were clumsy and grudgingly consumed in good humour till she hired a cook to teach her in refining her culinary skills). Then, two months back, Big Brother came home from a short official stint to Nainital, with a young, wisp of a girl in tow.

'He introduced her to me as Meenakshi Joshi. Her parents had died in a bus accident when she was very small and she had been brought up by her maternal grandparents ever since; her father's parents had refused to accept her for she was the only child of her parents and that too, a girl. Her maternal grandparents had readily accepted her and promptly dropped her father's surname, replacing it with their own.

'But they were old and destitute. Her mother had been the tenth and last child born to her parents, when they were themselves in their forties and fifties. By the time Meenakshi came to live with them, they were well into their sixties and seventies. Despite their abilities having been mellowed down with their advancing age, they took good care of her, as if she were their own daughter. With their meagre savings, they had provided for her education till class 10 and had been planning for her marriage when they had suddenly passed away within a month of each other, in August that year.

'Meenakshi was left in the care of one of her mother's brothers, as he was the only one who would take in an unmarried, grown-up niece: who would pay for her dowry? But that uncle of hers had a sinister motive. She had been accepted by her uncle and aunt as a servant and they treated her as such—she slept in their kitchen, as they did not have any spare room and did not want her to pollute their only daughter, by staying with her.

'One night, her uncle tip-toed into the kitchen and lay down on the mat spread on the ground, next to Meenakshi. He wanted to have his way with her and after muted protests did not deter him, she shrieked forcefully, bringing all family members into the kitchen. By the time her aunt arrived, the uncle had undone his *lungi* and was standing next to the hearth with his limp willy hanging down like a "wrinkled, dead mouse without its tail,"—her exact words when she had described the scene to me.

'Meenakshi's uncle accused her of seducing him, in front of his wife. He said that he had come into the kitchen to wet his parched throat and Meenakshi had pounced on him, demanding sex. She had said, "I don't know how my aunt had believed him. He has this huge paunch, a face pock-marked like craters of the moon and spindly limbs. I had always wondered how my aunt had agreed to marry him and then bore him four children. He is the most undesirable person I have ever seen in my life. And she believed every word of his; the lying, blubbery, poaching, chauvinist pig."

'Meenakshi's aunt had beaten her black and blue and declared her a seductress. Her condition worsened, as if that were possible, and she was not allowed any freedom, not even to venture out of the house for routine chores, kept confined within the four walls of the house.

'Her uncle, having been frustrated from having his way with her, in his malevolence, hatched an infernal scheme to teach her a lesson. He arranged her marriage to a 45-year-old widower from a lower caste—he was a Shudra—so as to avoid giving dowry.

'The news came as a deathblow to her. She had been raised by her grandparents to give high regard to the social mores, especially strict adherence to the rigid caste system. Her beliefs were dogmatised by their influence and she would never accept marrying outside her caste and that, too, to a man old enough to be her father. She worked out the sinister purpose behind the arrangement and on the day of her wedding she ran away from her uncle's house, taking advantage of the heightened activities and chaotic conditions associated with the event.

'The day Big Brother was waiting for his train at Kathgodam Railway Station, he encountered her in a dishevelled condition, as she had walked all the way from her village near Nainital and was extremely hungry. He took pity upon her and while she ate, he listened to her narration of her sorry state of affairs.

'He brought her with him to Lucknow, to stay with us till a decision could be taken on her future. That was two months back.

'She has been very cooperative since then and has virtually taken over all household tasks from me, insisting that I should study and not waste my time on domestic chores. Big Brother also maintained that I should let her run the house as she deemed fit and concentrate on my studies. Slowly she began drawing close to Big Brother. One thing led to the other and as time progressed, unaware to me, they started falling in love. I only realised much later, when one morning I saw her coming out of Big Brother's room in a dishevelled state, normally associated with someone who has just risen from sleep, than the room of younger brother, which was her dwelling when she had arrived here.

'I was overjoyed for Big Brother, that he had finally found his soulmate and when he announced that he would be marrying Meenakshi, I hugged her in a tight embrace and kissed her, welcoming her into our family. I was the happiest person during the reception ceremony, organised for his colleagues, after their marriage at the registrar's office; tears of joy did not stop their flow from my eyes till the party was over. My father had refused to come and bless the couple, though Mother had sent her gold bangles for Meenakshi through an emissary from our village. Younger brother arranged for their honeymoon at Srinagar.

'Oh Sanjay! She became the biggest mistake of my life. Big Brother came back from the honeymoon a changed man. He was full of these dogmatic ideas about caste and linkages between different castes and started evangelising about how evil inter-caste marriages are, how we should follow the well-established social structure and not interfere with what our elders decree and our scriptures lay down as our way of life. He started sounding like Father. Even in his deeds he started following what he preached; never allowing lower caste people inside the house, always ensuring that the sweeper, the maid, and the workers who come to do odd jobs and repairs leave their footwear outside the door, wash their feet with the holy water kept at the entrance, and then enter the house. They are never allowed inside the room where we keep our idols of gods and goddesses. Meenakshi cleans the room herself, not even allowing me to do the job. I have been admonished many times for making friends with girls from other castes. They are not allowed inside our house.

'Things came to a head a week back. As the day of our meeting was approaching, I started dreaming only about you. You were a love song that kept repeating in my head, never letting go of your hold over my thoughts. I saw you everywhere I looked: your smile, your flat cheeks, your sensitive fingers, your broad nose, your tousled short hair, that twinkle in your eyes whenever you saw me, that splay-footed gait of yours. I could never get you out of my mind even when I was studying, especially when I was studying. The black lines on the pages would blur and in their stead I would see you lying in that cave as I had rested atop you. I was so much looking forward to this visit and I had finally made up my mind that I would tell you at last how much I loved you.

'Last week I went down with fever, it was the chill. My feverish body shook with involuntary spasms every now and then, and my delirious heart was calling out your name. I don't know when the refrains of my heart became vocal and your name came out of my mouth, and how she heard it; it was not impossible for her to hear since she constantly flitted in and out of my room to check on my condition.

'In the evening when my fever abated and I woke up to sanity, Big Brother and Meenakshi stood glowering over me demanding to know who Sanjay was and why was your name on my lips in my unconscious state.

'Oh Sanjay! It was so miserable. All my denials would not convince them and when Big Brother reminded me of all the sacrifices he had made for me, I could not hold it in. I remembered my vow to never disappoint him and divulged the truth about us, except the cave—that would have broken him to pieces. But even without mentioning that, the mere fact that I had been indulging in a secret love affair without his knowledge tore at his heart. My repeated insistence that we had not been indulging in a romantic relationship did not assure him, and I read in his eyes the extreme sense of betrayal he was feeling. It was as if the light had gone out of his life. He did not speak to me for the next two days.

'He did research on you in those two days. The fact that you are from a lower subcaste—"an inferior brahmin", Meenakshi had said loudly—ate at him, when I told him that I loved you. How could he give his sister to a person from a lower *gotra*? That was blasphemous in Meenakshi's eyes, now my brother's, too. Gone was the tolerance towards an indulgent sister.

'The final nail was struck by my younger brother two days back, when he found the link between our families.

'He had gone to some office in New Delhi which keeps genealogical records of famous Freedom Fighters. He connected your grandfather's ancestry with our family legend and established that when our ancestor, six generations back, had run away from Cawnpore back in the mid nineteenth century, he had sought shelter at a village that had belonged to your ancestor Trilok Singh, a prominent feudal lord who owned that and many surrounding villages. Upon hearing of a fugitive on the run, Trilok Singh had put him under lock and key and had been awaiting the police to arrive to arrest him and put him to the gallows. No amount of pleading would persuade your ancestor to let him go free. But before the police could arrive, my ancestor managed to break open his temporary prison cell's window and escape. He had arrived in the terai region unhurt, ten days later.

'That was a slight which was unpardonable in my brothers' eyes.'

'But that was so long back, over a hundred and thirty years ago. How could it matter now?' I blurted out, flabbergasted at this sudden turn of events.

'Exact same words I had thrown back at them. But they wouldn't budge. "A betrayal is a betrayal. No amount of good deeds by future generations can erase the treachery of an ancestor. Thank heavens he came out alive from that. And that is where the truth lies," younger brother had said.

'Two days back they took my life away from me. Both of them told me to forget you, to not even acknowledge your existence, to not even think of meeting you again, to not dream of a future with you.'

'Why don't you leave them? I will convince my parents to keep you with them till I am capable enough to marry you.'

'Sanjay, Sanjay. Please don't ask that of me. I was stuck between a rock and a hard place. I didn't know whom to choose then. On one side were my brothers—the very reason I am what I am today, the very purpose of my life. Had it not been for them I would have been living a desolate life in some godforsaken village in the Himalayas, suffering a miserable existence living a life of drudgery and servility, if not dead. On the other hand were you—the love of my life, the only person, apart from my brothers, who has given me so much happiness and joy, whose mere thought brings a smile to my lips and gladdens my heart, the one person whom I can depend upon to love me endlessly, till the end of my days. But love also means sacrifice. I am sacrificing my love for you at the altar of my obligations towards my brothers. I chose them.'

I was in a daze. All sensations left my body as if to congregate in another being, afraid of the explosion that will succeed the implosion of my heart. Tears were raining down my cheeks in a deluge. The knot in my throat refused to budge, trying to restrain the shards of my heart which was breaking into thousand pieces. There was only one thought in my mind which kept repeating like a stuck LP record: 'Two people, two people, two people. . .'

Two people: one a frail girl totally unrelated to me and the other a philandering feudal lord far removed, so far removed—six times over—that his memories had faded in the sands of time, leaving just his name standing tall like a dead monarch at the top of our genealogical tree, shooting down branches of his progenies, his ghost having been consigned to whatever world is inhabited by its kind. These two persons have decided my destiny. For the first time in my life I felt so helpless.

'What about me?' I wailed after I had regained some semblance of normalcy from the turmoil raging in my heart.

She said after a while, 'Sanjay. I am so sorry. I never expected to fall in love. At the very beginning I consented to meet you at your request because you seemed a breath of fresh air in my dreary life. You became the avenue through which I could reach out to the outside world, with my domineering father and doting, omnipresent brothers occupying my inner domain, which at times became too oppressive. I started liking talking to you about my life and listening to your life story. But everything transformed when we moved to the open world atop the Water Tank Hill. You showed me that there is another world existing, so far removed from the real one, far more exciting than the ones residing in those books and novels I used to cherish. You, with your fanciful ideas while recreating the English literary works, with the manner in which you would replace character after character, inventing entirely new stories, and largely with your beliefs and values which reflected the purity of your soul—you grew on me. I felt that you had at last filled a void which I had never realised existed within me. What started as an itch festered into a wound which seeped from the outer surface and silently wrapped my heart with an aching grip. The only times my insides won't crave was when I was in your presence. After that fascinating tale of the giggling girl and the fancy planet you created, I fell in love with you. And then the cave happened last winter.

'The intimacy we shared in that cave—you must have surely worked out long time back that it was a deliberate act on my part. I wanted more of you, to feel you, to kiss you, to hold you in my arms with all my might, to melt into you. Maybe somewhere deep inside me a demon was raising its head and telling me that that was the last time I would be meeting you, maybe my subconscious mind had had a premonition of the future unfolding where I would be separated from you forever. Whatever be the reason, I wanted that intimacy as part of my compact with you, as a final seal of my love for you, on my heart. I did not want to go the limit, just to feel you intimately, as I was not sure of what contraceptive method should I be adopting. I would have loved to make love with you. So I had intentionally asked Bindu not to accompany me that morning, had faked stepping into a hole and fell while climbing the trail. It was risky, we could have ended up with broken bones and engendered a scandal of mammoth proportions. I had not expected that my fall would lead to a slide down the slope, but I had never for once doubted that you would let go of my hand, except I was not sure whether you would be able to halt the skid. When I had climbed on top of you, after we had come to a halt, it was heavenly. Later, when I saw how embarrassed you had felt wrapping your arms around me, I realised that you held me in such reverence, with such unsullied piety that if I appeared to be too straightforward you would balk and walk away. So I had to convince you into believing that it was you who was leading me into it, than the other way round. Don't get me wrong Sanjay if I sound too uninhibited. I was 20 years old and I was with my love. I was having these urges for some time and wanted to at least satisfy some of my physical cravings with you, if not make love. And I am thankful that I gave in to my desires. It is the one memory I will cherish all through my life and carry it with me when I leave for my heavenly abode, where I will confront my Maker and ask him why he had destined my fate in such a manner, why he had given me so much elation and then snatched it away as if I was a child who had had too much candy. When my time comes I will definitely demand from him his reasons for fabricating this greatest turmoil in my life. Yesterday, while I was shedding silent tears into my pillow for the second consecutive sleepless night, I had for a moment thought that had I been married at twelve it would have been better than having to spend the rest of my life pining for you.'

'No Pratima. Never feel that way. Had you not come into my life I would not be what I am today, my world would not have been so colourful, as it has been the past four years.'

'But I never realised that I was living in a dream world. Reality struck like a thunderbolt last week and I diminished. Had I any premonition of my outside interest in you morphing into love, which would then lead to this, I would never have commenced this journey of love, hope, and despair. Oh Sanjay! I am so sorry to have dragged you into all this; I should never have met you in the first place. I shouldn't have given a chance for love to bloom in your heart. I should have kept you away. At least you wouldn't have had to go through this pain. Please don't cry.' She sobbed and wept and cried her heart out as I tried to pick up the fragments of my own shattered heart, bit by tiny bit, to somehow assemble the two-lovers-kissing-shaped organ which controls our emotions.

Time stalled, the seconds hand on the wall clock moving relentlessly in jerky motions on its circular journey, futilely trying to indicate passage of time. Amidst the soft 'tick-tock' of the clock informing me that time had indeed not stalled, I collected my thoughts and my senses surged into me from whichever dwelling they had gone into hiding. I tried to retrieve the lost ground with one last ditch effort.

'Tell me this is all a fancy story you have cooked up to get back at me for all those occasions I had trumped you with my fantasies, tell me this is all untrue, that you said it in jest, tell me that the shock of my sudden appearance made you say something crazy and you manufactured this wild illusion of a wisp of a girl and those ancestors of ours, that the photographs of a married couple outside in the corridor are cut-outs from a magazine to give credence to your fantasia, tell me that . . . tell me that the truth is that your brothers will walk in this very moment from one of the other rooms and will accept my proposal, agreeing to give your hand into mine when the time comes. Tell me anything but this.'

She turned her head towards the front of the house at the pitter-patter sound of a moped coming through a half-open window. 'Oh my God! I did not realise that time has passed so fast. What should I do now? They are back from their movie. Oh Sanjay, where will you hide? No, you can't hide, that would be too cowardly. You will have to confront them. Thank heavens younger brother had left yesterday. You will have to face them and please, for heaven's sake, don't create a scene. He is a reasonable person, just talk to him as if . . . as if . . . oh whatever, just don't make a fuss.' And she walked to the door, her long *kurta* swaying in long swishes and her hair bouncing. There was no lemony perfume in her wake (she really wore it just for me!).

She opened the front door of her house and I heard her exclamation, 'Big Brother you are back early. How was the movie? . . . there is someone here. . . Please listen to him. Promise me you will not be angry . . . just hear him out.'

In walked the handsome man from those photographs. In person, he was tall and gaunt and looked older than his 30 years. He was dressed in a checked blue-green sweater, the bow of his red and white striped shirt collar sticking out of the neck of his sweater. He had a pleasant-looking face, now scowled in suppressed fury, his large, black rimmed spectacles shooting off reflections of the solitary tube light in the room, thus hiding the expression in his eyes. His nose bore a striking resemblance to Pratima's, the same straight bridge and sharp pointed tip, but he had flaring nostrils making it appear bigger than Pratima's. His hair was oily and combed with a side parting snaking in a jig jag line towards his crown.

He marched in with a sense of purpose, halted in front of me and said in a soft voice (he had all the makings of my favourite teacher, Giri Sir), 'And you must be. . .'

I was standing and shot out my right hand, 'I am Sanjay Tivari sir. It's a privilege to have finally met you. I had come to meet Pratima. I presume I have overstayed and it's time for me to take leave.' There was no need now to deliver my rehearsed line, 'I had come to return this book to Pratima which I had borrowed from her before the summer vacations during an accidental meeting in the school library and could not get a chance to return it by the time she left Ghorakhal.'

'No, you stay', turning to a girl barely out of her teens, with soft features sitting on a slight frame—a replica of the garlanded, grimacing bride in the photographs in the hallway—he said, 'Meenakshi dear, kindly get two glasses of water for these poor souls. From the looks upon their faces, both of them have done nothing but cry their hearts out.' Turning towards a trembling Pratima, he said, 'Chhutki, go wash your face. And don't look scared. I am not going to eat him.' Finally facing me, he said, 'You can wipe those tears still lingering on your face son. How old are you? You seem too young to be falling in love.'

'Going to be 17 next month sir,' I took out a handkerchief from my trouser pocket and wiped the remnants of the tears and their streaks stuck on my flat cheeks. His soft voice and caring attitude gave me a glimmer of hope. 'Pratima has told me everything. I do not have to tell you how much I love her and what good care I will take of her for the rest of her life. I will be at NDA next July and four years hence I will be an officer, just like your brother and since I would be over 21, I will marry her the very next day, that I promise.'

'Not so fast son, not so fast. You have presumed from my soft manners that I would readily accept you. Had my Mohit been here, he would have killed you for spending time with our sister alone in my house. I won't "how dare you" for that. Yes, Pratima has told us about your infatuation and that she also loves you. But she must have also told you that she has nothing to do with you henceforth.'

Pratima walked in with a glass of water and placed it on the table in front of me. Meenakshi was nowhere to be seen, probably asked by Pratima to leave us alone. Sensing something building up inside me, her brother gestured for me to take a seat. All three of us sat down in a hush.

After some time elapsed, I replied, 'Yes sir, she has told me that and much more. She has also told me that she still loves me and she is leaving me because she has to sacrifice her love for her brothers. I understand her compulsions and respect her decision. I just want to know if I can say what I have to, to hopefully effect a change in your decision.'

He looked at me sincerely and said, 'I am a reasonable man. The way you speak, you sound way beyond your years. Go ahead, have your say.'

I shifted in the couch and composed my thoughts for a minute. 'Thank you sir, for giving me this opportunity. Firstly sir, I wish to erase the impression you have developed, maybe because of my age, that I am infatuated. No sir, I am not. I am in love as much as you are with your wife, if not more. I have been in love with Pratima for the past four years and it has only grown over the passage of time, not diminished. Despite not being able to see her in the past seven months, I have not looked at another girl during the entire period I have known Pratima. I am formally asking for her hand in marriage. The day after I get commissioned into the Army I will marry her.'

'But you are not from our caste,' he objected. He looked around as if searching for his wife. Her hold upon him in such matters was obvious.

'We are the same caste sir. I am a Brahmin too,' I said emphatically.

'But from a lower *gotra*. We don't marry our daughters and sisters into a family from a subordinate subcaste,' he casted about again for his wife, shifting uncomfortably in the settee he was seated upon.

I sniffed an opportunity and ploughed on, 'I do not believe that such a highly learned and worldly-wise man like you would hold on to such dogmatic and outdated customs. We are in the modern world. And it is not as if I am from a lower caste.' And his wife strolled in; she must have been standing outside the door the whole time, eavesdropping on our conversation and must have come to a decision that her husband was losing ground. She walked up to the settee and perching her diminutive form next to Big Brother, held his hand. I couldn't believe that this pint-sized individual wielded such immense power so as to change the course of my future. I could feel that my chance was slipping away.

'Don't you go questioning my beliefs, they are steadfast and unalterable.' He retorted in a stiff manner, regaining his dwindling confidence as his wife slowly patted his knuckles: 'she is a cold one,' I thought. 'And there is that episode from the past involving my predecessor from the nineteenth century.'

'But that was way back in the past. How can such an issue affect my future?'

'But it was a betrayal of trust, planning to turn over a fellow Indian to the evil Britishers, to be killed mercilessly. Had your ancestor, Trilok Singh, had his way, I wouldn't be existing today.'

I said in an exasperated tone, 'Is there anything I can say, anything I can do which can change your mind.'

He slid his hand out of his wife's grip, stood up and paced the length of the room a couple of times, lost in thought. He stopped in front of me, having made up his mind.

'No son,' and my world crashed. 'I respect the candid manner in which you have put across your arguments. Under different circumstances (he looked at his wife) I would have agreed to your proposal. But we cannot go against our rituals, exorcise our past, and detach ourselves from our ancestry. The circumstances of our birth decide our destinies. Who are we to change what God has ordained for us?' He added after a pause, 'Moreover, you are too young for Pratima. By the time you are 21 she will be 25; too old. How many marriages happen where the bride is older than the groom? Very rare.'

My age again! Why do I fall for older women? First *BB Mausi*, now Pratima.

I stood up and stared at him for some time, locking my eyes with his. I leaned down and touched his feet. Straightening up, I said, 'I have been wanting to pay my obeisance to you for a very long time, for all that you have done for Pratima. Thank you for not throwing me out at the first opportunity and for lending me your ears. It felt as if I was speaking to her father. Thank you also for calling me son, it felt so nice coming from you. You are her real father. I respect your decision. Had it not been for your perseverance and kindness, I would have never met Pratima and known the joy of her company. These four years have been the best years of my life. And if you ever feel that we had betrayed your trust in her, I want to assure you sir, that what we had was the purest form of love a boy and girl could ever have. If there were someone to blame for it, it is definitely not her but I. She is the light of my life, as much as yours and I would never do anything that would harm her. I know that you have her best interests in your heart and whatever future you decide for her, I request that you include her too, before arriving at the decision. She is the most wonderful person I have ever met in my life and I would like her to have a destiny which she desires and not what you impose upon her. I give you my solemn promise that I will abide by your wishes and will never meet or communicate with Pratima again in her life. Having said that, I also request you to give me permission to bid my final farewell to her, alone.'

His wife opened her mouth to protest, but he laid a soft hand upon her shoulder and beckoned her to leave with him. As they walked out of the door and closed it, Pratima got out of her chair and sat next to me on my couch. I turned towards her and held her hands.

'That was the most wonderful sentiment I have ever heard Sanjay. Are you really sure you are 17? When did you grow up to be so mature? I will miss you Sanjay. Till Meenakshi walked in I was sure you would win the argument. But she spoiled everything, and I had requested her not to interfere. Big Brother was dithering and would have given in had it not been for her. Oh Sanjay! It would have been so magnificent to spend the rest of my life with you. I would have been the luckiest woman alive.'

'We can't go there now, Pratima. That's over for us. But you are not. You will remain in my heart for the rest of my life and even beyond. I will never forget you. You are the most fascinating girl I have ever met and I don't think I will meet another one like you, ever. But I have to accept what fate has dealt me. Our story ends here, without that "lived happily ever after" cliché. I hate that overused, hackneyed phrase anyway. I don't know how I will continue existing hereafter.'

She placed a cupped palm over my lips. 'Please don't do anything stupid. You are young, you are beautiful, you are so pristine with such purity in your heart, you contain such noble values. You will one day meet your life partner in the future and both of you will live a wonderful life together. I will not be that soulmate, that's my destiny. Go make your life worth living.'

'I am not going to kill myself, if that's what you feared. I am not craven enough to hide behind death. My heart has broken today but I will try to mend it. Thank you Pratima for making me believe that I too can love. I love you and I am leaving you. I have not said often enough how much I love you. But then, you knew that well enough from my eyes. I wish I could kiss you one last time. But I will not do that here, not in your brother's house and not now. That will be betraying his trust.' I lifted one of her hands and placed my lips upon her knuckles, feeling the soft texture of her skin on my lips, 'That will have to do.'

We sat for some time lost in our thoughts of a future which did not contain the other person.

The clock struck seven and a gong sounded seven times from some clock tower out in the streets or maybe from inside the university campus. I jolted out of my reverie, slowly retrieved my hands from her grip and stood up.

'I guess it's time for our goodbyes. Adieu, my sweet love. Live a life full of joy and happiness and don't shed a tear for me. If at all you remember me, relive all those happy times we spent together and not the sad happenings of today. Can I get a farewell hug?'

'Oh Sanjay! You are so good. How will I ever live without you?' With that she got up and melted into my arms, embracing me in a tight squeeze, shedding silent tears into my chest. I closed my arms around her and inhaled the sweet aroma of her body. I planted a kiss into her hair.

Reluctantly, I let go of her but she held on for dear life. I had to pry myself out of her embrace. I cupped her lovely face in my palms and kissed her forehead.

'Bye Pratima. God bless you and your brothers.'

'Farewell Sanjay. Be happy.'

I walked out of the living room and out of the house. She followed me and halted at the threshold. I reached the bottom of the steps leading out of the gate and turned around. She was holding the twin panels of the door. I forced a smile upon my lips. She smiled back, but it did not reach her eyes. It seemed as if the light had gone out of her eyes.

She closed the door slowly. I stared at the amber panels of the door with Lord Ganesh carved on the wood, shining with the reflection of the yellow neon light on a lamp post nearby. The closing of the amber door signalled the end of my love affair. I was at a crossroads now, with the signal telling me to start stopping: stop and do what? My life had ended here; I cannot stop for nothing now.

I looked up at the heavens, 'You are merciless. You have ruined my life and to add spite You have sent Your emissary in the form of this god of auspicious beginnings to preside over my end. What wrong have I ever done to You that You are punishing me in this manner? How will I continue living now? What is there left for me? What further journey have You planned for me that You have sent Lord Ganesh? Tell me Oh God! What do I do now?'

I regretted that I hadn't told her that I would indeed be writing that half-ending story I had promised to her so long back. I vowed silently that I would do it in her memory.

I caught a tempo back to Sainik School Lucknow and at around midnight reality struck like sudden lightning and I spent the night shedding tears, suppressing my sniffles and sobs lest someone noticed me crying. Close to dawn, exhaustion, borne out of so much crying, seeped in and I missed the bus to *Kanya Putri Paathshaala*.

I reached the venue for the second paper of the NDA entrance exam, by a combination of tempo and cycle rickshaw, arriving an hour late. After much cajoling and proving with my blood red eyes that I had not got a wink throughout the night spent in studying and had got late due to falling asleep in the morning thus waking up late, I was allowed to take the paper. I promptly put my head down upon the desk and spent the next two hours lost in my dreams of Pratima fighting off a demonic Meenakshi, her grimacing mouth breathing fire, brandishing a flame covered sword trying to cut Pratima to pieces, I was staring helplessly as her two brothers had tied me to a post; somewhere in the background a turbaned, moustachioed, giant of a man, surrounded by scantily clad damsels, was guffawing, his head hanging back, as a body swung in the wind from the gallows in which an enfeebled fugitive had been hung. Time and time again the pretty invigilator would wake me up with a shake and urge me to answer the paper. Every time I would nod and pick up my pencil, and go off to sleep again. I did not attempt to answer a single question.

I left Lucknow after depositing my unanswered paper with the lovely invigilator, who was being bombarded with requests for her address from some of my classmates. I ignored their queries and concerns for my treacherous condition. I caught a train to Shaktinagar after travelling to the school by that cycle rickshaw-tempo combination to collect my belongings.

Once home I could not reply positively to Father's questions of how I had fared in the entrance exam. Dissatisfied with my round-about replies, he left me to my own devices with Mother complaining that I should have put in more effort.

I spent the winter vacations lost in my thoughts, always replying to my parents' enquiries in monosyllables, if the nods and shakes did not satisfy them. I spent hours after miserable hours lying in bed, staring at the ceiling, my mind blank. There were no emotions surging in my heart, just a big dark hole where my soul lay in deep slumber. Often I would shed silent, unbidden tears, which my parents ascribed to as my reaction to my poor performance in the entrance exam. I was no joy to my brother and we even stopped our routine fights, to the immense relief of our mother. My parents fretted about me but I was inconsolable and after a few attempts they gave up on springing life back into me. I wore a sullen look throughout the vacation.

After rejoining the school, I broke contact with all of my classmates and preferred to trudge up the hill to sit at the water tank on top, every Sunday and whenever I could get time off the school's routine on the other days. One Sunday, Bindu came up to the water tank and complained that she had not seen me for so long, as I was never wandering the corridors of Raman Block, preferring to remain in my classroom during the intervals between classes. After the lament, she scrutinised my face closely and suddenly realised that something was not right. She wouldn't accept my repeated assertions that nothing was wrong with me. When she won't let go till I told her the truth, I relented and narrated the entire episode that occurred at Pratima's brother's house in Lucknow. By the end of it, I had my head upon her shoulders and my eyes were leaking tears. She patted my head and expressed her condolences, as if I had lost someone very close to me. She became my sole companion who dragged me out of the morass I had plunged into. Invariably, on each Sunday thereafter, she would climb up the hill and we would perch on the water tank's roof, talking about Pratima and the times we had spent with her. We laughed, we shed tears, we joked, we wept, we took delights while recounting happy episodes, we went into the depths of sorrow when we desired her presence; as we sat recalling her life from 6 years old till she left Ghorakhal. I told her everything I knew about Pratima's life and retold the stories I used to regale Pratima with, when Bindu herself used to lounge under her favourite pine tree, reading or snoozing.

On other days, when Bindu was not with me, I would go to the cave and lie there, thinking about how it felt to touch Pratima's body and reliving alone that time we had spent together there. I longed the most for her then. I missed the most the scent of her lemony perfume, which she wore only for me.

I barely managed to scrape through the eleventh class final tests and flunked again in my second crack at the NDA entrance exam that summer. One look at my gloomy visage, when I arrived home after the entrance exam for my summer vacations and my parents knew that I had not fared well again. Father shook his head and muttered something about a good-for-nothing son. Mother berated me for wasting away my life. Brother sniggered and snickered in a corner.

Two days later, I met the true love of my life and my future changed forever.

PART TWO

1

Sharmajee

The cold was extremely severe. That winter of '83 was unbearably frigid and the wind bit hard and deep, even in the plains of Shaktinagar, something to do with the alignment of our planets earlier in March of that year. I was home for my winter vacations; my heart singing a merry tune, my eyes glimmering with glorious images of Pratima in elegant poses and exotic dresses, my ears ringing with her cackling, deep laughter, my soul firm in my resolve to marry her, and my mind dreaming of wonderful scenarios of blissful domestic existence, with her as my soulmate. That cold December evening, Father had just returned from his daily errands, home at last after a hard day's toil, back to his hearth seeking the warmth of paradise amidst his family.

Suddenly, the doorbell pierced my dream world with its incessant, desperate shrieks—'treeee. . .'—it went on and on, till I opened the door a fraction to be cursed with a vision of a hellish black curtain amidst the dense whiteness of the thick fog. The curtain was actually a human covered in black, head to toe, with his head and face hidden inside a monkey cap, the morose, yellowed sclera of his ferret like blinking eyes giving the sole indication that there was a living being of mammoth proportions, hiding in all that black. His belly stuck out like a pregnant woman about to go into labour, its round curve pushing into the door handle, even though he was standing well away from the door. Intense hatred instantly boiled inside me at the sight of this ridiculous creature from hell.

'*Namastey*, what can I do for you?' I asked of this spectre from whichever hellish domain he presided over; his very appearance was suggestive of ill intent, the way he croaked his reply, the way he stood as if he owned the turf, the way his eyes conveyed malice, the eyeballs dancing all over as he tried to peep over my shoulder to survey the realm beyond. His immense girth had rudely parted the white world of fog and its white tendrils were making desperate attempts to regain their lost territory and win more of the same, by stealing into the confines of our warm, cosy home.

'Is TivariSahab home?' he squawked. The insouciance of his tone peeved me no end.

'Who may I say is calling?' I asked with my own note of exasperation.

'I am Sharmajee and I have come to meet him on some urgent *bizziness*,' he pronounced the reason for his visit as in dizziness. I slammed the door on his face; so repulsive was his appearance, so suspicious his nature, and called for Father. The white snakes of fog drifting in were another reason for me to shut the door in a hurry.

The single bedroom in our house was shared by all four of us humans, a Dunlop-mattressed double bed, and the evening-time folding cot. Crowded by all these animate and inanimate occupants, hardly any space was left in the room for moving around. My brother, Kaalu, was curled up in one corner of the eight-foot-wide double bed, snoozing under a blanket. Upon my return, after witnessing the grotesquely fat stranger—I had followed Mother's diktats and not talked more than the mandatory 'thirteen' words to him, thank God it was not a Friday—I dropped on the six-inch thick foam of Dunlop and resumed the conversations with my now-here-now-there, imaginary Pratima. Two minutes later, Mother broke into my reverie and ordered me to serve water to the 'Gentleman.'

There he sat, sprawled on the rickety, easy chair Father had acquired from his father. He had taken off the monkey cap, revealing a reluctant bunch of black hair sitting atop his crown, its sparse, stray strands swaying with each shake of his head. That small cluster of fluff was enclosed by an empty brown circle, with a few strands running along the fringes of an egg-shaped bald head. To top that, this I noticed when he turned his face backwards, he had a long clump of hair twisted in a number of tight knots hanging from the back of his head (a hallmark of an orthodox Brahmin—some of my cousins have it, too). I suspected he must also be twirling coils of the sacred thread, *Janeoo*, around his ear, while relieving himself. I have seen people, including those cousins of mine and their fathers, coiling the sacred thread around their right ear with two rotations, before defecating in the open or urinating in full public view, the length of the thread worn from the right shoulder to the waist. The practice is supposed to squeeze two nerves behind the ears, a process which opened up the body's internal passages and orifices, enabling easy disposal of the waste. It is a common malady afflicting Indians cutting across all religious, caste, creed, class, status, and societal lines—keep me, myself, my house, my children, clean; the rest of the world be damned. Thus we have my fellow countrymen, and women too, spitting all over, shooting off streams of red-as-blood betel juice or hawking and hurling projectiles of thick, viscous phlegm, without a care for where their discharges would descend; strewing garbage in the streets and public places without regard to the diseases that may sprout from their refuse; defecating and urinating in full public view unmindful of exposure; disposing wrappers, plastic packets, papers, peels, and pips wherever convenient, with a damned-if-I-care attitude. The same Indians, when they go abroad, to Singapore or the US, are careful not to be caught spitting or littering lest they be fined or worse, jailed (but never be mistaken that they want to leave an impression amongst the *firangs* (foreigners) that they are civilised); they even give up their regular tobacco-chewing fixation when out on such foreign jaunts. However, once they are back in India, they let off a glad-to-be-back greeting of a fat glob of thick, juicy, phlegmy spit, the moment their feet touch the hot tarmac at the airport—MY INDIA, MY PRIDE, MY PLACE TO LIVE, MY RIGHT TO KEEP IT DIRTY. What an irony of existence?

And, has anyone noticed that our women are not permitted to wear *Janeoo*! It is as if the male-dominated Brahmins have ruled that women do not need a smooth passage, even for their waste. That it is the norm for our women—to suffer 'hard stools', sorry I meant hardships, throughout their lives.

Our visitor—looked like a staunch Brahmin—had taken off his massive overcoat and through the faux-wool jersey I could clearly make out his man-breasts, which shivered whenever he made a movement with his arms or chest. His humungous belly almost threatened to acquire enough kinetic energy to push the centre table aside, as he leaned forward to dip his dirty-as-night-soil, long-nailed, crooked, pudgy fingers, to scoop up the tomato sauce, generously served in a large bowl by Mother. His other facial features included a bushy brow, flaring ears sprouting with dark hair, round jaws converging on a sunken chin, plump cheeks with stray clusters of little brushes of hair dotting it—his alopecia seemed to extend from his pate to his cheeks too—a thick neck which seemed nonexistent, what with the layers of thick, quivering chunks of brown flesh leading down from his sunken chin towards the shoulder. His calcium deficient, yellowed, crooked teeth looked like the remains of the kernels of a partly consumed cob of corn.

I desist from describing his physiology below the belly as, firstly, I could not any further bear to look at such a sad representation of the Homo Sapiens, and secondly, thankfully, the lower portion of his body was hidden beneath the high centre table, which also served as our dining table, and which was adorned with numerous bowls of tomato sauce, diced onion, sliced tomatoes, and crushed garlic.

This was Sharmajee, a specimen beyond comprehension. He was an engineer with the hydrothermal department of the National Thermal Power Corporation Limited, NTPC. His was a supposedly prestigious designation within the public sector enterprise and he had his chunky fingers in the dealings my father's security agency had association with. He wielded great influence upon Father's affairs and that was the primary reason for his regular, nocturnal visits to our house. Tomato sauce, dipped in onion and garlic, was his gourmet fetish. He relished the sauce, but to add variety, he garnished it with onion and garlic and an odd tomato. As a result, he was as smelly as the breath of a vulture.

Sharmajee was a character by himself. A spinster-in-breeches (he was a bachelor but his manners were those of a spinster), he stayed in a similar two-room house like ours and dined copiously on the packed meals from the local eatery (*dhaba*). But, since the *dhaba* did not include free tomato sauce in the menu, he made our house a regular stopover before he retired for the night. My mother had been alerted by Father, of his tomato sauce-dipped-in-onion-and-garlic fixation and hence the lavish spread on that first night I had laid my eyes upon him. He was a moderate rum drinker, in a sense; he got tipsy after the first drink and uncontrollable post the second peg. Any more beyond that and he became a certified drunkard. But despite all his failings, which were numerous, he invariably left after his second drink, that is, when he was in an uncontrollable state. Father would thereafter walk his swaying body out of the house, kickstart his Lambretta scooter, shush him at times from belting out out-of-tune, drunken songs, ensure that he had firmly perched himself on the seat of his ride and send him off with a genial push on his generous rump. Sharmajee immensely enjoyed that push and off he would be on the 200-metre ride to his digs. There have been many nights when Father had had to rush, after that genial push on his generous rump, to pick up Sharmajee after he had driven into a lamp post on his 200-metre journey.

I witnessed only one occasion when Sharmajee really got drunk at our house. It was the Holi holidays in March of '84 and I was on a spot of leave at home. He had come to our house to wish Happy Holi—without any gift; after all he was an officer and my father only a *bizzinessman*. But Father was up to the task; he knew Sharmajee's true worth and indulged him not only for help with his official dealings but also because he was single and lived close by, and of course, he was a fellow Brahmin. Sharmajee's sole purpose for the visit was to slurp on the four bowls of tomato sauce, dipped in onion and garlic, which were dutifully served by Mother. He was doubly delighted when Father opened a bottle of scotch whiskey. As the evening wore on, in his enthusiasm he had two pegs of whiskey to go with the earlier single peg of rum. By the time he finished his second whiskey, he was on cloud nine. Such were his utterances thereafter, that they are not fit for general consumption and repetition here. Suffice to surmise, he had used choice words to portray each of the superiors in his department and what he intended to do to their near and dear ones: their mothers, sisters, and wives. Those superiors who were lucky or unlucky to have none of these had their fathers and brothers roped in, in his diatribe. Father, realising that Sharmajee's circle was fast closing in and having soon exhausted his superiors he would home on to his neighbours, including us, quickly finished his own drink and half-walked, half-carried him to his house; scooter ride for the 200-metre distance was out of question, what with Sharmajee in such a 'glad' state.

During the remaining days of my two-month long winter vacations of '83–'84 and subsequent summer vacations, he became quite friendly with me. He would invariably invite me to his house, on his free days, for a game of chess or a dash at the carom board or a go at the other board games he kept in his house. It was fortuitous that Mother always insisted that my brother accompany me, whenever he called me over to his house. For, the true motives behind his invites to play those indoor games were revealed during the summer vacations of '84.

On that day, he proposed to take me on a sightseeing tour of the hydrothermal plant located in the centre of Shaktinagar. My mother, as always, included my brother in the party. During the trip, my brother, hampered by a cricket injury to his leg, started lagging behind, and noticing his crawl, Sharmajee increased his pace midway through the trip. As we rounded the corners and left my brother in the lurch, out of sight, he started touching me, at times fondling, at times caressing, at times rubbing my behind, at times brushing his hands against my cheek and such like intimate gestures of utter disgust. To me these acts of his were not only inappropriate and irritating, but they also reminded me of my school days as a much younger kid. Combined with his smelly odour and that garlic laced breath, his actions evoked total revulsion inside me. I made a hasty exit along with my brother lest he took the next step of forcing me into an isolated room to indulge in his homosexual fantasies. He did manage to crassly whisper, 'Come to my home in the evening,' before reluctantly letting me go.

I proceeded for my school and the Water Tank Hill the next day and forgot about this singular incident where Sharmajee revealed his true colours.

What a fiend he was—taking advantage of my father just because he was in a position of influence. My father, after a lot of searching around, had at last secured a vocation which earned him a decent living to feed his family, ensure proper education for his sons, luxuriate in his addiction of a pack-a-day of his nicotine fix and the three-pegs-of-rum evening ritual, nourish his passion for the Yezdi motorcycle which he rode on his errands and which all four of us shared when the family visited the local market or went movie-watching at the open air theatre; my brother perched on the fuel tank, I squeezed between Mother and Father. And to top it all, Sharmajee tried to take advantage of me. The word rape occurred to me—I was a skinny adolescent, with miniature, almost nonexistent biceps, which popped up with so much reluctance and shyness whenever I tried to boast of my muscles to my equally scrawny brother. I was endowed with very little visible masculinity and even though I had outgrown the effeminate manners of my early-teen years, I was not of a build that I could take on a fat oaf like Sharmajee, if it ever came to defending myself in a physical confrontation.

Post vacations, the school activities, my own scholarly pursuits, and above all, Pratima's delightful company made me forget the bitter experience of that day in a jiffy. The next few vacations at Shaktinagar I deliberately avoided him whenever he visited our home, for his regular fix of tomato sauce and two pegs of rum. On those rare occasions, when my parents would insist upon my sitting with them to give him company, there was lasciviousness in his stare whenever he looked at me.

2

The Settlement with Twin Tall Chimneys

Back in '82, Father had finally been successful in opening his own enterprise and earn money, take Mother away from the draconian diktats of my grandmother, and ensure good education for his younger son in a convent school—all courtesy the ever-faithful Arjun Thakur. In mutual collaboration, they had opened a jointly managed security agency, composing initially of retired Army men from the villages and towns of my home district. Laden with freshly stitched khaki uniforms, their personal belongings stuffed in the Army style tubular kit bags issued during their prior Army life, sixty patrons of his security company had arrived at Shaktinagar in August of that year, to be employed by NTPC for ensuring safety of their numerous assets and office buildings. Father was the overall organiser of the security agency's activities in the field at Shaktinagar, whereas Arjun Thakur managed the affairs at New Delhi, coordinating with the head office of NTPC there. The security agency's chief supervisor at Shaktinagar was Urba Dutt Uncle, a genial, retired subedar from the Army, whose bicycle became my constant companion during the vacations, till Father bought a shiny red Atlas for me in '83.

Till the thermal power plant was established in the area, there was a little hamlet in its place, which went by the name of Kota and whose original inhabitants were tribals, sustaining on the meagre resources of the surrounding jungle. Shaktinagar came up, consuming Kota in its wake, in order to exploit the abundant natural resource of coal from the nearby mines of Jayant, Duddhichua, Nigahi, Kakri, Khadia, and Bina. The huge Govind Ballabh Pant Sagar Lake was conveniently located close by, to provide water for converting heat and vapour into electricity and the NTPC moved in with its directors, engineers, managers, supervisors, doctors, nurses, shopkeepers, janitors, drivers, orderlies, clerks, peons, contractors, and other minions from all over the country, to establish a semblance of a town.

The settlement was divided into three distinct colonies, as per the class and status of the occupants. The first colony was established at Kota Basti in mid Seventies, which consisted of single-storey apartments constructed in never-ending rows, each house comprising two rooms, a tiny bathroom, a tinier toilet, a small kitchen, a store room, and an open-to-sky verandah. For larger families, two such dwellings were joined together, by breaking the intervening wall, to convert them into a four-room apartment. The first market was established at Kota Basti and the apartments near the market, with more and bigger rooms, were constructed for people of higher status. Father was way too low in the pecking order and we had to make do with the two-rooms-tiny-bathroom-tinier-toilet version. And, despite Sharmajee's presumptuous haughtiness, his station did not merit him a status above Father's, in terms of allotment of dwelling units. He was also allocated the lowest of dwellings meant for those employees of NTPC occupying low rungs in the corporation's rigid, jealously guarded, and unyielding hierarchy—a typical Indian trait. In actuality, all structures in India—be they political, governmental, public, private, or family enterprises—are individual microcosms of our world, reflecting the larger social framework within which reside our differences of religion, caste, class, creed, state of domicile, linguistic, gender, and whatever other distinctions a mind can dream of, and each occupant of the lower rung has always been discriminated against by those privileged to be higher than them, who themselves are trod upon by those a notch higher than them—a vicious, vicious pyramid where everybody dominates others and is in turn dominated by others, except the pyramid of our Indian society does not have a top stone. There is no let up in this setup, but there was a serious shortcoming in this structure—while each echelon down or up the framework has someone below him to dominate, the poor sod at the lowest rung—the *Bhangi* outcaste, the beggar, the *Shudra*—did not have anyone to treat as inferior, to gloat over. Millennia ago a permanent remedy to this dilemma was discovered, when, cutting across all religions, castes, class, and status, women were recognised as the humans to be constantly and routinely kept under the thumb by men, to be dominated upon and condescended with derision.

When the swell at the newly established Kota Basti increased and more people started moving in, Jwalamukhi Enclave came up, four kilometres away from Kota Basti. This new colony contained bigger houses, some duplexes too and a larger market—all for the privileged lot. Later, an open air theatre was also built there. The much revered *Jwalamukhi Mandir* is also located near this colony. When the directors, managers, engineers, supervisors, doctors et al. started moving in with their families—some of them left their pretty daughters back at the cities and towns they came from, to the unmitigated chagrin of us adolescent young boys bursting with unrestrained hormones going haywire, shooting all over the place—a third colony came up, a further four kilometres from Jwalamukhi Enclave, which contained duplexes and bungalows, in addition to multi-storey apartments; a bigger and shinier shopping arcade with a glittering restaurant, aromatic eateries, and shimmering shops; a convent school; a Kendriya Vidyalaya; and a cinema hall with a cinemascope screen, in contrast to the thirty-five-millimetre screen of the open air theatre at Jwalamukhi Enclave.

The pride of place in the settlement of Shaktinagar was taken by the massive hill which dominated the entire settlement and sat like a deity surveying the goings-on of his supplicants. This hill rose 400 metres into the air and provided a panoramic view of the entire settlement from its large flat plateau on top. The plateau could be reached using a metalled road through Jwalamukhi Enclave. There are a few rock strewn pathways and trails from Kota Basti side too, to the sheer delight of the trekkers amongst us. The hill is barren, with brambles and bushes and shrubs and brushwood and cacti and thistles and nettles and thymes, dotting its slopes and the base. It ran a distance of four kilometres at its base, from Kota Basti till the end of Jwalamukhi Enclave. Its plateau top had been cleared of all vegetation, barring a few banyan trees towards its secluded southern end. A helipad, a view point, a huge water tank, and a colony for the Russians, who had come to establish and run the thermal power plant, were constructed on the plateau top.

In the dead centre of this settlement of cackling colonies, screaming markets, whispering shopping arcade, musical cinema hall, sat the thermal power station with its boilers, its turbines, its water pumps, its electrical generators, its condensers, its conveyor belts, its pulverisers, its superheaters, its precipitators, its transmission lines, its step-up transformers. The cooling towers, which belched out white clouds of steam, stood at one corner of the plant. From the opposite corner, two tall chimneys rose more than 200 metres into the atmosphere and spewed out filtered smoke—sometimes greyish white, sometimes blackish gray, sometimes whitish gray, sometimes greyish black—into the sky. The upper storeys of these chimneys came into view from twenty kilometres away and were visible from all corners of Shaktinagar, except the leeward side of the Helipad Hill. At nights, their mouths glimmered with an ethereal red glow, as if a demon was feeding lost souls into a hellish blaze deep inside their bellies.

3

Arranged Marriage

June of '86 saw me again faring poorly in my second crack at the NDA entrance exams. After bearing the nasty comments of Father and the berating of Mother, I squeezed out of the house to roam the vacant streets of Kota Basti, wandering aimlessly from morning till evening, lost in thoughts of 'what-would-have-been' scenarios. Pratima's loss and my flunking the entrance exams were eating into my adolescent heart and I was at a loss as to what remedy would take me out of my gloom. Over the next few days, nothing could make me snap out of it—not Father's apologies for his earlier impulsive reaction and scathing comments, not Mother's care and delicious meals, not my brother's pleas of letting me bat throughout our cricketing practices.

The third day of my vacation, I decided to watch *The Good, The Bad and The Ugly* and with the video cassette of the Clint Eastwood-starrer Western film firmly held in my grasp I was on my way back from the video parlour, when I spotted a brand-new scooter in front of our door. The two-wheeler bore a swastika sign made by red vermillion on its front instrument panel cover, a ribbon was tied around its front panel and plastic sheets were still covering its seats, indicating its newly bought status; another hallmark of every Indian, who never removes the plastic sheet covers from his newly bought vehicle's seats for years, till they fade into insignificance and their remains had to be reluctantly removed—the hubris of every middle class Indian never allows him to cease in showing off to his neighbours that he is better off than them—more Indians die of heart diseases due to this aspiration of being better than the others than the bad cholesterol which blocks the blood vessels.

As I entered the house, lo and behold, there was Sharmajee, lounging on his usual rickety easy chair—I always admired the chair's tenacity, it never uttered a squeak whenever he thumped down on it with his 100 plus kilograms of body mass and never protested whenever he fidgeted and rubbed his wide bottom on the soft cushions. The cushions of course needed constant replacement every three months, as the daily visits of Sharmajee used to flatten them like pancakes in those ninety days.

He hollered, 'come Sanjay. How was your school? It is so nice to see you after such a long time. You remember our visit to the thermal plant long back; I still carry fond memories of that trip (the slimy scoundrel!). *Bhabhiji*, these samosas are good,' with that he dipped a huge *samosa* into a bowl of tomato sauce and chomped on a morsel, simultaneously licking the tomato sauce dripping down his fingers—yuck!

Beside him sat a demure, delicate girl, dressed in a pale green, chiffon sari with wavy designs, her *pallu* covering half of her luxurious, shining black hair, which was piled high in an elaborate coiffure. She was very pretty. 'Who is she? Did she come with Sharmajee? Or is she visiting Mother? What a pretty girl?' I was already feeling a strong emotion building inside my heart. Then I noticed the vermilion streak in the middle of her forehead—a thin red line starting at the base of her hairline and vanishing into the dense black jungle of her delightful tresses—the large *bindi* on her forehead, the assortment of glass bangles adorning her forearms: all signs of a married woman, and my heart sank. 'She is married. To Sharmajee? Oh no, that is not possible. She cannot be married to this buffoon, champing away on the sauce-dipped samosas. How on earth did he get so lucky, getting married to this beautiful damsel, this young and nubile maiden, this desire of youthful fantasies, this shy, virginal delight for sour eyes?' She looked like she would not be more than a year or two older than me.

And Mother confirmed my suspicions by addressing her, 'Meena, your husband loves his food. Why don't you too take a *samosa*? You are so thin. You should eat something. Eat these *jalebis*, try this sandwich. Your tea is getting cold.'

Sharmajee chimed in, 'Yes Meena dear. Take something; otherwise, people will accuse me of not treating my wife properly. You have no fat on your body, gorge yourself and grow some flesh on your bones. I don't like thin girls (he does like 15-year-old boys, the cad! Memory of that long past visit to the plant flooded my mind). Treat this place as your own home. Bhabhiji is very kind; she is like your elder sister. Sanjay, she likes playing badminton a lot. Why don't you play with her? Bhabhiji I will get the rackets and shuttle tomorrow.'

At this, the pretty girl looked up and stole a glance towards me. My heart skipped a beat. She had such lovely, soft brown, almond eyes. The small button nose on her round face added to her charm. Even though Mother and Sharmajee grumbled about her skinny physique, she had a full and well-proportioned face. Her red lips, sans any lip gloss, were like ripe cherries. Her slender jaws lined up to a slightly protruding chin. She possessed a long neck which ran endlessly, till it culminated at protruding collar bones and there was a delightful dip where her neck met the clavicle; something was glistening there—it was her sweat which had lodged itself inside the dip—how I wished I could morph into that salty globule and rest within the cosy confines of the soft unblemished skin of her long neck. Immediately wiping out the charming vision, she followed my gaze and with a swipe of her hand sent the bead into orbit, in a trail of tiny droplets and adjusted her sari to conceal the object of my interest.

As she got up to leave, after Sharmajee had consumed all eight samosas, two bowls of tomato sauce, half a kilogram of jalebis, ten sandwiches and four cups of tea—this man had some appetite—I could not help notice her voluptuous figure. Skinny, my foot! She had Maushumi Chatterjee features, including the conical canines, as she flashed a dazzling, surreptitious smile towards me from the door, when no one was looking. I couldn't believe it!

'Oh! What a shame. She must not be more than 18 years old and she is married to this 30-plus, fortyish, specimen of a human, who has pervert sexual proclivities. How can she bear him?' My heart went out to her.

That evening, after a long time, my brother and I sat in a huddle, before and after dinner, discussing this odd pairing of the Sharmas. After prolonged deliberations and desperate sighs and lamenting upon the sorry plight of dainty, pretty girls like Meena being stuck for life with crackpots like Sharmajee, we arrived at a combined conclusion that life indeed was not fair, 'specially for people like us who will never be able to get girls like Meena. They are already in short supply, particularly in these dusty, overpolluted, full of grown-up couples 'who have left their daughters at their respective hometowns', environs of Shaktinagar. And what with the

Sharmajees of the world always lurking around the corner, we don't stand a chance of ever landing with such a beautiful wife.'

With that repentant, self-pitying sentiment, I retired for the night, launching straightaway into a dream world of slender jaws, slightly jutting chins, numerous images of soft brown, almond eyes (like the ones Rajesh Khanna drew in *Safar*), cherries morphing into lush red lips, that dip at the lower end of her neck at times filling up with a dazzling translucent fluid and at times being slurped by a rough, leathery, serpentine tongue, at which instant the liquid acquired the hue and consistency of tomato sauce and the dip in the neck turned into a circular bowl. After flitting in and out, Sharmajee acquired centre stage towards the middle of the night, in the form of a giant, his face shining with a sheen akin to petrol spilled on water; he possessed menacing fangs and sabre-tooth canines as he advanced, in his naked glory, upon a cowering, whimpering Meena, his treads reverberating and sending seismic waves along the ground surface, his hairy breasts bouncing like crazy-balls with each step, his belly threatening to give way to the eternal pull of gravity and drop to the ground, leaving a gaping hole in Sharmajee's midsection—thankfully the overhang of his hirsute belly hid everything immediately below it. But when Meena gave a heart-rending shriek I woke up with a start, as she had screamed after gazing at whatever was hanging down there, below the overhang.

'Oh! Thank God! It was a nightmare. Meena is safe.'

But how could she be safe? She was his wife and he could do whatever he desired with her. 'What did she see down there to make her scream like that; was there a serpent's forked tongue between his legs?'

I groped under the pillow for the wrist watch Father had gifted me one summer back, for having achieved first-class grade in the tenth class board exams. It had a radio-luminescent paint coating its minute and hour hands, as well as the digits—popularly known as radium dial watch. There was one straight line pointing towards '12' from its centre—the minute hand had mounted atop the hour hand, indicating that it was twelve o'clock at night. That delightful dream followed by the nightmarish nightmare had left me empty of emotions and I did not stand a chance of summoning any more sleep, from whichever corner it had vanished to. My mind drifted and meandered, floated and fluttered, hovered and lingered, sailed and strolled, wafted and wandered, as I searched for logical reasons that must have led to this awkward marriage.

As the night aged and my parents and brother shifted and tossed and turned in their respective slumbers, I finally got it—this was an arranged marriage. Sharmajee belonged to Bihar and such arrangements in that state and other states in India, stretching North to South, were routine. He must be from a higher *gotra* amongst the Brahmins and she from a lower *gotra*, belonging to a poor family.

Arranged marriages are a strange phenomenon, developed and nurtured on the Indian subcontinent for centuries, with a zealous fervour. It is also common in most parts of Asia and Africa. It establishes a rigid, formulaic approach towards man-woman relationship, in which parents and other well-wishers decide who will spend her lifetime with whom, for eternity. In the olden days, leading up to my grandfather's first marriage, the bride and bridegroom happened to see each other for the first time, only on their wedding nights. And even till this day, in certain rural and semiurban societies, marriages are fixed by third-party individuals—distant aunts on the mother's side, diligent uncles on the father's side, and such like. At times even the ubiquitous local barber was entrusted with the responsibility of fixing marriages—he was the 'matrimonial site' for the illiterate millions who populated the rural realm of our country. I couldn't help recollecting an incident and its aftermath, which occurred a few years back in the late Seventies and which, if not for the alert eyes of the barber, would have led to a totally different future for the principal protagonists involved.

It so happened that, on a hot June afternoon, in the simmering heat, a couple of marriage parties were waiting at Etawah Railway Station, after consummation of their respective marriage ceremonies, and the two sets of brides and bridegrooms were on their way home, along with the respective groom's party. There was the usual hustle and bustle at the platform, characteristic of any railway station in India; the chaos of hurrying humanity, the sweat of waiting anxieties, the dust of shuffling feet, the song of buzzing flies, the stings of blood-thirsty mosquitoes, the squeaks and squiggles of sneaky rats, the horrid smell of baking poop, and flowing urine, the desperate cries of hawkers and peddlers, the shifty eyes of the wily pickpocket, the furtive glances of the local drunk before he pulled out his country liquor pouch for a swig. The brides and grooms of both parties, dressed in similar attire—red glossy sari for her and spotless white kurta pyjama for him—were standing amidst their respective huddles, a few feet apart. The train came chugging along, lumbering in the heat and drew onto the platform. It halted in a cloud of steam and the crowd went into a frenzy of eager passengers desperate to grab the window seat; people jostled with each other to vie for the door, some lugged their luggage through the bar-less windows to dump on the seats before they were occupied, small children and diminutive women were pushed through the windows to seize the births—the womenfolk did not even mind that the men fondled and groped and grabbed and poked amidst the furore, as their entire effort and concentration was focused on grabbing the empty seats and lying down on the birth to reserve it for the entire family. Such delirium was, and still is, a routine feature of any railway station in India and there were those omnipresent petty thieves who relished such moments of chaos and clamour to help themselves to some free money from the hapless passengers preoccupied in boarding the train and securing a seat for themselves, all the time mindful of the numerous number of packages, counted countless times, that comprised their accompanying baggage.

Amidst the commotion of the flurry of activities that ensued when the locomotive hooted and hissed and brought the blundering bogies to a halt at the platform, the brides got exchanged from one huddle to the other. As everyone in the respective parties, including the groom, was more attentive to getting their own belongings and the much aspired for dowry items dumped into the train, the brides, who had their saris pulled low over their faces and who themselves had never been able to get a good look at their respective grooms, during the exhaustive and cumbersome marriage rituals, followed the group they believed to be theirs. The shouts and smells emanating from the members of both the parties were similar, the grooms wore the same nondescript crystal-white attires and had remarkably unremarkable features which could not help differentiate one from the other, and one thing led to the other resulting in the brides boarding the train unnoticeably interchanging their respective cluster and exchanging their husbands. Since no member of the wedding parties had ever had a peak at the brides—the marriages having been arranged by a maternal aunt, who had routinely passed away a few days before the marriages, on one side, and on the other, by a barber well known to the bride's family—the brides settled down comfortably in their respective in-laws' households over the next few months and the husbands, counting their blessings on having bagged a most suitable wife, got sucked into the newfound pleasures of stolen moments of nocturnal carnal activities. They never suspected anything amiss—why should they? They had married their respective wife and she was theirs to please.

Fate struck once again, in the form of the barber who had brought the earlier marriage proposal to one of the groom's families. Now he came with a fresh proposition of a bride for the younger scion of the family and as he sat sipping the hot cup of tea, dutifully served by the young wife of the elder son, basking in the adulations being bestowed by the mother for having found her such a conscientious, mindful, and pretty daughter-in-law for the elder son, he was taken aback when he saw the face of the young girl. Initially he imagined that there was a third son in the family and he took her to be the wife of the nonexistent third sibling. Further enquiries revealed that she was indeed the very bride whose proposal he had brought to the family previously; but she was not the same girl! He created a ruckus and was insistent that she was not the girl whose proposal he had brought earlier. To prove his case, he produced an album which contained the original bride's photograph, amidst prints of a number of other girls—he did carry photographs of each prospective bride but never showed them to the potential grooms or their family members. A commotion erupted and in the thick of blame-gaming the younger son recalled that there was another marriage party which had boarded the same train all those months back.

Frenetic enquiries ensued, and after days of consultations and deliberations and to-and-fro-ing and name-calling and brick-batting, another huddle assembled, mostly at the behest of the barber-cum-marriage fixer-cum-marriage portal. This fresh group comprised members of all the four families, including the brides and grooms involved. Since marriages in India have more to do with contracts between families and little with the affairs of the heart and soul of the boys and girls involved, it was settled that the wives would now revert to their original, 'fixed' partners. Now the husbands butted in and protested:

But she is soiled . . . she is no longer a virgin (virginity of the newlywed wives is more treasured by the men in India than the girls themselves). . . I cannot accept a wife who has slept with this man. . . What if she is pregnant with his child?. . . What if she starts comparing my willy's size with his?. . . Mother just accept this one as your daughter-in-law, she is so dutiful, so attentive to you and father. . .

Their laments went on similar lines—nary a remark of love, heart, soulmates, and such like was ever uttered by either of them.

The matter was ultimately resolved by the patriarchs of the husbands' families and the wives changed husbands once again. Each of them delivered a baby girl within the next nine months and thereafter the wives' lives turned into hell—the birth of the girl-child was blamed on her for having carried the seed of the other 'husband' when she was reverted to her 'original' family.

4

Dhal Gaya Din, Ho Gayi Raat

I spent the next few days in deep frustration. Sharmajee's house was a short distance away and as much as I could try, I was not able to get a glimpse of Meena. He still frequented our house for his customary bowls of tomato sauce and the two pegs of rum, but he never brought along his wife with him. He would arrive straight from his workplace, sometimes after having downed a swig or two of country liquor at some seedy joint, and sit talking of this and that with Father, till he had had his fix and his fill before departing pompously, strutting like a jenny in heat. I avoided sitting in our living room whenever he was present. One day, Father called me over and lectured me on the importance of preparing well for exams and not to waste my time in sundry pursuits like cricket and girls. Sharmajee smirked during the monologue of Father and gave me a sly look with a wicked gleam in his eyes (the cad!) when I finally left their presence.

By the third day after her first visit to our house I became eager for a glimpse and conspiratorially suggested to Father that my brother and I should start playing badminton, as I wanted additional practice to make it to the school's team. Truth be told, I never played badminton at school. But then Sharmajee had never lived up to his promise of getting badminton rackets and shuttle for Meena to play with me. As for Meena, she never ventured out of the confines of her house. I was desperate for a sight and thus this masquerade.

Newly purchased rackets in hand, their taut strings twanging as I ran my finger tips along the grid, we commenced my 'practice sessions' that evening. What tricks a desperate mind can play! I selected a piece of ground which was in direct sight from her house, as our 'court'. During the play, I selected to keep myself facing her house. With each passing minute, I moved our 'court' closer to her home—since there was no 'net', the drifting of our 'court' became easier with each shot. By our second game—the first one was easily won by me—we were playing right in front of her house. I imagined that she would be sitting by her window and itching to come out and play with me.

She never came out and I shrugged in disappointment as the sun bade its final goodbye to another day of frustration.

Repeating the same trick the next evening, I did not wait long after we had drifted in front of her house. Sweating profusely, I wiped my brow and face with a hand towel and rang her doorbell.

She opened her door and I lost my breath, my knees folding over as if the caps and joints had dissolved into a mush. Her tousled hair, hanging down till her waist in slithering waves, lent a bewitching quality to her appearance. Her soft brown eyes were looking at me with a hint of amusement and 'was that anticipation? God, she is absolutely stunning when she gets out of bed!' I wanted to lose myself in that dense forest of her mane. She waited for me to say something; her lips parted in a pout, making me want to love them. Her conical canines peaked through the gap when she smiled and I imagined running my tongue against their pointed tips. I placed a hand on the wall flanking her door, to prevent myself from toppling over.

'Can I have a glass of water please, Mrs Sharma?' I half gasped, half croaked to her.

'Wait here,' and she came back a few moments later with a steel glass in hand.

I drank the cool elixir in loud gulps and wiped my lips after handing over the empty glass back to her. 'Thank you. Why don't you come and play? Sharmajee forgot to bring the rackets and shuttle, so I bought them myself. Please play with me.'

Her eyes lit up and she threw a dazzling smile at me. 'Wait, I will be out in a moment.'

I trilled and looked around; her house was in a secluded spot with the sole neighbour being an old couple occupying an apartment across the street. The other houses were a good 100 metres and beyond.

Five minutes later, she emerged, her hair piled high in a bun, multiple pins and clips shining with the sun's reflection. Her supple frame was clad in a tightly wound sari which set my heart racing, as each of her curves stood out, as if she were wearing a figure-hugging dress. I promptly shooed away my brother to go complete his homework and 'leave the racket with Mrs Sharma, better call her Aunty. Now off you be. Tell Mother I will be late.'

And thus started our badminton games, we became badminton partners. My brother was consigned to the tram lines at best, at times he would not accompany me for the 'practice sessions'. To Mother, I would be, 'Sharma Aunty is a better player than Kaalu and I am learning a lot from her. Playing with her is improving my game and I am sure I will be able to make it to the school team this year.'

Meena had no game at all; she was not even a novice. But who was interested in the 'practices'. I was more into Meena. The desolation of Pratima's loss was finally finding an escape route and I had been successful in pushing her into a corner of my heart, whenever I was playing with Meena. In my efforts to woo her, I tried the antics of Jeetendra in *Humjoli*, where he badminton-danced to the tunes of '*Dhal Gaya Din, Ho Gayi Shaam*'. I imitated his mannerisms, sans the ensemble of his crotch hugging white trousers and black belt, to the extent that each of my shot was accompanied with a click of the tongue, to produce that '*tuk*' sound in the song.

The next day, after hearty chuckles at my clumsy impersonation of Jeetendra's sequences of shakes, twists, and jerks, she dangled an invitation: 'Why don't you come over to my house when he is not home?'

I retorted without thinking, 'I will be there in a few minutes.'

'I will make tea.'

I sprinted to my home, poured a bucket full of water while still wearing my shorts and T-shirt, peeled off the soggy garments and hung them on the wash line in our verandah, dumped talcum powder on my face and neck (away from Mother's eyes), pulled on a fresh pair of shirt and trousers and after a hurried exchange of—'Mummy, I am off for a walk'; '*take Kaalu with you*'; 'I can't, he is busy studying'—I was in front of her house in a jiffy, my heart swooning with nervous anticipation. Glancing around to ensure that no one was there to witness my entry into Sharmajee's house—it would erupt into a scandal of mammoth proportions, with Sharmajee's young wife being alone at home—I pushed on the door. It was ajar and I entered her house.

Her living room—or what could be termed as a living room since there were only two rooms, the other being her bedroom—was redolent with the familiar aroma of fried *pakoras*, spices, Brooke Bond tea, and an unfamiliar perfume. She had also spruced herself up in the short intervening period; she was a multitasking genius, having changed her attire as well as prepared the snacks and tea. She welcomed me in an elegantly draped purple sari, splashed with spidery yellow waves flowing down the length of the chiffon which moved this way and that with each delicate movement, a sleeveless golden blouse which dazzled the smooth fair skin of her shoulders and arms, her hair undone and flowing in silky threads down to her slim waist which was just visible through the sheer fabric of her sari that could barely conceal the pit of her navel; my fingers trembled with excitement as I imagined dipping my tips into that delicious dip in her taut belly. My nasal nerves discarded all other senses and just concentrated on enjoying the intoxicating aroma of the unfamiliar perfume and talcum powder emanating from her.

The jumbled folds of her sari at the waist, where it was cinched in, betrayed the hurried manner in which she had prepared herself in the fifteen minutes she had at her disposal. But the pains she had taken in sprucing herself for our tête-à-tête, including applying lip gloss and foundation on her cheeks, registered on my subconscious, which took to form as the evening aged and the tea cooled.

She walked up to me and said, 'Come Sanjay, sit down there,' pointing towards a bamboo settee; seemed to me like a lovers' couch, with just enough space for the two of us to snugly fit in, its curved frame and soft cushions meant for the two of us to be in a lovers' embrace. She broke into my fantasy and, after putting a latch on the door, sat next to me, maintaining a reluctant gap of six inches between us. I started getting the shakes, with her sitting so intimately close to me. Goose pimples popped and sprouted in delicious sequences all over my body and I shifted in my stance, my leg rubbing against her thigh. She was saying something but I was not there at all. I was somewhere else altogether. The room had lost its dimensions; there was nothing except Meena, saying things I could not comprehend. She handed me a cup, but I could not hold it, my hands shook visibly, spilling the contents and I placed it on the table. She sounded worried, and after an exclamatory remark, she held my hands. That touch brought me back to reality, the four walls emerging as if I was waking up from a dream and I realised that she was enquiring about my well-being. Nothing else made sense; I went by my instinct and lifted her hands up to my lips. 'They are so soft, so delicate, the skin so fair, the nails are so well groomed with a deep red polish on them.' She palmed my face and gazed deep into my eyes, with those soft brown eyes of hers. I saw the twin reflections of the tube light in her eyes and searched for my image in them. I leaned into her and kissed her forehead. I closed my eyes feeling my way down her face with sweeping motions of my burning lips, my nostrils flaring with the dormant desire of an adolescent heart bereft of love for so long, the love itself heating up my body, the tips of my fingers were numb as if dipped in icy crystals, singeing sensations were racing along my skin as if I would burst from the heat building up inside me. She let out delicious sighs and our breaths mingled in a sweet fragrance as I pulled her towards me. 'God! She feels so delicate, don't press her too hard you might crack a bone.' But I gave in to my desire when I closed my lips around her cherries and crushed her into me. We were locked in our embrace and kiss for a long time. She pulled my shirt out of the waist band of my trousers and ran her dainty fingers along my chest. The sweetest of sensations coursed through me as soothing tingles ran along my skin. The goosebumps did not abate, I breathed in short bursts and an ache mushroomed in my throat and in the area below my diaphragm.

The sensations lasted no more than a couple of minutes, but I was so immersed it felt like an eternity before we broke to catch our breaths. Suddenly, it seemed like she had come out of a trance. Her body went rigid as something made her stop herself and more significantly, to stop me from any further adventures. One hand on my chest, now outside the shirt, the other on my forehead, she pushed me away gently and pleaded with me, in a desperate whisper, to leave.

No badminton the next two days. Mother wondered about my 'practice sessions'. Brother would not play with me. I imagined I had upset her—to her I must have seemed like an uncouth groper, my first day alone with her and I had already started kissing her. She had only asked me over for a cup of tea, but was there not something more in her invitation, 'Come . . . when he is not home.' Was I stupid to read too much into it? Well, I had to find out. I could not keep still.

5

My English Lessons

Two days after our last badminton game, Sharmajee went away on a tour—he had mentioned it during his visit to our house the previous night. That evening, I picked up a notebook and announced to the house that I had to seek clarification in English subject and since Sharma Aunty was good in English, she would be able to explain verbs better to me. Mother agreed and off I went.

When I rang her bell, she let me in without a remark. I sat down on a chair and noticed, for the first time, the other occupants of the room. In addition to the usual furniture and an Allwyn refrigerator, there was a small shelf along a wall on which sat a few classics; *Wuthering Heights, Mother, War and Peace, 1984*, and some heavy stuff on spiritualism and psychology. She appeared to be a fan of Swami Vivekanand. I presumed that these were hers, as it was beyond her husband to have ever attained any mental ability to venture into such intellectual excursions, and I had not seen these books during my earlier visits to the house, when Sharmajee was a bachelor. The room looked tidy enough and had a fresh look to it.

She sat opposite me and I enquired if she would be able to explain transitive and two-place transitive words. She went into her bedroom and returned with a thick volume, which I recognised seeing on the table of our English teacher at school, MC Pandey Sir. She commenced her tedious explanations. By the time she was into noun phrases, prepositional phrases, direct and indirect objects, I had grown delightfully confused. I was more into her soft brown eyes and small button nose, than the examples she was illustrating, like 'the players gave their team mates high fives' and its variant 'the players gave high fives to their team mates.' I was more like, kiss me, kiss me, kiss me, please, please, please.

271

By the time she reached tritransitive and ambitransitive verbs, I was reliving those sensations I had experienced earlier. Somewhere in my befuddled brain I was also marvelling at her expertise in English, which was rivalled only by MC Pandey Sir. When she reached valency, my muddled mind failed in differentiating 'Does your dog bite?' from 'That cat bit him' from 'Can you bite me a piece of banana'; all this biting was getting on my nerves and before I knew it I had her index finger inside my mouth. An inspirational impulse had taken hold of me by then. The fountain pen she was holding had suddenly started to leak, smearing her slender forefinger in blue and I had the sudden urge to lick her finger clean—I imagined her as my Noelle Page and I became her Constantin from *The Other Side of Midnight*—and the connected episode had entered my fantasy world; I had to live my fantasy.

Soon her mouth was coated in blue as I kissed her with a hunger I had never felt before. There were blue streaks on her neck where I bit her and a blue circle in the dip of her neck where I sipped at a bead of perspiration, relishing the tangy, salty, inky taste. One thing led to the other and we discarded our torn clothes with 'the biting cats and dogs' and I carried her weightless body into her bedroom—she stitched the buttons on my shirt later and threw away the shredded vest. I did not lose my virginity at my first attempt. I was so excited, so nervous, so thrilled, so eager, so inexperienced, so out of control, so abrasive, so not knowing what to do, so generally useless in the act, that I spent myself and squirted all over her belly and thighs, well before the act. I hung my head in embarrassment as she pulled me down and kissed me softly. 'This is your first time. It happens. We will try again. Be calm. You are like a cat on a hot tin roof. Stop shaking like a leaf in a storm.'

When we did it the second (or first) time, I was lost to the world. All my senses were dulled, except that I was only aware of her; the way she moved, the way she gasped, the way she bit her lip, the way she sighed with absolute delight, the way her breaths quickened.

The sensation was divine.

I did not know much about sex, except what I had read in the pornographies we shared at school; the *Mastram* Hindi booklets sold at railway stations, bus stands and small roadside and pavement shops, which contained sex stories written in uncouth and vulgar Hindi language (they later made a movie titled with the same name, which premiered at the Mumbai Film Festival in October 2013, ahead of its theatrical release in

May 2014)—the books acquired a cult status amongst the sex-starved, small-town youths of the Eighties and Nineties. The other outlets we sought as adolescents, at the all-males environment of the Sainik School, were the Indian sex stories in *Human Digest*, with their highly erotic tales of lusty housewives, incestuous affairs, horny neighbours, voyeurs, lesbians, and other crazy fantasies. But what I enjoyed the most were the fantasies of women in *My Secret Garden* and *Forbidden Flowers*, written by one of the pioneers of feminist erotica, Nancy Friday, who argued, through her tales of eroticism, that women should get over the guilt and fear that wanting to reach orgasm made them Bad Girls, that the social norms which caricatured an ideal womanhood were outdated and too restrictive and they did not represent the true inner self of a woman, that openness about women's hidden lives would help free them to feel the enjoyment of being themselves, that it is healthier for both women and men to be equally open, participatory, and free to be accepted for who and what they are—these were the very sentiments that were after my own heart and in addition to enjoying the erotica, I marvelled at the hidden intent and message behind these stories. For visual gratification, we used to go to Bhowali at nights, absenting ourselves from our Houses when we were sure that the Hostel Superintendent was out of station, to watch X-rated movies at a seedy video parlour, which screened adult English movies for select audiences at a first floor room of a house, rented for the specific purpose of showing Hindi movies during the days and English movies at nights, with Wednesdays and Saturdays reserved for the *Blue Movies*—it did not come cheap at Rs 20 per show. The experience left us ecstatic and we secretly enjoyed the grunts and harrumphs, the thrusts and jerks, the spasms and pants, and the final squirts in *Deep Throat*, *Debbi Does Dallas* and such like titles.

But Meena was totally different. I expected to experience something similar to what I had felt while watching those characters in the movies, writhing and pushing into one another—but not this. With her it was not sex, but an art form. She had transformed the very act of copulation into a work of art—she was so delicate, so deliberate, and so sensuous that I never knew I had so many nerve points which could send me into thralls of ecstasy. Meena brought an innovative novelty in her lovemaking and exposed me for the fool that I was. I was enthralled. What I felt was similar to what Vishwamitra must have experienced after his dalliance with

Menaka—we had one thing in common though, our abstinence before the revelation; mine natural, his self-enforced.

Afterwards, as the world around me started taking shape once more, I noticed the rumpled sheets slithering in tendrils between our legs, the pillows pushed towards a corner in a haphazard pile, our torn clothes streaking in snaky lines from the living room to the bedroom door. We lay in each other's arms, our limbs entwined like writhing snakes in their throes of ecstasy, our combined sweat damping the sheets under our soaked bodies, her faced roiled in ecstatic delight, the yellow light of the sixty-watt Philips bulb lending a golden hue to her unblemished fair skin, the rickety Usha fan barely able to circulate the turgid air as it went on and on in its slow-moving circular rotations, emanating a squeaky noise as if rats were scratching against polished steel.

Then I noticed her lying beside me, her long strands of hair splayed luxuriously around her head, her nostrils still flaring, her panting mouth letting out shuddering gasps, and the first thought that struck me was, 'What if she becomes pregnant with my child?' I had disturbing visions of Sharmajee coming for his first sight of a pudgy, infant version of himself in his newborn, to be confronted with a visage of a strangely familiar likeliness of someone he knew, and suddenly the infant child's flattened, elongated cheekbones reminded him of me. To confirm his suspicions, he turned the child over and was greeted with an angry, red question mark on 'his' son's right bump. Realisation dawned on him in a rush of adult grievance. However improbable these likenesses of me to be found in her child, I couldn't shake off the feeling of discovery from our progeny. By now I was beside myself with worry, anxiety, and fear and I blurted out, 'Does Sharmajee use condoms?'

She was not expecting this as a pillow-talk topic. No woman would want to be reminded of her burden while sweet-talking with her paramour. And I must have struck a nerve somewhere, for her eyes darkened, her mouth curled into a sneer (till then I never knew that a sneer could make a face even more beautiful), her nostrils flared noisily, and she retorted harshly, 'You need to leave. It's late. He will be back home shortly.'

'Oh! I didn't realise it's so late (the clock showed it to be almost eight o'clock—I had spent close to two hours for my English tuition; how would I ever explain that to my parents?). Can I come again, say tomorrow?'

'As you wish' was her curt reply.

Later, as I was tying up my shoelaces and she was draping herself in her plain 'sleeping sari', she seemed to have lost whatever fervour was disturbing her earlier and implored me in a passionate tone: 'Sanjay, I want you to come here again . . . it was wonderful what we did today and I am extremely grateful to you. . .'

'My English is still weak and needs improvement. I am appearing for an essay writing competition when I return to school. Don't you worry, my parents will understand.'

'Okay, but we will have very less time. His shift ends by 8:10.'

'Oh, that's no cause for any anxiety. Haven't you noticed that his first stop after work is some seedy country liquor joint and my father's place for his tomato sauce and two pegs of rum?'

'Okay then. See you tomorrow.' With that, she gave me a hug and a peck on my cheek. When I tried to kiss her lips, she hesitantly declined by pushing me away and whispered, 'Go now.'

I explained to my parents that I had gone for a walk after forty minutes of tutorial with 'Sharma Auntee'. I smiled inwardly when I called her that, her face alight with orgasmic delight swimming across my eyes. I was filled with absolute joy and delight, at not only having lost my virginity (I could boast of that to my classmates at school, but could not relate to with whom), but also at having done it with the object of my desire and not at some seedy brothel with a professional, which is often the case with our twelfth class seniors who often boasted of it. Even though it was Meena who had derived pleasure from the experience rather than I giving it to her, I was particularly pleased to have given her satisfaction, which was in sheer contrast to those boasts of our seniors at school who only revelled in their own sensory delights. With a professional it is always a five minutes' job done in an unseemly hurry and they know how to shorten those 300 seconds into two minutes, especially with teenaged greenhorns from an all-males residential school whose sole exposure to such matters is giving hand-jobs to themselves, or to each other, in the school's toilets or under their blankets. Mine was not a five minutes' job. After that initial bungling, Meena had taken matters into her own hands and she had prolonged the experience for close to forty minutes. I was pleased with myself that I could hold on till that long, but it was all her doing. Since I had lost all my senses

I could not recollect all that she did in the process, but whatever it was, she was able to derive pleasure herself. The next time I decided to keep control of my senses to see how she went about it. With a fair amount of jealousy, loathing, and hatred, I imagined her doing the same with that buffoon of a husband of hers. No, she couldn't be doing that with him. She must be acting inert with him, cold as a slab of ice. I couldn't bear the thought any longer and shook my head off furiously, banishing the very thought of him from my imaginations. And sure enough, as his image faded from my mind, I heard the clattering, rickety, knocking sound of his ancient scooter outside our door. I entered our bedroom as Sharmajee entered the house for his tomato sauce gourmet fetish and two pegs of rum fix, back from his tour.

The remaining days of that vacation I spent many delightful evenings with her. Those few hours each day with Meena, all by myself, filled me with contentment, with a joie de vivre I had never experienced before, with an unexpected elation, with a sense of belonging. By the fifth day, I became obsessed with her—she remained in my thoughts all through the day, replacing Pratima progressively. I couldn't shake her off as the days passed, even when I was conversing with my parents or my brother; they even took to calling my condition as absentmindedness. I started forgetting my day-to-day chores. I once forgot to fetch the milk from the milkman and got two litres of mustard oil in its stead. Many a time Mother caught me with a book in my hand but staring at the wall, smiling to myself. She went on to complain to Father that I was going loony. When questioned about the incident, I muttered that I was mugging up Archimedes' principle and the law of buoyancy and as for the smile, well, I was imagining the naked Archimedes racing through the streets of Syracuse shouting 'Eureka, Eureka. . .' and I was thinking of his jostling and juggling bumps and his dangling willy as he went about his business.

Over those next few evenings, she opened her heart to me, telling me about her trials and tribulations in life. Later, I had always taken it as a proof of her acceptance of my presence in her life, that she had been so candid while recounting her life story.

She was born in an orthodox Brahmin family in Patna. Her father was a rich landlord whose farms were cultivated by his minions and serfs at a nearby village and the earnings from the agricultural produce had not only made him a millionaire, but his staunchly held beliefs had also earned him a healthy reputation of a devout, practicing Brahmin devoted to God and religious dogmas. Her house, a double-storey bungalow, rang of Hindi and Bhojpuri devotional songs all through the day, and prayers and sounds of bells emanated from the huge temple constructed in the courtyard of the building, the air redolent with the sandalwood aroma of constantly burning incense sticks. She was the third of five children born to the Shukla family and, even though she never felt privileged in the company of her three brothers and lone sister, she was never overly discriminated against.

Recalling Pratima's childhood miseries, I interrupted her and asked, 'How was it like living as a girl in a male-dominated environment? Was female infanticide prevalent? Were you ever forced to marry as a child?'

'Child marriage was rampant but I was never forced to accept that fate. Yes, female infanticide used to take place. It was more prevalent in the villages and small towns, including some cases which occurred from time to time in the state capital too. What was more common place was female feticide. Prenatal sex determination clinics were mushrooming and there were so many pliant doctors, greedy medical practitioners, misogynist midwives, even quacks, ojhas (exorcists), and hakims, who became partners in the gendercide and were ready to abort a foetus, if it was determined as a female. Since the enactment of the Medical Termination Pregnancy Act in 1971, abortion has not been considered illegal and people often used the excuse of ill health of the mother to get rid of the female foetus. Some fanatics were quite vocal about their real intentions and would tell the doctors that they did not want the child since she was a girl. I know of women who refused to have the child aborted and were subsequently drugged into unconsciousness and had their foetus removed surgically. I was amazed at many of the young wives who took immense pride in giving birth only to sons. In my childhood innocence, I used to wonder which would-be mother would ever want to abort her unborn child. But they were all party to it—the husbands, the wives, the mothers-in-law, the fathers-in-law, even the girls' parents.

'But my father must have given up the practice sometime before I was born, as by the time I was conceived, the doctors had warned him that due to the multiple abortions, my mother had had to undergo in his relentless search for sons, any further pregnancies, if aborted, would be fatal for her. So he accepted his fate and had to bear the burden of two daughters with a son thrown in between. Mother finally took the vow of celibacy after my sister was born and Father accepted the reality that God was not too kind to him after all.'

'He was deeply religious. How could he have such a convoluted mindset with regards to girl-child? After all a child is a gift from God.' I asked. This was incredulous. I could understand Pratima's families misogyny but here was a devout, God-fearing Brahmin who, instead of accepting God's gifts, treated his wife as a receptacle of screaming, Y chromosome bearing male progenies. There was indeed so much to learn from this world.

'Since he is deeply religious, he sought justification and based his beliefs on our scriptures, which permit preference for sons. As per him, it is written that *Pitra Dosh* has to do with the debt of the son's ancestors up the paternal lineage. The mother and her ancestors never figure in determining the Karmic Debt of our forefathers. The rituals conducted to rid us of our ancestors' sins and mistakes are done by the sons. This preference for sons has found deep roots in our society, through our Holy Scriptures and Vedas, and the associated rituals will always remain perennial. I don't renounce the preference for sons, but to kill a girl-child or abort a foetus just because it has different chromosomes—that is criminal and should be punishable with death. Look at the ritual of only the son or a male descendant, lighting the pyre of a deceased. It establishes the primacy the son enjoys in each Hindu family? Why can't the daughter do it? Because the Garud Puran, one of the eighteen Mahapurans, insists that the eldest son should perform the last rites of the deceased.' She walked over to her stack of books lining one wall of her bedroom and pulled out a thin volume of Garud Puran in Hindi, with Sanskrit Hymns.

I continued where she let off, 'And Hindi movies glorify it—"*Mat Jaa Beta, Too Chala Gaya To Meri Chita Ko Agni Kaun Dega* (don't go son, if you go away who will light my funeral pyre)".'

She chuckled and showed me the passage in Garud Puran where Shri Krishna extols upon the greatness of a son to Garud, 'Sons and grandsons (son of son and not daughter's son) of the deceased should carry the mortal remains and with full rites light the funeral pyre.' 'What about the role of the daughter? Nothing. The daughter is meant to be 'given away', and even when she is unmarried or without a brother, tradition has still favoured a male relative, however distant, to perform the funeral rites, thus maintaining this key religious duty within the masculine domain, exclusively. See! Son, son, son . . . our religion permits it and fanatics convolute it and start killing their daughters. I am not saying our religion allows female infanticide, leave aside encourages it, but what will a man, who wants only sons, do, if his wife births girl after girl. He may shun her, take a second wife, or continue procreating with the existing one. At some point during his desperate search for sons, he will start disposing off his new born daughters, if he has not commenced the process with the first child already, because with no son he will not get *moksha* (liberation from the Karmic Cycle of death and re-birth) and his *Aatma* (soul) will wander for eternity in whatever realm they thrive in.'

(Even today, in the 'modern' twenty-first century, this condescension of daughters continues. When an ex-cabinet minister, Gopinath Munde, died on 3 June 2014 and his funeral pyre was lit by his daughter, Pankaja Munde, it had led to a huge controversy in certain dogmatic circles of our society).

'I will have my daughters do it when my time comes. I am confident that my *Aatma* will wait for you and find succour in your arms when you arrive in that realm,' I declared, a deep emotion building inside me. I looked at her huge stack of books placed in neat rows floor upwards, reaching up to head height, larger, thicker volumes at the base and the paperbacks on top. It ran the entire width of one wall of her room. I wanted to change the topic, as I was not ready right then to venture further into a territory which reminded me of my vows and Pratima and her travails. Not now, maybe later.

'What about your education? I see these books lining your wall and outside in your living room—surely your husband is not this well learned. You seem to be well educated for a Bihari.'

'Don't you go stereotyping me?' She said in a feigned admonishing tone and poked a delicate elbow into my ribs; that was delicious. 'I agree Bihar has got a low literacy rate, particularly the female literacy is pathetic, to say the least. But that is true of the villages and small towns only. In the bigger towns and the capital city, girls are encouraged to go to school and be educated, up to a point. There are number of girls-only schools and some co-educational institutions, too, where girls can study up to classes 10 or 12. Some, with sheer perseverance or out of the benevolence of their fathers even go on to graduate from a college, with a degree in hand. It is an entrenched belief amongst the upper class families there that a literate girl will get a good husband. Why that pensive smile on your face?'

'I was just wondering at the irony of people of two different societies having such divergent viewpoints with respect to bringing up their daughters. It is such a revelation. I used to know a girl whose parents did not allow her to go to school because they feared that if she got educated she would remain a spinster because she would then become more educated than the eligible bachelors available in their social group. None of her relatives ever allowed their daughters to study and married them off at 12 years of age, and her father did not want to start a trend that would brand him an outcaste. But she had her brothers as her saviours. They fought with their parents for her just rights and disowned their father recently. How about your brothers? Did they ever stand up for you? I don't have a sister so I don't know how brothers behave with their female siblings, other than what I just told you about Pratima.' I had no intention of saying her name, not just yet in the infancy of our relationship, but it came out with the flow.

'I would like to know more about this Pratima of yours and the other girls in your life.' I blushed and hid my face inside her breasts to prevent her noticing my cheeks having gone red. Was that a note of envy in her voice? I was not sure. 'My brothers and we sisters lived in our own different worlds. So much so that sometimes I used to wonder whether we were products from the same seed and had shared the same womb. They are a pampered lot, especially the youngest one, since he had come after me and had displaced the desolation that had descended upon our house from the day I was detected as a girl in a sonographic image of me as a 14-week-old foetus. They flitted in and out of the house at odd hours, always in a hurry, always embarking on some mischievous adventure; their friends were uncouth and threw vulgar comments at girls—one of them had even groped my sister when she was just 9. My male siblings lost their purpose in life in their teens due to the numerous occasions Father shrugged off their transgressions and overlooked their peccadilloes, and Mother spoiled them by piling extreme love and affection upon them. The manner in which Father never bothered whether they were studying at all for their exams, the way Mother never told Father that they were routinely failing in their exams and the visits Mother used to go on after each final exam to bribe the school officials to promote them to the next class; all these made them take their highly privileged lives for granted. However, they were dead-ended when they appeared for the board exams, the youngest one could not even reach there. To make the other two pass the tenth class exams Mother would have had to persuade Father to sell his entire property. I often used to rue at the irony and wonder, 'What is it with my parents that instead of telling their sons to work hard and study, they are willing to waste money to bribe lowly clerks to ensure that their prides of heart remained literate ignoramus.' Only the eldest passed the tenth board exams but flunked the twelfth exams, after which he took up a job as a security guard in some bank at Patna. He is in his thirties and my father is finding it extremely difficult to get a suitable bride for him. None of his upper caste, rich acquaintances would ever deign to give their daughter to a security guard and Father would never agree to stoop to levels where he would have to accept a daughter-in-law from a family which is lower in status; that one will die a bachelor, though not a celibate as he has had a very active libido since he was 13 and has despoiled numerous maids and other low caste women who visit our house on some errand or other, married and unmarried, all kinds, eunuchs even, and has deflowered number of young daughters of the low-caste flunkeys working our lands in the village; no preference for any particular age, even 5-year-olds have been his objects of desire and he has at times dallied with 60-year-old widows and spinsters. I have lost count of the number of brothels he has frequented over the years. It's a miracle that he has not contacted some venereal disease yet; the day is not far.'

I was chuckling at the brashness with which she had described her brother's carnal proclivities and the choice of words used by her. 'How do you know so much about his libidinous ways?'

She too chortled and said, 'I have my ways. Since the time it became apparent to me, as a 9-year-old, that my parents had placed my brothers atop a high pedestal they did not deserve, I have been keeping an eye on them—my school and college friends, their brothers, their brothers' friends, local gossipers at the general store and such like have been my sources for all the shenanigans my brothers have been indulging in. Plus, on so many occasions, I have flicked money off my parents to pay for the abortion of unwanted children planted by my eldest brother into the wombs of unmarried girls of our underlings in the village; I had felt so miserable when a poor labourer had begged me for money to help him abort the foetus in his young daughter's belly, poor girl, she had just reached puberty and was so flimsy—I had carried her in my arms to the hospital for the abortion, as if she were a toddler; thank God she survived. I suspect he has even poked his dick into some young boys too.'

'Where do you breed such rascals?' I immediately bit my tongue as I had been drawn in by her candour and realised that I may have overstepped my limits by calling her brother by the moniker he deserved.

She did not seem to mind my outburst or must have agreed with my assessment, for she replied to my question in a neutral, wry tone. 'My parents' house is a breeding ground and a clearing house for such specimen Gabbar Singh would have been proud of and would have readily recruited into his gang of dacoits. Rascal is too soft a term to describe all three of them. If Salim-Javed had known about them, they would have replaced that iconic dialogue with, "Bete *So Jaa, So Jaa Nahin Toh Ghanshyam Aa Jaaega*," (in a perfect intonation of Amjad Khan's tone from the movie *Sholay*), Ghanshyam is my younger brother. All of them are demons in human form.

'But you should hear my father singing paeans, extolling their "virtues" (she crooked her forefingers and flipped them up and down, making two inverted commas in the air). According to him, my eldest brother is learning the ropes right from the roots upwards as he wants to open a security agency after sometime. Security agency my ass, he can barely manage to keep his job due to his incapability in comprehending the very concept of decent human behaviour—the oaf almost lost his job last year for fondling an 8-year-old son of a bank employee.

'Father's second son is in the Army: "He is a true patriot, son of the soil, a brave soldier. You will see, one day he will win a gallantry award"— Father goes on and on, endlessly, in similar vein. Truth be told, my second brother gave 50,000 rupees, surreptitiously slipped to him by Mother, to bribe a lowly clerk in the Army Recruiting Office at Patna to join the Army as a barber, since he was not able to pass any of the tests for a soldier. So he entered the Army to cut hair in his *paltan* (battalion). In reality, this I found out from a colleague of his who is from our village, since he couldn't wield a pair of scissors properly and lopped an earlobe of a fellow soldier, he has been handed a pan—imagine the scion of a rich, Brahmin landlord clearing night soil of his colleagues. But in Father's eyes he is a true *Fauji* (soldier) guarding the nation's frontiers with a rifle in his hand and fire in his eyes, whereas, the lone weapon he has ever handled is a broom and the only fire he has ever encountered is the one his colleagues light under him, in condescending jest, when he squats to shit. Sins of our past do visit us. Fortunately, for him, Father had been able to hoodwink a poor sod in faraway Ballia in Uttar Pradesh, who works in Bombay, to give his daughter in marriage to this *Fauji* brother of mine; her clueless father was told that the *Fauji* is an officer in the Army and the poor fellow fell for it, even went to the extent of selling a parcel of land from his ancestral property to meet the excessively exorbitant demand of dowry from my father. The girl now lives a servant's life in the house. My mother disposed off the services of the maid and cook, who had diligently served us for so many years, the minute my sister-in-law entered her new home. She has lost all of her vivacity and weight in the past one year. I am not sure she will survive another year.'

'Doesn't her husband do anything for her?' I shuddered, imagining the sorry plight of the poor girl.

'He is in Jammu and Kashmir and visits home every six months or so. During those month-long visits, his sole interest in his wife awakens when the lights dim and she enters his room to submit to his demands for copulation—he virtually keeps her up all night, and her mother-in-law does not let her rest during the daytime. My brother doesn't even leave her be during her menses, taking her from behind to satiate his lust. Oh Sanjay! I fear for her life. She will die there. I was the only person in the house in whom she used to confide her secrets, narrate her woes, and cry her heart out. Now that I am here, what will become of her?'

I kissed her warmly and spied moist droplets in her eyes. She closed them and I placed my lips at one corner. A drop trickled and I sipped it, loving the tangy taste. She sniffled and squirmed to settle into my embrace and I closed my arms around her. We lay in silence for some time, listening to the 'ricket-ricket' of the meandering ceiling fan. Sweat was pouring from our bodies in the searing heat, the fan as good as absent—it was moving in mournful rotations as if grieving the death of a loved one. When she shifted and moved closer into my embrace, our conjoined skins gave off delightful squelching sounds, like a baby suckling from her mother. It felt heavenly hugging her wet body.

We separated after some time, with reluctant sighs, not able to bear the heat emanating from the other's body any longer. She had regained her composure and I asked, 'What about your youngest brother?'

She smiled a demure smile and I kissed her with a longing I had never felt before for anyone. 'God! She is bewitching.' Now that I had overcome the formality of our association, I couldn't get enough of her. An ache mushroomed in my belly and I looked deep into her eyes, searching for her soul.

'The most pampered one? His birth had been a cause for celebration never seen in my village for a long time. It had seemed as if the pall of doom spelled by my birth had been lifted by the arrival of this jet black baby with a crooked nose. He grew jutting, pointy teeth and to hide them he adopted a permanent petulant pout in his preteen years. Overall a ghastly visage, but he was indulged in so much as if he was the very avatar of *Kaamdev*. Drawn in by his coal black complexion, Father named him Ghanshyaam, treating his arrival as a blessing from Lord Krishna. He never reached tenth class and changed schools frequently, as his academic inadequacies and malicious conduct came to the notice of the principal of each school within days of his admission at a school and Mother did not have the balls (I chuckled at the pun) to bribe the principal—either their prices were sky-high or some of them were incorruptible, clean as a whistle. He remains an illiterate, uncouth youth with obscene manners, carrying a demon in his heart. When my 9-year-old sister had reported to Father that one of his friends had groped her, he had told Father that it had been her fault, that she should not have been so pretty, that had she not been his sister he would have done more than just touch her.'

'What was your father's reaction to that?' I asked unbelievingly, horror struck by such attitude of a brother.

'He had shrugged his shoulders and told my crying sister to not be seen when my brother's friends were at home. He did not even admonish his beloved son for his vulgar comment and that friend of his was at our home the very next day and for many days thereafter, his shady eyes always searching for my younger sister. Fortunately for her, I invariably kept her locked up inside our room and taught her how to fend off such predators.'

'Were you ever victimised by any of them?'

'Once, when I was 12. He got his just deserts. There was this brute who had tried to touch me. I grabbed his testicles and squeezed them in my fist with such ferocity that he had tears in his eyes. Then I bit his ear and tore a chunk off his lobe—the clot still carries half a lobe and is shameful to mention its real cause; "A rat ate it in my sleep," he lets it be known. I took to carrying a razor blade with me since then and warned my brothers that if any of their friends tried to act fresh with me, I would snip off his balls and feed them to the pigs. My sister used to carry a small penknife with her, till she got married about a year ago.'

I thought, 'She is a feisty one. She may look delicate but she has a fire inside her.' I wanted to immerse in her flame and drown in her heat. A desire arose within me to join her in her fights, to lend her support in her claims for justice. There was something in her manners that was contagious.

'What does your younger brother do now?'

'He is a loafer. Loiters around, lives on the largesse doled out by my parents, wastes his time with his equally notorious friends, eve teases colony girls, warms the prison cells off and on for minor transgresses, forces Father to buy him luxuries, like an imported Mercedes car, Rolex watches, alligator skin shoes. Why, he even tried to buy himself a role in a Bhojpuri movie— the casting director had kicked him out of his presence, openly repulsed by his overly made up black skin and blood red lips—God, that clown thought that red lips on his black face was a fashion statement; some well-wishers he has got.'

She chuckled and I happily joined her, relieved that she had overcome her bleak mood of some time ago. 'In his blind love and *putra moh* (love for son) for the youngest child my father has lost most of his ancestral property and has even gone in debt to moneylenders. If ever there was a perfect reincarnation of the blind emperor Dhrithrashtra (from *Mahabharat*), he is the one. You don't have to go far, just a look at my father and you will understand what compulsions let Dhrithrashtra overlook his villainous sons' demonic conduct in stripping their cousins' wife in open court.

'Enough of my indolent brothers and their shenanigans, and my parents' overindulgence. You are up and ready and I want more of you. Gosh! Did you ever go soft? You are such a delight,' and she climbed over me and moments later she sent me propelling into some exotic, sweat soaked heaven of her own making—sweat had never felt so divine.

6

Her Quest for Education

Over the balance of the vacation, we met often. Our dates always started with an erotic excursion where we would lose ourselves to our senses. We made frequent love during each date. Each of our lovemaking lasted twenty to forty minutes, as she would lessen the tempo whenever I neared ejaculation and in delightfully painful movements make me hold on till it became impossible for me and I would finally let go in spasms of heavenly ecstasy. She never groaned or grunted or 'Oh me God-ed', as they showed in the movies. Whenever she experienced orgasmic delights, she sighed with pleasure—I felt her sighs and each had a different quality to it; the way her breath left her mouth, the way her lips quivered, the way her breath entered my mouth, the way her tongue tasted, the way her eyes closed, the way her legs wrapped around me, the way her hands roamed my sheared head. There were soft sighs, hungry sighs, delighted sighs, hot sighs, surprised sighs, contented sighs, reluctant sighs, ecstatic sighs, and the quivering sssss-sighs when thousands of tiny electric jolts rocked her nerves. When she was engulfed by these unearthly sensations, she would clutch my head and pull me into her as if she wanted me to merge with her or arch her body and wrap her legs and arms around me, pushing herself into me as if she wanted to dissolve into me. For me it was a journey where reality merged with fantasy and I got lost in a world of exquisite sensations. Before her I did not even know that there were parts of my body that had nerve endings which when titillated would send me into ecstatic raptures. The humble nipple, about which I had read that it was the most useless organ of a male body, after the appendix, became my most treasured pleasure zone; her hard bites on those tiny protrusions of my chest sent me soaring into an exotic world. Her soft nibbles on my earlobes would generate such waves of delight that I refused to return to the real world from wherever I was transported to. And she taught me how to use my fingers and mouth to such great effect that I felt that their sole purpose in life was to stimulate her and send her into spasms of sighs and gasps.

As it turned out, the biggest problem for me was finding excuses for being away from my home for a prolonged duration of three to four hours every other evening, without arousing suspicion. My 'English lessons' lasted the next two sessions after which Father remarked one evening, when I was returning from my 'third lesson': 'You have had too many tuitions from that pretty tutor of yours. Kaalu is complaining that you have not been playing with him for some time, been busy with your English lessons. Stop these tuitions, your academic session has not yet started and you don't need to study much English in twelfth class. And you don't have to participate in any essay writing competition. I will speak to your teacher, Vikram Singh, and he will ensure that you pass the English tests. You have to concentrate more on passing your last chance for NDA entrance exams this December. And give Kaalu company, too.' That had got me worried. Not only because my 'tuitions' had been noticed with some disbelief and suspicion, but that I was being told to stop my ventures. I had to come up with some other justification for my long absences. Something Father had said in his short admonishment gave me a glimmer of hope, but for the world of me I could not recall what it was. I turned the matter over and over in my mind that night as I lay in my bed, my heart growing increasingly despondent at not being able to meet Meena henceforth. I drifted into a fitful sleep late into the night, letting off disappointing sighs. I woke up with a start, from a dream of Father restraining my naked body as the devilish Sharmajee, emerging from that first dream like a sceptre, carried away a screaming Meena shouting my name in pitiful wails, hanging from his flabby shoulders. I lifted my head and surveyed my surroundings fearfully, wondering whether Meena's name had escaped my lips. I heaved a sigh of relief when I noticed that my parents were not there. But where were they? In the eerie silence of the night, interrupted by Kaalu's soft snores and his chapping lips as he mumbled some oddity in his sleep, I heard soft whispers from the adjoining living room. I smiled at the possibility and. . .

It struck me—that faint chance I had been mulling over, before sleep engulfed me. Father had said to concentrate on my NDA entrance exam, to be held in that December. Yes, that is what I would do. I had to get out of my gloom. I still felt down whenever I was home, the twin memories of Pratima's permanent loss and Meena's temporary absence not letting me shake off the blues. In the calm of the night I worked out the plan and deliberated upon how I was going to approach my father, laying it out in front of him.

The next evening, after playing the dictated cricket game with my brother, I walked up to Father and told him that I could not concentrate on my preparations for the NDA entrance exams within the confines of our small house and needed to go on long walks to clear my mind and in the process would sit under a lamp post or some other suitable place and study the Guide Book.

'What is wrong with our house? Find a suitable corner and study.' He appeared suspicious and I couldn't shake off the incredulity with which he studied my face.

I explained that the frequent bickering of Kaalu was affecting my nerves—and he wailed in pain again to prove my point; I had deliberately hit his ankle with the leather cricket ball during our evening cricket game to make him complain to our parents, thus facilitating me in executing my plan. Also, Sharmajee talked and belched and farted and harrumphed so loudly during his nocturnal visits; how could I be expected to concentrate amidst such a chaotic environment? Mother always had incessant demands to fetch something or the other from the local grocery store, for which I was like her favourite lackey. To escape all these disturbances and hurdles for my future I needed to be out of the house in the evenings for three to four hours at a stretch.

Then I threw in the punch line: 'Don't you want me to have a bright future? This is an ideal time for me to study. When I rejoin school I will get too busy with the twelfth-class syllabus. Since the NDA entrance exam is based on the eleventh class syllabus, I have to brush up on that, too. I have identified my weaknesses in the last couple of days and I promise you that I will sharpen my rough edges and pass the exam this time.'

That gave him a cheer and he agreed with my proposal.

The next part of my scheme was easy—Sharmajee. His work hours were till late in the evening, well after the sun bade goodbyes to us mortals, and his first stopover after work and an occasional visit to the seedy country liquor joint, was to our house, for his tomato-sauce-dipped-in-onion-and-garlic gourmet fetish and two pegs of rum fix. I had already laid out to Meena that she should not keep any bottle of tomato sauce in her house: 'Say that you are allergic to the smell of its preservatives and the garlic seasoning included in it, and that the very sight of its colour brings to your mind dreadful visions of a close friend of yours bleeding after an accident, as she lay shedding her lifeblood with a similar consistency of the tomato sauce, and that its mere presence in your house will urge you to throw up and you are afraid that one of these days you will discharge your entire lunch and evening snacks all over him.' After a pause to allow her chortles to subside, I had added, 'I hope you don't like tomato sauce. You will have to tone that down a bit.'

When I was with her I had to merely keep my ears open for the throaty clitter-clatter of his ancient Lambaretta scooter, indicating his arrival; the new Priya scooter he had got in dowry had been sold off by him for the cash it had fetched.

The final point in my agenda was entry into her house. I couldn't enter from the front; it was in direct line of sight from my house and after my last visit I had seen a flicker of reflection in the curtains of a window of the house occupied by the old couple living across the street from her house, while I was leaving her.

I picked up the MBD Guide Book for the NDA entrance exam and after bidding solemn goodbyes to my parents, promising them that I would be back in four to five hours, after walking up to Panchsheel Enclave and studying in a secluded corner at the park there, I went to the rear of her house to reconnoiter. Her backyard had a thick copse with a banyan tree nestling somewhere amidst the large population of mango trees. Birds of all varieties spoke in various tones and languages to their paramours, singing melodious love songs—I soaked in the warbles of the red-winged bush lark, the chatter of the oriental magpie-robin, the pipes of the nightingales, the coos of the Indian cuckoos, the whistles of the Indian ringneck parrots, the croaks of the ravens, the twitters of the sparrows—mothers dropped elixir from their beaks into the gaping mouths of their newborn chirping chicks, bees hummed soft musical tunes as they returned to their hanging honeycombed lairs after a day of feasting on the sweet nectars of the flowers of Shaktinagar, crickets creaked as they hopped and leaped in their eternal search for the choicest morsels amongst the fallen leaves and seeds, ferrets scurried around chasing each other in their ferrety version of 'Catch Me If You Can', frogs ribbited and gibbeted as they jumped all over running after the hopping and leaping crickets, their tongues flashing in and out for a delicious crunchy meal, grasshoppers chirped in fright and launched themselves vertically into the air to avoid the dangerous sticky tongues of the amphibians and turning into a green feast themselves, rats eeked in alarm imagining the shifting shadows to be the slithering form of their perennial nemesis, squirrels scooted up the trees, their bushy tails quivering in excitement as they returned to their dwellings inside the tree trunks to celebrate another day of survival, with their loved ones.

Amidst this musical cacophony and delightful sightings, I reached the rear wall of her house and looked around. The wall was well concealed by the dense foliage of the grove all around and I did not suspect that anyone would be able to observe me as I scaled it to meet my inamorata in secret. Even if a casual observer did happen to see me atop the wall, which was six and a half feet high, I was safe in the knowledge that he would assume me to be a thief breaking into a house which was not his and with the 'damned if I care (*Sannu Kee*)' attitude, which pervades all Indians, he won't even bother to investigate further or report the matter to the authorities. At least one enduring Indian quality of my countrymen was in my favour. A country's inhabitants, who revere a prince, giving him the status of God and for whom they had coined the epithet *Maryada Purushottam* (One Who Follows Rules Ideally) for his virtues and generosity, do not think twice for their fellow humans. Well, *Sannu Kee*. With that shrug I propelled myself up and scaled over the wall, slithering onto the top and down into her open-to-sky verandah. I spied a shadow flit into the kitchen and a moment later she emerged into the verandah. Taking up a fencer's stance, she held a long, narrow, steely knife pointing towards me like a sword, its pointy end glinting as the sun's rays shot off it and veered into thousands of invisible reflections. She looked delicious in her warrior's posture; head held high, chin jutting out, her tiny nostrils flaring, her eyes breathing fire, her hair fanning behind her as if acting as her shield, her sideward pose making me notice with sheer delight the up and down movements of her round chest, her hand shaking with fury, making the knife's sharp tip draw concentric circles in the air. 'God! She is amazing. Instead of me acting as her saviour she will willingly take on the role and be my guardian angel and will definitely beat me to it. That fire in her eyes—I want to burn in it and be consumed by her desire.'

The effect lasted a few seconds and her face glowed when she instantly recognised me in the smeared mess I had become from borrowing the powder out of the whitewashed wall, while I had slithered up and down the wall and in the process had coated myself in white.

'You scoundrel! What took you so long?' She threw away the knife in a clatter of steel and mosaic floor, hitched her sari and petticoat up to her thighs, ran, leapt into my waiting arms, straddling my waist in a desperate grip of her legs, and thrust her tongue into my mouth. It moved around, flitted in and out as if it was the blind hand of a mountaineer groping for purchase from below an overhang. Her breath, redolent with the taste of milky Brooke Bond tea and glucose biscuit, was too appetising to resist and I drank it in thirsty gulps. I savoured each poke of her tongue's thrust and caught it with my teeth as she pulled her sari out of the drawstring of her petticoat and flung the five-yard length of cotton fabric behind her. It landed on the floor in a graceful, flowing, billowing motion, settling down in waves of red, orange, and green. As she undid her petticoat to lift it over her head, I unhooked my trousers and pushed my V-Brief and pants down. She descended on me with a hot sigh and I braced my back against the wall, unmindful of the white lime rubbing into my pristine, angry-red-question-mark blotted skin.

Ten minutes later I carried her into her bedroom and lay my head on her stomach.

'Why did you come in this way?' she asked, running her fingers in my hair, their tips futilely searching for a strand to hold on to in my closely cropped head, as she sat propped up on a set of pillows.

I told her about Father's assumptions. 'He called you "that pretty tutor of yours". My heart had stopped as I thought that he had become suspicious.' She shot me a worried look when I told her that he had forbidden me from any further English tuition. When I came to my dream, my sudden waking up in the middle of the night, my parents' absence and their muted, walled-in whispers emanating from the living room, she exclaimed, 'Eeeeesh! Were you spying on your parents?'

'I was not spying on them. I had woken up from a nightmare where your husband. . .'

'Don't call him that, not in my house, never in my presence. Try avoiding talk of him. Even then call him as "he" or "him". It doesn't seem nice.'

'Okay, my sweetheart. I had woken up from a nightmare where my Father was holding me back from rescuing you as that devilish "he" was carrying you away and you were screaming for my help, and suddenly I found the room empty except for the silent snores and chapping sounds of my brother. I was wondering where my parents had gone when I heard these murmurs from the other room. Anyway, I did not give much thought to it and concentrated on how I was going to convince my father to let me be absent for three to four hours every other evening.'

I told her about my conversation with Father that evening, my minimum worry of 'him' ever finding out about us, my apprehensions of entering her house through the front door, and the welcoming tunes and delightful sights of nature in the copse her house backed into.

After a thought I said, 'You know when I saw my parents early in the morning, going about their morning routine, I felt something akin to pity for them. Our house is an exact replica of yours, very small for all four of us and they have to allow us to sleep with them, since we can't afford more than one desert cooler. They have to have their private moments. So they remain awake till both of us knock off cold, deep in our slumber and in the dead of the night they have to slip away to the other room and lie on the floor. No wonder Mother enjoys her afternoon siestas. Father must be making up for his lost sleep at his office or being an ex-Army man he could afford to do with lesser hours of rest. What about your parents? Didn't you ever notice them . . . you know?'

'My sister and I had a separate room for ourselves and before my mother took her vow of celibacy I was too small to notice anything. I think my mother took the pledge because she was afraid that if she became pregnant again and the child turned out to be a girl, my father would dispose off her child, since aborting the foetus would have killed her, too. By then rumours had been floating around about rampant incidences of female infanticide in the adjoining villages and she did not want to have a child who would be killed at birth.'

'Why did they not think of contraception?'

'In one of her rare candid moments, some eight years ago, I had asked her about pregnancy and how it happens, in a daughter-mother chat. She had then confessed, after prolonged, discreet questioning on my part, full of intentional double entendres, that my father had never been keen on using contraceptives and pills or any other means on her part would have been fatal. But like all men in my family, he has a keener libido. After my mother's bed turned cold, he started seeking outlets in the streets. His brothel visits commenced and somewhere down the line he started keeping a mistress—a dark hued, ugly, fat widow of one of our flunkies who was killed in a freak accident. I have often thought of the possibility that, though she is not much to look at, he must have set his eyes upon her when her husband was still alive and would have had him killed to enjoy the fruits of his plump wife all by himself. After her mandatory grieving period he had had her shifted to a two-room apartment he had procured at the other end of the city. He started spending entire nights and sometimes days away from home and Mother got suspicious.'

'How do you know so much about such affairs?'

'I have my sources. Plus Mother had erupted like Mount St Helens when, after hiring a private detective to confirm her suspicions about his frequent long absences, she had confronted Father with explicit photographs and burst into a tirade I had never heard before in my life. When she is in that mood even the soundproofed walls of the Cabinet War Rooms at the Imperial War Museum in London wouldn't have been able to restrain the flow of her sound waves and confine them within their walls. The whole house and many adjoining houses had reverberated with her high-pitched screams as she berated Father for keeping a keep. I had never seen him so subdued and ashamed of himself. She had warned him that if he ever had a mistress again, she would kill her and herself. He had to immediately throw that widow out and she added in good measure that he could dip his—she had used that vulgar Hindi term which is also the surname of that Austrian Formula One driver Niki—into whichever prostitute or call girl he took a fancy to, he could even do it with eunuchs and boys for all she cared, but he could not spend one night out of the house. She even stipulated a time: "You will be back home by twelve o'clock from whichever dirty hole you had poked it in or else you will find my dead body in our bedroom, hanging from the ceiling." My father, since then, visits brothels like my elder brother. They must have shared the same woman a number of occasions, though separately, may be immediately after the other had left. Imagine my fathers' and brother's sperms, floating in mutual harmony inside some miserable whore, trying to show-off to each other who is the better specimen—the creator or the creation. I get such a thrill out of thinking that one of these days I am going to ask you to write an anonymous letter and post it from your school, suggesting to them to organise a threesome—father and son humping the same woman at the same time and spraying inside her. I will pay the woman a king's ransom to get pregnant. I want to see whose features the child will inherit, whose sperm was faster and better during the fertilisation: father's or son's.'

'Why are you so caustic while talking about him? Your brothers I can understand, they are the very dregs of humanity and deserve no kind word. But why are you so sore with your father? After all he allowed you to live and provided for your education.'

'Oh Sanjay! You don't know him. He is too steeped in his convoluted, corrupt orthodoxy and is not responsive to any reasoning. He allowed me to live because Mother wouldn't have survived another abortion and she definitely would not have allowed him to kill me as an infant. She is the only member of the family before whom he cowers like a blundering, bumbling child. But for both of us, his daughters, he had laid down conditions; we would both be allowed education in a Hindi medium government girls' school till class 10 so that we could fetch one of the sons of his acquaintances as a husband, who would have a steady government job or be an heir to a businessman father, who would inherit the shop or whatever other enterprise. I latched on to his fixation of a suitable husband for me. After wasting seven years in the government school I was becoming increasingly frustrated. I had discovered a natural talent for English in me as an 8-year-old and the environment at the school was stunting my growth. I wanted to converse in English to improve my vocabulary, but none of the other students nor the teachers, not even the principal, could speak a complete sentence—they all had this heavy Bihari accent and would muddle and fuddle their verbs. I wanted to study at Mount Carmel High School.

'So like you, what you did today, I chalked out a strategy using the wife of the DC (District Collector) as my prop. After passing my class 5 exams, I told Father that the DC's wife spoke such *Farraataa* (fast and unhesitatingly) English and that she was so well educated because she had attended an English medium school. She was a graduate too. I impressed upon him that if I studied in an English medium school I could also hit a jackpot and get him an IAS (Indian Administrative Service, the most sought after government department job in India in the Eighties and Nineties) son-in-law. He would then become the talk of the town and would wield tremendous influence amongst his friends and relatives. Piling on the sugar icing, I further added that if my future husband got a posting at Patna, Father would be exalted to an emperor's status. I said, 'you will be the esteemed father-in-law of one of the most powerful and prestigious men in the district. You will be the pride of Patna. All your acquaintances will bow before you, seek your blessings, whisper requests beseeching you to put in a word for favours from your son-in-law. Father, imagine strangers on the streets approaching you and touching your feet as you walked around, doling out untold benefits to your minions. You could get your grains sold at the highest price, you could hoard your farm produce to sell them later at whatever price you wished to fix, and no one—not the police, not the cooperative—would ever have the nerve to even touch you. You will be as powerful as the DC himself.'

'I could see my reflection in the sudden gleam of his eyes. He was literally shining with the glow of false pride. He had leaned back in the sofa and closed his eyes. I saw his daydream as if I was sitting inside his head— Shri Bindeshwar Shukla, his head held high as if someone had stuck a rod down his throat; his chest puffed up as if his spine had suddenly acquired a convex curve; his spotless white kurta and dhoti reflecting the sun's glare with such intensity that people did not even deign to look towards him; his new shining black sandals kicking up dust, leaving a cloud in his wake as he marched with the purpose of a rhinoceros bull approaching a cow in heat to copulate; one minion holding a gaudy parasol over his head, his hands shaking in fear, as my father barked instructions to hold the tiny umbrella straighter, lamenting that the sun was tanning his swarthy skin; another lackey carrying a tray piled high with juicy *paans* covered by a muslin cloth to prevent the fat flies buzzing around his sweat soaked face, from partaking a sip of the *paans'* juice; yet another flunkey lugging a huge, shiny, brass spittoon into which my father shot streams of betel juice from his red mouth, with the precision of a clumsy archer, the sprays landing all over the mouth of the spittoon and the forearms of the flunkey, the container's belly sloshing with the juices of the *paans* consumed earlier.

'He came back from his vision reluctantly and asked me, "What exactly do you want, child?"

'I told him that I wanted to study at Mount Carmel High School till class 12 and thereafter graduate from Patna University in English Literature. By then I would be ripe to be plucked by any IAS officer he selected for me, well qualified to match up to his standards and I also added that my qualification might also help in bringing down the prevailing dowry-market rate.

'He had looked at me with anxiety, but then the vision resurfaced with a violent surge and after smiling, as if in a dream, his eyes grew soft and he said, "We will see about graduation later. But you can study at that English medium school till class 12."

'I had touched his feet, and inspired by a rush of sibling affection, I tried to venture further; and to test his intention, with hesitant anticipation, I entered troubled waters and asked him to also consider my younger sister with similar favour.

'He had replied in a condescending tone: "Don't you go about meddling with my resolve child. Don't try to take advantage of my benevolence. Consider my kindness as a blessing. But that girl! She is not as brilliant as you. You have a great future ahead of you, so you will be an intermediate pass from an English-medium school. That one is too mediocre. Let her rot in that *govermint* school and I will find a suitable husband for her. Off you be before I change my mind about you."

'Thanking my stars, I left his presence in a hurry.'

'What happened when you passed your twelfth class exam?'

'Not so fast, Sanjay. This sweat is killing me. Let's make some more of it and drench these sheets with our water, before I resume. Come on, get up from my belly and stop sucking at my belly button. Don't you drink water?' She playfully hit my head, which was busy in her belly, my tongue inside her navel, with a pillow, chuckling all the time.

Thirty minutes later, she continued her narrative.

Similar sequences repeated like a pendulum over the next nine visits before my vacations were over, and over all future visits whenever I was home on vacations—make love immediately on arrival—no tearing of cloths like the first time, since she got fed up of stitching back my buttons and I got tired of explaining the rips on my shirt to my mother and the absent vest, of course—talk and listen, make love again, talk and listen, make love again, make and drink tea, take a bath, make love, talk and listen, make love again if there was still time, and finally bid tearful goodbyes as if we were not going to meet again. I had read somewhere that too frequent lovemaking within a short span of time drains out a man. But that may be true of those who indulge in rambunctious acts involving savage thrusts and throaty grunts and frequent jerks and heavy movements and scraping nails and tonguing tongues. Meena and I never moved an extra muscle than what was necessary. Our lovemaking was supremely sublime with soft touches, feathery caresses, delicate movements, desperate sighs, sweet kisses, tiny bites, delicious nibbles and lots and lots of delightful squelches, primarily due to the heat and the almost nonexistent ceiling fan. With her I could have gone on and on till eternity without breaking a sweat—the sweat metaphor may not be applicable during the severest of severe winters, but in summers, we swam in each other's perspiration, so intense was our lovemaking and so delicious the smell and taste of her sweat.

7

The Delicious Soreness Between the Legs

After her admission into the missionary school, she laid down two objectives for herself—one, to get her father to agree upon letting her sister, Teena, also study at her school and second, to get a graduate degree for herself. And she applied herself to these tasks with the gusto and zeal of a warrior.

The two sisters were never allowed out of the house, except for infrequent forays, when Meena would be tasked to fetch a *masala* or a vegetable or milk or curd or such like items required in the preparation of the dinner, from the corner grocery shop, since the servants would conveniently vanish at the most desperate moment—the sons were too privileged to be sent on such menial jobs and anyway, they were never home before it was time for dinner, engaged as they were in their mischief and roguery in the company of their equally malicious friends. Meena used these visits to the grocery shop to pick up tidbits about the shenanigans of her brothers and would note down their acts of transgressions, upon her return, in a diary she maintained for this purpose—'Rogues' Accounts', she had named the diary, which she kept under lock and key always, the key securely tied around her waist so that nobody could notice it under her salwar suit. The diary came in very handy later, when she had confronted her father after her twelfth class exams.

Since the sisters never ventured out of their house, except the trips to their school and back, they kept themselves busy with girlish games and studies. On occasions, one of their friends would visit her house, accompanied by their brothers or cousins, and would spend time with them. Birthdays of the daughters were occasions when only the sisters 'Happy Birthday-ed' each other, as none of the other family members would even bother to remember the occasion. If any of their friends dropped by with a wish and a gift, the parents would take the gift, thank them, and inform them that the birthday girl was not home. The gift was never delivered to the daughter but thrown out with the garbage. In complete contrast, the sons' birthdays, their name-days, anniversaries of their *mundan* ceremony and other such yearly recurrences of any particular joyous event in their respective lives, were celebrated as if it were a festival. On such occasions, the front facade of the house used to be decorated with strings of little lights, as done during Diwali, and inside the house tender lines of smoke and aroma of the incense sticks wafted amidst the chants of the priests brought in to perform *Havan* (holi ritual)—specially on the sons' birthdays—beseeching the blessings of the Almighty for long life and prosperity of the male progenies. A party in a five-star hotel in the evening was a must, which was attended by her father's acquaintances and their families, when the boys were small—the daughters were never allowed to go to these family parties. As the boys came of age, the venue of the parties shifted from hotels to farmhouses outside the city or hired-for-one-night apartments inside the capital, her father's decent friends and their docile wives were replaced by rowdy teenagers and adolescents, the soft drink bottles and vegetarian snacks were supplanted by tankards of beer, bottles of scotch, weeds of marijuana, smoky effluents of hashish and barbeques, the soft music at the hotels was forsaken in favour of loud renditions of Hindi film numbers and Bhojpuri songs with vulgar lyrics, performed by hired singers and scantily clad dancers. As the night wore on, residents from the city's brothels, with not a stitch on their plump bodies, would join the inebriated revellers to continue the party into the wee hours and even much later, sometimes till noon of the next day. Into the orgy, eunuchs and little boys and girls were also thrown in for those desiring variety or some who had different inclination.

'Where did the money come from for such debauchery?' I had asked in bewilderment, shocked that there are people existing who would put even the erstwhile Maharaja of Patiala to shame.

'Our Mother! Especially for the younger son, she would start pestering my father for cash days in advance, even going to his Munshi at the village to wheedle money from the coffers, where Father used to keep his extra cash. For her youngest son, she used to pay exorbitant amounts of money for the best apartment in the city, the most expensive imported scotch, the choicest of drugs, dancers with the skimpiest clothes and to top it all, the priciest call girl in Patna; for her Ghanshyaam. Not for him the dirty whores from the city's red light areas carrying all sorts of diseases between their legs. But the biggest irony is, he still had to do with the permanent residents of the brothels, he never had an opportunity to screw any of the high-society "clean" call girls.'

'What do you mean?' I asked impatiently, not wanting her to pause.

'One of my friends at school had an acquaintance who worked as a call girl to supplement the pension of her widowed mother—the extra cash was needed for her brother's education. When she was told to go to a birthday party and entertain the scion of a reputed family, she had insisted on seeing his photograph; she always did that—she could get her way, since she was very pretty and people were ready to pay thousands of rupees, just for an hour with her. The moment she saw my brother's photograph, she threw it into the dust bin and told her agent-cum-fixer to never again ask her to service such uncouth clients.'

'Is he so repulsive?' I did not have any clue about call girls and their network and this sounded interesting.

'He is the very incarnation of Krur Singh from *Chandrakanta*, if they ever convert Devaki Nandan Khatri's magnum opus into a movie or a TV serial—black as the blackest coal, lopsided nose, poking conical teeth, a menacing gleam leaping out of his eyes. That one has a mean streak too. The only time he got a real call girl, she ran away within minutes of being ushered into his room. It turned out he had placed some god-forsaken demand before her, which that girl had considered too demeaning and had thrown his toy at his face before making a dash for it. She had escaped from him by a whisker. Word spread and he has since been shunned by all call girls. But the money offered by my mother sent the agents salivating, so much like the dogs that they were. She was ready to pay up to 50,000 rupees for a night of some depraved fornication by her son. So, the girl who had treated the photograph and its owner as garbage, came up with a devious solution. "Get a whore from the slums, from amongst those who service the rickshaw pullers and the like, spruce her up, pay her 500 rupees—it will be more than what she makes in a month—and tell her that she would be paid after the client is satisfied. And double the rate to his mother promising her that you would be getting the best from Calcutta for her son. And for this salacious advice you can pay me half of what you get from that fat mother of this . . . this . . . whatever, he doesn't deserve a mention even. Lastly, no clients for me for the next one month." That is the day and Shuklaji's much pampered son gets a lowly prostitute at over a lakh rupees for his lavish parties. The usual going rate of these prostitutes from the slums is fifteen to twenty rupees from each lowly client which includes rickshaw-pullers, labourers, *bhangis*, and the like. I don't know, and have no intention of knowing, what he does with them, but I have heard that none of them ever goes back, once she has tasted his medicine. The only reason he gets fresh meat is because of the never-ending supply of cash from my mother. The last I heard, she had paid five lakh rupees for his twenty-third birthday orgy last year and the agency had to pay 50,000 rupees to arrange a "call girl" from a village who charges two rupees per customer—she is a beggar who sells her emaciated body as a side business to earn extra money. She would have come out battered from the experience but her future has been made secure. At least his debauchery is benefiting some poor souls. God does have his mysterious ways.

'Once he had told Mother that he wanted a young boy and a young girl to satiate his urges. She had enquired and found the boys and girls at our village unsuitable and the matter scandalous, if conducted locally. So she had sent him on a week's holiday to Bangkok, with two of his friends, their expenses too paid for by her, to indulge in whatever perversion they had planned. One night all three of them were raped with beer bottles, as they refused to honour their commitments to the Thai prostitutes. The very next day they limped back to India and had to be admitted in a hospital to have the pieces of broken glass removed from the walls of their asses.'

'How do you know so much about these affairs? And don't tell me you have your sources. I want to know. I would also like to know how a son can be so candid with his mother in such matters. Hell, I can't even ask for money from my mother to buy a condom, if I want to. Not that I would ever like to make love with you wearing that latex covering.'

She chuckled at my aversion for all things elastic covering my 'loveliness' and said, 'My mother knows that her sons have inherited only one enduring quality from their illustrious ancestors, going back many generations—their propensity to philander and whore around. She is fully aware that the men in her family have wandering libidos and unruly urges. While the older ones, including her husband, could find their pleasure houses, her much loved Ghanshyaam required delicate handling. Whenever he used to be rotting

302 | *Mamta Chaudhari*

in jail for molesting some hotshot's wife or daughter, she would berate him in front of the entire prison staff, telling him again and again that if he ever felt these urges he should let her know and she would arrange the "best" for him. I don't know what inspires them, but my parents have their own convoluted conviction when it comes to rearing their brood. When I came to know about the pact between my mother and her Ghanshyaam, I had requested a close friend at school, whose father is in the CBI (Central Bureau of Investigation, the country's premier domestic investigating agency), to get me a listening device, which I had installed in my parents' bedroom to eavesdrop on this strange mother-son duo's private tête-à-tête, the ideal feed for my "Rogues' Accounts". Plus they had got suspicious of. . .' She stopped in mid flow.

'Suspicious of what,' I said eagerly, fascinated by this tale of debauchery, of quirky parental responsibilities, of strange urges, of extreme villainy, of an over indulgent mother, of a lustful and indolent son. 'Suspicious of whom'—was what slipped into my mind as she stared blankly at her row of books. 'There is more to her than meets the eye.'

I broke into her reverie and leaning over, whispered into her ear, 'Say something.'

She snapped out of it and smiled wryly. 'Enough about my brother. Leave him be. All three of them are the very dregs of humanity, as you so forcefully said earlier. I will tell you about us, my sister and self. Two bosom friends you must have never heard of before.'

She had converted their virtual imprisonment into an opportunity. Desperate to get her sister educated in an English medium school, she initiated her English lessons as soon as she herself started attending Mount Carmel High School. The two of them would spend hours inside their locked room, studying. Meena tutored her sister, in addition to learning her own lessons. She was not brilliant, but she had one thing going for her, her perseverance and die-hard spirit. She rarely slept during the day and required merely six hours of rest during the night to rejuvenate, and she spent every waking minute either absorbed with her sister's tutoring or immersing herself in her own studies, except the times when her mother made her run errands or when she had to learn cooking from the family cook.

Her diligence bore fruit and she excelled in all her exams and also ensured that her sister came first in her exams at the mediocre Hindi-medium government school. Teena, though educated formally in Hindi medium, was familiar with the books of Mount Carmel High School, sixth class onwards, as Meena used her own books from two years back to teach her. In her tenth class, Teena had topped the Bihar School Examination Board. Meena in her turn topped the class 12 ICSE board exam in Bihar, a few days later.

The day after the results of her performance became public, her father had at last relaxed his stoic facade and distributed sweets in the colony—this was the first instance in the ancestry of the Shukla family that a child had topped an exam in the entire state. And the bonus of their younger daughter's performance too brought extreme delight to the girls' parents. Meena decided to seize the opportunity and availing of the exultant atmosphere at her home and in her exuberance, she had brought up her earlier request of further studies. Her father had dawdled and procrastinated, till she dangled the carrot of an IAS son-in-law again. By that time his circle of social friends had started diminishing and many of his earlier acquaintances had vanished, so much like a fart in the wind. He had started losing his land property to his younger son's profligacy, and as a consequence, his rich and prosperous friends had started avoiding him. None of the sons of his remaining friends were in any worthwhile position to be a suitable son-in-law. He appeared to be relenting when she brought up the case of her brothers. None of them would ever earn a graduate degree in their lives, what a shame for Shukla family. She was the bright star who would erase the disgrace her brothers' notoriety had earned for their family. She started narrating the numerous misdemeanours and crimes of her brothers, which she had committed to her memory from her 'Rogues' Accounts' the night before, and which had dealt a heavy blow to her father's reputation. With an IAS son-in-law, he could hold his head high again and not cringe with embarrassment for his security guard eldest son, his sweeper second son, and his felonious youngest son. Slowly, in a painful crawl, sense wormed into his rigidly obstinate brain and at last he relented to her taking an English Literature course from Patna University.

'For my sister I had a different strategy and an unexpected ally—my mother. A friend of mine, four classes senior to me at school, had recently got married to a dashing young Captain in the Army and after spending six months with him, she was full of praise for her life as an Army officer's wife. When she started singing the paeans, I took her to my mother's room, as I sensed a godsend opportunity. I also explained what I wanted her to say. In front of my mother, after exchanging the formal pleasantries, she commenced her spiel by saying how lucky she was to be married to an Army officer. Then she launched into her experiences on the excellence of Army life—the colourful dresses of the ladies, the respect officers gave to the wives of their comrades, the glitter of the mess and club functions, the charisma of the official functions, the chutzpah of her husband when he kissed her openly during a dance, the pleasures of having her husband all to herself, especially during Sundays when he would be home all day long, the long honeymoon of six months. She had continued, "The feeling of floating amongst the clouds never abated during our six months of togetherness. The sole drawback was the first night after his looooong absence of fifteen days on some desert training exercise. All these *Faujis* return from their sojourns hungry as a bear, so starved they become in their loneliness in the deserts. He had arrived home late at night and we didn't catch a wink all through the remaining part of the night. I spent the next few days with a delicious soreness between my legs. After the shock of that first night I became used to it, so much so that, now I look forward to his return after his absences. I am eagerly awaiting my return, as my poor Captain is all alone, pining for me. Look Aunty my heart is beating so fast, this anticipation will kill me one day. I can't wait a minute to be back with my hero spending our first night, after my own prolonged period of absence, without any sleep. Aunty, being an Army officer's wife, is the next best thing to Lord Indra's favourite *apsara* Rambha." She had always been too forthright. I had never told her to talk about her coital extravaganzas, but my mother seemed to enjoy my friend's brazenness, especially when she had mentioned that "delicious soreness" bit, my mother had smiled wistfully, as if struck by a long forgotten memory.

'After she had left, I cultivated my mother by extolling the virtues of an Army officer and the privileges her younger daughter would enjoy. She became my accomplice, as I used to continue my litany on an hourly basis, daily and just like the advertisements, which, with replay after replay, make a humble male underwear appear like a crotch enhancer, my repeated praises made her visualise her youngest child living the life of a princess.'

After her father had acquiesced to her request, Meena had put forth her sister's case. In this she was joined by her mother who knew a relative from her mother's side, whose youngest son was training at NDA. He was of similar caste, his family had huge acres of land near her hometown of Hazaribagh and they were very reasonable—they did not demand much dowry in their elder son's marriage, they had only asked five lakh rupees and a motorcycle for their doctor son. For the younger one, whose price had not been made public yet, their advertised requirement was a convent-educated girl, with a graduate degree. All this information had been gleaned by Meena and told to her mother to strengthen her case.

Here Meena had picked up the refrain: 'I appealed to him, "Father, he is the ideal choice for Teena. In six years he will emerge in the marriage market as the most eligible bachelor. In that period our Teena would have also completed her graduation. You will be the father-in-law of two illustrious sons-in-law—an IAS officer and an Army officer. All the sins of your past will be washed away in the glory of reacquired prominence. You will regain your earlier exalted status. Your sons' misdeeds will be eclipsed by your daughters' accomplishments through marriage. All those friends who had forsaken you in such terrible hurry will come scurrying back, begging you for accepting them again in your circle. All we have to do is get Teena into Mount Carmel High School and two years later she can join me at Patna University."'

Her father had taken one full week to mull over it. In that one week, the Captain's wife came every day, to sing praises of the Army life and eulogise about her good fortune to have been able to grab such a wonderful husband. One day Meena had her brag about her life having had taken a turn for the better, in front of her father, and how her own father was the toast of his social circle, earning respect from all and sundry; even strangers touched his feet and smeared their foreheads with the dust under his feet. Meena's father had announced that very evening that he would be going to Mount Carmel High School the next day for admission of Teena in that school. And she better do well there if she wanted to be a graduate. He also asked his wife to keep a close watch on that NDA boys' parents—'No need to approach them now. We shouldn't appear too eager. Some people get put off by that. I will go with our proposal when the time is ripe.'

'And that's how I came to earn a graduate degree a year ago and my sister got her Army man and is completing her graduation from Hazaribagh. That was my life. I would like to know about you when we meet next. All of this has left me drained. Come on fill me up before you leave,' and she pulled me on top of her.

'And what about your IAS man?' I wanted to ask, but was overwhelmed by otherworldly sensations as she started sliding her tongue around my new-found nipples.

8

The Miracle

It took long in its coming, but the miracle happened in the third week of my vacation.

My initial attraction for Meena had more to do with my physical desires than the need of any emotional anchor. Till I had met Meena, the jubilation I had experienced in that cave with Pratima, one and half years back, was still fresh in my mind. Most of the intervening period back at school I had spent long brooding hours lying down in that tiny, rock-enclosed space, reliving the intimacy I had shared with Pratima, letting out desperate, sorrowful sighs, tears streaming down the corners of my eyes in long twin lines, the drops accumulating on the black rock surface both sides of my head, failing to seep into the ground to disappear, the rock refusing to yield to their desperate pleas to merge with the surface. When I used to get up to leave the cave, the tears would remain there on the ground, as two small dark pools separated by the span of my head, their surfaces glistening with the sorrow of witnessing the dying sun. Everything withered when the sun went down—the cave, the pools of tears, the place where Pratima had lain on top of me, the corner where she had sat leaning her back into me and had promised that one year later we would renew our love and salvage my heart and my soul.

When I had come on vacation in that summer of '86 I carried with me vivid memories of the cave and Pratima was still occupying my heart like a wound that refused to heal. Seeing Meena and her voluptuous body had awakened dormant desires deep within me. All my efforts to woo her, after that first meeting at our house, had been in an attempt to meet those desires. After making love with her for the first time, my need multiplied manifold and it felt as if I just wanted to keep on making love, whenever I was with her. Whenever I was not with her, Pratima took hold of me and would never let go. She was there like a permanent ache eating my insides, draining me of all emotions. The sheer contrast between the purity of my platonic love for Pratima and the purely physical nature of my relationship with Meena, at times baffled me and kept my heart from getting too deeply involved with Meena. I intended to keep her on the surface as a surreal reality. And maybe in some deep recess of my heart, somewhere, there was a ghost of a chance of reconciliation with Pratima and renewal of our love affair. Moreover, there was the fear of the social stigma of an illicit relationship with a married woman.

I had never considered Meena as my salvation when I commenced on this journey of ecstatic delights. She was just for my physical needs and not to mend my shattered heart. I did not need her shoulder to cry on. But adolescent hearts can be fickle, especially when a grown-up, exquisitely beautiful, matured woman gives her all to you.

From the beginning she had this look with which she would regard me thoughtfully in her pensive moods—it was a delightful mix of gratitude, adoration, and devotion. That look gave me the confidence to overcome my own guilty feelings. In later years, when her adoration turned into love and we would contemplate a future in which we were together forever, that look gave me the strength and sense of purpose to take on the world, come what may.

Meena grew on me. Over a period of two weeks she entered my heart and opened it up, petal by slender petal, till it blossomed like a lotus flower and somewhere down the line, at some point, unaware to my senses, she sat on it, occupying centre stage, consigning Pratima to some remote corner, where it became extremely difficult for me to access her and she became a distant memory. In silent and slow procession, Pratima's memories started fading, her beautiful face invariably dissolving, changing into that last dreadful vision of the amber door.

It was miraculous how I got over my Pratima fixation and when Meena started occupying that space in my heart reserved for Pratima, I knew that it was time to confess my love for her. I did not want to delay in letting Meena know about my true feelings, once bitten twice shy.

In addition to hearing to her struggles through her life, I also learned to listen to the real Meena. Through her narration she laid bare her innermost thoughts, the values she cherished, the secret force that drove her, her views on the society at large, and gave me a peek into the real Meena, as the days went by.

Besides her external charm, she had many qualities which I found irresistibly alluring—her intellect, her faith in herself, her cherished principles, and the way she spoke my name.

She was very sharp and intelligent. On my second visit, when she went to her kitchen to make coffee after our cycle of making love, followed by talk and listen, further followed by making love, I walked up to the stack of books piled in neat columns, covering one wall of her bedroom, floor till head high. The books carried numerous titles encompassing varied subjects from philosophy and spiritualism to English literature to Marxism and communism to biographies and autobiographies of famous historical personalities. There were tomes of Ramayan and Mahabharat in Sanskrit, Hindi, and English; a King James Bible; and an English translation of the Koran. Hindi and English translations of the Bhagavat Gita were kept in an alcove next to the stack, where she had placed her Gods and deities. There were travelogues and journals on different countries in Europe, Africa, and South America. As I was examining the titles printed on the spines of the books, she entered the bedroom with two cups of coffee and holding a steaming cup, the curls of vapour masking her beautiful face when she blew into the beverage with a sexy pout, she explained the importance of each book's contents and how her life was moulded by absorbing the messages contained in every one of them, especially the accounts of historical figures and Swami Vivekananda. During her discourse I ran my eyes and spied *Thus Spoke Zarathustra* by Friedrich Nietzsche, *The Communist Manifesto* by Karl Marx, *Being and Nothingness* by Jean-Paul Sartre, *The Prophet* by Khalil Gibran, *The History of Spiritualism* by Arthur Conan Doyle, *Imperialism: The Highest Stage of Capitalism* by Vladimir Ilich Lenin, *Das Kapital* by Karl Marx, numerous plays of Shakespeare, *Great Expectations* by Charles Dickens, *Emma* by Jane Austen, and many others. I removed an interesting book from a middle row and flipped through the pages of the James Murphy translation of the autobiographical manifesto of Adolf Hitler—*Mein Kampf*. I read the opening lines of Chapter 2: The Years Of Study And Suffering In Vienna—'When my mother died my fate had already been decided. . .' She also dipped her head and spoke into the second paragraph, 'I wanted to know his ideology, what insanity drove him that he ordered the killing of such a large portion of humanity. There is a second volume lying somewhere in one of my trunks.'

'You have got more books?' I asked incredulously.

'I have two trunk-fulls kept in the storeroom,' she said, after I had finished my inspection of her collection. 'And it keeps growing. He gives me a small portion of his earnings to indulge in my fantasies and I buy books every other month.'

She said that the books kept her sharp and her mind alert. That's true.

Later, when we had finished with our life stories, she would talk on topics ranging from the tragedy in Shakespeare's *Othello* with its central theme of love, jealousy, and betrayal; the fierce commitment of Mahatma Gandhi in his struggles to ensure that the downtrodden and the discriminated segments of the society in South Africa and later in India were treated with basic minimum human dignity, which had been denied to them for centuries by their imperious overlords—the whites in the southernmost country of the dark continent and the upper caste bullies in the Indian subcontinent. She was particularly fascinated by the zeal of Swami Vivekananda, as he went about reviving Hinduism and introducing the Indian philosophies of Vedanta and Yoga to the Western world—she specifically revered his 'sisters and brothers of America. . .' speech to the members of the Parliament of World's Religions at Chicago in 1893. She practiced her religion with sincere devotion, without getting mired into the jingoism so favoured by her parents, and she was equally attracted to the philosophy of universal brotherhood preached in the Bible and Koran—'Something which we lack. We have this rigid caste system which is the single most social stigma ruining our country today. People from the upper castes look at the Harijans with such disdain, as if they are from another planet. My father never ventured out of his room till the time the person who used to come to clean our latrines, *Bhangi* he used to call him, had left the house, his treads sprayed by the other servants with *gangajal* (water from the Ganges river, also considered as holy water). Later, when my sister-in-law was forced to take on the task, she was never allowed to enter his room and had to bathe in cold water fetched from the Ganges before entering the kitchen, even during the winters, the poor soul. No Mahatma Gandhi, not even Lord Krishna himself, will ever be able to change the stereotypes of our culture.

Even the Gods have been copyrighted by our different castes; Lord Krishna is the only God of the Yadavs, Jats have their Lord Hanuman and the poor Harijans, they are not even entitled any God, since Purusha did not birth them. They are even denied entry into temples. People from North to South have these different versions of Lord Krishna and Lord Shiva.'

Her depth of knowledge was amazing. She was far more intelligent than Pratima. Where Pratima's knowledge was restricted to what she could learn and absorb from reading the books, Meena's awareness about the world and what made it what it is was bolstered by the acumen to relate what she read with what goes on around us. Pratima, with all her magnificent brain and eidetic memory, would never be able to stand up to the array of topics Meena would pick up to study and thereafter refine the knowledge thus gained with her experiences of the outside world.

She held staunch beliefs with regards to the status of women and the downtrodden in our society. She spoke of her father with contempt and disdain because of the way he had treated her for a year, for his misogyny which led to her forced marriage to the repulsive Sharmajee—the reasons for which she revealed later. The condescension, with which her father and brothers treated women merely as objects of desire, had strengthened her resolve and moulded her character. She used to often meet the victims of her brothers' carnal fantasies to help them in getting the foetus in unmarried girls' wombs aborted or take them to hospitals for treatment of their injuries suffered during her younger brother's orgies—she used to skip classes for these forays, since she was not allowed to venture out of her house otherwise. She used to help out with her sister-in-law in domestic chores and lent her shoulder for her to cry upon, when things got unbearable. She had once asked her mother to hire a servant to assist her daughter-in-law, in at least cleaning the latrines and sweeping the house, but the mother-in-law had not relented from her stance that it was the duty of wives to serve their husbands and in-laws. Her mother had quoted Garud Puran and said, 'It is even written in our Holy Scriptures that the principle *Dharm* (religion) of a woman is to obey the orders of her husband. Since her husband is not here that responsibility delves upon us. And anyway, your father is in dire straits, losing money like a sieve and soon we will not be able to afford servants. It is better that she gets used to it well before that time comes. Let her be. It took me two years to get used to your grandmother's diktats. This one is frail, she may take longer.' 'But she will die well before that mother.' 'Have you ever heard of anyone dying of hard work? Had that been the case you would have never been born.'

They say that the fastest way into a man's heart is through his stomach. Meena entered mine through her voice, especially the way she called my name. She said 'Sanjay' with a lilting, melodious, singsong tone. The first syllable was spoken as a mere formality, like someone pronouncing 'Sun'. It was in the second syllable that she poured magic. The 'j' phoneme emerged from the depths of her throat, as if being pulled out of her heart. The short second vowel and the 'y' were pronounced as the phoneme produced by the vocalic digraph 'ae' and extended in a long continuation of 'ae' 'ae' 'ae' 'ae' . . . -s ending with a gasp, which sounded like the soft breath an infant takes while turning in her sleep. That gasp in the end added a silent vowel to my name—as in the name of the mythical blind king's personal narrator of the killings taking place at far away Kurukshetra in the epic Mahabharat, when read in English: Sanjaya. She often spoke my name thus and I would invariably lose myself in the breath of her gasp.

Two days before my departure for Ghorakhal, we were sitting on her bed, my back braced upon a cushion of pillows—she had ten of them—her bare back pressing into my chest, our feet playing hooky-dookies on the damp sheets, her head under my chin, dancing tendrils of her hair waving in and out of my nostrils, tingling my hairs inside—the fan had improved its circulation as she had had its motor greased, 'not to get a good sleep but to reduce our sweat, I was getting fed up of cleaning the sheets every other day.' Our fingers were playing '*Chor-Police*' on her belly and chest, the tips sometimes hiding in the depths of her navel, sometimes chasing each other over her torso—up and down, up and down—once in a while dunking into the sweaty world of her armpits. She felt ticklish at times and squirmed against me in luscious wiggles. We chuckled and giggled during the little game of our fingertips. After some time spent in hiding, escaping, and hunting, my fingers got tired and thirsty and plunged into the moist domain between her legs, seeking solace there.

Letting out an urgent sigh, I spoke to her jasmine-scented head, 'Meena, my sweetness. I don't know about you, but I have fallen in love with you. I love you from the bottom of my heart.'

She addressed her chest sceptically. 'I hope that's not the lover-going-away-for-next-six-months speaking. I know that a lot of you teenagers forget your heartfelt confessions, the moment you are out of sight of your paramours. Not that I would mind that of you. You have given me enough joy and happiness to last me a lifetime in these twelve times we have been together. Even if you forget me and treat me as a stranger, the next time you come home in December, I won't take it amiss. I would lump it and treat it as just my luck, like so many other events in my life.' Her tone had a wishful yearning in it by the end.

I felt offended. I retrieved my hands reluctantly from their earlier resting place and leaned down, pulling her up in the process. Lifting her chin with the crook of my forefinger, I touched my cheek to her cheek and said to the emptiness in front of us, 'Don't you know me enough by now. I will never forget you, even if Brooke Shields comes up to me and proclaims her undying love. I have given it a great deal of thought and have realised that I cannot live without you. Whatever be your status, married or not, I love you and want to spend the rest of my life with you. I will think of a way to rid you of the clutches of your hus . . . of him.'

She did not say anything for a long time, searching for a reply amongst the spines of her books staring at us in appreciative contemplation. Having come to a conclusion finally, she skid forward, turned around, pulled me, and the damp bed sheet stuck to my bare hips towards her, wrapped her legs around my waist, closed her arms around my back, and kissed me with an urgency of desperation. 'Oh Sanjay! What will I ever do without you?' (But she did not say I love you too!)

Then I told her about the portions of my life with Pratima, that I had left out when I had told her about my time at Ghorakhal earlier; the last winter, our first kiss, the sensations she had aroused in me by her touches, the intimacy we had shared in the cave, how Pratima had explained to me the various erogenous zones of her body and how I had spent one year without meeting her, waiting for our rendezvous at Lucknow. I spoke about how despondent I had become, how miserable my life had been the past six months, how, short of committing suicide, I had ruined my life; barely managing to pass my eleventh class exam, flunking twice in the NDA entrance exams, barely speaking one complete sentence to my parents, having no friends from school to speak of, except Bindu.

'But you changed everything. Had you not come into my world, I don't know where my life would have been heading. You have now become my sole purpose of life. I will move heaven and earth to win your love and when the time comes I will make you mine for eternity. I have decided to do one thing at a time. Come December I will clear my NDA exams and in July next year I will join NDA. Four years hence I will be a commissioned officer in the Army and like Rana Pratap take you on my Chetak, away from the vicious clutches of your husband and the prying eyes of the society.'

The blood rushing into my head during that declaration had also been surging into my loins and we made passionate love again.

Later we lay in each other's arms, our sweaty limbs entwined and I asked the question that had been festering inside me like an open wound: 'How do you know so much about the art of making love?'

She was silent for sometime then looked at the clock, satisfying herself that there was enough time and having concluded that since it was confession time, it was her chance to come out with the truth, she said, 'Sanjay I don't know how you will take it. I did not want to tell you earlier because I enjoyed what we had going between us and I feared that if I opened up further, letting out the entire truth, you would turn away. But now it doesn't matter. Even if you think of me otherwise and decide to have a change of heart, I will live the rest of my life with your memories.

'Sanjay, when I was younger and became aware of my desires during my university days, I found a way to satisfy those urges. I fell for a much older, married professor at the university and indulged in a torrid affair with him. It was not that I was promiscuous, but the lascivious ways of the men in my family gave me the encouragement—I thought if men could do it why not me, too. But as it turned out, I selected a totally unsuitable choice. I had been warned by the other girls who had fallen victim to him earlier. But he was handsome and had this charm which led me to him like a magnet. It was much later when my father had incarcerated me that. . .'

'What incarceration?' I interjected.

'I will come to that later. I learned much later that he was fond of collecting trophies—the number of girls he had slept with in the university. I had been on his radar for a long time and he snared me at the first opportunity he got. The circumstances of our first meeting are inconsequential, since I myself was so eager to meet him. We had a long drawn affair for up to a year.

'We used to meet often at hotels—small hotels with dingy rooms which were used by many in Patna for similar clandestine affairs. I used to see many middle-aged, plump women flitting in and out of the smelly, musty rooms, before or after some portly gentleman with a broad grin on his face or a young adolescent with shifty eyes and a sly smile, came out. I used to spend fifteen to twenty minutes with him of which five to six minutes were spent in intercourse. Despite his libidinous nature he was a lousy lover. Most of the times it was a short wham-bam-thank-you-ma'am job, lasting not more than two to three minutes. He always wore condoms. On the few occasions when he used to be in an amorous mood, he would give me pleasure and teach me new ways.'

She glanced at my face, shame written all over her face, and having mistaken my shocked expression, she said, 'Oh Sanjay! I am so sorry. I shouldn't have started on telling you this. It was a terrible mistake,' she made to get up.

I wrapped my arms protectively around her slender body and smelled the sweet scent of jasmine from her hair. I dipped down my head and sipped at the sweat dripping down her neck. After sometime, I said, 'You know, we boys are very crazy. Till we get married we dream of having sex with whichever girl we meet. My case may be an exception. But majority of us want to have physical relations with the first unmarried girl we meet and make friends with. I can say that for a fact when I speak of my schoolmates. But when it comes to marriage, all of them want a pure, untouched virgin for a wife. The situation is paradoxical. If the wishes of all these boys were granted, where would they get the virgins from? So the elders in the upper caste societies allow their boys to take their pleasures from the lower caste girls or at best turn a blind eye to such goings-on. "Boys will be boys," they remark with an insolent smirk. All to preserve the chastity of their own daughters so that their sons can marry own caste, pure, chaste virgins. That is the hypocrisy of the society we live in today.'

I cupped her face and looked directly into her eyes, 'I don't subscribe to such crass mentality. I go where my heart takes me in matters of love—that is how it should be. I wasn't there in your past, I couldn't do anything to change that past and I can't do anything about it now. But you are my present and I want you in my future too. We will try to erase the memory of that past together, without letting it contaminate our present and future.

After today, we will never talk about this sordid period of your life, not even in jest.'

'Oh Sanjay! Why couldn't I find you earlier?' But no 'I love you' still. I will wait; I had five years for that.

I said, 'But I have a feeling that there is something more sinister here. You have yet to finish your story. Why didn't you get your IAS husband?'

Despite taking all precautions—that's another reason she had placed that listening device inside her parents' bedroom—during her final year of graduation, one of her fathers' friends saw Meena and the professor moving into a hotel room surreptitiously and had later confronted her father, claiming that she was promiscuous. As a consequence she was incarcerated for a year, not allowed out of her room at her father's house, her meals dutifully brought to her by her younger sister or sister-in-law. Her sole consolation was that she was allowed to take her exams to attain the graduation degree—'My father wouldn't have accepted that after putting in so much money he wouldn't have a graduate from his family.' She had accepted her virtual prison sentence as justified punishment, and also, she did not have the nerve to take on her father then. Up until then she had got her own and her sister's dues through her guile and working on the situation to her advantage. But now she had nothing going for her; she had been a fool to get into that premarital relationship and she had to bear its consequences.

'But I was not going to let my sister suffer because of me. My father, steeped deep in his orthodoxy and fearing another scandal, thought that since my sister spent most of her time with me, she would also ape my "evil ways"—his words—if she had not already done so. So he wanted her to be sent away soon, even before she could complete her graduation course. I had not wished that for her when I had planned her life—a stupid husband from amongst the brood of one of father's bigoted friends, who would work her to death. I wanted that NDA Cadet, who had by then become an officer, for her. I wrote an urgent letter to him, sent a photograph of my sister to him, arranged a meeting between them in the garb of a college trip to Gaya and when she met him, he fell for her. She is way prettier than me, despite that reverence in your eyes. He also agreed to persuade his parents to let her continue her graduation course, after marriage, till she joined him a year later. From what my mother had told me about them and how he wrote in his letters, it seemed his parents are normal people who hadn't dismissed their servants the moment their eldest daughter-in-law joined the family. His elder brother stays with his parents and I was fairly certain that my sister would remain happy with her in-laws. Then I worked on mother through Rashmi, that Army Captain's wife of the "delightful soreness" fame, who came for a visit at my behest, and over a ten-day period worked her magic on my mother again, convincing her to persuade my father to take the proposal to Hazaribagh. Teena married her Army man a year back.'

'What about you?' I asked, marvelling at the remarkable achievement of this amazing woman, who despite being imprisoned herself, organised a marriage against all odds. What an amazing woman. This saga of love and sacrifice, of sisterly love, touched my heart, like nothing has ever done since. It brought to my mind the relationship Pratima was so privileged to have shared with her brothers.

'My father is a vengeful man who never forgave me for my indiscretion. He searched and searched, to punish me. And then found the perfect candidate for consigning me to purgatory for life. He had actually let out a hoot of laughter, liberally laced with mirth, when he had seen my prospective groom's photograph and uttered "teach her a lesson, the whore", or something to that effect—this from a man who never thought about it twice before fucking a whore himself, what misogyny we propagate. In reality he killed two birds with one stone—he was in big-league debt to my father-in-law and drove a hard bargain during the dowry negotiations (it turned out eventually that in effect her father-in-law paid bride money to buy a wife for his incapable, only son), winning a waiver on the interest amount and he was also happy to avoid a scandalous revelation, had my dalliances become public—he had also been paying a handsome amount to keep his friend's mouth zipped, the one who had found out about my affair earlier. I was married two months back and was transferred from one hell to another, till I met you and my life has changed forever, since then.'

I reiterated my promise. 'Meena, my sweetheart. I will love you for the rest of your life and other six lifetimes. I will free you from your bondages very soon. Give me some time to attain the ability to bring about the changes I have promised.'

'Oh Sanjay,' she gasped and sobbed and cried and melted into me, as I closed my arms around her.

When I was leaving she said with a wistful and earnest tone, 'Sanjay, you will be going away day after tomorrow. I want to spend the entire day with you tomorrow, even though I believe my "full moon time" might commence tonight. Will you come at ten? I know that you would find it difficult to explain your long absence to your parents, but you will go away for almost six months. I desire you so much.'

'My parents want to take me to Renusagar for the day, to meet Father's distant uncle. I don't know how to inveigle out of that. I am sorry darling, but this may be our last time together till December. Goodbye, my love,' I said wistfully to her sad eyes.

She called her time of the month as 'full moon time'. I wanted to find out how she intended to spend the time without making love.

9

The Demon Surfaces

The next day I woke up to another hot day, the sun simmering with some unexplained vengeance, turning the slate of the polluted sky above Shaktinagar into a dull, grey canopy, which could not be penetrated by our gazes. A few wisps of cloud held promise, but floated away after a few moments, as if carrying a lover for a clandestine rendezvous with his beloved. Desire burned in my heart with an intensity far greater than the sun's, to meet my own paramour, although I did not have the luxury of being carried by the clouds.

My parents left early for Renusagar, a town eighteen kilometres away, and said that they would be returning late in the evening; I feigned a mild ache and a runny stomach, and to give credence to my charade, I visited the toilet thrice, since waking up. After my brother had left for his school in the school bus, I locked all the doors of our house and clambered over her wall to spring a surprise upon her by my unexpected visit. Dirty utensils and crockery, with a plate containing remnants of a meal of congealed *daal* and fat rice grains, littered her verandah next to the basin. 'That is a first one,' I thought, since she always kept her kitchen and utensils clean—many times we had shared the chore of cleaning the utensils, crockery and cutlery after consuming our tea and snacks and the occasional meal. There was a rancid smell of vomit erupting from the basin—I refrained from looking into the basin to inspect the contents which emitted such a horrid offense to my olfactory nerves. Her bedroom door was wide open and I could hear soft sighs emerging from inside the room. She had not heard me jumping into her house, by now I had perfected the manouvre and could be as noiseless as a cat on the prowl. Without making any sound I took off my sneakers and tip-toed towards her bedroom, after peeking into her living room to make sure that the front door was locked.

She was sitting on her bed, knees pulled up, elbows resting upon her knees, forehead perched on the forearms. Her body shook with occasional tremors, as if she was hiccupping or drawing frequent deep breaths. I stood at her bedroom's threshold admiring and wondering at her dishevelled state. After some time I cleared my throat to declare my presence.

'Eeeeh!' she shrieked shrilly, jerking her head up. 'How did you . . . when did you . . . how come you. . .' She sprang to her feet and ran into me, hugging me tightly, deliciously pressing her face into my chest.

'I decided to give you a delightful surprise. I couldn't sleep a wink last night. I am having a stomach ache and have been passing watery discharges since the morning. My parents gave me some medicines and left for Renusagar an hour back.'

'Are you?'

'No my sweetest honey. That was the charade to escape being in the company of my geriatric distant relative. But what's the matter with you? Why are you shaking like a leaf?'

She was trembling in my arms and I also heard her sobbing into my chest. She clung on to me as if her life depended on it, silently crying with soft sighs, her tears damping my shirt. When she did not utter a single word for some time, I put my forefinger under her chin and lifted her face. What I saw left me dazed and shocked. Her eyes were bloodshot, tears streamed down her face, mingling with the stains of the tears shed earlier, her lips curled in a soundless wail, her hair dishevelled and running helter-skelter, with strands sticking to her cheeks, glued to the tears raining down. She looked so bereft with grief that my heart went out to her.

I enveloped her in my arms and whispered into her head, 'Tell me what happened? Did he beat you? I will kill the bastard.'

Her head shook a negative reply on my chest.

'Did he threaten you?' A negative shake again.

'Did he somehow find out about us?' A firm negative shake.

'Then why the tears, my doll?' I lifted her face again and put my lips on the tears flowing in a continuous torrent, relishing the salty taste.

She again rested her cheeks, speaking into my chest and the tremors in her voice pierced their way into my heart, 'Oh Sanjay, Sanjay, Sanjay! He is a pervert.'

'What . . . what do you mean?'

'A pervert . . . a homosexual maniac.'

A scene from the distant past flashed through my mind, as I recollected how Sharmajee had fondled me, pressing his fat girth into my chest, trying to rub his groin against my stomach, scraping his stubbled cheek against my face, his stale, garlic-ridden breath blasting my nostrils as he had whispered lewdly, 'Come to my home in the evening,' and my brother was lost in the maze of machinery which made a hellish noise as the assorted levers, rods, bearings, lathes, hammers and tongs, grinded and squeaked against each other. I shook my head vigorously to shake off the nightmarish vision.

The morning aged into afternoon and she told me about the demon who had surfaced from the murk he was dwelling in all this while.

Last night, after I had left, he arrived quite drunk from those two drinks at my father's house—'Your perceptive father restricts him purposefully to two pegs of rum, as he knows that anymore and he would be out of control.' But as soon as he had entered her house, he pulled out a pouch from his trouser pockets, which contained a lemon-hued liquid sloshing in the thin plastic. 'Country liquor,' he had said, 'that Tivari doesn't give me more than two pegs, he is so stingy. Get me a glass of water. Today I will drink to my fill.' When Meena had got him his water, he gulped down a measure and ordered her to get him food fifteen minutes later.

'He also grabbed hold of my hand and pulled me down beside him on the couch. I wriggled out of his grasp and explaining that I had to warm his food, I came into the kitchen. After warming the food and placing the daal, rice, and egg curry in casseroles, I returned into the living room, more to check that he had not passed out, than to listen to his ramblings. He was mumbling into his half-empty glass and when he looked up I saw a drunken, devilish hatred in his eyes. He berated me for not performing my wifely duties, for not granting him his due in bed, and lamented about how all of his friends boasted of raunchy nights in bed with their wives, whereas here I was, his "Sati Savitri" wife who had taken a vow of celibacy and did not entertain him.'

To avoid creating a scene, Meena had got up after a few minutes of listening to his inebriated banter and went into the kitchen to bring his food. As he shovelled mouthfuls with his fingers, he continued his tirade— 'Yesterday that idiot Mishra was telling me that he had sex three times a night, every night, in the first six months of his marriage. And you have not even given me one night of pleasure,' he had raved in accusatory tones.

'Who is this Mishra?' I asked.

'He is a lecher and his colleague. He had come to our house a couple of times to eye me. I had got so fed up of his malicious looks that one day, while serving tea, I held that pointy knife under the tray and brought the edge of the tray so close to his face that the knife's tip had virtually grazed his chin. You should have seen his face. He literally soiled his pants and has never been here ever since.'

I chuckled, 'You are some goddess. I am grateful that you did not castrate me the first time I kissed you.'

'You are different from others, Sanjay. Don't you ever compare yourself with others? You are the most wonderful thing to have ever happened to me.'

Last night, she had replied to his complaint by asserting that he had never shown any interest in her since their wedding night. On that night too he had been so drunk that he did not even come to her bridal chambers, sleeping off the night with his friends.

He had blasted, 'How dare you accuse me of being disinterested. I have always wanted it, but you lie flat like a slab of ice and expect me to do everything.'

'I had replied, "Don't you dare me by accusing me of that. Look at you. You are so fat and your thing is such a teeny-weeny thing you can't even get it in."

'"How do you know it is small? Have you seen other men's? Have you been fooling around in my absence? Has that bastard Mishra been visiting you behind my back? Or are you going to him, you slut?"

'"Don't you dare call me a slut!" I had shouted at him. "It was you who had failed all the time. We tried it thrice in the past and they all ended in utter disaster. Accept the fact that you can't put it in."' Her confession, that she had never done it with that devil, washed over me like a wave of relief.

'I can feel that,' she raised her head; her body curled inside my arms, and she looked deep into my eyes, a wry smile on her lips. At least she had lost her sense of desolation. But her eyes were still wet.

'What, my sweetheart,' I bent down and touched my lips to her eyes, sipping the tears, as they escaped the corners.

'Sanjay we have been together thirteen times, we have made love umpteen times, so many times that I have lost count.'

'I have kept a count of all of them. We have made love forty-six and a half times, the half is for my first attempt.'

'You do know how to pep me up,' she chuckled, 'so in all those forty-six and half times and the forty to fifty hours we have been in each other's company, I have been privy to all your emotions and feelings. I feel that immense love you have for me, I know that your lips quiver when you are deep in your throes of passion, I know that your nose crunches with envy when you realise that I have more knowledge than you on certain subjects, I know that you twiddle your thumbs when you are impatient, I know that you shake your thighs vigorously when your nerves are shot, like that first day when you had come for tea, and just now I sensed a wave of relief washing over you—your muscles lost their tension, the hair on your forearms rose slightly, your heartbeats slowed down a wee bit. Don't love me so much Sanjay.'

'You can't even begin to imagine how much I love you my sweetness. But we digress. Do continue my lady.'

'Do you wish me to continue? It's a sad episode, one more to add to all other such previous events in my life.'

'But I do know that this one will lead to a happy ending, my darling. And don't you dare think of sad events. I am here and now. I will give you happiness for the rest of your mortal life and then some,' I proclaimed chivalrously.

She sighed contentedly and continued her tale, as if on cue. 'My raised voice shut him up and he continued scooping morsel after shabby morsel into his mouth with his dirty fingers. He kept on mumbling incoherently, his voice slurring and spittle drooled out of the corners of his mouth, with un-chewed rice. After sometime, the pitch of his voice picked up again and he began ranting again about how I have denied him pleasures, how wrong he was in imagining that his nights would be full of sweetness, how wrong I was that he had no interest in me.

'Suddenly he let out a huge burp and covering his mouth with both hands he rushed and staggered towards the basin and threw up his half-eaten meal and the mixture of alcohol he had consumed earlier. He returned with specks of vomit dotting his mouth and a wet slimy trail wiggled down the front of his shirt. I was bent over the table, picking up the dishes, when he grabbed me from behind and demanded his right of a husband. I pushed myself away from his grasp, my hands holding on to the plates and glass and told him to go to the bedroom.

'By then I was pretty certain that our sole neighbours, that elderly couple living across the street, must have been awakened by our domestic crisis, what with him shouting so loudly and I did not want them slandering me, spreading rumours of a domestic rift. He was drunk and I knew that I could get it over with in a jiffy, without much effort.'

I was staring incredulously at her. 'Don't get me wrong, Sanjay. I was in a difficult situation. Had I not agreed, he would have raised a ruckus and I was afraid that he would end up raping me, so full of himself was he.'

'Did he?' I asked with violent rage. 'Tell me, did he? I will kill the son of a bitch.'

'"No, I will do it right here," he said,' she continued, after a shake of her head in response to my query.

'"Okay," I said, "go wash your mouth and throw away that shirt. Later lie down on the floor."

'"No, right now. Bend over."

'"What do you mean bend over? Why should I bend over?" I gingerly put the plates and glass on the table.

'He grabbed hold of my behind and started slapping it with both hands: "Bend over right now and lift up your sari. I will show you how I can put it in."

'A dreadful chill coursed through me. What is this man up to? Why is he slapping me in such a manner? Then I recalled how, my sister-in-law and some of my married friends back in Patna, used to tell me about their sordid experiences during their time of the month, when their sex-crazy husbands would demand copulation even during their menses and would take them from behind. Shaking with dread and afraid of his sudden brutish manners, I pushed him violently into a chair and ran into the kitchen. Grabbing hold of the pointy knife, I rushed back into the living room, stepped up to him lying sprawled in the chair and put the pointy end just below his right eye.'

'Don't tell me? You did that? What an amazing girl you are, my darling?' I kissed her tenderly on her lips.

'Well, now you know that I am not a girl at all. But I was afraid as well—he must weigh above 150 kilograms, he could have easily swatted away that knife, pinned me over the chair, and had his way. But more than that, I was filled with an inconsumable rage that he could have the temerity to do to me whatever he wished, that he could defile me in whatever manner he desired, that he never considered my feelings, that having escaped the living hell my father had consigned me to, I would have to live another hellish existence with this oaf. I couldn't allow that to pass. I had to take matters in my own hands. There was no one else who could set things right, but me. My rage overcame my fear, regardless of the consequences of his turning the tables on me.

'"What are you?" I hissed into his face, disregarding the foul reek of his breath. The blood drained out of his face. I could see naked fear in his eyes as he sat shaking like a leaf. He was scared to death, with that knife ready to plunge into his eyes. He tried to move his head.

'"Don't you dare move an inch or I will carve that eye out of its socket," I threatened with a bit of drama—his craven reaction and the dread in his eyes gave me confidence. "Answer me. What are you?"

'He finally found his voice and wailed, "Please don't kill me. My eyes . . . please. I am sorry, very sorry . . . I did not know what I was doing . . . I was very drunk . . . please don't plunge the knife into my eyes . . . I . . .I . . .I. . ."

'I looked at his grotesque, wretched face, tears glistening in his eyes as he started weeping. "But you didn't answer me. Are you a . . . a . . . pervert." I moved the knife away from his face, but kept it poised to strike, close to his neck, lest he be fooling me.

'He wept silently for long, head hanging down like a mongrel caught soiling the carpet. "I like boys," he confessed after some time.

'I walked over to the settee, settling down in it, still holding the knife in one hand, pointing towards him. "What do you mean you like boys? Are you homosexual?"

'He nodded into his chest. "It all started when I was eleven. There was this elder cousin, Bhuliya, the son of my father's cousin."'

10

The Divine Gift

'Come over here, Motu,' Bhuliya whispered into Sharmajee's ears.

Sharmajee had spent most of his growing up years in the company of his robust male cousins, at his native village during vacations and at his grandfather's bungalow in the town of Chhapra, when he was attending school. He had no brothers, despite Sharma senior's many trials and errors, which resulted in three daughters, and numerous miscarriages and abortions, and ultimately Sharmajee's mother had opted for sterilisation after her fourth child. As an 11-year-old, he was very chubby with soft pads of flesh covering his body, especially all over his upper body and around his buttocks, as a result of which he was the butt of jokes in his cousins' company. Their rude jokes often left him frustrated, as the pranks usually culminated with Sharmajee's clothes torn off his body, which left him red-faced with shame and embarrassment. During such moments, one fully grown cousin, with brutish manners, started taking more than brotherly interest in him. After the other cousins would leave, this burly cousin, Bhuliya, would approach Sharmajee, by now shivering with shame and muted rage, utterly helpless in his nakedness, and take him into his arms to console his younger cousin. That consoling took the notorious form of caresses and fondles and soon enough, after a few days, on his twelfth birthday, Bhuliya gave a special treat to Sharmajee in an abandoned hut, a short distance from his house where the other children were celebrating the occasion, with that whispered entreaty. After feeble protests and at the same time, inviting manners, Bhuliya introduced Sharmajee to the pleasures of 'brotherly love'.

That first instance had resulted in severe pain but, with liberal application of lubricants, the experience turned into pleasure-seeking ventures in no

326

time at all. So much so that soon Sharmajee started seeking Bhuliya out to enjoy the adventures. Bhuliya was ever eager to satiate his own desires and exploited his younger cousin to the hilt. It had become a win-win situation for both of them.

But it all ended with Bhuliya's marriage two years later. Sharmajee had by then become more rotund, but for Bhuliya, his plump, newlywed wife's curves and softness became more enticing than Sharmajee's gruff manners and growing muscles. Bhuliya was from a village outside Chhapra, who had never been to any school and knew only one form of coital relationship; that which he had enjoyed with his younger cousin. His wife, brought up in a male setup without a mother or sister to advise her on her wifely duties, knew nothing about how to copulate. So, even after marriage, Bhuliya continued in the manner which he had become accustomed to with Sharmajee. Bhuliya's parents were increasingly becoming frustrated with their daughter-in-law's inability to conceive, even after overhearing their son's efforts every night from the adjoining room. They had even declared their daughter-in-law barren, without giving it a thought that their son may not be knowing which hole to pour his seed into. Blissfully unaware, Bhuliya and his wife went on with their lives, with she having to bear the cross of a barren, till his 'good-natured and well-meaning' aunt, after a couple of interviews with the wife, suggested that the couple seek divine intervention from a 'god-man' in a neighbouring village, who with his 'miracles' had converted the empty wombs of many mothers into a fertile ground of cackling babies—she herself had been a recipient of such a divine gift, eight times over up until then, since her husband had proven to be an impotent imbecile, pretty early in her married life. (She went on to give birth to twelve of the 'god-man's' children and one of her husband's, later).

Bhuliya, with his young wife, paid a visit to the miraculous 'god-man', who, after dutifully performing the holy rituals and demanding an exorbitant amount to invoke divine intervention, one night asked for the girl to pray alone with him for a vision—'*darshan*'—of the Creator who would put his seed inside the barren girl's womb. Many such 'eyes-only *darshans*' later, till the wife announced that she had missed her cycle, did the grateful Bhuliya's parents dole out another bagful of cash to the 'god-man' for his invocation of divine impregnation. Nine months later a bonny son was born

328 | *Mamta Chaudhari*

to the contented mother. Had it been a daughter, another visit to the 'god-man' for another divine gift would have been in the offing.

(Bhuliya's aunt was a different matter. Having realised pretty early in her married life, most probably on her wedding night itself, when her husband's pecker wouldn't awaken for the world to acknowledge its presence and for Bhuliya's aunt to appreciate its prowess, the sheer powerlessness of her husband's inability to perform his husbandly tasks led her in search of a suitable replacement, as if she wanted a mechanical part in her oven to be replaced. After she discovered the 'god-man' and his divine impregnation scheme, she not only enjoyed the seeding part but also the subsequent ploughing and harvesting of the crop too. So much so that she was back for her private 'darshan', even after her menses halted, to indicate that she was with child. And she would again ask for fresh seeds immediately after her earlier child was born. For her bewildered family members, her devotion to the 'god-man' and her sincere belief in the divine impregnation earned her the reputation of Kunti, the mythical mother of Pandavs, all of whose children, including the one born out of wedlock, were the fruits of her *tapasya*—her six sons were children of her mystical union with the gods; Sun (Karna), Dharmraj (Yudhishthra), Vayu (Bhima), Indra (Arjun), and the Ashwini Twins (Nakul and Sahdev). In our real world, in the rural part of Bihar, our Kunti, Bhuliya's aunt, after five sons, six daughters, and one transgender—who had been plucked by the eunuchs on the very day he was born when they saw that the child was gifted with both male and female genitals—had to suffer the ignominy of disfavour from her own modern day '*Sant*' (saint). Well into her forties, the muscles in her walls had loosened after the birth of her twelfth 'divine' child and the 'divine impregnator' complained that he could feel nothing whenever he entered her and that due to lack of any friction he was never stimulated. Bhuliya's aunt, who had enjoyed twosomes to sixsomes with her '*Sant*', in the company of Bhuliya's wife, the maidservants at his *ashram*, his disciples—*Chelas*—and other minions of the '*Sant*', couldn't handle the pressures of a loveless and sexless married life, after her '*Sant*' threw her out of his *ashram*. Her body's urges knew no restraint and after dallying with some unworthy minions of her household and her husband's hired farmhands, she discovered the benefits and joys of the Vacuum Erection Device, which she had got imported from the US. Now, at last, she has found coital bliss in her conjugal union, as every night her earlier impotent husband can keep it up for at least half an hour and as a result, she again got pregnant, just before her menopause set in, and gave birth to a sweet girl in her fifties, giving rise to speculations that she had indeed been blessed with such fertility that she could bring children into this world till eternity. Much later, when we were discussing my chances of an alternate profession, I told Meena that I disagreed with her claim that the most suitable alternate profession for me was as a gigolo. I said that for men like me, there could not be a more suitable profession than turning into a '*Sant*', to enjoy the benefits of a gigolo and that the sainthood would provide me divine permission too. The sexual peccadilloes of the Great Indian Gigolos of the twenty-first century, '*Swami*' Nityanand and '*Sant*' Asaram (the Bapu suffix people have ascribed to him is a blasphemy and the geriatric, libidinous imbecile should be languishing in a dungeon with the keys thrown away for eternity; unless of course his female disciples have also been 'divinely impregnated' by him, thereby earning him the sobriquet of a father—that should be apt for his gifts) have shaken the faith I have ever had in these and other saints. I have always been fascinated by the way the general populace places so much sanctity on these god-men, even when the newspapers and televisions hound and denigrate them. It does not matter how many of these people are arrested, the belief that it cannot be them, they are so famous, persists among the general population, including the upper caste and class society, especially them).

11

The Wrestler and Sharmajee's Penchant for Youngsters

Sharmajee, after Bhuliya's marriage, was increasingly becoming frustrated and kept on pestering his cousin, who finally introduced him to the secret club which functioned in the city, with exclusive membership for similarly inclined men in their twenties to fifties. In that secret underworld of shady gay men, inhibited by societal censure, reputation spread by word of mouth. Sharmajee instantly acquired a well anointed repute of a docile, effeminate participant, well versed in the art of even sating a male corpse; some of it was a bit farfetched, no doubt. His fame was also enhanced by his plump features and ready availability to any comer. While most of his 'partners' were from his hometown, his name was spoken of with glowing tributes amongst the practitioners of this vile form of sexual ventures, from afar. Once he travelled all the way to Calcutta to fornicate with a renowned wrestler. The wrestler must have heard of Sharmajee through the grapevine—'Heard of this podgy little Bihari boy,' one of his 'partners' must have whispered in the wrestler's ears, 'all of 16, plump as a ripe plum, flesh soft as a cow's distended udders; he has been going around in Chhapra. Would you like to ride him?' The information was passed on from a friend of a friend of a friend of one of the exclusive members of the secret club, who would have taken extra pleasure in Sharmajee and must have boasted about it with the others. Sharmajee had pilfered money from his father's pockets for the trip to Calcutta and cooked up a school-organised trip for a quiz competition as an excuse. He had heard a lot about the proclivities of the wrestler and was looking forward to a night of pleasure and gratification. But the experience had left him shattered. The wrestler was as brutal inside his bedroom as he was in the wrestling arena with his opponents. Sharmajee had returned to Chhapra in bruises and had a lot of explaining to do to his father.

After that bitter sexperience, Sharmajee started seeking boys so that he could be the male in the partnership. After a lot of cajoling and some amount of threat, he persuaded the house servant's son to be his 'partner'. Sharmajee lost his 'virginity'— so to speak—to the servant's son. Thereafter, he gradually broke his relations and terminated his dalliances with the other members of that secret club and only looked for contentment in youngsters. Stealing money from his father had become a habit and he would pay his 'partners', who invariably were destitute; the servant's son, the young servant who replaced the elderly flunky after Sharmajee reported that he had been stealing money from Sharma senior's pockets (this was after the servant's son had refused to satiate his desires any further), the milk boy, the newspaper boy, even a beggar at the railway station who had caught Sharmajee's fancy.

Fate and circumstances struck a hard blow on Sharmajee's future when he was nearing graduation. By then he had established a comfortably prolonged relationship with a young nephew of his father's friend, who had always been suspicious of his ward's effeminate manners, which had been further aroused when he was spotted in the company of Sharmajee. Sharmajee had enrolled at one of the engineering colleges in Patna for his graduation, and being far away from his father's prying eyes had emboldened him in taking undue risks while indulging in his passion. Where earlier, he used to conduct his illicit affairs secretly hidden at his hometown, at Patna, he was seen routinely flaunting his newfound 'friendship' with a scion of a reputed family—his father's friend's nephew. The 'friendship' was advertised by Sharmajee as a mentorship to a young engineering aspirant and as a result, they spent considerable amounts of time in each other's company, apparently in the form of a mentor-student relationship, blissfully unaware of the growing suspicion taking root in the mind of the observant uncle of the youth. The 'couple' was often spotted at various eateries and *dhabas* of Patna, sharing notes on structural integrity of buildings, discussing different models and such like in the company of thick tomes, just to keep up the charade. In reality, the boy was a dim-wit, who would never be able to grow enough gray matter to pursue any engineering course. After one such 'serious' discussion, they proceeded on their separate journeys, back to their respective abodes. But that was just a trick. Midway to their destination, they changed course and headed for the dingy hotel room booked by Sharmajee earlier in the day. This was how they conducted their dalliances, unmindful of any intrusions or suspicion. On that fortuitous occasion, the boy left the *dhaba* with the name and address of the hotel memorised in his dim-wit brain and a local ruffian hired by his uncle followed him surreptitiously. The uncle's suspicions had been confirmed the previous night when, after much needling, his nephew had expressed a genuine lack of interest in any subject connected to engineering. And when the hired goon reported from the hotel's telephone, after having spied the boy entering room number 24, followed a few minutes later by a plump, round fellow in his twenties, the uncle took no time in converging on an unsuspecting Sharmajee with a posse of hired hooligans. The subsequent beating Sharmajee was subjected to left him just short of his death—he would have departed from his miserable existence on Earth had he not been his father's son. Courtesy the respect that uncle had for his father, Sharmajee's nearly dead body was carted all the way from Patna to Chhapra in an Ambassador car and unceremoniously dumped at his father's doorstep. When his proclivities were revealed to his conservative, religious-minded father, Sharmajee wished that he had died back at Patna in that thrashing. His studies were abruptly suspended for a year, which he spent at his native village, working as a farmhand with the low caste minions of his landlord father. His year-long ostracisation ended when he promised to his father that he would never again engage in homosexual acts, which was substantiated by his good conduct in the village, where he had never indulged with any of the teenage sons of the other farmhands. He was allowed to complete his bachelor of engineering degree course, after which he secured a job with NTPC and got his posting to Shaktinagar, occupying one of the lower echelons of the corporation's rigid hierarchal structure. Once away from his father's strict edicts, he had reacquired his taste for young boys and had found fresh victims amongst the young boys of the tribals who were engaged in various vocations as un-indentured labour, milk boys, tea stall and liquor joint waiters, and such like. He paid them generously out of his salary and till his marriage he was living a blissful existence.

He had reluctantly agreed to marriage, bowing to pressure from his father, who wanted to attain respectability after the shame that his son had wrought upon the family by his unnatural proclivities. His father was also getting fed up of Meena's father's inability to pay usury on his dues and had reluctantly agreed to waive off the interest on the loan he had given to him, as he had thought that it served his son right to have a 'soiled' woman for a wife—he knew of his daughter-in-law's secret before Meena's marriage, that friend of Meena's father was on Sharma senior's payroll too.

After his revelation Meena had barred his entry into her bedroom; he has to make do with a folding cot, a thin mattress, and a dilapidated pillow inside the living room or the verandah henceforth. She had further decreed that he could have as many boys as he wanted but could never, even in his wildest of dreams, ever think of touching her or else he would be at the wrong end of her kitchen knife with either his tongue sliced off or one off his eye balls lying discarded on the floor. She had added to good effect what she had done to the ears of her brothers' friend as a 12-year-old and said that it was not beyond her to nip off his testicles and feed them to the cockroaches and rats. And she never wanted to hear of a scandal about his sexcapades or else she would castrate him and leave him pecker-less.

'I lay on my bed awake till dawn. Sometime, deep into the night, my rage cooled and reality struck like a thunderstorm. My life was ruined. I had moved from one hellhole to another. From a domineering, misogynist father I had been transferred to a pervert, homosexual fiend. What a life! I couldn't go on living like this. My life till now swam like a kaleidoscope. I was desolate, thinking of my future as a bleak landscape. I dozed off into a nightmarish slumber as the sun heralded a new dawn. I did not notice him slink off for work. He just left a note, saying that he would be going out and would not be back till late. No sorry, no apology, no nothing. The night's events returned to me like a jolt from the blue. I was despairing hopelessly when you came. I haven't even brushed my teeth. Kissing me must have been horrible for you, all that stale breath.'

I leaned down and kissed her mouth passionately. 'No sweetie pie. You taste as sweet as sugar. Your kisses will never taste anything else. Come, I will brush your teeth and bathe you. I have always dreamt of making love with you, covered in soap.' Her 'full moon time' was a bit late, it seemed.

Later as we lay in bed, she sighed wistfully, 'I feel sorry for him, however reprehensible his behaviour last night.'

'Why feel sorry darling? He is a fiend.'

'No, don't you say that. It was not his fault. Somehow I feel that it was that brute cousin of his who was at fault, to have initiated him into all this.'

'That's the woman in you speaking, always finding excuses for a man's shortcomings. Nobody is forced into homosexuality. It is the choices a man makes in his life which define his future.'

'Care to explain?'

'Boys in our country, especially those from small towns and villages, live in a male-dominated society. Except for his initial few years spent in his mother's care, a boy is surrounded by males all through his life. There are boys-only schools, boys-only boarding schools, men-only organisations like the defence services, men-only clubs, and so on. It is no mere coincidence that at some time or the other, these boys will get attracted to each other. There are always pretty boys in boarding schools who catch the fancy of their seniors. But that doesn't mean that they all turn into homosexuals. The orientation of a man is not dependent on his circumstances, but his choices. Because being homosexual is unnatural. Even animals know this. Take an animal, say a lion, who has lived his entire life in captivity. Till he attains adulthood let him live a lonely existence. Thereafter, put another lion and a lioness to give him company—both of them also bred in solitary captivity. This is the first time that all three of them are in the company of another being of their species. They don't know whom to mate with. But after some time the lions will start duelling with each other to claim mating right with the lioness. They know that the lioness is for mating and to do that, one of them has to be killed or the other will be killed. That's nature. The lions don't kill the lioness to mate with each other. That will be unnatural.'

'But I have seen dogs screwing dogs.'

'That's why it is called a dog's life. Have you ever noticed female dogs behaving around males? They strut around as if they are the very reincarnation of Cleopatra. Each female dog is chased by many males. What would the poor males do? The betas to omegas hump each other while the alpha male gets the girl, so to speak. But other intelligent animals are different—they choose wisely. When an animal can choose between what is natural and what is unnatural, men can also do the same. So he had a choice. Even though he was exploited as a teenager, he could have forgotten about it, after Bhuliya started seeking pleasures in his plump wife and would have continued to live a natural life, would never have been shunned by his father, would have married in his twenties to some other girl and you would not have been contemplating a living hell today.'

'But then I would have never met you.'

'Then it's just as well that he is what he is today. I don't know how else we would have met.'

'That's destiny for you. You are a boarder too, did you ever experience homosexuality in your school.'

'I was a victim, too.'

'Oh God! Don't tell me! Who was this fiend? Was it bad? Did he . . . you know? I shudder with dread thinking about it. My poor boy!' She climbed over me, kissed me hungrily and said, 'Tell me about it.'

'It was bad and not so bad. When I had joined the school, I was a pretty boy. I had this fair skin and plump cheeks, which lent some effeminacy to my features. And there was this brute, one class senior to me and too advanced in his years. Even in class 7 he looked like a 15-year-old, and I was only 11 and a half. It is possible to get admission in schools with fake dates of birth. In fact, many boys in my school have two dates of birth: one actual and the other for the school admission forms. Since most of the small towns in our country have not yet learned how to keep records of birth nor do the authorities issue any birth certificates, a father just requires a certificate from a local government official attesting the date of birth, to get admission in schools. Money would be exchanged under the table and a greedy and pliant official would reduce the son's age by three years. That simple!

'This overaged lout took a fancy to me and would often corner me, rubbing his lips against my cheeks, grabbing my behind, licking my cheeks, pressing his groin into me, fondling my privates, guiding my hands between his legs and such like.'

'Didn't you report to anyone?'

'I did not tell anyone; not my classmates, not my hostel matron, not my teachers, not even Dwivedi Sir. There were many reasons for me not doing that. The first time he did those things to me, I complained that I would report it and he threatened me with dire consequences, squeezing my neck to give me a taste of those consequences. He was tall and strong, I was plump and weak. I grew afraid of him. There was also the associated shame and embarrassment, if it ever came to light. My classmates would snicker at me and brand me girlish. I did not want to suffer the ignominy of being caricatured a pansy.

'Things came to a head one day, when I was taking a bath. Suddenly there was a loud crash and the door flew open. He had kicked it open with a single strike, breaking the latch. I had just finished bathing and was drying myself, when he entered the bathroom, kicked the door shut and grabbed me from behind. He tore off my underwear and loosened his grip a bit, to pull his pants down. I grabbed the opportunity, turned around, kneed his groin with all the strength I could muster and scooted out, covering myself with the towel. I ran into the dormitory and saw that there was no one there; he had chosen his time well.

'He had by then limped out of the bathroom, holding his crotch, his face grimacing with pain and rage, and staggered towards me. Wrapped only in a towel, I ran out of the dormitory towards the hostel matron's residence, located some distance away.

'Fortunately she was home and I rapped frantically on the glass panes of her door. She opened the door, saw me draped in a towel, and demanded an explanation for my odd appearance at her entrance. She was a sweet girl in her twenties and had always been firm but understanding with us freshmen. I told her that I was in trouble, that a senior was after me, giving her his name. She glanced towards the dormitory, saw him ambling out of the dorm's door and shouted in a shrill voice, 'Hey you pervert. Come here.' He immediately took off like a scared rabbit and she took me inside her home. She soothed my nerves with a cup of milk and I narrated the entire episode to her, including his past attempts at sodomising me. She patted my cheeks lovingly, took me back inside the dormitory, and stood at the entrance while I dressed. When she asked as to why I had not reported the incident, I gave her my reasons and she had sympathetically tut-tutted and tousled my hair. Then she told me to write down all the events on a piece of paper; that was a very smart move on her part, as it turned out later. Taking the paper, she assured me that the brute would never trouble me henceforth and that she would have him rusticated.

'My father later told me the sequence of events that followed. Kamlesh Shukla, the matron, had immediately reported the matter to the House Master and Dwivedi Sir, but she did not let them in to the fact that she had everything written down in my own handwriting. The House Master told her not to tell anything about the incident to anyone in the top hierarchy. Dwivedi Sir had remained silent initially. But he had got hold of four of his favourite class 11 students, who gave a nice beating to my tormentor and threatened him of broken limbs if he ever approached me again. That had put a scare in him for some time and he tended to avoid me, though he would snicker at me from afar and snigger to his classmates. A month passed and nothing happened.'

'What? They didn't throw him out?' She exclaimed, not believing the apparent apathy of the school authorities.

'There was school politics in play all this while. Sainik Schools have a strange setup. The teachers and administrative staff are all civilians. They serve in the same school for long, some till their retirement. Whereas, the management of the school, that is, the three top positions of principal, headmaster, and registrar, are manned by transitory defence services officers, who serve for two to three years at a time. This led to a lot of consternation amongst the teachers, who aspired for the top slots but couldn't get there due to the government's policies. Hence there was a coterie amongst the teachers who kept the top three men isolated from the happenings in the school and rumblings were stamped down ruthlessly, depending upon whose interest was being served. Why, when I had joined the school some of the teachers had even instigated the students to organise a students' strike for the first time in the history of the school, against the top troika's policies. The school had been shut down for almost a week, with the students and teachers divided into two groups—I was part of the anti-strike group, because its leader was from my hometown (he later joined the dingy and dangerous world of state politics of Uttar Pradesh). There was no neutral party in that strike.

'This brute's father was a hot-shot in the local politics of Ghazipur. He had warmed a lot of hands in getting his son admitted to the school and his well-wishers at the school were paid handsomely to keep his son in the school, despite his notorious acts. He was a terror to us sixth-class students, as he used to always beat us, at some pretext or the other. Once, he had a football player, from our class, kick our bent backsides, and a few of us had been badly hit in our scrotums. Our House Master indulged him, since he was one of the beneficiaries of the munificence of his father. When he came to know that the boy had been beaten up at the instigation of Dwivedi Sir, he decided to defend the thug. He ensured that my misfortune was not reported to the troika at the top, who would have immediately rusticated the ruffian—after all they were upholders of all that is sacred, good, and morally and ethically correct and would never have accepted a maniac studying in the school. Also, the reputation of the school and their own careers would have been at stake, if the Sainik Schools Society, which manages all the Sainik Schools in the country, one in each state, came to know about the incident. To the hostel matron—who was desperate for the job, which provided for her poor parents and ensured education of her younger brother—the House Master threatened that she would lose her job with a single negative report from him. Dwivedi Sir was concerned that if he reported the matter, he would be given the cold shoulder treatment by the other teachers. So the whole incident was hushed up.

'But the matron was a smart girl, God bless her. She was brilliant in fact. After observing the behaviour of the brute and sensing that he was gaining in confidence after his initial deference, post the bathroom episode, and also, she was getting increasingly frustrated at not being able to prevent him from thrashing us sixth-graders, no doubt allowed by the House Master, she consulted Dwivedi Sir, revealing to him that secret record of the incidents she had kept to herself all this while. She had then posted that paper to my father, adding the salutation, "Dear daddy" and my name at the end, in her own hand.

'Father arrived at the school immediately on receiving the letter, in full fury, and confronted the trinity, threatening to write to the Sainik Schools Society and the Army Headquarters if the ruffian was not thrown out of the school. He took me home and gave them an ultimatum of fifteen days, after which he would have acted upon his threats, if no action was taken by the school.

'Fifteen days later, when I rejoined the school, the House Master had been changed, the brute had been withdrawn from the school, and I attained the status of a hero amongst my classmates. They had all hated the thug from Ghazipur and believed that I had had him unceremoniously thrown out of the school for the beatings we had to endure. If only they knew.'

'That was intriguing,' she said after a moment of silence. 'Let's get back to your theory—the one of choice. I think I get your point. It's all about choices, life is about choices. Had I not chosen to enter into a premarital affair I wouldn't have been married to him? Had I not married him, I would have never come here? Had I not come here, I would not have met you, and had I not met you, I would have never met my destiny? That's it; what better example of one making one's own destiny. I was destined to meet you, so my choice decided my fate. And I am so happy that my destiny led me to you. I want to savour the sight, sound, and smell of you, forever.'

We went silent for some time, lost in our thoughts. She broke our reverie with 'but why did he choose this orientation?'

'Who?' I asked, before realising that she was talking of Sharmajee. She mockingly threw a pillow at me, 'You know who.'

'He enjoyed it, I guess. I am amazed you got him admitting to being a homosexual in such candid detail. It is so difficult to imagine. Attagirl! You are my girl. You are the only woman in the world to me. You are truly amazing—pulling a knife upon your husband. No one, truly no one, would believe me if I told them. I am so lucky to have fallen in love with you.'

'I think you are evading my question. Come on; tell me why did he choose such a preference?' She pounded my chest playfully.

'I told you, he enjoyed it.'

'What? Bothways! That's too pervert.'

'Then he is too pervert. I think he enjoyed being the passive one initially. But it all must have changed when that wrestler happened. That must have led him into thinking, "Why not enjoy the young soft flesh myself." And when he first did it—lost his virginity so to speak—with that servant's boy, he must have felt the thrill more enjoying than what he was being subjected to earlier. And remember, he was not attractive to the fairer sex at all. He would have never got his pleasures from girls; that's why boys like boys. So, to satisfy his urges, he sought an outlet and found one easily. Why, he even tried to seduce me.'

'No!' she exclaimed. 'You. . .' she slid out of my arms and stood up, looking down at me from head to toe. 'Hmmm. I can imagine. You are beautiful.' She jumped down upon me, the bed letting off painful shrieks; she was so weightless I did not feel anything at all. 'Tell me what happened.'

I told her about the visit to the plant, the way he tried to always keep me out of my brother's sight, the way he groped when my brother was lost in the maze of machinery, the way he had whispered, 'Come to my home in the evening,' the way he had given my bumps a squeeze.

'Oh my darling, that was horrible,' and she started stroking me in long, silent motions.

I had gone drowsy by then and she whispered, 'Sleep my Sanjay. I will keep busy with My Sanju.'

That afternoon, my dream world and the real one existed in a wondrous, exotic mix. In my dreams I was stranded on an island filled with naked, virgin Amazons, found my Meena among those wild women, reigning as their queen, and we made wild love, all the while being watched with erotic curiosity by the other maidens. I drowsily came out of my slumber to the real world, breathing in Meena's hot breaths as she lay on top of me, replicating the actions of the other Meena, the Queen of Amazons of my dreams. The wild sensations traversing my nerves were divine. The whole afternoon and evening was filled with eroticism. I wanted time to stand still.

As the sun rode itself below the horizon, decorating the skies with amazing orange, red, yellow, and magenta-hued bands, she said in an exhaustive tone, 'You know, I am happy that you escaped his clutches, what with his penchant for young boys. But even if he had been successful, you wouldn't have been uncomfortable.'

'What do you mean by "I wouldn't have been uncomfortable"?'

'I meant you wouldn't have felt any pain down there.'

'Do you mean he has a gnawed, half-eaten short pencil, for a willy? Like the ones poverty-struck parents give to their kids—cutting the whole pencil in three parts—and the child gnaws away on the wood of these short parts and the length of the pencil shortens with each sharpening, till its end no longer rests in the crook of the thumb and the forefinger, but the father would still not dole out the second one-third pencil till the earlier one is so small that the child could not even hold it between his fingers. Or is his, one-fourth part?'

She was giggling endlessly. 'Something like that. But My Sanju is what I want.'

Her hands roamed around and she said, 'How do you manage to keep him up all the time?'

'It's you sweetheart. You keep my blood flowing the whole time. You are so lovely that I can never imagine a time when I could not be up to it. You are so bewitching that my blood boils just by your touch.'

'Don't love me so much, Sanjay.'

'Why, my darling? Why shouldn't I love you . . . so much?'

'Never mind,' she evaded the question. 'Let's enjoy the moment.'

When I returned home late that evening, my parents were already there, worrying about me. They were taken aback, seeing my tired and haggard look from those umpteen times I had made love that day, which I attributed to the hike up and down the slopes of the Helipad Hill, and that was also the reason for the late hour, as I had been feeling bored around midday and not realising that it was too late to commence the hike I had still gone, just to shake off the lethargy, and yes mother's medicine had overcome my dysentery by then. That almost convinced them—but what about the uneaten portion of lunch, left unconsumed by me? That had left me dumbstruck, since I couldn't have gone on a hike without having eaten something. Then inspiration struck. It was similar to a bulb lighting up in the deep recesses of the brain, as they show in that comic strip of *Chacha Chaudhary*.

'Just before I left the house, I had this intense craving for *samosas* and *jalebis*. So, I forgot the lunch and went to Bhajan Lalji's sweet shop, ate the delicacies there, and also took some *pakoras* for the trek. I met a group of kids on the plateau and shared the *pakoras* with them. We got chatting and I did not realise the passage of time till it was too late.'

'Was there a girl?' Father enquired with a smirk. I looked down at my toes to hide the blush reddening my face. The delightful sight of Meena lying supine on her bed swam across my eyes, and I nodded, adding in protest, 'But I was not interested in her, none at all, I swear.'

Where did I get all that money from, for the *samosas, jalebis,* and *pakoras?*—this from my brother, the brat, being flippant but there was an undertone of real resentment in his voice. Why did he have to ask that question? Father had not given me any money when my parents had left for Renusagar in the morning, I couldn't say that I had borrowed the cash from the cash box kept buried deep inside the Godrej almirah, as the keys to both the almirah and the cash box were always with Mother, I couldn't have borrowed the money from any of the neighbours as Mother would surely ask them the next day, while returning the cash, I did not want to drag Meena into the affair and borrow money from her and Bhajan Lal was too true to his trade—a stingy merchant—and would never dole out freebies, even to the scion of the respectable Tivariji. Before any further delay, which could give rise to any suspicion, I blurted out to their expectant faces, 'I begged Bhajan Lalji to give me the *samosas*, *jalebis*, and *pakoras* on credit.' Father asked, 'How much did it cost? I will pay him tomorrow.'

Cooking up all those lies and coming up with one seemingly reasonable explanation after another, marvelling inwardly at my own ingenuity, I had not anticipated the next query coming up during my interrogation. I had thought that the simple explanation of a trek up the Helipad Hill would be enough to satisfy their curiosities. But the unconsumed lunch and that brat of a brother of mine, with his innocent sounding query about the money, had landed me in a thick soup. That's the thing with lies. You land up in a vicious spiral, digging up excuse after excuse, and traversing in circle after circle you realise much later, that the last circle would never close, that there would always remain a huge gap in the end which could never be bridged, whatever new lie you come up with. This statement of Father's had put me in a jinx.

An image immediately sprang up in my head, of Father, the next day, handing over money for the items his son had purchased on credit the previous day and Bhajan Lal refusing to take the cash, vehemently claiming that he had not seen Tivariji's son in a long time, relentlessly maintaining that he would never give anything on credit to anyone: 'Even if Madhav (Lord Krishna) stood in front of me I would insist on instant payment, Tivariji, what to talk of your son.' And then Father would not rest till he got the entire truth out of me. That was not going to happen; getting me to spill my beans. But I decided to continue the charade, to grope for an opportunity to get out of the spiral.

'It's fifty rupees. It is only seven now. Give me the money. I will run over to Bhajan Lalji and pay him his dues.' I did not entertain the possibility that Father could enquire about the credit without having to pay Bhajan Lal the money himself. One of these days he might just happen to be visiting the shop and might goad Bhajan Lal for giving items on loan, when it was a well-known fact that he never gave credit, 'Not even to Madhav, Bhajan Lalji,' Father may chide him thus, 'And here you gave credit to my son. What about your jealously guarded reputation?' Then the whole lie would fall flat on my face. But I left that one for another day.

'Don't you run off anywhere,' Mother held my arm in an iron grip, 'I am not finished with you yet. You did not even think of your brother, leaving all the rooms and the front door locked.' I glanced at Kaalu. He was smirking with a smug look inhabiting his face, clearly relishing my predicament. 'Poor boy had to climb over the back wall, so small that he is, eat his cold lunch and snooze in the open verandah, all the time exposed to the hot, fiery sun. You didn't even bother to consider his plight?' How could the cold lunch be my fault? Served him right, the young devil that he is, to sleep under the scorching sun. She looked at Father and said, 'Darling, I think he is telling a lie. There is a girl involved, is my guess.'

Another flash of inspiration inspired me! Why hadn't I thought of that all this while? So absorbed was I in not getting Meena dragged into the entire affair that I had not thought of this line before. It would keep Meena out of the spiral and there would be no further enquiries to verify it. It would also give me a chance to finally close the circle. But I could not risk another gap. If I had to make this one convincing I would have to play the part carefully—one of these days my inspirations were going to run dry and land me in deep trouble, *Chacha Chaudhary* or no *Chacha Chaudhary*.

Buoyed by the stimulus, I once again dug my chin into my collar and stood silent, staring at my toes, so that they could not see the lie in my eyes.

'Come on son. Out with it. What is the truth?' Father demanded.

After a few moments of silence I mumbled into the 'V' of my shirt, 'I am sorry, Daddy,' and to my shock and horror I noticed the tear stains painting the front of my shirt, where Meena had wept her copious tears in the morning.

'Come again,' Father said.

'I am sorry. It was indeed a girl.'

'See, I told you so!' Mother exclaimed, 'He is seeing a girl.'

'Come on darling,' my parents always addressed each other with that endearing word, 'he is over 17 now. He deserves to go out,' Father seemed to be defending my case.

He laid a reassuring hand upon my shoulder. 'Then why the lie, son? You should have told the truth at the first instance. We don't mind you going out with a girl. It is not criminal in any way.'

'I did not know how you would react, thus the lies.'

'So, there were no *samosas*, *jalebis*, and *pakoras*.'

I shook my head.

'I knew it. That Bhajan Lal is a miser. He wouldn't even give credit to his dying mother. I was wondering what made him give you credit? How did you manage to go up the mountain without food?'

'I am a strong, grown-up man now. I don't need any food to climb up this hillock.' I gestured with defiance at the huge mountain which presided over the settlement like a towering god staring down from heaven. I had by now grown in confidence and could boast of climbing the mountain with no effort, food or no food.

'Who is the girl? Do we know her parents?'

Here came the gap in the circle. I had to be very careful while bridging it. One slip and I would end up in the spiral of endless lies again.

I fended for a girl. I did not know any daughter of Father's acquaintances— hell I didn't even know if any of them had any daughter—except Mr Yadav, who had a buxom, thick-around-the-waist daughter of my age, who looked like she had never known teenage years. If I told her name, more than the fact that Father would find out about the truth the very next day, I was worried that he would be disappointed with my choice. So, I silently sent a prayer of thanks to *Chacha Chaudhary* again and said, 'She is not from around here. We became friends on the train while I was coming home for the vacations. She studies at Lucknow and her father works at Renukoot (a town fifty-six kilometres away) with HINDALCO. She had told me that she would be coming to Shaktinagar today. Her father had some work here and she accompanied him with a couple of her friends. We had arranged to meet at the Helipad Hill. She had a picnic lunch and that's what I had. I am sorry that I had to lie to you earlier.'

Father gave me a hug and said reassuringly, 'Don't lie in the future. Are you serious about her?'

'No, she is just a casual acquaintance I met on the train, that's all.'

'Well, if anything serious develops let us know. We would like to meet her parents, too. What caste are they?'

'I think they are Rajputs. Her surname is Chauhan.'

There was a sudden tightening in his grip, his body seemed to stiffen and the genial nature of his tone became gruff, as he said, 'Then it is better that she remains just a friend.'

I felt ashamed of having had to cook up a story of a girl from Lucknow. I did not give much thought to Father's change in demeanour, when I had mentioned the fictitious girl's caste.

That night I thought a lot about my situation. What had become of my life? I had to come up with myriad excuses for going to meet my Meena. Sometimes, I felt overwhelmed with the burden of lies I had to tell. Meena had invaded my heart, my soul, my life, and my uncertain future. I loved her, heart and soul, and had confessed as much to her so many times. But she had never reciprocated. Whenever I broached the subject, she would appear evasive or just stare blankly at the ceiling, saying nothing. When I spoke glowingly of a future in which we would live as husband and wife, she would respond with, 'Wait for the future sweetheart.' Sometimes I wondered whether she loved me at all. Or did she even know the concept of love. She surely never loved that professor, definitely not her husband, and she wouldn't say that she loved me. Maybe I will have to live with, 'I adore you so much, Sanjay.' But I vowed that night that I would marry her, come what may. Remembering the summer of '83, I decided again that I would join NDA next summer and four years later, after I became a commissioned officer, my first act would be to elope with her, Sharmajee or no Sharmajee.

I slept fitfully, my dreams full of Amazons with the buxom, thick-around-the-waist daughter of Mr Yadav leaning over the queen's throne, forcing me to enter her from behind, the other Amazons bickering and demanding me to hurry up with the queen. Her hair turned into red flames and all the remaining Amazons straddled me as they descended upon me en masse. In another dream, I was donning a second lieutenant's uniform, streaking down the streets of Lucknow on a blood-red Kawasaki Bajaj motorcycle, Meena hanging on to my waist, her hair sailing like a black mast behind the bike and when I turned around to look at her overjoyed face, I saw the revolting multiple chins of Sharmajee's moon-face with speckles of vomit and spittle dotting the regions around his mouth, a short, pencil-shaped phallus jutting out, screaming 'I am not a cuckold' repeatedly.

12

Her Quirky Quirks

On the evening, when I had declared my love for her, she lay on top of me and sighed with contented pleasure, after a sensational, orgasmic journey. By now she had taught me enough about how to titillate her erogenous zones and arouse her sensations. She whispered in a passionate tone, 'My Sanju,' and pressed her puckered lips over mine.

'Booot ooo looog ooo oooing mooo foool nooom,' I spoke into her mouth.

'What was that?' she drew her head back, chuckling.

'I was saying—but I like you using my full name, with that melodious, breathless gasp at the end.'

'It's not you, my sweetness. This is the naming ceremony. I have named him My Sanju,' she glided her hands between my legs.

'That's a sweet name.'

'Since it is the smaller version of you—though not so small—hence your name in short and the possessive determiner 'my' denotes my proprietary right over it. Don't you go fooling around when you are away?'

I placed my hand over her head and declared, 'I promise to the peril of my life that I will never put My Sanju anywhere else—that's a solemn pledge. And,' I cupped her face in my hands, 'I love you with my heart and soul.'

'Oh Sanjay! What will I ever do without you?' with that she wriggled down, put her face on my chest, and wept warm tears. I shed some tears, too.

She had many crazy quirks, some adorable, some I simply loved, and some I never liked at all. She called them her kinks, her eccentric habits, which reassured her that she was different from the others, that she had an identity all by herself.

346

She insisted on remaining in the buff throughout my stay. It gave her a sense of freedom, she said, which she had never experienced earlier in her life. Our time together was what she looked forward to every waking minute and she did not want to spoil the effect by being confined by our clothes.

Who could deny her that, given her circumstances? She had fought for freedom all through her life—freedom from being labelled a burden the day she was born, freedom from being sidelined once her younger brother was born a year after her, freedom from being denied higher education just because she was a girl, freedom from having to strive harder just to prove that she was better than her brothers, freedom from having to repeatedly insist on a better station in life for her sister, freedom from being consigned to an existence of servitude and penury, freedom from having to depend upon the pittance meted out by her father and later her husband, freedom to live life on her own terms, even if it included a premarital affair with a much older married man and a scandalous, adulterous relationship with a younger boy-man, freedom from being tied, for eternity, in a loveless marriage with a homosexual pervert who had a proclivity for defiling her body (who could vouch for him not approaching Meena's boudoir again, vehemently demanding his husbandly rights to sate his unnatural desires; the very thought gave me shudders of morbid terror), freedom from having to bring up her child in an environment reeking of male chauvinism, and inculcating in him the concept of respect for women, if he was a male or preventing her from falling into the mire of worthlessness and servility, if she was a female.

'And I like it that I keep you in a semiaroused state all the time. I am amazed that you find me so attractive. I have always regarded myself as too skinny. Thank God for that. You never go soft when you see me like this. I detest that wrinkled, droopy sight, so I don't wear any clothes when I am with you.'

That was true enough. She was so exquisitely proportioned that I could never believe my luck at having her all to myself. She was an *apsara*, an angel, and a nymph, all rolled into one. Even ancient sages, deep in their meditation, having renounced all material desires, would have been roused out of their trance at her sight. Her Creator must have spared an entire day in making her. Her slender shoulders were so nimble that I never tired of nibbling at them, leaving tiny pink marks on her unblemished skin. Her breasts were neither big nor small, they had no sag and did not veer to the flanks; they were two delicious orbs sticking straight out with their slightly wrinkled, pinkish brown nipple and swollen areola a permanent invitation to my lips and tongue. Her ribs did not as much as poke out, but merged with her skin, giving an impression of a strong frame. The lines of her waist delightfully curved to give her an hourglass appearance; her belly was tight and taut with nary an ounce of flab or fat on it. She had the flattest of flat stomachs I have ever seen—even amongst the cadets at NDA—it was not emaciated, but evenly toned; her secret—pranayam and yoga. Whenever she exhaled and pressed her stomach in, during her breathing exercises, I feared that she would crush all those intestines, kidneys, spleen, and other internal organs nesting below her midriff. I could spend hours lost inside her navel, where my tongue went on its eternal quest for elixir. The lush triangle of black hair between her legs hid the object of my desire, and after I had shaved it off, revealing a pinkish area, her Mound of Venus deliciously curved outwards. She had full, round hips, which swayed and dipped and dupped whenever she sashayed in and out of her bedroom. The flesh in her shapely thighs was ample enough to add to her voluptuousness; not the thunder-thigh version of Sri Devi and neither the cigarette style of the size-zero crazy, twenty-first-century girls. Her dimple-free knees, slender calves, and dainty ankles completed the appearance of an apsara. Every part of her body was divine perfection, and there is not a mortal alive whose blood would lose its vitality, especially in the nether regions, when his eyes are blessed with such a vision. I am a lesser mortal and how could I deny 'My Sanju' his right to remain alert all the time.

'And I love the perfection of your body,' she added. I was not sure of that. In recent times there had been a considerable improvement in our diet at the school, plus I had the added privileges of extra helpings, being one amongst the seniors. Our new registrar, a young captain from the Army, had a penchant for throwing around utensils, full of *daal* and vegetable curry, if they did not meet his exalted standards of culinary excellence and did not suit his palate. After a few episodes of clattering aluminium containers, splashes of watery, yellow-as-runny-stool daal and flying chunks of half-cooked potato and hard cauliflower stems, no florets to speak of there, smeared in black, rubbery gravy; the cooks at the students' mess had been put to the task and they had recently started producing such culinary delights never known in the school's history. As a consequence, I had stopped resembling a concentration camp escapee, my cheeks had filled up some, and a few centimetres of flab had given a new shape to my previously nonexistent belly. My hips had acquired a semblance of the hemispherical orbs they should be, rather than the flat pancakes they had assumed to be their destined existence. Now that I had acquired a likeness to my original 'good-looking in a good-looking sort of way' looks, who could fault her in seeing in me the very incarnation of Adonis, especially compared to the obscenely obese cretin she had for a husband.

I for myself had only one singular fetish—painting her toenails. Each time, after exploding in a delicious orgasm inside her, I would lay sprawled across her legs and buried deep between her feet, I would apply thin lines of nail polish on her nails, painting them with different colours. My initial attempts proved to be clumsy and I smudged her feet often. As I gained expertise, I even started painting varying patterns—circular, spiral, horizontal, vertical, and myriad other shapes, whatever caught my fancy. I used a magnifying lens and sharp-pointed brushes, needles even, to get the patterns and shapes right. She kept a generous supply of nail polish containers, contributed handsomely by me too, through my meagre pocket money.

13

The Most Elegant Attire

Somewhere during the middle of my vacation, she finished her life story, less the revelations which came later.

When it was time for me to tell her about myself, I commenced from the mid nineteenth century. I wanted to tell her everything in a chronological sequence and not the hop-forward, step-back, hop-forward-again version of the news-reel-jumping style I had used with Pratima.

I told her about Trilok Singh, my mid nineteenth-century ancestor, who had imprisoned a fugitive and how the prisoner had escaped to the terai region before the police arrived. I told her about my grandfather, his Freedom Fighting days, his twin marriages, his Shajhanesque declaration, his generosity and concern for his family, friends, and animals, his visionary inceptions, his six sons and lonely daughter and their progenies, my father's army life, my birth and its effects, my accident (she fussed over me a lot, kissing my right leg again and again) and subsequent recovery in grandfather's company, his days in a vegetative existence, his enduring vibrancy and positive energy which used to wrap me like a cloak whenever I was at Shanti Bhavan, his absolute joy when his only daughter got married, and his relieved demise four days later.

I told her about my maternal grandfather, his desire to secure education for his four girls, my parents' marriage and how they broke the age-old practice of not conceiving me on their wedding night, about my cynosure status, as an infant and toddler, amongst the women at both the households, about my visits to Jaswantnagar, my puppy love for *BB Mausi* and my eavesdropping on her secret conversation with her sister. I narrated how, in her own subtle ways, she had made me see only the best in women and

350

how, since then, I have viewed women in a light different than the other boys and men in my family.

I told her about Father's search for a job after leaving the Army, his extremely loyal friend Arjun Thakur, our move to Dalmiapuram, my daily bus rides to Tiruchirapalli, the evening when my 7-year-old self had felt that my parents had abandoned me, Father's reasons for our move to Hospet, my bunking classes to see 'Amitam' Bachchan movies with Mother, the young college-going boy who took me to the other movies at the behest of Mother, her desire and success in learning English so that she could devour all the gossips and scandals in the English film magazines, Father's mad ride after he had been stung by a scorpion, our 'Once In A Lifetime Trip' to Bangalore, Jog Falls, Mysore, and Brindavan Garden, the accidental appearance of a badly bruised Manfred Potter at our house and his subsequent recovery, my Coca Cola sojourns in the company of my brother, after flicking money from Father's pockets, the fright of my life when Father had wielded that steel-studded belt and beaten those crooks in his office, his compulsions in leaving the well-paying job and returning to Shanti Bhavan, after selling his car and other possessions.

I told her about Father's hunt for work again, our penurious existence, Mother's travails at the hands of her mother-in-law, our schooling at a convent school, Mother's struggles in making both ends meet, her father's fortnightly visits and the secret transfer of money from father to daughter, my preteen loves for Hasina and Neelima, my crush on the Sanskrit teacher, the preparations for and clearing the entrance test for Sainik School Ghorakhal, the dancing circles and purple pen of my botched medical examination, my horror at being admitted at a Hindi-medium government school, my subsequent move to Ghorakhal, my relationship with the Dwivedi siblings, my infatuation for the hostel matron, and my first sight of an angel.

I also told her about the pretty younger twin who used to play with my younger brother, making me go green with envy, as I had to make do with her plain featured elder twin.

'Do you always fall for the first beautiful girl you meet? You do love women.'

'What is there not to love in them? And I am a sucker for a pretty face. I have always been fascinated by women. Unlike a man, she has an adorable appearance, soft silhouette, spotless silky skin, bewitching beauty, captivating countenance, alluring aroma, charming curves, glossy tendrils of hair, alluring almond eyes one can drown into, elegant eyelashes, pretty pert nose, luscious lips, delicate chin, long neck, soft shoulders, slender arms, dainty fingers, svelte figure, lithe waist—though some are blessed with an abundance—everything a man cannot have. Look at you, I cannot imagine another being with such long lustrous locks sitting atop your head like a crown, with velvety tendrils flowing down your back, a few stray strands either shielding your almond eyes or caressing your cheeks as the breeze whips your tresses around. What more divine vision does one need? Despite what our Holy Scriptures, the Bible, and the other books say, God created women after his own image and when I see a girl I catch a glimpse of my Creator. What else do I need? You are the ones who give life and are yourselves nurtured into anonymity. What an irony? I pity our race for failing to appreciate the colossal contribution your lot makes in the lives of us men.'

'Oh Sanjay! Where do you get such poetic flow from?'

'From a girl so marvellous I once thought I would never be able to live without her.' Then I told her about Pratima; her birth, including how she was almost abandoned, her struggles in life, her doting brothers who shaped her destiny, her brilliance, her photographic memory, and above all, her unsurpassed beauty. I narrated the stories we used to regale each other with and the g-shaped girl from Vodrumeepfijiksha. 'She inspired me into creating such fantasies that I find it hard to imagine that I am the same person who could work such miracles with my imagination. I have lost the capacity since the day we parted.'

'You loved her so much! What led to your . . . separation?'

'The circumstances of my birth decided my destiny. I had decided in '83, more than a year after we had met, that she was the one I would spend the rest of my life with, though she is four years older than me. She took a bit longer in arriving at her decision and when we met for the last time at Ghorakhal, just before her twelfth exam, she more or less committed to me.'

I told her about Pratima's father's decision to marry her to that peon from Nainital, how he had decided to sell his daughter to a homosexual to clear his debt, how her Big Brother threatened imprisonment and lynching to put the fear of death in her father, how she left Ghorakhal with a promise to meet me a year later at Lucknow, how her brothers discovered her love for me and how she had to chose between her obligations to her brothers and her love for me, after it emerged that my ancestry and *gotra* were the principle hindrance to our union. I ended my story with the closing of the amber door.

Later, we made deep passionate love, with tears flowing down my eyes and she sipped each of the damning outpourings and heralded the end of my love affair with Pratima. That night Pratima took her final leave from my heart, to only return more than four and a half years later.

The next time I told her about my ruminations as a 13-year-old, at Golu Devta's temple and the subsequent discussion, including Pratima's prognosis of a scrofulous society in the future. I only left three incidences out of my entire narrative: the intimacy I had shared with Pratima in the cave, the desolation I had felt after the closing of the amber door, and the two pledges I had taken in front of Golu Devta—it was too early in my relationship with Meena and I was not sure whether I should share such intimate secrets with her.

'But you are wrong about the sari. Women in the Indian subcontinent were never forced to wear a sari as the lone apparel. It was more of a necessity than a choice. And, sari is the most elegant attire for a woman, anywhere in the world. It can be worn in more than eighty different ways—each of our states and regions have different styles to drape the strip of cloth, varying from five to nine yards of length. Which other singular dress can have such versatility? And it caters for all ages, shapes, sizes, girth, height, moods, and desires. The more daring among us can wear it low down the waist with a low-cut sleeveless and backless blouse, to show off a lot of our fair skin. The conservative ones can wear it covering their entire body and head. Those endowed with an abundant waistline can wear it in a manner which hides their prosperity without making it too obvious. Shorter girls can tuck the width inside their petticoats to achieve the right length for their pleats. The pleats can be tucked into the waist inside the back to allow free movement of the legs. It can be worn tightly draped to accentuate a slim figure or worn loosely to avoid a lecher's eyes. And the blouse, it adds to the allure. It can be tailored to allow the right amount of peek, sleeveless to highlight the slender lines of our upper arms, full sleeved to cover those bad spots on the skin, low cut to show off the cleavage, as a choli for the more modest ones, a tight-fitting one to boost up the sag and reveal a generous midriff and backless to showcase a nimble back. There is no other dress in the world which is as adaptable as the sari.

'Its origins can be traced back to the Indus Valley Civilisation; numerous mentions of it can also be found in the Jataka tales and older scripts. The very term sari and its accompaniments can be traced back to our history— Sari itself is derived from the Prakrit word Sadi and even has a mention as *Sattika*, describing the women's attire, in Jataka tales. The *Choli* is derived from the ancient Tamil ruling clan, the Cholas, and the *Pallu* originated during the Pallava period and is named after that ruling clan from the third- to ninth-century Tamilakam. Our first- to sixth-century sculptures depict goddesses and dancers draped in a sari. As per our ancient traditions, the navel of the Supreme Being is considered to be the source of life and creativity, hence the sari is worn leaving the midriff bare, even though for sometime navel exposure became a taboo due to prohibition by some Dhramashastra writers who opined that women should always cover their navel.

'It was more of a dress borne out of convenience keeping in view the climatic conditions in our country, especially in the Deccan Plateau and further south, where the long hot summers prevented wearing of heavy garments. Since ancient times, women have been wearing sari-like garments for lower body and shawls or scarf for the upper body. The one-piece sari is a modern invention.

'Sari provides protection from the leers of predatory men. A sari can reveal as much as a woman desires and at the same time cover all her vital assets. When a man sees a woman wearing a sari draped in a pious manner, he is reminded of his mother and sister. Women in ancient India were considered as the epitome of all that is beautiful on earth, they were regarded with immense respect and held in reverence. This was not the case all through our history. When the invaders from the Middle East came, to initially plunder and later conquer India, they must have been amazed at the way the women in our subcontinent appeared in minimum clothing, with bare upper bodies, in complete contrast to the way they were used to, in treating their own women, all covered in black. And, as is the wont of any invading army's soldiers, they considered the native women as easy prey and indulged in rape and abuse—in recent times our own General Maneckshaw had issued a diktat that no Indian soldier would indulge in rape and pillage during the '71 operations and he subsequently came down heavily upon the defaulters, including dismissing some senior officers from service. Every victory in wars, since the dawn of man, has turned into an orgy of rape and plunder. Men became animals. Their predatory manners were subsequently picked up by the locals—when the invaders left after their plunder, the natives exploited in their wake. A woman, once considered beautiful and pure, now turned into an object to satisfy the men's lust. What could women, whose protectors had been killed by the invaders, do but be defiled? How did women save themselves? They committed *Jauhar* to avoid being exploited by their husbands' victors and save their honour—there have been many Rani Padminis in our history who resorted to the ultimate sacrifice, forfeiting their lives. And there was that draconian tradition of *Sati*—that was truly barbaric, making an ordinary woman commit suicide, even if there was no danger to her life after her husband's untimely death. Thank God we had a Raja Rammohan Roy. Had *Sati* not been outlawed in 1829 and subsequently banned in our country in 1861, we would still be having this cruel custom. But it still goes on in some villages in certain parts of our country. They will have to have a law to ban it entirely.'

(Even after it was banned by Lord William Bentinck in areas under British control, through the tireless efforts of Raja Rammohan Roy, under the Bengal Sati Regulation, 1829, it continued in the princely states till 1861, when all states banned it. But the evil practice still continued in modern times, as a widow, who self-immolated at her husband's funeral pyre, was considered virtuous and attained the status of *Sati Mata*; there are temples of *Sati Mata* in Rajasthan and Madhya Pradesh. The lethargic Government of India, as always, woke up only when an 18-year-old Roop Kanwar was immolated at the funeral pyre of her 24-year-old dead husband on 04 September '87, to glorify *Sati*, which led to the passage of The Commission of Sati (Prevention) Act, 1987, then too after a huge public outcry).

'But how could women save themselves from their own men who had turned predators? These men preyed on the weaknesses of women and considered them as objects of desire. So, the women decided to become less desirous—they thought, 'Cover yourself up entirely and people will think you are least desirable.' They chose the alternative of shielding themselves and covered their entire body with the sari and blouse. In South India, till the mid twentieth century, women from many communities wore only the sari, leaving the upper part of the body exposed. The blouse evolved as a form of clothing only in the tenth century. But the defenseless and hapless women could not do enough to prevent themselves from the lewd nature of men—they continued to be preyed upon.'

'But why cover yourself from your own family?' I asked, still disturbed by the *purdah* system prevalent in the country.

'Because predators do not live in the dark streets alone. When I was growing up, I was told never to venture out of the house after dark, not to go to isolated places, never take a route which has a lonely stretch, never look a stranger in his eyes; never do this, never do that. I never saw a movie in a cinema hall till I went to the university. Women then rarely went to the movies. There was fear everywhere. Predators roamed the streets looking for easy prey. Animals will remain animals. When they did not find prey out in the streets, they came homeward bound.'

'But they have their wives for that,' I said, incredulous at such a mindset prevailing among my 'countrymen'.

'I am not talking of pure lust. There is something else to it. What prompted those invaders to rape the women of their rivals? It was not sexual gratification alone. By abusing the women, they were demonstrating their ultimate power. They were telling the vanquished that they were as powerless as a rodent in a serpent's jaws. A man who can't protect his women is considered the worst kind of craven. These predators enjoy establishing their power over others, men or women.

'When a child is raped by a man, he establishes his power over her parents or relatives. Whereas a woman is raped to overpower her, it has the sinister purpose of condescending her and to show her that her rightful place is below her tormentor, both in the figurative and real sense. Rape has never been about lust alone. There are other means to satisfy those urges. When a young boy is ditched by his love interest he takes offence and rapes her to put her right. When a man sees a woman dressed in a manner that he feels is not prescribed by his religion, he has her molested and blames it on her provocative dress sense.'

She wriggled out of my arms and walked over to her books. She brought forth the Garud Puran and the King James Version of the Bible.

'This condescension of women draws its authority from our religious scriptures. Take the Garud Puran: "A woman's principal *dharm* (religious duty) is to obey the orders of her husband"—my mother's oft repeated refrain to pile miseries upon her daughter-in-law. On widowhood it says, "A woman who does not take the refuge of another man after her husband's death, will enjoy the association of Goddess Parvati in heaven." Men found their justification to kill widows here.

'Take Christianity: Genesis 1: 29, Chapter 2, Verse 22—"And the rib, which the LORD God had taken from man, made he a woman and brought her unto the man." Verse 23, same chapter—"And Adam said, this is now bone of my bones, and flesh of my flesh: she shall be called woman, because she was taken out of Man." A woman by herself has no existence; she is there because she came out of man and hence she will forever remain his to please. God did not object to Adam's claim then and neither does he interfere with Adam's successors' attitudes today.

'Genesis 3: 6, Chapter 3, Verse 6—"And gave also unto her husband with her; and he did eat". And what does her man say. In verse 12 of the same chapter, he accuses her of wrongdoing: "The woman whom thou gavest to be with me, she gave me of the tree and I did eat." As if he did not have any say in the matter, despite claiming proprietary right over her.

'And how does God punish her? Verse 16—"I will greatly multiply thy sorrow and thy conception; in sorrow thou shalt bring forth children; and thy desire shall be to thy husband, and he shall rule over thee."

'Rule over me my foot, I will kill the man who ever lays that claim over me.

'I have nothing to say of a religion which permits multiple wives and prescribes that their women be stoned to death. How much more morbid can you get than that?

'No religion has a female entity as the Supreme Being. Only males. Hinduism does have goddesses, but then we have more than 84,000 gods and goddesses, for everyone to choose her or his salvation. But the holy trinity is an all-males club. The ultimate recourse for mankind is the Holy Books, and as they proclaim superiority of men over women, the men in turn claim it as their birthright. Since religion permits it, things will never change. Men would always want to exercise their power. Whenever they feel threatened by women, they would resort to means to keep them suppressed.

'Since the beginning of time, when man and woman started living as couples and raising families, duties were assigned based on differences in physiology and propensities—women to tend to the hearth, bed, and the progenies and wait for their men; the men in turn would go out and fend for the family. The fender, since he provided for the family, became the superior one. The woman, who slaved day in and day out, was the inferior one. Every religion observes one day in a week as a day for worship and rest—Sunday or Friday. Men rest and lounge around. But there is no rest for the homemaker. All days are the same for her.

'But despite all this, a woman has many positives—our tenacity, our superior brains, and this thing between our legs.

'Most women avoid intercourse post menopause. But men have never-ending desires. After my mother took her vow of celibacy, my father started frequenting the city's brothels. My mother's only conditions are that he will never take a mistress and will not rape anyone. Thank God for that. He has kept his promise till now, except that lone incidence of that widow. But other men—they couldn't find their release in the streets. They never had enough money for the brothels and many ran into debts with the pimps and brothel owners. They then started visiting their close and distant relatives and preyed upon the unmarried daughters there—preteens even.

'I have three distant cousins who were routinely molested by their uncles; one of these uncles was the girl's mother's first cousin.'

'Their parents never objected?' I asked bewildered.

'When these girls complained to their mothers, one of them was married off promptly and the other two were told to keep quiet about it. And the worst of it, the predatory uncles were still allowed inside the houses and continued exploiting the other two girls till they were married. One of the uncles was that first cousin who took advantage of his superior status and the girl's mother grudgingly permitted free access to him. The other uncle had a powerful hold over the girl's father, something to do with his business having gone sour, and that uncle had used his influence to bail him out.

'It was not about lust, it was the same old game, what those victors played over the vanquished—the game of exercising power. That gave them the high and not the two-minute humping of a young girl. She was the tool using which the uncle demonstrated his power over the girl's parents. Once the girls got married, the uncles stopped visiting their parents' homes again, moving on to other pastures.'

'What about their virgin status?' I asked, recalling that Indian husbands value their newlywed brides' hymen more than their own foreskin.

'That was easy enough, so easy that it is laughable. On their respective wedding nights, their mothers gave the girls a small rubber pouch filled with some animal's blood or some other red fluid. During intercourse, all the girl had to do was grunt in pain and pierce the pouch, spraying its content on the sheets. Virginity proved.

'In certain cultures in Africa, the Middle East, some South East Asian countries, and I have heard even in our country—God only knows what goes on behind those closed doors—they remove young girls', even infants', clitoris and labia and sew up the remaining part with thread, thorns, or catgut, leaving a small hole for passage of urine and menstrual blood. All to ensure that the girl does not succumb to her desires before marriage and her virginity could be proven on the wedding night. To top it all they have given decent sounding names to such mutilations, proclaiming divine permission—Sunna circumcision and Pharaonic circumcision. On the wedding night, the stitches are removed by a midwife, in the presence of the groom and his relatives. In some cases, it is sewed back to ensure that she remained faithful and loyal to her husband. Some don't even bother removing the stitches, forcing themselves despite the stitches; it gave them the assurance that she was a virgin and loyal. What about the loyalty of the husband? Should we put a lock on it? Why do women only have to bear the cross of virtue? Why did Draupadi accept that she would be wife to the other brothers of Arjun, too? Why did she not tell Kunti that what she had decreed was immoral and unethical? Why do women have to suffer the lot?

'What gave my father the authority to decide my destiny? Where is my individuality? What am I? What is a woman? What are we—humans or in-betweens? In prehistoric times, women, by virtue of our inadequacies, were entrusted with bearing and rearing the brood and keeping the hearth warm and the bed warmer, whereas the men hunted and brought in food. But when did it degenerate into slavery? Why do men treat women as if we are something to be acquired? Our rajas and maharajas kept harems for their pleasures. The common man treated his woman as a slave, hers to do what the master wished. Why should we have a Sati Savitri, why not a man who offers his life for his love? Even Lord Ram did not go after Ravan for Sita; it was his hubris—how come another man, a devil incarnate at that, could take his wife away from him. His love for her fell flat after they returned to Ayodhya—in his wisdom she was guilty until proven innocent. Even the *Agnipariksha* was not enough to absolve her and she was banished to the forest. Look at Draupadi, had it not been for Lord Krishna she would have been standing naked before the entire court while her husbands, sworn to protect her honour, stood impotent, hanging their heads like limp dicks. What are we conveying to our younger generation? That women are material objects, to be possessed and abused in whatever debased manner they could imagine. That we are perpetually inferior.

'There are two women I admire the most in my life—Phoolan Devi and Kiran Bedi. It's a paradox I know, one is deemed evil and the other was the first woman officer in the Indian Police Service. One was a bohemian who challenged the writ of the upper caste male chauvinist pigs and got her own back, even after suffering such colossal setbacks in her young life. The other followed her "urge to be outstanding" and joined the police to improve the system. We need more Phoolan Devis and Kiran Bedis to take on the fanatic bigots and then maybe, just maybe, we might have a just society. At least we are not as bad as some Middle Eastern countries where a woman is not even allowed to venture out of her home without a male relative accompanying her. Men put the fear of other men inside their women. Why not put the fear of God inside those men? Because their God is a male Himself and would allow the men to condescend the lesser species, as if it is his divine right to treat women as property. I do not fear the physical damage that the men who letch at me would inflict on me. When people look at me lecherously, it is the psychological scarring I dread the most, because men believe that what they desire is permitted by the society and if they cannot have the woman of their desires physically, they can always use the scriptures to make her submit to him.'

'What do you think when I look at you?'

'You are different Sanjay. The very first day when I had laid my eyes upon you and you had looked at me hesitantly, I knew that you were different. You do not look at women like others. You have a purity that I have never seen in a man. There is reverence and adoration in your eyes when you look at me. And there is a hint of pity. You don't have to do that; don't ever feel sorry for me. I may be a victim of my circumstances but I am fully capable of taking on this world of misogynists. I am not someone who would take things lying down. Yes, having you by my side would help. The attitude of my father has given me enough strength. My only regret is that I did not have this strength six months back. Being with you has strengthened my resolve.'

Who could have not been infected by that sentiment? I left for Ghorakhal, firm in my resolve that I would be her saviour and her partner in her battles with this world full of bigotry and prejudice against women. I have never loved a girl more.

14

The Hirsute Sardar and the Petrified Girl

There comes a time in a person's life when everything starts falling into its rightful place. Mine came in the year following my first sight of the love of my life. The power of love can make you perform wonders. Despite the difficulties of calculus, I was able to muster more than 70 per cent marks in the twelfth board exams. But the icing was my performance in the NDA entrance exams that December. When the results were announced, just before the Board Exams, I had scored the highest marks in the country and a letter from the Chairman of the Union Public Service Commission, addressed to the school's principal, congratulating me on my superlative performance, was kept displayed on the School Notice Board for a month.

All this while Meena was with me—as a memory when I was away from her and as an inseparable extension of my existence whenever we were together. That winter vacation after my NDA entrance exam I spent numerous wonderful evenings with her. During those stolen occasions, she regaled me with stories from the books she had read from her endless treasure trove. We also read to each other the books we enjoyed. To add to the entertainment, I enacted scenes from Amitabh Bachchan movies, though without the bell-bottoms I must have looked more like a clown.

After the board exams, I insisted upon Father to let me join a Services Selection Board, SSB, coaching institute at Pusa Road in New Delhi. In New Delhi, I stayed with Arjun Thakur and his family and enjoyed the duck curry and chapatti prepared lovingly by his wife for the entire duration of ten days; heated and served for every meal. Having prepared myself adequately during the ten-day stint, I sailed through the psychological tests, physical tests, group discussions, group tasks, extempore speech, and interview of the tough selection procedure at Allahabad. I met my nemesis again in the medical test: the colour-blindness test book. The army doctor, having realised that the book was beyond me to decipher, tested me on identifying the four primary colours peeping out of the pinholes on a rotating cuboid, where I was successful and was declared temporarily fit to join NDA—a slight problem of varicocele was discovered by another doctor. I had to undergo a surgery to seal off the dilated vein and ensure even blood flow through the other healthy veins. The same doctor, who set me forth in pursuit of my calling, by coincidence, also brought forth my firstborn upon her birth twelve years later.

Meena visited me in the hospital while I was convalescing after my surgery. She fussed and fretted over me, more than my mother, and was becoming increasingly worried that the cause for my testicles shrinking must have been her overexuberance. After some time, it became my duty to console her. I replied that even if that had been the case, I would readily suffer 100 such shrunken marbles, but would have never missed even a single moment of our intimacies. That had brought a smile on her lovely face, her conical canines twinkling, and when I ran my hands over her belly, I noticed a thin, uncharacteristic flab. When, exultantly and anxiously, I asked her whether she was pregnant, she replied that the growth was due to my prolonged absence, which prevented her from burning those excess calories. I promised that I would leave no stone unturned in ensuring that all those calories evaporated, the moment I was out of the hospital.

After I returned from the hospital, I had only five days left before my final medical exam, prior to being declared fit and leaving for training at NDA. I spent all those five evenings with her and by the end she had not only lost that flab but also improved my dexterity. Our calisthenics reached new dimensions as she had procured a colourful, glossy reproduction of *Kamasutra* and our lovemaking acquired new meaning.

NDA training was a revelation. I spent the first five months at NDA Wing, Ghorpuri, where the first-termers trained in isolation. I never knew that I had such reserves of stamina and endurance within me, to undergo the tough, physically intensive training as a cadet. What Sainik School could have prepared me for NDA? It is a misnomer that Sainik School training is adequate for NDA—balls it is. I was amazed at the versatility and virtuosity NDA engendered within me. The constantly busy schedule kept us on the move always—crammed as it was with physical training, drill, equitation, swimming, sports, weapon training, extra-curricular activities, academics studies for the graduation degree and thrown in between this entire muddle, were the three to four hours of glorious sleep. The ordered routine hid within it an endless maze of permutations and combinations and juggling with time, as within the schedule were thrown in punishment runs, caring for the Academy's cleanliness, project works for the BA degree, so on and so forth. Even Sundays were not entirely free—there were the morning cross-country run practices, fifty-kilometres long many days, hikes, and punishment runs for frequent defaulters; my name invariably and mysteriously was always on this list, every Sunday. To any outsider, the NDA routine might resemble a mad scramble, but to a cadet there was a method in this madness.

The Academy builds a culture where outdoor activity becomes second nature to a cadet. Cadets are constantly put in pressure-cooker situations to prepare them for the future challenges as leaders of men, so that when we became officers we could handle high amounts of mental and physical stress. The gruelling schedule instils in us a sense of purpose and devotion to duty which no other training could achieve. Being relentless and ceaseless in pursuit of one's goal is the principle character trait revered at the Academy— you may be forgiven if you are not talented enough to complete a thirty-five-kilometre run, with full battle loads, in three hours, but all hell would break loose if it was perceived that you had not tried hard enough.

When I came home in December '87, for my meagre four weeks of vacation, I basked in the glory of pride in Father's eyes and suffered the 'ch-chs' of Mother for my having gone so thin to 'almost become nonexistent'. After those first few minutes of attention and departure of Father for his errands—my brother was by now studying in St Francis' College at Lucknow, which had no 'long' winter vacation—I told Mother that I had to go to Renukoot to meet a 'course mate' from NDA. I was keen, since Sharmajee's scooter was absent and I wanted to spend the next ten hours in Meena's arms. Promising that I would be back by dinner, I set off to meet my love, after such a long period of absence.

As soon as my feet landed in her verandah, she ran up to me and exclaimed, 'What happened to you? How long have you been sick? Where has your flab vanished? Where are your cheeks? Your flat cheekbones have become more pronounced.' Then, as she ran her hands all over me, she remarked at each change my anatomy had undergone, 'Oh my God! When did you grow these bumps on your biceps . . . I can iron my clothes on your stomach . . . the way your shoulders are sloping my fingers are panting in their efforts to trudge up the slope . . . take off your shirt, I want to see whether you still have your nipples . . . why is your spine so straight, is there a rod in there? Why are there caves in your hips, did they erase your beautiful question mark too? Oh! You have become my David, though at his full height of over fourteen feet you would look grotesque. Why are you hiding this beautiful body, take these off. Even though it is my full moon time, I still can't wait to see the complete you.' With that she started unbuttoning my shirt and unbuckling my belt.

I enjoyed her company more during her full moon time. She talked and talked, with short breaks to work magic with oil and her fingers, as she massaged my body, head to toe. It sounded heavenly now, after the toll my muscles and bones had taken during the past five months.

While she acted my personal masseuse, delicately removing the knots from my newly developed muscles, I regaled her with tales of my days and nights at Ghorpuri—the novelty of staying in a horse-stable-turned-into-barracks, whose roughly textured walls still carried remnants of the musty odour of horse urine and sweat; the barks of our drill instructors which sounded so much like staccato bursts of a machine gun fire—for the first few days I did not understand a single word they bellowed in their throaty shouts, pulled from deep inside their bellies; the patriotic songs we used to belt out at the top of our voices, in the middle of the night, as a sozzled and besotted Colonel Hoshiar Singh, the Wing Commander and bossman, and winner of the Param Vir Chakra in the '71 war, sat atop his car's bonnet, relishing our collective croons with a wistful expression belying his thoughts; the euphoria of my first drag of cigarette, as the multiple chemicals laden white smoke travelled past my tongue, went through the trachea and dumped its nicotine and tar into my lungs to mix with my blood and give me my high; the humungous quantities of hams, sausages, and other gastronomic novelties I had never heard of before and which we consumed with such bulimic fervour; my clumsy attempts at eating chicken with a knife and fork—they even made us eat soup with a fork once—I gave up eating chicken for two months, till I had mastered the art of slicing the flesh off the bone without launching the entire piece into some sorry sod's unsuspecting face; the camaraderie I shared with my course mates, which was the sole crutch that helped us limp through the gruelling training regime; the umpteen gallons of water I had had to gulp down in the swimming pool during my futile efforts in staying afloat, while the swimming instructor left no opportunity go waste in tugging me and my tiny, crotch-embracing swimming trunks down under the water and the latter down my legs—there had been many instances when my red-coloured trunks would be floating just out of reach and I had to flap and paddle across to grab at it in order to emerge out of the pool without baring my question-marked bottom and my limp pecker.

The biggest disadvantage of NDA training was the short vacations; four weeks after every five months. That left me with barely 24 days at home. I soon ran dry of excuses for making my Meena trysts, especially during the summers when my younger brother was also home on his vacations. I worked up strategies of watching movies alone at the new cinema hall and going for long walks to ease my mind. I refused to go to Shanti Bhavan with my parents, insisting that they take Kaalu to meet his uncles and cousins. Whenever they were away on those long trips to Shanti Bhavan, I spent entire days with Meena and even many nights, with her intoxicated 'he' snoring in the next room in a drunken stupor, his entry into her bedroom prohibited by the knife hanging at her door.

When I came to her in June '88, after another five months at Kharakvasla, the main NDA where we had moved to after our first term at Ghorpuri, Meena refused to recognise me. When she saw the gleam in my eyes, the overjoyed reaction on her face more than made up for the longing I had felt, living away from her. She ran into me and enveloped me in a fierce hug, her soft body smelling of roses and lime. After a looong, hungry kiss, she said, 'For a minute there I missed my knife. What has become of you? What do they do to you there? Where is your flesh? It's all muscles and bones. God! Do people have muscles like these in reality? I only see these in photographs of those contestants for some stupid bodybuilding competition. You have become even more delightful. I want to eat you right now. Why are your clothes still on?' Riff-rap-shred-ping-smack and moments later we were down on the floor, my bare back burning from the hot concrete of her verandah, my entire body enflamed with renewed desire. Prior to returning home late that evening, I had to borrow one of the huge

XXXL-sized shirts of her husband and some money from her to buy a new shirt from a local garment shop; my original shirt, having suffered massacre at her hands, was of no further use even as a dishcloth. I think she must have consigned her shredded blouse and bra to the flames and cut her petticoat into smaller strips—that was the first time our frenzy had resulted in so much damage to our couture. Henceforth, I never wore a vest and carried a fresh pair of shirt and trousers, whenever I went to meet her on the first day of my vacation—there was no saying what fate my clothes would meet in our passion. The most difficult part was to explain to my parents why the muggers took only my shirt and at times trousers, and not the cash or watch. I merely shrugged and said that they had looked so desperate and so naked with their shrunken, sleepy willies never holding any promise of waking up, that I had felt pity on them and handed over my clothes before they could aspire for better things. While they wore my clothes, I made a run for it and bought fresh clothes from a nearby shop.

In our frenzy on her verandah floor my back had turned red and hot, which I only noticed after my own heat had exploded inside her. When we moved inside she had me lie on my stomach on her bed and applied a soothing balm on my burning back. She tut-tutted and said, 'My poor Sanjay. Never again on hot concrete. Next summer I will sprinkle my verandah with cold water and spray crushed ice before you jump in.'

I winced at the burns and said, 'We could have waited till I had carried you in here. It's only a few paces from your verandah.'

'Oh Sanjay! Seeing you there, standing lean and tall with your rock-hard muscles, I couldn't resist myself. What do you think I do when you are away for five months? I pine for you every minute and long for your arms around me, to feel you inside me. I hope you don't go about seeking adventures at Ferguson College and MG Road in Pune.'

'No, my little daffodil. You are the only one for me. And anyway, I haven't passed my drill test, so I cannot go on liberty from the campus. I haven't enjoyed the delights of Pune in the last one year.'

'What else was new at Kharakvasla?'

'Joining our long list of tormentors—the drill instructors, the PT instructors, the divisional officers, the weapon training instructors, and even the medical officers—are our seniors; a long line of third-termers, our frustrated immediate seniors who do not think twice before dumping their wrath upon us, our supposed to be benevolent fourth-termers whose sole ambition in life is to goad our third-term seniors to pile untold miseries upon us second-termers, the fifth-termers who dream nothing but to be the sixth-termers and the sixth-termers for whom we are their favourite lackeys. Our day starts at four in the morning and we get a mere ten minutes' period to vacate the bathrooms for our seniors. Thereafter, we wait for tea, not for ourselves but for our sixth-term overstudy—one sixth-termer for each second-term understudy. Muster starts at five and we stand at the parade ground for an hour, being inspected by each of our seniors, as if we were prospective brides, and nobody approves of what they witness, the bride never gets a nod of approval: 'your buttons are twisted', 'your shirt has less starch', 'your shorts are dirty', 'your belt is loose', 'your garters are too long', 'your stockings are short', 'there is too much hair on your head', 'rub that stone on your cheeks to scrape those studs you left from your morning shave', 'your bootlaces are not tied properly', 'there is nothing wrong with you—that's a first one—but what the hell, still get into *Murga* position', and down we would bend, our hands holding our ears through our legs— it is the most uncomfortable position one can ever be forced into; knees bent at an impossible angle of sixty degrees, our rumps pointing towards the heavens, the hands coiled through our legs to grab the ears with our fingers, our eyes looking straight ahead: we couldn't let go of the ears or lower our bumps, that would invite a kick, and who would want to risk their manhood. I have been doing it from my school days and have gained quite an expertise in turning into a rooster, but I pitied the civilian guys—the non–Sainik School, the non–military school and the non-RIMC (Rashtriya Indian Military College) types—they were the ones who got the most kicks and busted balls.

'We are issued with bicycles, but they are meant for exclusive use by our seniors, who are too busy—a euphemism for apathy, so to say—to get their damaged bicycles repaired. So we sprint from place to place, the training areas being a kilometre or more apart from each other—the equitation training arena is five kilometres away. For us second-termers, there is no other mode of travel—no marching, no running, no jogging—it's only sprinting, with our knees touching our nipples. After the two morning periods of drill and PT, we have a breakfast break of one hour, during which we have to bathe, change into fresh uniforms, eat our breakfast and move to our classrooms for the academic lessons. There are timings for everything and since I hadn't mastered the art of cleansing myself in a flash, I did not take bath for the first fifteen days. It was only when my seniors could not stand my stink, even while standing six feet away, that I was given five minutes to scrub myself, under supervision. I will tell you about the bathroom escapades later.

'Breakfast was whatever we could gulp without chewing, before our seniors arrived in the mess. Invariably it used to be two fat slices of bread with sugar, jam, butter, cheese, cocoa powder, and black pepper—to make all that sweetness taste better—packed between the slices. Eight to ten bread slices, with butter and jam, used to find their pride of place inside our khaki shorts—stiff as a cardboard due to the starch they were dipped in—with the melted butter seeping through the thin muslin cloth of the inner lining of our pockets and dripping down our legs as we sprinted to our classrooms. There we consumed the balance of our breakfast. The classrooms were where we made good on our lost sleep, slumping our heads down upon the desks the moment our haunches perched on the wooden seats of our chairs. Some academic instructors, like Ms Suman Thorat, were benevolent enough and let the entire class snooze and snore, while she diligently continued teaching the heads staring at her with nonexistent eyes.'

'How old is this Ms Suman Thorat of yours?' she asked with a touch of jealousy.

I teased her, 'She must be just out of college and she is so pretty that I have still not got over my crush on her.'

She poured the remains of the iodine bottle over my still burning back, not an ideal remedy, and feigned indignation: 'You rascal! And what happened to that "you are my sole purpose in life, my doughnut"?'

I yelped as nails dug into my back and she picked up a pillow to wipe off the iodine, which had done its intended job and whose molecules were relishing my predicament, giggling with hilarious giggles, as they seeped through my burns. When my skin turned redder, a worried frown creased her forehead and she applied an icepack and Burnol to cool off the burns. I turned over to look into her eyes which had, all of a sudden, gone moist.

'I am sorry Sanjay.'

'No need for that my love. I have suffered worse than this. And I now know that some things do make you go green with envy for me. Why don't you say it, that you love me, that I make your heart go swooning?'

'Oh Sanjay! Why didn't you meet me two years earlier? Where were you when I needed you the most?' She wept hot tears which fell on my warm cheeks and she buried her face into my neck.

Still no confession! Why do my girls take so long? I decided to wait; I had all the time in the world.

Later when her emotions cooled, I told her about my post lunch travails, when we were made to undergo all sorts of 'toughening' exercises for our mistakes from the morning muster—the front and back rolls on the hot tarmac of the parade ground, the bending over on all fours upon the sweltering concrete behind our Squadron (the building containing the single-room dwellings, with combined toilets, where we lived), the sprinting around the sprawling edifice of our Squadron in circles and circles and circles, the lifting of cycles over our heads, and other similar activities which continued till late into the evening. The dinner experience was similar to the breakfast one, except we could not carry any of the *daal* or curries inside our pockets. But some smart alecks still managed to scrape away a few chapattis and pickle, to be consumed in their cabins after midnight. One month into the term, our, second-termers', complaints against the treatment meted out to us by our seniors during the meals led to the commandant ordering that a separate row of tables be placed at the cadets' mess for exclusive use by the second-termers. That lasted fifteen days, as on the sixteenth day, the commandant entered the mess and went enquiring from the second-termers about the novel experience of eating without interference. I was dipping into my breakfast with a relish akin to someone who had gone hungry for the past three days and when I had stuffed my mouth full of bread, jam, butter, sugar, and eggs, I found him standing right in front of me and asking me as to how the food was. The stuff in my mouth was so humongous that I could not gulp it down in a hurry and chewing would have taken eons, so I blurted out an answer and out flew the bread and the eggs accompanied with its assortment of jam, butter, and sugar. Fortunately, the commandant was standing a fair distance away; else he would have also smelled of eggs all through the day. The next meal onwards we were back sitting with our seniors who took their revenge with a vengeance. I did not suffer due to the hunger pangs thereafter as much as from my fellow course mates for being the sole cause of the renewed torture during mealtimes. Many were the occasions when I was subjected to hostile stares and beatings by my mates for my blundering at the dining table.

Post dinner, our 'toughening' exercises resumed with rolling under the carpets lining the long corridors of our Squadron, rolling under the rows of showers in the bathroom, with the faucets raining down alternate scalding hot and icy cold waters on our backs as we traversed the cavernous bathrooms with our rolling bodies. We finally reached our beds, dead as logs, well past midnight, to catch our forty winks before being up again within a few miserly hours.

'Are they humans?' she asked incredulously.

'They are better than your brothers, at the least. And it's all for our toughening.'

'You said something about telling of your bathroom experiences later.'

When I had entered the bathroom, after those first fifteen days of fetid existence, I noticed that there were no bathing cubicles, just eight showers in a row, under which we had to stand and bathe in full view of the others. As I walked under one such shower stall, the third-termer who had been tasked to supervise my cleansing, ordered me to take off my briefs.

Fearing the worst, I said, 'But you are here sir. What do you want of me?'

'You damn idiot. I am not a homo. We bathe naked here. That's the tradition. Take those goddamn undies off before you enter the shower.'

I took off my flimsy V-briefs and a few minutes after I had turned my back to him, I heard a gaggle of giggles, cackles, and murmurings behind me. I turned around to face a bunch of my course mates pointing at my behind, now facing the wall. I smiled at them and said with a smug expression, 'That's my birthmark and so many girls have licked and kissed it that I have lost count. If any of you want to get that lucky you better get branded, only on your puny asses it would look like a malicious hook than my beautiful, inviting, intriguing question mark, and instead of licks and smooches you will get kicks on your bumps. Now scamper off you gofers and let me scrape the dirt off my valley.' With that I turned my dimpled, question-marked butt towards them and shoved my hand between my cheeks to rub off the grime nestling there, feeding off my skin and hole for the past fifteen days. My butt remained the butt of jokes for the next few days, especially amongst my seniors, whom I couldn't tell off as I could my course mates. But word spread around about the countless girls who had tasted and swooned over my birthmark and slowly the jokes dried up.

She chuckled and turned me over. 'Why didn't I ever think of that,' and ran her tongue along the angry red question mark—it appeared as if it lost its anger when traces of her saliva covered it in its sheen. How I wished that she had a mirror installed on her ceiling so that I could see the red question mark cooling into a shade of pink. 'It doesn't taste any different than the rest of you, but it felt good. I will have to make it a habit. Remind me if I ever forget. It does make your backside look even more gorgeous than Mel Gibson's or Sylvester Stallone's. Was that a boast or many girls have molested you?'

I agreed with her oft repeated observation that the only derrieres that came close to mine in perfection were those of Mel Gibson and Sly Stallone. But where the Australian's and the Italian's faded into insignificance was when the inviting Question Mark came into the equation. I never thanked Miss Mary and her impetuous slap more.

After she had had her fill of my Question Mark, I turned over and lifted her atop me. 'Except my family members and you, nobody else knows about it. Not even Pratima. And you are the only one who has been so intimate and tasted it with such relish. It felt wonderful.'

Then I told her about the hirsute Sardar.

'The timings for bathing on weekdays are fixed—the breakfast break in the mornings and a thirty-minute window in the evenings. On Sundays there are no fixed timings. One can take bath anytime of the day. The Sikh cadets, who take long hours washing their hair, utilise the afternoons of Sundays to indulge in the exercise. I have a course mate, a giant of a Sardar, his six-foot-two-inch frame covered in dark bushy hair, head to toe. He has a long unruly mane which takes him almost an hour to shampoo. He had chosen one unfortunate Sunday afternoon to indulge in his fortnightly shampoo drill. Unbeknown to him, a senior cadet had two visitors in his cabin, an eventuality not permitted in the Academy, since visitors are meant to be entertained only at the cafeteria or the market place inside the campus. But which senior will not assume thwarting the rules as his divine right. And one of his visitors was a pretty lass from Ferguson College, with whom he was getting cosier, as the visit wore on. The other girl was his sister, who, after hours of holding it in, declared that she wanted to use the bathroom. Her brother, by now drowning deep into the depths of the Ferguson girl's doe-eyes, pointed towards the bathroom, where our tall Sardar, belting out the 'oohs' and 'aahs' of *Love in C Minor*, had covered himself in a thick foamy lather by then. Dreaming of his village belle, he had stirred up a stiff, glorious erection too. He was jerking his pelvis in tune with the imagined beats of the iconic musical piece by Cerrone, twirling round and round, when the clueless girl, who had probably imagined the sounds as though emerging out of some loud speakers placed in the bathroom, for the entertainment of the cadets, entered, to be confronted by a scene straight out of some wild fantasy of a porn movie. As the two confronted each other, there ensued a silence for a few long beats. Soon, as if waking from a nightmare, she let off a shriek and the Sardar did the only thing which came to his mind—he leapt for his towel hanging on a peg close to where the girl was standing and covered his face, leaving his member in full, erectile glory, appearing as a lone sentinel standing at attention, guarding some secret portal. To any outsider, the tableau in the bathroom would have been somewhat akin to what Larry Collins and Dominique Lapierre so delightfully described in the delectable *Freedom at Midnight*, about the custom followed, till the twentieth century, by the Maharaja of Patiala appearing before his subjects once a year, wearing only a diamond breastplate, with his organ in its full and glorious erection, as if it was radiating magical powers to drive the evil spirits away from the land, and being cheered by his citizens, acknowledging the size of the Maharaja's formidable asset. Except that, our tall Sardar at Kharakvasla was adorned in a thick, frothy foam of white lather and instead of the cheers of an adulating crowd, he was being greeted by the screams of a terrified girl who must have been surely petrified by this vision of a hirsute man, all covered in white, hiding his face, with his member in a mighty glorious erection, the only point of similarity with the erstwhile Maharaja from his native state. Needless to say that the two girls beat a hasty retreat from the Academy, to the utter disappointment of their host, who had by then worked up enough courage and determination to kiss the Ferguson girl, and who now targeted his pent-up ire upon the hapless Sardar—he suffered miserably for his indiscretion in displaying his wares in public view. No fault of his, since the senior cadet was the one at fault for inviting the girls to his cabin and thereafter letting his sister visit the bathroom without checking it first. But then an NDA cadet is a breed apart; give him a girl and he goes bonkers, and this particular one was besotted with his sister's friend.'

I spent the ten most wonderful hours of my life with this most exquisite girl. We made lunch together; the rice had to be cooked twice, as the first batch was dispatched by an angry pressure cooker in thick streams of starch and overcooked rice grains, shooting up to the ceiling and spattering the walls, since we forgot to turn off the electric heater after the mandatory three whistles, engaged as we were, pitching and yawing and rolling in the roiling waves of our passion on the floor outside her kitchen.

15

The Kiss

We were in her living room and she sat snuggling in my lap, on the lone furniture that could take the two of us together—her two-seater couch. I was home on vacation after having completed one and a half years of my NDA training. As I finished my one-hour long, nonstop monologue, narrating the incidents of the five months gone by since our last meeting, I smelled the *mehndi* in her hair, the aroma mingling with the sweet fragrance of jasmine and I was in bliss.

'My sweet Jasmine, why don't we go out? I am fed up of meeting you within the confines of these four walls.'

'Where do you want to go?'

'Let's see. You are alone tomorrow, it's a Wednesday, Father will be away at work, Mother will be busy with her friends and chores. Hmmmm . . . Let's go picnicking to Helipad Hill. I will scout for a lonely spot in the morning, before we leave.'

'What if someone happens upon us there?'

'So what, you rarely venture out of your house; hardly any of his acquaintances knows you. I have never been here for more than two months at a stretch—there are bare minimum people who know me in this dump. And even if someone does recognise me, I can always come up with some excuse. I will say you are a casual acquaintance I just met or you are a distant cousin staying somewhere close by. No, not a cousin, one is enough for me to engage in oedipal fantasies.'

'You and your girls,' she chuckled and pounded my nose with a delicate fist. 'Don't you think it will be a bit risky?'

'Oh! I love risks. Please come, my darling. I feel so claustrophobic here.'

'So now you have started feeling claustrophobic. After two and a half years, this house constricts you? Come on enough of your NDA adventures. I have been waiting for you for so long, it seems like an eternity. Do you want to come to the bed or this couch would do?'

'This couch is so snug and inviting.'

The next day I woke up early and after my reconnaissance for a suitable spot—I used Father's motorcycle for the purpose—I announced that I was keen on exploring the surroundings and would not be back till late in the evening. I had a hefty breakfast to allay Mother's worries about my missing the lunch.

It was a glorious winter morning, the sun shone with its full might, bathing the sleepy settlement with an unearthly brightness. I met Meena at the base of the hill, a leisurely distance of a kilometre from our respective homes. She looked delicious, draped in a parrot green chiffon sari sprayed liberally with red polka dots, the five-yard-long silk tightly wound around her svelte frame. Its hem was hitched up to permit liberal movement of her feet, allowing a peek of her dainty ankles, above a pair of green rubber pumps adorning her feet. She was carrying a green woolen shawl in her arms. A shiver of desire raced through my nerves when I sighted her bare arms and shoulders, as she was wearing a blood red, sleeveless blouse and after confirming that there were no onlookers, I folded her into my arms and nibbled at her bare shoulders. She dropped the hamper she was carrying and nestled into me. After a long moment of delightful bliss, she separated from me and said, 'It feels so unreal. Why didn't we think of this earlier? Shall we go or do you want to ravish me out here? I am all for it.'

'It sounds tempting but the ground is very rough here and we wouldn't want to encourage voyeurism in this stupid, sleepy town. Come on let's get moving before My Sanju becomes impatient.'

I picked up the hamper and, holding her hand, climbed up the hill, using the narrow creek running down its slope for our trek. A third of the way up the slope I had to let go of her hand because, after the initial gradual gradient, the slope became steeper and the trail narrower as we climbed higher and higher. I moved ahead of her, always ensuring that she was not more than two paces behind me. Two hundred metres short of the summit, I heard her shriek from behind, and turning around, I saw her sitting on a rock, looking down at her right leg. Her pumps were thin soled and a thorn had got stuck in her great toe. I tenderly removed her shoe and since the thorn had made deep inroads I picked it out with my teeth. There followed a thin trickle of blood and after putting her shoes into the hamper I picked her up and carried her up to the top. She was not too heavy and my training at NDA had given me enough strength to carry her forty-eight kilograms of weight without breaking a sweat. At the top, I sat her down upon a moss-covered boulder and she gazed at me with an intensity I had never seen in her beautiful eyes before. It seemed as if she was drinking me in through her eyes. I knelt down to look at her toe—there was just a tiny pin prick of clotted blood. I closed my lips over her toe and sucked at it with suckling noises. I gazed into her eyes, trying to fathom her intense look. She stood up with me and winced when she gingerly put weight on her right foot—it had probably gone to sleep—staggering in the process. I caught hold of her and folded her into my arms. I could feel tiny tremors rocking her body. She brought up her face and kissed me with a hunger she had never revealed earlier. Where on earlier occasions, I was the one who often hungered for her kisses, this time it was she who put her mouth to mine. Earlier our kisses were more of a prelude to our lovemaking, desire clearly apparent in the way we nibbled at each other's lips, the very act reflecting our lust. Now she thrust such energy in her kiss that I felt overwhelmed by her intensity. It seemed as if she was clutching at straws before she was consumed by the eddies of her emotions. She put so much passion in her hunger that it felt as if she wanted to enter my soul through my mouth. I was pleasantly and delightfully taken aback by her kiss, as I crushed her shaking body into me; she seemed so fragile I feared I would break a bone or two. But she was oblivious to any pain or discomfort in our tight embrace, as she caressed the stubs on my crew-cut scalp with one hand's fingers and cinched the back of my neck in a fierce grip of her other hand.

We broke out of our trance when I heard a clapping sound. I turned suspiciously towards its source and saw an elderly Russian couple sitting under a tree some distance away. They beckoned us over to join them. I immediately took them up on their offer and led a protesting Meena to the shade of their tree. We conversed in halting English and some smatterings of Russian; I knew a bit of the language as I had selected Russian as my Foreign Language to be learned at NDA. After a few, drawn-out exchanges of '*Kak Vas Zavoot?*', '*Menya Zavoot Sanjay Tivari*', '*Menya Zavoot Nikolai*', I sensed Meena's discomfort, which she demonstrated with repeated fidgeting and apparent listlessness, throughout the conversation. I bid the couple 'Dasvidaniya', with some reluctance, as I had started developing a liking for them, primarily because of their lavish praise on 'such a loveleee . . . couple.' But before they could start prying into our 'blissful marital life', I decided to disengage rather than conjecture on a conjugal relationship with my 'wife'.

We moved to a shallow depression on the far side of the plateau, away from any prying eyes and shielded by the thick trunk and dense foliage of a low hanging tree. As soon as we were under the overhang of the tree's broad leaves, she fell into my arms and I staggered into the tree's trunk. She kissed me again with the same passionate hunger and said at last, 'I love you Sanjay,' with that familiar lilt to my name's second syllable and the gasp at the end. I picked her up and sliding down the trunk of the tree, I coiled her in my lap. Till that moment I had thought that she regarded me as someone who filled a void in her life caused due to Sharmajee's proclivities and his inadequacies in performing his husbandly duties. Despite her endearments and proclamations of 'where were you Sanjay when I needed you the most', I had doubted that she would ever fully open her heart to me. 'I love you Sanjay'—I was dying to hear these words from her lips for the past so many months. Now that she had said it, I was filled with the greatest of joys. My heart brimmed with an elation I had never felt before, not even with Pratima. It seemed as if my sole purpose in life had been fulfilled, that now, even if Yamraj (God of Death) came down and asked for my soul, I would readily give it up. She placed her head against my heart and I buried my nose into the bun of her hair. We sat frozen in that posture for a long time, till I was pricked by the rough bark of the tree biting into my back and the blood refused to flow into my buttocks. I shifted some and she wriggled in protest, ensconcing herself deeper into my embrace. Slowly, as I undid her bun—I never liked her hair coiffed up like that—she poured her heart out, stating how she had come to love me over the past two and a half years, bit by delicious, tiny bit. Hers was not an impetuous emotion, she had given it a deep thought, as this was the first time she was experiencing such a feeling. She had never fallen in love before, not even with her scandalous, two-timing professor, and she wanted to be sure of herself before she could let it out to me.

'My sweet Sanjay! The place where I come from, women are treated as a sort of second-class citizens, so much like dirt. Rare are the households where the birth of a girl is a festive occasion. This is true of our entire country, I presume. Our growing up years are markedly different than that of our brothers. They get all their wishes fulfilled, whereas our childhood desires are quelled even before they could be expressed. When we are grown up, we are married off, often against our wishes and thereafter we fulfil the desires of our husbands and their parents and later on breed and bring up their future generations.

'I was one of the fortunate ones who could study to obtain a graduate degree, that too through frequent trickery and entreaties to my father. For that I am grateful to him. But by the time I had tied the nuptials I had resigned myself to a life of subjugation and servility.

'But destiny had something else in store for me. You arrived into my life like a breath of fresh air. I revelled in your infatuation, luxuriated in the notion of being the object of your desire, took secret pleasure in indulging in a naughtiness which showed two fingers to the social mores; adultery became an adventure for me. During those moments when pangs of guilt assaulted me, I would confront my inner soul by reflecting upon my predicament of being mired in a loveless marriage with a homosexual, who did not have even an inkling of a woman's needs and desires. For him I am just a vassal whom he had got into a union with, just to please his father and assure his inheritance.

'You transformed me, with your youthful enthusiasm, your zest for life, your high-spirited zeal in taking a formidable risk, your insatiable passion, your high ambitions. I had never met a person like you before. I loved the apparent contradiction in the real you—a morally upright person of strong character, a boy-man who has a very vivid perception of right and wrong—and yet you did not hesitate from entering into a relationship with me. I might say you even encouraged me into it.

'But above all else you are a good person. You were always decent with me, you never forced yourself upon me, you have always been attentive to my needs, you even love my cooking,' she chuckled for the first time, 'God! How much I admire you when you gobble up the crap I prepare, you relish it so much. I have never been able to prepare a decent meal, but you had nothing but praise for my meagre skills. It was as if I could never do anything wrong in your eyes. Initially I had thought that you were infatuated, but vacation after vacation you had eyes only for me and you grew on me. Any woman would count her blessings for having you as her companion. You have shown nothing but genuine respect for me. I have never known any man having such deep respect for women. In our society grandmothers, mothers, sisters, daughters, nieces, aunts, girls-next-door, all are treated with such disdain and condescension. Today, your acts of ensuring that I never fell back more than two paces during our climb—any other man would have never bothered whether I kept pace; of taking out that thorn with your teeth—any other man would have dug in another thorn to pry it out; of carrying me up the slope—any other man would have left me to limp my way up; all these reinforced my belief in you.'

She leaned into me and placed her head against my chest, tears streaming down her face by now. 'Sanjay, you have a very good heart. I love you with my heart and soul.'

I had heard her launching into long diatribes earlier, but never had I listened to such an emotional outpouring from her. She had me tongue-tied for a long time. This was the first time a girl had proclaimed her love to me in such an emotionally charged manner and also added high virtues to my character, that aside on encouraging her into adultery notwithstanding. I was somewhat embarrassed that she saw a virtuous man in me, worthy of such high praise, worthy of love even. My dream was fulfilled.

'Say something,' she whispered after an unending period of silence. With the cheerful chirping of the birds providing a melodious background score, the hiss of the wind blowing through the broad leaves of our tree, the roar of the twin chimneys, letting out silvery wisps, disturbing the calm ambience; I lifted her face and leaning down sipped her tears. Their salty tang brought fresh tears to my eyes and reluctantly letting go of her I slid further down and lay on the dry grass. She melted into me and I closed my arms around her supine body, as we conjoined together in a snug embrace. It felt even more intimate than when we used to lay together in her bedroom.

'Marry me,' was my first reaction.

'What? That is impossible,' she retorted with apparent incredulity.

'Not now my silly sweetheart. Look, two and a half years from now I will become an officer in the Army. Then we will elope and marry. And we will live happily ever after—howsoever clichéd that may sound. We will be together.'

'Oh Sanjay, Sanjay, Sanjay. I love you, love you, love you. You raise such high hopes, you conjure such wonderful dreams. It is possible, but I cannot just up and leave him. I will have to get a divorce to be able to marry you.'

'We have two and a half years to make that happen. We will work something out sweetheart.'

I propped myself up on my elbow and looked at her. She closed her eyes to enjoy the warmth of a ray showering her body. The sun was glistening off the small pool of sweat in the dip of her neck—a sweet nectar beckoning me. But I liked the radiance reflecting off it and despite my craving urge I restrained myself from sipping at the bead. After a long moment, when she shook her head to ward off some undesirable thought, the liquid dribbled down her neck, breaking the spell. I leaned down to kiss her glistening lips. I tasted her breath, redolent with an aroma of her toothpaste and sweet milk. 'I am the luckiest guy in the world to be loved by this remarkable woman,' was my first thought as I closed my lips upon hers and nibbled hungrily at her lower lip, as if there were no tomorrow. As my arms closed around her in a tight embrace, I could feel her deep emotions through her soft trembles; the confession had been a relief to her and she was in the throes of an unfamiliar sensation. The world ceased to exist and I was floating in a weightless existence, my mind full of undreamt possibilities. There emerged a maddening kaleidoscope of the present and a future where Meena and I are joined in marital union, in a world free of the moralities of a society that spurned our relationship.

We spent the next few hours in a glorious vision of a life full of infinite possibilities; marriage, house, home, conjugal bliss, children—lots of them—new adventures and what not. Time seemed to fly by and when the evening sun threatened to herald dusk, hunger pangs brought us back to the real world and we devoured the food she had brought in her hamper. Even though it had gone cold, it tasted delicious, what with our hearts filled with such optimism.

Despite her protests, I carried her all the way down the hill to the base, and leading her to the copse behind her house, I showed her how I entered her house. The sun had set by then. I assisted her in climbing over the wall and spent the better part of the night with her, until she reminded me that my parents would have turned the town upside down by then, in search of their precious son, who had gone missing since he had left their house in the morning. I reluctantly agreed to leave half an hour later, the time was half past two in the morning. After opening the lock of her front door and handing over the lock and key to her, I entered my home to face my anxious mother, who hadn't slept a wink. She fretted over me, made a lot of fuss about my carefree attitude, and seemed to have bought into my tame explanation of having gone to Renukoot to meet my 'course mate' and since we were meeting after 'such a long time', I didn't realise the passage of time because of which I could barely manage to catch the last bus, which dropped me at Anpara, the driver insisting that he won't go any further as there were no other passengers and I had to walk the twenty-kilometre distance in the dead of the night to reach home so late—'No great shakes there Mummy. It was as if I was at NDA and undertaking the Route March at Camp Greenhorn, sans the rifle and the heavy pack.' Father was with the police, frantically searching the small settlement for me, scouring the plateau and slopes of Helipad Hill and visiting the usual trouble spots frequented by youngsters—the open-air theatre, the park, Jwalamukhi Temple, the sprawling thermal plant and such like—all the time fearing the worst, that I had been kidnapped. After assuring herself that no harm had come to me during my four-hour long trek from Anpara, she made delicious *Aaloo Paranthas* for me and slept relieved. There was no sleep for me that night and many subsequent nights, as Father, on his return at six in the morning, grounded me for the next full week—no more movies, no long walks, and definitely no visits to Renukoot to meet my 'course mate': 'Why doesn't he come here for once? We would also like to meet this colleague of yours,' he had retorted when I had finished with the reasons for my late arrival.

After that one week of solitary confinement, I met Meena again for many delightful evenings till it was time for me to leave. She came over to our house the evening prior to my departure for NDA and smiled demurely at Mother's grumbles about my earlier carelessness. She whispered a, 'I will miss you sweetheart, take good care of yourself, I have proprietary right over you now,' when Mother was out of earshot. That sounded so wonderful, like hundreds of jingles from wind chimes dancing softly in a spring breeze.

16

That Feeling Called Love

It is indescribable. Words lose their meaning while expressing it. It is more powerful than any word can convey. It is the most powerful force in the world.

I have this susceptibility to fall in love with beautiful girls at the drop of a hat—something to do with my childhood spent mostly in the company of women at both of my parents' households. But falling in love with a girl is way different than receiving love from her. Even with Pratima, I was never sure of her feelings for me—she only opened her heart to me on the day she had closed that amber door on me and sent me away.

With Meena, after having struggled with my emotions for the past two and a half years, I had finally been able to win her love. During the initial period of our relationship, that first year till I joined NDA, I used to suffer pangs of guilt for having entered into an impossible relationship with a married woman, much older than me—specially when I used to be in one of those, rarely ventured into, pensive moods. Those times I searched for justification and finally homed on to the proverbial 'Knight in Shining Armour' rationale—she had suffered a lot in her life and finally having been dumped into a loveless marriage, she had no further avenues to seek joys in her life; that I had been destined, by the unknown force which designs and controls us mortals' fates, to provide her the satisfaction her father had denied her by marrying her off to a homosexual fiend, that I was her sole ray of hope. Our initial trysts were more of mere dalliances to seek pleasures from the sexual adventures, to satiate our sensual desires—the illicitness of the affair added to the risky adventurism I craved, as much as Meena's body. When I had first met her in the summer of '86, I was 17 and a half, and at that age, we adolescents are a very dangerous breed. At the cusp

384 | Mamta Chaudhari

of adulthood, our hormones croon crazy numbers and perform macabre dances. I had been led by my hormones then, desperate for sex with her from the word go. At the beginning it was all about lust, satisfying my desires. All those adult movies and jerking off all by myself had awakened the dormant animal inside me, the type that sought solace in the arms of a beautiful woman and hunted for pleasure between her legs. Even then, there was a sobering little mite, a tiny bit, which made me see the real Meena in her, and not just an object of my desire. But the baser instincts had brushed my sobering thoughts under the carpet. And as time flew by, with her opening up her heart and soul to me, the way she put her full faith in me, in no time my lust for her morphed into an affair of the heart for me. My heart, broken as it was after Pratima's brother had shut me out of her life, got drawn towards Meena like a bee to nectar. She became the very purpose of my life and it was my yearning for her that defined my choices in life—I joined NDA for her.

She was a contradiction, her very life a paradox even, and I couldn't have enough of her. I cannot think of one woman who is such a mixed bag—a teenaged girl who bit off the earlobe of her molester and coached her younger sister on how to defend herself; a daughter who spied upon her parents to overhear their secret conversations; an unmarried adolescent who had no qualms about entering into a premarital affair with a much older, married professor; a sister who moved heaven and earth to ensure that her younger sister got her just dues while she herself accepted her own fate with a guilty forbearance; a woman who threatened to gouge out her fiendish husband's eyes; a wife who, despite being so religious minded—she worshipped her idols with sincere dedication—had no misgivings about conducting an illicit affair with a boy-man much younger in age; a hero-worshipper whose ideals were the vertically opposite personalities of Phoolan Devi and Kiran Bedi. I never tired of counting my blessings for having met and fallen in love with such a wonderful woman.

What ultimately cinched my heart and occupied my soul was her attitude towards her failures. Long back, during my first vacation with her, after she had let me know the events which led to her unfortunate marriage, I had asked her, 'Don't you regret your affair with the professor?' She had replied with an evident candour, 'Why should I? I was young and infatuated, I confess. But that does not imply that I was not aware of what

I was getting into. I had taken the decision to involve in a scandalous affair knowing full well the consequences. But one doesn't take decisions in life based solely on cold logic. The heart rules in such matters. I was besotted, he was handsome and there were those other girls who boasted of having slept with him. Plus I thought, foolishly as it turned out, that I could make him fall in love with me. But the fiend had had many girls before me and he wouldn't have left his wife from a rich family for some infatuated student. So the affair which, for me, started with such great promise, fizzled into an exercise in which satisfying our physical desires became our primary motive. And I have never felt any regret. Now, whatever the world may call me—an adulteress, a seductress, a nymph even—but for the world of me I will never call what we have between us a regret. I feel so fortunate that you found me and that you revere me so much. How much more luckier can one get?'

There is no feeling greater than love. After creating humans, when God thought of creating the six emotions of anger, fear, surprise, disgust, happiness, and sadness, he must have taken the essence of all these and created the most supreme emotion of love. And there cannot be a greater emotion than the love between a man and his paramour. Especially when the love started as an adolescent infatuation and over a period of time matured into a mutually reciprocal feeling. When Meena acknowledged her love for me on the Helipad Hill, my heart, my soul, my entire being had leapt with boundless joy.

After her confession and her 'I have proprietary right over you now', whispered declaration, at NDA she became a delightful distraction during the boring academic classes; she was a beacon of soaring, shining light during our long, lumbering route marches at night; she was the cushion of a duck's down when I was put through countless sessions of rolling on hard, rubble strewn surfaces, as punishment for my transgressions; she was the icy cool touch during the hot, searing afternoons when we would be doing bend-stretches on scorching concrete surfaces to build our muscles— angry hot blisters on our palms were collateral damage, an occupational necessity; she was the fragrance of the monsoon rain falling on parched earth after a scorching summer season, during our training camps, where we went unbathed for a week, deliriously enjoying the camaraderie of stinking companionship; she was the lilting score of a musical melody when my ears would be reverberating with the barks of our seniors and drill instructors;

she was the soothing balm on my tiring muscles during the fifty-kilometre-long, cross-country practice runs.

I often dreamt of those sweet mornings when I would wake up next to her, feeling her soothing warmth, kissing her lips, drinking in the stale breath of her unwashed mouth, relishing the drool which had dried up on her cheeks during the night, dipping my soul into the cloud of glossy hair splaying the pillows thrown unkempt during our slumber, softly caressing every inch of her body to a point of arousal that she couldn't wait to make love again, sharing the toothbrush, showering together, rubbing the sleep out of each other's body with thick, soapy foam, preparing breakfast of eggs and toast as she lounged on the couch, both of us having not bothered to put on our clothes yet—in my dreams, the eggs were sunny side up and she would deftly place the fried eggs between the buttered toasts and eat the sandwich, letting the yellow yoke escape the confines of the piled twin bread slices and run down her fingers; my cue to lick the golden, viscous fluid off her fingers, while she chewed on the sandwich, both of us relishing the taste of a blissful life of love and longing, of desire and delight, of togetherness.

17

And He'll Be There

Meena and I rarely argued, so enamoured was I. We held varying opinions on the character traits of our respective heroes and would often differ on the way various events and personalities were depicted in the books we read and discussed. Sometimes, when I vehemently defended my point of view, she would get ruffled and would not speak to me till it was time for me to leave. Then, as I got ready to leave, letting out an exasperated sigh, she would collapse into my arms and we would forget our differences and make passionate love again. But before I finally left she would teasingly bring up the matter again and try to convince me to accept her viewpoint. Invariably she succeeded, since I was never staunch in my opinions and would give in to her ultimately—love has that effect and anyone who does not believe it is a miserable fool.

(I am in my mid forties now and have been successful in holding on to my wife of twenty years because of the immense love she has bestowed upon me all this time, as I never impose my opinions upon her and accept hers with some initial reluctance).

Once, after having read Mahatma Gandhi's autobiography, *My Experiments With Truth*, I brought up the contradictions in the great man's character—an opinion I still hold on to staunchly—when he wrote that he was enjoying coital bliss with Ba while his father lay dying in the next room. She had defended Gandhiji vehemently: 'In the same book he also writes the remorse he had felt all his life for that one moment of blind lust. The Mahatma called it "being blinded by animal passion". He remained eternally repentant and considered that episode as a blot he was never able to efface or forget. It weighed on his conscience so much that he found it unpardonable that he was gripped in a moment of lust when his revered father lay dying next door. That singular episode coloured his attitude towards sexual control later in his life.' She also attributed his sole blundering into blind passion, to his young age and bouncing hormones, 'which full-blooded youth could ever resist his young wife's charms. Take yourself, you can't even wait the moment you enter my house and want to make love with me so many times—not that I am complaining, I absolutely love it, the way you crush me into you with such passion.'

I was equally amazed that he experimented with his sexuality too and was disappointed that, as a 77-year-old, the Father of the Nation slept with his naked, teenaged grandniece, Manubehn. 'That's totally misconstrued. Firstly, the allegations are yet to be proven—that is so Irving Wallace-esque in its assertion, the way he wrote about Mahatma Gandhi's sexual experiments in his book, *The Intimate Sex Lives of Famous People*. But even if it is true, it is reflective of the greatness of the man and not an aberration in his character. He had become a celibate pretty early in his life, at 38, and he constantly experimented with himself to test his baser instincts. It was his spiritual experiment to test his celibacy. His was a perennial quest to eliminate the animal residing inside him, to become one with his Creator. In addition to his sexuality, he constantly challenged himself and others, reinterpreting the prevailing religious traditions, confronting the prejudiced societal and religious conventions, which relegated women to a lower status—do you recognise a feminist in him—he is a kindred spirit. Next you will start questioning his sexuality, reading too much into the Mahatma's calling Hermann Kellenbach his "soulmate".'

'Well, unlike us, soulmates need not be physically intimate, too. Let's leave the German be.' I said, unwittingly letting her win the argument again, as I had run out of ammunition with regards to Gandhiji's sexuality.

But I was not going to let her off so easily. 'He subdued his wife's self will and moulded her into his view of the ideal, Hindu submissive wife.'

She retaliated, again defending her hero vehemently. 'But he did teach her to read and write and acted as her reforming companion in addition to being an active sexual partner.'

The one serious argument we had, had more to do with my obstinacy and my desire to speak the very words that Erich Segal had written and which I had found so heart rending that I had etched the phrase upon my heart. It was the summer of '89, six months after The Kiss on the

Helipad Hill. I was into the second day of my vacation and Mother said that Sharmajee had gone to his hometown, 'with that sweet wife of his,' after my innocent enquiries about Father's drinking companion—I had noticed his absence the previous night. That turned my *Kheer* sour and I moped and moped for the next seven days. Kaalu and my parents gave up on me and left for Shanti Bhavan three days later. Once again, I begged to be excluded from the family reunion and they relented after some initial suspicions—I was no more allowed a 'course mate' at Renukoot and had to come up with a graduation project work on 'Production and Distribution of Electricity', for which I would wait for Sharmajee's arrival next Monday and go on a tour of the thermal plant, in my scholarly pursuits, so essential to get good grades.

On Monday, I spotted Sharmajee's scooter parked outside his house; it had been inside the house during his absence. My penchant for risky ventures had given me adequate confidence by then. I walked up to her door and upon being confronted by the ever expanding Sharmajee, I said, 'I have got this project work on "Production and Distrubution of Electricity". Will you allow me to go through your books on electricity generation. After sifting through your collection, I would leave with the ones I need. I would also like you to take me on a tour of the plant, like the last time,' that invitation of a tour and the possibility of an orgy inside a secluded room, amidst the cacophony of steel machinery, had eased the suspicious frown which had creased his forehead after I had entered his house. He glared at me and I saw the gleam which lit his eyes as he went into a dream sequence of poking his tiny willy into my hole. I breathed easier only after he kick-started his ancient scooter to leave for his office.

Inside her living room I turned and stared at her, my mouth curled in a petulant pout, as she closed her door. I had a package in my hands, its contents procured and prepared painstakingly by me at NDA in the past two months. She came up to me from behind and wrapped her arms around me, her soft breasts pressing into my back. She whispered, 'I missed you a lot, my sweet darling.'

I was silent, still feeling resentful, my heart vaulting with conflicting emotions. She slid to the front and closed her lips over my pout, waiting for me to press her into me. I pulled back and said, 'You didn't think of me for one moment.'

'What's the matter Sanjay?'

'I get only four weeks and already one week has gone by. Why did you have to be away at this time?'

'His father had a stroke and we had to go visit him. I am the only daughter-in-law, I couldn't shirk my responsibilities.'

'What about me? You didn't even consider that I would die, without even suffering a stroke, if I couldn't see you.'

'Don't be childish. I couldn't have said no. It would have raised questions I would have found difficult to answer. He is not suspicious but why give rise to speculations?'

'You could have come back earlier. Alone. You knew that I would be home by last Monday.'

'I couldn't. It was difficult enough for me to come back with him. I was asked to stay there till his father got better. I am here only for you. I have to be back at Chhapra in three weeks.'

'Then go back now. I have nothing to do with you. You have no feelings for me.'

'I love you Sanjay,' a note of exasperation crept into her voice, 'and no one can deny me that, not even you. If you want to leave, go now. But I will wait for you every day and night, till your vacations are over. You forget that I am a married woman and that someone else may also have demands on my time, if not my body.'

I turned towards the door and sat in her couch placed next to it. We stared at each other for long. Reading the petulance in my face, she gave in and slipped into my lap, 'I am sorry, Sanjay.'

'God! I would have died if you hadn't said that.' I lifted her chin and kissed her passionately. 'Love means not ever having to say you are sorry,' I repeated the very dialogue from the beautifully composed and heartrendingly poignant *Love Story*, written by Erich Segal. The package in my hands contained a video cassette of the Ryan O'Neal-Ali MacGraw starrer film version of the book and the book itself, in its hardbound avatar. There was also an audio cassette of the song 'Where Do I Begin?', based on the theme music of the movie, in the sublime voice of Shirley Bassey, which had taken me long, painstaking hours to fabricate, re-recording the song again and again on both sides of the tape, twenty times, from the album *Something Else*. I had prepared this special cassette for Meena, as the music and lyrics, so beautifully composed by Francis Lai and Carl Sigman, reflected my true feelings for her.

I carried her into her bedroom, where I laid her down on the bed and inserted the special cassette into her Philips cassette player. The player was our single-most, constant companion during my visits, its love songs muffling our cackles, chortles, and conversations. As the lofty voice of Shirley Bassey filled the air, I removed her garments in tune with each stanza and we made love to the music, our passion heightening as the song reached its crescendo of *And He'll Be There*, repeated every three minutes, nine seconds.

Where do I Begin?
To tell the story of how great a love can be
The sweet love story that is older than the sea
The simple truth about the love he brings to me
Where do I start?

Like the Summer Rain
That cools the pavement with a patent leather shine
He came into my life and made the living fine
And gave a meaning to this empty world of mine
He fills my heart

He fills my heart with very special things
With angels' song, with wild imaginings
He fills my soul with so much love
That anywhere I go, I'm never lonely
With him along, who could be lonely?
I reach for his hand, it's always there

How long does it last?
Can love be measured by the hours in a day?
I have no answers now, but this much I can say
I'm going to need him 'till the stars all burn away
And he'll be there

He fills my heart with very special things
With angel's songs, with wild imaginings
He fills my soul with so much love
That anywhere I go, I'm never lonely
With him along, who could be lonely?
I reach for his hand, it's always there

How long does it last?
Can love be measured by the hours in a day?
I have no answers now, but this much I can say
I'm going to need him till the stars all burn away

And he'll be there

Later, with Shirley Bassey crooning in the background, I got busy with painting her toenails in blue, yellow, and magenta spirals, and she said, 'I wrote to my sister about you.'

'And?'

'She wants to meet you.'

'Did she express any concern . . . you being married and all?'

'She was very happy for me. We share a very special relationship. We are more friends than siblings. She understands me and my compulsions, and she just wants to meet the man who has made me so happy after all these years.'

'That's interesting. I would definitely like to meet someone who considers me a grown-up. Will we be meeting her Army man, too?'

'Yes, they are at Banaras with the Gorkha Training Centre. Will you take me there tomorrow?'

'Why not? I am alone here; we can take my father's Ambassador and spend some wonderful time at Banaras. I have always wanted to take you out of this overpolluted dump of a town. I will pick you up from behind this house at five tomorrow.'

That evening, buoyed by another mischievous impulse driven by my maddeningly passionate risky adventurism, I invited Mrs and Mr Sharmajee to my house and served him a cocktail of rum and whiskey, four *Patiala* pegs at that, and two bowls of the customary tomato sauce too. During the course of the evening, Meena explained to her husband that she would be going to Banaras to meet her sister for the next few days and would be taking the early morning bus for the trip. He did not even bother to enquire how she would be going to the bus stand from their house, so full of himself was he. Later, he slipped into an inebriated inertness before he could finish the fourth glass and lay sprawled on the mattress I had placed on the floor of our living room. Meena and I spent the night in her bedroom, leaving Sharmajee to his drunken dreams of teenage boys and inch-long peckers, in my parents' living room—I had actually taken a peek while we were arranging his inert body on the thin mattress and Meena had slapped my hand wickedly when I had remarked on his weedy thing, hidden deep within the dense growth of his pubic hair (there was no effect of alopecia down there); it was pathetically tiny and shrunken.

The next day, after leaving her house reluctantly at four in the morning and depositing a barely awakening Sharmajee at his house, I waited near the copse behind her home. She was a bit late and climbed into my father's car at half past five. I had taken her change of clothes earlier and had packed them with my clothes in a Safari suitcase. Having saved a couple of thousand rupees out of my pocket money from NDA days, I was confident that my NDA Identity Card and a few honest Mahatma Gandhis printed on 100-rupee notes would tide me over any difficulties with my nonexistent driving license, if any of the cops demanded it en route or at Banaras—advantages of living in a corrupt India.

'What if your sister is more beautiful than you? Will your brother-in-law mind if I flirted with her?' I said jokingly, as the twin chimneys vanished from the rear-view mirror.

'You scoundrel!' inflections of her Bihari accent slipped effortlessly and naturally whenever she addressed me thus. 'You might be in the Army now, but he is totally besotted with her. It is not beyond him to take offence and leave you mangled, if you even show an inkling of interest in her. And yes, she is much more beautiful than me.'

She turned out to be correct on both counts.

Our stay at Banaras had been arranged at a sprawling guest house inside the Army Cantonment and a lunch invitation to her sister's house was awaiting us when we reached there, six hours later. The bathroom contained an inviting bathtub, already filled with warm water; the Army does look into the little details. The lunch was forgotten as we immersed ourselves into the warm bathtub and collectively erased the fatigue—borne from lack of sleep the previous night and the long drive—out of our tired limbs. We would have exhausted ourselves from all that rubbing and scrubbing, frequently interrupted by our desires, had a Gurkha soldier not interrupted at four with incessant shrieks of the doorbell, to remind us of our luncheon engagement.

Fifteen minutes later, I did a double take when Pratima opened the door to Meena's sister's house. After the initial shock passed over, I realised that she was not Pratima, but had a striking likeness to the most beautiful girl I have ever met. Teena was much more beautiful and radiant than her elder sister, and the handsome and tall Army man holding her waist looked like he would follow her to the very ends of the universe and not bat an eyelid in the process.

Teena hugged Meena for an eternity, as I stood admiring this first meeting between the sisters, after Meena's marriage. After having wiped each other's tears, Meena introduced me to the couple. They gave me a once over and it looked like they approved her choice; no grudging acceptance there, it was more like 'where had you been hiding all this while?' The Army man welcomed me into their lives with a warm hug and an 'I am proud of you' remark. It seemed they knew much more about Meena and me than I had presumed. In a world full of bigots, who frowned upon such a relationship, not to talk of those who would stone my Meena to death, I felt grateful for the two people in the entire world who accepted Meena and me for what we were.

We talked of this and that and other things during our late lunch; all the while Teena gave me appraising looks and whispered sweet nothings into her sister's ears. My besotted, eager ears caught snatches of 'where did you find him?', 'you two are made for each other. . .', 'father would surely die of heart attack when he hears of this. . .', 'I wish you had met him earlier. . .'. I basked in their adulation and was already feeling like I was going to be called 'Mr Meena'—the surname became difficult. I would have given my right hand to just be named 'Mr Meena aka Second Lieutenant Sanjay Tivari'. I wished I could marry Meena at the Kashi Vishwanath Temple, then and there.

When the topic of our post-lunch discussions veered towards our future, I revealed my intention of marrying Meena immediately after I was commissioned on 08 June '91. Teena argued that there was the issue of Meena getting a divorce before I could marry her. I replied that I had given it some thought and was confident that, if Meena filed for it, she could surely get her marriage annulled. Teena's husband pitched in and said that he would consult a lawyer and put in his entire effort to ensure that that eventuality materialises. That led to a sceptical exchange of looks between Teena and Meena. I sensed a shadow of apprehension pass over Meena's face at some imagined uncertainty, should an alarm bell have given me a ping then; now that I think of it, I kick myself for having been so naive and stupid to have ignored that warning sign.

Meena refused their invitation for dinner, citing tiredness, and we slept off the next twelve hours in each other's arms, dead to the world, tired from all that travel and the noon calisthenics in the bathtub.

The next day, Teena and Meena went shopping, an indulgence Meena had been denied since her incarceration by her father—I had felt so miserable when her eyes lit up on seeing her sister at our doorstep with the offer. An olive green jeep, belching blue smoke out of its exhaust, was parked behind Teena to take them shopping. I sent a silent pledge to the heavens that I would take my girl to the shoppers' paradise in Paris once she became mine forever. Teena's husband took me on a tour of the Training Centre. I witnessed the young recruits doing drills in the scorching heat, their heads pruned down to the scalp, leaving just a tuft of black studs sitting atop their nuts like a black Jewish skull cap, so much like us, NDA cadets. In their classrooms, most of the soldiers-to-be snoozed and snored to make up for hours of lost sleep, in minutes. I visited the firing range where the youngsters, some so young that they hardly looked to be in their teens, ran all over the grounds more and fired the weapons less. The firing practices had more to do with building their stamina and upper body strength than gaining the expertise to ping the bullseye. I decided to show off my marksmanship skills, and after changing into a borrowed pair of fatigues—it fitted me snugly as the recruits' physiques and mine bore a striking resemblance, although the trousers were a bit short—I fired the 7.62-millimetre self-loading rifle, scoring 29 points out of 30 with my ten bullets. Teena's husband did not stop singing my praise till I left Banaras and felt overwhelmed by his unending accolades.

After another sumptuous lunch at Teena's house, this instance, at a regular time, I took the sisters to the famous temples and other holy sites of Banaras. I thanked the Jyotirlinga of Lord Shiva at Kashi Vishwanath Temple for having sent Meena into my life as a divine gift, promised Lord Hanuman at Sankat Mochan Temple that I would love her for eternity, beseeched Goddess Durga's blessings at Durga Temple to make my dreams come true, redeemed my pledge of never taking dowry to Lord Ram at Tulsi Manas Temple, and took a holy dip with Meena in the Ganges at Dashashwamedh Ghat, seeking Bhishma's mother's approval of our union.

The Army man joined us late in the evening, when all four of us went to see the *Ek Do Teen* diva, Madhuri Dixit, in *Tezaab*. I almost kissed Meena when Anil Kapoor started serenading with Mads in the soulful number, *Kehdo Ke Tum Ho Meri Varna*. That was the first time I experienced an epiphany. I started weeping when Mads joined Anil Kapoor with *Dekho Kabhi Na Aisa Kehna. . .*, imagining what my life would have been without Meena. The Army man sympathetically passed me his hankie when my sniffles alarmed Meena. But she seemed to understand for, after a while, she leaned on me and, taking my hand, she placed it on her shoulder and deftly settled her cheek on the back of my hand. Sometime later, I felt her warm tears on my hand. We spent the balance of *Tezaab* wiping each other's cheeks and whispering sweet nothings to each other.

I had my first sip of beer at his house, where we had another lavish spread of chicken, goat, and partridges for a late dinner.

That night, Meena and I spent the first four hours in the bathtub and the remainder of the night plus a couple of hours post-dawn on the floor, the carpet, the couch, and even the dining table—the bed was for sleeping, and we did not have any time or inclination to indulge in that inert exercise, so passionate had we become after all that had taken place during that day. In the morning, the Army man and Teena came to see us off on our journey back to Shaktinagar, and witnessing my bloodshot eyes, he suggested that, since I had not slept even for a minute in the past twenty-four hours, I could leave in the afternoon and still reach Shaktinagar on time, before dusk. I replied that, even if I spent another twenty-four hours with Meena, I would not be able to catch a wink. He guffawed and slapped me hard on my shoulders. I further added that I was as well trained as he is and could go seventy-two hours without a wink and that I would add an additional twenty-four more hours for Meena. He winked and said, 'These sisters don't realise how lucky they are to have us in their lives. You love your Meena more than I do my Teena. And I envy you for that. Best of luck to you, young man!'

I have never felt so joyous than in the familiarity of Teena and her husband's adoration and adulations.

18

The Worst Evil of All

I completed my gruelling three years of training at NDA on 09 June '90 and passed out from the grand portals of one of the finest military training establishments in the world—if hard pressed, one could draw comparisons with Sandhurst and Westpoint, but that, too, would be a bit overdrawn. My parents and Kaalu had driven down to Kharakvasla for the Passing Out Parade in Father's favourite Ambassador car. On our way back, we went to the hill stations of Panchgani and Mahabaleshwar, and roamed the Juhu Beach in Bombay (now Mumbai).

The high point of our trip back to Shaktinagar, via Shanti Bhavan, was the visit to the famous Khajuraho Group of Monuments. Belying popular perception, the temple sculptures contain less than 10 per cent eroticism based on sexual themes, with the majority of the monuments being temples dedicated to Lord Shiva. I saw each of the twenty surviving temples, spread over an area of six kilometres squared. I was awestruck by the towering majesty of the 116-foot–tall spire of Kandariya Mahadev Temple. The 2.5-metre-high lingam in the square grid design of Matangeshwara Temple left me mesmerised by its sheer size. The architecture of the temples, consisting of twin platforms, various *mandapas* (halls), the ambulatory for circumambulation by the pilgrims, and the huge tower topped by the *Amalaka* and the *Kalasha*, was a marvellous representation of the Nagara-style architectural symbolism of the late tenth– and early eleventh–century India, pioneered by the Chandela dynasty. The very symbolism of the places of worship of the two schools of Hinduism and Jainism built together at the same time suggests a tradition of acceptance and respect for diverse religious views in the society during that time—the very quality that we are losing sight of in the modern twenty-first century, dominated by religious intolerance and bigotry. Perhaps our present-day political leaders can take a leaf out of the books of the Hindu kings Yashovarman and Dhanga to comprehend the concept of universal brotherhood. I fail to understand why so many of my countrymen cannot come to terms with this wonderful concept of brotherly love, irrespective of all those differences in religion, caste, creed, race, state, language, and sex. I think the makers of our constitution did not ever bother to carry forward the message of 'Unity in Diversity' and explain it to my compatriots living in the villages and small towns that are the very essence of India, where the masses of the country live, thrive, and propagate ideologies of hatred and discrimination. Our country remains, sixty-seven years after independence (today in 2014), as diversified as it was when Jawahar Lal Nehru spoke of his 'Tryst with Destiny', all the way back on the night of 14 August 1947, on the eve of our independence. Then, we had those 565 maharajas, nawabas, rajas, and rulers, who divided our great nation; today, in our 'united' country, we have so many discriminatory criteria, that anyone who feels different can easily identify himself with a minimum of one antagonist social group, where he can find a way to vent his anger and carry on living in bigotry. What a shame! And to think that we are the very country where Gautam Buddha, Mahaveera, and Guru Nanak had birthed such great religions, which have always treated all humans as equal.

The temples of Khajuraho were also targeted during their time, and underwent desecration and destruction at the hands of different Muslim dynasties that controlled Central India during the period from the thirteenth till the eighteenth century, the most notable of them being Sikandar Lodhi's temple destruction campaign in 1495. In addition, an overgrowth of vegetation and forests took over the temples, till they were discovered in the nineteenth century. The combined effects of man and nature, as a result, left the remains of twenty temples standing out of the original eighty-five temples. The temples' remoteness and isolation were instrumental in ensuring that they did not meet the fate of Somnath, and it was only in the 1830s that they were rediscovered for the global audience by the British surveyor, T.S. Burt. Historical records also reveal that, over the intervening centuries, the temples were secretly used by yogis, and thousands of devotees also used them to conduct pilgrimages during the annual Shivratri festivals celebrated in February and March, a practice that continues till today, in the form of the Khajuraho Dance Festival. The temples were later systematically documented by another Britisher, Alexander Cunningham, who categorised them into three distinct groups: the Western Group around Lakshamana Temple, the Eastern Group around Javeri Temple, and the Southern Group around Duladeva Temple.

Khajuraho is one of the four holy sites devoted to Lord Shiva, the other three being Kedarnath, Kashi (Banaras), and Gaya. As per Hindu mythology, Khajuraho is the place where Lord Shiva got married; hence, the name of the place is ascribed to Kharjuravahaka, meaning Scorpion Bearer, another symbolic name for Lord Shiva, who wears garlands of snakes and scorpions when in his fierce form.

The Jain temples of Khajuraho are located towards the east–southeast region and are enclosed within compound walls constructed in the early twentieth century. Of these, Parshvanath Temple contains an inscription dating from AD 954, which mentions the Chandela king, Dunga, as the reigning king. It also includes the famous magic square, also known as the *Chautisa Yantra*, a four-by-four grid of squares that contains all the numerals from 1 to 16 and in which each row, column, and diagonal add up to 34. The other old surviving Jain temple is Adinath Temple. Shantinath Temple is more modern, incorporates within itself sections of several temples, and has numerous shrines.

More than the religiosity, I was fascinated by the eroticism depicted in those less than 10 per cent sculptures, as any hot-blooded normal adolescent would be. On the second afternoon, when my parents were enjoying their ritual of siesta at the hotel, I slipped out with my brother and sketched all the positions depicted by those statues involved in the calisthenics of improbable possibilities. Some of these seemed easy to carve and sketch but extremely difficult to practice. Later on, when Meena saw those sketches, she exclaimed, 'No, not that, never,' upon seeing one particular position, which we gave up at our first try. I still possess that sketchbook and use it frequently to spice up my married life whenever it threatens to totter towards mundanity. That 'No-Not-That-Never' position we have left for the gymnasts and the Rubber Man, Reed Richards, of the Fantastic Four fame to emulate and practice because our bodies are not supple enough to get into that impossible position.

I left my parents and Kaalu in the company of my uncles and aunts at Shanti Bhavan. The moment my feet landed in Shaktinagar, I was climbing into her verandah, along with my baggage—no time to waste by dumping my dirty laundry at my home even.

After I had relished her spasms of ecstasy in the sequel to that 'No-Not-That-Never' trial, Meena gave me a wonderful piece of news when she said that Teena's husband had contacted a lawyer friend of his who had assured him that Meena could get a divorce on the grounds of nonconsummation of the marriage—easier said than done, in case her husband claimed that he had, on the contrary, enjoyed numerous raunchy nights of sexual gratification.

On the second evening, after an unnaturally long hour and a half spent in eroticism, which culminated in an explosion of sweating squelching bodies entwined in divine ecstasy, I propped myself up on an elbow as she lay panting. Her tresses spread out in long wavy wavelets on the pillows. I picked up a strand and started whirling the silky thread around her nipple, making concentric circles on the areola. After a few failed attempts, I succeeded in covering the pink surface of her areola with a sea of black circles.

As I closed my lips on the encircled nipple, she said, 'Sanjay,' my tongue flickered at the gasp in the end, 'What is it with you? I just can't . . . I don't know . . . I just can't fathom you. You are such a bundle of contradictions.'

'And I thought you are the one carrying a mixed bag of inconsistencies.' I grinned at her—how much more divine can life be!

'I maybe, but, presently, we are on you. I can't figure out what drives you. You have this high sense of right and wrong, yet you never balked from a scandalous affair with me. With all your other girls, especially Pratima, you were platonic, but with me, you had sex in your mind from the very first day. You have such high regard for women, and you treat my body as a place of worship, but initially, before you realised your love for me, you were only interested in satisfying your lust.'

She let out a gasp of deep longing when my teeth pulled her nipple with a tiny, tiny as a dwarfish dwarf's pinkie's touch, bite. 'You continue like this and I will morph into an insatiable nymph.'

'My sweetness, these soft breasts of yours are the sole reason of my existence. I don't even know how I live when I am not with you. I can't have enough of you when I am with you; away from you, my life turns into a living hell. What would I ever do if my teeth and tongue are not engaged with these wrinkled extensions of your mammary glands? I pity our children. When your breasts start lactating, they will have to fight with me for their nourishment, as my hunger for your milk will know no end. God, forbid, if we ever have twins, one of them is surely going to suffer malnourishment.'

'You rascal,' she feigned indignation in her tone, 'if you ever dare deny food to my children, I will never speak with you. My breasts are my breasts, and once we have children, they will have sole proprietary right over their secretions. If you grow desperate, you could have your fill, but once their tummies are full and these globes have shrunk, then you will get only a few pitiful drops. Not before that. And with twins, you can forget all about ever touching my breasts with your mouth, till their weaning. Your tongue will have to make do with my navel and below. And your teeth, well, they can be put to better use, such as chewing your food, than nibbling on my tiny protrusions. Get your head away from there. I also want to see the dark circles around my nipple. You are such a magician. How can you conjure such marvellous patterns?'

I thought that question to be rhetorical and continued in my amorous fashion, 'Has anyone else seen you this naked, ever?'

'My earlier sexual adventures were more in the league of lift up the sari and lie down on the bed. I have not felt the need to ever undo my blouse, except when I was alone or with my sister. With you, it is entirely different. With you, I feel like even shedding my skin to reveal the Meena that resides inside my heart and soul. But I am still waiting for my reply.'

'I sometimes doubt the intentions of my Creator. I don't know why he has made me this complicated. I have never known a moment of happiness except when I am with you. Even when I am with you, the moment you are out of my sight, I start fearing the worst: that I will lose you forever. It may sound morbid, despicable even, but even when you are in the toilet, I want to sit next to you. Think of my plight. Just imagine my apathetic existence at NDA or even when I am out of your house. I live a life of longing, pining for the sweetness of your scent, for your arms around me, for feeling your softness, for everything you have. Before your kiss at the Helipad Hill, I lived each minute in deep frustration, as if the desolation of your refusal to acknowledge my love would never fade. But after that kiss, everything changed. I started feeling as if I had been transported from some dark hellish realm into a brightly lit heaven. And I go completely crazy with your quirky quirk of being completely nude in my presence. I am ready to give my right hand just to win the privilege of being with you forever. Once we are married, I don't know how I would ever be able to leave our house for a single minute without you. I think I will be a goner once I am in the Army.'

'Oh Sanjay! You say such sweet things that I feel like crying. Why are you so complicated? Why do you love me so much? I, too, sometimes feel that I would lose you. Why have we been chosen to live such a life of fugitives? Why do you have such respect for me, knowing full well that I do not deserve such reverence?'

'I, myself, don't know. Right from my childhood, I have been surrounded by women. My mother's and other women relatives' early and pervading presence have never been withdrawn and, as a consequence, I was late for my proper initiation into the all-male world. Since the time I can recollect, *BB Mausi* had always been telling me stories of heroes who had been virtuous towards women. She always maintained that I should show and develop respect not only for those women who were related to me but also for any woman I encountered—as a kid, I was made to touch the feet of every woman who visited my grandfather's house, irrespective of whether she was related to me or not. Later on, when I became aware of the charms of Hasina and Neelima, and had those churnings for the Sanskrit teacher and the hostel matron, I was drawn in. Pratima, with her ethereal beauty, changed it all. Even though I had started masturbating very early in my life, I never had any desire to have sex with her. I sought and got my pleasures in the pornography of the adult movies we saw at Bhowali, jerking off in the dark, spilling into my pants. Even inside a cave with Pratima, I never wanted to go all the way. What I had was enough for me—in fact, I enjoyed more when she was in the throes of her own ecstasy rather than the feel of her hands on my . . . you know. I believe my masturbation has left me with a feeling that sex, for me, is merely a mechanical exercise. I feel more ecstatic when you sssss-sigh with pleasure.'

'Continue in a similar vein and you might turn into a blessing for women. If you ever decide on an alternate profession, I know a few women who want gigolos for sexual gratification.' She chuckled, 'I can even run a publicity campaign for you—"Available! The ultimate desire for womanhood, this avatar of Kaamdev. Come, one and all; age, caste, creed, size, and colour are no barriers. Enjoy the pleasures of his love-infested arrow, which will not only pierce your besotted hearts but will even send your souls soaring into an exotic heaven of his making, where even Yamraaj would never deign to deny your hearts' desires". How does that sound for a blurb?'

'Except for the age and colour bit, and maybe the size, too. No old spinsters, no dark ugly ducklings, and definitely, no Aunteejis with hot air balloons for the waists for me—I won't even be able to enter her in the missionary position, and if she got on top, my groin would be crushed into a paste of bones, flesh, and blood, copious amounts of blood at that. But I think it would be better if I turned into a god-man as an alternate profession and enjoyed the privileges of a "saint" as well as a gigolo. Remember Bhulia's aunt and wife?' We discussed the possibility of my renouncing all materialistic desires, including discarding my robes, and acquiring 'sainthood' to enjoy the benefits and privileges of the Great Indian Gigolo, divinely impregnating women desirous of children and whose mortal partners were not able to maintain an appropriate disposition of their principle asset or whose tadpole-shaped cells are not potent enough to penetrate the tough exterior walls of their wives' eggs. Learning Sanskrit was the sole obstacle we mutually agreed upon as the principle impediment towards my being called a 'Sant'. Well, that's the story of human existence— one can never be perfect and get all of his desires. I finally consented to serve in the Army till I retire in my fifties. The mention of my golden jubilee sparked another discussion on how we would look like when we reached that age—would we become pudgy, would wrinkles line our faces, would I retain my virility, would she lose interest post-menopause, would my smoking make me incapable of maintaining My Sanju as a sentient being still skilful of superlative performances, time after time.

The future has never looked rosier than in the company of my Meena. I joined her in her wild imaginings as she got on top of me.

Later on, 'Your parents are very proud of you. Your mother once told me that they were already looking for a suitable match for you and that your price has been fixed at five lakhs.'

'I don't think they are ever going to realise that dream, not with what I have in my mind. What do you think will happen when we announce our marriage? Will they put two and two together and speculate that I had an affair with you all this while, that my English teacher not only stole my heart and soul but also denied them those five lakh rupees? Will they ostracise me, banish me out of their lives forever?'

'I don't know Sanjay. I wish that would never happen. I shudder at the very thought that I could become the cause of a rift between you and your parents. They love you so much. They have such high hopes for you.'

'What about my hopes and love? Shouldn't my love achieve its culmination? Should I be denied my "happily ever after" denouement? We should only think of ourselves, my sweet doll. In this world full of selfish desires, why should we deny ourselves our simple pleasures? I don't desire much, just to be with you forever—is that too much to ask for?'

'I know Sanjay. Nothing in this world, not even a boon of eternal life, would ever make me happier than when I would be able to write my name as Mrs Meena Tivari.'

'When we were at Banaras, I had been so drawn in by your sister's approval of us that I would have given my right hand to just be called Mr Meena.'

'Oh Sanjay! Don't love me so much. Why do you always say the very things that tear up my heart?' She wept silent tears as I held her close to me, wishing that our bodies and souls would merge and be one with the Almighty.

Later on, 'Your parents will be mighty disappointed of not being able to fetch those five lakh rupees.'

'I think my brother can make up for me by joining the IAS and marrying into a political family, for all I care. He can even sell himself for double that amount. That would make them prouder and happier, and would somehow overcome their disappointment of my falling in love with you. But even if you had never come into my life and I had to marry some other girl chosen by my parents, they would still have been disappointed with the outcome.'

'Meaning?'

'I have this thing against dowry.' Then, I told her about my twin pledges made to Golu Devta as a 13 year old, which I had held back all this while.

Being born in a patriarchal family myself, where the birth of a son is celebrated with festive gusto, whereas a daughter's arrival remains barely noticeable, I knew that my parents were looking forward to a hefty dowry. My becoming an Army officer in a year's time was surely going to raise my value a lot. But I was not going to put myself on sale. I loathed to be caricatured as a commodity in the marriage market of our country—I could visualise an unpalatable advertisement for me:

> *'A suitable groom, Class I Gazetted Officer in the Army, safe in a secure government job, belonging to an upper caste Brahmin family, available. Those Hindu Brahmin families that can afford Rs 30 lakhs and above in dowry need only apply. Unwed girls are mandatory—age, colour, and size no bar. Even divorcees and widows qualify, provided the sale value is met.'*

(I may have gone way overboard with that Rs 30 lakhs tag. I realised my true worth in my parents' eyes during my 'girl-seeing' spree—another ritual connected with our arranged marriage tradition, which I so detest but had to accept as an inalienable reality when it came my turn to choose a bride for myself, after repeatedly failing in my earlier quests for love: that of the prospective groom going for the selection of his soulmate. The girl would be all decked up in her fineries and jewellery, and put on show, so much like the cows on sale at the Pushkar Mela, the only difference from our bovine cousins being that, among the Homo Sapiens, the female of our species also carries a tray of tea for her husband-to-be and his parents—so Bollywood-esque that I have never hated a cliché more. In my case, my parents had insisted on my seeing the girl, even though I had already told them of my decision after one look at her photograph. But, for some unfathomable reason—which was disclosed later on—my mother kept on pestering me for a personal visit, till I relented. I went with Vijay, an elder cousin, to a village called Ajitmal, for the ceremony. I had felt such a pity for the girl that I almost agreed to say yes after Mother's repeated entreaties upon my return, despite my heart insisting on saying no. What got my goat, so to say, was when Mother, in frustration, let it out involuntarily that the girl's father had finally agreed to meet our price of Rs 1 lakh. 'What the f__k,' my heart had exploded, 'I suffered four years at NDA and the Indian Military Academy, IMA, to be sold for just Rs 1 lakh.' Had my grandfather been alive, he would have forced his son—my father—to bend on his knees and would have given him a nice spanking on his bumps with his cane—so what that my father was in his middle age—for belittling the Tivari name. Surely, my numerous ancestors' ghosts, right from Chaudhari Trilok Singh, would have squirmed in agony for this generation of Tivaris, who would stoop so low as to sell their son for such a meagre sum. What a downfall—from a feudal lord of 1,162 villages to being grateful to a girl's father for 'finally agreeing' to buy a Tivari scion for Rs 1 lakh only. It felt as if my cost was written on a bankers' cheque, with that suffix 'only' added to indicate 'nothing more'. That was the day, and I have only 'seen' one girl since, that, too, at the insistence of my mother, as she wanted to be sure that my 'yes' this time, after a mere glimpse of her photograph, was sincere. She is my wife today, and I have never been more grateful to God. The dowry thing was another issue. Even if I had not made my promise to Golu Devta, I would have still walked off the *Mandap* (the enclosure where the marriage rituals are held) had my parents insisted on that one lakh rupees during my marriage. She is my true soulmate—she, too, had rejected an unsuitable prospective groom before agreeing to marry me, despite my 'good looking in a good-looking sort of way' looks. I salute both of my grandfathers and my father-in-law for the nobility of their hearts, for providing opportunities to their daughters and for caring for their women—something that has been denied to one-half of the humanity by the society at large, for eons. It does not take much effort, just a peek inside one's soul and attitudinal change in our mindset. But, in reality, it would take a tectonic shift of humongous proportions to bring about that change. Does Utopia emerge in anybody's mind?)

There was a rebel streak, too, in me. The experiences of my early years had revealed to me that girls, too, have an identity, unlike the popular perceptions and beliefs in the small towns and villages of the country. Hasina, Neelima, and Pratima were not just girls, but individual human beings, each with a distinct identity, their respective personalities characterised by the brilliance of each of their minds and the purity of their hearts. They were intelligent, they had independent thoughts, they were driven by an ambition similar to that of any man, they loathed the idea that a woman's sole duty was to bring forth and nurture the future generations of male scions. My philosophy in life forced me to go against the grain, and I revelled in the thought that I would break the stereotype.

I continued after that short preamble. 'For me, dowry is the vilest evil ever engendered by mankind. Imagine, a man spills his seed inside a woman, and the damn chromosomes decide the entire family's fate and future. Who gave man the authority to tweak with what nature decides? As if it was not enough to consign one-half of the humanity to hearth and bed, man created this draconian tradition. I don't know about other countries, but my countrymen have developed it into an art form, and use it as an excuse to pile miseries upon women and their parents.

'Many of my fellow countrymen allow a foetus to grow into a baby if its cells contain the Y-chromosome, else it is flushed out. Even if it is allowed to grow inside its mother's womb, the moment it comes out without a weed between its legs, she is discarded at some hillside or dumped into a gutter.'

(The practice continues in the twenty-first century. In December 2014, I read of a newly born infant girl discovered near a garbage dump in Bhopal, left to her miseries by her 'modern' parents. Her barely alive body was found covered in a swarm of red ants, as if they were hired to finish the job by her devilish parents. I refused to believe my equally bigoted friend's argument that she might have been born out of wedlock. He had no answer to my reply when I asked, 'Have you ever heard of infant boys being dumped likewise?' What can one Narendra Modi do? He can't sit inside the grotesquely twisted hearts of my fellow countrymen and change their attitude towards women).

'Many are still allowed to live, after all, a man needs a woman to establish his superiority, but women carry this burden of inadequacy throughout their lives. And, to add to her woes, man decided to be more condescending and forced fathers to suffer for having bred a girl. How much more illogical can one get—a man needs a woman to survive; otherwise, God wouldn't have taken Adam's rib to create her, but the same man forces another man to pay up for giving the star of his eyes to another man's son. Why can't my parents be satisfied with just welcoming another person into their lives? No, they want their pound of flesh, too, in the form of the poor girl's father's hard-earned money. Who is the alpha male here—the one whose sperms carried the Y-chromosome all those years back. We have created a social structure where the alphas dominate the omegas by virtue of having bred only males. The one whose sperms were so "weak" that they made a girl and who was not craven enough to kill her at birth, if not earlier, has to suffer the consequences of her birth throughout his life. In my hometown, and in many other small towns and villages that make up our great country—great is a satire here—many brides' parents have to continually dish out money to their daughters' in-laws throughout their lives, even after they had paid the dowry in full during the marriage. Which father would like to live a life of such subservience, so to ease their own burden, they commit gendercide? And, to seek spiritual justification, they wrote the Holy Scriptures in a manner that women are depicted as occupying a lower pedestal, under the very feet of men, to be always treated with disgrace. Do you wish for me to continue my tirade?'

'I have never seen you this passionate before. I am loving this, we are kindred spirits. For the umpteenth time, where were you all this while when I was looking for a soulmate? Please do continue, Milord.'

'All this while, I was searching for you, my sweet daffodil. And I am so grateful to God that I found you before it got too late. Marry me today.' I couldn't stop the deluge of emotions threatening to overwhelm and drown me. 'Let's go to Jwalamukhi Temple and say our solemn vows. Later, we will go to Banaras and register our marriage.'

'Oh Sanjay! Don't love me so much. We will have to wait. Come on, it has been over an hour, I am wet and you are ready. Make love to me with similar passion. Your talk has awakened the dormant animal inside me.'

Later on, 'Dowry has never been so cruel all through the history. Being a transfer of property at the marriage of a daughter, it had noble intentions when it was conceived,' she said as I got busy framing her sweat-soaked face with her lustrous hair. 'Throughout history, it has undergone many changes, but the principle theme had been to ensure that the daughter got her share of her parents' ancestral property. Its modern-day, degraded avatar reflects the progressive degeneration of the attitude of men towards women.'

'I will tell you about the degradation. After my vow, I conducted a lot of research on the subject, primarily to convince my parents when my time came. History has not always been so unkind to women. Even though dowry is deemed to be an ancient custom, its purpose has been to guarantee financial stability for the wife in the event of widowhood or if the worst happened and she was cursed with a negligent husband. In societies, where division of labour ensures that most of the work is done by women, a bride price is given, as in sparsely populated regions where shifting cultivation takes place. It is paid as a compensation for the loss of her labour to her family. This practice is not uncommon in certain tribes among the Garo and Khasi societies in the north-eastern states of India, where they follow a matriarchate system. Among them, the ancestral property is inherited by the youngest daughter, and the groom goes to live in the wife's house. Among the Lushais, Zemi Nagas, and Kukis, wives are bought by paying a marriage price in the form of their most prized currency, the *mithuns* (*gaur* or *gayal*, a bovine animal found in abundance in Northeast India, South and Southeast Asia). The system is typical of how that society is structured, where a boy, except when working in the fields, is free to go hunting, fishing, drinking, singing, dancing, and making love to his heart's content, whereas a girl helps her mother, from dawn to dusk, in domestic tasks and caters to the needs of the menfolk. No wonder an unmarried girl there is considered a valuable asset, and her parents demand a price to part with her. Some of these tribes have another extraordinary custom that, after the death of the husband's father-in-law, the widowed mother-in-law marries her son-in-law, and he becomes the husband of both the mother and her daughter.

'Getting back to history, the Code of Hammurabi in ancient Babylon described dowry as an already-existing custom. Daughters, upon marriage, got dowry from their parents as a lifetime security, since they could not inherit from their father's estate. It remained within the control of the wife, so much so that her dowry was inheritable only by her own children.

'In India, the origins of this custom remain disputed. Historical eyewitness accounts suggest that dowry in ancient India was insignificant and that daughters had inheritance rights.

'The famous Sri Lankan social anthropologist, Stanley J. Tambiah, claims that the ancient Code of Manu sanctioned dowry among the Brahmins, since it was considered to be more prestigious, and bride wealth was restricted to the lower castes, who were not allowed to give dowry; he suggests that this practice persisted till the first half of the twentieth century. Another historian, Michael Witzel, cites ancient Indian literature to suggest that this practice had not been significant during the Vedic period, as women, then, had property inheritance rights, either by appointment or when they had no brothers. These analyses are based on inconsistent *smritis* from India and not on eyewitness accounts.

'The famous Greek historian, Arrian, gives an eyewitness account from the conquests by Alexander the Great, in the third century BC. In his book, *The Invasion of India by Alexander the Great*, he wrote,

> *They (these ancient Indian people) make their marriages accordance with this principle, for in selecting a bride, they care nothing whether she has a dowry and a handsome fortune, but look only to her beauty and other advantages of the outward person.*

'In another book, *Indikka*, he goes on to write,

They (Indians) marry without either giving or taking dowries, but women as soon as they are marriageable are brought forward by their fathers in public to be selected by the victor in wrestling or boxing or running or someone who excels in any other manly exercise.

'These two sources suggest that dowry was absent or was infrequent enough to be noticed by Arrian. Another famous historian, Al-Baruni, who wrote a memoir on Indian culture and life, as observed by him during his sixteen years of stay in India, from the early to mid eleventh century AD, 1,200 years after Arrian's visit, had this to say in his *Chapter on Matrimony in India*, in about AD 1035:

The implements of wedding rejoicings are brought forward. No gift (dower or dowry) is settled between them. The man gives only a present to the wife, as he thinks fit, and a marriage gift in advance, which he has no right to claim back, but the (proposed) wife may give it back to him of her own will (if she does not want to marry).

'He further goes on to claim that a daughter, in eleventh-century India, had inheritance rights from her father, at fourth part of her brother, which she took with her on marriage. But she had no rights to income from her parents or any additional inheritance on her father's death after her marriage.

'It is unclear when and how the inheritance laws in India changed after Al-Baruni's visit to India, more than ten centuries back. It is also unclear when, why, and how quickly the practice of dowry demand by grooms began, whether this happened with the arrival of Islam in the late eleventh century or with the arrival of colonialism five centuries later, or both.'

'I will tell you about that.' She interjected. 'Why do you think ancient Indians were so poor in maintaining proper historical records? Because they were always fearful of the judgements of future generations. Deconstruction of history is the easiest of vocations. One man's Napoleon is another man's despot. The ancient Indians, especially the much learned and revered Brahmins, knew that they were treating their women disgracefully. But instead of correcting a wrong, they left no account of the ill treatment meted out to the women of their time. They created these goddesses, the apsaras, the angels, and other virtuous female human beings, and hid the common man's woman under a shroud of anonymity—never heard of, never read about, always to suffer. Hence, there is hardly any account of dowry in our surviving records. What Arrian and Al-Baruni witnessed must have been stage-managed to showcase the best of India to a foreigner. Don't underestimate the Brahmins—they can pull the wool over anybody's eyes, what were a couple of foreigners to them. The tradition continues even today—don't you notice these upper caste people extolling virtues of secularism and inclusiveness and, at the same time, exploiting the downtrodden at every given opportunity.

'In our patrilineal society, dowry, over a period of time, became a common practice due to the inadequate male-biased inheritance laws, especially in South Asia. The only nation in our neighbourhood that abhors this heinous practice is Bhutan, where daughters neither take their father's name at birth nor their husband's name upon marriage. There, inheritance is matrilineal, and women can hold rural land as well as businesses. Polyandry, like Draupadi, and polygyny are socially accepted, with the latter practice of having several wives at the same time being more prevalent. Sometimes, a prospective groom has to work in the bride's family's household to earn the right to marry her.'

I picked up the refrain there onwards, 'But in India, this practice of dowry has assumed draconian proportions. It puts immense financial strain on the girl's family; hence, she is treated as a burden and is often killed before or immediately after birth. It is such an irony that, despite having a prohibitory law in the 1961 Dowry Prohibition Act and the Indian Penal Code Sections 304B and 498A, dowry is demanded and given in an unabashed manner. So much so that husbands and their parents have been killing their brides for her parents not meeting their demands.

'I could, for once, understand the rationale behind dowry, if someone could convince me that the money and property so gained has been used for the betterment of the wife's life. In our joint family system, the dowry is not merely the property of the husband, but his larger family of parents, brothers, and sisters, too, claim proprietary right over it. A father takes dowry in his elder son's marriage to provide for the education of his carefully bred younger male progenies and, also, for the dowry of an unfortunate girl born in the family and who, somehow, managed to survive, despite all the efforts of her parents to get rid of her before she came of age. It is the reason and result of our son preference. Look at our mythology, even the epics—is there ever a mention of women whose virtues have been sung for being anything other than a dutiful wife, an obedient daughter, a subservient sister and, yes, how can I forget the ubiquitous nymph? This discrimination against daughters stems from this worst evil of all. That's why I have vowed that we will only have daughters and show the world how a small town boy can thrive in this corrupted environment of misogyny and flourish with his girls. And I will be eternally grateful to you if you would agree to be their mother.'

'I bow to you, *Jahanpanah* (emperor), and pledge that I will only give you daughters. Why don't I become a first one and abort a male foetus?' She was getting carried away with the force of our discussion.

'I will support you wholeheartedly with that, I promise. That is surely going to get my parents' goat and rule out any reconciliation.'

'Can we stop talking about your parents and their predicament in our future? Can't you think of a better purpose for your tongue? No, not my navel, you scoundrel; there is no sweat left there. Don't you drink water?' as my tongue searched for the tangy globules inside the delicious dip on her belly.

'I can't help it. Your belly button contains my elixir. But your desires are what I want to fulfil. I do have a better use for my tongue.' I grinned and slid further down.

19

The Letter

It came as a surprise, one March afternoon in '91, during my final six months of training at IMA, as she had never written a letter to me earlier.

My move to IMA at Dehradun in July '90 was more of an anticlimax after the high of the senior-most term at NDA. Back at NDA, I was the boss, enjoying all the privileges divined for the sixth-termers—the late waking-up; missing classes at any whim that caught my imagination; bossing over the juniors; sending my second-termer understudy to fetch tea, cigarettes, donuts, and pastries from the Gole Market; not bothering to strain any muscle during the game periods in the evenings; visiting harsh punishments on the hapless juniors; haunting Ferguson College every Sunday to solicit a partner for the now-famous NDA Ball—no success there—loitering in the Squadron; wearing only the dressing gown: we had a strange 'tradition' of wearing casual apparels within the Squadron—second-termers had to wear the entire night suit under the gown; third-termers could afford to not wear the shirt but had to don a vest and the pyjama under the gown; fourth-termers could be without the vest; fifth-termers graduated to even removing the pyjama but had to wear an underwear beneath the gown; and sixth-termers, well, we could even afford to roam around naked, who was there to object to that? We were God's own after all, but decency forced us to adorn a gown with nothing underneath. Those with Dharmendra-style gowns from *Raja Jani* could flaunt much more than what Dharmendra did with Hema Malini.

But, at IMA, we were back to being juniors—the microcosm of our society; there is always somebody above you, one can never reach the very top. We were again herded, very much like sheep, and had to move in orderly formation from place to place. There were the drill instructors, the PT instructors, the weapon training instructors, the officers, and the ubiquitous seniors to torment us again. One major difference from NDA was that we were gentleman cadets, GCs, now, as if prefixing the 'cadet' with that epithet would, overnight, convert us from rowdies into an honourable person. NDA cadets take very long to metamorphose into GCs, and by the time few of us managed to achieve the impossible, we suddenly realised that we had already become officers and gentlemen, without comprehending what that second term meant.

I had still not been able to master the art of converting into a GC when that warm March afternoon, I received a letter with her neat cursive handwriting spelling out my address on the envelope. The circumstances of my clandestine love affairs, both with Pratima and Meena, had never permitted me to realise my dreams of sending them love notes, written on the backs of bills, napkin papers borrowed from restaurants, the silver wrappers lining the insides of cigarette packets, and such like stationeries. I had never had an opportunity to write to either of them for fear of my letters falling into wrong hands. They also never felt inclined to write to me when I was away due to the same reason. Hence, my surprise at this unexpected communication from Meena. Elated, I slipped into my cabin with the bulky envelope to read her missive in leisure.

And my world came crashing down, exploding like an atom bomb.

There were ten pages in all, each of them decorated with numerous tiny smudge marks—many words were obliterated by the smudge, not unlike the ones we encounter when taking down notes out in the rain. I ran my tongue over one of the smudge marks; it tasted of ink and paper, and a faint remnant of salt, as an aftertaste.

My Dearest Sweetest Sanjay, the Love of My Life, (she began thus)

As I sit amidst the scattered baggage, crates, and bins containing the meagre possessions of my household, and take a hiatus from the frenzy associated with the preparations accompanying my permanent move to Chhapra, I want to pen my final thoughts concerning our relationship, which lasted for four and a half most enchanting, enticing, exhilarating, and wonderful years of my life.

As tears streak down my face and leave their sorry smudges on this epistle of love, I cannot help but wonder what would have become of my life had I not met you that fateful day, when I had come visiting your house on my first day of arrival at Shaktinagar. That summer of '86 changed my life for good. I recall that moment with a clarity that is only associated with reflections on momentous incidents which lead to tumultuous changes in a person's fortunes and future. I had never felt it opportune to relate to you my feelings of that fortuitous day when I had first set my eyes upon you. I will be very candid in accepting that I had seen in you what you were then—a young 17-and-a-half-year-old boy-man, shy of manners, bursting with untamed energy, a bit of a bully while dealing with your younger brother, supremely attentive to your mother's wishes and orders, and foremost, you exhibited a shade of narcissism, bordering on introversion. But I could see from the way you were trying to catch my eye that some stirrings had commenced within you. I could have never prophesied, in my wildest of imaginations, that this young, shy, 17-and-a-half-year-old boy-man with slightly elongated cheekbones (what caused it, I had then speculated) would take me on a journey of such wonder, joy, and ecstasy.

By the time destiny had conjured our fateful meeting, I had become a broken, crushed, and discarded wreck of a beautifully carved piece. During my incarceration, I had completely broken down. My sister was my sole window to the outside world during that nauseating period of desolate existence, bringing me news of all the happenings in our college (where I only went for my exams) and the immediate neighbourhood. After that year spent in solitude, I had felt that my marriage would, at least, release me from the clutches of my father, and I would be able to breathe the fresh air of liberty and adventure. But the initial few months of my married life revealed that my expectations were just a figment of some delightful imaginary world. The short time I spent as a wife and dutiful daughter-in-law at Chhapra turned out to be a transfer from one hell to another. He never showed any interest in me, as you are well aware, and at his parents' home, I had felt suffocated, since his father did not look eye to eye with him and treated me like an invisible presence, totally ignoring my existence. His short grunts and gruff rejections of me, whenever I addressed him to enquire after his daily needs, left me bereft of any emotion, and I had consigned myself to a life of bleak survival—so desolate had I become in those two months at Chhapra. Even my mother-in-law and her three daughters took after the patriarch and rarely treated me as an equal. The claustrophobically constricting environment at my in-laws' household was psychologically dislocating me—I had forgotten what sound emerged from my throat when I laughed; I never had an occasion to reflect on a happy happenstance and smile. To add to my woes, my father-in-law had still not accepted him back and often threatened to disinherit him from the family's bequest.

When he had finally taken me to Shaktinagar, after much forceful persuasion by his father and my own insistence, I had let out a sigh of relief. I could bear that I would never be able to seek physical satisfaction from my marriage, but having my very existence being ignored was getting too much to endure. Since I was not aware of his orientation then, despite those botched three occasions, his reluctance to have physical relations with me left me puzzled. But I was equally grateful that he showed no interest in me, as his size and manners gave me the dread whenever I thought of him forcing himself upon me.

Here, at Shaktinagar, the very first day I saw that look in your eyes, I had a premonition of some tumultuous change in my life. The next few days, I sat at my window and awaited your arrival. When you started your badminton game, I had wondered how to join you. You cannot imagine the joy I had felt when you asked me to play. Your antics, your poor imitations of Jeetendra, your attentiveness to my wishes, your eagerness to please me filled me with eternal gratitude. I learned to laugh again.

The invitation for that first cup of tea was just that: an innocent invitation to return the favour you had bestowed upon me by bringing that sliver of joy into my despondent life. Your advances during tea that day took me by surprise, but I admit that I did not want to discourage you. I had been hungering for physical intimacy, for kisses and caresses, to immerse into those long-forgotten sensations, and your adolescent self was replacing what was nonexistent for the past so many months of my life. But I was not ready to take it any further than a kiss and a caress, and I had to put the brakes after those few moments of intimacy.

Oh Sanjay, I have never in my life felt as miserable when I saw the disappointment on your face after I had asked you to leave. The moment you walked out of my door, I felt like tearing myself into pieces, so regretful had I felt for rejecting you. But that quality of yours, of persevering against all odds, which you had honed to such perfection, proved to be my saving grace.

The next few days I spent in constant yearning, and I grew increasingly anxious when you did not try to meet me, did not show any inclination for badminton, did not even venture to my door—I expected you to barge in any moment and crush me into your arms. In my longing I often dreamt of touching you, feeling every inch of your body, kissing you—I wanted you to make me feel what a young woman should rightfully feel. I had even contemplated going over to your house and try to have a few words with you.

Some prescience indicated to me that you would come to me on the fourth day. I had spruced up the house and tidied the rooms, which were, most of the time, kept unkempt, and awaited your arrival that evening. When I heard the bell's trings, I knew that it was you, and I opened the door with hope and eagerness to let life enter my house.

Whatever you might think after reading these pages, I want you to believe that I will love you till eternity and beyond, if ever such an epoch exists. I may reside in my body, but my soul belongs to you. I gave it to you a long time back when you stood in front of my door with an eager anticipation alighting your face that day. Yes, my sweet darling, Sanjay, you stole my heart that very day, and I will repent it till the end of my days that I held on for so very long before finally opening my heart to you on the Helipad Hill.

I give you my soul as a recompense for the love you have given me all these years—not that I ever consider being in love a bargain. You have filled me with so much love that each pore of my mortal body permeates your essence. I consider myself extremely lucky to have met you and to have been loved in return, to a point of obsession. No girl would have ever been desired by her soulmate with so much passion and devotion.

Your arrival into my life had opened a whole new world for me. Until that moment, I was languishing in the throes of sheer despair and misery, brooding over the quirks of fate that had led to my wretched reality—it was seeming as if there was nothing to look forward to in a future that held no appeal for me. And there you were, standing at my doorstep with that queer look of triumph on your face, your eyes gleaming with an expectant realisation of some new adventure, your restlessness evident from the way you fidgeted, seeking entry into my soul. The mere sight of you had taken my breath away, and realisation dawned on me that, finally, I had met my soulmate. I must have been mad looking for salvation in a 17-and-a-half-year-old you; somewhere deep within me, I felt a guilty reminder that I was walking into a disaster, that in my somnambulance, I was leading a young boy into a morass from where there would be no escape, that in my desire to relive my passion, I was using a conduit that might not be able to put up with the pressures of a relationship, which he wouldn't even be able to put a name to. But I have suffered enough, I had reasoned then. I longed for an opening; all that had happened in my life earlier had been clogging me up. As you sauntered in, my heart had fluttered with an uncertainty, an expectation, and an unexplained desire. It was only when you had explained that you wanted tutoring in English that reality struck; you wanted something from me, and here I was thinking of my own selfish desires. When you did that Noelle Page–Constantin Demeris act, I fell head over heels for you. When your inexperience became evident, I revelled at the thought of being your teacher in things other than clearing the literary incongruities of the English language. I wanted us to not only be lovers but soulmates.

But, to come to terms with my own guilty feeling, I decided to keep it at a purely physical level, despite opening up my heart during the retelling of my life. I loved the time we spent together—742 hours and 56 minutes in total. I did keep a record of it, on the flyleaves of Hitler's Mein Kampf— that sod came of some use after all. Although on that one occasion, you used the word dalliance, I resented the use of that term. For me, it was more than merely satisfying my physical desires. It may have started as a purely sexual adventure, but truth be told, when you gradually opened up yourself, baring your heart to me, I had started believing that I had reached my life's objective. You were not merely the singular object of my physical needs, but when you said that you loved me from the bottom of your heart, you also became my emotional anchor and soulmate, in the truest sense of the word. Ever since that fateful day, I have always bowed my head in gratitude to God for having destined my fate in such a miraculous fashion that our paths crossed—grateful may not be enough to carry the weight of the feelings I have for you. With you, I was fortunate to catch glimpses of a world beyond the wildest of my dreams.

When you announced that you had been selected for NDA and that, four years later, you would deliver me from the shackles of an unfortunate marriage, my heart had wept with joy. The past seemed to evaporate, and

I immersed in a rosy vision of a future where we would be together forever. I started believing in the possibility of change in my fortunes. What I had held back for so long, my true feelings for you, came out in a torrent on the Helipad Hill, after you carried me up the slope. It was then that I realised that, if I did not confess my love, I would implode with the pressure of my bottled-up emotions. I kissed you with an intensity and hunger I had never felt before. And, when you started painting a picture of pure bliss in our joint future, I had thought no girl could ever get more fortunate.

But, when the forces of reality strike at the doors of fantasy, everything comes crashing down like a house of cards. What was I dreaming of? I, a married woman, thinking of settling down with a man poised on a path of a brilliant future? Won't I become a hindrance to your ambitions? Your parents would never accept me. You promised marriage, and I could not even guarantee a stable life. Our future together would be a saga of constant struggles, of insurmountable hurdles, of unreliable quests in the face of daunting challenges. What society would accept us as legitimate, bless our union, welcome us with open arms, and permit a blissful life? These thoughts often took me into a familiar territory of desolation, and I often got mired in doubts.

Then, we went to Banaras, where Teena's husband and you gave me a glimmer of hope again with your determination to get my marriage annulled. My hopes soared, and I started dreaming of improbable possibilities again. By approving and supporting you, Teena and her husband gave me strength, which had started fading with the passage of time.

Everything came to a head when I went to Chhapra after you left for IMA in January this year. My father-in-law was dying, and his impending mortality had wrought changes in the attitude of my in-laws towards me. All this while, they had been treating me like an outsider, but this was the first time that I was welcomed as an intimate member of the family.

And, when my mother-in-law told me about the provisions of my father-in-law's will, the earth dissolved and vanished from beneath my feet. Oh, Sanjay, I have never felt so lonely in my life, not even when I was serving my virtual prison sentence at my home. I had fainted when I realised the implications of his will. My father-in-law has never been able to reconcile with the fact that his son is a homosexual, and to ensure that he never indulges in his proclivities, he has put in a condition that his son would only inherit the ancestral property if he remains married to me—to me! I couldn't believe what I was hearing when my mother-in-law amplified that 'married to me' was the most important clause my father-in-law had insisted upon. She further added that her son would be deprived of his inheritance if he ever separated from me.

God could not have been crueler. I wanted to reason out with my father-in-law, to explain to him how my life would become a living hell if he did not remove that condition. But he had passed away before I could petition him with my request. I implored my husband to give me divorce on the grounds of nonconsummation of our marriage, but he refused and said that he would lie and testify in court that he had enjoyed his husbandly privileges inside our bedroom on numerous occasions, that I would have no proof to refute his claims. I threatened to kill myself; he had smirked at that and said that he would be happier, as he could still retain his inheritance. I talked to Teena's husband, and he said that it would be well nigh impossible to secure a divorce without my husband's approval and that annulment, on any ground; domestic cruelty, nonconsummation, violence, etc., needed irrefutable proof. And since I had been living with him all this while, separation could not be taken as an excuse for seeking divorce. I considered eloping and living with you, but he cautioned me that that would jeopardise your career—the Army would never accept me as your wife when I was already married to somebody else, and you would be ostracised even before you commenced your career.

My heart shatters imagining what recourse you will take after reading these words, but this is the only way forward for us. Anything else is unimaginable. We have to consign those to the realm of dreams and fantasies. Oh, Sanjay! I don't know how to break this to you, but it is the end of the road for us. In this real world, we cannot be together forever.

With each word I write, a fragment of my soul departs in search of my true love. As Pratima had so rightly surmised, love does mean sacrifice. I love you so much that I am sacrificing myself at its altar.

I want you to believe me when I say that this can be done no other way. We can never be tied in a marital union. I can't put you through the ignominy that my association will bring upon you. I will even give up my life before any harm can come to your personal honour and character. And that's what will come to pass if you insist on living up to your promise of living happily ever after together with me. I want you to live happily ever after—there is nothing I would desire more in this world. But with someone else. Not with me.

Sanjay! The society we live in is too hypocritical and feels insecure whenever someone like us goes against the norm. Nobody will understand the true love we share between us. I can live an eternity with the stamp of a seductress, a temptress, an adulteress even, but I cannot let you bear the consequences of my actions.

I don't know what fate has in store for me in my future. After today, I won't even care.

But I have one sole desire—to care for a child. I would have loved to have your child, but that would have given rise to a scandal I could do without, since he had let it be known to his family—during my tirades for divorce in front of his mother and sisters—that he had never had sex with me and that now he had no further desire. I, for myself, would have killed him or even committed suicide before ever accepting his child. I even refused in-vitro fertilisation when my mother-in-law suggested it.

My eldest sister-in-law was widowed a few months back, and since she gave birth to twin daughters, a couple of months before her husband's unfortunate demise, his family has abandoned her, and she now lives with her mother and sisters. She wants to spend the rest of her life in the City of Widows, at Vrindavan, in the company of others who have similarly been abandoned by their respective families, and live for her Madhav. I have decided to adopt her nine-month-old twins—they are the loveliest 9-month-olds I have ever seen. I want to be their mother and raise them as my own children. Madhav has taken you away, but he has granted me a boon in them. I will eternally pine for you but will endeavour to find contentment in them.

I have another responsibility—that of taking care of my aging mother-in-law and my sisters-in-law, one of whom is a 29-year-old spinster, and the other, a 10-year-old child living inside a 25-year-old autistic woman. My mother-in-law is the sweetest and gentlest lady I have ever come across. We have grown closer to each other with each passing day. I have even started revering her. And my sisters-in-law need me more than I need them. I intend to find solace in them. Living with them for one month has led me to realise the futility of life. I can't live without you and I want to live for them. I don't know any other way of putting it.

Will you ever forgive me? I don't know. Am I right in seeking your forgiveness? I do not know that, too. But what I am absolutely sure of is that I will never be able to forgive myself for having kindled a hope in your heart and then extinguishing it in this manner. This is the only sin I have ever committed in my life—the sin of making myself fall in love with you. Had I continued our relationship in a purely physical sense, maybe your heart would mend itself, but now, I am not sure of that. I can't even begin to imagine what will happen to you. I feel the fragments of my heart piercing my soul into million pieces, and I cannot assemble those pieces. What about you—will you ever be able to live a normal life? You have failed twice. What man can live through two heartbreaks?

Oh, Sanjay! I ask of you to forget me. Please forget me. Please don't come to Chhapra. I don't know what infamy would befall upon us if we ever meet again—I will not be able to control myself, and the consequences will lead to your downfall.

Our relationship has remained a secret so far, and I implore you to let it remain thus.

For many years, perhaps my entire life, I have let my heart rule over me. Now, I want my mind to decide for me.

I will pray to my God everyday to make your life happy. I have nothing to ask for myself from Him. You have filled my life with such joy that it will last me till eternity. But, for you, I want him to give my portion of happiness, too. And let your sorrows be mine—I will ask of him that, too.

Live your life to the fullest, Sanjay! And take my advice—love is not for you. You will fall for the wrong girl again. Go with your parents' wishes, and marry a sweet girl of their choice, who will give you more happiness than I could have ever given you.

> *Whatever may happen in the future,*
> *I will remain yours forever, my Sweet Darling,*
> *Your Meena*

Her letter wrought utter devastation—the feeling was akin to what Hiroshima's soul must have felt when Little Boy had exploded in its heart on 6 August '45. A sad ghost closed its fist around my shattered heart. I was stoned to death by grief that had rained down on me in a deluge. Even though she had clearly given her reasons, I still couldn't believe that she could mean it. And I couldn't even grieve at my heartbreak. I had not let any of my course mates at IMA know of my love affair, as I did not want any of them to belittle my love for Meena, which is invariably the case with our generation when someone reveals an affair with a married woman. Their sex-starved brains just concentrate on the physical aspect of the relationship; they do not appreciate the involvement of the heart, as most of such cases are seen in the light of the sexual desires of an adolescent youth taking recourse to engaging with a married woman to satisfy his lust, and of course, the cuckold is always the butt of jokes. As a consequence, I had to suffer my heartbreak all by myself.

But time, the universal healer, had an ally in my case—the gruelling training regime at IMA. The busy daily routine left nary a time for contemplation. The physical exertions during the daytime left me with barely enough energy to hit the sack and be lost in a deep slumber, for the nights. Most of these nights were dreamless, but there were some nights when Meena would appear in myriad avatars: as an angel descending from the heavens, bearing some secret message from the Gods above; as a doting wife pining for my return from some faraway realm, where I would be fighting my battles with some imaginary foe; as a caring mother of my children as they fought with me to seek her attention—nothing was more blissful than my children screaming for her as I carried Meena to fantasyland, buried deep inside my arms; as a lover eloping with me, leaving a gaping world of malevolent demons wielding stones; as a demure damsel waiting for her knight to execute a brave rescue from a dragon-infested prison; as a sex siren executing a Menaka-style performance to stir passions inside me while I sat meditating a la Vishwamitra. Sometimes, Pratima, too, would emerge, out of some remote corner of my heart, and my senses would flip-flop, draining me of all emotions as I seesawed between Meena and Pratima.

20

Two Flickers and a Sudden Darkness

I somehow managed to complete the remaining portion of my training and realised one-half of my dreams—that of becoming a second lieutenant in the Indian Army. But the occasion did not engender any joy in me; I could not share in the exuberance of my parents and brother. The only bright spark during the Passing Out Parade was Eesha, the 14-year-old daughter of Arjun Thakur. She had come to Dehradun with my parents to witness my commissioning. We had started knowing each other well during my ten-day stint in the spring of '87, when I had stayed at Arjun Thakur's house in Delhi while attending the SSB Coaching Institute at Pusa Road. I had seen Bindu in Eesha then, and over a period of time, she had replaced Bindu, after I left Ghorakhal. She assumed the place of a sister whose absence I have always felt as an emptiness in my life. Over the years, we had written to each other often, and she also sent me my sole *Rakhi* during every *Raksha Bandhan*. So, on 08 June '91, I was glad to rejoice in the joy of Eesha, and when she clapped as I marched past the spectators' stand in the Academy's Parade Ground, resplendent in the glorious olive green uniform of IMA, my heart swelled with immense love. I was so taken in by her exuberance that I insisted on her pinning the lone brass star of a second lieutenant's rank on my right shoulder, a privilege that the other jubilant GCs of IMA reserved for each of their proud parents. My parents and brother jointly pinned the star on my other shoulder.

Even Father's gifting me a black Kawasaki Bajaj motorcycle did not help in lifting my spirits, so morbid did I feel, when I was at Shaktinagar for four weeks of leave before joining my artillery unit at Amritsar. Her house was vacant, as it had been earmarked for demolition after Sharmajee had moved out of it, and I spent three long evenings pining for her in her bedroom. I scaled her rear wall and walked into her dust-ridden barren boudoir, and lay on the cool concrete of her floor, where we had spent so many amorous hours, whenever the soft cushions of her mattresses lost their appeal and we wanted the hard feeling of the mosaic floor for our passionate lovemaking. Even after three months of her departure, I could smell Meena's fragrance in the dust of her house. In my desperation, I crawled through all the places we had made love and professed our feelings for each other—the living room, where the two-seater couch never protested even once; the tiny kitchen, where the one-foot-by-one-foot slab was enough space for my bumps to be perched on; the tinier bathroom, where Meena's soapy body made such lovely sounds whenever we pressed into each other standing up, our bodies moving with the rhythm of the water dripping from the shower; the vast expanse of her verandah, where I spent many cool summer nights when the electricity abandoned us and we would lie on a thin mattress out in the open, my bare bumps providing a feast of endless supplies of blood to the mosquitoes who gorged on my pristine buttocks, enjoying the gastronomic equivalent of a Thanksgiving dinner, as my senses refused to acknowledge their stings till Meena indicated with her ssss-sighs and entwined arms and legs that her nerves were trembling with a million-watt electric current; it was then and only then that the mosquito bites would bring me back from our exotic world to the reality of Shaktinagar, with its numerous garbage dumps that bred and groomed these tiny insects with the sting of a Jewish merchant, so relentless are they in their search for an elixir. Her storeroom still contained the oily patches, where I insisted that Meena always remain on top, as I did not want the spotless skin of her back to ever be blemished by those black marks of sundry oils and grease.

By the fourth day, my patience was at its tether, and in sheer desperation, I announced that the pollution of Shaktinagar was getting on my nerves, depriving me of even a single pure breath of oxygen molecule, and that I wanted to be out. My parents, who had been wondering about my morbidity, which I had alluded to my not getting commissioned into the Infantry, the branch of the Army where I wanted to serve, agreed with my proposition that a few days at Shanti Bhavan, in the company of my uncles, aunts, and cousins would do me a world of good. I took a train to Allahabad, and from there, I changed into the Ganga Kaveri Express and disembarked at Chhapra at half past twelve in the afternoon the next day.

After a few enquiries, I got the address of the respectable Sharmaji, 'who had unfortunately passed away in his sleep in January, God bless his soul. He was the very personification of all that is sublime and graceful in this world full of chaos and disorder. You will find his bungalow in Nagina Colony. I had been to his house often when he was alive. That son of his is a nincompoop, but his daughter-in-law is the reincarnation of Sati Savitri; I wish my son had married such a girl,' so said the octogenarian who gave me Sharma senior's house's address. My heart soared with delight when I heard such high praise for her from a complete stranger, and I was filled with renewed determination to make my dreams come true. That evening, I stood under a streetlamp across the street from her house and re-read her words 'I have another responsibility. . .' I have not felt so miserable in my life ever since, torn between my desire and societal censor. Firming up my heart against the inevitable and burning with an uncontrollable urge, I crossed the street and rang the bell. A geriatric old lady, leaning heavily on a stick, her back bent as a bow, opened the door for me. After I told her that I had come from Shaktinagar, she assumed that I had come to meet Sharmajee and allowed me to enter her house. Over a cup of tea, I saw a parade of the remaining occupants of the house: Meena's widowed eldest sister-in-law, draped in a plain white sari, without a blouse, her head shaved down to the scalp—'She will be leaving for Vrindavan tomorrow, now that the papers of the adoption of her twins by Meena have been finalised'; her plain-looking second sister-in-law whose pock-marked face, squinted eyes, and awkwardly curled lips would never have fetched a suitable husband for her; the child-woman, her youngest sister-in-law, who had recently learned to walk on her legs, having spent her entire twenty-five years of existence, so far, in therapy and crawling on all fours—'She still finds it difficult to go to the toilet. Had it not been for our Meena, I don't know whether she would have found the desire to continue living, having spent her entire life dependent on her father for all her needs. After Sharmaji's demise, this girl would have also died had Meena not taken on her responsibilities. Now, she lives only for Meena and our Meena, God bless her, she cares for her like her own child—brushing her teeth, washing her after she visits the toilet, bathing her, changing her clothes, caring for her during those terrible menstrual cramps when she cries all night, feeding her tiny morsel after morsel whenever she is swept with emotions. Meena has started taking her out for strolls in the evenings, now that she has attained the capability to walk on her two feet. God has been overly kind to us for having given us Meena. Come, I will take you to my granddaughters, Bunny and Chikoo.'

I followed Meena's mother-in-law's shuffling gait to Meena's bedroom, where, in a crib lay sleeping the two prettiest girls I have ever seen in my life. They had such sublime contentment written all over their chubby cheeks that my heart gave way and I cried silent tears at my own selfishness. One of them turned over in her sleep and wriggled into the body of the other twin, and I heard the gasp that Meena had added to my name. I turned my face away to hide my guilt.

Back in their living room, her mother-in-law said, 'My son is not home. He is rarely home these days, and that is as well for all of us. I don't want him ever touching our Meena. He enjoys the company of his cousin, Bhuliya, and his other nefarious friends. Meena has threatened him with dire consequences if he ever gets his friends and Bhuliya home. He sleeps in my husband's study upstairs, and it suits us all well.'

I said, 'I have not come to meet Sharmajee.'

'I knew that you cannot be his friend. That devilish son of mine can never be fortunate enough to have you as a friend. You look to be so gentle and well meaning. If you have not come to meet him, then what can we do for you, my son?'

That 'my son' was the final straw. I could not bottle up my emotions any further. I cried and wept copious amounts of tears, as the elderly lady and her three daughters, including the child-woman, crowded around me.

'What's the matter, brother? Why are you getting so emotional?,' asked the curled lips.

'I . . . I . . .' I sobbed and sobbed for long. Later on, having regained control, and in the process, my befuddled mind having found a suitable excuse for my uncharacteristic outburst, I explained, 'My mother was very fond of Meena. During the period of Meena's stay at Shaktinagar, they had grown quite close to each other. She has often told me that had Meena not been married, she would have asked her to be my wife. Now that Meena has left Shaktinagar, my mother feels bereft and has asked me to convey a message of gratitude. I have come here to seek her forgiveness as I had been very rude with her when we had last met, accusing her of stealing my mother's affections. I had then felt that she was coming in the way of my mother's love for me, as if Meena's presence was dividing my mother's love. I never realised that love is boundless. I only understood last night, when it dawned on me that she loved me with the same intensity as I loved her and that I would also have to sacrifice some of it. Please let her know that I understand her sentiments, and I promise that I would never deprive her from living up to her responsibilities, as my mother would never do it with respect to her children. Please also tell her that I respect her decisions and have great regard for her unselfish nature.' With those double entendres, I got up to leave. They stared at me, bewildered with the contents and meaning of my statement and request.

The child-woman seemed to be the only one who could grasp the reason for my outburst and the meaning of my explanation, for she walked me out of the house, and standing beneath the lamp post across the street, she said, 'Had Meena *Bhabhi* not been away to attend a marriage, I think she would have run away with you. That would have killed my mother for sure. Meena *Bhabhi* never talked about you with me or anyone else, but from the forlorn look in her eyes, I knew that there was someone whom she pines for every waking minute. I have often heard her murmuring your name in her sleep and, also, whenever she is alone and desolate. She loves you a lot, Sanjay *Bhaiya*—I hope you don't mind me calling you brother. Maybe it is because I am a child in a woman's body that I feel this way, or maybe I am made that way, or maybe I do not understand the difference between right and wrong in human relations—whatever be the reason, I don't find fault in whatever you had between the two of you. But that was in the past. We are not so much her future as she is ours. Please don't deprive us of that. Please don't take her away from us. You must be wondering how come an autistic girl can be so understanding. I am what I am because of her. She taught me how to walk—not the doctors, not the therapies, and certainly not the medicines. She spends ten hours daily with me. She teaches me from the books for eight hours of those ten. She assures me that I will be able to get my B. Ed. degree in ten years and teach others myself. My mother took to bed the day our father died and would have still been bed-ridden, if not dead, except for Meena *Bhabhi*'s care. My eldest sister can now spend the rest of her days in her passion for Lord Krishna, as she is secure in her knowledge that her twins will not be deprived of their mother's love. In fact, she says that she herself wouldn't have loved her children with such devotion as Meena *Bhabhi*. She has kindled hopes in my unfortunate second sister's depressed heart. She has already started sending out feelers, and I am sure that, within a year, she will be able to find a gentle widower or a divorcee for my sister. For Chik-Bunn, she is their entire and only world. They don't miss their mother, as she is their mother now. She may not have milk in her breasts for them, but her boundless love is enough nourishment for them. Haven't you noticed the healthy glow on their cheeks? But you have the power to change all of that. Till the time that you are an invisible presence around her, she will remain with us. Till your ghost doesn't materialise into your mortal form, she will never leave us. But the moment she sees you and touches you, even a feather touch, she will abandon us. From what I have seen of you in these brief moments and have heard from your sentiments in that brief explanation, I can surmise that you have a noble heart. Do you want to turn selfish now and deprive six souls their reason to continue living? Please leave, *Bhaiya*, and never come back, I implore you. I assure you that Meena *Bhabhi* will be safe with us.'

'I wish . . . I wish. . .' I was at a loss for words at this torrent of emotions from the child-woman. God has mysterious ways—what no grown-up could have expressed, this autistic woman had done so eloquently. I tried to lighten up, 'To hell with my wishes. If wishes were to come true, Aunteejee would be flaunting balls. Two girls have told me that love means sacrifice. You mistake my love for Meena. I agree I came here in my desperation for a last look of her. But eloping with her had never been my intention. I love her so much that I would have never interfered with her generous nature. Even if she had consented to leave today, I would have taken all of you with me and cared for you till the end of my days. But that can never happen—it is too utopian.'

'I don't know what utopian means, but I think I can get what you mean. In the real world, that is not possible. Human relations are not made that way. We can't choose where we are born, and we have to bear the consequences of our birth and our choices in life.'

'You and I are kindred spirits. Just promise me one thing. Do you know about your brother's orientation?'

'Yes, she told us all about that knife under his eye. We have started hating him like a sore since then.'

'Then, I am assured that she will remain safe. But it is not beyond him to turn on his sisters, if he feels that you are powerless, though.'

'You don't have to worry on that score. None of us sisters is afraid of spending time in jail. All of us carry knives whenever he is home, and if he even lifts a finger on any of us, Meena *Bhabhi* included, we would plunge the pointy end into his heart. He knows as much and I am sure that he will keep his . . . his . . . whatever that thing is between his legs, just there, buried deep inside his pants. Bhuliya has already lost one ball when he tried to act fresh with my plain-looking sister.'

'No. . . ? What happened?'

'Actually the bastard had his eyes on Meena *Bhabhi*. But, since he was not able to make much headway, despite my brother's encouraging gestures, one evening, he got piss drunk and groped with Rashmi *Didi* when she was alone. She screamed, and Meena *Bhabhi*, who carries a knife all the time, put the knife's pointy end at his jugular vein and pulling down his pants removed one of his testicles from its sac with the knife that Rashmi *Didi* had on her and, later, fed it to the rats. The bastard barely managed to live because she insisted upon my terrified brother to take him to a hospital. Since then, word spread around and everyone in Chhapra is scared of this avatar of Kali. Girls in the city now roam around at night without any fear of molestation, with their knives hanging down their waists.'

'She will become a reformist. I shudder thinking what would happen if she ever decides to enter politics. I think she would ensure that all rapists are castrated if not hung from the nearest lamp post. We need more of such women to reform our society.' I glanced up at the neon light perched on top of the lamp post and imagined one, two, three . . . even five rapists' inert bodies hanging limply, nylon ropes strung around their spindly necks, the pull of gravity extending their necks into an elongated string (so much like Najibullah's castrated body hanging from a traffic light in the streets of Kabul on 27 September '96).

'Go, Sanjay *Bhaiya*. Live your life, and let us live ours.'

'Give me one last promise. Tell her that I came to express my undying love for her and not to take her away. She wrote her compulsions in her letter, but now, I know her reasons. I will never want her to be selfish as she has never been anything but benevolent her entire life. I will remember her till eternity, and she does not have to seek my forgiveness. We shared some of the most wonderful times together, and I do not regret having fallen in love with her. Tell her that . . . tell her that. . .' I was at a loss again, and I let the unsaid words hang like a curtain between us.

The 10-year-old child inside a 25-year-old woman parted the curtain and slid into my arms. I hugged her tiny body tightly, clinging on for survival. She kissed my cheek and said, 'There is no need for any more words. I know what to say. I wish she had married you. Any girl would be lucky to have you as her husband, and she is one woman who deserves you. But we can't deny what fate has in store for us. Goodbye, *Bhaiya*. And don't worry, your secret is safe with me.'

She slipped out of my arms and I turned towards a man who was urinating noisily close by. The light of the streetlamp flickered twice and died. The sudden darkness signalled the end of my second love affair.

I turned towards her to ask her name, but she was already across the street, and I caught a glimpse of Meena, as she had returned from the wedding and was entering her house with her sister-in-law. I saw her radiant face in the light of her living room—she looked as beautiful as the first time I had seen her. My heart leaped a thousand leaps, and I turned my face upwards to face the gods.

I shook my fists in defiance, at the twinkling stars, the smiling half-moon, and the silent Supreme Being gloating at his triumph, 'I will never let you take me down. I am the Phoenix. I will rise again out of the ashes of my love's pyre. Wait and see. You have denied me twice. I will find love again. You can't deny me the one thing that sustains me. I thrive upon love, and I will find it again.'

I also promised that, against the wishes of Meena, I would write about the sublimity of our love story, and let the whole world know what true love is.

With those twin pledges shoring up my sinking heart, I climbed aboard the Vaishali Express the next day after spending the night at the railway station. I was homeward-bound and wanted to seek solace amidst the multitude of Tivaris thriving at Shanti Bhavan.

There I found my reason for continuing living.

PART
THREE

1

The Younger Twin

She took long. Way too long in coming into this world. If one puts even a shred of faith in urban legends, it is believed that she enjoyed the warmth of the dark world of her mother's womb so much that she lay lodged inside that cocoon for another fifteen minutes, after kicking out her elder sibling, with whom she had shared the tiny space for the past nine months. And in the process, as she lay ensconced alone, she not only fed on additional nutrients through the umbilical cord, the last remnants of the genes that personified the legendary beauty of her mother also transferred into her, solely. As a consequence, where the elder twin was scrawny and plain-looking, the younger one retained a healthy glow and grew from a chubby baby into a lovely girl.

The Chauhan twins lived in a palatial bungalow across the street from Shanti Bhavan. Theirs was a joint family of humungous proportions. On the day they were born, the Chauhan household comprised two sets of grandparents (both twins again born two generations back and who also married twin sisters); countless number of uncles surviving in varying stages of single and married status; two elderly spinster aunts, who had reached their respective expiry dates some years previously and were now destined to continue their celibate existence into their next lives; multiple amounts of screaming and bawling cousins aged from their teens to barely a couple of months old—there were a few sets of twins there, too, some identical, some fraternal—a lawyer father with a roving eye; an exquisitely beautiful mother who had once, not so long ago, sent even my father's heart soaring the day she had married the lawyer; and one elder sister born five years earlier. A younger brother followed three years later, after which their still-beautiful mother, exhausted after three births, four children, and numerous abortions, went the Mahatma Gandhi way, an eventuality that forced their lawyer father to shift base to the High Court at Allahabad in search of new paramours, now that the bed at home had gone cold.

The latest instalment of Chauhan twins was born three years after me. I do not recall having ever met them before I was 6 and a half years old and had left for the South with my parents. It was only when we returned to Shanti Bhavan permanently, after our Southern sojourn in the autumn of '78, did she spring into my life, and it was then that I started noticing Anju, the younger twin, for the first time.

Our colony in Etawah consists of numerous residential houses owned by *septua cum octogenarian* patriarchs of upper caste Brahmins and Thakurs. Most of these family elders, steeped deep in the age-old traditions, still considered anything foreign as taboo, including the English language, which they abhorred, and consequently got their sons and handful of daughters educated in Hindi-medium government-aided schools. I think it had more to do with the lesser fees charged by these government schools, than the chauvinism they so brazenly professed, to be the sole reason for their ignoring the only English-medium convent school in town. The lawyer father of the twins had witnessed his brothers and cousins ruining their children's lives by insisting that they study in government schools, which suffered mostly from poor management and poorer remunerations for the teachers. As a consequence their sons could never acquire the skills required to get jobs as they grew older. Most of the scions of these wealthy, upper caste families fared poorly in competitive exams for jobs in our country and permanently languished as frogs in the well of Etawah. The very idea of education at an English-medium school was an anathema to them. So much so that, when I had finally qualified for Sainik School Ghorakhal in '80, the occasion became a cause for celebration in my colony, and my achievement was publicised on the front page of the local newspaper, *Din Raat*. That advertisement in the local newspaper belied the hidden undercurrent in the society—while they never allowed their own sons to ever be educated in English-medium schools, the success stories of children studying in such schools were always looked at with admiration, coupled with some degree of resentment.

But, like my father, her father was also made of sterner stuff and appreciated the value of good education. He had put all of his three daughters and the only son in St Mary's Convent School, where my brother and I had also joined after our return from Hospet. While her elder sister studied in my class, she and her twin were in my brother's class, and their brother was three classes further down, in upper kindergarten.

Father, on his return from the South, had become the talk of the town, and his two sons, who spoke such good English, had acquired cynosure status among all those who visited our house. Our reputation spread far and wide, and Shanti Bhavan, which was just twenty-five metres from the Chauhan Bungalow, became the twins' favourite destination, and the sisters became our constant playmates. They used to often come over to our house, and we would play stupid boy-girl games, which usually got boring after enthusiastic starts. Then, we would sit and talk mundane boy-girl talks, which made no sense to man or beast. For me, those were the highlights of our time together, as I could then listen to her talking about her family, her trials at school, her difficulties in understanding maths, her domineering younger brother, her father's fixation with all things concerning caste, her mother's legendary beauty and the numerous suitors she had had as a young maiden before her lawyer husband stole her heart—her parents' was a self-arranged marriage. I relished those long monologues of hers, delivered in an equally monotonous tone of a 6-year-old girl, as on other occasions, my brother had complete proprietary right over her time. I used to often complain to Mother that Kaalu did not allow me to play with Anju. My mother's oft repeated reply was, 'We can't tinker with nature. She was born younger, so she will play with Kaalu. You are elder, so you will play with her elder sister. Period. No more hankering on this issue. Understand. If I ever see or hear of you playing with Anju, you will be grounded, and they will be banned from entering our house.' So I had to make do with her scrawny, plain-looking freckle-faced elder sister, who came into this world fifteen minutes earlier and consigned me to admiring Anju from afar.

I started seeking salvation in Hasina and Neelima as a consequence of having to share Anju's time with Kaalu. My reed-thin, black-hued younger brother piled upon my miseries by never allowing Anju to spend her time alone with me. Even when we sat talking, he made sure that I sat the farthest from her, with he and her sister perched between us. It later emerged that the scheming little twerp was acting on the orders of my mother.

Later, when I left for Ghorakhal and the delights of my platonic love with Pratima engulfed me, she moved to Allahabad for her studies. We rarely saw each other whenever I came on my vacations to Shanti Bhavan. Sometimes, I caught glimpses of her enchanting face during my youngest uncle's and eldest cousin's respective marriages, and other festive occasions. Those times, I used to feel strange stirrings erupting within me, but by then, I was besotted with Pratima and had eyes for no one else, not even Anju.

When Meena came into my life, I had stopped visiting Shanti Bhavan altogether, preferring to spend my entire vacations in the welcoming arms of the love of my life at Shaktinagar. Anju had never again entered my horizon till that fateful day in June '91.

I was into my fourth day of arrival at Shanti Bhavan after the light at Chhapra, with its sudden darkness, had extinguished my reason for continuing living. In the past seventy-two hours, I had immersed in the adulations of my large family, suffering the pecks and hugs of my numerous aunts and cousins. The Freudian feelings of affection, which had nothing to do with being filial or sisterly, from my youngest aunt and that cousin, who had bared her all when I was a 12-year-old, aroused me no end. Their kisses were the hottest, and their caresses, the craziest. My cousin even kissed me full on my lips, her fiery tongue sending me into raptures as it searched for embers inside my mouth, when she entered my room and found me alone on the very first day of my arrival. She rubbed her chest and groin against me vigorously, and I was taken by surprise when her hands deliberately brushed against the hardness between my legs. Mistaking my erection for an invitation, she pulled my trousers down before I could even protest, and wrapping her fingers around it, she started sliding her hands up and down, sending shivers jolting through my nerves. With a desperate and reluctant groan, I peeled off her fingers one by one, before things got out of control and asked her to leave me be, hardness and all. The balance of that day, I avoided being close to her alone, and despite her assurances that there was no danger, as she was married now and even if she got pregnant with me, it wouldn't matter, I did not give in to her suggestions. She left Shanti Bhavan the very next day, even though her husband was due to arrive two days later to take her home. God! A woman spurned . . . very dangerous.

The youngest aunt was a different matter altogether. I had been her husband's closest friend during their marriage and had once even accompanied him to Gwalior to fetch her, after she had spent her first mandatory time with her parents, post-marriage. Over the intervening period, we had drawn closer, although I had rarely shown any real interest in her, since by the time her marriage was a year old, I had fallen deeply in love with Meena and never visited Shanti Bhavan, till now.

This first visit, after so many years, was a pleasant surprise to everyone at Shanti Bhavan, and I forgot about Meena in the flattery heaped upon me by my aunts and cousins. Every day, I was feted by one uncle or the other, and my aunts never tired of feeding me copious amounts of food and desserts. I was being overwhelmed by the famous Tivari generosity, and when my youngest aunt, one evening, whispered into my besotted ears to meet her alone in her room the next day, when my uncle would be away, I was taken aback. By way of explanation, she said that she had a surprise for me. Filled with anticipation, that night I dreamt of delightful surprises and angels descending from heaven bearing hopeful messages, along with Meena's various avatars.

I entered my aunt's room at exactly three the next evening, and there she was. After Pratima and Teena, I had never seen such a beautiful face. Meena's memory seemed to be fading in front of Anju's radiance. I had long forgotten how she looked, since the last I had seen her was almost two years back, during my eldest cousin's marriage. As I looked at her lustrous hair, I tried to recall her name, and it was only when my gaze shifted to her mesmerising eyes that I blurted out, 'Hello Anju. It has been such a long time.'

'Hello, Sanjay.' She put a similar lilt to the second syllable of my name as Meena used to do, and my eyes welled up with Meena's blurry image swimming in shallow pools of tears—at least the gasp at the end was missing, else I would have broken down. 'Why no "How are you"? Has training for the Army taken all manners out of you?'

After wiping a tear with my handkerchief, I said, 'Oh! Sorry, Anju. My mistake. I was taken by surprise seeing you here. You look so . . . so . . . radiant; it took my breath away for a second there. How have you been doing all this while, Anju?'

She smiled a demure smile, 'That's more like it. Yesterday, when your aunt told me that a surprise was awaiting me in her room, I had not imagined that the surprise would be you. I must admit that I am delightfully surprised at meeting you here after such a long time. I have been keeping well. How about you?'

'Now that she has left us to our own devices, I must say that I, too, never expected that my surprise would be you. She has played her cards very well. She can open a matchmaking column in the local newspaper now. I am equally surprised at seeing you here. Till now, I had not been feeling quite myself, but I have a premonition that, after today, my life will never be the same again.'

'How many girls have you used that line to before? You really have grown up. Is it the Tivari genes or have you become a flatterer all by yourself?'

I chuckled, 'As far as I know, the other male Tivaris have only one singular purpose in their lascivious minds and approach their objects of interest with a purposeful determination akin to a rampaging bull elephant in heat. I tend to be more sublime in such matters.' She laughed at my poor simile of a lustful Tivari in the form of a blundering pachyderm. I immediately fell in love with the thousand jingles of church bells her throat emitted. God! She has such a wonderful laugh. I wanted to spend my entire life just listening to her laughter.

We went silent after our initial exchange, and I utilised the time studying her, from head to toe. She was wearing a peach-coloured *salwar* suit, her yellow stole adding the requisite contrast to her ensemble. Her hair fell in glorious wavy tendrils down to her shoulders. She had such beautiful round eyes that I could see my very soul inside them. Her lips were curled naturally in a sexy pout, as if she would give me a kiss any minute. What is it with all my girls and their smiles? Her smile was also accompanied with cute dimples, and I resisted the urge to touch them. She appeared to approve of what she saw in me. I approached her casually and sat down on the bed beside her, holding her hand. Her fragrance was divine, and I breathed in her lemon perfume—lime had never smelled so heavenly.

I studied the lines of her hand and the ridges in her palm. She, in turn, studied my face. 'Why do all you Tivaris have such broad noses?'

'Something to do with our grandfather's genes, I presume. He never wanted the world to ever forget what a handsome nose he had, so he had commanded his genes to leave their nose-making imprints in each of his progenies. And this damn protrusion never stops growing. When I reach my father's age, you will not be able to distinguish us from our noses. That's the reason why, in old age, all Tivaris look the same. Look at my eldest uncle and my father—they almost look like twins separated at birth by three years and two miscarriages. Had all of my grandfather's children been alive, you would have had twenty senior Tivaris and their forty to fifty junior Tivari likenesses to choose from.'

She chuckled, 'God! That would have been some spread. All kinds of Tivaris in varying shapes and sizes, many with round waists and moon-faced visages, some reed thin and emaciated—except you, who are so perfectly chiselled—with one thing in common running like a thread among all of you—your broad noses with equally wide orifices. Had my mother not met my father, one of your uncles or even your father would have inhaled her and made her his wife. Did you know that your father was besotted with her and had it not been for the caste difference, we would have been brothers and sisters? But we would have never been born.'

'I am glad that she is a Thakur, else I don't know how else we would have come into this world. And I shudder at the thought of such a big nose marring your pretty face.' I was already falling in love with this delightful chirpy fantasy of youthful minds.

I continued, 'I once read about this concept called multiverses, where there are multiple universes, in each of which there is a parallel Milky Way galaxy and the same solar system as ours, with multiple Earths existing in their individual dimensions. If, on this Earth, your father married your mother, and she gave birth to you, in another parallel Earth, in that alternate universe, my father would have married your mother, and half of you and half of me would have been born to them. Maybe, he would even have some half-half name like San-ju. That's serendipitous; both our names can be combined to arrive at this wonderfully wonderful sounding short name of mine.'

'Why should it always be a he?'

'Sorry. I am the last person on Earth you can ever fault for being a misogynist. I respect women more than you lot regard one another yourselves. I hate such stereotypes and despise people who treat women as dirt. I wish one of these alternate Earths has a society where women are treated as equal.'

'Oh, Sanjay! I am so sorry to have misunderstood you. I never knew that, over these past years, you would have been influenced by experiences that have been so different than what I have been through. In the society where I grew up, both here and at Allahabad, women have always been condescended upon and pitied by our masters, the male members of our family.'

'I have also grown up in a similar society. There has been no difference there. Except that the women and girls in my life have paved my beliefs towards a different path. I feel wholesome in the company of women; men's company is too claustrophobic for me with their single-track mindset focused purely on behaving with the fairer sex with an air of puffed-up superiority.'

'That sounds interesting. Will you tell me about these women and girls in your life?' She shifted closer and almost slipped into my eager arms. Her fragrance assaulted me with such ferocity that I drowned in a sea of lemons.

I grew hesitant. I was not sure of myself—whether I should take her into my arms and bury my face into her lustrous curls or should I tell her about my puppy loves for Hasina and Neelima or my childish infatuations for the Sanskrit teacher and the hostel matron at Ghorakhal, or my sincere love for Pratima, or my physically intensive and soul-stirring love for Meena. I decided that disclosures about Meena would have to wait till I have finally won my soulmate's heart and soul, and that could only be my wife. I had never felt so unsure of myself before. Not when I had confronted Hasina for laughing at me; not when I had asked Pratima to stay till I had finished my soup; not when I had closed my lips around Meena's cherries to taste their sweetness that first day at her house when she had invited me for an 'innocent' cup of tea; and not with Teena when I had stood in silent contemplation outside her door at Banaras, as she had run her eyes over me before nodding her approval of me. With them, I had felt sure that whatever action I had contemplated would win them over to me. But, with Anju, it was different. She was supremely confident of herself, but accompanying that fearlessness was a note of reticence in her eyes and shyness in her manners, which put a caution inside me. It felt as if whatever further course I took would be met with instant disapproval. So I held on, not responding to her moving closer towards me nor to her query about the other girls in my life.

Rightly reading too much in my hesitation, she said, 'It seems such disclosures will have to wait for another first day. Let's leave intimate thoughts to that next first day. Tell me, what do you like doing whenever you are not cramming books?'

I said, blurting into a familiar terrain, 'I like seeing movies in my spare time.'

She turned out to be a kindred spirit—she also liked movies. Unlike Pratima, who rarely saw movies, and Meena, whose movie world revolved around Rajesh Khanna's romantic renderings of the clichéd 'lived happily ever after' endings, Anju was a true connoisseur of the art of acting. But there, our similarities hit upon a fork in the road; she veered towards offbeat cinema, whereas I was well and truly into Amitabh Bachchan. Her favourites dated back to the Twenties and Thirties, and included movies till the late Eighties. Her repertoire read like a virtual landscape of parallel cinema—from V. Shantaram's 1925 silent film *Sawkari Pash*, which portrayed a poor peasant and his travails when he migrates to the city to work as a mill worker, to his portrayal of women in the Indian society in the 1937 film *Duniya Na Maane*, to Chetan Anand's 1946 social realist film *Neecha Nagar*, which won the Grand Prize at the first Cannes Film Festival, to Satyajit Ray's neo-realist *The Apu Trilogy* of the mid and late Fifties, which promoted an authentic art genre—'the three films, *Pather Panchali*, *Aparajito*, and *The World of Apu*, are listed among the greatest films of all time'—to Bimal Roy's award-winning *Do Bigha Zamin* from 1953, which paved the way for the Indian New Wave. She also liked 'middle cinema', which reflected the changing middle-class ethos in India, often depicted in Hrishikesh Mukherjee's movies, which carved a middle path between the extravagance of mainstream cinema and the stark realism of art cinema. Basu Chatterjee's *Piya Ka Ghar*, *Rajnigandha*, and *Ek Ruka Hua Faisla* also appealed to her for their plots on middle-class lives and their trials. Her personal favourite was Guru Dutt's heart-rending portrayal of a struggling poet and his inamorata, *Gulabo*, another sterling performance by the diva Waheeda Rehman in the 1957 film *Pyaasa*, which, with its depiction of the hypocrisy, corruption, and materialism of the world, had left such a mark on its viewers and critics, that even in the early Nineties, people from my father's generation do not tire of singing praises of Guru Dutt, whose performance as the poet Vijay was so outstanding, that the movie was featured in the *Time* magazine's 'All Time 100 Movies', compiled in 2005 by critics Richard Schickel and Richard Corliss. Of the recent films, she liked *Jaane Bhi Do Yaaro*, *Aakrosh*, *Sparsh*, *Chakra*, *Bazaar*, *Ardh Satya*, *Mirch Masala*, *Salaam Bombay!*, and *Arth*. Her favourite actors were Naseeruddin

444 | *Mamta Chaudhari*

Shah, Om Puri, Ravi Baswani, Pankaj Kapur, and Amol Palekar, and her favourite actresses included Smita Patil, Shabana Azmi, Dipti Naval, Neena Gupta, and Vidya Sinha. After listening to her, I felt bereft of any comment. I had been so immersed in Amitabh Bachchan that I had never realised that there was a world of cinema existing that portrayed the injustices of our morbid world with much more clarity and realism than what the Angry Young Man could fight against in his glitzy world of commercial cinema. I decided to defend my hero but vowed to see all the movies that she had named.

She scoffed at my Amitabh Bachchan's inadequacies, which she listed with such nonchalance bordering on insouciance, that I could not believe my ears listening to my favourite actor's deconstruction. She countered each of my argument with 'He carries the Angry Young Man image too far. He can never match the versatility of Naseeruddin Shah in, say, *Jaane Bhi Do Yaaron*' and such similar scathing comments.

'But Naseeruddin Shah is too broody in his portrayal of dark characters. Even in *Masoom*, he is very morose.'

'He would still have acted better than Amitabh Bachchan in many movies like *Namak Haraam, Sholay* even, *Aakhree Raasta*, and *Main Azad Hoon*, among many others. I agree that Amitabh Bachchan looks better in action sequences, although Naseeruddin Shah in *Jalwa* proved that he could do action movies, too.'

Realising that the Angry Young Man was taking a serious beating for the first time in his life, I changed tack: 'So why don't we pitch them together in a film?'

'That's an idea nobody has thought of yet. Maybe because they both represent different genres. But let's try. Which movie would you have liked both of them working together? Remember, none of them would ever accept a side hero's role, and Amitabh Bachchan is notorious for asking directors to reduce other actors' screen time and space.'

Stung by this scathing criticism of my favourite star, I said, 'That's a lie and a rumour spread around to malign Amitabh Bachchan. But let's, for the time being, take it at its face value. That would mean that the only roles suitable for them would be a hero's and a villain's role for Amitabh and Naseeruddin, respectively.'

'Okay. I don't think that Amitabh Bachchan would ever consider playing a villain if he does not convert into a hero later, remember *Don*. Or like *Agneepath*, he would like the movie to be an out-and-out villain–oriented film.'

'Hmmmm . . . Which movie has a dark brooding villain? *Zanjeer*—no, nobody could have replaced Ajit. *Namak Haraam*—problem of side hero and no villain, but Naseeruddin Shah could have enacted Somu's character very well. Naseeruddin Shah could have easily replaced Amitabh Bachchan in *Kasme Vaade*. I think it will have to be *Laawaris*, with Naseeruddin Shah playing Amjad Khan's Ranvir Singh to Amitabh Bachchan's Heera. An added advantage would have been that Naseeruddin Shah's benign presence in the movie would have tempered Amitabh's over-the-top acting and fiery dialogue delivery.'

'There will still remain the question of sharing screen space. Amitabh would not have allowed Naseeruddin adequate screen space, with Ranjeet also being a villain. I think if we replaced Prem Chopra with Naseeruddin Shah in *Do Anjaane*, then we would be able to judge who is the better actor among the both of them? I am sure Naseeruddin Shah would come out trumps.'

I was getting tired of these mental calisthenics, and having not seen many Naseeruddin Shah movies myself, I soon ran out of fresh arguments to defend my hero. I had to give up, vowing to renew our rivalry another day, when I had a fresh lot of ammunition in my magazine.

Over the period of next few days, she revealed her other passion—Hindi novels written by Gulshan Nanda and Munshi Premchand. I was particularly enamoured by her deep knowledge and associated passionate concern for the social issues raised by the former in his romantic novels—from the widow's plight in *Kati Patang*, to the heart-rending story of unrequited love and rebirth in *Neel Kamal*, to the trials and tribulations of a courtesan (*tawaif*) pretending to be a rich Thakur's wife in *Khilona*, to the bigamy portrayed in *Daag: A Poem of Love*, and to love across centuries, intermingling the past and the present in a delightful mix, in *Mehbooba*. A total of twenty-one novels of Gulshan Nanda were converted into films, of which six movies won the Filmfare Award for Best Story for *Kaajal*, *Neel Kamal*, *Khilona*, *Kati Patang*, *Naya Zamana*, and *Mehbooba*. We also discussed which of his other novels should have also been made into movies.

We differed on many—I wanted *Palay Khan*, *Gaylord*, and *Gunah Ke Phul* to be made into movies, whereas she desired *Gunah Ka Rishta*, *Lakshman Rekha*, and *Patthar Ke Honth*, which have good stories and which could be converted into movies. Ultimately, we both agreed on *Ghat Ka Pathar* being the ideal movie-novel from Gulshan Nanda's humongous repertoire.

On Munshi Premchand, the *Upanyas Samrat*, she regretted that not many of his novels and stories were made into movies, whereas his stories touched the social issues with such immense depth and understanding. Her all-time favourite was *Seva Sadan*, which highlights the plight of a married woman Suman who, after being forced into a loveless marriage, leaves her home to become a courtesan in one of Banaras's many *kothas* from where, due to social ostracisation, she joins a widows' home and finally joins Seva Sadan as a manager and teacher at the orphanage for young children of former courtesans. The story reflected what I felt and cringed about every waking hour of my life—that women still have to strive to control their own destinies. I found a kindred spirit in Premchand and wished that his ghost would visit me in my dreams to show me the correct path. That night, I thought of the parallels between Meena's life and that of Suman, both of whom were forced into a loveless marriage, and how Meena, after seeking love in me, met obstacles in the society's views on adultery and finally found her mission in life in her husband's mother and sisters, whereas Suman, after many hardships, ultimately carved a distinct identity for herself without the trappings of a marriage and a family. The parallels and contrasts in the lives of my love and my heroine (I had adopted Suman as my heroine—my ideal woman who fought and fought till she got her due; she had replaced Scarlett O'Hara from *Gone With The Wind*) left a void inside me, which I found hard to fill, except with the torrent of tears that wet my pillow till the wee hours of the morning, when there were no more tears left in my bloodshot eyes to shed any further. When Anju asked me about the cause of my sleepless night, I replied that Suman's story had touched my heart, without elaborating further. She appeared to have accepted my feeble explanation, although I could read scepticism burning in her eyes when I tried to evade her further enquiries.

Her tirade on dowry, as depicted in *Nirmala*, also gave a glimpse into what drove Anju and her beliefs. I felt sorry for Nirmala and her plight, and tried to find justification for Mansaram's love for his stepmother, Nirmala, who was a year younger than him. The story was later converted into a TV episode in the serial *Tehreer Munshi Premchand Ki*, which was directed by Gulzar and in which the Marathi actress Amruta Subhash played the main protagonist, Nirmala. Another of her favourites, my own personal favourite, was *Godaan*. The story revolves around a poor peasant, Hori, who is morally upright with simple desires—buying a cow was his life's ambition; his wife, Dhania, who accepts beatings from Hori but still stands by her beliefs, and tries to make Hori see the truth and the reality of facts, who is not lost in the rigmarole of clichés and ideals and who, despite struggling throughout her life herself, helps the needy, irrespective of caste and creed; their son, Gobar, who aspires for a life of comfort and who, after impregnating Jhunia, runs away to Lucknow, fearing the wrath of the villagers because she is from a lower caste, leaving a pregnant Jhunia to be cared for by his parents and who, later, returns and takes Jhunia with him to the city; the greedy moneylender and village priest, Datadin, who is so vile and steeped in hypocrisy that I felt sorry for being a Brahmin myself; his son, Matadin, who is pure in heart, and despite his father's many efforts to purify him after he had an affair with Seliya, a lower caste girl, he finally settles down with her, after discarding his holy thread, *Janeu*, and liberating himself from the shackles of Brahminism (I felt so thankful that my father never forced me to wear the thread); and Miss Malati, the foreign-educated doctor-turned-social-reformer, who spurns marriage to the love of her life, Mr Mehta, because she wants to serve the poor and the needy (I found traces of Meena in Miss Malati, too). I simply loved *Godaan* for the simplicity of its story told by weaving the narratives of so many diverse characters that represent the microcosm of our society. It was the first time I felt happy and contented with the 'lived happily ever after' cliché, when Miss Malati finds her calling in her commitment to charitable deeds. The novel was made into a Hindi film in '63.

Another of his books made into a film was *Gaban*, the movie version of which was made by Hrishikesh Mukherjee. The story focuses around the lives of a middle-class young couple and their aspirations. It captures the social and economic conditions and conflicts of the North Indian society in preindependence India. Again, a depiction of our society in its stark reality, which forces a young man to embezzle with government funds to reach a higher status in his life. The police is also shown in poor light in the book.

2

Who Made Whom?

I was seven days away from joining my unit, and the past seven days, I had enjoyed the company of Anju every single day. Most of those days we spent in my aunt's room, but the last few days, she has been coming to my room instead. Unlike Meena, with whom I could barely spend three to four hours every other evening, Anju would spend entire days, morning till evening, with me. Many times, we would forget lunch, and when our stomachs used to start grumbling in desperate protests, some cousin of mine would get me lunch, which I shared with her. No one else in Shanti Bhavan knew that I was spending time with Anju, except my matchmaker aunt, who never divulged the secret to anyone else, except her husband, of course.

One day, after our discussions on Premchand and his novels were over, she asked me, 'Are you now ready to tell me about your girls?'

'Are you now ready to be embraced by me?' I blurted out without thinking—I have never been more ready for being enveloped by her sweet lemony fragrance.

'You silly, was that the reason you were so hesitant the first day? I would have died waiting if you had delayed it a moment longer—my heart has been aching for your touch since the first moment you walked into my life again. I had started imagining that the girls in your life were for your intellectual enrichment and that you were actually more interested in boys.' With that, she slid into my arms, and I pressed her into me, feeling the roundness of her curves as her breasts crushed into my chest. She had soft beautiful curves around her back, and I felt each one of them with my fingers as her hands explored the nearly barren realm of my scalp. I inhaled her lemony perfume and tilted her chin upwards. She submitted her lips and I kissed her. The touch felt heavenly, and Meena started dissolving like a checkerboard, fading into nothingness. 'Nooooo . . . Meena, don't go away. My heart beats because of you. Don't leave me bereft of all emotions. Please stay, Meena, please, please, please. . .'

She must have felt the sudden quickening of my heart's beats for she whispered softly, 'What was she like?'

'There were two of them. Both older than me, both wiser than me, both as beautiful as you are, both as intelligent as you are, and both left me in the end, as they valued something that I could have never been able to give them.' I caught a flash of jealousy coast through her eyes, and I immediately regretted my words. I tried to make amends, 'I have vowed to never meet them nor write to them. It's a solemn vow, and I intend to live by my words. I have never promised in vain, ever.'

Her body immediately relaxed in my arms and I heard her heave a sigh of relief, as if a ghost she had kept bottled up inside her had suddenly been released. I felt happy and contented. I had found my love again. I will show God that I can live again. Meena was wrong after all, love will make me whole again—Anju's love.

'Will you walk away if I said that I loved you?' It was she who asked the question of me, and I had thought that how come my heart had spoken.

'Oh Anni!,' for that was the name her mother had given her when the midwife had informed Mrs Chauhan that her second child was refusing to leave the safety of her mother's womb eighteen years back—*Aa Nahin Rahi Hai, Aana Kaani Kar Rahi Hai* (she is not coming out, she is dithering). Her mother had then called her 'Anni' in jest, a name everybody else had forgotten and that had sunk into her family's history unnoticed ever since, to be revived now by my besotted heart.

'I love you, Anni. Thank you for saving me.' I said, with a deeply felt emotion rending my voice.

'Why do you say that, my love?' She spoke the endearment with such passion that the sound of it reverberated in my empty heart, till the pear-shaped organ, which not only indicates that a being is alive but also controls the very essence of human life, our emotions, filled with her image. Slowly, as my slowing heartbeat indicated the passage of time—with each 'lub', Meena left from the abode where she had made her permanent home in my heart, and with each 'dub', Anju occupied the space vacated by Meena.

'I . . . I. . .' my voice choked and I started weeping. We lay down in bed, and she clutched me so tightly that my breaths stopped. Slowly, with her bosom pillowing my head, I gained control over my emotions and inhaled the sweet feminine fragrance emanating from her chest.

'Whoever said that physical tribulations are the worst kind had never fallen in love? There can never be anything worse than failed love, to turn your life into a living hell. I have failed twice, not counting the other time when I was jilted by my *Mausi* as a 9-and-a-half-year-old. Do 9-and-a-half-year-olds understand the concept of love as a 19-year-old should?'

'What did you feel for me when you returned to Etawah all those years back and when your brother would never let me play or sit with you?'

'Thank heavens you too noticed that. I had always felt so resentful that I had thought I would kill him one day. I confess I was besotted with you even then. Tell me, I have always been assaulted with this recurring doubt—did you ever feel even a tiny bit of attraction for him?'

'Your brother? Never. I would die of self-pity before ever feeling anything close to attraction for him. He was in my class, and just because he scored better marks in the tests, he used to feel as if he was God's own. He was too condescending towards the girls, especially those who did not fare well in the exams. He dared not behave in that manner with me because he knew that I was better than him. So he took it out on me at your home, whenever I wanted to be with you. My mother had warned me against you, saying, "The elder Tivari is too fair and girlish. Be careful of that one. Kaalu is masculine, play with him only. If I ever hear of you getting too pally with Sanjay, you will never go there again." What else could I do? I had to abide by her diktats or never have the opportunity to even lay my eyes on your sweet face, flat cheekbones and all. Oh Sanjay,' the same lilt when she ended my name with an extended ae . . . ae . . . ae . . . ae. 'Oh Meena! Please go away. No, please stay. Please, please, please. . .' 'It was so miserable to look at you and not be able to open my 6-year-old heart to you. I fell in love with you then. Now, you know that 6-year-old hearts can fall in love.'

'It sounds so *Laila-Majnu-esque*. My mother also told me to never play with you. I have a theory on that and I will bet my right hand if anyone could prove me wrong. Your and my mother never wanted us to grow close to each other when we were younger. Else we would have fallen for each other and there would have been hell to pay, what with our being from different castes and all. Had we started loving each other then, I don't know what would have happened. Why, she even encouraged me in my infatuation with Hasina, because she always knew that it was transitory and would keep my mind and heart away from you.'

'Who was this Hasina?'

'A wonderful girl who took great pains in improving my Hindi vocabulary and diction.'

I told her about Hasina and Nilima and my childhood crush on my Sanskrit teacher.

'These two girls, after *BB Mausi*, taught me to respect girls and their craving for knowledge. They were way too intelligent and their perseverance knew no ends. They worked hard to achieve their goals in life—to excel in the exams. They pursued it with a vigour that was absent in the other boys in the school. Even Vidya and Preeti got immensely motivated by them and all of them would beat me to the fourth or fifth position in the class tests and exams. I aped them. I developed this habit of completing my homework in the class rather than at home, not because I felt it challenging, but so that I could spend more time at home with you.

'Both Hasina and Nilima had excellent calligraphic skills. Nilima wrote in this beautiful font with perfectly rounded *o*'s and *a*'s, her *y*'s and *g*'s ended in spirals with long tails; her capital letters were beautifully crafted and she gave a delicious slant to the verticals of her *b*'s, *d*'s, *l*'s, and *t*'s. Her *w*'s and *u*'s looked like tiny Chinese cups, with the two ends ending in long serpentine coils. It was a treat to watch her writing, whenever she got in the mood.

'She once recited the poem *Jhansi Ki Rani* (written by Subhadra Kumari Chauhan) and when she came to that part,

> *Bundelon harbolon ke munh hamne suni kahani thi*
> *Khoob ladi mardani woh to Jhansi wali Rani thi*
> (This story we heard from the mouths of Bundel bards: Like a man she fought, she was the Queen of Jhansi)

'I actually had a vision of Rani Laxmibai galloping on her horse Badal, clad in a Sowar's uniform, her adopted son Damodar Rao strapped to her back, her sword raised triumphantly in the air, her eyes on fire, her mouth open with a blood-curdling scream emanating from it, as she charged in fury, at the sepoys ranged in front of her. I had goosebumps sprouting all over me the first time I heard her sing that poem. It was mind-blowing.

'Where Hasina was pretty, Nilima was plain looking—big eyes, sharp nose, freckled face, a toothy smile, and an unremarkable chin. But I look at these illiterate girls dotting the by-lanes of Etawah and even the most beautiful amongst them cannot match the grace of the 10-year-old Nilima. Every boy in school found her attractive because of the way she carried herself and the attitude she displayed in class—qualities which can only be engendered through good education.

'I once challenged her to come up with the longest word in the English language. I was sure of beating her this time, as I had recently learned that *floccinaucinihilipilification* was the longest unchallenged word which in the dictionary means "an act or habit of describing or regarding something as unimportant." Its first recorded use was in 1741, by the English poet William Shenstone, in a letter, when he used the sentence, "I loved him for nothing so much as floccinaucinihilipilification of money."

'The next day, she came up with the forty-five-letter word *pneumonoultramicroscopicsilicovolcanoconiosis* and said that it was the longest word published in a dictionary. She went on to explain that it is a lung disease caused by inhaling fine ash and sand dust. The disease is otherwise known as silicosis.

'Deflated, I had argued that hers was a technical word whereas mine was a word which could be used in an everyday sentence. I further amplified that my word could be used as a verb in simple present and past participle like in 'I don't want to floccinaucinihilipilificate your views', sounds funny though.

'But her logic was that even though her word was technical and can only be used as a medical terminology, it was still the longest word as per the *Oxford Learner's Dictionary*. I had to accept defeat again.

'Now that I think of that episode, I have to concede that she was trying to make a point. When I had challenged her, I already knew about my word. She, on the other hand, conducted her research—her father being a doctor possibly helped—and she came prepared for the challenge the next day. She demonstrated an insatiable hunger and quest for knowledge. She was not going to take it lying down from us boys. She must have poured over her father's medical books, probably spent a few hours in the school library, but she had found the challenge exciting, and there was an intense desire to best me at my own game. Amazing quality in a 10-year-old girl from a small town in the backwaters of Uttar Pradesh, a state notorious for denying education to its girls.

'There must be many such Nilimas languishing in the small towns and villages of our huge country, but we don't even know of them, because we have never given them an opportunity. How can we? We don't allow them to flourish. Our men are so scared of their women that if they allow them to be educated, they fear that the women would better them at their own game.

'Human brains are made separately for men and women. At the genetic level, female brains usually do not contain Y chromosomes, whereas every cell in a male brain contains a Y chromosome. Size-wise, male brains are bigger, giving rise to the argument that men are more intelligent than women—if that be the case then elephants and sperm whales, who have brains three to six times the size of the human brain, should be far superior to men in the intelligence department and we should have been ruled by the pachyderms. Then there are the differences in the nerve tissues in the male and female corpus callosum, which connects the left and the right cerebral hemispheres of the brain, and since it is thicker in female brains, they seem to have language functioning in both sides of the brain, thus giving women better linguistic and fine motor skills, like handwriting, especially till they reach puberty. Men may have more gray matter, about 6.5 times more, but women have 9.5 times more white matter, the stuff that connects various parts of the brain, further reinforcing their dominant language skills. Also, they are faster and more accurate at identifying emotions. They are more adept than men at encoding facial differences and determining changing vocal intonations. They are better at controlling their emotions.

'To understand the functioning of human brains, we need to go back to the caves. Thousands of years back, when humans started living as families and assigned responsibilities to each other, based on the physical characteristics of men and women, because of their better bone structure and musculature, men assigned for themselves the task of getting the food for the family. They started roaming the grasslands, the steppes, and the jungles, hunting for food; they became the hunter-gatherers. Since hunting involved skills in terms of locating the prey and closing in on it from different directions, men's spatial abilities have become far more developed. An apt example of this is when men and women are involved in navigational tasks—women rely more on landmark cues—like go to the railway station and turn right, whereas men navigate via depth reckoning—like go north, then west.

'Now take the women amongst the cave dwellers. Due to their child bearing and rearing abilities, they were consigned to looking after the domestic front. They were required to keep the hearth warm and the bed warmer for the men when they returned with the food, after their physical exertions. Division of responsibilities were clearly defined—physical activities and the mental processes required to hone the physical skills associated with these activities were for the men; the women, on the other hand, had to look after the children, live back home in communities, cook the food when the carcass was brought in, and tend to the cave to keep it clean and welcoming. What did they do the whole day? They talked and talked and talked—to themselves, to their children, to their neighbours. The modern woman of today is more gossipy and manipulative with information. She uses language more when she competes, since it would have given her a survival advantage back during that cave-dwelling period, especially in relation to any rival to her partner's affections. Today we have mothers-in-law who manipulate their sons to gain advantage over their wives by feeding the husbands wrong information. The wife in her turn tries to get her pound of flesh by filling his ears against his mother.

'But Nilima's attitude has changed my thinking. Why are we so stereotypical in our approach towards women? They have qualities; we should provide them opportunities to refine those skills and to rouse those dormant abilities. And what better way than to provide better education to the girls. Why should we let your lot languish in the doom of ignorance when you can shine in the brightness of knowledge? Illiteracy is a curse, lack of knowledge is a blight; women should be encouraged to pull themselves out of the mire of ignorance.

'Men try to suppress women by denying them this opportunity. There is always the fear that if they got better than men, then they would start demanding their rights, they would start questioning the well-preserved, derogatory, inhuman traditions of dowry, widow-out-casting, sati, and so on. This fear is more prevalent amongst the upper-caste male society. Why are our Holy Scriptures and hymns written in such an unfathomable language—the Rigveda has not been completely deciphered yet, it is so complicated? Because their authors did not want the common man to ever be able to communicate with the Almighty, without using the priests as the conduit, else the Brahmins' importance would fade. In similar vein, the downtrodden in our country are discouraged from sending their children to schools. Keep them mired in poverty and they would be forced to use their children for labour and not be knowledgeable ever. Without knowledge, they would never demand their rights. As a result, many politicians go to the villages begging for votes during elections and not one of them promises to make schools there, because villagers in our country don't aspire for their children's education, their needs have not yet reached that level of refinement, even after forty-four years of independence. They merely want water to drink and irrigate their fields. Their souls need no nourishment because that invisible essence of their miserable lives has already been crushed into nothingness by their masters.

'The predicament of women and the lowest caste and casteless men in our society is similar. But why fear women? Look at Kerala, their women have the highest literacy rate in the country. Have their better-educated women, who have also donned the hunter-gatherer garb, absolved themselves of their homemaker role? I don't see any turmoil in that state on this count. The Keralite nurses, who work in the hospitals in North India, look after their children, cook food for the entire family, send their husbands to office and children to school, maintain their homes, and also add to the family's income. Men should consider themselves lucky if they have a wife who works. But look at the bigotry—a working woman is viewed as loose by our hookah-sucking elders; they should suck each others' you know what, that would at least give them a high.'

She chuckled and said, 'I never knew that a Tivari scion from this heap of a dump of a town of ours would have such noble thoughts.'

'There is more of it where it comes from. I think that by denying education to women, we are denying our next generation, male and female, chances of a better life in the future. An educated woman, even if she does not work, can be instrumental in the grooming of her children—you won't need additional tuitions for the children if their mother is knowledgeable. Men are so parochial. A father looks at his daughter as a burden, as someone else's responsibility. So he does not bother to ensure her education—why waste meagre resources? When a young man takes this same illiterate girl as his wife, he sees in her a provider—provide him food, provide him his next generation, provide him his two minutes of release by opening her legs at night. He sees no other role for her in his life. And that's how life goes on. Sorry for my vulgarity.'

'It's okay, Sanjay. Vulgarity at times is necessary to understand the inner workings of vicious minds. No one could have articulated it in a more sublime manner. Can I touch that heart of yours? I want to feel its beats. Never have I come across such a noble one. Its rhythms must be different from others.'

Having noticed nothing different in the regular lub-dubs of my heart, despite placing her lips on my bare chest, she asked, 'What was it like at Ghorakhal?'

'You keep that going—opening my shirt—and we will end up shaming ourselves. I don't want to do anything till you are ready. Holding you in my arms is blissful enough. Kisses galore and caresses send me shooting into an exotic world.'

'You naughty', she poked a tender elbow into my ribs and repeated her question, 'What happened at Ghorakhal?'

'Oh, I fell in love there. What else could I do, you were not there. I had to fall for someone. I love female company and got fortunate to fall in love with one of the three most wonderful girls I have ever met in my life.'

'Was she beautiful?' God! Why was she so envious of the others? I will never be able to understand the inner mechanisms of women's brains; even God would find it herculean.

'My sweetest darling, there have been many girls in my life. Two of them have been exquisite and have made my life worth living, and also a living hell after they left me. When I was with them, I never aspired for another heaven. When they left me, I imagined I would not be able to survive another day. But I am still here, well and truly alive. What more assurance do you need that I am yours and yours alone?'

'I am sorry, Sanjay. It is just that . . . we girls are different. When our object of desire is not with us, we imagine horrible scenarios. There are so many beautiful girls out there that I feel that I will lose you again.'

'Now that we have found each other again, I promise that I will never leave you. When I was deeply in love with Pratima and Meena, I never had eyes for anyone else. They were the only ones for me. Henceforth you are the light of my life, everybody else fades into insignificance. And no more "I am sorry", my honeybee. You might not sting but I want to be your nectar. I read somewhere that love means not ever having to say you are sorry.'

I told her about my crush on the hostel matron, my delirious condition at Ghorakhal after that dreaded vaccination, and Pratima's entry into my life. She shuddered when I said that she had barely managed to survive and marvelled at her childhood triumphs. She kissed me passionately when I told her about my ruminations and my twin pledges made to Golu Devta. She muttered her sympathies in sympathetic tones when I told her of the devious schemes of Pratima's father, through which he tried to initially absolve himself of her responsibility by dumping her with Bhago and subsequently tried to get rid of her burden at various stages of her growing up years, including attempting to sell her to a fiend who wanted to keep her as a sex slave. 'Are there men existing who can be such devils?' she exclaimed disbelievingly, 'there must be some special school where people like Pratima's father and that devourer of women must be taught these specialties. They must be awarding diploma certificates to the best among them—diploma for girl-child killers, certificate for most number of such kills, cash rewards for serial rapists, accolades for deflowering a girl before she reaches puberty. Gosh! What society do we live in?'

'I have learned that it takes all kinds of people to make this world interesting. And you don't need to go to any school to learn the tricks. Go to any village in North India and sit at the feet of the revered elders, sucking hookah and reliving their lives—the younger generation is learning from these suckers.'

'Thank heavens for her brothers. They are her real saviours. How did you fit in all this?'

'They never knew about me till it lasted.' I told her about the Water Tank Hill and the times when Pratima took it upon herself to enhance my education. I regaled her with my stories and the deconstruction of the English classics. She marvelled at my ability to conjure the giggling girl. When I came to the watershed year of '83 and my vow to marry Pratima, she was so immersed that I felt she would have been happy for me to be married to Pratima. When I came to the last winter of '84 and the intimacy I had shared in the cave with Pratima, she climbed on top of me and expressed her desire to make love. I told her to wait, that the time was not right, that we should not initiate something driven by a maddening rush of passion, which we would repent later. She suggested using condom; I refused, saying that I did not do condoms. Her passion cooled and she thanked me later for not rushing into it. I told her that I loved her so much that I would never let her feel ashamed of us. She kissed me with a hunger I had never felt before inside her.

'When I went to meet her in '85, I was full of hope of a glorious future. Little did I know that my world had changed and that she would no longer be mine. When she told me that her newlywed sister-in-law, a staunch believer in caste-ism and all its trappings, had found out about me when she was delirious with fever and repeated my name in her unconscious state, I knew that it was all over for me.' I told her about the ancestral linkage between my family and Pratima's family and how that, coupled with the disadvantage of my being born in a lower subcaste, spelled doom for me. 'My entreaties with her big brother, to accept me for what I am and not for who made me, would have convinced him, if not for his wife. Pratima and I parted at her amber door, and Lord Ganesh, carved on the door's panel, paved a fresh path for me, which came into prominence six months later.'

I told her about my two failed attempts at the NDA entrance exams, about Bindu, and how we relived our respective lives with Pratima at the Water Tank Hill, and my lonely pining for her in the cave. When I came to Sharmajee and his advances and the other homosexual predator back at the school, she remarked that I was way too pretty and that she was happy that I had not been defiled.

She expressed concern when I told her about Meena and my attraction for her. 'Didn't you feel guilty of forcing her into an adulterous relationship?'

'My sweet doll, listen to her entire story, then sit in judgement. I will come to the guilt part after I finish with her trials and tribulations.'

I told her everything about Meena; I wanted her to feel that I would never hide anything from her, so I covered our lovemaking in great, vocally-graphic detail, including the games we used to play.

She 'ch-ched' a lot when I narrated the debauchery of Meena's brothers; she pitied Meena's sole sister-in-law, who had to submit to her husband's lust even during her menses. (The last I heard from Meena she had survived her ordeal and was a harassed but happy mother of two bonny boys). She laughed with glee when I told her about how Meena had bit off the earlobe of her molester as a 12-year-old and carved out Bhuliya's one ball to feed it to her grateful rats, who had gone berserk during their feast. We almost made love when I reached Banaras and the bathtub.

'Sanjay, do you love me as much?' she asked when I had finished my narration, with my last sight of Meena from across her street, as the light from her living room had bathed her in a lovely profile of an angel.

'Yes my dearest Anju, as much, if not more.'

'Weren't you apprehensive of Teena's disapproval of your relationship?'

'Meena's confidence in her sister was so infectious that the thought never occurred to me. I was only worried that Teena or her Army man might not approve her choice. After all, we had long outlived our guilt, so even if Teena or her husband had objected to our being together, we had our ready explanations, hers of her fight for freedom and mine of defiance.'

'Care to explain your defiance theory.'

'I object to both the society and the scriptures sitting in judgement on adultery. What society, whose society . . . this society? I despise the men who constitute our world of misogynist Brahmins proclaiming what is right and what is wrong. What gives them the right to recognise a sin and punish her? Do these people agree with what stares back at them from the mirror? What gave Meena's father the right to punish her, when his own sons were indulging in premarital affairs, when he himself visited brothels? Wasn't he committing adultery, too? Why is adultery a one-way street? Why should only the woman suffer?

'A father who does not admonish his youngest son for being lustful towards his own sister has no moral grounds to incarcerate and consign his other daughter to a living hell. Whatever be her temptations, Meena had indulged in premarital sex because in her subconscious, she had thought that it was an accepted norm, since the men in her family were unabashedly enjoying orgies. A mother who spends lakhs, so that her unmarried younger son could wallow in his gory fantasies in India and abroad, lost her claim to motherhood when she willingly participated in the imprisonment and subsequent exile of Meena.

'Meena was never promiscuous like her father or brothers, at least two of them. When men are promiscuous, they visit brothels, promiscuous women sit in brothels. That's very well, promiscuity breeds choice. Meena's choice was coloured by the environment in her house. What was wrong in her seeking physical satisfaction before marriage?

'But her father upholds all that is misogynist in our society—he is an orthodox Brahmin and he will live what he preaches. When Meena's affair came to light he ostracised her, incarcerated her, and forced her into a loveless marriage to a homosexual pervert. What was Meena to do? It was not within her to accept what the so-called mentors of our bigoted society dole out to her.

'When I first met her, I saw a vulnerability in her which I wanted to erase, there was this huge hole in her life which I wanted to fill with my soul. My heart ached at the mere sight of her. She was a victim of her circumstances and I revelled in being her saviour, her knight in shining armour—which young adolescent heart, fed on movies and tales of valour, could ever resist that? We had initially started our love affair in a purely physical sense, to satisfy our desires. But she grew on me and I on her. She had told me that she fell for me on that first day itself, I may have taken a bit longer in falling in love with her—remember, I was coming out of a heartbreak myself. But once I had lost my heart and soul to her, I never felt any regret. In fact, I took untold delight in the thought that I was showing two fingers to the very society I had come to detest. That was the most wonderful feeling.'

'Where does God fit in all this?'

'God doesn't even begin to figure in it at all. I said scriptures, not God.'

'What is the difference?'

'The difference is in what you perceive to be true. Since times immemorial, man has always been twisting the truth to conform to what he wanted to hear. In the process, a few of them wrote some words and called them the message of God and they themselves became messengers of God. They imposed those messages on others and claimed that what the scriptures contain, written for and by themselves, mind you, is the absolute truth. But I have a different take on the subject. If one agrees with God's existence then the scriptures are wrong. If God does not exist, the scriptures lose their authority. Joseph Heller would not have found a more apt Catch 22 situation.

'Take the first premise.

'God exists. He created the only universe, those millions of galaxies, those billions of stars, our sweet solar system, and after spending one-third of his time in contemplation, he created our lonely Earth, the only planet in the entire known universe where life thrives. Our Earth, which has been in existence for the past four and a half billions of years, give or take a few millions, after the initial tumultuous period of its formation, started breeding life, as we know it, some two billion years ago, not counting the chemical graphite and microbial mat fossils found in Greenland, which date back to within a billion years of the Earth's formation. The first vertebrate land animals came into existence some 380 million years ago. Humans' earliest predecessors, the Hominids, appeared two million years ago. God did not create the world in six days, unless one day was equivalent to an epoch, a hypothesis I fail to agree upon. He experimented a lot before finally homing on to the humans to give them these capabilities and capacities much greater than the other beings. For 165 million years, he let the dinosaurs rule the world. But when they turned into marauders, destroying large swathes of his beautiful world and devouring his other creations, he destroyed them sixty-five million years ago and millennia later created humans after his own image and sent them to rule and multiply. He has existed for all those billions of years and we humans came to know of his existence a few thousands of years back, give or take a few centuries—if ever there have been late bloomers, we are them. Come to think of it, all the major religions of the world came into being in the last 4,000 to 5,000 years, with the first of the surviving religious texts, the Pyramid Texts, composed in the period 2494 to 2345 BC, in Ancient Egypt. Before that the ancient burial rituals give some indication of even Neanderthals believing in the existence of an Almighty, right from 223,000 BC onwards.

'Who created whom then? Did God create man or did man create God? That is the dilemma. If we try to answer the first question, then man does not have proprietary rights over God and can't claim that we are the chosen ones. God created humans after his other experiments failed. Some might say that he was waiting for the opportune moment before making humans the dominant species on Earth. If that be the case, why did humans wait for so many years before recognising God's existence?

'Because early humans did not feel the need of God to justify their own existence. So why did humans create God? Do you get the paradox? Humans needed God to justify something else. They had created these divisions of caste, creed, colour, and multitudes of other distinctions to rule over one another. First, they wrote some words in some vague language whose knowledge they restricted to a chosen few, who they said were their medium for communication with God. The language was so complicated and secretive that the common man could never communicate with God on his own. These Brahmin communicators with God, to justify their existence further, created Messengers of God, whose followers propagated the message of God and in the process subjugated the balance of humanity to a life of servility. One half of humanity, the women, automatically qualified as inferior beings, to be ruled over by men. When Adam proclaimed that the woman was beneath him, as she came out of his bone and flesh, God agreed with him. Who made women the oppressed half of humanity? Not God, but the people who wrote the scriptures. God, who created the most beautiful creation on Earth, would never be so cruel as to decree that she be stoned to death.

'I am not saying that I am an atheist. I am a true believer, I believe that God exists. But my God is benign, he is invisible, he is there, he is not there, he is inside every soul on Earth, he is the very essence of life; whereas their God is malevolent, he is in the cross, in the idols, in the statues, and in the posters, he is omnipresent, he commands every soul, he is life, and he is death, too. Therein lies the difference between whom I believe in and whom everybody else believes in—what God represents. For me, he represents life; for them, he represents life and death. We Hindus have gone many steps further and created Gods governing every aspect of human existence and even of death. In a way that suits me—to everyone his own God, pick and choose. The only Supreme Being I choose is the one that does not exist amongst the pantheons of Hindu Gods and Goddesses. Because my God is difficult to fathom by bigoted minds. He lives here, in my heart and in every living heart; he dwells in my soul and every other soul—I see God in the beggar whom everybody despises, in the sweeper who comes to clean our latrines and whom we are told to not even lay our eyes upon or else my mother makes me wash myself—have you seen *Ganga Ki Saugandh*, where even the shadow of Pran's outcaste *Chacha* falling upon the village priest defiles him—I see God in the mongrel in the street everyone kicks around, in the poor imbecile who hounds *Lala*'s teashop, begging for tidbits to survive and whose frame is used by the colony kids to improve their marksmanship with stones. That's my God, I chose Him. If you read deep into our scriptures, that is what their essence is. Religion and its scriptures are the very tools of goodness and love, but in our desire to be better than others, to proclaim our superiority over others, we have turned them into instruments of hatred and bigotry. Over the centuries, more people have been slaughtered in the name of religion than the combined power of all atomic bombs made possible. Our religious books contain, hidden deep within them, the powerful message of non violence and tolerance, but the preachers of these scriptures had overlooked this very essence a long, long time ago. They have weeded out this primary message of universal brotherhood, consigning it to oblivion and divided humans into haves and have nots. Long time ago, religion forgot the central message of God, which is contained in all the religious books, that of promoting good and avoiding evil. During the Crusades and numerous other times in the past, humans used religion as a pretext to kill other humans. Which God would ever allow that to come to pass? My God would never permit that, for him every human is an extension of his self; how could one be different from the other. He does not permit a human to kill another just because she is different and believes what is true for herself.

'Since times immemorial, humans have been beseeching God to come to Earth and deliver them from evil. In *Satyug* and *Dwaparyug*, he obliged us and took the form of Lord Ram and Lord Krishna to fight evil. Why not now, when the world is once again being ruled by evil? Because, back then he believed in us, in the goodness that personified human existence back then. He recognised the evil in the Shiv-worshipping Ravan and came in the avatar of Lord Ram to slay the ten-headed demon. But today, he refuses to acknowledge our prayers because our beseeching reeks of corruption. Every prayer is laced with selfish desires—grant me a promotion Oh God and I will donate 100 rupees, give me a son and your temple will get an idol in return. Oh God, don't give a car to my neighbour and I will be your slave for eternity, get me a wife with one crore rupees in dowry and I will give 10 per cent share to you. My God laughs and pities us when he receives such missives. He is not going to deliver us from ourselves. Why should he? He has given us enough abilities to be rid of the evil from within ourselves. It's we who refuse to believe in that. We created virtues and sins, in the name of God, and ruled that those who sin are evil. But what is sin—any activity we do and are not caught doing it, is not a sin. It is only when someone gets caught that the sin is identified and the sinner punished. Else the 'sinner' continues sinning because the sin has not been identified by the others. Isn't taking undue advantage of the downtrodden a sin? But our society thrives on it; corruption has become a way of life for us Indians—the same Sarpanch who orders that a newlywed bride be killed to preserve the 'honour' of the community, would never think twice before siphoning off the money meant for the betterment of the same community.

'A man sins because of the circumstances. If a soldier kills another human being on the battlefield, he receives the accolades of a hero; but if the same hero kills a man in a brawl over some prostitute, he is sent to the gallows. In similar vein, if a woman, forced into a loveless marriage, seeks love in someone else, why should she be punished? No one should sit in judgement on the sinners but the sinners themselves.'

'You mean to say a sin should not be punished?'

'Punish the sinners, yes, but look at the circumstances first. I like the confession system of the Christians. What can be a greater punishment than forgiveness? Forgive a sinner and he will spend the rest of his life consumed with guilt. But in our world, eager for swift judgement and corporal punishments borne out of intolerance, bigotry, and misogyny, women will always be the losers. Who will defend them? I have known women being raped and killed by their close relatives. Does honour killing ring a bell? The girl's parents kill her for marrying against their diktats.

'Meena was a kindred spirit. Her entire life, she did what she did because she was growing increasingly frustrated in the claustrophobic environment she was living in; her home, her father's societal circle, her mother's indulgence in her sons, her father's refusal to allow her and her sister proper education, the corruption in the minds, and lives of all those around her and above all the all-pervading straitjacketing of the common man by the very people who promised betterment of the down-trodden, people who were the bastions of her society, like her father. She hated them all. I saw a bit of myself in her, and that is the reason I fell for her.'

My leave period got over with that tirade. I had Father send the Kawasaki Bajaj to Amritsar by train and an hour before my departure; she came for a last visit. As we held one another, she said, 'Sanjay, will you forget me when you are there at Amritsar?'

'My sweetie-pie, I love you from the bottom of my heart, and it will take a Menaka to ever make me forget you. You may not have replaced Meena yet, truth be told, but she has started fading.'

'Will you ever forget them?' there was more than hopeful anticipation in her tone. I felt pitiful at her insecurity. I decided to be truthful.

'Will I ever forget Pratima and Meena, in particular? Very difficult to answer, Anju. They have been the biggest influences in my life; they made me what I am today. How can I ever forget that? Pratima personified perseverance against all odds, and in her struggles, she was supported by her brothers. Meena, on the other hand, fought for justice, for herself and her sister, alone; hers was a lonely battle. I will go with Meena any day. Where Pratima's dilemma was her love for her brothers in leaving me, Meena answered to a higher calling. The two loves of my life have left me bereft of several heartbeats, but they have enriched my soul with their ideals and beliefs shaped by their individual struggles against a society so deprived of ideas, and I will remain eternally indebted to them. But just that. I love you now and you are the only world for me henceforth.'

3

The Quest Continues

I joined my regiment at Amritsar Cantonment in July '91 and commenced a journey which is unparalleled and which has given me so much that I will remain eternally grateful to the Army. It has given me an opportunity to carve a niche for myself in a world full of mediocrity; it has given me fame and fortune I could have never dreamt of at my small, nondescript, unheard of, famous for political conspiracies and lynching, hometown of Etawah.

I could have never asked for a higher calling than serving my nation in the Army. It is not only my bread and butter; it is the very essence of my soul and has defined my adult life. Patriotism may not be the sole preserve of the defence services and I have never presumed myself to be a bigger patriot than the tea shop owner who gets up at four in the morning to prepare the elixir for his early-morning customers. But what the Army's ultimate lesson for me has been to be humane towards others. The only time I have ever drawn comfort is in the company of the soldiers who make up this great Army of ours. One look in their eyes and the microcosm of our society stares back at me, with all that is worth living in this divided and divisive world. The soldiers of my unit come from all over the country, professing different religious ideologies, hailing from societies which preach the divisions of caste as the gospel. But their behaviour, when in the barracks, is the very antithesis of what the elders of their respective villages propagate. In the profession of soldiering, there are no differences of religion, caste, creed, colour, race, or so many others—we cannot afford it, else we would never have been able to build the camaraderie on which any army thrives. In their day-to-day lives, the men respect each other's beliefs and ideologies and pray to one Almighty in a *Sarv Dharm Sthal*, a place where all gods and their prophets are represented. We never allow the prejudices of religion and caste ever enter our daily lives.

(When Babri Masjid was demolished in '96, I had felt such a pity for my country, which could not take a leaf from one of the bastions of tolerance—the Indian Army).

I spent the first month of my service life living in the barracks with the men, despite a room being available in the Single Officers' accommodation in the Officers' Mess. That was the time I got close to them: waking up every day at four in the morning, getting in line at the cook house to be served tea out of a huge *degchi* (utensil), doing intense physical training with them from six to seven, bathing in the community bathroom along with them after PT—all of us clad in underwear to hide our privates, no NDA-type bathing rituals here. Breakfast of *Puri-Sabji* was followed by cleaning the gun barrels, counting the numerous grease nipples on the 130-millimetre artillery gun and the multitude of vehicles of different shapes and sizes, getting under the same vehicles and staring at the axles and shafts and drums, without understanding one word of the Havildar who went about, in a monotonous drone, explaining the different mechanisms that propelled the metal monsters, which had replaced the long-suffering bulls and horses of yore, a few centuries back. Lunch in the cook house was succeeded by an hour's break for rest and that was the time all three of my loves would invade my soul. I wept silent tears for Pratima and Meena and would dismiss the anxious queries of the soldiers, resting in adjoining beds, with a shake of my head, which sent trails of droplets in arcs of wet tears—after sometime, they gave up on me, leaving me to my own devices, thinking that I was feeling homesick; 'missing his mother, poor *Sahab*,' Havildar Ram Singh had muttered once. I took these jibes and other similar jokes of my men, in my stride. In my hour-long mulling over my past and lamenting on 'what would have been' scenarios of varying proportions, I took solace, and my hopes rose whenever I thought of Anju. After the hour-long break, as the men went about their tasks of cleaning and maintaining the vast estate occupied by the unit, I spent the time preparing for the Young Officers', YOs', Course, where I would get my first opportunity to prove my worth to the other officers and, especially, the men of my unit. Till that happened, I was just a 'new Second Lieutenant *Sahab*' in the unit. My performance in the course would decide the place I would occupy in the hearts of my men.

Unlike popular perception, Army life is not about fun and frolic and an occasional war to kill the enemy's soldiers and win glory for the nation, respect for the Army, and medals for self-gratification. It is a saga more of sweat and less of blood. And as officers, we have to excel in all endeavours. There can be no letup in our intellectual pursuits to enhance our knowledge. Knowledge is what makes an Indian Army officer unique—knowledge of one's profession, of the enemy's way of war fighting, of the world in general, of what constitutes the universe of fighting soldiers, of everything in particular. When I had joined NDA four years back, I had thought that I had left behind my student's life of cramming up the various theorems and principles contained in the school syllabus books—at NDA, I had been a BA student and had sailed through the three years without much flow of electrical currents through the nerve centres of my brain. When I finally got commissioned, I had imagined that I would now be able to spend my time in new adventures requiring not much investment of my gray matter, except the occasional indulgence in my hobby of reading fiction. All of my wild imaginings of lesser and lesser studies were consigned to some dark recess of a huge dustbin, with no worthwhile hopes of retrieval in the forthcoming near future, when Captain Anand Mishra, my Senior Subaltern entrusted with the responsibility of converting me from a fresh GC into a mature officer, thrust a heavy training manual, containing 300-plus, A4-size pages, with an innocuous sounding title, the moment I had stepped off the train at Amritsar Railway Station and he announced in a Patton-esque baritone, 'This is your bible for the next five years. Mug up every word in the next nine months, prior to your departure for the YOs' course. Your test on the first chapter on Fire Discipline is scheduled on the twentieth of this month—each word counts.' That was fifteen days away and the first chapter was thirty-four pages long, the words numbering in the thousands. What had I landed up in, I wondered. I barely managed to score in that first test.

The evenings were when I found my elixir. The games period of one hour, from five to six, became the one event I looked forward to every day. Having never been a keen sportsman myself, I had to strive hard during my NDA and IMA training days to learn the rudimentaries of playing basketball, volleyball, hockey, and football: the sports preferred by the men in all army units. In my unit, most of the men were from villages where sports, as a culture, was absent—the hard, daily grind of struggles for survival took prominence over every other facet of existence in the dreary lives of the millions living in rural India. As a consequence, these soldiers were as clueless as me in the finer niceties of these sports and my evenings would invariably turn into jostling with the men, our sweat commingling and our hands slithering off each others' torsos, than in pursuit of the balls. But the fun was in rubbing our sweat-soaked bodies with each other, as the balls evaded our clumsy feet, butter-fingered hands, and useless hockey sticks. I had taken to wearing a waist belt over my sports shorts in basketball to preserve my modesty, as it was not beyond Ram Singh and Charan Singh and the likes to pull down my shorts while I was poised to score a basket. The first time it had happened, my sweat soaked, unsuspecting shorts had insisted on taking my equally soggy V-brief undies along for the ride, and all those present had guffawed at the sight of my unblemished, question-marked buttocks and my well-proportioned pecker. I had joined in the jest then, since I had scored two points from that throw, despite Ram Singh's finagling. I got my own back when Ram Singh's loose shorts and his huge, striped underwear did not accompany him in his leap, the forces of gravity assisted by my generous pull forcing them to come sliding down his leaping legs, revealing a pair of sinewy, flat-as-pancakes butt cheeks and an impish, shy-as-a-newlywed-bride penis, for the world to gawk and pity. In that males-only world of testosterone-driven mass of humanity, the size of my pecker became the talk of the town for the next few days. My underwear clad groin was subjected to many furtive glances during my morning and evening baths—I even allowed a generous dekko to some insistent stares—and even the small size of one of my balls did not dampen their enthusiasm and admiration. Word also spread around amongst the officers and one month later, during my initiation into the officers' fraternity, in the form of my dining-in party, in a drunken frenzy, I had allowed a peek to some of them eager for a look, within the safe confines of the bathroom.

The nights were long, way too long. Ram Singh, with the generous assistance of some of his brethren in the Officers' Mess or the Junior Commissioned Officers' Club, would be successful in siphoning off an occasional bottle of Old Monk rum and hefty chunks of chicken and goat liver and kidneys, and would host the 'new Second Lieutenant *Sahab*', blessed with handsome assets, to a gorgeous, rum-soaked meal of delicious liver and kidneys, *tadka daal*, fat rice, and paper-thin chapattis. Later I would slip into a rum-induced sleep at around eleven and immerse myself into my dream world of a beautiful Pratima kissing me passionately atop the Water Tank Hill, a giggling, g-shaped, Vodrumeepian avatar of Meena making love to me inside a spacecraft, and numerous such delightful dreams of a wonderful mix of ecstasy and sublimity. Sometimes Anju, with her exotic curls, would saunter in from some remote corner and try to shove off either Meena or Pratima or both.

Anju puzzled me—with her obsessive desire and pronounced jealousy. I had no doubt in my mind and heart that I loved her. But did she love me, too, despite her earnest endearments and 'I love you, too, Sanjay' confessions? Vijay, that elder cousin of mine, had once warned me that she had many suitors, both at Etawah and at Allahabad, and that one of them, from Allahabad, was way too serious in his wooing of Anju. I had dismissed it then as rumour mongering and attributed it to Vijay's jealousy prompting him into poisoning my ears. But even a wee bit of poison can colour the blood. As the days passed by, I was increasingly being assaulted with doubts. She never wrote to me, even though there was no danger of her letters ever landing in wrong hands, as there were only right hands in my unit. I despaired at my predicament; both Pratima and Meena had never been envious of my past affiliations and infatuations—Meena had even been overly sympathetic when I had cried into her chest after narrating the episode of the amber door closing on my face. But this was the first time I was encountering a jealous girl, who had worries about my affections for her, as well as resented my past associations with the other girls in my life. I had never met a girl like Anju before—so lovely, so well read, a movie buff to boot—she had a vivacity bordering on a tenacious hold over my emotions, her desire for me was so infectious, and she had these tiny black moles on her breasts, number of them. During my dining-in party, after downing the mandatory beer-jug-full cocktail of a heavy and unpalatable mix of unadulterated rum, whiskey, and gin topped up with frothy beer, I had blundered into my commanding officer, CO, Colonel Ram, and slurred into him, opening my shirt and indicating the various spots on my chest where my girlfriend had those black beauty marks.

Within a week of my joining the unit, we moved to the vast deserts of Rajasthan for firing and field manoeuvres. I stayed in a small tent, sleeping on the washerman's narrow-as-a-nymph's-waist ironing table—I had not yet been issued with my foldable camp cot—and ate from the field kitchen, where the open utensils were assaulted continuously with sand storms, as a result of which, the food contained numerous grains, courtesy of the violence of Mother Nature, hiding ensconced, like tiny pebbles, in a sea of nourishing *daal* and rice. The tiny sand grains crunched between my teeth with each bite, arousing that sickly feeling I used to suffer when Giri Sir, back at school, scratched the black board in the class with the blunt end of the chalk stick or, worse, his fingernails, creating that squeaking sound which reverberated in our ears with their high-frequency screeches, whenever he felt like torturing us for being too rambunctious in class.

I fired my first artillery shell on 17 July '92, propelling the sixteen-and-a-half-kilogram heavy, ogive-shaped projectile, sixteen kilometres away, to explode in a shower of thousands of fragments of the shell casing, raining down hell and havoc on the flat desert land. If there had been any living being present, it would have been pulverised into nothingness with the force of the explosion and its outer body shell punctured with hundreds of holes from those flying fragments of steel.

On the last day of my month-long period of stay with the men in the barracks and the tent, I was dined-in at the Officers' Mess, after we returned from our sojourn in the arid lands of Rajasthan. That formal initiation ceremony—a sort of baptism—brought back the 'what would have been' scenarios with a vengeance, when I met the other officers' wives for the first time. My longing for Meena grew severer as the evening wore on, as amidst the shimmering chiffon, the glittering bangles, the glossy lips, the shiny eyes, the rouged cheeks, the coiffed hairdos, the clacking stilettos, the graceful manners, I saw Meena cackling heartily at their jokes, commiserating with them, whispering secrets about my bedside manners, exchanging recipes of my favourite *Gatte Ki Sabzi*, lamenting about the ever-increasing prices of vegetables, recounting her recent visit to Hall Bazaar to purchase the famous Amritsari suits, explaining why she never had an opportunity to visit the Golden Temple to pay her obeisance, as her husband had to stay with his men, complaining that it is during the night times that she misses me the most, tossing and turning in her bed all alone in the single officers' quarters that was her new home now, cursing my CO for making me stay in the barracks when his newlywed wife pined for him all by herself—'He could have at least let him come to me on Sundays. My poor Sanjay has withered into a weed without me'—throwing surreptitious glances towards me as I downed beer mug after beer mug of that obnoxious cocktail of rum, whiskey, and gin topped up with frothy beer, constantly worrying at my worsening condition as the evening aged and I got sozzled with each passing minute and gulp, chortling and shaking her head as, in an inebriated state, I approach her, kneel down clumsily in front of her, and, kissing her knuckles, ask her for a round of the dance floor before my CO could claim the right for the first dance with my lovely Meena. I cried into my food at the dining table, sitting sandwiched between Mrs Pundreek and Mrs Kapoor, and they took my yearning for Meena as a reaction to the eloquence being sung by my CO in his opening speech, welcoming me into the unit. That night, I had drunken dreams of Meena fading into nothingness, stilettos and all. The following day and the next many days, I spent hours in a haze of insignificance.

In mid October, as agreed upon with Anju earlier, I came on a leave of thirty days to celebrate Diwali with my parents, at Etawah. For some unexplained reason, she did not turn up at Etawah, neither for Dussehra nor for Diwali, and I spent the festival of lights brooding in a darkness of the unknown and the unknowable. Vijay added fuel to the fire raging inside me by suggesting that she was spending the Diwali night in the arms of that serious suitor at Allahabad. I almost took off for the city of the confluence of Ganga, Yamuna, and the fabled Saraswati Rivers. Instead, I decided to visit my brother at the Birla Institute of Technology and Science, Pilani, where he was pursuing his civil engineering degree course. I stayed in his hostel room and both of us marvelled at Sachin Tendulkar's genius. He was batting like a dream, carting and pummeling Alan Donald and co, to all corners of the stadium in the one-day international match played between the visiting South African team and the Indian cricket team at the Eden Gardens in Calcutta, and which was being beamed on a flickering television set in his hostel's ante room at Pilani.

But when I was back at Etawah, my heart again yearned for Anju and I often gazed at her door from the confines of my living room and imagined her suddenly emerging from her front door to come over and meet me.

I could never unravel the enigma that was Anju. We met again at Etawah just before I left for my YOs' course. I had gone there for a week-long leave, before heading to the School of Artillery at Devlali. She pledged her undying love for me and I assured her, after sensing her discomfort, that I would never look at any pretty girl at Devlali during the next six months I would be spending there. She did not explain her earlier absence during Diwali, muttering just a vague reference to her father insisting that she spend the festival with him and his latest love interest. That did nothing to boost my confidence and I was reminded of Vijay's insistence of a rival paramour.

I rarely went to Shaktinagar till my marriage, it contained too many memories, and I knew that the moment I stood in front of Meena's now-demolished home, I wouldn't be able to stop myself from catching the next train to Chhapra. Shanti Bhavan became my permanent stopover during my leaves and I tried to find solace in Anju's arms. We never met anywhere else except Shanti Bhavan; small towns are notorious for scandals and their repercussions, and we did not want anybody to throw dust on our relationship, especially an inter-caste one in a caste-driven social milieu. Only my youngest uncle and aunt knew about us, and they could be depended upon to keep a secret.

What a fate? I fell in deep love thrice in my life and all three of them had to be conducted as clandestine affairs. Sometimes, when deeply frustrated, I wondered about the day God had created me. Maybe, when he was busy conjuring me, he was with his own paramour; that explains why I fall for every pretty face so easily. At that very moment, his superior, the Supreme of the Supreme Beings, must have happened to be close by and my Creator, in addition to creating my soul, must have had to simultaneously conduct his dalliances with his consort, in secret. What else could explain my predicament?

In that week-long delightful company of Anju, I got over Meena. Her smile, which dissolved her cheeks into numerous dimples and lit up her eyes, was enough to make me forget Meena's cackles and chortles. Her restraint was a sheer contrast to Meena's open and frank attitude towards everything in life. Her shy nature and hesitation in gradually opening up to me was refreshing, after Meena's affability and zeal with which she used to make love to me. Anju did not so much become my emotional anchor, but bit by painful bit, Meena started drifting from the centre stage she had occupied for so long inside my heart, to some remote recess, from where she would occasionally spring up like a jack-in-the-box. Slowly and gradually, I assumed control of the box's lid and by the end of that week, I was successful in only recalling Meena whenever I felt the need of her presence to perk me up from whichever gloom I might descend into. No longer were the memories of Meena accompanied with a silent sob and a wet tear, but with a smile and a spark. Such memories were usually summoned by me purposefully, to reminisce the good times I had spent with her. Gone were the pangs and the heartaches and in came the glories and promise of a bright future again.

But that did not come in a rush—the promise of a bright future. When the week ended and I left for Devlali, I felt an emptiness in my soul, which had not yet been filled by Anju's presence for the past seven days. I longed for something else. For the first time in my life, I wanted a routine love affair, where I could propose to a girl in public and not inside a room, hiding from everyone else, where we could go to restaurants and order lavish dinners, where we could go see re-runs of *Tezaab* and whistle at the gyrations of Madhuri Dixit, where we could go to a circus and enjoy the acrobatics while I secretly ogled the Russian beauties in scanty bikinis, where we could go picnicking to the picnic spots where lovers go and steal kisses behind thrilled bushes, where we could stroll hand in hand into dark alleys to caress and exchange hot kisses, where we could write to each other and pour our hearts out in those sweet, inane, love notes. I tried to enter into that form of love affair twice in the next six months and met with disastrous failures both times.

It all started with Swati.

She was a lithe, lissome, slim, and tall dusky beauty—if ever I fell for a dusky hued girl after *BB Mausi*, she was the one. She was very tall and when in heels she could have easily topped my meagre five-foot-eight-inch frame. She reminded me so much of the odd pairing of Nasstasja Kinski and Dudley Moore in the Hollywood movie *Unfaithfully Yours*, not that I drew any inspiration from the five-foot-three-inch-tall, round-nosed, scruffy-haired English actor. When I had spotted her at a party in the Panther Defence Officers' Institute (a club for entertainment) back at Amritsar, before my departure for Devlali, I had recalled the last scene in the movie, where the tall Kinski girl carries the impish Moore in her arms like a baby, to enjoy their 'happily ever after' bliss—I wanted Swati to carry my not-so-tiny self in a similar fashion, into our version of a 'happily ever after' world. The next day or a few days after my sighting her, my CO called me into his office, and after admonishing me for some imaginary misdemeanour, he informed me that Colonel Joshi, Swati's father, who was also at Amritsar, had asked me to accompany him on a trip to Jallandhar. Sandwiched between Colonel and Mrs Joshi, in the cramped back seat of a Jonga, I was bombarded with questions about my background, by both of them. I told them, in sincere tones, about my father's life in the Army, our Southern sojourn of three years, my schooling at a 'mundane' Sainik School, my joining NDA four and a half years back, and about my father's struggles before finally turning into a businessman. I don't know what turned them off—maybe my crushed, sunken cheeks, or my belonging to a nondescript, now gaining notoriety for goonda-ism and Mulayam Singh Yadav's brand of divisive politics, town of Etawah, which was equally famous for its close proximity to the notorious Chambal Valley dacoits, or my schooling at an equally worthless, in their eyes, Sainik School, or my father being just a businessman—whatever be the case, that was the day and ever since then I have never been interviewed by any colonel as a prospective groom. The Sikh driver of the vehicle must have also been disappointed at my inadequacies and would have been surprised at Colonel Joshi's desperation in his search for a groom for one of his two daughters, for he almost vaulted the vehicle into the canal running parallel to the highway, to avoid a bone-crushing collision with an onrushing monster of a bus belonging to the Punjab Roadways, which are notorious for being driven by maniacs high on dope and not civilised humans. The results of my interrogation, during that trip to Jallandhar, were never made public, but I got a feeling that the time had not yet come for me to give up on my own efforts. Another of my senior, Captain Ash—who had fallen in love with his first name so much that he had posters of the famous sprinter, Ashwini Nachchappa, pasted all over the walls of his room—came to know of my not-so-routine trip to Jallandhar, and deciding to play the matchmaker, he informed me that Swati was studying at the Ferguson College in Pune and that I could meet her there when I would be at Devlali.

So, one Friday, taking advantage of the free Saturday and the succeeding Sunday holiday, I took off for Pune from Devlali, zooming at 100 kilometres-an-hour speed, perched precariously on my faithful Kawasaki Bajaj for the 204-kilometre trip. There I roomed with Vishal Chaudhary, another classmate of mine from Ghorakhal, who had taken us all by surprise when he had announced back at school that he wanted to become an Army doctor and had joined the Armed Forces Medical College at Pune after leaving the school. The next day saw me standing outside the gates of the famed Ferguson College, where two years earlier, as a 21-and-a-half-year-old cadet, I had spent countless hours in search of a partner to dance with me at the NDA Ball—I ruefully recalled that I had been a failure then. But this Saturday was bright and sunny and I was full of hope. When I enquired after Swati Joshi and her whereabouts, the Nepali gatekeeper blasted me with high-sounding words that there were thousands of students at the college and that one particular Swati Joshi, howsoever lovely she might be, would have never been registered by his marijuana-clouded brain. Undaunted, I walked to the main office building of the college, and after some indiscreet inquiries, I was directed to a notice board, which contained the list of students who would be taking the forthcoming exams. There, after running my eyes over hundreds of names printed on number of pages in a never-ending list, I saw her name listed amongst the botany course students. A further few enquiries later, I was standing outside the laboratory where she was trying to fathom the world of plants and their uses. She came down from wherever she was busy amidst her botanic world and must have been surprised to see my crushed cheeks, for that was where her eyes landed the moment she stood face to face in front of my delighted, bright-as-an-infatuated-five-year-old eyes. After the few sentences by way of my introduction, I suspect she must have decided that my 'good looking in a good-looking sort of way' looks held no great appeal for her, for she rejected, in a determined sort of way, my offer for a dinner that evening—out went my dreams of a routine love affair of lavish dinners at fancy restaurants. And in she went to her plants.

But the experiences of my short, 23-year-old existence had taught me that perseverance, if nothing else, pays in matters of the heart. So, refusing to take it lying down or standing up—if that sounds better—I enquired further about her place of stay and learned from a benevolent clerk at the main office of the college that a certain Swati Joshi, daughter of a colonel who regularly paid her fees on time, stayed at a hostel, even though she had a grandmother living in the city. I walked over to the first building located close to the college that advertised itself as a girls' hostel. I could have blundered into notoriety had a shriek from an ancient-looking, *bidi-*smoking, geriatric hostel minder not halted my steps at the hostel's main gate. I had not realised that being a male member of the vast species of the Homo Sapiens, I could not enter the exclusive domain of the females of my species without proper permission, and that, too, accompanied by a close relative of the one particular female who was the object of my interest. He further informed me that there was no Swati Joshi staying in that particular hostel, and when I assured him that this specific girl was known to be staying in a hostel and that I was not a wandering loafer but a serious suitor, he gave me the address of a locality where there were number of girls' and working women's hostels and said that I would be able to find her there. I reconnoitered the locality, homed on to the hostel where Swati Joshi was listed as an occupant and chalked out a course of action, as diligently as a general planning a battle campaign.

The next day, I was standing in front of her hostel since seven in the morning to ensure that she would not vanish without my noticing her. At eight, assuming that it was a decent-enough time for a college girl to wake up on a Sunday, I rang the bell at the hostel's gate and announced to the suspicious lady warden that I had come to meet Swati Joshi. She remained unconvinced till I assured her that I knew Swati from Amritsar, where her father was a colonel and that he was the one who had asked me to meet her and enquire after her well-being. Reluctantly, she picked up the microphone of the hostel's public address system and I heard tinny echoes of her announcement, 'visitor for Swati Joshi' repeated every five minutes, till she came down in a hurry, thirty minutes later. A good sleep does wonders to a girl, and I almost took her into my arms when I saw her dressed in a navy blue salwar suit. She looked more radiant and lovelier than the previous day and my heart skipped several beats, as I watched her climb down the stairs, the ends of her stole gracefully trailing behind her, jumping down the steps. I was mesmerised by her sight and couldn't get a word out, till she exclaimed, 'You again? What now?' My heart sank with those words. All my plans made the previous evening evaporated with that single volley of accusatory questions from her and I managed to blurt out that I had not been able to sleep the whole night, that I wanted her to go out with me, that I wouldn't mind even if it was for a fifteen-minute cup of coffee in a nearby coffee shop, that I wanted to speak to her, that I had come all the way from

Devlali just for her and that I did not want to feel disappointed like I did the day before. Maybe it was my manners, or my desperation, or my sunken cheeks again; but she still refused my offer. 'Not even a five-minute chat?' my despondence was clearly evident in my tone. 'We have been doing that for the past ten minutes and nothing worthwhile has come out of it,' she turned around to re-enter her world, leaving me desolate in mine. 'Just five minutes alone, and we might come to know each other better. Maybe you might change your mind then,' I rushed to face her and forced her to halt in her strides; my desperation had by now taken the hue of reckless obduracy. She said with a finality, which sounded like a judge banging down the gavel to pronounce a death sentence, 'Look, I don't know you. Just because you saw me in some party at Amritsar doesn't give you the right to invade my privacy. I appreciate your perseverance but that alone is not important in a relationship. Please don't come here or at my college again,' and with that death knell, she walked into her hostel, leaving me bereft of any emotions.

But I did not let that singular episode bog me down for long. After the mandatory mourning period of thirty minutes over the loss of an opportunity to pep up my love life, spent in a pitiful retelling to Vishal Chaudhary, I was fresh and eager for new adventures of the amorous kind. On returning to Devlai, I discovered that I had attained notoriety for my philandering ways amongst my colleagues and one of them, Second Lieutenant S. Bhattacharya, took it upon himself to play the role of Cupid. He told me of a girl called Charu, from Bombay, who had expressed a keen interest in meeting young Army officers. She regularly listened to the Forces Request programme on the All India Radio, sending frequent requests for love songs and repeated entreaties to imagined Army officers. He gave me her address and I promptly wrote to her a five-sentence missive, by way of my introduction and my desire to meet her. I got a reply back within seven days in which she wrote that even though my letter had come as a surprise, she would also like to meet me—just two lines. There was something amiss in her reply but I could not put my finger to it. I wrote back, saying that I had a three-day break coming up within the next few days and further added that I would like to spend that period at Bombay and get to know her better. This time her reply took me by surprise.

Bhatta, that is what my earnest matchmaker goes by, was and is a queer fellow. He is famous for his blundering manners, even his gait is so lopsided that he trips over himself while walking. His answers to the questions during our classes could be categorised into the only category reserved for nincompoop replies. He thought of himself to be a maverick, in the class of Tom Cruise in *Top Gun*, but we all knew, those who had had opportunities in the past to have suffered him, that in reality, he was more in the league of Peter Sellers from *The Party* and that he would have also blown the bugle endlessly in the opening scenes of the movie, without any prompts from the director. Now, in his matchmaking haste, he had conjured that first reply, purportedly written by Charu. On closer inspection, I realised that the postmark of the inland letter indicated that it had been posted at a post box in Devlali and that the handwriting was not cursive enough to be that of a girl's, which was confirmed when I saw his notebook.

The second reply, now definitely written by Charu, expressed surprise at the candour in my 'second' letter and she also mentioned that she was very wary of communicating with strangers, but that since I was in the Army, she could still feel safe and that my offer of meeting her at Bombay had piqued her interest to such an extent that she could not wait for the day when we would be face to face.

Bhatta guffawed stupidly at the idiotic prank he had played on me and took sole credit for the way events had finally turned out. He congratulated me on my success and offered to host me at his parents' house in Bombay, during my three-day long stay there. I thanked him for his generous offer and in turn decided to take him to Bombay on my Kawasaki Bajaj. We rode together to the city of dreams and barring a minor hiccup, when due to a flat tire we had to drag the motorcycle for a distance of five kilometres before the tire could be repaired, we reached Bombay and Bhatta's house in Bandra, safe and sound and in good health.

Buoyed by an equally healthy optimism, I rang the doorbell of Charu's father's fifth-storey apartment near Haji Ali's mosque at nine, the following morning. Her mother opened the door and let me enter her abode, after confirming that I was the same Second Lieutenant Sanjay Tivari whom Charu had invited for a cup of tea. I spent the next few hours in the delightful company of Charu and her elder sister. We were rarely interrupted by her mother, who came into the room only once, bearing three cups of tea and a plate of biscuits. Charu turned out to be very chirpy, her nose crunched when she was deep in contemplation and her smile was radiant enough to brighten up the room and my heart; the only difference from the other girls in my life being that her 1000-watt smile was not accompanied with attendant dimples. I loved the sight of her pearly white teeth whenever she beamed a la Madhuri Dixit smile, minus the dimples. She was interested in genetics and we discussed a lot about the mysteries of nature and how natural selection is being tweaked by us humans in the form of genetic modification. We also discussed about the implications of mutation of genes and how science fiction movies were turning lizards into monsters and turtles and rats into benevolent do-gooders, with the turtles named after the Renaissance era artists, Leonardo (da Vinci), Michelangelo, Raphael, and Donatello. By the evening, she had shown enough concern for me and even went to the extent of inviting me to Haji Ali's mosque, whose muezzin's calls for the evening prayers were clearly heard by us, in order to make me denounce my smoking. I had politely declined the offer, but rejoiced in the note of serious concern that had crept into her voice. After a late lunch, I came back to Bhatta's home to a sumptuous dinner of rice and fish curry, served copiously and consumed with relish using my fingers.

The next day, she asked me to take her to a friend's house—it was actually a show-off event. She wanted to parade me in front of her jealous friend and display her trophy find. We went to her friend's house by my motorcycle. Charu disappointed me by sitting at the very end of the seat, and throughout the thirty-minutes ride, I longed for her to lean into me, to feel the pressure of her chest on my back and the touch of her thighs against my leg—I even sat back, to no avail, the Kawasaki Bajaj seat was way too long—and the only feel I got was that of her right palm perched tentatively on my right shoulder. When we reached her friend's apartment building, we discovered that the ancient lift had gone kaput and initially I held her hand to help her climb the stairs for the first three floors; thereafter, when she declined to climb any further—Bombay girls need some serious working out—I asked her to climb onto my back. After the first few minutes of reluctance and also realising that her heavy breathing would take longer to return to normalcy, she obliged me and what I missed on the ride I realised on the climb. But I would not call that heavenly, as by the time we had reached the tenth-floor apartment of her friend, I was heaving and sweating like a racehorse after winning the derby. Once inside her friend's house, I never minded playing second fiddle, for I revelled in being admired for my looks after such a long time and especially, after the rude dismissal by Swati. For the first time in my life, after Teena's 'you two are made for each other' admiration, was I referred to as 'he is so good looking', in their quiet whisperings; it was a huge, humongous—truth be told—relief when Charu's friend had not added the 'in a good-looking sort of way' suffix, in her murmurs.

That evening, we went to Fashion Street and I bought a red tank top, with yellow polka dots, for her; my eyes were actually set on a bikini with a similar design, but my dreams of seeing her gyrating to the tunes of *Itsy Bitsy Teeny Weeny Yellow Polka Dot Bikini* vanished into thin air, when she quashed my suggestion of a gift of the shiny and tiny two-piece set, saying that she did want to fall into the dilemma of which piece to remove, if the lifeguard at the swimming pool insisted that they only allowed single piece swim suits. The next day, I went back to Fashion Street again, before returning to Devlali, and did buy that bikini, along with a cassette of the iconic Brian Hyland song. When Bhatta raised a questioning eyebrow and remarked 'within two days? That's very fast. What will it be the next time? I cannot persuade my parents to vacate my house!', I had dismissed his insinuation and said that Charu had refused that gift the previous day, settling for a tank top instead, and that I was now interested in seeing which piece would Anju remove first, when she danced to the tunes of the song—my fantasies knew no end and my imagination was flitting between Charu and Anju—the delights of too many riches.

Charu did not so much as kiss me goodbye on the third morning, but she did relent to my constant persuasion and gave me her telephone number. That proved to be my downfall. Over the balance of my course, we exchanged many letters and I often spoke to her over the Graham Bell invention, spending more than an hour each time, to the chagrin and frustration of the other customers of the lone PCO booth at Devlali; so much so that they used to vacate the booth whenever I came for my eight-o'clock, long-distance chat. One night, after downing one too many of the Peter Scot whiskey shots and inspired by my bragging of amorous nights at the iconic 'Taj Mahal Palace' hotel near the Gateway of India, in the company of a sensuous Charu, for which I was constantly goaded by my sex-starved, equally inebriated colleagues, I summoned Charu at eleven, when her suspicious mother answered the incessant rings of the telephone. In my intoxicated state, I badgered her to come to Devlali and spend her evenings and nights with me, amidst the vast expanse of the firing range, and when she refused to come, I lamented that she did not love me at all, that whatever she had written and spoken earlier was just a trap to lure me into a fruitless dream, that she was playing with my emotions with no concern for my heart—whiskey works in its own mysterious ways and makes a man throw all reason to the wind. That wind not only carried my empty words but also spelled doom on my fledgling attempts at a normal love affair. The next day's sober Sanjay Tivari and his attempts at reconciliation faded into insignificance when she refused to come to the phone to listen to my desperate pleas of sincere apology. She never answered my letters, too, and after a few months, my dreams of reconciliation fizzled out.

4

The Chetwode Motto

I realised my full potential as an officer upon my return to my unit after the YOs' course. I had been graded 'Above Average, (A)' in the course and was adjudged the second best student, although that position is, at best, an also ran, since, in the Army, only the winners count, the others are consigned to the dustbins of history. So, my second position in the YOs' course held no meaning and was lost in the sands of time in no time. But my 'A' grading was what was appreciated by all and sundry, and I was feted to a grand feast, *Bara Khana*, by Ram Singh and co. It was in the company of my men and amidst the daze, induced by the fumes of Old Monk rum and soda, that I discerned the true meaning, and the hidden essence of the Chetwode Credo, which all officers in the Indian Army vouch for, live by, and would give our lives for. The motto, inscribed in the much revered Chetwode Hall at IMA, is the ultimate oath imbibed by the heart and soul of each officer of the Indian Army at the very moment when we leave the hallowed portals of the Academy's Chetwode Building located behind its Parade Ground. The credo epitomises our outlook towards our future life, up until the day our mortal bodies would be consigned to the flames of our pyre, and when our immortal souls would depart for the Unknown. Its words give me goosebumps even today, whenever I feel the rare necessity to remind myself of my duties, in my moments of doubt; it is similar to the feeling I get when I listen to the stanza, *Hindi Hain Hum, Hindi Hain Hum, Watan Hai Hindostan Hamara*, from the iconic Muhammad Iqbal song, *Saare Jahan Se Achcha Hindostan Hamara*. The credo is embedded in us thus:

The Safety, Honour and Welfare of your country come First, Always and Every Time

*The Honour, Welfare and Comfort of the men you command come Next
Your own Ease, Comfort and Safety come Last, Always and Every Time.*

I have often wondered at the emotional outbursts Field Marshal Philip
Chetwode must have been experiencing when he spoke those very words in
his inaugural speech to the Gentlemen Cadets of the *Pioneer* Course on 10
December '32. Sitting amidst the *Pioneers* and imbibing the essence of that
credo were the legendary GC Sam Manekshaw, GC Mohammed Musa, and
GC Smith Dunn, each of whom rose on to become chiefs of their respective
Armies in India, Pakistan, and Burma, respectively. Our own General Sam
Manekshaw was the chief architect in the liberation war of Bangladesh
where he liberated the hapless but determined Bengalis from the demonic
clutches of Pakistan in '71 and thereafter rose on to the coveted rank of
Field Marshal, a rank he held proudly all through his mortal life and history
granted him immortality for his deeds. Even as a 90-year-old, he never let
his shoulders stoop, or his gait falter, or his uniform develop even a solitary
wrinkle, or his baton slip—his life, and demise, aptly epitomise the adage
'Old Soldiers Never Die, They Just Fade Away'.

'Well, revered Field Marshal Sir, you will never fade from our hearts, you
will always remain an inspiration for generations of soldiers, irrespective of
the country we belong to, and will forever remain a beacon of all that is worth
living and worth dying for, in this world full of corruption of mind and soul.'

The other, earlier Field Marshal, the First Baron Chetwode, Philip
Walhouse Chetwode, had laid the greatest emphasis on the safety, honour,
and welfare of the country, which is every patriot's duty, irrespective of
whether he or she is in the Army or in any other vocation. But when it
came to the soldiers, their comfort replaced the safety part, since on the
battlefield, the safety of the men has at times to be undermined due to the
necessity of achieving the mission, which is paramount to ensure the safety,
honour, and welfare of the country, the principal bounden duty of an officer.
As Indian Army officers, we have to be fiercely committed in ensuring the
dignity of our soldiers by upholding their honour, ensuring that they are
well looked after and that their comforts are taken care of, whether on the
battlefield or during the peacetime training for war, including that of their
families. For our own self, we as officers have the ultimate responsibility.
We are the ones entrusted with the task of originating the battle plan, and

that can only be achieved if our minds are free of clutter. That is where our own ease and comfort play a big role. And safety of officers finds a way in because if an officer is not safe on the battlefield, who will execute the plan and think of reactions to adverse situations? I liked the beauty of the words and their essence dawned on me with each sip of the rum and soda that evening—it was an epiphanous experience, if ever there has been one.

As the feast progressed into the dark hours of midnight and I sat mulling over the credo, I was struck by an irony. Our great country is full of a civilian bureaucracy populated by stereotypes who carry the divisive mindset of our society to their workplace—why shouldn't they, they live in the same society, some might argue. But my take is different. Adopt the Chetwode motto as an Indian ethos; accept it as our way of life. When I see these dignified dickheads, who comprise our IAS 'Officers' and who take such great pride in self-categorising themselves as 'Class 1 Gazetted Officers', a league denied to Indian defence services officers, since the domain is too exclusive to be opened to the very people who have sworn to give our lives for this great nation of ours, when I see these denizens of that exclusive realm behaving in such condescending manner with the common man of the country, an RK Lakshman epithet for the millions who populate our country, I am filled with such immense remorse. This anguish leads me into wondering what would have happened if the Britishers had not come to India to teach us the modern ways. Our 565 rulers who, before 15 August '47, had divided the country into as many kingdoms and princely states, would have never let our nation be united, so steeped were they in their divisiveness and discrimination. We would have continued to languish in the dark world of ignorance. We hate the Britishers for having kept us in the shackles of *Ghulami* (servitude) for so many centuries, but we fail to admire the immense work some of them had contributed into making India what it is today. The very bureaucracy which they had created as the Indian Civil Service, ICS of British India, to provide a select group of people possessing intellect and commitment to 'serve' the common man and which Sardar Vallabh Bhai Patel had so staunchly defended as the backbone of the administrative machinery of the country, when there were cries for dissolving the ICS in the days leading to and succeeding our independence, the same hallowed set of people instead of serving, now rule over the common man. They have degenerated to such an extent that the IAS has become a cosy, dark cartel of people who have converted their responsibilities into their divine right to rule and condescend. How I wish that Baron Philip Chetwode had been a civilian and had spoken those words at some ICS convocation ceremony; then we would have adopted his credo as every Indian *Officer*'s Credo. Replace the words 'The Men You Command' with 'The Common Man' and the credo would become a motto by which every Indian *Officer* should live and die for. It's an irony that it took a Britisher to tell us the essence of living by our ideals.

(And we Indians still have not learned, even sixty-seven years later. Our bureaucracy still suffers from a feeling of insecurity and a false sense of superiority—after all they are not so superior, they too have to bend over backwards, and forward, to wipe the spit off a Mayawati's shoes—the microcosm of our society, again.)

Even the Pakistan Military Academy at Kakul has the same motto, with the words 'the honour of men you command' replaced by 'the safety of the men you command' and some other minor modifications in the other two lines. These words are inscribed in the hallowed portals of their iconic Ingall Hall. That is why the Pakistanis have been reluctant in claiming the dead bodies of some of their soldiers in all the wars fought between India and Pakistan—the honour of their soldiers, even dead ones, has never been their primary concern. And it is also an irony that despite having pledged to ensure the safety of their men, the Pakistani Army still continues in futile military adventurism, forcing their soldiers to die in their pursuit of their long-cherished dream of Bleeding India With A Thousand Cuts.

The credos of both the armies, despite the minor change in the concern for the men, are more or less identical. In addition to carrying forward the British legacy, it also proves that the values eschewed by the common people of both the nations bind our countries in an invisible embrace, and it is our political leaders who have caused so much death and destruction in the four wars our two countries have fought with each other and in the ongoing proxy war, which continues unabated with no end in sight. 'Where are the visionaries? We need them now, God. If ever their need was felt it is now—humanity is being dragged towards oblivion by the very leaders, religious and political, who had sworn to let us thrive and prosper, to lead us into a utopian world. Save us, your most cherished Creation, Oh Almighty!' Will my prayers be heard, ever?

5

The Blundering Continues

My failed attempts at reigniting my love life were turning into blunderings of a recently blinded man, who, with every step, thinks that light will return into his suddenly turned dark world. These bungling steps led me to Kavita—someone who, ironically, does not even know that I exist and whom I fell in love with at my first sight of her. There is never a dull moment when I encounter a pretty girl.

On my return from Devlali, I saw her divine figure, dressed all in white, playing tennis near the officers' gymnasium inside Amritsar Cantonment. I was drawn by her white uniform, her knee-length skirt, her toned legs, her graceful strokes, her healthy cackles, her lean figure, and her beautiful face. I immediately took to tennis, spending hours trying to learn the searing overhead serves, the delicate lobs, the full-blooded ground strokes, and the sweet volleys—and here I thought that the volley dwelled in the sole domain of volleyball. All of this to no avail, for my shots invariably sent the balls into hyperbolic orbits, much beyond the constraints of the small tennis court—with me the balls decided to be subservient to their own minds. It led me into thinking and believing that John McEnroe, Jimmy Connors, the lovely Chris Evert, and my lovelier Kavita were all magicians, wielding the tennis racket like a wizards' baton, a la Harry Potter; though JK Rowling was nowhere in the horizon then, but what the hell, I am writing this story in 2014 and can afford such similes. Even hitting the tennis ball against a wall did not improve my skills, as most of my shots sailed over the wall to disappear into the shrub land beyond. The ball boys often gave up on their searches for the yellow balls hiding in the green undergrowth, and I would end the evenings paying for the cost of the numerous yellow balls consumed by nature's gift of green. One day, I gave one last, forlorn look to the cemented tennis court and decided that tennis would never become my forte. My dwindling finances were threatening bankruptcy and I had to give up on tennis, but not on Kavita. After Swati's 'please don't come here or at my college again' ultimatum, I was wary of the direct approach to my love interest. I decided upon a more direct tack, a straight-to-the-heart-of-the-matter route. I reasoned: why go the roundabout way wooing the girl, that's too time consuming, fraught with innumerable dangers and pithy rejections, go on the attack like a true soldier, and launch a direct assault on her centre of gravity—all her defences will become redundant. My military mind, having firmed up in my determination, now chalked out a course of action worthy of even Patton.

Kavita happened to be the daughter of one Colonel Balan, who had replaced Colonel Joshi, Swati's father. When I told Captain Ash about my feelings for Kavita, I was immediately branded a threat to all colonels with daughters of marriageable age. (Now that I am 46 years old and a father of two lovely daughters, I can understand how those colonels of my youthful days must have felt with their daughters amidst a sea of suitors—after a 17-year-old adolescent, the next dangerous breed is a 23-year-old, young Army officer. Be careful all you colonels who take such great pride in being called 'true gunners', because we have only daughters. If ever I have cursed myself for my vow to Golu Devta, it is when I see these youngsters ogling my firstborn at Mhow, the only place on Earth where there are more than 2000 Army officers at any given time, most of them bursting with untameable hormones in their twenties, many amongst them, even though married, never tire of reliving their younger days of voyeuristic bachelorhood).

One evening, I decided to pay a visit to Kavita's father and ask for her hand in marriage!

What made me contemplate such a course? Even God would find it difficult to come up with a reasonable answer to that question. When the inner workings of a woman's mind are unfathomable for him, what chance does he have of deciphering a young man's heart, which has taken so much shattering by the tender age of 23? Who knows how a young man's heart beats—the constant lub-dubs, in their rhythmic repetitions, hide within those beats some insanity which made me decide to propose to the father. Well, that is why I want to go to that parallel Earth in an alternate universe—remember the concept of multiverse—to find out what actually happened. On this Earth, I was intercepted by Major Ravi before I could even reach my motorcycle, and he happened to know Kavita's father more intimately than me—I didn't even know his full name.

At four in the evening, I stepped out of my room, dressed up like a dandy metrosexual, replete with a red tie and shiny black leather shoes, at a time when the other officers were dressed in white shorts and canvas shoes. Major Ravi accurately judged that I was poised to launch into a new adventure which could only lead to some catastrophe of unmanageable proportions and promptly took me to my CO. My new CO, a tall, Sikh colonel, who had replaced Colonel Ram a few months back, was the very image of an officer who had skipped many generations of warriors and had landed into the late twentieth century with the values, beliefs, and mannerisms of a Napoleonic era general. He was taciturn at the best of times, never smiling—his stoic, stern face gave an impression that even when told that he had been blessed with a son, his grim, tight lips would never part to reveal a set of shining teeth—a strict disciplinarian, haughty of manners and a divorcee for the past many years. I think the last quality was what brought my house of cards down.

After I had explained the reason for my unusual attire for that time of the day, he first gave me a dressing down and later, when it dawned on him that it would take more than that to make me budge from my determined stance, like a benevolent father, he started listing out the minuses of my intention to marry Kavita at the very moment when my unit was poised to move to the mountains of Sikkim, where I would not be allowed to take her with me. I countered that she could stay with her parents or my folks, during my tenure of two years at a location where wives are not allowed to stay with their husbands. What if she said no to my proposal, he tried this tack. I was prepared and said that I would take my chances, that after my recent experiences in similar situations, where I had failed with my other girls, I was sure that my fate would allow me this one chance of success, the law of averages evens out many downs with an occasional up. But as the evening progressed, I was getting increasingly weighed down by the force of his arguments, and my flimsy counterarguments started losing their initial fervour. By eight-o'clock, we arrived at an understanding that I should wait till I completed my Sikkim tenure before approaching Kavita or her father, for her hand. He did not even let me go to her or her father to tell them that they would have to wait for me till then.

Poor me! Later, while at Sikkim, Major Ravi informed me in sympathetic tones that Kavita moved to Bangalore a few months after I had left Amritsar and that a further year later she married a Non-Resident Indian settled in the US. Till today, she doesn't even know that I exist and that I had almost blundered into an unexplainable venture, all those years back. I shudder thinking how Colonel Balan would have reacted to my proposal, had Major Ravi not intercepted me—most probably he would have kicked me out of his sights and his house, for good.

6

I Will Require More Time to Think It Over

That November saw me in Anju's arms again, my head hiding in her breasts, her moles blinking at my predicament. I did not tell her of my three failed attempts, else she would also have thrown me out. A few days before my departure for Sikkim, she proposed to meet me at Agra, since she had to go there as part of a college excursion. I jumped at the one chance of living my dream of a normal love affair and come December 10, I was standing in the grounds of Taj Mahal waiting for her.

We entered the sanctum sanctorum of the white, marble Mausoleum of Love with hope for me and trepidation of an uncertain future for her. Amidst the diffused light entering from the screens in the balcony openings in the corners of the ceiling, I looked at her and tears welled in my eyes at the prospect of how she would respond to what I had in my mind. As if driven by an impulse, I proposed to her, 'Marry me, Anni'—the octagon-shaped interior chamber seemed to lose its shape, the corners dissolving into ghost-shaped onlookers. My high-decibel proposal invited sheepish looks from the other admirers of the monument dedicated to love, most of them young couples trying to find the meaning of life in a dead couple's final resting place. Many young girls waited with bated breath for her response and even followed us out into the gardens. Like her birth, she took long in everything in life and this time, too, took a very long time before coming up with 'I will require more time to think it over', as we were leaving Shahjehan and Mumtaz to their uninterrupted slumber. We went to the gardens outside the mausoleum.

After her 'I will require more time to think it over' reply to my proposal, she had remained silent while I drifted between despair and hope. In the gardens, too, she was lost in her own thoughts, and realising that her gloom might turn into my nightmare, I tried to draw her into a world full of hope: 'There is only one thing in the universe which is the sole elixir of life.'

'What is that?' she said, after shaking off the doubts clouding her brain.

'Love, my darling, true love.' Soft, shuffling sounds indicated that we were still being hounded by eager couples desperate for knowing her reply. Their murmurs and whisperings were getting on my nerves, and turning around to face a foursome, I hollered at them, 'She said she requires more time. It won't happen today.' When they heard the disappointment in my voice, they nodded sympathetically and started peeling off. One of them, tearing away in a hurry, shouted back, 'Best of luck, pardner.' I nodded my acceptance and turned to hold Anju's proffered hand, I could feel the desperation in her squeeze.

'The origin of life on Earth is a very complex contemplation.' I continued. 'Was it Darwin's ghost back then which, with each passing epoch, goaded some being or the other to mutate and become a new being, even requesting the contented, tree-dwelling apes to come down and start walking on their hind legs? Or was it some invisible force, a primordial entity, a huge giant, or maybe even the humble corn, which propelled fully grown beings into an empty void, to rule and be ruled? But I am sure of one creation myth, that there is one Permanent Soul, the soul of the Supreme Being, from which all the other souls take their form. All these souls remain dormant within this Permanent Soul, waiting for their time to be released into this world. During their time inside the Permanent Soul, each of our souls lives with a matching twin—a male and a female equivalent of all beings on Earth. These twin souls are released into this world by the Creator at different times and at different locations. And our Creator gives us one single purpose for our mortal existence: to search for our twin soul, and once we find each other, we attain *Nirvana*. All our trials and tribulations, our choices and rejections, our searches and losses, our misjudgments and corrections are conjured by him to enable us in reaching that objective. To assist us in identifying our twin, he has given us the most powerful force he has ever created—Love. Love is what assists us in finding our lost twin soul. And I think I have found mine in you.'

'Where do you get all these ideas from?'

'I read some and my mind and soul derive their independent meanings from what I ingest from the books and what I observe in the world around us. What comes out of my mouth is what I believe in to be true, after all that ingestion, digestion, regurgitation, and repeat ingestion.'

'I wish I had such an imaginary mind like yours. But how can you be so sure that we are each other's twin soul?'

'How else can you explain my earlier failures in my search for my true love? Every time I felt I had reached my *Nirvana* stage, I lost her. Except, with you, it is different. I think you are my twin soul. I have never felt this strong love for anyone else before.' By now my eyes had gone misty.

'Why is it that every girl desires the most perfect Mr Right for herself?' She appeared to be changing the topic of our discussion, most probably judging that I was overflowing with my emotions and would soon start crying.

'Because that Mr Right is the one with whom she had spent an eternity inside the Almighty's Soul, before coming to Earth.' I would not yield.

'Are you my Mr Right, Sanjay?'

'I feel I am the one. God has made us meet again; there must be a purpose to it. I threw my heart for Pratima and for Meena, but never met my Maker. None of their souls matched with mine—not Pratima's, not Meena's. I want to spend the rest of my life with you and meet my Maker in our union.'

'What if it does not prove to be true? What if our souls were never made for each other?'

That put me in a quandary. I had believed that my short monologue on love would convince her and remove the lingering doubts from her mind. But it seemed that my 'twin soul' theory would have to wait before its hypothesis could be proven.

'I guess I will wait for your answer,' I said with an air of pessimism and we strolled out of the gates of the Taj Mahal to take our separate rickshaws to our respective destinations; she had politely declined my offer of sharing the journey back to the hotel where she was staying, fearing that someone would notice us there.

That night I dreamt of lost souls and the most powerful force in the entire universe. How can you dream of such abstract feelings, but then who can prove that there are no twin souls? My last dream was of her saying 'I will require more time to think it over'.

That 'more time' took one additional year, when I was able to finally squeeze a fifteen-day-long leave from the ever-diminishing quota of leave in our unit, as the CO had grown very stingy in granting leave to officers and being the junior-most officer, my turn came in December '93 to enjoy a fortnight long respite from the extremely cold climate of Sikkim.

This time, we discussed about our combined future a lot. She was increasingly becoming despondent due to our belonging to different castes. My repeated assurances that inter-caste marriages were no longer frowned upon did nothing to allay her misgivings. She was more worried about the reactions of her family members, as they were true believers of the rigid caste system which bound a man to his family for life.

The origin of caste system in our country dates back almost 3,500 years. Our Vedas, from as early as 1500 BC, mention the caste system. *Manusmriti*, the Laws of Manu, defines the rights and duties of the four *Varnas*. The *Varnas* delineated a system of social diversification based on spiritual development, not by birth but by *karma* (duty). Our ancestors created *Varnas* as a way of life to define each person's value and his duty towards others. The *Varna* had more to do with the abilities of a person in a chosen vocation. But the priestly class exploited it and made it hereditary, calling it *Jati*. Where earlier, each member of a particular *Varna* drew his or her identity from the occupation he or she was engaged in; later, our Brahmins ensured that each person acquired his or her social status purely by virtue of birth.

Despite these divisions, some of our old texts and scriptures have looked at humanity through a common prism. Our ancient sages wrote in Yajurveda: 'The universe is the outpouring of the majesty of God, the auspicious one, radiant love. Every face you see belongs to him. He is present in everyone without exception.' The Isha Upanishad says thus, 'The Lord (The Divine) is enshrined in the hearts of all.'

Roots of the *Varna* system of social division can be traced back to the Hindu belief of reincarnation and its implication that rebirth of a soul depends on the virtuousness in its previous life. A truly virtuous Shudra in previous life can be rewarded with rebirth as a Brahmin in the next life. Social mobility in mortal realm was very little in this rigid system. It is only in the Unknown that souls moved among different levels of human society. But on Earth, during his entire lifetime a person had to strive for virtue to attain a higher status next time around.

Some learned professors also claim that, in earlier times, people had options to change from one *Varna* to another, depending on their abilities. As per noted sociologist Professor MN Srinivas, through the process of Sanskritisation, a person from a lower *Jati* could learn the habits and culture of a higher *Varna* and belong to that class. It was easy to achieve a status of Kshatriya by fighting and winning, and getting the Brahmins to validate it.

Brahmins, however, remained an exclusive domain. No person from any of the lower *Varnas* could ever become a Brahmin, even though they may have all the qualifications. And likewise no one from the outcastes, who were considered nonproductive people, could cross into the fourth *Varna*, the Shudras; they were segregated and disallowed—these are the dalits of today. The Rigvedic *Purusha Sukta* provides the divine reasoning for this division and the religious basis on which today's upper-caste people treat those from the lower castes with such disdain and apathy. In its tenth Mandala, it says thus, about the emergence of man's many varieties out of the different body parts of Purusha, the primordial giant:

The Brahmin was his mouth, of both his arms was the Rajanya (Kshatriya) made.
His thighs became the Vaisya, from his feet Shudra was produced.
(translated by Ralph TH Griffith)

This system of division dominates three key areas of human life: marriage, meals, and religious worship.

Marriages follow a rigid rule of being consigned to within a *Jati*. Inter-caste marriages are very rare, so much so that any inter-caste marriage, in our small towns and villages, becomes fodder for our tabloids and dominates the realms of public discourses for many days.

Brahmins always enjoyed the upper hand in the sole activity in which humans and animals share a commonality of interest and an unquenchable desire of ambition—our unrelenting pursuit for food. But unlike humans, most of the denizens of the animal kingdom do not share our animosity, when it comes to sharing the food with the other members of the same species. The alpha may insist at being the first one to gorge on the kill, but slowly and grudgingly, he allows the others their share of the banquet. But us humans—we are a breed apart. Our Brahmins take great pride and assume it as their divine duty to hand over meals to others, even ones from the lower caste. But if a meal has been touched by a lower caste person, God's sole representative on Earth would be offended and his purity would be polluted by that touch. I have always been touched by the tolerance practiced in the animal kingdom when it comes to sharing of water. Come water time, the shores of any water body are lined with unending rows of animals of various varieties: zebras, giraffes, lions, tigers, wildebeasts, deer, monkeys; the preys and the predators together, standing or leaning in different postures and enjoying the sips of the elixir of life. But in the human domain, go to any village and you will find that the public well gets polluted, all by itself, if an untouchable even touches the rope attached to the bucket to draw water.

Religion remains the sole domain of the Brahmins. Because they wrote the hymns and the rituals themselves, they became the common man's telephone for sending his messages to God. They even prescribed that the incantations have to be delivered in a particular manner else they would never reach God. The poor common man accepted their diktats as divine proclamations and never challenged the norms. A Shudra accepted it as his fate that his God would always go hungry since he would never accept his sacrifices. An Untouchable searched for his God in the mortal domain without realising that, since he could not enter a temple, there may not be a God for him at all—'Purusha' never gave birth to him, how could he dare claim a God for himself. He was rightly selected by God to remain outside the caste system, as his mere shadow would contaminate others, including God Himself. Even in the afterlife, he had no hopes of reconciliation, as he had no right of cremation at death.

Our scriptures provide the authority, and we are no one to change the system. There are numerous references of the quadruple division of our society in the epics and other texts; in the Valmiki Ramayana, in the Mahabharata, and in Kautilya's Arthashastra, too.

The division based on hereditary concept had been abolished by Lord Krishna, who had categorised people based on their nature and actions (*Guna* and *Karma*), and not on genetics. He said that knowledge was higher than defence so the learners and thinkers were categorised as

Brahmins; that defence was higher than commerce, so the warriors were in Kshatriya category; that commerce was higher than production and thus the traders became Vaisyas; and the engineers, craftsmen, farmers, et al., who were the mainstay of society, were called the Shudras, a notch above the Untouchables, who were never granted any status—it was only in the twentieth century that Mahatma Gandhi took up the cause of the Harijans and got Untouchability prohibited under the law, but it continues in the form of its various avatars of discrimination in many parts of our country. Lord Krishna had disposed of the word *Jati* and its 4,000 variants and brought in *Varna* with its four variants. The effect of this sort of division led to the members of many *Jatis* registering themselves to a higher *Varna* without letting go of their *Jati*—*Varnas* got added to *Jati*.

The Bhagavad Gita has been very elaborate on the concept of *Varna* and *Jati*. In his discourse with Arjun, Lord Krishna said, 'I am the Self seated in the hearts of all creatures. I am the beginning, the middle and the very end of all beings.' He further extolled, 'I look upon all creatures equally; none are less dear to me and none more dear. But those who worship me with love live in me and I come to live in them.'

When Arjun queried him about the *Varnas*, he said, 'Birth is not the cause, my friend; it is the virtues which are the cause of auspiciousness. Even a Chandala observing his vow is considered a Brahmin by the Gods.'

On the creation of *Varnas* and their importance, he said, 'The fourfold division of castes was created by me according to the apportionment of qualities and duties. Not birth, not sacrament, not learning, make one *dwija* (twice born) but righteous conduct causes it. Be he a Shudra or a member of any other class, he that serves as a raft on a raftless current or helps to ford the unfordable deserves respect in every way.'

But humans couldn't remain satisfied with this meagre division of such a large population base. How could we? In a world full of such a mix of varieties, how could humans be clubbed in mere four groups? So they went ahead and added three zeros to Lord Krishna's fourfold division of humanity. They created 4,000 *Jatis* and still not satisfied with that, they made each *Jati* a conglomeration of numerous subcastes (*Gotras*). Mankind started enjoying the fruits of division, and discrimination became the prime mover of this juggernaut of divided humanity which now thrives on prejudicial practices to sustain itself.

But for the time being, if we disregard our scriptures and purely concentrate on anthropology, historian Romila Thapar has this to say on the origins of caste-ism in India:

> When the Aryans first came to India, they were divided into three social classes—the warriors or aristocracy, the priests and the common people. There was no consciousness of caste, as is clear from the remarks such as 'a bard am I, my father is leech and mother grinds corn.' Professions were not hereditary, nor were there any rules limiting marriages within these classes, or taboos on whom one could eat with. The first step in the direction of caste (as distinct from class) was taken when the Aryans treated the dasas (slaves) as beyond the social pale, probably owing to a fear of the dasa and the even greater fear that assimilation with them would lead to a loss of Aryan identity. Ostensibly the distinction was largely that of colour, the dasas being darker and of an alien culture.

What happened that everything got corrupted? We categorised people into *Jatis*, 4,000 of them. Many *Jatis* constitute a *Varna*. Four classes were manageable, and the *Varna* system also provided opportunity for advancement, upward mobility was inherent in the division of society. But 4,000 castes! With its obsession with denoting particular communities based on rigidly practiced and jealously guarded customs and rituals, with its strict adherence to hereditary passage of profession and its inclusive marriage rights, caste-ism divided our society into so many exclusive domains, and we practise this distinction through all activities in our life and even in our death—those young lovers who seek bliss outside their castes are killed by their own family members.

Marriages moreover, follow their own logic.

Indian arranged marriages, and to some extent, love marriages, have to follow these rigid rules which govern more than just the union of a woman and a man. A marriage is also a coming together of two families. In a society where even eating with a lower caste is considered taboo, how could an inter-caste marriage survive? How could two families from different castes eat together during the marriage ceremony? So, inter-caste marriages happen outside the bondages of society. The girl and the boy elope and 'live happily ever after' till either the girl's or the boy's brother or father or some other relative discovers and kills one or both of them—invariably it is the girl, since she carries the burden of family honour. At times, the parents, with the passage of time, come to some sort of reconciliation and the couple is allowed to continue living with little chance of being accepted back permanently. There have been cases where the reconciliation has led to a reunion with either the girl's or the boy's family, invariably the boy's, since he carries the hopes for the future of the family name, especially if he is an only son.

7

The Long Train Journey

Keeping in view her family's rigid stance and my father's staunchly held opinions on all things concerning caste (that incident of the fictitious Thakur girl from Renukoot all those years back surged back into me with a vengeance), I had only one desire—elope and evade. I wanted her to come to Sikkim with me and I had already planned her stay in anonymity, at two places, Chungthang and Mangan—I had identified one two-room dwelling at each of these towns and, fortunately, the houses were owned by septuagenarian widows with no interest in life other than a companion to talk to. The houses themselves were located at the outskirts of the towns, way down the slopes and were accessible through meandering footpaths. The remoteness of the towns, buried deep inside the mountains of Sikkim, provided the security Anju would need. Her father or brother were sure to lead search and destroy parties, once our elopement grew into a slanderous scandal, and I did not want them to ever be able to think of the little dumps of Chungthang or Mangan as a suitable destination for a newlywed couple. There was a secret letter in the custody of my youngest uncle who would send the missive to the local newspapers at Etawah, Agra, and Kanpur, once we became famous. The printing houses will be paid handsomely, again by my uncle, to gleefully announce the elopement of ex-Second Lieutenant Sanjay Tivari and Anju Chauhan, both belonging to different castes, and further add that Sanjay Tivari had resigned from his Army profession and was last sighted in the company of a certain Amitabh Bachchan, since he wanted to pursue a career as an 'extra' in all Bachchan movies, even acting as his double, though his height would have to be enhanced with the help of some high-heeled boots. Had Rommel thought of all the contingencies in similar fashion, he would have won the war for Hitler and I would have been living in an egalitarian society where every man's true worth would be recognised by the rank he held in the Army. No other qualification would have been required of me, and free of all societal restraints, I would have been the husband of Pratima, Meena, and Anju—polygamy had never appealed to me so much.

My mind mulling over such thoughts, trying to find the true meaning of my version of love and immersing in an utopian world of blissful, polygamous existence under a despotic regime; time flew by and soon I realised that it was time for me to return to my unit.

On the penultimate day prior to my departure, Father had planned a trip to a village called Manikpur, located twenty kilometres from Etawah, where a distant cousin of his had invited our family for a meal comprising *Handi Daal* among others, the *Daal's* recipe being as secret as the battle plans for Operation Overlord. I feigned illness, my nicotine-stained nails helping in the visual diagnosis of jaundice and leaving me in the company of Threptin biscuits and a large jar of orange juice, they left for Manikpur. I waited for my answer.

She came with her answer and spelled my doom.

When she arrived, she looked as if she had not slept the whole night. Though outwardly she was as radiant as ever, I could see dark circles of dejection under her eyes.

'Sanjay,' there was no lilt in the way she spoke my name; I knew there and then that there was no further hope for me. 'I don't know how to say it. If I elope with you the male members in my family would never rest till they find us and kill us.'

'Why do you think that's going to happen? Your father likes different women, irrespective of caste. If he does not mind his body getting smeared with the fluids of lower caste women, how can he object to our souls meeting in a union blessed by God.'

'Thakurs regard wives as trophies. I will marry not because of love, but because I am beautiful and can be flaunted as an acquired possession. Why do you think I am paraded in front of the visitors who come visiting our house? I am being asked to exhibit myself so that the best Thakur scion can see in me an object for display. Why do you think my two aunts have never been married? They are too plain looking. And I think a similar fate is going to befall my elder twin too. But when it comes to coital relations, nature has bestowed immense tolerance in male Thakurs. Our men can enjoy their pleasures with lower caste women, but when it comes to the Thakur women, we can only let a *Chhota* Thakur enter us. Any other cock would defile us and dishonour our family. And, as you said earlier, each one has his own God. As per my father and brother, our God would never accept you. For them you would defile me if I married you and hence they will kill you and me, too, for bringing such dishonour to our family name.'

'I never knew Honour Killing had roots here, too.'

'Two decades back, an aunt of mine had run away with a *Kayastha* Srivastav boy. They lived in hiding for a year and she gave birth to a lovely girl. Thinking that, hearing about the news of the birth of a child, her family would at last accept her decision to marry outside our caste, she wrote to her mother with the news of the child's birth—poor sod mentioned her gender, too. Upon getting her letter, my grandmother sent my father and her other sons to bring her head, and they added the little infant's head, too, in the booty. The Srivastav boy was hung from a telephone pole in the middle of his village with a message of eternal hatred—'Those who seduce Thakur girls will meet similar fate.' I don't want that fate to befall you, my love.'

I was immensely touched by her concern for me, but the despondence pervaded my soul—'How could she do this to me? Oh God, not again. How will I live now onwards, my heart will stop beating any moment? Where is my twin soul? How will I find her? Where is my *Nirvana*; will I languish in this mortal world for eternity, without any hopes of salvation?'

I tried to retrieve the situation. I laid out my plan before her. 'You will stay at Chungthang. There is an old lady who will rent her two-room house and you will stay there. I will be able to visit you often. Within a year, if God is kind to us, we will welcome a set of twin girls into this world. Please come with me. Be the mother of my children. I love you so much Anju, my Anni.'

My CO had recently got married again. Though I doubted that his new wife would ever deign to stay in a two-room house in some dinghy place called Chungthang or Mangan—he would be headed for a second, lightening quick divorce in no time if he ever suggested that to her, who traces her roots back to six generations of *Faujis* who have served in the Indian Army since the mid-eighteenth century; one of her ancestors was amongst the survivors from that dreadful retreat from Kabul in which Pratima's ancestor's paramour's husband had perished. Wheels of life meet me at such consequential moments. But I was sure that my CO would view my predicament with sympathy and would allow me to spend time with my new wife, the moment I brought her to Chungthang and explained my situation to him—he would in fact be happy that I had finally gotten over my Kavita fixation. And Chungthang was just a five-hour journey from my unit location.

But Anju's predicament was different. She was more worried about the men in her family ultimately finding us wherever we would be hiding. She countered my plan of supposedly resigning from the Army, by saying that they would somehow find out about my reality from my parents, who would willingly or unwittingly, depending on how much they would hate me then, let them know about my whereabouts. And who is to stop the newspapermen from spilling the beans, after the news had run cold, and they may divulge the truth after some not-so-gentle persuasion. I was at a loss of words at her apprehension.

But I was relentless in my obdurate insistence and threw arguments after forceful arguments at her. I said that Chungthang is a godforsaken place nobody would even dream of as a location where she could be staying, that I was in the Army and nobody, not even her father or brother, would ever dare to even touch my wife, that I would position a soldier or two near Chungthang who would keep close watch and guard her 24x7x52, that my uncle would be keeping me updated on the goings-on in her father's house and I would be forewarned well in advance of any mishap being contemplated by her family, that Vijay, my other cousin, was staying at Allahabad and would keep me informed of the events taking place there at her father's place—I would have to make him my confidante, though. I also assured her that my father was surely going to get over his initial resentment and he may not later love his son as much, but he would never contemplate an electric pole as my final destination. He was not going to ever tell her father about me and my location or my profession.

After a light lunch of Threptin biscuits and orange juice, we made deep, passionate love for the first time in our lives, and finally relenting, she promised to meet me the next day at the railway station. I spent the night in delightful anticipation and planning for my elopement.

The next day, I spent the whole morning gazing at her door across the street. When my time arrived to leave for the railway station, she had still not left her house. I climbed on the rickshaw for the short ride to the station and she still had not indicated her departure. I scanned the crowd at the railway station, but she was not there, too. I secretly bought another ticket for her. The train trundled onto the platform and there was still no sign of her. I climbed aboard my second-class compartment and glanced in anticipation towards the station's entrance, expecting her breathlessly running for the train. The train hooted twice before its bogies started moving for Sikkim. I leaned out of the door and searched for her over the heads of my parents, who had come to see me off. No, she had not come, she will never come, she never intended to come.

I was left stranded again. As the train continued its relentless journey towards the east, I lost the faces of my parents in the throng of ever-diminishing figures standing on the platform. At last, when they were consumed by the distance and dwindled from sight, I sighed and went into the bathroom to weep and cry my heart out. I had lost again to God. Meena was right after all, I will never find true love.

Where Are They Now?

Meena. I couldn't keep track of Meena for many years. I had to keep my promise to her sister-in-law. A few years back I met Teena's husband during a field exercise in the deserts of Rajasthan. Over tearful recollections, warmed by the fumes of whiskey, he brought me up-to-date with the happenings in my true love's life. Her husband had died a miserable death, two years after her return to Chhapra—he succumbed to all that cholesterol he had accumulated over the years and as a consequence each of his organs gave up on him. His death took long in its coming and he had screamed and screamed in pain, till his breath left him after seven long days of suffering. None of his family members were close to him during the whole time he lay dying in his father's study room. Meena's Chikoo and Bunny have grown into the loveliest twins ever seen in Chhapra. She never opted for politics but took up a teacher's job at a children's school, rising up to the principal's post within four years. Her youngest sister-in-law is also a teacher in the same school, though she could never outgrow the child inside her and remains a spinster. The second sister-in-law got a husband, a wealthy widower, and is now a mother of two strapping sons. The eldest sister-in-law still lives for her Madhav at Brindavan. Her mother-in-law passed away a happy and contented old lady in her nineties, a few years back. Meena now rules the Sharma household like the matriarch that she is. And Chhapra still remains the only town in Bihar where girls can roam around the streets at night without any fear of molestation, courtesy of the knives they still carry around their waists.

Pratima. I rarely get any news of Pratima. Appu once told me that she is a grandmother now. I saw a bit of her profile on Facebook sometime back. She became a teacher at a local school in Lucknow after her graduation. Later, she obtained the mandatory B. Ed. degree. Five years hence she got her doctorate in English literature and is now a professor at Lucknow

University. She married a Joshi boy, as per the wishes of her brothers and her sister-in-law, and gave birth to two sons, from one of whom she has two granddaughters. She never responded to my friend request and we still remain incommunicado with each other.

Anju. She gave her reasons for not coming to the railway station much later. That evening, after she had promised to elope with me, she had a visitor in the form of my brother—the truth behind my jaundice had been divined by my mother, somehow. She had sent Kaalu to put the fear of God in her, and he threatened Anju with dire consequences if she ever thought of marrying me or forcing me into marrying her. Faced with twin threats, Anju's heart ultimately gave up and she never came to the railway station. A few months later, before I could again come on leave, she married a Thakur scion, who was also in the Army. He did not take her as a trophy wife; that was my sole consolation. He loves her a lot and is totally devoted. But the same cannot be said of her mother-in-law. After Anju gave birth to a daughter, she had to suffer numerous abortions and some miscarriages, too. But I think Golu Devta granted her my boon, too. Despite all trials, she gave birth to an autistic girl a few years back and her mother-in-law finally gave up on her search for a grandson. Anju teaches at a school for disadvantaged children, where her younger daughter is a student, too, in Allahabad. She lives in her in-laws' place in the city, where her husband settled down post leaving the Army. Her elder daughter is a student at the Delhi University.

Bindu. Bindu married the son of an acquaintance of Father's, despite my father's vehement protests with Dwivedi Sir against the ill-fated marriage. One dreadful day, her throat was cut by a servant in Delhi, where she was staying with her husband. His hand in the murder was suspected but never proven as the servant was never caught. What a loss! Fortunately, she did not leave a motherless child in this world. Her father, after retirement, made a school at Haldwani in her memory, where their eldest son is the principal. Rekha *Didi* married into a wealthy family at Rewa; she is related to me now, as her husband is a distant cousin. The youngest Dwivedi son joined the Army and is a strapping young officer. Dwivedi Sir and Aunteeji still pine for their younger daughter.

Haseena and Nilima. I lost track of these two brilliant girls long time ago. Except, I attended Nilima's marriage to a doctor settled in the US, in

March '94. She lives there and is often visited by her father, the doctor who had treated me all those years back as a 3-year-old. Haseena, well, I don't know what happened to my Hindi teacher.

The Sanskrit teacher and the hostel matron. The Sanskrit teacher never returned to Etawah after her marriage. The hostel matron left Ghorakhal when I was in class 9; married an Air Force officer, I believe.

Swati. The girl who never understood my desperation is lost to me.

Charu. I never kept in touch with her after she rejected my repeated offers of reconciliation.

Kavita. She still remains blissfully unaware that I exist on this Earth and that I had almost proposed to her father for her hand. Some tennis player she was.

BB Mausi. BB *Mausi* still remains my first love, or my first half-love. She lives in Kanpur with her husband's huge family and is eternally grateful to her brother, my younger-by-eight-months uncle, who gave her his infant son. I still am not on talking terms with her husband.

I. I am a 46-year-old colonel in the Army, currently writing this memoir of unrequited love amidst the mountains of Jammu and Kashmir, the hill slopes reverberating with the booms of the thousands of guns the Pakistanis are firing at us. I am on a night's rest before I join the assaulting troops for another go at the enemy dug in atop a hill close to the line of control. Vodka and soda are my constant companions during my musings. Tomorrow might be my last day and I want to leave this tale of love, as I had promised to Pratima and had sent a pledge to Meena. I married a girl from Bhopal, in an arranged marriage, and found love again, post marriage. She is my twin soul. I lived up to my promise to Golu Devta and he in turn granted me the boons I had prayed for. I insisted on no dowry during my marriage, to the utter chagrin of my parents, who, ever since, have never forgiven my wife for not bringing dowry with her. And to add to their woes, she brought two lovely daughters into this world. They are my little princesses and I dedicate these memoirs to them and my wife, of course. But I will never forget all those other girls in my life, ever, the ones who have made my life worth living and their memories worth cherishing. My wife knows all about them, that's why she is my twin soul.

It gives me a pleasant thought that in all those parallel Earths in those other multiple universes, there are a number of me's who would have married the different loves of my life, in their own versions of existence, and are presently experiencing their blissful company. One of these days, one of these me's is going to call a conference of all these other Sanjay Tivaris, along with their respective spouses, and then, and only then, would I be able to meet all my loves and share in their experiences.

That's a goosebumpy thought, though!

Printed in the United States
By Bookmasters